Face Behind the Mask

Sins of The Father: Book Three

By Leo King

Illustrations by Staci Reed & Nathan Morimitsu

Grey Gecko Press
565 S. Mason Road, Suite 154
Katy, TX 77450
www.greygeckopress.com

Printed in the United States of America

Also available as an eBook

Library of Congress Cataloging-in-Publication Data
King, Leo
Sins of the father: face behind the mask / Leo King
Library of Congress Control Number: 2014951633
ISBN 978-1-9388216-3-9
First Edition

To the magnificent writers of Team Armageddon for making this trilogy possible.

Face Behind the Mask is the third and final volume in the *Sins of the Father* trilogy. Sam's story begins in *The Bourbon Street Ripper,* continues in the second volume, *A Life Without Fear*, and concludes in *Face Behind the Mask.*

Acknowledgements

Back in August of 2011, I started my first draft of *The Bourbon Street Ripper*, then called *Untitled Mystery*. It was a completely different story, with less mysticism and more grit, and Sam was the killer.

Yup, Sam was originally the killer.

But as the story grew, and as I worked with a critique group, it evolved. Soon, what was one book became two, and what was two became three. Without even realizing it, I was writing a trilogy.

Sins of the Father had been born.

This trilogy has done what is called genre-bending, starting as a mystery and turning into a supernatural thriller, and ending in what is almost urban fantasy. I loved doing it, but it's been stressful, and I don't plan on doing it again.

Now for the part where I acknowledge those who have contributed to this book. Only I'm not going to do it the normal way—that's boring. Instead, I'm going to thank each of them directly, right here, right now:

Jason, thanks for running GGP. You've given us all something to dream.

Hilary, thanks for being so patient with me. You've made me a better writer.

George, thanks for being a great sounding board. I feel I can bounce any idea off of you.

Shannon, thanks for being so insightful. You really seem to understand my characters.

Erik, thanks for being so engaging. I always feel like you offer something unique.

Dominick, thanks for being so supportive. You go out of your way to make me feel great.

Kristina, thanks for being so awesome. Talking late at night has gotten me through three books.

Gini, thanks for mentoring me. You've shown me just how far I can go.

June, thanks for all the kind words. Meeting you showed me just how much I'm loved.

To every aunt, uncle, and cousin in my big Nawlins family, thanks for supporting me. Really, I couldn't do it without such an awesome family.

Mom and Dad, thanks for believing in me. You guys made it possible.

Sarah and Ryan, thanks for supporting me. You both give me something to strive for.

Janna, thanks for loving me. Without you, my words would lack soul.

And thanks to every friend or fan not mentioned on this page. I'll get you next time!

Lastly… see ya in Valhalla, Jake. Save me a flagon of mead!

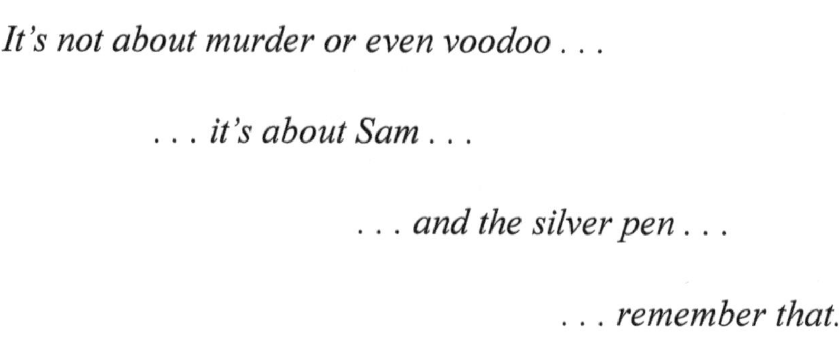

It's not about murder or even voodoo . . .

. . . it's about Sam . . .

. . . and the silver pen . . .

. . . remember that.

— Leo King

Contents

Contents

Prologue

Date: **Wednesday, August 26, 1992**
Time: **10:00 a.m.**
Location: **Tulane University, Doctor's Lounge**
Downtown New Orleans

Seated on a leather couch, his back straight as a board, Dr. Lucius Klein sipped on a cup of dark-roast coffee. His arms stayed at strict right angles, and he stared straight ahead. He was silent, his expression contemplative.

An older doctor with thinning hair sat beside him. "You know, you don't have to wait for her to wake up. We'll contact you and your associates directly."

Dr. Klein peered at him the way a professor would regard an unruly pupil, and he spoke with his German accent. "With all due respect, Dr. Hoffman, I am not here to visit her."

Dr. Hoffman rubbed his forehead. "Right, so why are you here again?"

"I'm here to stop someone else from seeing her."

"Who?"

On the other side of the doorway came the gentle squeak of wheels. Dr. Klein narrowed his eyes. "Here comes ze quack now."

The door opened. In came a gray-haired man in a wheelchair, pushed by a pale woman with both lips and hair the color of dark blood.

"Dr. Lazarus. You are too late, as usual." Dr. Klein sipped his coffee loudly. "Samantha will be mine."

Dr. Lazarus glared. "She's not your property."

"I beg to differ. I am ze only one who can save her."

"The only thing you want is to increase your standing with 'those people,'" said Dr. Lazarus, a fierce look in his eyes.

With a slap to his knees, Dr. Hoffman stood. "And on that note, I'm out. But, gentlemen, I will say this: Miss Castille is currently my patient, so until either of you get a judge to say otherwise, she's my responsibility. We'll all be lucky if that poor girl isn't dead by tonight."

He left without a backward glance.

Dr. Klein snickered, raising his cup in a mocking toast. "Do you hear zat, Dr. Lazarus? Dear, sweet little Samantha could die soon."

Clenching his fists, Dr. Lazarus grimaced and then sat back. "You are a fool. You can't possibly understand what's going on with that girl. She's cheated death already. She'll pull through again."

"Bah, how? Because of ghost und goblins? Preposterous. How you ever became a doctor amazes me."

Dr. Lazarus's expression darkened, if only for a moment. Then he shook his head. "You've never learned to accept that life contains things beyond your understanding. No matter. You can't have Sam. The world needs her more than you will ever imagine."

Putting down his cup, Dr. Klein smirked in a particularly unfriendly manner. "Oh, I disagree. Und this time, I have the ability to keep you away from Samantha for good."

"Oh? And how will you do that?"

"With me," a new voice said.

Another doctor, a younger one in a white coat, entered the lounge. The light glistened off his oily black hair and his small, rectangular glasses. His smile was as wide as it was condescending.

He leaned down over Dr. Lazarus. "A pleasure to meet you. My name is Dr. Ignatius Kindley. I'm an associate of Dr. Klein's. We work for the same—well, benefactor."

As Dr. Lazarus looked him over, his eyes slowly widened. On Dr. Kindley's lapel was an ornate golden pin with the crest of a red cross and a golden crown.

"That crest. It's the symbol of—"

"Indeed it is." Dr. Kindley kept smiling. "We've been out of the game for too many years. So now it's our move. I do so look forward to seeing who emerges victorious in the final round. Will it be us? You?"

He pushed up his glasses.

"Or perhaps the gods themselves."

Part One

Chapter 1
Nothing But Darkness

Date: **Friday, September 11, 1992**
Time: **4:00 p.m.**
Location: **A Dark, Silent, Lonely Place**

Sam Castille floated in a cold nothingness.

Am I dead? Is this heaven? Is this hell? Is this nothing at all?

Nothing but darkness surrounded her.

Everything that I went through. Everything I did. Was it all for nothing?

Nothing but silence answered her.

I've never felt so alone. So terribly alone. Is this what it's like . . . to be dead?

Nothing but numbness consumed her.

Then that silent, dark, cold void began to break. A slit of light cut across the blackness before her. As it widened, sensations started filling her being. She heard a steady tone beeping in time to the beat of her heart. She smelled her bitter sweat. She felt a contrast of chilly air and a warm fabric.

Suddenly, her vision filled with blinding light, and she felt unbearable, hot pain along the left side of her body. But the void of nothingness was gone, replaced by a world of shape and sensation—the world of the living.

Sam opened her eyes.

For a long time, she just lay there, taking in the ceiling of a very unfamiliar room. At first, she thought she might be paralyzed, like when she suffered from locked-in syndrome, but she was able to move her head to look around. The movement was painful. The skin of her neck felt tight and hot.

She was alone in what looked like a hospital room, the fluorescent lights above uncomfortably bright. Along the wall was a sink and near her bed was a privacy curtain. The door was open, leading out into a hallway. To her side was a steadily beeping heart monitor. Her left arm was heavily bandaged up to her neck, a catheter was inserted in her right arm, and both were bound by leather straps. Gauze was taped to the left side of her face. She was covered in sticky sweat and a stale odor.

Panic welled up inside of her as she remembered the last time she was bound in such a manner. Dallas Christofer, the new Bourbon Street Ripper, was torturing her. He had managed two cuts before Rodger Bergeron, the only detective left on the case, had arrived and stopped him. The two had fought, and Dallas had overpowered Rodger, but then Sam had freed herself and helped Rodger destroy the copycat killer.

As those awful memories assailed her, she realized she was straining against the straps. The veins in her arms began to pop out, the straps creaking. Just as she felt the straps start to give, she relaxed, panting. She wasn't in the Castille Mansion. She wasn't being tortured. She was in a hospital. She was safe. But where was she? And how had she gotten there?

Sam closed her eyes and focused on remembering what had happened. All she could recall was a fire in her townhome right after learning that Rodger had died.

Then she remembered that Michael, Rodger's partner, had been killed a week before that.

And then she remembered that Richie, her boyfriend, had turned out to be Dallas. He had committed suicide when he had realized what he had done.

The memories opened a floodgate within her heart. Before she realized it, tears were running down her face. They burned.

Oh, God. Everyone is dead.

Rodger. Michael. Richie. My poor, sweet Richie.

They're all dead. I'm the only one left.

The heaviness crushed her heart.

Turning her head to the side, she saw raindrops hitting the window. More memories returned. It had also been raining the night Rodger and Michael had first visited—the night everything began.

Tears continued to flow painfully down her cheeks. She was the only survivor of Vincent Castille's madness.

Vincent.

Just thinking of him, the original Bourbon Street Ripper, pulled her heart from the presses and plunged it into fire. Even knowing that Vincent was actually her father wasn't enough to extinguish the inferno of hate. From beyond the grave, he had managed to mastermind everything. The serial murders, the random deaths—all were him using Dallas and voodoo spirits called *loa* to continue his evil work.

But for what reason? Try as she might, she couldn't remember why Vincent did it. She only knew it was something horrible.

A voice came from the hallway. "All right, time to check on Miss Castille."

That drew her from her thoughts. Seeing the shadow of someone approaching, she quickly straightened and closed her eyes. She wasn't ready to speak to others just yet. A moment later, she felt someone standing over her.

Cracking one eye open, she saw an African American nurse taking notes on a clipboard. As the woman turned, Sam shut her eye again. She then felt the nurse move around her. She smelled of sanitizing lotion and chewing gum.

"Hmm. All seems normal." The nurse mopped some sweat off Sam's brow.

As Sam lay there, however, she also began to feel other presences, ones she couldn't see, hear, or smell. Were these the voodoo *loa*? Were they perhaps even ghosts?

Memories of what had happened continued flooding back.

Did Vincent really contact me from the spirit world?

Did I really make a pact with the queen of the loa*?*

Did I really fight my way out of my home as it burned around me?

"Checkin' the blood pressure." The nurse attached a strap to her right arm. Within seconds, it tightened.

Memories returned with every breath. Soon she was certain of what had happened that night. Most of her life, she had thought she was mad. It turned out to be a powerful possession.

When she was five years old, Vincent put the *loa* Marinette inside of her. Now Marinette was dead, killed by her own hand.

Now, I have Bridgette, the Loa Queen.

"Not bad." The nurse released the blood pressure strap and moved to her other side.

Sam frowned. Despite knowing she had made a pact with Bridgette that night, she couldn't feel her. It was like the *loa* queen was gone.

Bridgette, can you hear me? It's Sam. Let me know you're OK.

Nothing. Not a single whisper or nudge.

The last thing she could recall was passing out on her front lawn. *I was badly hurt, wasn't I?*

As Sam struggled to remember, the nurse started unwrapping the bandages from her left arm. Searing pain shot through her like venom. She jerked upwards and screamed. "Holy shit that hurts!"

The nurse fell back, hand to her chest. "Good heavens! Don't scream at me like that. Oh, Lord, girl. You 'bout gave me a heart attack." She leaned against the wall, catching her breath.

Sam was still shaking from the sudden jolt of pain when another nurse—a young, strong-looking guy—rushed in. "Ester, is everything OK?"

Ester waved him off. "Yeah, Marty, it's all right. Go . . . go tell Dr. Hoffman that Miss Castille is awake."

Sparing Sam a glance, Marty left. As Ester came back over, Sam tensed the muscles in her left arm. Another hot slice of pain shot through her nerves. She hissed and relaxed, but the pain barely ebbed. "What happened? Did I get burned?"

Ester's lips turned down. "Yeah, hun, you got burned. Pretty badly."

Seeing pity in her eyes made Sam feel a surge of indignation. *Who the heck is she looking at like that?*

With a "tch," she craned her neck. "So, where am I?"

"The burn unit at Tulane." Ester held the clipboard to her chest as if it were a shield.

"Tulane Hospital." Sam flexed her left arm. The pain was a throbbing, constant, inescapable heat. "What day is it? How long have I been out?"

Ester cleared her throat. "It's September 11th, hun. A Friday. You've been out for 'bout two weeks."

"Two weeks." Sam laid her head back down. "Unbelievable."

That movement made the left side of her face hurt. Instinctively, she tried to touch it, but she was stopped by the leather straps. She wrinkled her brow. "So, Ester, why am I tied up?"

"To stop you from hurting yourself," a new voice said from the doorway.

A middle-aged doctor with thinning hair, wearing green scrubs, entered the room. Sam felt like she had seen him once before. Marty stood nearby, his arms folded. His expression was both curious and wary.

"You must be Dr. Hoffman."

Dr. Hoffman took the clipboard from Ester and examined it. He then smiled in a way that looked pitiable. Again, she felt an indignant surge well up within her. It was humiliating to be regarded in that way.

"How are you feeling, Sam?"

She stared at him, feeling more incredulous every second. "I'm bewildered and confused. I wake up and I'm hurting like the Devil's been cooking me. I'm tied up to stop me from hurting myself, whatever that means. I smell and feel like crap. And I've got people looking at me like I'm crazy. You tell me how I should feel!" Her neck muscles strained with discomfort.

He leaned forward and rested his hands on the side rail. “Yes, I can see how that’s confusing. You know, Sam, this is the third time in your life that I’ve treated you. The last time was a few weeks ago. You had passed out while driving your car. And before that, when you were five years old, your grandfather brought you here after you suffered a collapse.”

“Don’t call Vincent my grandfather!” Sam yelled with such force that both Ester and Dr. Hoffman stumbled back. Marty started to come forward, but he stopped when Dr. Hoffman held him back.

“Let Miss Castille speak. She obviously has a lot to get out.”

Tears again threatened to spill from her eyes. “That damn bastard. He took everything from me. He stole my past. He stole my future. He stole my life. He’s nothing to me!”

Dr. Hoffman slowly approached, holding out his hands. “I’m sorry for bringing him up. Given what Vincent has done, I can’t blame you. I just wanted to point out that I’m familiar with treating you. I’m on your side, Sam.”

She nodded, just wanting the conversation to end. All that pain was tiring.

“So let’s talk about your injuries, OK?”

She nodded again, just wanting to slip back into sleep. Emotions this painful were even more tiring.

“All right. Your townhome had caught on fire. You fell out of the attic. When you did, you suffered deep second- and third-degree burns to your left extremities, the left side of your torso, including your left breast and buttocks, and to the left side of your neck and head. You’ve been spending two hours a day in oxygen treatment.”

She felt sick to her stomach, trying to imagine her torn-up, burned-up body.

“When you landed, you broke over a dozen bones. Actually, it’s a funny story, because at first we thought it was every major bone in your body, but it must have been a mix-up with the X-rays. After stabilizing and moving you here, we did a second set of X-rays. You got away with only broken legs and a few cracked ribs.”

She bit her top lip and sucked. *No . . . that’s not it.* Her ability to heal was enhanced. She already knew that from previous experiences.

Again, Dr. Hoffman rested his hands on the railing. “Your first few nights here were pretty rough. We honestly thought that you were going to die. But you pulled through. Three times now, you’ve sustained life-threatening injuries and survived. You are truly remarkable.”

Sam continued to suck on her upper lip. She was sure that there was more to it. Vincent had revealed something extremely important. *I feel as if I wasn’t in any danger of dying. Why is that?*

"Anyway, even in a coma, you've been pretty reactive to pain. Every time we've applied Silvadene to your burns, you've nearly broken a nose or cracked a collarbone. So we've restrained you."

She snorted. "Less for my protection and more for others, eh?"

He continued to regard her with pity. "Sam, I'm sorry. I'm afraid I can't remove the restraints just yet. Much has happened since your accident, and you've gained a lot of attention. A few people need to talk to you before your personal psychiatrist can see you."

She gasped. "No, not Dr. Klein. He threatened to hurt me. He threatened to torture me!" The heart-rate monitor quickened until it was a flurry of beeps. Sounds around her started to mute and sensations started to grow.

Ester and Marty traded looks. Dr. Hoffman cleared his throat. "Please relax, Miss Castille. Your psychiatrist is Dr. Lazarus. Don't you remember firing Dr. Klein? He's been complaining about it for weeks to anyone who'll listen. But anyway, Dr. Lazarus will want to know that you're awake."

She relaxed, her heart rate returning to normal, and with it the sounds and sensations of the room. She remembered that Dr. Lazarus was much more open to the idea of her being possessed. "Sorry. I'm OK. I just hate Dr. Klein."

"I can understand that. For now, though, Ester needs to change your bandages. I'll come check up on you later. Until then, please try to remain calm." Glancing back once more, he left.

Her ears burned. She felt like a scolded child. *Hurt and torture me—Jesus, Sam, shut the hell up! You sound like a damn lunatic.*

Ester gingerly approached. "Sam, I'm gonna to give you some morphine while I change your bandages and clean n' treat your burns. It's still going to hurt, though. Marty's gonna keep you steady, all right?"

Sam glanced toward Marty. He was handsome, probably in his early twenties and built like a lumberjack. Suddenly, she wondered how good he'd be at pinning her to a wall while having her. Her cheeks grew hot and she pushed those feelings aside. What was wrong with her? The man she loved had died just a few weeks ago.

Then the world started to swim. Ester had added morphine to her IV. Sam leaned back, smiling goofily. Tears in her eyes turned the light into specks. Then the specks turned into butterflies. "Yeah, I feel it. Good ol' morphine . . . lovely Miss Emma . . . delicious. This is the stuff. Go on, Ester. Hit me."

Through her semi-daze, she saw Ester nod. Then she felt Marty's strong hands resting on the right side of her hip and chest. She rolled her head toward him and winked. "Hey, there, kiddo. If you wanna have some fun, wait until we don't have an audience. Wait until—"

Then, some of the most excruciating pain she had ever felt shot through her left arm. It was just as relentless as when Dallas was slicing into her. Almost against her will, she looked. Ester had removed the bandages. Her entire left arm down to her hand was nothing more than charred meat that stank like bad barbeque.

She thrashed against her restraints. "Fucking stop! The morphine isn't helping at all!"

"Ma'am, you need to relax," Marty said forcefully, pushing harder.

Ester pulled back. "Hun, you need to stop. You're only going to hurt yourself."

Sam eventually calmed down enough for Ester to remove the bandages from the rest of her body, including her face. The pain was a constant, hot throbbing. He left leg was a gnarled mess that she could barely recognize.

I'm a freak now . . .

The treatment didn't get any better. The pain from having her wounds cleaned was bad enough to make her weep. She somehow endured, gritting her teeth and crying out until her throat hurt.

When she was finally done, Ester said, "Sam, I'm going to put the Silvadene on now. This is going to hurt, but I need you to be brave like you've been so far."

"OK," Sam said in a small voice. She was already hoarse. She just wanted the pain to end so she could go back to sleep. But as soon as the Silvadene hit, her mind went blank, unsure how anything could register as that painful and not kill her. Despite Ester's pleadings, she struggled harder than before. Marty was barely able to hold on.

Then, quite suddenly, the morphine high start to lift, and the instinct to survive overtook any rationality. Clenching her fist, she let out a guttural shriek and pulled her right arm against the restraints. The leather strap easily popped free. With another roar, she pushed Marty off her. He landed against the wall and collapsed.

Snarling, she grabbed Ester and pulled the terrified nurse closer until their noses were touching. A part of her she didn't recognize had risen to the surface, something arrogant and angry. She could smell the nurse's fear. Somehow, it was a delicious ambrosia.

"You will never touch me again, you goddamn little insect."

She pushed Ester to the ground and then passed out.

Chapter 2
Enter Dr. Kindley

Date: **Saturday, September 12, 1992**
Time: **11:00 a.m.**
Location: **Tulane University Hospital**
Downtown New Orleans

As Sam slowly awoke, she again felt the spirits, patches of coolness flitting about the warm, muggy September air. Some were very small, like children. Others were the size of adults. And others were no larger than clothespins.

Then she felt another presence, one that was warm, very close, and very familiar.

When she opened her eyes, she saw a woman in an overcoat standing next to her. One of the sleeves lay limp at her side. She looked at Sam with a mixture of sadness and concern.

Sam's eyes focused, and she recognized Lieutenant Detective Dixie Olivier.

"Hey there, Sam. How're you feeling?" She touched her arm softly.

It was enough to make Sam feel a little better. "Dixie? Oh, you have no idea how good it is to see you."

She tried to sit up, only to realize that additional restraints—leather straps crossing over her torso—had been added. She sighed. "I guess I shouldn't have thrown such a fit, right?" She didn't need an answer—what she had done to Ester was repugnant. And where had all that arrogant rage suddenly come from?

An answer came anyway.

"Yeah, you pretty much blew everyone's trust with that little escapade." Dixie gently stroked the right side of Sam's face.

"Sam, what's happening to you?"

Sam turned away. Dixie's kindness hurt more than any of her burns. *I don't wanna feel anymore.*

"You wouldn't believe me if I told you. You'd think I was crazier than Dallas."

Patting the stump that used to be her left arm, Dixie said, "I think I've seen more than enough to know what is and isn't crazy."

Sam felt a compulsion to push Dixie away, one that was almost overpowering. But then she remembered Rodger saying that she could be trusted. *I guess I can give it a shot.*

"It's Vincent. He's the reason Dallas became the copycat killer."

Dixie regarded her inquisitively. "I think you should explain yourself, Sam."

"Eh, probably a good idea," Sam said. At this point, it felt like talking it out was the best way to come to terms with it. "After I heard about Rodger's accident, stuff started happening. Weird stuff. Crazy stuff. I thought I was losing my mind."

"What happened?" Dixie asked in a low, conversational tone.

"Oh, where to begin? My reflection turned into some sort of ghost monster. The equipment in my office started working by itself. The fireplace in my study lit up with a pale green flame. There were two skeletons playing cards in my kitchen while little black clothespin creatures were making coffee."

"Yes. That does sound crazy. But, please, go on." There wasn't a hint of condescension in her voice.

Sam focused on the window. It was still raining. "So Vincent's voice starts talking to me. He tells me how he's been using *loa*. You know what *loa* are, right?"

"Yes. Voodoo spirits. But they're just superstition."

Looking back, she cocked an eyebrow. "You know I was possessed during the fight with Blind Moses at the wharf, right? By a *loa* named Marinette?"

Standing up, Dixie rubbed her head. "Right. So, for the sake of conversation, what was Vincent doing with these *loa*?"

Sam bit the side of her lip. She knew Vincent was doing something extremely important, but she just couldn't remember. "All I know is that Vincent was using the *loa* to influence Dallas to commit those murders. He also used them to kill Michael and Rodger."

Dixie didn't say anything. At the mention of Michael, her expression grew solemn. For several minutes, she looked lost in thought. Finally, she said, "Well, I'm no expert in these matters, but it sounds like you had a serious psychotic episode."

"Go to hell." Sam whipped her head to the side, her heart aching again. "I knew you wouldn't believe me."

She then felt Dixie's hand on her shoulder. "Whoa, whoa. I didn't say that. I just said that's how it sounds. I'm sure that whatever you experienced, it was absolutely real to you. I'm not sure what happened to you, Sam, but I don't think you're lying."

Slowly, Sam looked back at Dixie. The other woman was smiling tenderly.

Gradually, Sam smiled back. It felt like Dixie was indeed on her side. "So what happens now?"

"Well, Ouellette is talking to Dr. Hoffman. I'm sure you'll need to undergo a psychiatric evaluation. After all, you did attack two nurses."

Sam huffed, annoyed at the entire situation. "Well, they shouldn't have taken me off the morphine when they were cleaning my wounds. I wouldn't have lost my shit."

"They didn't," said Dixie, shaking her head. "You somehow managed to burn away its effects, which has everyone scratching their heads. Please understand this, Sam. How you've been healing and are able to resist drugs like morphine . . . well, it isn't human. If I hadn't seen you fight Blind Moses, I would think this whole thing is a hoax."

"Yeah, but now?" Sam tilted her head to the side. The bandages on her face pulled tightly, sending a shock of pain through her.

Dixie chuckled. "Sam, there is very little you could do that would surprise me."

"Thanks, Dixie," Sam said, feeling better about her situation.

Suddenly, Dixie's expression grew considerably more serious, and then she leaned down toward Sam.

Sam blinked. *Wha—? Is she gonna kiss me?*

Instead, Dixie rested her forehead on hers in an abrupt display of affection. Sam froze up, the sudden emotion catching her off guard. She didn't know how to respond.

"Listen, Sam," Dixie whispered. "I can never say enough to apologize for falsely accusing you. I did you a great wrong. If it takes the rest of my life, I swear I will make it right. No matter what, you can trust me."

Sam didn't move. This unexpected action and statement stopped her thought processes. All she could do was whisper back, "Um, thanks."

"Do you two need to get a hotel room?" a rough-sounding voice asked from the doorway.

Dixie stood, her cool demeanor back in place.

Sam blinked again, certain she had a "deer-in-the-headlights" expression.

Then she saw who was at the doorway. *What's he doing here?*

Standing there in his usual suit and tie was Commander Ouellette. He had a particularly unpleasant look, sour even for him.

"Sorry, Commander," said Dixie. "I was just—"

"Close it, Lieutenant. I don't particularly care whether you were about to suck face with Miss Castille or not. I need to speak with her alone, and I need you to head downstairs. The DA wants this whole thing to go smoothly."

"Sir! But I think we should tell—"

Ouellette glared at her with the kind of look that would wither a flower. She clenched her jaw and then said, "Yes, sir."

Confused, Sam quietly watched them.

Dixie then gently touched her hand. "I'll be in touch, Sam. I promise. Remember what I—"

"That's enough, Lieutenant."

"Fine." She left without another word, stomping out.

Slowly, Ouellette closed the door and approached. "Sam, I'm breaking protocol doing this, and I'm taking a risk. But because of who you are and who I am, you've got one shot to tell me your side of the story."

Sam stared but said nothing. As far as she was concerned, years ago, he had tried to frame Edward, the man who'd raised her like a father. Trust was not something she had for him.

"Look, I know you don't like me, and to be honest, I don't care. I don't like what the Castilles have become. But I find myself in the unique position of being able to help you out, so start talking."

She continued to look at him with suspicion. Ouellette, someone she had hated most of her life, was now asking for her side of the story. The utter gall of him.

Then he let out an exasperated sigh. "Look, Sam. You need to tell me what really happened in your townhome or life is going to get very uncomfortable for you. And this time, no one is going to bail you out."

The exhaustion of defeat was once again growing within her. "You're going to think I'm crazy."

He leaned forward. His gaze was focused and unyielding. "Try me."

With a sniff, she said, "Vincent Castille was behind the copycat murders."

His eyes narrowed. "And what do you mean by that?"

She locked eyes. "The night Rodger died, Vincent's . . . ghost . . . came to me and told me that he was using *loa* to manipulate Dallas and others into finishing his killings from twenty years ago."

Ouellette's expression didn't change. She started to sweat, unable to get a read on him.

Finally, he straightened up. "Did he say why he was doing this?"

Sam couldn't tell if he believed her or not. "I think he was doing a voodoo ritual or something. I . . . I'm sorry, I'm having trouble remembering. It was definitely a ritual. A voodoo ritual with *loa*." Her brow furrowed.

He folded his arms. "You mean like with the Knight Priory of Saint Madonna?"

She nodded, remembering that Vincent had run the original Knight Priory and that some of the oldest and most powerful families in New Orleans were members. They were the ones who had put Marinette inside of her at his behest.

"Yes, them," she said.

Ouellette grimaced as if recalling something painful. "Go on. So Vincent's ghost was performing a ritual? How'd he do that? He's been dead since the seventies."

"He used something—a focus—to influence the world."

That seemed to get his attention. "A focus? Do you know what it was?"

Again, she struggled to recall that detail. She knew that the form of the focus, just like the ritual's objective, was important, but it was no use. She just couldn't remember.

"Sorry, I got nothing."

"Sam, you know you sound bat-shit insane, right? You say that your murderous father continued killing after his death, and yet you don't know why or with what."

Glaring at him, she spat, "Like your opinion of me matters. You've never liked my family, and you've never liked me. We're done here."

He continued, matching her intensity. "Yes. We're done. And I think this is the end of the immortal Castille family line."

As he started to walk away, she suddenly felt a spark of clarity light up. With it came the disturbing realization of exactly what Vincent had done. Murder after murder, suffering beyond suffering, all for the sake of a dark, long-forgotten ritual that would ensure life without the fear of death.

"Vincent made me immortal!" she blurted out.

He stopped in his tracks and looked back. His expression was genuinely perplexed. "What did you say?"

Her voice shook. The revelation had been as horrible as she had feared. "Vincent committed all those murders years ago and then influenced Dallas to commit his so he could complete a ritual to bind Baron Samedi to himself. He did this so the Baron wouldn't dig my grave."

Ouellette's expression became unreadable. "So, you mean . . . ?"

"I, um, can't die." Just saying it made her feel nauseated.

"I need to get going." Turning away, he shook his head and then left.

Sam tried not to throw up. *All that suffering was for me . . .*

For several hours, Sam lay there and thought about the ritual. She hadn't wanted to face why the murders were committed then, nor did she want to now. Each time she closed her eyes, she saw the victims, their broken bodies excised of tissue and organs, their faces frozen in screams of fear and pain. Even Edward, the man she knew as her father, was tortured to death in front of her. All of that suffering for one reason—to make her immortal.

She felt sick to her stomach.

I don't want this.

I can't even free the Baron and die in peace.

Bridgette is probably gone, too.

Everything I touch gets ruined.

She was deep within her self-deprecation when Dr. Hoffman came in with two orderlies. At once, both men detached her from the heart-rate monitor and hooked the IV bag to the side of her bed. She started to feel anxious.

"What's going on? Where am I going?"

Dr. Hoffman grinned cautiously. "Well, Sam, after what happened, the hospital's not comfortable keeping you here. We're transferring you to a unit where you can get better attention."

She watched warily as the two orderlies finished making her bed mobile. "Can you at least unlatch me?"

He patted her foot. "As soon as you get settled in your new room, the restraints will be removed. We'll come get you once a day for your oxygen treatment, of course."

That didn't make her feel particularly better. A minute later, they wheeled her through the hallways of the burn unit and then the intensive care unit. No one spoke to her.

Finally, they reached a closed metal doorway. Dr. Hoffman clicked on a wall intercom. "This is Dr. Hoffman with Samantha Castille, here to see Dr. Kindley."

A loud buzzer rang, and then the metal doors opened.

Huh? I'm in an area that's locked down? What the . . . Then it hit her. She knew exactly where she was going.

"Are you serious?" she said, trying to sit up. "You're transferring me to the psych ward?"

"Calm down, Miss Castille!"

"Wait! Don't I get a hearing or a lawyer or something?"

"Dr. Kindley will explain everything. I promise."

On the other side of the door, they were met by a doctor in his mid-forties with short, oily, black hair and a smile like that of a salesman. On one side of his white jacket was the name tag, which read "Dr. I. Kindley," and on the other side was a white button with "Would You Kindly?" written in red crayon. On his lapel, he wore an ornate golden pin with a crest on it—a red cross with a golden crown.

Sam focused on the crest. She'd seen that before, but where?

"Ah, here we have the newest member of our family," Dr. Kindley said as he signed something on a medical clipboard and then handed it to Dr. Hoffman. "There. All done. Thank you for personally walking her down here."

Dr. Hoffman sighed with audible resignation. "Just take good care of her, OK? She's had a very hard life. She's a good girl, trust me."

With a forced laugh, Dr. Kindley patted him on the back. "Oh, she'll be as happy as a lark here. Well, best let me see to my patient. Good day, Dr. Hoffman, and all that."

Glancing back at Sam, Dr. Hoffman offered an apologetic look.

"No, don't leave me here," she pleaded.

He quickly left without another word.

Then Dr. Kindley leaned into her view. "I'm Dr. Kindley. Welcome to the Tulane Psychiatric Intensive Care Unit, Miss Castille. May I call you Miss Castille? Good. Thank you."

She glowered at him and then looked down the hallway. A dozen or so patients were shuffling from one room to the next or congregating in a large, open space at the end of the hall. They all wore white hospital gowns. Some mumbled to themselves. Some hummed. Some argued with people who weren't there. One even stood along the wall, arms spread out as if on a cross, completely motionless. The whole area smelled like stale urine.

I'm in the nuthouse. How could this happen?

"Are you ready to meet your social worker?" asked Dr. Kindley. "She'll explain everything to you. Come on, gentlemen, please bring Miss Castille along."

The two orderlies wheeled Sam away from the other patients and into a room with a single table and chair. They set her up in a corner.

"What about my restraints? Can those come off?"

"All in good time, Miss Castille." Dr. Kindley continued acting as if the world was a picnic.

Then they left her alone with only the sound of the air conditioning rattling in the ceiling above. She struggled a bit with the restraints before settling down, finally closing her eyes and drifting off. She awoke a little while later when a woman in her late fifties with pale skin and light-colored lips, wearing a business suit, holding a briefcase, and sporting a gray bun of hair, entered the room.

"Samantha Castille? I'm Veronica Dumont, your social worker. I've been assigned to your case." Veronica sat down at the table, opened up the briefcase, and took out a thick folder.

Sam eyed it dubiously. "What's that? My file?"

"Yes," Veronica said. "Can I be perfectly honest with you, Miss Castille?"

"I'd appreciate that, since no one else has been," Sam said.

"All right. I was asked to be your social worker because no one else would. Your case came through our office, and suddenly everyone had a sick child or a doctor's appointment. I won't mince words with you, Miss Castille. We're all pretty distrustful of you."

That made Sam's jaw drop. "But what about Dixie? And Ouellette? And Dr. Hoffman? Don't they trust me?"

Sitting back, Veronica said, "Dr. Hoffman is terrified of you. That nurse you hit, Marty, suffered a broken sternum. You're lucky you didn't kill him. Both Ouellette and Dixie Olivier were sent here to give the judge's order directly to Dr. Hoffman."

Sam felt her confusion and frustration rising. "What judge's order? What're you talking about?"

"Your commitment, of course. You've been committed for six months to the PICU—the Psychiatric Intensive Care Unit—for acute schizophrenic episodes and intermittent explosive disorder. Anger problems."

Sam laid back and gazed blankly at the ceiling. So this was what Dixie was trying to warn her about. The sick feeling grew in her stomach once more. *Why didn't she just come out and say it?*

She knocked her head back against the pillow. *All those kind words. They were probably said out of guilt. She doesn't really care!*

Tears rolled down her cheeks. As the moments passed, the tightness in her chest and the pain in her gut continued to rise. There was no one left for her to trust.

Veronica cleared her throat. "I need to ask you a few questions, Miss Castille. Do you have any living relatives we can contact?"

The pain of Dixie's duplicity gnawed at Sam's heart. She didn't want to discuss her family. "No. I think I'm the last of the Castilles in New Orleans. I wouldn't even know how to contact my cousins or whatever."

"Do you have any bank accounts we should keep an eye on for you? To make sure no one uses your money while you're here?"

"I have a checking and savings account at Whitney Bank. I know my lawyer, Kent, was overseeing my estate before he went psycho and tried to get me killed."

"Yes, about your estate," Veronica said, opening the file. "You may want to get an attorney to help you sort that out. There is a clause that says that if you were to be committed, you'd forfeit your inheritance."

It was old news, and Sam was sick of discussing it. It was the entire reason Kent Bourgeois and his son Nick had helped Dallas: so they could get her money. Kent had even married Aunt Gladys, Vincent's younger sister, so he could inherit it. The whole situation disgusted Sam to the point where she was ready to just give up that money, all five billion of it.

"So who gets it now that I'm legally crazy?"

Veronica shrugged. "I don't know exactly. The whole thing is a mess, which is why I suggest legal counsel."

"I'll think about it. But now I have a question for you, Miss Dumont. Why the hell am I committed without a hearing? Don't I have rights? I'm pretty sure you can't just declare someone legally insane on a whim."

Closing the file, Veronica spoke in a hushed voice. "Well, I was instructed not to tell you, but I feel that you deserve to know. Someone with a lot of political influence pushed your commitment through in less than a day. Likely greased some palms and such. He'll be monitoring your progress with Dr. Kindley. If you don't respond positively, I'm told he's going to recommend a longer commitment with personal treatment from him."

Nausea started welling up in Sam's stomach. There was only one person she knew who had gloated over his political connections in New Orleans. Sometimes, during sessions, he'd even boast that his benefactors were the people who actually ran the city behind the scenes.

"Oh, God," she said, feeling weak. "Please tell me, tell me it's not him."

"I'm sorry, but it's your old therapist, Dr. Klein."

Sam screamed until the orderlies rushed in and sedated her.

Chapter 3
You Want My Story?

Date: **Wednesday, October 7, 1992**
Time: **10:00 a.m.**
Location: **Tulane Psychiatric Intensive Care Unit**
Downtown New Orleans

"So then I came home from my African safari, and my wife was in bed with the repair guy," the short man said to the ring of patients.

Dr. Kindley nodded, an action that seemed more rehearsed than sympathetic. "And how did that make you feel, Mr. Lafont?"

Sam closed her eyes and groaned. She tuned out the short man, whom she'd nicknamed Livingston, as he talked about how it had sent him into a downward spiral of problems.

God, kill me now.

She had been under Dr. Kindley's care for several weeks, and while most of her physical injuries had healed—once more drawing surprise and unease from the doctors around her—her commitment continued to stand. Every appeal had been dismissed, and Veronica had finally advised her to wait until her formal hearing at the end of the six months. It was all Dr. Klein's fault. She hated him so much.

"Also, with Dr. Marcus Brody dying yesterday, I'm pretty bummed. He was a good friend. Very helpful on my expeditions."

She frowned as Dr. Kindley scribbled on a clipboard. While the other patients in her therapy group had welcomed her, even blindly accepting her quick healing, she had pushed them all away. She just couldn't relate to their personality quirks, like Livingston's belief that the characters of movies like *Raiders of the Lost Ark* were real.

I'm so alone.

"We've talked about that before, Mr. Lafont," said Dr. Kindley. "The man's name was Denholm Elliot. Dr. Brody was the character he played."

"Right, right. I still get the two confused." Livingston waved it off.

Dr. Kindley's eyes skimmed the group before settling on her. "Would anyone like to comment on Mr. Lafont's story? He really opened up today."

Sam stared back, her eyes narrowed. There wasn't an ounce of sincerity in his body.

Fortunately, another patient, a woman whom Sam had nicknamed Miss Prissy, started talking in a high-pitched whining voice. Again, Sam tuned everyone out, inspecting her burns. They had healed, but scars covered the entire left side of her body. The ones on her face were the least noticeable, while the ones on her arm were the worst. Her left leg was still in a cast, so she had to use a pair of crutches to walk.

Sighing, she picked at a scar on her arm. *Just call me the Bitch of Frankenstein.*

Sudden laughter drew her out of her thoughts. Miss Prissy's shallow face was blushing furiously while everyone, even Dr. Kindley, was having a good bit of fun. For a moment, Sam felt outside of herself, the isolation almost overwhelming.

She had given them all sarcastic and somewhat demeaning nicknames, which she had kept to herself. There was a tall, bald older man who always carried a bible, Preacher Man; a witless-looking sod who would randomly go catatonic, Gormless; a man who looked like he used a children's playground as single's bar, Stinky Palms; a woman who had a reputation for hitting on anyone with a pulse, Lay-Me; and a guy who looked just like James Woods. Everyone was sharing the bonding moment. Even Miss Prissy started to chortle.

Everyone, that is, except Sam. *I just don't belong.*

"So, Miss Castille, what about you?" Dr. Kindley wiped away a tear that wasn't actually there. "You've been here a month and still haven't shared anything."

She suddenly felt all eyes in the room upon her. Scanning the faces of the other patients, some smiling pleasantly and others peering with suspicion, she shook her head. "Don't have anything to say. Pass."

Miss Prissy reached over and patted her knee. "Oh, come now, Sam. As Martha Stewart says, 'Without an open-minded mind, you can never be a great success.'"

"Right," Livingston said. "Besides, you listened to me prattle on about catching my wife cheating on me with Shaft. The least you can do is share something in return."

"'But to do good and to communicate forget not. For with such sacrifices, God is well pleased.' Hebrews, chapter 13, verse 16," Preacher Man said.

Sam was sure she had walked onto a sitcom. Gathering her wits, she sat up and folded her arms underneath her chest. "Sorry, everyone. I'm just not comfortable telling my story. It's just too . . . um, crazy."

Dr. Kindley hummed. "Come now, Miss Castille. No one's story will be ridiculed. And what do we say here about 'crazy,' everyone?"

He pointed to a string of multi-colored letters that decorated a side wall of the room, spelling out "Crazy is only in your mind." Everyone except Sam read it aloud at the same time, like children in an elementary-school class.

"So you see, Miss Castille, we all want to hear what you have to say. And I'm sure that your social worker, Miss Dumont, would love to hear that your therapy has been going well."

She tried to keep up the faux pleasant expression, but indignant feelings welled up inside. Who did he think he was to challenge her like this?

Then he cleared his throat. "Well, everyone, we should move on. Miss Castille is obviously too preoccupied with how she's going to convince the judge she's making progress for her to share anything."

She caught a nasty glint in his eyes along with the threat. For just a second, her pulse quickened and her vision reddened. Sounds around her started to deepen and lengthen, and the world began slowing down. Then, just as quickly, she pulled back, feeling the color drain from her face. The last time that had happened, she had just made her pact with Bridgette. She couldn't feel the *Loa* Queen inside her, yet she could feel those effects. What was going on?

Dr. Kindley must have taken her reaction as submission. "Well, now, Miss Castille, why don't you share with us the events that brought you here?"

"Oh, good," Lay-Me said as she wiggled forward. She brushed back her long, brunette hair, which revealed the rope-burn scar around her neck. "Sam's finally going to tell us her story!"

"Yes, tell us everything," Stinky Palms added. "Every succulent little detail."

Sam heaved a heavy exhale. "OK, you want it? You're gonna get it!"

She sat up, stretched, cracked her knuckles, and began. "When I was five years old, my grandfather, Vincent Castille, put a *loa* named Marinette inside me because of the weak heart I inherited from my mother, a lounge singer at the Jean-Lafitte Theater. Vincent, who turned out to be my biological father, was so distraught over the idea of losing me that when I was ten, he became the Bourbon Street Ripper and tortured and murdered over a dozen people, including my aunt and his own son, the man who raised me as his daughter, before being arrested and executed."

She leaned back and rested one leg over the other. "Twenty years later, my nephew, who is also technically my cousin, becomes the New Bourbon Street

Ripper, and besides continuing Vincent's murder spree, he convinces my lawyer and my lawyer's bastard son to frame me for it. He was able to hide from the police because he developed an alternate personality, a sweet guy I ended up falling for and having some righteously kinky sex with until such time as the killer's personality took over and tried to torture me to death."

Everyone in the group gawked at her. She gestured dramatically. "Fortunately, I was saved by my surrogate uncle, the lead detective who also caught Vincent twenty years prior. Unfortunately, in the process of all this, my uncle and his partner, who was the smartest man I'd ever met, and my nephew . . . cousin . . . lover . . . all died. And after all of this, I find out that everything that had happened was by the design of Vincent's ghost, who was actually performing a complex, twenty-year-long ritual to bind Baron Samedi to him so the Baron couldn't dig my grave. Good thing I made a pact with Baron Samedi's wife, right?"

She ended her "story" by standing up and holding out her arms. "So now I am possessed by the queen of the *loa* and basically immortal until I find a way to destroy Vincent and set Baron Samedi free. The end."

Then she sat down, folded her arms, smacked her lips, and then smiled in a ridiculous pursed-lipped manner.

Everyone looked around in silence. You could have heard a mouse hiccup.

Finally, James Woods said, "Sam, I know what you're going through. Last night, the spirit of Ben Franklin came to me and said he needed to borrow my body to march on the Federal Government and push stronger gun control." His expression was completely serious.

"Right," replied Livingston in an equally sincere tone. "Well, I've been communicating with the Ghost of Christmas Past, and he's pissed about how the holiday is going all commercial."

Lay-Me snorted. "You are so full of shit, guys. I've got the spirit of Cleopatra inside of me, and she's been telling me it's time to make another Caesar!"

Preacher Man stood up, pointed at Lay-Me, and blurted out, "Flee fornication! 'Every sin that a man doeth is without the body. But he that committeth fornication sinneth against his own body.' 1 Corinthians, chapter 6, verse 18."

That pretty much ended any sense of civility in the room.

Lay-Me got up and started yelling at Preacher Man to "take his bible and stick it where the gerbils are hiding." Miss Prissy rocked back and forth, reminding herself exactly what Martha Stewart would do in this situation. James Woods got up and ripped down the "Crazy is only in your mind" letters while complaining that the music was unacceptable, even though there wasn't any. Stinky Palms started to pleasure himself. Gormless fell over. And Livingston stood on his chair and started shouting at the top of his lungs for everyone to shut up or Hitler would hear them.

Sam took in the mayhem and then glanced at Dr. Kindley. He was glaring at her.

She smirked. *Kiss off, asshole.*

Later that evening, Sam was in her dormitory room, which she shared with Miss Prissy and Lay-Me.

"Oh my God, Sam! That was beautiful!" Lay-Me sat on the edge of her bed, giggling. "I don't know who was serious and who wasn't, but when it got so bad that Dr. Kindley had to call for orderlies to break up the session, I nearly died laughing."

"It wasn't that funny," replied Miss Prissy from a desk near the window. She was on the fifth iteration of a letter to the Boston Pops, having discarded the others because "the i's weren't dotted properly." She continued, "After all, as Martha Stewart says, 'Without a sense of teamwork, I think it's really hard to build a great business.'"

Lay-Me blew a raspberry. "Seriously, Ursula. Stop quoting Martha Stewart or I'm going to make you eat your own letter."

Miss Prissy harrumphed loudly.

Sam remained silent, laying on her back and studying the ceiling. Dr. Kindley hadn't spoken to her since the session had ended, only nodding politely. Somehow, that was much worse. She was sure that he was going to try to retaliate.

Her thoughts were interrupted as Lay-Me leaned over her. She had a particularly cat-like smile, which reminded Sam of Cathy from the old comic strip of the same name.

"Whatcha thinking about?" Lay-Me's voice rang out cheerfully.

"Um, nothing really," Sam said. Despite Lay-Me having a reputation as a nymphomaniac, she was one of the more lucid and friendly people in the unit, but Sam had never really tried to chat with her until today.

"Uh-huh." Lay-Me sat next to her, so Sam scooted over to give her room. "You know, you really should learn to trust people more, Sam. Not everyone is out to screw you over."

Blinking, Sam rubbed her head, feeling her emotional defenses rise. "Meghan, don't take this the wrong way, but I've had a pretty unhappy life filled with a lot—and I mean a lot—of betrayal. So keeping people at a distance is all I know to do."

"No reason to be a bitch," Lay-Me said. "You think you're the only one with problems? Get over yourself, Sam." She lay back on her own bed.

Miss Prissy hunkered quietly over her letter.

Sam rolled on her side, her eyes resting on the only empty bed in the room. Her fourth roommate, a young, mousy, gaunt-faced girl nicknamed Little Squeaker, had been transferred. Little Squeaker had been shy and never opened up, and Dr. Kindley said he couldn't treat her. So now she was gone. Sam didn't want to end up like that. She needed to at least try to make a few friends.

Sitting up, Sam cleared her throat. "Sorry. I'll try to be more open."

Lay-Me winked. "Apology accepted. So, can we be friends?"

"We can try, yes," Sam said, pushing back her defensive feelings.

"Then can I ask you something, Sam? Because I really gotta know."

"Um, sure. Go ahead."

Lay-Me tossed the book to the side and then swung her legs around, leaning toward her. "Tell me, did you really sleep with your nephew?"

Sam felt her face heat up. "I shoulda known it would be about sex."

"Hey, hey, you promised! And I really wanna know."

Memories of her and Richie—and the passion between them—made her chest swell and her body ache with need. The sudden rush of desire took her by surprise, and she remembered her reaction to the hot male nurse. She wondered if it was Bridgette's doing that she got aroused so easily now.

She fanned herself. "Yes. Yes, that's right. His mother and mine were twins. But we didn't know it while we were doing it."

Lay-Me whistled. "Damn, that's messed up. So . . . what did you all do? How good was he? Was it as 'righteously kinky' as you said?"

Her mouth slowly opening, Sam stared at Lay-Me, who was waiting with bated breath. Miss Prissy's ears were burning red, and she was obviously trying to eavesdrop without appearing like it. The entire situation made Sam feel good, even if only for a moment. It was the closest thing to a "sex chat with the girls" she had ever experienced. She wondered if that was what a normal life would have been like.

Clearing her throat, she reached over and tweaked Lay-Me's nose. "Sorry. A lady never kisses and tells. And despite what you may think, I am a lady."

Miss Prissy snickered, and Lay-Me, who looked like a child denied candy, shrugged and went back to her book. "Buzzkill."

Then Sam saw what Lay-Me was reading. It was *The Pale Lantern* by Richard Fastellos. Turning away from the others, she pressed her hand to her chest. Just thinking about Richie was like a vise squeezing her heart. That pain was compounded by the knowledge that until she destroyed Vincent, Richie and the other ghosts would be unable to move on.

I promise, guys, I will never stop fighting.

Lying back down, she thought of Richie, Rodger, and Michael until she finally fell asleep.

It was late at night when Sam awoke to someone moving behind her. For a moment, every muscle in her body tensed up like a serpent ready to strike. Then she heard Lay-Me whisper, "Hush! You'll wake Ursula up!"

In the quiet of the dorm room, she could hear Miss Prissy sleeping soundly.

Sam grunted, still half-asleep. "Meghan, what are you doing? I nearly kicked your ass. I nearly. . ."

Her voice trailed off as she felt a hand run down her back and then cup her rear end. Her eyes widened, and her pulse quickened.

"I know you've been through a lot, Sam, and you never touch yourself. So I figure you need to relieve some stress."

Rolling onto her back, Sam arched an eyebrow. Lay-Me started stroking her stomach, avoiding her burns with expert precision.

"Meghan, you know I'm straight, right?"

Lay-Me tittered and leaned down, kissing her nose. Her breath was sweet like peppermint, and her voice was low and husky. "I kinda guessed. But you're putting out some serious 'sex me up' signals. You don't have to do anything. Let me do all the work."

Am I? Why am I like this now?

Lay-Me cupped Sam's chest and squeezed. "Have you gotten bigger? Feels like it."

Sam inhaled through her teeth and arched her back, feeling her skin heat up. But even as her body reacted, she felt a growing sense of unease. This was not something she wanted. "Come on. Knock it off."

With a sultry expression, Lay-Me slid her hand into Sam's underwear and then ran her long hair over her face. "Don't make me molest you, Sam. You're beautiful, and I like you. You trusted me and opened up. I really appreciate that. Let me thank you in the way I know how."

The fire continued to grow within Sam. Unlike with Richie, there was no emotion, just raw physical desire. *What's going on with me?*

Then she felt Lay-Me's hand slide between her legs. "Oh, Sam, you're so wet . . ."

In an instant, Sam felt that unease blossom into panic. She slapped Lay-Me's hand away so fast, it echoed. "Don't touch me!"

Miss Prissy snuffled in her sleep and rolled over.

For a few seconds, Lay-Me just sat there. Then her bottom lip started to tremble, tears forming in the corners of her eyes. "I'm . . . I'm sorry . . . I just wanted . . . I just . . ."

Sam sat up and took several deep breaths, her long blond hair falling over her face. Her entire body was on fire, her libido in overdrive, and she couldn't figure out why. Part of her wanted to pounce on Lay-Me and use her until there was nothing left. The other part felt so freaked out that she wanted to run. She had never been like this before.

"I thought it would help. I'm sorry, Sam, OK?" Lay-Me sobbed softly.

Watching her, Sam felt a deep pity. She didn't think the other girl could help herself. Maybe it was the only way she knew how to connect with others.

She hugged the other girl. "It's OK, Meghan. I'll forgive it this one time, but never touch me like that again without my permission. OK?"

Lay-Me nodded.

Sam flipped her hair out of her face and then wiped Lay-Me's tears away. "I'll come to you if I ever want anything like that. Otherwise, we're just friends."

"All right. Sorry. I won't do it again. Promise."

As Lay-Me went to bed, Sam rolled to her side. After a while, she reached down and gently touched herself. She was still incredibly excited. Was it because of Bridgette? The *Loa* Queen was also a *loa* of sexuality. *But if she's causing this, why can't I feel her possessing me?*

Chapter 4
A Cup of Coffee

Date: **Friday, October 9, 1992**
Time: **12:30 p.m.**
Location: **Tulane Psychiatric Intensive Care Unit**
Downtown New Orleans

"Hey, Sam. You OK? You look awful." Meghan sat down next to her in the cafeteria.

Sam shrugged, poking at her lunch of meatloaf and mashed potatoes. For the second day in a row, she hadn't slept well and was unable to eat. Her stomach had hurt to the point of nausea both mornings.

Meghan stuffed spoonfuls of mashed potatoes into her mouth. "If you're sick, you should tell Dr. Kindley. He can get you a normal doctor's visit."

"I guess." Even though Dr. Kindley had yet to retaliate over the outburst in group therapy, Sam was certain he'd mention it to Veronica during their checkup later that day. "But only if I still feel bad by tonight."

Truth was, she felt like she could throw up at any moment. The smell of the ketchup-stained meat and salty powdered potatoes just made it worse.

"Well, well, now. If it isn't little Sammy and little Meggy," a voice said with a thick Cajun accent.

Meghan looked up and then grimaced. "What the heck do you want, Herpes?"

"That's Herpin, little Meggy. Orderly Herpin."

Herpin, who ran their section, stood over them both. He had a reputation for treating patients with the utmost contempt. Sam couldn't grasp how anyone like him would be employed by a place as prestigious as Tulane.

"Sorry, Orderly Herpes." Meghan spoke in a nasal voice and then giggled, elbowing Sam.

As he glared at Meghan, his mustache bristling, Sam gagged. She really wanted to throw up. His odor was like spicy garlic, and today it was particularly overpowering.

Then he tapped her plate. "Hey, little Sammy. You aren't looking too good. And you've hardly touched any lunch. What's wrong, our food not good enough for you?"

She glowered, indignant feelings rising within her. The last thing she wanted was to have him around making her want to puke.

With a resounding slap of her hands against the table, she stood and locked eyes with him. Everyone in the cafeteria stopped and stared. "You wanna know what's wrong, you jerk? This crap you feed me has been making me sick for two days straight. I can't keep any of this slop down. And then you give us tapioca pudding in the evenings for dessert. Really? Tapioca pudding? Do I look like I'm seventy-five? And don't even get me started on the Salisbury steak you served for dinner last night. The only cow in that meal was the milk I drank, which I might add was one day away from turning. And your stinky garlic-ass self isn't helping! Seriously, dude, do you shower?"

Even as she ranted, she couldn't place where all this frustration and indignation at being treated so commonly was coming from. It was like a part of her that had always been asleep was waking up—on the wrong side of the bed.

Several of the orderlies were heading over, and most of the patients were standing slack-jawed. Herpin was prickling like a porcupine.

Meghan tentatively said, "Um, Sam? The orderlies don't decide what to serve . . ."

But Sam ignored everyone. "But all of this could be forgiven if you just served me some decent coffee."

The words flew from her lips like spittle. She couldn't stop now if she wanted.

She poured the contents of her Styrofoam cup onto the floor. "You call this crap coffee? The motor oil my dad and Rodger drank back in the seventies was better than this dredge. How a hospital in New Orleans can serve such crap is beyond me. I haven't had a decent cup of Community coffee and chicory since I got here, and quite frankly, Orderly Herpes, this coffee stinks almost as bad as you do!" She tossed the empty cup over her shoulder and dusted her hands off.

Then she realized that everyone in the cafeteria was either staring in shock or glaring in anger. *Oh, crap, I did it again!*

Herpin gaped incredulously at her and then raised his hand. "You whore, I oughta—"

"Orderly Herpin, stand down!" Dr. Kindley stood at the entrance to the cafeteria, looking cross. "Herpin, you are to clock out and go home at once. I will call you tonight."

Growling threateningly, Herpin stormed off, never taking his eyes off Sam.

Meghan stuck her tongue out. "Yeah, go stick it in your ass, Herp—"

"Miss Dubios, that is enough out of you. One more outburst and I will seclude you from the general population. Sit down now."

With a suddenly meek expression, she sat down. "Sorry, sir."

He then smiled at Sam. That fake smile she detested. "Miss Castille. Please come this way. I wish to have a word with you."

She clenched her jaw. Meghan squeezed her hand. "Hey. You be careful, OK?"

"I will. Don't worry." She grabbed her crutches and hobbled after him. Two orderlies escorted her to his office, where a rather strong-looking male nurse and Veronica were waiting.

Dr. Kindley motioned for her to sit next to Veronica. The nurse closed the door and stood guard, arms folded.

"Miss Castille. Do you know why you're here?"

Sam sniffed. "Because a psychotic doctor told a judge that I'm a whackjob."

He looked bored. "You mean Dr. Klein?"

Veronica cleared her throat. "Sam believes that Dr. Klein is manipulating the system to keep her here against her will."

Sam pointed as if to say "what she said." Despite being unable to get her commitment overturned, Veronica was a trustworthy advocate.

Tapping his fingers together, Dr. Kindley said, "Dr. Klein, well . . . I may not agree with his methods, but he has been Sam's psychiatrist for over twenty years. There is no one who knows her profile better."

"And yet she is utterly terrified of him," Veronica added.

With an obviously fake whimper, Sam sucked on her bottom lip. She then raised her voice to sound like a little girl. "He's a bad man, Dr. Kindley. I think he wants to toucha muh boobie."

When everyone else in the room peered at her, she settled down. "Sorry." As much as she wanted to lash out about her situation, this wasn't the time or the place for it.

Dr. Kindley folded his hands together and rested his chin on them. "Miss Castille, the reason you are here is because you burned down your house, tried to commit suicide, and seriously injured a nurse in the burn unit. In short, you have a very violent nature and are constantly endangering yourself and others."

Another sudden wave of nausea hit, and she fought to keep from vomiting.

"However, two days ago at group therapy, you said something very interesting."

As the nausea subsided, she asked, "Um, what did I say?"

"You said you were possessed by the Queen of the *Loa* and are immortal."

As Veronica regarded her with a confused expression, Sam felt another wave of nausea.

"And I think that pinpoints the nature of your delusion, Miss Castille," he said.

Sam swallowed the urge to throw up, mumbling, "It's not a delusion! I really am immortal. I really do have the Queen of the *Loa* inside of me."

Dr. Kindley leaned forward. "Then prove it. Make me, a doctor, throw away everything I know about reason and rationale to believe in ghosts and voodoo."

Closing her eyes, she once more felt for Bridgette. All the signs were there: She felt regal, she felt sexual, and she felt indignant. But she couldn't feel the *loa* queen within her like she could with Marinette.

She finally opened her eyes. "Sorry, I can't."

Veronica sighed and rubbed her face. "Lovely. Just lovely. Another roadblock."

Sitting back, Dr. Kindley opened Sam's file. "As I thought. Now, Miss Castille, I'm going to prescribe a new round of medication to help with the delusions and symptoms of paranoia. Also, we're going to move you out of group therapy and into private therapy for a period of two weeks. You'll still be allowed to mingle with the other patients, but if you cause any more uproars, I will seclude you. Understood?"

"Fine." Sam scowled at Veronica, who was still rubbing her face. *And what's up with her? Is she going to betray me now?*

Then he tapped the intercom on his desk. "Bring it in." A few moments later, an orderly entered holding a tray with a Styrofoam cup and several packets of non-dairy creamer and sugar.

She craned her neck. "What's that?"

He motioned the orderly toward her. "I believe that good will is the best way to incentivize. To show you my good will, I am giving you a cup of Community coffee with chicory. If you continue to behave, you'll get one cup a day instead of that 'motor oil' you detest so much. You may drink it however you wish."

"Are you serious?" She couldn't believe it. She examined the cup as if she expected it to try to eat her.

Veronica patted her gently on the knee. "Until we can come up with a new plan, Sam, I think it's best you stay on his good side. Go ahead and take it."

She glanced over at Veronica, perplexed. It was like her attitude had changed the moment the conversation had shifted to Bridgette. Now instead of fighting

Dr. Kindley, she was almost biding her time. *There's something funny with her. What's she really about?*

Looking back at the coffee, she exhaled. "OK, fine. Thanks." She took the cup, held it to her nose, and inhaled deeply. The smell of coffee and chicory, her favorite drink in the world, was heady and strong.

A moment later, she threw up.

The coffee spilled to the ground along with her vomitus. She fell to her knees. It was the scent of the coffee that had done it. And as everyone around her rose to their feet, a light clicked in her head. *Oh, my God!*

She'd been sick every morning. Food she usually loved made her sick. She fell back, eyes widening, as the realization sank in. She and Richie had made love so many times, and not once with protection. How could it not happen?

I've been so screwed up that I hadn't noticed my period never came.

Then she touched her stomach. Within seconds, she felt a small but powerful spark moving through her fingers. Once more, the world around her became muted, but instead of her senses traveling outward, they traveled in. And deep within her womb, she felt it.

A pair of heartbeats.

"Oh, my God! I'm pregnant!"

It didn't take long to test Sam for pregnancy. Of course the test came back positive, and when the ultrasound revealed two sets of embryos attached to two different placentas, it confirmed what she had suspected—that she had twins. Despite knowing that she was holding the products of incest, she felt a sudden and immense joy. She wasn't sure if it was biological, emotional, or what—and she didn't care. In the blink of an eye, she had become a mother.

"Do you have names for them yet?" asked Meghan as she moved one of her bishops, capturing a pawn. The other patients from her group crowded around them in the common room as they played. In the background, another group was watching the first *Halloween* movie. The room had been scented with a pumpkin-spice candle to celebrate the upcoming season. A few of the nicer orderlies walked around, and the atmosphere was quite festive.

Sam shook her head, holding her left hand protectively over her stomach as if it were the only thing keeping her unborn children from becoming a dream. "I haven't given it that much thought, actually. I was thinking of waiting until I find out if they're boys or girls or one of each, ya know?"

From the television, the *Halloween* theme started playing.

"You shouldn't wait too long," said Miss Prissy. "I mean, as Martha Stewart says, 'When you're through changing, you're through.'"

"Oh, cut it out with the Martha Stewart quotes, Ursula," said Livingston, who then reached over and tapped one of Sam's knights. "You should move this one. He's ready to battle."

"Gracious, Lou! Let Sam play the game herself," said Miss Prissy.

The group around the television gasped as one of the movie's scarier scenes played out.

Livingston blew a raspberry. "All right, but I'm next to play. I tried playing checkers with Brian, and you can guess how that went." Nearby, Gormless stared blankly at a checkers board that lacked any pieces.

As everyone chuckled, Sam felt her spirits lift inch by inch. Even if it was only due to her pregnancy, it was nice to finally feel like she belonged.

She made her move just as the group around the television squealed. Michael Meyers hacked away at one of the many victims in the film. Meghan looked disgusted. Then she slapped Livingston's hand as he reached for one of Sam's pieces.

Once the screaming settled down, Stinky Palms said, "Yeah, half-naked, nubile teenagers aside, is it really appropriate to be showing that movie in here? Just saying."

Preacher Man snorted. "'Then said Jesus unto him, Put up again thy sword into his place: for all they that take the sword shall perish with the sword.' Gospel of Matthew, chapter 26, verse 52."

With a snarky laugh, James Woods patted him on the back. "I'm with Drake on this one. Hey, you guys! Turn it down! We've got a pregnant woman over here."

Sam's ears burned, and she tried to meld into the chair as he pointed at her like she was the most important person in the world. Someone in the group apologized and turned the sound down. People were really looking out for her now that she had a pair of meatloaves in the oven.

Even Dr. Kindley had been going out of his way to accommodate her. She had been moved into her own private room and put on a specific, healthy diet. Also, Veronica said that she would ensure Sam's file reflected a hormonal imbalance in correlation with her psychotic episodes. *Maybe this means I can be happy now? I'd like that.*

The game finally ended with Sam winning, Meghan declaring that she preferred checkers over chess, and Livingston and Stinky Palms getting into a disagreement over who would play next. But then the orderlies declared that it was fifteen minutes to lights-out and everyone needed to get back to their rooms.

As the patients started shuffling out, Meghan handed Sam her crutches. "Hey, need any help getting back to your room?"

Sam pulled herself to her feet, shaking her head. "Nah. I'm good. Thanks again for playing with me, though."

"You're welcome. See you tomorrow then, girl!" Meghan blew a kiss and skipped off.

By now, the room was mostly empty, with one orderly putting away the television. As Sam limped toward the exit, she heard a voice say, "They killed her."

She stopped in her tracks. Looking around, she saw that the room was empty save for the lone orderly and Gormless, who was still at the checkers table. He was motionless and drooling, having a catatonic episode.

Blinking, she approached. "Brian? Did you say something to me?"

He remained silent, a puddle of drool forming on the checker-board.

"Right. Now I'm hearing things. And I can't take anything but Tylenol for nine months." She turned back around to leave.

Then she heard someone again. "They killed her. She told me."

Her brow tense, she spun around. "You know, Brian, it's really poor taste to pretend like you're . . ."

But Gormless wasn't there.

Coldness descended over her. Leaning down, she examined the checkerboard. In the puddle of drool was a small charm on a chain—a pink mouse, one she knew she had seen before. Wiping it off, she scanned the room just in time to see Gormless shuffling out. With a soft sigh, she pocketed the charm and limped back to her room.

Once inside, she sat on her bed and took out the charm, dangling it between her fingers. Nostalgia suddenly coursed through her, and she rested it on her bedside table. *I need to hold Mom's charm now.*

Opening the drawer in the bedside table, she took out a red, plastic high-heeled shoe charm on a chain. It had been melted so badly, its original form was almost lost. The golden lettering for "Comus" was mostly indistinguishable. But despite the damage, just looking at it calmed her down. It was the only possession she treasured. It was a keepsake from her mother that she'd had to beg and plead with Veronica to get back.

She squeezed it gently. In her scarred left hand, it felt natural. It was times like this when she wished she had known her mother, who was said to be soft-spoken, gentle, and kind. *Oh, Mom, how would I have turned out if you had raised me?*

Then she realized she was crying. Wiping the tears away, she pressed it to her belly, her throat still tight. "Feel that, little ones? That's your grandmother. I won't make the mistakes my parents made. I'll be there for you. I promise. Mama will be there when you need her the most."

Drying her eyes on her sleeve, she lay down and stared at the charm.

It was late at night when Sam awoke with a start, still holding her shoe charm. The lights to her room were off, and the hallway lights were dimmed for nighttime as usual. She shivered, a chill all around her. Pulling her robe on, she hobbled to the doorway, intent on finding an orderly and complaining about the temperature. But it was warm and cozy in the hallway. The difference between there and her room was like night and day.

"What the hell?" She slipped back into her room. It was frigid and eerily silent.

Going back to her bed, she rubbed her face, trying to make sense of what was happening. The silence of the room was broken by a scratching sound beside her. She examined the bedside table. The pink mouse charm was slowly inching across the wooden surface, making scratching sounds, until it reached the edge and dropped to the floor. She watched for a moment, transfixed, before exhaling nervously and picking it up. Immediately, she felt a shiver in her shoulders and the sensation of being watched. Something was here. Something spiritual. And it wanted her attention.

She held onto the charm and hobbled over to the bathroom. Leaning over the sink, she splashed cool water on her face, taking a moment to recollect herself. *Don't stress over it. You've been feeling spirits all around since the fire. You'll figure it out.*

With a yawn, she gazed at her reflection. There were dark circles under her eyes. *I need more sleep.*

Then she patted herself dry and turned back into her room, coming face-to-face with a white, translucent apparition staring back at her with hollow, lifeless eyes.

Gasping, Sam stumbled back, falling square on her butt onto the toilet lid.

"Christ, what the hell?" She hadn't seen a spirit physically manifest since the battle in her townhome. This time, however, instead of a monstrous *loa*, it was what she figured a ghost would look like: pale, translucent, and misty. Hopping up, she inspected it closely. It was a girl, no older than her late teens, with a shaved head and a gaunt face. Her eyes were sunken in, and her mouth was sewn shut. Her body faded into mist at her torso. Sam could swear that she had seen this girl before.

"Who are you?" she asked, barely above a whisper.

The apparition pointed at Sam's hand, the one wrapped around the pink mouse charm.

Instantly, she knew who it was. A girl who had once owned that very same charm. A girl who was quiet and shy and never really fit in. A girl who went missing without any explanation other than that "she couldn't be treated." Sam flipped the charm in between her fingers.

"I know you, you're . . ."

But the apparition was gone. However, Sam didn't need confirmation. She knew who it was: Laura Levron. Little Squeaker.

"My God. She's dead. Little Squeaker is dead! They killed her!"

Chapter 5
One and the Same

Date: **Sunday, October 11, 1992**
Time: **9:00 a.m.**
Location: **Tulane Psychiatric Intensive Care Unit**
Downtown New Orleans

"What did you find out?" Sam asked Meghan. In the corner of the common room, the two quietly pretended to play checkers.

"Well, I had to do a few favors to get the information. The official statement is that Laura was transferred to the Evergreen Sanatorium. It's a long-term mental rehabilitation facility." Meghan kept her voice hushed, leaning in toward Sam.

Sam frowned. "That doesn't make any sense. Wasn't she from Lafayette? Wouldn't it have been easier to transfer her to Acadia-Vermillion Hospital?" She wished that she herself had been sent there. Then she'd be under Dr. Lazarus's care.

Meghan shrugged. "I think neither one of us have a freaking clue what's going on."

Rubbing her face, Sam groaned. "Something's not right. The whole story stinks. I'm convinced that they did something to her."

"Right, like that makes sense. Look, I know that some people here are shitwads, but what you're talking about is plain illegal. You're assuming a lot just from a mouse charm and something Brian drooled out."

With a grunt, Sam leaned back. She couldn't just say she'd seen Little Squeaker's ghost. "Well, I'd be more comfortable if we could look at her file. You said you could help me out with that, right?"

Meghan hummed, abandoning the fake checkers game. "Sam, come on. This isn't like *The Pale Lantern* or something. We can't just go traipsing around Dr. Kindley's office. If we get caught, we'll be in serious trouble!"

The reference to Richie's book made Sam laugh. When Meghan wrinkled her brow, she said, "It's just ironic that you're using something written by the father of my children as a basis of comparison, hun."

"Well, little Sammy, what's got you so giggly-giggly?"

Sam stopped as someone slapped her with a wall of stink. Covering her nose, she watched as Herpin stood there, grinning down at her. Bits of broccoli peeked out from between his teeth. She had hoped Dr. Kindley would have fired him for the cafeteria incident, but he had only been suspended for a few days.

"God, Herpes, you stink!" Meghan covered both her nose and mouth. "Where do you bathe, the city landfill?"

"You're cute, Meggy, really cute. I just want you two to know that I've got my eye on both of you. So, behave, ya hear?" He patted them on the shoulders and stalked off.

Closing her eyes, Sam pushed back the impulse to retch. It took her several seconds to calm down her stomach. "I really can't stand that guy. Please don't tell me you've ever traded favors with him."

Meghan snickered. "As if I would. Besides, the staff here is too afraid of getting canned to screw a patient."

Sam leaned back and deeply exhaled. "Well, that's a relief . . . Wait a minute. What kind of favors did you do to get the information about Laura?"

"I'm told I have a very talented mouth." Meghan winked.

"And that's what I get for asking."

"Well, Miss Dumont, I think we can say Miss Castille is on the road to a full recovery. But it will take time. I know she's anxious to get out of here, but we're at a point in the treatment where rushing it will be detrimental to her healing. Wouldn't you agree, Sam?"

Dr. Kindley's voice stirred Sam from her thoughts, mostly regarding Little Squeaker.

Looking away, she nodded. *He knows I'm not paying attention.* The Styrofoam cup of coffee and chicory steamed in her hands. She sipped it. It was still hard to get down at times, but drinking it reminded her of home. It helped that she liked to drink it black, which was the healthiest way.

Veronica, who was seated next to her, had been taking notes during the session. "I agree. But I also think that Sam is doing remarkably well. It seems that discovering she was pregnant sparked a very positive change in her. And I think we'd be remiss to ignore that."

"I agree," he said, playing with the gold pin on his lapel. "Sometimes, the sudden responsibility of parenthood can have a positive transformation on a person. I have high hopes for her."

Sam sipped her coffee again.

"Sam, what do you think?" Veronica was looking at her.

She offered a rehearsed, pleasant expression. "Yes, I feel optimistic about things, just like Dr. Kindley said." It was a canned response that required very little thought. She had since learned to just tell him what he wanted to hear. But she knew he'd hurt Little Squeaker. She was going to get proof and ruin him.

Dr. Kindley motioned for the nurse to open the door. "Wonderful! Well, I think we're done for today. Miss Castille, Miss Dumont, I'd like to see you both again tomorrow at the same time, and again on Tuesday and Wednesday. After that, I think we can go to once every other day. We'll have her back in group before the end of the month."

Finishing her coffee, Sam reached for her crutches. As Veronica passed by, she patted Sam's arm and spoke in a low, hushed voice. "We're all on your side, Sam. Don't worry. It will work out in the end."

Then she left, leaving Sam to wonder again what she meant. That was a bit cryptic.

She was halfway out of the office when Dr. Kindley stopped her. "Miss Castille, I'd like to speak with you a moment, if I may."

Cautiously, she backed up, realizing that she was alone in the room with him. She was pretty sure that was against the rules. He sat on the corner of his desk, resting his hands in his lap and smiling in that fake manner she hated so much.

"Yes, Doctor?"

He cleared his throat. "Your little friend, Miss Dubios, was very busy last night. She put one of my men in a very compromising position—three or four, actually."

Uh-oh. Meghan got busted!

"Your friend was inquiring about a former patient of ours, Miss Levron. I just wanted to assure you that she was a legitimate transfer. She wasn't responding to the treatment here, and I felt she'd do better at a different, longer-term facility." It was like he was daring her to disagree.

She masked her growing concern for her friend. "Well, I'm glad you cleared that up, Doctor, but I didn't have any doubts about your judgment. I'll be sure to set Meghan straight. I'll miss Laura, but I'm sure she'll get better at . . . where did she go again?"

Dr. Kindley chortled coldly. "Oh, that's not really any of your business, Miss Castille." Then he headed back behind his desk and picked up a folder stuffed with papers. "And don't concern yourself with Miss Dubios, either. After her last little escapade, I no longer feel that I can treat her, either. She'll be transferred as well, at the end of the week."

Sam felt a sudden chill. Her jaw tightened and her body tensed. He was going to send Meghan to the same place he'd sent Little Squeaker. *They're gonna kill her!*

Opening his desk, he put the folder away. She watched him, taking note of which drawer. He caught her gaze and smiled even more broadly. "That will be all, Miss Castille. Keep up the good work. I'm sure you'll recover soon."

Her gaze drifted back to the drawer. She had to look at those files tonight.

"Of course, Dr. Kindley. Have a nice day."

Hurriedly, she left the office and searched for Meghan. But it was too late. She was already gathered for group, and the orderlies wouldn't let her enter the room. Her stomach sank as Meghan waved to her from the circle of chairs and blew her a kiss.

"Love you, Sam!"

Dr. Kindley brushed past her. "Miss Castille, you look exhausted. Would you kindly go rest in your room?"

The heaviness in her gut only grew as she hobbled back to her room. Tearing up, she lay down, facing the wall. Meghan was running out of time, and her only chance of surviving was for Sam to find proof of Dr. Kindley's deeds and pass it to Veronica. *I need to do this tonight or Meghan is dead!*

She felt herself spiraling into a vortex of self-doubt, and she stopped it by repeating, "I'm better than this," over and over again.

When the last tears had fallen, she rubbed her face against the pillow as if it were Richie's chest. After a few moments, she realized she was both flushed and frustrated. The stress was gnawing at her. With that revelation came a desire to relieve the tension inside her.

Well, I haven't done it in days. I might as well while everyone is busy.

Throwing on the covers, she opened her robe and slipped her hand between her legs. She was already smoldering, and more than anything, she wanted to feel another person within her. Closing her eyes, she started to expertly move her fingers. Within seconds, the rhythm was perfect, and she was moaning softly and steadily. She'd gotten the whole thing down to a science.

Richie, I miss you so much. Where have you gone?

She wanted nothing more than for him to be there. But the last time she saw him, he was with Michael and Rodger's ghosts, trying to hold back Vincent's guardians. One of them just happened to be the ghost of Edward Castille.

I need you, honey. I love you. Richie!

When she reached her peak, she silently cried his name. Then she wept until she fell asleep, hugging her pillow as she had once hugged the man she loved.

It wasn't until after dinner that Sam was able to talk to Meghan alone. She had decided not to tell her friend about her impending transfer, figuring that if they could get the proof she needed, it would be stopped. So she only insisted that she get into Dr. Kindley's office that night. Even though Meghan tried several times to convince her to abandon the plan, Sam wouldn't hear of it. Meghan finally agreed to break in after the graveyard shift had started.

And so, late that night, Meghan led her through the hallways, using the same paths she used for her secret trysts. Sam's injured leg significantly slowed their progress, so it took them nearly an hour to avoid the orderlies and reach Dr. Kindley's office. They both hunched down in the alcove by the door, hidden in the shadows, except for Sam's leg sticking out into the hallway.

"This took way too long," she whispered.

Meghan stuck out her tongue. "Yeah, well, I've never had to sneak around with a pregnant woman on crutches. It's amazing that we didn't get caught because of how loud you move. Oh, wait, it's not amazing. I'm amazing."

Sam felt her ears burn. "Sorry."

"By the way, if your plan is to trip anyone walking by, you're doing great."

She tucked her leg in. "Sorry again."

With a sigh, Meghan took out a small key and unlocked the office door.

That made Sam blink. "How do you . . .? How do you have a key to Dr. Kindley's office?"

"You don't think Dr. Kindley keeps me around because of my award-winning personality, do you?" Meghan fluffed her hair.

Immediately, a nagging feeling arose in Sam's gut. Something wasn't right. Why would Dr. Kindley transfer Meghan if they were having sex?

"Hey, Meghan?"

"Mmm. Yeah, Sam?"

"Is there something you're not telling me? About you and Dr. Kindley?"

"What, other than I go down on him sometimes?"

"Meghan, please." The very thought of that repulsed Sam.

Then Meghan got very quiet. "You don't trust me. Is that it? You think I'm just some stupid slut who doesn't care about anything other than sex, sex, sex." She backed away, her face tightening. She looked genuinely upset.

"Look, Sam, I've screwed up a lot of things in my life. I lost the guy I was engaged to by sleeping with his father and brother at the same time. I've screwed every one of my bosses to get bonuses and perks. And I once hosted a gang-bang with the Saints' defensive line. I know I'm a useless piece of trash."

Tears trickled down her cheeks. "But, damn it, you are the only person to force me to connect as a friend and not a lover. Everyone else here—and I mean everyone—fucks me and then discards me. But not you. You care about me. That means something. I won't betray you. I promise!"

Sam felt a lump form in her throat. It grew as Meghan poured out her heart. *God, I never knew.* She was so wrapped up in her own problems, she forgot that others were suffering, too.

She pulled Meghan into her arms. "I'm sorry I doubted you. I'm just scared. Everyone I've ever trusted has betrayed me." She kissed the top of her head.

"Well, I'm not everyone," Meghan said, rubbing her face against Sam's chest. "You stupid bitch, I won't betray you! Now go in there and get Laura's info so we can get out of here."

Getting up, Sam entered the office and quietly hobbled over to the desk. She located the drawer she recalled Dr. Kindley using earlier that day. She was surprised to find it unlocked. Opening it, she took out the first folder.

It had the name "Laura Levron" on the cover. Underneath it was another folder with the name "Meghan Dubios." And underneath that was a folder with the name "Samantha Castille."

This was it. Something here had to incriminate this son-of-a-bitch. She felt her heart start to race as she opened the first one.

She wasn't expecting what she saw.

Photographs. Dozens of photographs that were taken from the streets, from windows, and from the doorways of hospital rooms. Dozens of photographs of a woman getting in and out of cars, moving about her house, sitting on her back patio, riding the streetcar, and more.

But these were not photographs of Meghan, or even of Little Squeaker.

They were all photographs of her.

What the hell?

She opened the next folder, and it was more of the same, photographs and photographs of her, surveillance on her as early as the 1980s. Her in college. Her in her townhome. Her out with Jacob. Her out with Richie. Her going to Angola with Rodger.

Everything was of her.

What's going on?

Hands now shaking, she opened the last folder. In it were notes, reports, maps with her walking routes, spreadsheets with her every movement throughout the day, and discarded receipts at places like coffee shops and restaurants. Some of the papers were decades old, faded in the middle and torn around the edges. Someone had spent the last twenty years tracking her almost every day.

"What the hell is this?" Sam asked out loud, her voice quaking. "What the . . ."

Then she saw it. In the right-hand corner of each folder was the same crest Dr. Kindley had on his lapel. Underneath it were the words "The Knight Priory of Saint Madonna."

"No fucking way!" She fell back on the chair. It was too much, too surreal, too positively awful to be real. This had to be a bad dream.

"Hey there, Little Sammy," came Herpin's voice from the doorway.

He cackled wickedly, holding some sort of a baton. Behind him, another orderly restrained Meghan. She struggled. "Let me go! Sam, I had no idea this would happen! Sam, I swear it, I—"

Herpin backhanded her in the face hard enough to knock her out. "Shut up, slut! You were just supposed to keep an eye on her, not get all cozy. Useless whore."

He then advanced on Sam. "Dr. Kindley told me not to hurt you unless you resist, seeing as how you got two incest babies in there."

She pressed back against the bookcase behind the desk, her hands shaking and her heart pounding against her chest.

His expression grew more menacing. "I beg you, though, please resist."

The look in his eyes was downright vicious. The instinct to protect her two unborn children melted away any desire to fight. She held up her hands. "OK. OK. Please, don't hit me. I'll go quietly."

As he cornered her, his sickening garlic stench started to make her gag. "Mmmm, your pussy smells good, Sammy. When I started working here, I thought little Meggy was the sweetest piece of ass. But you—yeah, you're a real whore fucking your nephew, aren't you?"

He rubbed his baton against her breasts and reached down to lift up her gown. She felt a swell of outraged pride well up inside her. It was overpowering. *This paltry little germ thinks he can just touch me? Who the hell does he think he is?*

Before she realized it, she had spat a rather phlegm-filled wad on his face.

The silence as he wiped the spittle away was deafening. When his face reddened, she knew she had made a mistake.

"You stupid cunt!" He smashed her in the face with his baton, the force sending her reeling to the side. She momentarily blacked out from the impact as teeth and bits of flesh flew out. Instinctively, she put her hands over her stomach to protect her children.

"You nasty whore!" He hit her again, this time in her left leg. Crying out, she stumbled forward into his grasp.

"Whoa, Josh, what the hell, dude!" the orderly restraining Meghan called out. Both were staring in horror at what was happening.

"Shut it, Steve," Herpin said as he pushed Sam against Dr. Kindley's desk. "This uppity bitch has it coming. Just hold that other skank back."

As she fell against the desk, objects spilling to the ground, he bent her over. Then he pushed her underpants down, lifted up her robe, and kicked her feet apart. His intention was very clear.

God, no. This can't be happening!

"No! Don't touch her, you bastard!" Having come to, Meghan jerked forward, only to have the other orderly pull her back. "No, no! Rape me if you have to. Tear me up! Just don't hurt her! Please!"

"Oh, shut up, you tramp," Herpin said. He ran his fingers over Sam's backside and slapped her cheeks. "You have such a nice ass, bitch. I'm going to enjoy ripping it up. Maybe if I go deep enough, your incest babies can lick my tip!"

When she felt him touch her rear, her entire body tensed. Seeing the panic-stricken expression on Meghan's face and the confused but fearful look on the other orderly, Sam realized that no one was going to stop Herpin from raping her. That realization, along with the deep-seated instinct to protect her children, ignited something within her that she hadn't felt in months. A fire within her: The same fire that had burned away the paralysis when Dallas was torturing her, the same fire that had burned within her when Vincent tried to re-possess her with Marinette, and the same fire that had burned within her when she accepted Bridgette's offer.

Bridgette's offer.

Time around Sam started to slow to a crawl as she remembered that Bridgette hadn't offered a mere possession. Their pact was something much more complicated. It was a symbiosis. A fusion of souls.

The fire within her flared into an inferno as she finally understood what had happened that night in her townhome. It was why she was so sensitive to spirits. It was why she could communicate with ghosts. It was why her sense of sexuality had spiked out of control. It was why she got so incensed when others offended her.

She finally realized where Bridgette had gone.

She didn't vanish. She's not inside me. She is me! We are one and the same. I am Sam and I am Bridgette. I am the queen of the loa*!*

And in that instant, her will to fight returned. With all her might, she focused on activating the power within her. Time had already slowed down to a crawl. Every molecule of air hitting her body, every drop of foul sweat from Herpin, every brush of his oily skin over her flesh, every scent from every person in the room, and every sound all floated into her in the finest detail. It was like that night in her townhome. She felt like a god.

Then she heard him unzip his pants.

Letting out a deep roar, she turned and, with a strength and speed that made him look like he was walking through oil, punched him square in the jaw.

It ripped right off.

Time and sensation returned to normal as Herpin, whose jaw had flown across the room, gawked at her, wide-eyed in fear, his tongue flopping around his neck, blood and spit pouring out. With a gurgle, he fell to the ground, writhing. A few seconds later, he stopped moving and let out a final burbling wheeze. His eyes went dark.

She sniffed and spat on him. "Never touch me without my permission."

Searing pain then tore through her body, like someone had set fire to her insides. She was barely able to cover her stomach in time as she hit the ground, every muscle seizing. Then she saw two men in black uniforms holding cattle prods. They had the same crest as Dr. Kindley's lapel pin on what looked like black military-style berets.

Every time she moved, they shocked her long and hard. She couldn't concentrate long enough to use her power again. She couldn't even contact the spirits around her to summon them.

Then Dr. Kindley entered the office. He seemed very displeased. "Unbelievable. You give a guy a second chance, and he tries to rape the Princess."

She shrieked as they shocked her again. Why had he called her "Princess"?

The other orderly was still holding Meghan. "Dr. Kindley, what's going on? What just happened?" His eyes were wide with shock and panic.

"Sorry, you're not a part of the inner circle." Dr. Kindley took out a pistol and shot the orderly in the head. "And you're fired."

Meghan squealed and fell into a huddled position.

Wiping the gun off with a silk handkerchief, he walked over to Sam. "I'm very sorry, Miss Castille, for what Herpin tried to do. But at the same time, I'm very glad. It was amazing what you just did. Truly amazing."

Feeling her control start to return, she tried to stand. One of the guards jabbed her again with the cattle prod. The electricity burned through her, causing every muscle to tighten and spasm. She whimpered in pain, holding her stomach, desperate to keep her children safe.

Dr. Kindley snarled at them, his professional countenance gone. "Cut that out! Remember, you hurt her children and you're dead."

"Sorry, sir. But to be safe, you should sedate her now."

One of the guards motioned toward Meghan. Two more guards had picked up her and restrained her. Her face was pale, and she had vomited on the front of her gown. "What about this one?"

With a dismissive wave, Dr. Kindley said, "Let Dr. Klein deal with her. She's seen too much to live."

As the guards pulled her away, Meghan yelled, "Sam! Help me! Please, help me!"

Sam's heart ached. *No!* she screamed in her mind. *Don't! She has nothing to do with this!* But she couldn't speak. They wouldn't let her.

"I wouldn't worry about her, Princess," said Dr. Kindley, filling a syringe with a clear liquid. "Dr. Klein's going to have a field day with you. If it were up to me, I'd keep you here. But sadly, I don't get a say. For now, I'm just a cog in the wheel, despite my perfect lineage."

She eyed him wildly. *What is that stuff? Don't, you bastard! My babies!*

While he leaned over her, finding a vein in her arm, she focused on the pin on his lapel. Now she knew that it was the crest of the Knight Priory. He was a member.

"Although, if I play my cards right, I'll run this whole thing before too long." He stuck in the needle and injected the syringe's contents.

She cried out, still unable to speak. Every part of her hurt.

"Don't worry, this won't damage your children. And if it makes you feel any better, I now believe you are possessed by Bridgette."

A murky blanket descended over her mind, and her vision started to fade.

"Too bad the others don't believe. They never have, no matter how long they've been watching you."

Sam lost consciousness with those words in her mind. The Knight Priory had been watching her for the last twenty years.

And now they had her.

Cold November Rain

(Dixie Olivier's Story)

Chapter 6
Blood Trails

Date: **Monday, October 26, 1992**
Time: **10:00 p.m.**
Location: **Desire Street**
New Orleans Ninth Ward

The nighttime air was cool and damp. At any moment, it could start raining. Lieutenant Dixie Olivier felt the pressure in the air. It covered her like a wet tapestry, pushing relentlessly on her ears and up into her sinuses. The coldness bit at the back of her throat, and the wetness made her hair clump in strands. But even worse, she felt it pinch the nerves along the stump of her left arm.

She massaged her stump, grimacing. It had been a little over two months since she had lost her arm at the New Orleans wharf during an arrest gone wrong. Even though it would be at least a few more weeks before she could be fitted with a prosthetic—bureaucratic red tape at its best—her physical therapy was coming right along. But no amount of treatment or medication could ease the phantom pains or relieve the bite of cold weather.

Detective Scott Rivette came up alongside her. "Hey, Lieutenant, you gonna be all right to handle this?" His hands were stuffed into his black duster, while his long hair was pulled back in a ponytail. A menthol cigarette rested between his lips, and his expression was one of concern.

She smiled. For a moment, he reminded her of a younger Rodger Bergeron. It was a welcome memory. "I'll be fine, Rivette. And please call me Dixie."

"Only if you call me Scott or Captain America." He puffed smugly on his cigarette.

"Ha! OK, then, Scott. Let's not start playing superhero with a crime scene." Then she jerked her head toward the shotgun house before them. About half a dozen police cars were circled around it, their flashing lights illuminating the block. Neighbors were sitting on their porches, watching from their windows, and even standing in the streets. Everyone's attention was focused on them.

"So what happened?"

He stroked his goatee. "Landry's inside with the crime lab unit. It's a massacre, Dixie. We haven't seen anything this brutal since, you know, the wharf."

Unconsciously, she touched her stump again, remembering the unadulterated slaughter. The assassin Blind Moses had killed almost every officer and SWAT member there. If it hadn't been for Sam's miraculous intervention, the fatalities would have been even higher.

"Um, did you want to go inside?" Rivette asked.

She quickly pushed those thoughts away, especially the ones about Sam. Thinking of her was too painful, and she needed to concentrate on work.

"Yeah. Let's go take a look."

With a nod, Rivette tossed the cigarette down and ground it out. Then he led her past the uniformed officers, who were either taking reports from the neighbors or assisting the crime lab unit. "Hope your stomach's empty."

The inside was pure butchery. The shag carpet had been soaked in blood until it was squishy, and the faux-wood–panel walls looked as if as someone had swung a red paintbrush around. One of the floor lamps—the white plastic kind found at places like Wal-Mart—was striped red like a macabre candy cane. Even a wooden console table, covered with family and individual photos, was covered in blood. The sheer ferocity of the attack made Dixie shake her head. Even after the wharf incident and the new Bourbon Street Ripper, carnage like this was still quite unsettling.

"What can you tell me about the victims?" she asked, taking note of the bodies. In the front room was a middle-aged African American man lying on a vinyl recliner chair. His throat had been slit, and his large, hairy belly and chest had multiple stab wounds. In the middle of the hallway was a teenage girl lying on her stomach. The backs of her knees had been slashed, and blood pooled around her neck—likely another cut throat. The second-to-last doorway was open, and a heavy-set woman was kneeling lifelessly against the frame. Her throat had also been slit, the front of her nightgown soaked red.

Along the way, Rivette read from a small notebook. "Let's see. They were all members of the Davis family. The one in the front was the father, Jordan. The mother, Brianna, was killed in the doorway of the master bedroom. The eldest son, Elijah, was killed in the kitchen. The eldest daughter, Kiara, was killed in the hallway. And the youngest son, Xavier, was killed in his bedroom."

Half paying attention, Dixie observed how the blood splattered. The streaks seemed to be originating from the back of the house, in the kitchen. *That must have been where the killer started.*

When they entered the kitchen, she caught sight of Landry, Rivette's portly partner. He was kneeled over the body of a teenage boy, helping Crime Lab take pictures. The boy was on his back, partially under a small dining table. His throat had also been cut, and there were puddles of blood at his feet. The acrid scent was everywhere. Gagging a little, she covered her nose and mouth with a scented handkerchief. The sweet smell of coconut soon filled her senses, and she returned to scrutinizing the room. Scene analysis was her forte, and this scene had a lot to tell her. There was such ferocity in these splatters. The killer had an inhuman amount of strength and rage.

Rivette waved at his partner. "Hey, Landry, anything interesting?"

Standing up, Landry wiped his brow with the sleeve of his jacket. He was already sweating profusely and smelled like an old pulled-pork sandwich. "Other than Halloween coming a little early this year? No, nothing special, Scott, Lieutenant. Looks like someone just decided to slaughter the Davis family."

"Just call me Dixie, please."

She continuously had to remind all of her subordinates to call her by her first name. While she was grateful for the promotion and the perks it offered, she hated the formality that came with it. So long as they listened when given an order, she wanted them to feel at ease around her.

"Right, Dixie, sorry." He bowed, and then returned to assisting Crime Lab.

"Looks like it's going to be another late night," Rivette said.

"Yeah. Seems that way." She returned to examining the room, scanning for anything that would tell the story behind the grisly murders.

Rivette started pacing in front of her. "It's damn disgusting, Dixie. We bust our asses every day, double since the New Ripper case. I can't even remember the last time I got a full day off. You'd think by now we'd get some slack. But nope, not at all."

"We've been over this," she said, starting to tune him out. "We lost too many men at the wharf. Until we get more qualified detectives, half-days off are the best anyone can hope for."

As he went on to complain about the mayor's recent round of budget cuts, she ignored him completely, focusing on the scene instead. Something was amiss. She could feel it. Nibbling on her thumb, which she often did when deep in thought, she examined Elijah's body. His legs were bent in an uncomfortable position, as if he had fallen back from being unable to support his weight. She knelt slowly, supporting herself on the table, her balance off due to the missing half of her arm. It was annoying. Once on her knees, she tilted one of Elijah's legs. As she suspected, the backs of his knees had been sliced. *That takes a lot of force. But why do that?*

Standing, she hurried into the hallway. Rivette followed her, still ranting. "And the worst part is that everyone in charge, from the mayor to Commander Ouellette, doesn't seem to understand that there are even more crazies now. It's like ever since the wharf, people aren't afraid to just wholesale murder each other."

"One second, Scott," she said, checking the rest of the victims. Both the mother and the sister also had the backs of their knees slashed, while the youngest son had been decapitated.

"None of them have defensive wounds. They never saw the killer coming."

"Hey, Dixie, are you listening to me?" Rivette seemed annoyed.

"Back off, Detective," she said, glaring at him. "My open-door policy does not extend to murder scenes. We can talk about your issues another time."

He held out his hands. "Sorry. I was out of line."

Landry, who had joined them, cleared his throat. "Dixie, it looks like we also have a kidnapping."

Dixie snapped her head toward him. "Excuse me?"

Flustered, he took out a handkerchief and wiped his sweaty, pork-scented face. "Yeah, there's pictures of her all over. Also, Xavier's room had a bunk bed. It's not uncommon for poorer families to bunk children together."

"Musta missed that," Rivette said, skimming the console table. He started wiping blood off one of the pictures. "My bad, Dixie."

She frowned. This was an added complication. "Are you certain there's another family member?"

"Oh, yes, positive," Landry said, drying the back of his neck. "Her name is . . . is . . ."

"It's Hannah," Rivette said, holding up a picture of a young girl. Her name was spelled with rhinestones glued onto the frame. "The blood was covering her face up, so I thought it was the older daughter. Sorry about that."

"It's fine. So, why are we declaring this a kidnapping?"

Instead of answering, Landry motioned for them to follow. He led them to the communal bathroom. "Check out the mirror, Lieuten—Dixie."

The sink was covered in watered-down blood, like someone had taken the time to wash their hands. Written across the mirror, in blood, was a single message that chilled her to the bone: The girl is mine.

Rivette snorted. "Just another night in the Big Easy, eh?"

The following morning, Dixie got to work early. As she cut across the open floor of the homicide division, she heard Commander Ouellette.

"Olivier. My office. Now." He stood at the entrance of his office, tapping his fingers on the wooden frame.

She stood there, holding the tote bag where she kept her lunch and most of her personal belongings, wondering what she had done wrong. Since her promotion, Ouellette almost never took that tone with her.

"Sure, Commander. Let me just put my bag down in my office and—"

"Or you could just get your ass in here now, Olivier."

She sighed and slowly counted to three, holding her tongue. Ever since her promotion, the commander almost always treated her as an equal. There were times, however, when he could still be an insufferable prick.

"Yes, sir," she finally said, stepping into his office.

"Close the door."

She did. "What's this about?"

"Take a seat." He then tapped the mute button on his speakerphone. "She's here, doctor."

"Ah, good. Thank you, Louis. Hello there, Lieutenant Olivier."

She immediately recognized the voice. "Dr. Lazarus. What can I do for you?"

She heard Dr. Lazarus shuffle through some papers. "So, I'll cut to the chase. Remember a few months ago when we spoke about Sam?"

Dixie sat up attentively. As painful as it was, Sam was never too far from her thoughts. "Yes, I do."

"Good. Then you remember agreeing to fully devote yourself to helping her when the time came?"

"Absolutely."

"Well, that time has come. Are you willing to help her?"

She looked up at Ouellette, and he motioned back to the phone. She couldn't read his expression at all.

Dixie bit her bottom lip. Three times so far, she had let Sam down. The first was when she had falsely accused Sam of being the new Bourbon Street Ripper, leading to the incident at the wharf. The second was when she had failed to recognize that Sam was suicidal, leading to her jumping from her burning townhome. And the third was when she had kept Sam's impending commitment a secret, choosing to obey an order from the police chief even though her gut said it was wrong.

She must think the worst of me. I have to make it up to her somehow.

"Yes. I'll do anything to help her."

"Good," said Dr. Lazarus. "I have worked out an arrangement with your commander. While you're working on your caseload, you'll also be helping me."

The urgency in his voice was so thick that she felt her heart beat faster.

"Doctor, is Sam in danger?"

There was a long pause on the other line. "I believe she is, Detective. I'll be in contact with you tomorrow mid-morning."

"OK." She leaned back.

"Thanks for allowing this, Louis," Dr. Lazarus said.

"You're welcome, Andre. Take care." Ouellette hung up.

Dixie continued biting her bottom lip. Ouellette's expression was still unreadable, the same focused one he'd had for most of the new Ripper case. "Um, Commander?"

"Yes, Olivier? What is it?"

"It's just that . . . tomorrow morning . . . if you recall?" She placed her hand over her abdomen.

He wrinkled his brow a moment, and then chortled. At once, his expression was relaxed, even fatherly. "Oh, that's right. Your ultrasound appointment. My apologies. I forgot."

She rubbed gently. It would be her first visit to the obstetrician since learning she was pregnant. "Right. So if Dr. Lazarus calls while I'm there, please let him know I'll call back, all right?"

"Of course. Don't worry. But about this Sam thing. There's something I need to get off my chest." He walked over to several rows of framed photographs on the wall: photos of fellow soldiers lost during the Vietnam War, photos of his son, and photos of every officer slain during the new Bourbon Street Ripper case. There was even a photograph of a squadron dressed in World War I clothes.

His expression softened as he scanned his personal wall of memories, his fingers sliding over the pictures of Rodger Bergeron and Michael LeBlanc. Dixie felt a lump in her throat as she gazed at Michael's photo. He had been her best friend.

Then Ouellette turned back to her. His expression was again unreadable, his stature and voice militant. "I don't personally dislike Samantha Castille. You could even say that I share a kindred spirit with her. She has an amazing will and could've been something truly special. But at this point, I've written her off as trouble. Every person who's become a part of her life has either died or suffered great loss. It's like her entire life is cursed."

He paused a moment and then exhaled deeply. "So I won't blame you if you tell Dr. Lazarus to piss off."

Dixie glowered. It had always been obvious that the commander never much cared for Sam, almost as if he were disappointed with how she had turned out. When they had visited Sam in the hospital, he'd spoken to her alone. Afterward, he had said, "It would have been better if that girl hadn't been born."

With a sigh, she said, "I'm sorry, sir, but I'm not ready to write her off. Every time she's needed me, I've failed her."

"Olivier, you're not responsible for what happened to her. It's silly for you to think you owe her anything."

"Call it what you will. I don't rationalize my emotions. I just care about her and want to help her."

"You hardly know her. Don't presume you're her friend due to guilt."

"And don't you presume to dictate the friends I choose."

He folded his arms. "You're determined, then?"

She nodded.

"You're going to help Sam no matter what?"

"Yes, sir."

Ouellette shrugged and then sat back down. "All right, but don't come crying to me when shit gets to be too much."

Feeling the rush of a victory over her hard-headed commander, she said, "I won't, sir."

He grunted, sorting through reports. "Good. Just work the Davis family case for now. You'll have your hands full with Dr. Lazarus. Of that I'm sure."

"Yes, sir." She stood up and gathered her tote bag.

"Oh, and Olivier?"

Stopping by the door, she raised her eyebrows. "Yes?"

Ouellette motioned toward her with an ever-so-slightly pleasant expression. "Congrats on the baby. I'm sure Gino and you will make fine parents. If you need anything, let me know."

Dixie felt better. Despite his being a prick, there were moments when Ouellette was genuinely kind. "Thank you, sir."

It was late in the evening when Gino called. Dixie had spent the entire day waiting to hear from the medical examiner on the Davis family murders, keeping busy by assisting her subordinates with their cases. So when he called, she was glad to finally hear the deep, sensual voice of her beautiful lover.

"Dixie. When are you coming home? Dinner will be ready soon." The sounds of sizzling and boiling were in the background. He was cooking, as he usually did on Tuesday nights.

She looked at the time. It was almost seven o'clock. "Oh, sorry, honey. I'll wrap things up and head home soon."

A pot clanked loudly, and then Gino muttered in Greek. A moment later he said, "That's perfect. I'll see you soon."

That made her giggle. He always managed to make her feel like a schoolgirl. "Everything OK, honey?"

"I am at war with the calamari. Sadly, my love, it is winning."

She held back a second giggle, imaging him batting at the food with a frying pan.

"I'll be here when you get home," he said.

"See you soon, honey." She felt great as she hung up, loving that he still ended every phone call with "I'll be here when you get home." It was like a kiss meant only for her.

For a few minutes, she just sat there feeling giddy. Then she picked up one of two photographs she kept on her desk, right next to her chess championship trophy. One was of her and Gino, and the other one, the one she picked up, was of her and Michael.

"Hey, you. So, tomorrow, I get to see my baby for the first time."

Her fingers traced the photo fondly. They were sitting at their favorite café and clinking two teacups together. She remembered that day. They had both been so happy.

"If you were alive, you'd be the godfather. You know that, right? You'd be the best godfather in the world to my baby. I'm sure of it."

A couple of tears dripped on the photograph. She spread them over the surface of the glass until it streaked. Even when the two of them had pulled an all-nighter one weekend and had ended up getting mind-blowingly drunk in the French Quarter, she had always felt safe with Michael. He would never take advantage of her or allow anyone else to. Over the years, she'd come to realize how much she cared about him.

The night you died, I tried to tell you how I really felt. But you already knew. And you let me down so gently, so lovingly. You were such an amazing person, Michael.

She held the photograph to her chest. "I miss you so much. Why did you have to die?"

Kissing the photograph, she set it down. The surface was now streaked with her tears and lipstick. In the silence of her office, the sounds outside muted thanks to her solid oak door, she took a moment to calm down and relax. Eyes closed, she slowly breathed in and out. In a minute, her nerves were once again as calm as a windless lake.

Then someone knocked on the door.

She opened her eyes. "Come in."

Rivette entered, looking haggard and smelling of menthol cigarettes. He held up a pair of folders. "I come bearing gifts of grim horror and blood, Lady Olivier." He bowed, his ponytail flopping over his face.

Despite having just had a somber moment, she laughed. "You ass! How dare you spoil a perfectly bad mood."

He dropped the folders before her. "A thousand ill-conceived pardons. Anyway, here is the medical examiner's report on the Davis family murders, as well as a profile of the missing girl, Hannah Davis."

Looking over the two folders, she grimaced. This would definitely make her late for dinner. "I have calamari and sex waiting for me at home. Anyone out there who can work on these?"

"Just Aucoin. He's typing up reports for the commander."

She shook her head. "No, Kyle's not a good choice right now. What about you?"

"Sure, I'll get right on that after the other six cases I have pending."

With an exasperated sigh, she threw up her hand. "Fine! I'll do it myself."

"Can I get you anything, Dixie? Maybe a cup of coffee?" He leaned over, smirking. The menthol smell was positively overpowering.

She wrinkled her nose and waved him away. "No, I'm good. But, ugh, Scott, do you really have to smoke those things? They stink worse than regular cigarettes!"

Leaning back, hands in his pockets, he said, "Ha! Hey, it's menthol. Pretend your nose is drinking a mint julep!"

"Just stop smoking them. For me, please?"

Snickering, he shuffled backward out of the office. "It's like you trying to get me to cut my hair, Dixie. Not gonna happen!"

She shouted after him, "Close the door, at least!"

When he was gone and the door was shut, Dixie opened the folders. It wasn't that Rivette didn't respect her—he just played around way too much. But she knew that if it came down to it, he'd have her back. She felt that way about all her subordinates, even Kyle Aucoin.

Although he's been going through hell since Cathy filed for divorce. Poor guy.

As negative thoughts started creeping back, she rubbed her forehead.

Come on, girl, focus!

With renewed determination, she opened the file on Hannah Davis. On the front cover was her school photo—a cute ten-year-old girl, her face shining with a smile that could light up a room. She had above-average grades and was active in her church. Nothing seemed out of the ordinary.

"Sang in choir. Never a hint of trouble. Just your normal, sweet girl from a lower-income family."

It reminded Dixie of herself when she was growing up with the Oliviers. Smiling, she finished reading the report. It seemed Hannah was very close to her paternal grandmother, Jada Davis.

"Jada died last Halloween in a nursing home. Hmmm. Some depression after her death. That warrants looking into. Maybe someone from there is the culprit."

She ran her fingers over Hannah's photo. "I swear, if some sicko hurt her, I will put the needle in his arm myself."

Putting aside the profile, she opened the medical examiner's report.

"I was right, no defensive wounds." Every victim had been knocked to the ground with a slash to the back of the knees. Except for the little brother, who had been decapitated, every family member had their throats slit.

She turned the page. According to the examiner, each cut was a single slice. The amount of force behind them was far greater than even a strong adult could normally manage. Leaning back, she nibbled on her thumb. Ever since the new Ripper case, strange things had been happening. Criminals were showing greater than normal strength, and the number of violent crimes had skyrocketed.

She closed her eyes, visualizing the murder scene. "But even with a violent, super-strong killer, there would be defensive wounds. It's human nature to fight against an attacker. Pure and simple."

But as soon as she said that, she opened her eyes. There was only one explanation that fit. And sadly, it was the most common situation when it came to murder.

"Even though most murders in New Orleans are currently perpetrated by strangers, the norm is that you are most likely to be killed by someone you know. That's why there are no defensive wounds. The Davis family knew their killer, and they were reluctant to fight back—even at the risk of their own lives!"

Chapter 7
Trying to Kill the Pain

Date: **Wednesday, October 28, 1992**
Time: **9:30 a.m.**
Location: **Tulane University Hospital**
Downtown New Orleans

"And if you look here, Miss Olivier, you can see the arms."

Dixie watched the screen, but it was hard to make out the details with her eyes so filled with tears. Gino sat next to her, his strong, olive-skinned hands covering hers as if they were a protective blanket.

"Do you see that, Dixie? That's our baby!" He squeezed her hand gently.

Tears flowed down her face as she laughed merrily, squeezing back. Despite promising herself she wouldn't blubber during the ultrasound, she did just that. "It's beautiful, Gino."

"Yes, it is." He squeezed again. "Is our baby a girl or a boy, Doctor?"

Dr. Cambre pushed her blond bangs behind her ear and directed the ultrasound technician to move the wand around. Dixie felt the cool metal slide over her stomach. Drying her eyes as best she could, she watched as the image of her unborn child shifted. Dr. Cambre moved over to the monitor and pointed out part of the baby's pelvis.

"We cannot be one hundred percent sure just yet. But I believe it's a girl, Miss Olivier."

Gino burst into tears. "A girl! It looks like we're going to have a little girl, Dixie." He cried freely, wiping his tears across his face.

Dixie gazed lovingly at the image of the life within her, her tiny head rising as if she knew she was being spoken about. *Yes, my little baby. Mommy and Daddy are talking about you. We're going to be so happy to meet you, little one.*

"She's nicely developed," Dr. Cambre said. "I'd say about fifteen weeks."

Blinking away her tears, Dixie glanced at her doctor. "Are you sure? I thought I got pregnant at the end of August."

The ultrasound technician finished, and the monitor shut off. Dr. Cambre came around and stood by her and Gino. "Fetal development is very predictable at this stage. The baby is certainly between fourteen and sixteen weeks. We wouldn't be able to tell the gender if it was any earlier."

That news made Dixie frown. She could have sworn she conceived the night of the incident at the wharf. *You mean I was running around with Rodger on the new Ripper case while pregnant? Plus, that means I missed a period and didn't even realize it. But I was very distracted during that time.*

Finally wiping his face dry, Gino said, "Likely, it was during our trip to Cancun. Is that detail really so important?"

She blushed, sitting up with his assistance. "Well, no, not really. I guess I'm just over-analyzing everything."

With the same joyful laugh she had fallen in love with years ago, he helped her to her feet. "Well, yes, Dixie, you do tend to overthink things. That's how you got fooled by 'Fool's Gold.'"

At the mention of the infamous anagram for "Nite Priory," which had confused and misled the entire precinct for weeks, she harrumphed. "You just bought me lunch at Arnold's for that, bub."

He knelt before her and kissed her hand. "As you wish."

It was close to two o'clock when Dixie returned to the office. Ouellette, who was going over a report with Landry and Rivette, cocked an eyebrow at her, looked at his watch, and shook his head. Still dressed up from lunch at Arnold's, she gave her commander a helpless shrug and then gracefully slid into her office.

I'm having a daughter, and my man just treated me out. Nothing can ruin my day.

She had just settled into her office when there was a knock at her door.

"Come in!" she said, almost singing it.

Aucoin entered, accompanied by a raincloud. In an instant, she felt the joy siphon from the air. Her former partner looked like he hadn't slept in days.

"Hey, Kyle. Everything all right?"

"You don't want to know." Every part of him, from his crew-cut to his shirt and tie, was in disarray.

It wasn't that she didn't want to know so much as she knew listening to him would bring her down. "Anyway, how can I help you?"

"Ouellette has me running reports for the field detectives. Do you need anything, um, looked at?"

"Can't say that I do. Sorry, Kyle."

He nodded and then started to leave. He was halfway out the door when she said, "Kyle, wait."

Turning around, he stared blankly at her.

Quickly, she scanned her desk for anything she could give him. Her eyes fell upon the file for the Davis family murders. It was an important case. She needed information soon, and Aucoin's reputation for hustling had become virtually nonexistent. She bit her upper lip and picked it up. Giving him a chance was the only way he'd ever be able to prove himself.

"I need you to check Social Security, welfare, and anything else you can think of. Get me a list of all living relatives and close family friends. Especially ones living in New Orleans. I suspect that the Davis family was murdered by someone close to them. Also, do a check on Jada Davis, the grandmother. I want to find out how her death affected Hannah."

With a grunt, he took the file. "Sure thing, Lieutenant."

As he started to leave, she said, "Oh, and Kyle. Please call me Dixie."

Without looking back at her, he said, "No." Then he left.

Once Aucoin was gone, she slumped back, exhaled, and then covered her face. She had been there for him when Cheryl had died. She had been there for him when Cathy had asked for a divorce. There was only so much she could do. *I love you, you big jackass, but I can't make you want to live.*

Dixie spent the next hour cleaning up her desk, which had gotten cluttered since she'd moved in two months ago. When she finished, all that remained was her case notebook, the files on the Davis family murders, her chess trophy, and her two framed photographs. She picked up the one of her and Gino and gazed longingly at it. They were posing on the beaches of Cancun the day before Ouellette called her back due to the new Bourbon Street Ripper case.

Gino looks so sexy in those swim trunks. My thighs are kind of big, though.

She puffed up her cheeks, imagining how big she'd get near the end of her pregnancy. When she realized just how ridiculous she looked, she said, "OK, I won't be that bad—"

Her phone rang so suddenly that she jerked and dropped the photograph. It seemed to spin and twist for a long time. Then it hit the ground, the glass shattering all over the floor.

"Crap!"

As the phone continued to ring, she grabbed the broken frame. A sharp pain shot through her fingers. When she pulled back, blood dripped copiously from her fingertips. On the frame, several shards of glass now shimmered with a crimson reflection. She looked around for some paper towels or tissues, but she didn't see anything, and she couldn't rummage around her desk with her one hand bleeding everywhere.

"Shit. Someone, help!"

Ouellette threw open the door, a dangerous look in his eyes. When he saw what she was doing, his expression changed to an annoyed scowl. He reached over and picked up the phone.

"Hello, Lieutenant Olivier's office." Ouellette handed her a handkerchief from his pocket. "Hello, Dr. Lazarus. Yes, she's in today, but she's away from her desk at the moment."

She grimaced, took the handkerchief, and squeezed her fingers with it. *Now how will you wrap up your fingers with one hand, genius?*

"Yes, I'll have her call you. In about an hour."

The blood was all over her desk. *Gross. Nick a blood vessel and it looks like you sliced a vein.*

"Yes, that's fine. Talk to you later. Goodbye."

Ouellette hung up. "You all right?"

Nodding, she held up the bloodied handkerchief. "Help, please."

To her surprise, he chuckled. It was one of the few she had ever heard from him. He knelt down, picked up the frame and the photograph, and laid them both on her desk. He examined her fingers.

"Looks like you cut a—"

"Blood vessel," she said along with him.

Ouellette wrapped up her hand. "You'll want to get those cuts treated with antiseptic."

"Yes, sir."

Her fingers tended to, he called the maintenance department to send a janitor for cleanup. Then he closed the door. "What's wrong?"

Dixie's hand was trembling. "The phone rang, and I dropped the photo. Nothing serious."

"But you're shaking like you had a panic attack."

She sighed. "It's just that when I cut myself, I couldn't bandage it. That's when I realized that with one hand, I'm pretty useless."

His brow wrinkled. "That's bullshit, and you know it. You're a brilliant detective with a mind as good as LeBlanc's. Who cares if you lost an arm? You got another one! So don't ever talk like that again."

She let out a sigh. "Yes, sir."

"Now, unless these shakes become a regular thing, I'm not going to demand you get counseling. But mind those nerves, OK? I don't need you catching PTSD."

The way he made PTSD sound like a cold made her smirk. "OK, sir."

"So take a few to catch your breath, and then go get those cuts treated. Afterward, give Lazarus a call back. Here's his number."

He tossed a business card on her desk. She snatched it up. The number was for Acadia-Vermillion Hospital.

"Thank you, sir."

"You're welcome." He turned to leave.

"Um, a personal question, please."

"Yes, Olivier? It's not like I need to go back to running a division or anything."

"Sorry, it's just . . ." Her voice was low as she asked, "How did you know I was in trouble? You're several offices down, and our doors are made of solid oak."

He looked at her like she had asked the color of an orange. "Because it's my goddamn business to know what's going on in my house. Now, Lieutenant, if you're done, go to the nurse and then get your ass back to work."

As Ouellette vanished out of her office, she rubbed her head. *The more I get to know him, the less I understand him.*

"Ah, Detective Olivier. Or should I say Lieutenant Olivier? Zis is a surprise!"

With a deep breath, Dixie entered Dr. Klein's office. She was certain he was standing at the exact same spot by the window as when she had visited with Rodger months ago. That only increased her sense of unease. But all the same, she kept up a pleasant expression. "Hello, Dr. Klein. Thank you for seeing me on such short notice."

"Please, sit." He motioned toward the same seat he had offered last time. As always, his motions seemed deliberate and rehearsed. Teetering a bit from her imbalance, she sat down. She just wanted to be done with him and leave. Her phone call with Dr. Lazarus had been short but to the point. Sam had vanished from Tulane overnight, and he suspected that she had been moved to a private facility run by Dr. Klein.

Dixie's task was simple, in theory: verify Sam's location and report it to Dr. Lazarus. He had also mentioned that her previous physician, Dr. Kindley, might know something. It was a long shot, but she knew she had to try. For now, she was just testing the waters. Seeing how easy it would be to get him to confide in her.

"So then, Lieutenant. Vat can I do to help the illustrious eighth precinct of the New Orleans police force?" Dr. Klein had taken a seat, and as before, his elbows formed right angles.

She inhaled softly. It was time to treat this like an interrogation—to play a role until she got what she wanted. "Well, to be honest, I've been having some problems lately. And I need some help."

When he raised his eyebrows, she quickly added, "Ouellette thinks I have PTSD. I fear my job may be in jeopardy."

It was a lie, but just as when she interrogated suspects, she'd use any method to get results.

He stroked his beard slowly, as if sizing her up.

This guy is such a creep. Gritting her teeth, she forced a smile, hoping it would look anxious.

Finally, he said, "Well, Lieutenant, I must admit this is a bit surprising. Last time we spoke, you made it very plain that you didn't vant my help. And then, if I recall, you tattled on me to your commander. Why is it I should help you again?"

She pushed every feeling down into her stomach and chuckled. "Sorry, I was out of line. But to be fair, I had just lost my arm in a fight, my partner was losing his mind, and I didn't know what was going on. Then you came at me from out of nowhere. What was I supposed to think?"

He stopped stroking his beard. "I suppose zat is understandable. We were all under a great deal of stress back then. But I am confused, Lieutenant. Didn't you end up running to that quack Dr. Lazarus? Why not go to him for help now?"

She exhaled in relief. Talking about Dr. Lazarus was a possible way in. Holding out her hand, she said, "That guy is a nutcase. I mean, he may be good at some things, but when I talked to him about Sam—antha, he started acting crazy like a Twilight Zone episode. I'm not going to trust my mental health to someone like that." She pursed her lips, reminding herself to refer to Sam by her full name when talking with Dr. Klein. He referred to Sam as her "other personality."

Resting both elbows on his desk, he leaned forward. "Well, then, I can see that you are a woman of reason. First, let's talk about your disorder. I can treat you, but first I must diagnose you. However, Lieutenant, I am very expensive und way beyond your salary. And I don't take insurance. Is your boyfriend, ze Greek, willing to pay my fee?"

It was painful to have him mention Gino, but everything was going how she wanted it. Once she had his confidence, it would only be a matter of time before she would be able to verify Sam's whereabouts.

"Gino would be happy to pay for my sessions. Also, you had mentioned special work for me a few months back. If that's still available, maybe an exchange of services." It was another way in, one she was hoping for.

Dr. Klein nodded. "Good. Then we will make the diagnosis today. As for my original offer from two months ago . . ."

She leaned forward, holding her breath.

" . . . I am afraid that the position is no longer available."

Her shoulders dropped. *No, come on! That would have made it so easy!*

Again, he raised his eyebrows. "You seem disappointed."

Feeling her cover slip, she quickly held up her hand and said, "Well, I'm not sure if my position with the police is secure. I think the commander is looking to replace me."

His eyebrows lowered. The feint was successful. Then he snorted. "Bah. Ouellette likes you, und you are clever. Besides, it is better to have me as your doctor instead of your boss, *ja*?"

Continuing to fake a smile so hard her lips quaked, she said, "Yeah, that makes sense. Thank you for taking me on."

It wasn't a solid win, but it was a good beginning. *I'll crack him. I swear it.*

He grinned like a vulture and started scribbling on a pad. "Good, then let's schedule your tests, *ja*? I'm anxious to see what's going on in that head of yours, Detective. Very anxious indeed."

She kept smiling until she thought her face would break.

When Dixie returned to the precinct, only Rivette was there, working on reports and looking devastatingly bored. "Hey Lieut—Dixie. Aucoin put something on your desk. Said it was really important. Then he left. He didn't look so hot. I think he's sick. Or dying. Or both. Kinda like me. These reports are killing me. See, I'm already dead." Then he went limp, feigning death with his tongue sticking out.

She appreciated his attempt at humor, sophomoric as it may be. Even though he often played around too much, his jovial attitude kept things from getting too grim. "Thanks, Scott. I'll be in my office if another crisis arises."

With a laugh, he spun around in his chair. "I'll try hard not to burn down the precinct, boss!" Propping up his feet, he returned to his work.

Reclining in her office, she just rubbed her face for a few minutes, smoothing out the stress lines that had been gathering all day. *I'm going to turn myself forty before this week is over.*

Finally, she turned her attention to her desk. There was Hannah Davis's file, along with a note from Aucoin that read, "Dix, you need to read this as soon as possible. Big stuff."

She blinked. That note was how he used to write back when they were partners. He also hadn't called her "Dix" in just as long. Opening the file, she started reading through it. There were several pages of new information.

"No relatives or close friends were anywhere near the family on the night of the murders." She started nibbling on her thumb. "So they had to have been committed by a stranger. But why didn't the victims fight back? It's like they knew their killer."

Turning to the next page, she read what Aucoin had discovered. "Oh, my God. Hannah's grandmother, Jada, committed suicide in front of her. She had been suffering from cancer, and the family couldn't pay for treatment. So Jada overdosed while the poor girl was visiting one afternoon. After that, Hannah was never the same. She blamed her parents for killing her grandmother. She even told a school counselor that she was having homicidal thoughts. But no one reported it. They thought she was just throwing a fit."

Dixie frowned. It was a problem with a lot of inner-city children: rarely did people take their cries for help seriously.

"But still, a ten-year-old girl having murderous thoughts? Any counselor worth her salt would have reported that."

Suddenly, an awful, ugly idea came to mind. She slowly lowered her thumb.

"Murderous thoughts? No way. It can't be."

Closing her eyes, she reimagined the crime scene. Every victim had been attacked with cuts meant to bring them down. Only the brother and father, who had been lying down, didn't have such injuries. "So why would the killer topple the victims to cut their throats?"

She opened her eyes. "What if the killer was short, like a child!"

Rushing out of her office, nearly tripping due to the lack of balance, she slammed her hand down on Rivette's desk. He had given up on the reports and was doodling pictures of his figurines. With a surprised yelp, he fell back. "What the hell, Dixie? Ya messed up my Green Ranger!"

She snatched his notebook. "You can draw later, Scott. Let's get in your car and go. I think I know where we'll find Hannah."

It was raining again when Dixie and Rivette arrived at the cemetery off Desire Street. The cool, misty precipitation sprinkled down on them as they looked around, flashlights out. The black iron gate was open, and the bulbs of the street lights were broken. The cemetery was in complete darkness.

Oh, this is creepy. She motioned for him to follow. Back-to-back, they slipped inside. As they crept through the rows of graves, she whispered, "It's possible that Hannah is dead from exposure or even suicide. But just in case, be ready."

He whispered back. "Be ready for what? A ten-year-old girl? Her kidnapper? You're giving me very little to go on, Dixie."

"Sorry." She struggled to keep her footing, her balance problem compounded by her shaking hand. "All I've got is a hunch. You'll have to trust me."

"OK. Well, please don't take out your gun when your hand is shaking like that. I don't want to get shot in the ass."

She said nothing. Firing a gun one-handed was difficult at the best of times.

Once they were deep inside, she shone her light around, searching for the family graves. Just as she turned to Rivette for help, a white flash caught her eye. It was coming from a small orb flittering toward a mausoleum.

What the heck was that white thing?

It flew right inside. The name "Davis" was on the brass nameplate.

Then she heard a soft voice hanging across the rainy nighttime air.

"*Cause nothin' lasts forever . . .*"

"Shit, Dixie, did you hear that?" Rivette sucked in his breath.

Anxiety jolted through her. "Yes. Hush. Listen!"

"*And we both know hearts can change . . .*"

She strained to catch every syllable. It was coming from inside the Davis family mausoleum. Moving slowly so as not to slip on the wet stone and mud, they crept slowly toward it.

"*And it's hard to hold a candle . . .*"

The sky briefly lit up with some cloud-to-cloud lightning. The gate inside the mausoleum was open, hanging on a single hinge.

"*In the cold November rain . . .*"

Leaning over to Rivette, she whispered, "Cover me, but stay back. OK?"

He grimaced, looking unsure. "OK, but at the first sign of trouble, you fall back. Ouellette would kill me if you got hurt."

"*We've been through this such a long long time . . .*"

Nodding, she tucked the flashlight under her left arm. The nerves on her stump prickled painfully. Drawing out her pistol, she slid into the mausoleum. *I can't shoot, but hopefully I can intimidate.*

The inside of the mausoleum, like most in New Orleans, was only big enough to hold a few adults. Even with the awkward position of the flashlight, it only took her a moment to find what she was searching for.

The name plate for "Jada Davis." It was still fresh, barely weatherworn.

"*Just tryin' to kill the pain . . .*"

Beneath it, huddled in the dark, was a ten-year-old girl wearing a white nightgown. Her dark skin was even darker with splotches of mud caked on it. She looked like she had been sleeping outside for at least a day or two.

Dixie cleared her throat. "Hannah? Hannah Davis?"

Hannah, who had been staring at the ground, stopped singing and looked up at her. Her eyes were bloodshot and her pupils were dilated. Her face, her hair, and her nightgown were covered in dark, dried blood.

In her hand, she held a chef's knife also caked in dried blood.

Her face was expressionless. "Hello, lady. Why are you here? Me, I'm just trying to kill the pain."

Chapter 8
Regarding Hannah Davis

Date: **Thursday, October 29, 1992**
Time: **11:00 a.m.**
Location: **New Orleans Police Department**
Precinct Eight, French Quarter

The rain was still coming down from the night before, a steady trickle that bounced rhythmically off the window of Dixie's office. With her eyes closed, she could hear every drop as it fell upon the glass pane. It was sweet, ethereal music that helped calm her frazzled nerves. Dr. Klein's analysis had come back, diagnosing her with an anxiety disorder. Her treatment would consist of one session a week and medication she couldn't take until after giving birth. It wasn't enough to go on to find out where Sam was.

But as she sat there, she wasn't thinking about her issues or even about Sam. Hannah was the only thing on her mind. She had been taken into custody without incident and had immediately become docile and despondent. She wouldn't even talk to her CPS social worker. Commitment was being discussed.

Someone cleared their throat, bringing her out of her thoughts. When she opened her eyes, Rivette was waving his hand in front of her face. He had a rather annoyed expression. "Nap time, Dixie?"

"Sorry, Scott. I did promise you a chance to air your grievances. What else is on your mind?"

He shifted back in his seat. "Mostly, it's just how we're terribly understaffed. I mean, you got Landry and me working all of Bergeron's and LeBlanc's old cases from before the new Ripper shit. Half the time, Landry goes off to do his own thing—I have no idea what the fat bastard is up to. Then you got Aucoin, and I'm sorry his life has fallen to hell, but he's not pulling his own weight at all. Breaux and Gravois are just as overworked. You're pregnant and will likely be put on maternity leave soon. And there are what, four other detectives in homicide left? Everyone has double and triple caseloads. Our territory is the freaking French Quarter. How can we stop all the bad guys, Dixie, if we just don't have the manpower?"

She frowned. As much as it pained her to admit it, everything he was saying was true.

Leaning forward, she rested her elbow on her desk. "Scott, you bring up valid points. I'll talk to Ouellette about getting some detectives from the other precincts to help out. Just please remember, it wasn't just this division that Blind Moses nearly wiped out. We lost most of the eighth precinct. That included our entire SWAT team. Remember them? Arsenault's Arsenal, the biggest, baddest group of cops in the city?"

He snorted. "Yeah, real badass. They got wiped out by a blind woman."

"You weren't there!" She slapped the surface of her desk, jumping up and leaning in his face. Her nostrils flared. "While you were cozying around Sam's townhome, playing with her copier, I watched men—good men—die horribly. Don't you ever poke fun at it again!"

Her outburst made him slide back. His eyes were wide as he held out his hands. "Sorry. I was out of line. It's just . . . what happened there sounds impossible no matter how many times I hear about it."

With a sigh, she sat down, hard. Her anger rapidly dissipated. "The entire thing was impossible. It's been two months, and I still don't know what to believe. Some people say it was a wonder drug, the *tkeeus*, which those two took. Others say it was voodoo. Honestly, Scott, not thinking about it is the only thing that lets me cope."

Nodding, he scratched his scalp and then tossed his long hair to the side. "Dixie Olivier refusing to think through a problem? This is coming from the woman who beat Michael in chess, am I right?" He motioned toward her trophy.

In spite of herself, she blushed. "It was a good match. But now you're comparing apples and oranges. Just because I'm good at games like chess doesn't mean I can figure out crazy stuff like what happened at the wharf."

"Well, I'm not one to patronize, but didn't you once tell me that the simplest solution was often the most correct?"

That brought back a memory of one of her barbed lectures to him and Landry years ago. She chuckled. "Occam's razor. You're misquoting it. It actually states that the theory with the fewest number of assumptions should be selected. But you're close enough."

Rivette waved his hand. "However you want to word it. In the case of both the wharf and Hannah, you've probably already worked out an answer. But knowing you, it sounds ridiculous in your head. But if it's got you assuming the least, then it's probably correct. Ya know, that kind of thinking has gotten me through some of my toughest cases."

"Really?"

He grinned. "I know I play all the time, I've accepted write-ups instead of cutting my hair, and I'm pretty damn annoying. But Ouellette keeps me around. Why?"

The question seemed rhetorical, but she answered anyway. "You work like a horse and, yes, despite being a man-child, your close rate on cases is as good as mine."

"Exactly, and all because of ol' Occam's razor, which I apparently have been misquoting for over two years. Go me." Getting up, he knocked good-naturedly on her desk. "But seriously, just go with whatever solution has the least assumptions. Because we all know about assumptions: they make an ass out of you and 'Mption,' and he doesn't appreciate it."

She rolled her eyes at his humor as he left. Then she sank into thought. *The fewest assumptions? That would require me to accept that crap like voodoo is real. I'm not ready for that.*

"Hey, Dixie, got a moment?" It was Landry, standing at the doorway.

"Yes, Paul?"

"You know how you asked me to come get you when CPS was here and Miss Davis was ready to be interviewed?"

"She's awake, she's been Mirandized, and she's with the CPS worker?"

"Yep. The commander wants to watch this one. Do you want Scott and me to sit in there with you? I mean, she is a murder suspect."

Standing, she scooped up Hannah's case file. "No. Just watch from the other side of the glass with Ouellette. She's only a kid. We don't want to intimidate her too much, or the interview might get tossed out of court."

"All right. Will do."

As he started to leave, she called out to him. "Oh, and Scott tells me you head off a lot without informing anyone. Is something going on? Anything you want to tell me?"

Looking back at her, Landry said, "Scott needs to mind his own business, or better yet needs to focus on his work instead of playing Game Boy at his desk. But since you asked, my mother hasn't been doing great lately. We're thinking of moving her to assisted living." His eyes kept shifting away.

She bit her bottom lip. It was obvious that he was hiding something.

"I am very sorry, Paul. I didn't know. Why didn't you tell me about it?"

He shrugged. "I didn't want to burden you while you have your baby to worry about. So don't worry, I told Ouellette everything."

Her head spun as heat rushed to her ears and blood rushed to her head. *Did that fat prick just use my pregnancy as a handicap?*

For a moment, she considered punching him right in the mouth. But even as she curled her fist, she stopped. He was normally the most mild-mannered and polite person in the division. He likely didn't mean it that way. Taking a deep breath, she asked, "So Ouellette has approved your sudden absences?"

"He has. You can verify it if you want."

"Oh, I will. Well, I hope it works out. If you need time off, just let me know."

Again, he shrugged. "It'll go right, or it won't. Thanks all the same."

She started to walk off, but then she stopped and stuck her finger in his face. "But let's get one thing straight. I'm your boss. And neither the chain of command nor my pregnancy is a burden. Say anything misogynistic like that again, and I won't suspend you, I'll kick your damn ass."

As she walked away, she heard him shuffle behind her and mumble apology after apology. *Good for you, Dixie. Good for you.*

Outside of the interview room, Dixie met with Ms. Liana LeBeouf, the CPS worker.

"I'll be keeping a firm grip on the interview process, Lieutenant," Ms. LeBeouf said. She was a pretty, mocha-skinned woman about Dixie's age, wearing a copper-red weave. "I've heard of your aggressive style. Any of that and the interview will be over."

Dixie wasn't planning on it. Not with Hannah. "I understand. Just remember that Miss Davis is a murder suspect who has waived her right to counsel."

"She's a child," Ms. LeBeouf replied. "She'll be given one anyway after arraignment."

Clicking her jaw, Dixie said, "If she is arraigned. She might just be committed after I talk to her."

That seemed to settle things for Ms. LeBeouf. Both women entered the interview room while Ouellette, Rivette, and Landry watched through the one-way mirror.

What happened to those massive caseloads? Suddenly not too busy to watch me work, right? Men!

As soon as she entered the room, Dixie's skin started crawling with goosebumps. The air was cooler, and it pricked at her skin. She couldn't help but shudder.

Ms. LeBeouf shivered as well, briskly rubbing her arms as she ambled over toward Hannah. "Hannah? It's me, Liana. This lady is Lieutenant Olivier. She wants to talk with you."

Hannah was sitting in a strange pose, balanced on the top edge of the back of the chair with her legs straight out and her heels resting on the table. Her hands, which were cuffed, lay in her lap. Her straight, black hair, now cleaned of the blood and dirt, rested over her face like a curtain. Except for her shoulders, which barely rose and fell, she was perfectly still.

The sight of her made Dixie's skin crawl ever more. *Creepy little girl, how are you not falling over?*

She carefully laid the case file on the table and sat down on the other chair, opposite Hannah. She cleared her throat. When there was no reaction, she spoke.

"Hannah? Hannah, are you awake?"

There was no response. Ms. LeBeouf came back around to Dixie's side. "Why is she doing this?"

Slowly, Dixie exhaled. "I'm not sure. Ever seen anything like this before?"

"No. Never."

Giving the table the slightest nudge so as not to unbalance and knock the child over, Dixie repeated herself. "Hannah? Are you awake, Hannah?"

Hannah leaned her head back just enough for her bangs to part and reveal her face. Then she opened her eyes. They were bloodshot with dilated pupils. Silently, she regarded them both unblinkingly. Ms. LeBeouf gasped as Dixie felt her heart thump hard in her chest. The air got cooler, and the prickling sensations spread through her body.

Good Lord, what's with this kid?

Dixie took a moment to calm herself down, breathing deeply and slowly. Miss LeBeouf paced between the table and a corner of the room. All the while, Hannah stared ahead with those bloodshot eyes, completely motionless. When Dixie felt her heart rate return to normal, she cleared her throat once more. "I want to talk to you about the night of Monday, October 26th. Is that all right with you?"

Hannah said nothing.

Dixie locked eyes with Ms. LeBeouf. "Please, Liana. I want to help her."

"All right," she said. "Hannah, hun. Please talk to us."

Opening the case file, Dixie took out pictures of the victims. She then turned them around and slid them over to Hannah. "Do you want to tell me what happened?"

Hannah didn't move, save to shift her eyes down toward the photos. Her lips parted into a wide, white grin.

Ms. LeBeouf snatched the pictures away. "Let's not do that to her. Something's wrong. Hannah, what happened? Here's your chance to explain, hun. We're here to listen."

Hannah still said nothing.

Leaning back, Dixie rubbed between her eyes. She was just about to stand up when suddenly, Hannah started to sing. It was that same hauntingly beautiful voice from when they found her in the cemetery.

"*I know it's hard to keep an open heart when even friends seem out to harm you.*"

Dixie glanced back at her. Hannah was again focused on her. As she sang, however, only her mouth moved—nothing else. The effect was even more unsettling.

It was the same song that she had sung last night. Dixie knew she had heard it before.

"What are you telling us, Hannah?" Ms. LeBeouf asked.

Hannah continued to sing, never blinking, never taking her eyes off Dixie.

"*But if you could heal a broken heart, wouldn't time be out to charm you?*"

Suddenly remembering the song, Dixie stood up. "Ms. LeBeouf, give me one second. I have an idea."

She stuck her head out into the hallway, holding onto the door frame to avoid falling over. Ouellette, Rivette, and Landry all turned to her. "Scott, you collect Guns N' Roses albums, right?"

"You're damn straight I do! Axl Rose is God!"

"Good! Get your copy of their latest album and play 'November Rain' into this room."

He did a two-finger salute as she went back inside. Hannah was seated as before, still motionless. Ms. LeBeouf looked utterly exasperated. "Lieutenant, what's going on?"

"I think she suffered a bad trauma. I'm hoping this song will help her become more lucid." The idea seemed logical enough.

As she sat back down, Hannah's eyes re-focused on her. She resumed singing.

"*So never mind the darkness, we still can find a way.*"

"That's 'November Rain,' right?" Ms. LeBeouf asked. "I heard it this morning while on the Causeway."

"It's still extremely popular," Dixie said. "I'm hoping hearing it will spark something in her."

Hannah continued to sing. "*'Cause nothing lasts forever, even cold November rain.*"

As the song started playing softly over the loudspeakers, Hannah's eyes and mouth closed, and she tilted her head back. With a moan, she slid down the chair until she was seated. Then she slid her feet down to the floor, sighing gently. When she lifted her head, her bangs had parted completely and were framing her face. Those bloodshot eyes and dilated pupils looked like something from a midnight horror movie Elvira or Morgus would present.

Dixie smiled softly, keeping her voice measured and gentle. "Do you like that song, Hannah?"

Ms. LeBeouf smiled as well. "We all like that song, Hannah. It's a love song, you know."

Hannah grinned again. This time it was far more malevolent. "You are one stupid bitch. You know that, right?" Her voice had a notable reverb to it.

Both the tone of Hannah's voice and what she said caught Dixie off guard. As Ms. LeBeouf inhaled, Hannah threw her head back and howled with cruel-sounding, almost inhuman laughter. "The song is about suicide, ladies. Do you think I like it for the rainbows and kittens?"

Brow furrowing, Dixie leaned forward. There was no way she'd lose control of this interview. "Do you think about suicide often, Hannah?"

"'Do you think about suicide often, Hannah?'" Hannah said in a nasal, mocking voice.

Ms. LeBeouf cleared her throat. "Hannah, please. Try to remember that we're here to help." Her voice was quivering.

Snorting, Hannah shot her the bird and nasally mocked her once more. "'Try to remember that we're here to help.' 'Hannah, please.' 'Hannah, please.'" Then she sniffed derisively. "Right, lady, like you and Ms. Stumpy McStump-Stump know what's going on." As she spoke, she rocked her head side-to-side.

Dixie tapped her fingers on the table, staring at the girl. Even Richie had never acted quite this brazen. *Let me try changing tactics.*

"Tell me about your home life, Hannah. What was going on in your house before the night of the murders?"

Hannah reclined in the chair and pursed her lips like a fish's. "It fucking sucked. The house was always dirty. Dinner was always deep-fried. And I could hear Elijah jerking off in his bedroom. Every. Damn. Night."

Making a repeated, exaggerated stroking motion, she moaned and spoke with a deepened tenor. "Oh, Monique! Oh, Keisha, baby! Oh, girl, your butt is so big! Flip page, fap-fap. Flip page, fap-fap. Spoooooooge!" She threw her arms up in the air as if scoring a goal.

She stuck out her tongue. It slid past her chin. "Bleh!"

Then she slurped it back up like spaghetti. "Makes me wanna puke!"

The room was completely silent as Dixie gaped. Ms. LeBeouf leaned over and whispered, "OK, this girl is very ill. I think we can go with emergency commitment to Tulane. Please, let's end this now."

"But you know what the worst part was?" Hannah leaned forward, her expression suddenly very serious and her tone quite formal.

Dixie shook her head. At this point, she had no idea what to expect.

Hannah's lips tightened, her eyes narrowed, and her voice lowered to just above a whisper. "When I finally killed those miserable shits, I didn't get to keep any of their life energy. All of it was used. Every last drop. Now how is that fair?"

The sudden confession made Dixie blink. "Hannah. You killed your family?"

"I did, indeed."

"Why?"

Hannah leaned back and checked her fingernails. "It was a slow Monday."

She scratched her chin. "So now here I am. And here you are. And here is the table in both of your faces."

Flipping back, she kicked the table, knocking both Dixie and Ms. LeBeouf to the ground. Dixie cried out, shifting her weight to fall on her back as the table took Ms. LeBeouf with it. Ms. LeBeouf squealed as she and the table crashed into the side wall of the interview room, an ear-splitting crack bouncing off the walls. Then she landed in an unconscious heap.

Instantly, Dixie cradled her arm over her stomach. "No! Stop, please! I'm pregnant!"

Hannah flipped up to her feet, her hair back over her face. "You think I give two flying craps about that? That's more life energy for me. I'm going to enjoy stomping your baby out of your hoo-hoo. Maybe I can make it shoot across the floor like a bloody bowling ball. Time for a seven-ten split!"

As she advanced on Dixie, the door burst open, and in charged Rivette, Landry, and Ouellette. Landry had a stun gun drawn and ready, electricity crackling across the diodes.

"Back the hell off her!" Rivette shouted as he rushed at Hannah in a shoulder tackle.

She slipped to the side, dodging him, moving far faster than she should have been able to. Then she spun on her heel and kicked him in the rear end. With a cry, he flew as if he had been hit by a car, hitting the back wall.

"Tilt! You lose!" She laughed maliciously.

Dixie screamed as Rivette slid down to the floor, teeth falling out.

God, no! This is not happening! This is just like at the wharf!

Then she heard Landry cry out, "Whoa! What the heck?"

Ouellette flew by them and in an instant was grabbing Hannah in a full nelson take-down. The two fell to the ground with the girl's arms pinned over her head and her legs trapped in between his. She thrashed and struggled against him but seemed unable to move.

Her eyes were wide and she looked panicked. "No, no, no! Don't obliterate me, please!"

Ouellette held her in place, drops of sweat breaking out on the side of his head. His voice strained as he said, "For God's sake, Landry! Are you going to stand here and wait for her to break free and kill me? Or are you going to stun her?"

Landry, who had been staring with his mouth open, stumbled forward. Just as he reached Hannah, the stun gun crackling with its charge, Ouellette broke the hold. The diodes pressed into her skin. Immediately, she let out a shrill shriek and convulsed violently. A moment later, she went unconscious, her body shaking.

Sitting up, Ouellette rubbed his hand over his bald head, wiping off the perspiration. "Goddamn, I am getting too old for this shit. Landry, when Rivette's arm heals, you're both getting retrained in unarmed combat. That was pathetic."

Dixie continued to lie there, protectively holding her stomach. *What just happened?*

"Yes, sir," Landry said. His hands were shaking as he added leg restraints to Hannah. "But, sir, how did you move that fast? I mean . . ."

With a dismissive sniff, Ouellette pulled himself to his feet. "You'd be amazed at what the human body is capable of doing. Besides, I've served in more than enough wars. I know how to fight."

By then, several uniformed officers and other personnel had arrived. Some went to help Rivette, others to help Ms. LeBeouf, and others to assist Landry. One of them called for an ambulance.

Ouellette gently helped Dixie stand. "Are you and the baby OK?" His voice was gentle, almost fatherly.

She nodded.

He walked her out of the room. "Just to be sure, go to the hospital right away and have yourself looked at. I'll give Gino a call and tell him to meet you there."

"Yes, sir." Once they were in the hallway, she asked, "Commander, what the heck happened in there? With Hannah? With you?"

"Hell if I know what's up with that kid, yet. Whole world is falling apart, it seems."

She bit her bottom lip. "What about you, Commander? Back there, I mean—"

"I already told you, Olivier." He sounded irritated. "I've lost too many good cops already. I'm not losing any more. If you wanna believe in hocus-pocus or super drugs or whatever, be my guest. But that shit in there? That's nothing compared to what my old ass would do if crap like what happened at the wharf happened again. No more meaningless deaths. Not on my watch. I'm taking a stand starting now."

As he helped her sit down, the anxiety from the attack started melting. "Something like how mothers get a boost of strength when their children are trapped under a car?"

"Something like that, only more fatherly, or grandfatherly, depending on how you look at it. But for now, get yourself checked out. Then go home and have Gino make you a nice cup of tea or coffee or whatever the hell Greek people drink to calm down. Also, please go visit Aucoin at home tomorrow and make sure he's not rotting in his own crap."

More of the tension drifted away. "Giving me the dirty work?"

"Oh, yeah. I'm not about to fire him—not yet—but I'm close to putting him on paid leave whether he wants it or not. Anyway, I'll get a patrolman to drive you to Tulane. And I'll call Gino to meet you there."

"Thanks, sir." It was odd, but for the moment, her commander reminded her of Papa Olivier. *I guess we're kind of his children, aren't we?*

Ouellette waved off the thanks and started to leave. Then he stopped. "Oh, and Lieutenant."

"Yes, sir?"

"Before the suspect went crazy, she did confess. I don't know if it'll stick, but what I'm trying to say is . . . good job."

Chapter 9
Concerning 'Krabinays'

Date: **Friday, October 30, 1992**
Time: **9:00 a.m.**
Location: **Kyle Aucoin's house, St. Bernard**
New Orleans East

"Thanks for seeing me this morning, Kyle."

Dixie followed Aucoin into the living room. The interior of his house reflected his own personal state—a complete mess. Packing boxes lay everywhere, half of them still open with the contents carelessly rifled through. Plates of mostly eaten pizza or empty microwavable meals hosted swarms of gnats and micro-colonies of ants. The smell of garbage was overpowering.

She covered her nose and mouth as she looked around the living room. Her gut and throat tightened in concert as she fought the urge to throw up. Still wearing his pajamas and a robe, Aucoin lumbered to a recliner and sat down heavily.

The sight of her former partner made her shake her head in disgust. *Jesus, Kyle. What have you become?*

"I'm guessing you're here to fire me, right?" He looked as tired as he sounded.

"No, you ass. Just checking in on you. Although I'm sorely tempted to report your condition to Ouellette."

He shrugged. For a few long, tense moments, they just stared at one another.

I can't let him be like this. She put down her tote bag and assessed the room's condition. It was just as bad as the trailer she'd grown up in.

"Just sit tight for now, Kyle. I'm going to do a little cleaning." She took off her jacket and pulled back her sleeve with her teeth.

"Don't be stupid. You're pregnant. And you have one arm. You don't need to clean up anything. Let me sit here in my own mess." He seemed more agitated every second.

"Not gonna happen," she replied, heading into the kitchen. It was as much of a wreck as the living room. She spent a few minutes searching through cabinets and on counters. Finally, she found what she was searching for—a box of trash bags.

"All right, Dixie. Time to get real domestic."

It took her over two hours to clean up the trash and get all the dirty dishes in the dishwasher and another hour to clear out all the insects, open the house, and spray enough air freshener to start cutting through the curtain of stink. When she was finished, the house was a cluttered but livable mess.

Aucoin just watched the whole time. As she finally sat down on the sofa beside him, sipping a glass of water, he said, "Thanks. I appreciate it."

Dixie's lips curled into a small smile. That was more like the man she used to call 'partner.' "You're welcome."

"So, why did you come here, Lieutenant? It wasn't just to clean up my house."

Resting her glass on the coffee table, she said, "I told you, Ouellette wanted me to check in on you. But also . . ."

She reached toward his hand, inches away on the sofa. "I just wanted to see you, Kyle. I'm worried about you."

He pulled back his hand. "Don't be."

That made her frown. "I spoke with Cathy last week. She's worried about you, too."

"Bullshit."

The silence after he said that was deafening. She quietly watched him, the ice in her glass clinking softly as it melted. A sharp, hot pain bit into her heart and renewed the tightness in her throat. Her face was reddening. It took all the willpower she had not to start screaming at him for acting this way.

After looking her up and down, he grunted and then grabbed a large notebook off the coffee table. Opening it, he took out a silver fountain pen. "Look, Lieutenant. I appreciate your concern, but I've got to deal with this in my own way, in my own time. I already told Ouellette I would take unpaid leave for this, but he's the one who decided to keep me working from a desk. That's all there is to it. So unless there's something really important, I want to enjoy my half-day off for the week." He started scribbling.

Locking her jaw in place, she counted backward from ten until she felt her pulse and temperature lower. When she opened her eyes, he was still writing in his notebook with that silver pen.

"Kyle, what're you doing?"

He capped the pen, slid it back in the notebook, and put both away. "I get ideas from time to time. Dark thoughts. Thoughts that I'd rather never share with anyone. My therapist said to write them down. Said it would be good for my recovery."

"OK." It was a reasonable explanation. And she hadn't seen any drugs or alcohol while cleaning, so it was unlikely that he was abusing anything other than himself. Everyone had been afraid that since he loved drinking so much, he'd slide into alcoholism. But instead, he had stopped drinking altogether.

But despite that, he refused to deal with any of his problems—the death of his daughter, Cheryl, and the impact it was having on his life, or his failing marriage with Cathy. He just shuffled from one day to the next like he was waiting to die. The thought of that made her sigh again. There was only one option now. It was time for some tough love.

"Kyle, I'm going to be completely honest."

He arched an eyebrow. "And?"

"I think you're being ridiculous the way you're pushing me and the others away. I know you're suffering because of Cheryl. I know you're angry because of Cathy. I can't even imagine how much pain you're in right now. But I love you. My years partnered with you were the best I've ever had on the force. Everything I know about being a detective I know because of you. So whenever you get out of that black hole you're in, no matter how long it takes, I'll be there. But until then, don't expect me to come helping you out again. You need to decide on your own to start living again."

Then she glared at him, putting on what she felt was her sternest expression. For a full minute, he quietly matched her gaze. Then he shook his head.

"I didn't ask for your help. In fact, I want you to stay away. I don't want you to see me like this, Lieut—Dixie—Dix. When, if, I'm ready to live again, you'll be the first to know, right behind Cathy. And I'm sorry, but I think that's about as much as you're going to get out of me right now."

Dixie tried not to succumb to the weight on her chest. It was all she could do to keep her emotions from running wild. *At least he called me "Dix." He wants me to know he cares.*

Finally, she stood. "All right. That's all I have, then, Kyle. Thanks for having me over. I'll see you at the office tomorrow."

He nodded and showed her to the front door. "Hey, one thing. I heard about what happened yesterday with Hannah Davis. I'm glad you and the baby are OK. What about the others?"

She stopped at the doorway. "Well, Scott was banged up, but nothing serious, thank God. The only one really injured was her social worker, Miss LeBeouf. It's a mess. She's threatening to file a lawsuit and to go to the *Picayune* with details on the crazy stuff Hannah did. I think the DA's placed a gag order on her."

"Probably for the best. And what about Hannah?"

"She's going to be committed on an emergency certificate later today."

"She's nuts, then?"

"Either that or possessed." She chuckled, finding the idea ridiculous.

With a smirk, he said, "You mean like Sam was supposed to be, right? Later, Dix."

"Later, Kyle."

When Dixie arrived at the precinct, there was a note on her desk to call Dr. Cambre, her obstetrician. Immediately, she felt her temperature plummet and the dampness of perspiration gather on her upper lip and brow. Was something wrong with her baby?

Locking herself in the office, she dialed the number as quickly as she could. She bit her bottom lip and fought back the rising tide of anxiety. Had Hannah managed to hurt the baby yesterday?

The other line picked up. "Hello, Dr. Cambre's office."

She felt the sides of her neck throb. "This is Dixie Olivier. Dr. Cambre asked me to call?"

"Ah, yes. One moment. I'll let her know it's you."

Almost immediately, zydeco hold music started playing, interspersed with a calm voice expounding the benefits of the Tulane Medical Facility. Dixie rocked back and forth, trying like mad not to succumb to the anxious feelings in her heart. What was wrong with her baby?

Finally, Dr. Cambre picked up. "Miss Olivier, how are you doing?"

"Doctor, what's wrong?"

"What's wrong? Oh! No, nothing is wrong, Miss Olivier. Nothing is wrong at all."

A wave of relief washed over Dixie like the tide. She leaned back. It was one thing to be told you have an anxiety disorder, but actually experiencing it was a completely different monster. At least she could get on medication once the baby was born.

"So what's going on then?"

"Well, I wanted to prescribe a prenatal vitamin for you," Dr. Cambre said. "And given the stress and danger of your job, I'm going to recommend that you stay out of the field as much as possible."

"Right," Dixie said. *As soon as this case is over.*

The phone call reminded her of the issue of when she had conceived. "I know we went over this already, but you're still sure that I'm fifteen weeks along?"

"Yes, as I said, I'm projecting April 7th as your due date."

Dixie hummed. Fifteen weeks didn't properly add up. "So I conceived in early August?"

"It had to have been late July."

That didn't make sense. "Is that so. Are you sure?"

"Absolutely. That reminds me, I'll also have my receptionist send you all the information on second trimester care, all right?"

Dixie nibbled again on her bottom lip. "I'll be on the lookout for it. Thanks."

Hanging up, she sat back and rubbed her forehead. "Gino was out of town until the beginning of August. So how did we manage to conceive in late July?"

After moment, she let it go. "I'm overthinking again, most likely."

For an hour, she worked on reports. It was nearly lunchtime when someone knocked on her door. "Yo, boss lady, may I come in?" It was Rivette.

"Yes."

Opening the door, he poked his head around the corner like a cartoon character. "Hey, you ready?"

She sat there feeling lost. "Ready for what?"

He came into the office and then held up his wrist and tapped it as if he were wearing a watch, which he wasn't. "Time to go bring Miss Davis to the wacky ward. You still want to do this, seeing as how she threatened to stomp out your baby? 'Cause Landry and I can handle it."

"Oh! Yes, absolutely. I want to make sure that nothing goes wrong. She's sedated, right?"

"Yes, ma'am, she is. All right, then, meet Landry and me out back in ten. We'll follow the transport to the hospital."

He closed the door as he left.

Leaning back, she closed her eyes. It was hard to accept that a ten-year-old girl could be a heartless killer, no matter what the circumstances were. But the facts—and Hannah's own behaviors—were pretty damning. And the warning signs for violence had been there—it's just that no one had paid attention.

No wonder Hannah loved "November Rain" so much. She identified with the sadness. Poor kid. I hope the doctor can help her.

Dixie scanned the name of the accepting physician. Then she gasped, hardly able to contain her excitement.

"Dr. Kindley? That's the other guy who may know where Sam is!"

The smell of the Tulane Psychiatric Intensive Care Unit lingered in Dixie's nose, body odor and urine hanging like a musk. It reminded her of the geriatric home where Papa Olivier's mother had spent the last of her days. Rivette and Landry seemed unaffected.

She wrinkled her nose in disgust, trying to ignore the odor. She figured it was likely oversensitivity due to her pregnancy, but that didn't make it any more enjoyable.

"How's the suspect?" Landry asked.

She regarded Hannah, who was cuffed to the wheelchair she'd been pushing. Hannah's head rolled in a small side-to-side arc as she burbled unintelligibly. Dixie felt the back of Hannah's neck. The skin was cool to the touch.

"Drugged." She gently rubbed it. Despite having almost been harmed by her, Dixie couldn't hate her. Something about Hannah's situation just seemed off.

"What did they put in her, anyway?"

Someone spoke behind Dixie. "Diazepam."

She turned to see a man in his forties with oily, short, black hair wearing a white physician's jacket and rectangular glasses. He smiled like a salesman would at his clients.

"Dr. Kindley at your service, Detectives."

He shook hands with Rivette and then Landry, lingering for several seconds with him. "Landry, yes? I believe I spoke with you on the phone, correct?"

Landry wiped perspiration from his forehead. "Correct, Dr. Kindley. This is Lieutenant Olivier. She's, um, my boss. She'll be handling things from here."

Casting her eyes toward him, she rubbed her bottom lip. *Well, that's odd. Paul's acting mighty suspicious.*

Dr. Kindley's smile broadened as he reached over and shook her hand, pulling her attention away from Landry. "Lieutenant Dixie Olivier? I read about you in the *Picayune* a few months back. You worked with Detective Bergeron on the new Ripper case, correct? Quite the heroine you are!"

She glanced over at Landry and then back at Dr. Kindley. "Rodger's the one who really solved the case, Doctor. I just helped. He and Michael are the true heroes."

Rivette looked around at them, his expression almost completely vacant. "Everything OK here?"

With a dismissive wave, Dr. Kindley said, "Yes, of course, Detective. I'm just congratulating a role model to all citizens. But that's in the past. This is the present. And presently, it seems you have a very troubled little patient who'll be joining our family."

Again, she rested her hand on Hannah's neck, gently touching the girl's chilly skin. She couldn't shake the feeling that Hannah was really a victim.

"Hannah Davis is her name, Doctor. We'll be transferring her to your care while the district attorney decides how they want to proceed."

"And of course, Connick will want a full psychological evaluation?"

"Yes."

Landry handed over a large manila envelope that was over-stuffed with papers. "Here's copies of everything the DA wants you to have. If you have any questions, you're to contact Mr. Connick directly."

Taking the envelope, Dr. Kindley skimmed a random paper. "Thank you, Paul," he said, striding down the hall. "Lieutenant, will you please come with me to my office? We can sign everything there."

"'Thank you, Paul,' eh?" Rivette eyed his partner, who shrugged.

Dixie squeezed Hannah's shoulder. The girl rolled her head back, drooling. "It'll be all right, Hannah. Scott, can you go outside and let transport know we're done here? Paul, assist the staff in getting her settled in. Make sure she's secure."

Rivette sighed exasperatedly, threw up his hands, and hurried away.

As two orderlies approached, taking the wheelchair from Dixie, she leaned over and whispered to Landry, "What's going on? How did Dr. Kindley know our first names?"

He shrugged again. "Just does."

The desire to slap him was growing. Before she could speak, though, he added, "Ouellette knows, remember?"

He said it so suddenly that she stopped. Then she heard Dr. Kindley clear his throat. "Lieutenant, are you coming?"

Landry rushed off with the two orderlies and Hannah. With a defeated sigh, Dixie followed Dr. Kindley to his office. *This isn't over, Paul.*

Once inside, he closed the door and offered her a seat by his desk. "Now, let's get to the crux of the matter, shall we, Lieutenant?" he asked, still smiling in a fake manner. "I read the report on Miss Davis's arrest and interrogation. The strength she exhibited—you've seen this before, haven't you? At the wharf?"

His question caught her completely off guard. She bit her bottom lip and said the first thing that came to mind. "I'm not sure I know what you're talking about."

Oh, that sounded stupid.

"Really? So you can't compare it to someone running up the side of a crane?"

Her mental guard had returned. "I'm just here to sign custody of the suspect over to you, Doctor. Any other line of questioning would be inappropriate."

Tapping his fingers on the surface of his desk, he said, "If you say so, Lieutenant. But I don't think this is a simple case of psychosis."

"What would you say happened to her, then?" He was giving her the chills. Something about him just felt wrong.

His grin got more wolfish. "I believe that Miss Davis's condition was caused by a more . . . external source. I've recently come into some fascinating reading material, so I'm still learning about it. I'm sure I'll have plenty of time to verify my theories."

Dixie was lost. The entire conversation had taken a completely different turn, one she wasn't privy to. "Say what again?"

"Oh, don't worry about it. Just the ramblings of a doctor with some new tools. Here. Let's get to business, shall we?" He slid over a clipboard containing the transfer form—filled out and waiting for her signature—and a ballpoint pen.

"Thanks," she said, signing the form. She slid it back to him. "By the way, are you the physician who treated Sam Castille?"

Dr. Kindley put it away and then leaned back. "Yes, I am. She was a remarkable woman. It's a shame that her commitment had to be extended indefinitely."

It was all Dixie needed. Maybe he knew where she was.

Leaning back in the chair, she focused on the conversation as if were an interrogation. "Yes, it was a heavy blow to me. We were friends, you know."

"Were you? She seemed to think you had betrayed her."

That struck Dixie's heart like a dagger. It was just another way she had failed Sam. Tapping into those feelings, she blurted out, "I didn't, really! It was all a huge misunderstanding."

Her outburst didn't faze him. "I can imagine. Your duty versus your feelings. Tough predicament."

This guy is good. Too good. She fought back a grimace, refusing to show any emotion but being distraught at having no contact with Sam. "I can't even apologize. No one will tell me where she is. It's frustrating."

He snorted. "Well, protecting a patient's privacy is part of our legal system. HIPAA is such a pain, isn't it?"

She nibbled her bottom lip, hard—all part of the act. "Can you at least confirm that she's getting the proper care? You must understand how that weighs on me."

For a long few seconds, he scrutinized her. She kept nibbling her lip until he said, "I'm sorry. I wish I could say she was getting treated properly. Sam's doctor is . . . well, he's an eccentric little man. I respect him for his intellect, but I don't think his treatments will help her."

Of course, that must mean Dr. Klein is treating Sam himself!

Feeling a rush of excitement and barely holding it back, she forced a choke in her voice. "Is she not getting constant care?"

Come on. Take the bait.

Dr. Kindley's voice grew thick with contempt. "Well, what she gets is constant. Her doctor sees her every day. But I wouldn't call his methods 'care.'"

She held back her reaction, but on the inside, she cheered. If Dr. Klein saw Sam every day, she must be within driving distance of New Orleans. But that revelation brought about a separate concern. Were these "methods" harmful? "Now, Doctor. If there's patient abuse going on, you're obligated to report it."

To her surprise, he laughed out loud. It was a particularly malicious sound. His change in demeanor was once again disarming.

"Dear Lieutenant. You really haven't a clue how this city works, do you? Maybe you should talk to your commander about the way the upper echelon of the Big Easy plays its games."

"Excuse me?" What did Ouellette have to do with this?

Standing up, Dr. Kindley opened the door leading out to the hallway. "But I've talked enough. You are a clever one, aren't you? Your little line of questioning got some things out of me after all. Let me give you some free advice: stay away from Sam Castille. The people that want her? You can't handle them. They'd crush you and your little perfect dream like the insect you are. You need to think about your future. About Gino. And about your child."

As he sneered at her, she rose so fast that she nearly fell over, catching herself on the chair. Then she glared at him, balling up her fist and shaking it under his chin. "How did you know about all that? Are you threatening me? Are you seriously threatening a cop?"

This time, he spoke barely above a whisper. "No. I'd never lower myself so far as to threaten someone who crawled out of a trailer park and is trying to play nobility. You'll always be on the fringe of my world. This chat has been droll, Lieutenant. Good day to you." His gaze from beneath his glasses was penetrating and unyielding.

She stood there a moment, sweating. Who was this guy? Then she scowled and left. On the way out, she imagined punching him so hard his nose caved in.

Now it was her turn to smile.

Out in the parking lot, Dixie found Rivette alone, smoking a cigarette. The smoky scent clung to every fiber of his hair and clothes. It was obvious he'd been chain-smoking. "So, I don't take a lot of things seriously," Rivette said, "but tell it to me straight. Is my partner up to something?"

"I don't know, Scott." Then she glanced around. "Speaking of which, where is he?"

"I thought he was with you."

Rubbing the space between her eyes again, she fought back the approaching shakes and sweats of another anxiety attack. *Now I know how Richie felt. How ironic.*

"Want me to go get him, boss?' Rivette looked concerned.

She shook her head. "I can't take any medication while I'm pregnant, so I'll walk it off. Just have the car ready, OK, Scott? Be my hero today."

He tossed his cigarette to the ground and stomped it out. "Sure thing, my lady. I'll even take you anywhere for lunch . . . except Arnaud's, or Commander's Palace, or Mulates . . ."

As he continued to list the most expensive restaurants in town, she felt her mood rise just enough to take the edge off. "Donuts and coffee is fine."

By the time she reached the common room, her anxiety had subsided, although her stump was prickling again. Rubbing it, she scanned the room. It had several tables and chairs, a television on one side, and a wall decorated with multi-colored letters that spelled out "Crazy is only in your mind." Several of the patients were gathered around a short one standing on a chair and telling a story. Nearby, Hannah sat in front of a small table with a Scrabble board. Landry stood beside her, watching the storyteller.

"And it was then that Sam said, and I kid you not, 'So now I am possessed by the queen of the *loa*!' Oh, ho, ho, you should have seen the way Dr. Kindley just sat there simmering. I thought his face would melt off like that Nazi prick Arnold Toht!"

The other patients started laughing riotously. One of them, an older woman with graying hair and a shrill voice, said, "It's only funny because you tell it so well, Lou. I could never make it sound that good. As Martha Stewart says, 'I've had my share of dirty underwear on the floor.'"

Dixie tapped Landry on the shoulder. He turned, giggling. Then he got a panicked look. "Crap, sorry, Dixie! It's just this guy—"

"Were they talking about Sam Castille?"

He nodded and covered his mouth, suppressing another chuckle.

"Excuse me," she said, heading up to the short patient.

He noticed her and bowed low, nearly stumbling off the table. "Hello, beautiful one-armed lady. Might you have time for another story of indelibly riotous Sam Castille?"

Even though it was an interrogation, she didn't project any forcefulness. Instead, she just offered her hand to him, playing the role. "I'm afraid, good sir, that I don't have time. But might I inquire as to where she went?"

He kissed her hand and said, "Oh, that? Everyone knows that, even that drunkard Marion. Poor Sam was transferred to the Evergreen Sanatorium. We shall all miss her."

The other patients bowed their heads. A tall, bald one, said, "Amen."

Slipping back, Dixie brimmed with triumph. Another piece of the puzzle had fallen into place. Nearby, Landry was sweating again.

Then an orderly arrived. "All right, Lou, everyone, that's enough. Let the detectives get back to work."

As the patients started leaving, she rubbed her bottom lip again. *Evergreen Sanatorium?* She'd never heard of it. That could be the answer, but she needed to verify it.

Landry patted her arm. "Hey, Dixie. We should go, right?"

"Yeah. Give me a moment to say goodbye to Hannah. Meet you outside."

He shuffled out without a word. Then she felt someone looking at her. It was Hannah. She was drooling, her dilated pupils completely unfocused.

Taking out a handkerchief, Dixie wiped her mouth. "I don't know what's going on, but we'll figure it out."

Suddenly, a flash, just like at the cemetery, caught her eye. For a brief moment, the same small, white orb from before floated over the Scrabble board. Then it vanished like mist.

Wh-what was that?

Leaning down and bracing herself on Hannah's wheelchair, Dixie examined the board more closely. While most of the tiles were in a jumble, a few had been moved into an arrangement. Hannah's hand was next to it.

The word made no sense to Dixie. Maybe it wasn't a word at all.

"What are you trying to tell me, Hannah?"

As Hannah burbled uselessly, rolling her head down, Dixie committed the word to memory: *krabinay.*

Chapter 10
A Game of Chess

Date: **Friday, October 30, 1992**
Time: **12:30 p.m.**
Location: **New Orleans Police Department**
Precinct Eight, French Quarter

"Olivier. Get your ass in my office this instant." Ouellette looked pissed.

Once more, Dixie was standing there, tote bag in hand, wondering what she had done. Then she heaved a heavy sigh, tossed it into her office, and headed into his. He closed the door behind them both.

"You mind telling me why you harassed Dr. Kindley today? I would have expected that from Bergeron or LeBlanc, rest their souls, but you?"

Just hearing that heated up her cheeks and ears. "He's the one who threatened me!"

He stood there nose-to-nose with her. She could smell the coffee on his breath. "Now, listen carefully, Lieutenant. I'm already in the shithouse with the DA because of Miss LeBeouf threatening to take Hannah's story to the *Picayune,* and I'm not taking any more heat. So stay away from Dr. Kindley." He stuck a finger in her face. "He's off limits."

Her nostrils flared, and she slapped his hand to knock it away. But it was like she had hit steel. It didn't budge at all. Instead she drew back her hand, shaking the pain away from the sudden impact. But she locked eyes with him again. "He said I should ask you about the people that run this city. The upper echelon, he called them. What gives, Commander? It's like you're hiding something. And that could hurt the precinct."

"Humph." Ouellette went around his desk and sat down. "Take a seat."

She did, steadying herself, never breaking eye contact. Her trust in him was wavering with every breath she took.

He rubbed his scalp and then his face. "Dr. Kindley is a member of the Knight Priory of Saint Madonna."

The moment she heard that, her eyes widened. That was the group that Vincent had led before becoming the Bourbon Street Ripper. "Are you serious?"

"Yes. He's one of the few purebloods left. And he's connected to all the most influential members."

"But Jonathon Russell said that after the night Vincent performed a ritual on Sam, the Knight Priory was never the same."

"That is correct."

"No, no. How can this be possible? Rodger and I assumed this meant the Knight Priory just fell apart."

To her surprised, Ouellette sniggered. "You think they'd disband the most powerful group in New Orleans—no, all of Louisiana—just because a crazy SOB does something akin to a Black Mass on his daughter? You can't be that naive."

Dixie's shoulders sagged. So they still existed.

Ouellette leaned back, his face pensive as if recalling an unpleasant memory. "The Knight Priory is no longer run exclusively by the old families in New Orleans—the purebloods. Most of its members now are businessmen and politicians, people who are hungry for power but don't have the heritage or respect for it."

The sickening feeling of disappointment crept through her. The damn Knight Priory just wouldn't go away. "Commander, can you please tell me how Sam fits into all of this? Or is Dr. Kindley being a member of the Knight Priory just a coincidence?"

He folded his hands together and rested his chin upon them. "Several reasons. The Castilles have always run the Knight Priory in the past, so there's the symbolism of the name. Symbolism's real important in these secret societies. The purebloods will likely want her to have children to continue the family line. And everyone wants that bitch's five-billion-dollar estate."

Sam's money was what had led Michael to Kent and gotten him killed. She shivered, the nerves in her stump tingling uncomfortably. "The whole world would be better if Sam just got her money back."

Ouellette leaned back again. "You'd have to have the best lawyers in the world to get her a dime of that fortune. She's basically screwed for life."

"I know you hate her," she said. "But can you at least show some compassion?"

"It's not that I hate her, Olivier. I just know how much trouble she is."

He seemed quite remorseful for a moment. After a few seconds, he sighed. "Look, I know this is confusing. You're being thrust into the middle of a terrible power game, one played by people with far better resources than yourself. I tried to warn you about this, and now you're in too deep and are struggling to keep your head above water. My advice to you? Focus on what Dr. Lazarus asked and then get out. You still have his card, right?"

"Yes." She patted her overcoat pocket.

"Good. Call him when you've done your thing and then tell him you're finished working for him. It's your best chance at a normal life."

"I'm not sure I—"

"Look, you have a big heart, Olivier. And I don't want to see you hurt. But you're a grown woman, and I can't tell you what to do. So don't be surprised if helping Sam ends up being your downfall. I can't stop the Knight Priory if they choose to go after you. Not like that. Taking them down will require many years of very careful planning, not the recklessness of one misguided but well-intentioned detective."

"Thanks. I appreciate the advice. I'll definitely consider it."

"You're welcome. Oh, and another thing."

"Yes, Commander?"

"Lay off of Landry for now. I have his fat ass working on finding something for me. An important tool I lost."

"All right," she said, wondering if it had anything to do with the "new tools" Dr. Kindley mentioned. "May I help at all?"

"Negative. For the moment, I only want Landry involved. All the right people trust him, and that's all you need to know."

Pushing with her good arm, she stood up. "One last thing. How do you know all this? And please don't give me 'It's my damn business to know.' I mean, how do you know everything about what's happening in New Orleans? The Knight Priory. Sam. The Castilles. Whatever Landry's doing. Everything."

The look in his eyes got distant, almost sad. "Someone's gotta fight the good fight, Olivier. I've got my own sins to do penance for."

"Is that why you're working with Dr. Lazarus?"

With that, he sat up straight, his expression militant once more. "Don't ever think I'm on Dr. Lazarus's side. Or the Knight Priory's, for that matter. It just so happens that currently I have the same goals as Dr. Lazarus. Now get on out of here. You have work to do."

She left without another word.

So whose side is he on?

It took Dixie over two hours to fill out the report on Hannah's transfer, partly due to typing with one hand. When she was finished and had handed the report off to Rivette, she locked her office and dialed into the police network. The modem's squawk as it connected pierced the otherwise peaceful atmosphere. A few minutes later, she was loading up her terminal browser.

I sure hope that one day they figure out how to make this crap faster, quieter, and more useful. Maybe even some pictures instead of just green text. Wouldn't that be an advance in technology? Won't hold my breath, though.

Once the command prompt came up, she did a search for "Evergreen Sanatorium."

A minute later, the results were on her screen. It wasn't promising. There were no private or public facilities with that name. According to the network, the Evergreen Sanatorium didn't exist. She rubbed her eyes, hoping this wasn't another red herring.

"Maybe the name 'Evergreen' is a clue. I'll search for that."

Doing a query for just the word "Evergreen," she sat back and massaged her stump. The phantom pains were really starting to annoy her. When she was done, she made a note to check on the status of her prosthetic. *You'd figure they'd rush it since I'm a cop. So much for looking out for me, City Hall. It's like when you forced Rodger to retire.*

The results finally came back. Two items were on the screen: the city of Evergreen, Louisiana and the Evergreen Plantation in Edgard.

"Well, the city is way up in central Louisiana. There's no way Dr. Klein could reasonably get there every day."

She pulled up the file on Evergreen Plantation. It was located on the west bank of the river, was about halfway between New Orleans and Baton Rouge, and was privately owned.

"A person could easily drive there from New Orleans in about an hour."

Dixie shivered and then closed her eyes. "I need to verify that Evergreen Plantation is the same as Evergreen Sanatorium. Dr. Kindley is off-limits, so my only chance is to try to get Dr. Klein to admit it."

It took her only a few minutes to call Dr. Klein's office and set up an appointment. As she waited on the phone for the receptionist to verify the time, she did a search on the word that Hannah had spelled using Scrabble pieces: "*krabinay.*"

"Yes, Miss Olivier. Dr. Klein is available today and will see you at 5:00 p.m."

She didn't respond at first. The search results had her distracted.

"Miss Olivier, are you there?" The receptionist sounded annoyed.

She shook it off. "Yes, five o'clock. Perfect. See you then."

As she hung up, she leaned back, staring at the results on the screen. Then she started nibbling on her thumb. "*Krabinay*: a type of malicious *loa* popular in the voodoo mythos."

She shook her head.

"Voodoo. It's coming back to voodoo."

As Dixie entered the occult store in Jackson Square, a sweet, feminine voice called out, "Hello, welcome to La Croix Voodoo Shoppe. How may I help you, miss?"

A chocolate-skinned woman wearing a rather immodest outfit—obviously meant to accent her curves—was leaning on the counter and smiling as pleasantly as could be. Something about her felt comfortable.

Dixie showed her badge. "Tania Patterson, correct? I'm Lieutenant Dixie Olivier."

Tania's expression slowly hardened, and behind her chocolate eyes, a flame lit. "Are you, now? So I see. What can I do for you, Lieutenant?"

About a dozen patrons and a handful of employees were in the small store. Everyone was focused on the two of them. As soon as she saw that, Dixie pursed her lips. *Humph.* It was best not to interrogate her in front of everyone. She didn't want to get a complaint registered against her.

Motioning to a black curtain covering a doorway leading to the back, she asked, "Mind if we have a moment in private? I wanted to talk to you about some things."

"Is that so?" Tania leaned back against the wall behind the counter and folded her arms. The sunshine around her was gone, and in its place was steel. Her eyes blazed with a steady flame. "You were at the wharf, weren't you? When Sam and Violet fought?"

Or we can do this out here.

Dixie held up her stump. "See this? Violet's the one who did this to me. I was hoping to spare you this in front of your customers, Ms. Patterson."

As if to accent the point, a few customers quickly exited.

Watching them leave, Tania grunted and headed through the black curtain. "This way, then."

The back of the store was well-lit. It looked like someone was disassembling an old carnival dark ride. Dixie stepped up the ramp to where the cart was. She ran her fingers over the railing.

"What's this?"

"It was the Voodoo Tour," Tania said, her arms folded under her chest. "But with Violet gone, I haven't had the heart to run it anymore. So I'm taking it apart. It's worth more to me as scrap anyway."

Patting the empty cart, Dixie turned around, only to catch Tania's eyes. They narrowed, as if Dixie were a prey animal and she was a predator. Almost at once, Dixie started to sweat, cold running through her. It was the exact same feeling as when she had faced Blind Moses at the wharf.

But how? How can this be?

She breathed heavily. Anxiety was coursing through her like a drug. "Please. I don't know what you're doing, but please stop. I need your help."

A moment later, Tania said, "I'm sorry. I don't even realize I'm doing it half the time."

Tania's eyes were now normal, although not particularly cheerful.

"How do you do that, Tania?"

"What do you want, Lieutenant?"

Understanding that she wouldn't get any more of an explanation, Dixie said, "I want to talk to you about *krabinay.*"

That got Tania's attention. "*Krabinay*? What in the name of Papa Ghede do you want to know about a *krabinay*?"

"Everything. Just tell me everything."

Instead of answering, Tania walked up the ramp and over to the doorway that led into the dark ride. On it was the painting of a skull smoking a cigar and wearing a top hat. She traced her fingers over it. "Tell me, Lieutenant, do you believe in monsters?"

Fully composed once again, Dixie asked, "What, you mean like the bogeyman? No. No, I don't."

Tania snickered and then turned around, hands on her hips. "I suppose that's one way of putting it. *Krabinay* are lesser petro *loa*. That means malicious, dangerous. Basically, monsters."

At last, some answers about this voodoo thing. "So *krabinay* are, um, evil *loa*?"

"Eh, I do hate that term—'evil *loa*.' *Loa* like *krabinay* embody rage, violence, and delirium. Those are negative traits, but not all-encompassing evil. A human would have to direct them to do evil. Otherwise, they're dangerous, yes, but not the kind that would hunt a person down in cold blood."

A headache was threatening to start. *Damn hormones.* Dixie rubbed her temples and asked, "OK, so if *krabinay* don't kill in cold blood, why would they kill a human?"

"Hunger. Self-defense. Lesser *loa* are little more than cognizant wild animals."

"And 'lesser' means weaker?"

"Oh, not at all. 'Lesser' just means common. Some lesser *loa* can be very strong. Such as the *krabinay*. They are sort of the catch-all monsters I mentioned."

"Right, so if in one of my investigations, a suspect mentioned the *krabinay*, what would that mean?"

With a contemplative expression, Tania folded her arms underneath her chest once more. "What kind of investigation, if I may ask?"

"I can only tell you what's been released to the news. It was a multiple homicide. Someone wiped out an entire family in a violent and gruesome way."

"Hmm. Did your crime lab tell you that the killer had amazing strength?"

"In a manner of speaking, yes."

Tania closed her eyes, silently moving her lips. Then she asked, "Were the slayings ruthless?"

"Yes, indeed." Dixie leaned against the cart.

When Tania opened her eyes, they were sad. "Lieutenant, are you talking about the Davis family murders?"

Dixie stepped back, blinking in surprise. "How did you know?"

With a sigh, Tania walked down the ramp. "I'm a priestess, Lieutenant. One of the neighbors on Desire Street contacted me a few nights ago. I couldn't enter the house, but I read its energy. A *loa* had been there, a strong one that left a malevolent signature. And hearing you discuss the investigation, I suspect that a *krabinay* was involved."

"What do you mean?"

"I think that your suspect is possessed by a *krabinay*."

Shaking her head, Dixie also went down the ramp. "This is ridiculous. I'm thinking it's a mental illness or something, not hocus-pocus. There's no such thing as voodoo."

She had started heading back to the front of the store when Tania said, "How else can you explain the wharf?"

Stopping, Dixie turned around and pointed her finger at Tania. "You listen. You just . . . listen to me."

"I'm listening." Tania slid her hands behind her back. "But you're not actually saying anything."

Dixie covered her face and counted to ten.

"You and I both know there's no other explanation for what happened at the wharf," Tania said. "And as for your investigation, what about the suspect's pupils? Were they perpetually dilated? Was their body cool to the touch? Did they act in a manner that was crude or even sexual?"

Now massaging the side of her head again, Dixie groaned. She couldn't believe she was even entertaining this insanity. "Yes to all those things. The suspect is a ten-year-old girl, and she nearly knocked me out. And don't ever tell anyone I shared that with you. I could lose my job."

"So it's Hannah after all? We suspected as much. You need to let me see her. We should be able to help." Tania rested her hand on Dixie's shoulder.

Who is "we?" Dixie removed Tania's hand from her shoulder, noting that it was also cool to the touch, like Hannah's had been. "I'm sorry. She's already been committed."

Tania groaned under her breath. "Life is never simple. Look, just please call me as soon as she can have a visitor. If she's possessed, I'll know. And then I can help."

"I'll think about it," Dixie said. "But I don't believe in voodoo."

"Ha! Lieutenant, it doesn't matter what you believe." Tania's tone had become patronizing. "If *loa* exist, they exist. If one's inside of Hannah, then your skepticism isn't going to change that."

As Dixie started to rebut, Tania held out her hand dismissively. "Don't argue. Just call me when you're ready to believe."

That uppity bitch. That did it for Dixie. Without another word, she left, feeling that she had completely wasted her time. *Forget this.*

"Thank you for stopping by today, Lieutenant," Dr. Klein said.

"Thanks for having me in on such short notice." Dixie was wearing her best fake smile as she entered his office. She hung her overcoat on the rack, taking her time to get comfortable and scanning the office for a conversation piece. All she needed was something to steer the discussion toward Evergreen.

He motioned to her. "You are having phantom pains, then, *ja*?"

Looking down, she realized that she was rubbing her stump again. Heat rose in her cheeks. "It's annoying. I'm off-balance all the time, and the tingling is driving me crazy."

"Well, then. Sit down, please, und we can talk about it." He motioned toward a brown leather recliner.

As she scanned the room again, her eyes fell upon a marble chessboard on the far side of the room. Perfect.

"Say, Dr. Klein. Do you like to play chess?"

He puffed out his chest. "I do enjoy the occasional game. Und I have even been champion in a fair share of tournaments. Do you play, Lieutenant?"

She nipped at her bottom lip, certain she could use this to get into his head and learn about the Evergreen Sanatorium. But she needed him to think she was an amateur, or he would be too guarded.

"I've tried it a few times. Could . . . could we play while we talk? It may help me clear my mind. I mean, if that's OK." She finished her lie with as cute an expression as she could muster.

Slapping his hands together, he strode over to her, grinning. "I think zat is an excellent idea, Lieutenant. Let us play a game of chess!"

It took them only a few minutes to get the chessboard set up.

"Since I am a gentleman, I will give you first move advantage," he said, gesturing toward the white pieces.

Dixie kept up her agreeable expression as she slid into detective mode. She had already noticed that he didn't have a timer and that his pieces were beautiful, hand-painted marble figurines.

This set is for decoration. He's a hobbyist at best. Tournament champion, my nub.

Centering her thoughts, she began playing.

First, she moved one of her pawns, and then he moved one of his. She rubbed her face, hoping it would make her look like a rookie. Then she moved another pawn, beginning her strategy. Sometimes you sacrificed pawns to ensure success.

He moved one of his knights. "You are taking an active role in your recovery from the anxiety disorder, Lieutenant. I find zat to be remarkable."

She examined his last move and saw that he was starting an early offense. Perhaps her ruse was working? Purposefully, she moved out a bishop and then nodded in an exaggerated manner. "Thank you. I want to beat this. I don't want to have to spend my life medicated or in long-term care. Both terrify me."

Capturing one of her pawns with his knight, he said, "Taking medication to treat an illness is a cornerstone of our society. Und there is nothing wrong with long-term care, Lieutenant, if it is warranted." He smirked from behind his beard.

She quickly inhaled. Now he was trying to get into her head. She rested her fingers on one of her rooks. But before she moved it, she recalled how she had been able to coax Dr. Kindley into revealing information by getting him to drop his guard. Perhaps allowing Dr. Klein to think he had succeeded in getting into her mind would open up a weakness.

Instead, she moved one of her knights and captured a pawn, leaving her piece vulnerable. "Maybe. But I don't want to be locked away from Gino or my daughter just because I'm having problems that aren't easily fixed."

His grin widened as he captured her knight with one of his bishops. "If you are talking about commitment, Lieutenant, zhen you need not worry. Commitment is reserved for someone who is a danger to themselves und others."

Leaning back and rubbing her stump for show, she scanned the board. So long as he continued to think he was in charge, her strategy had a good chance of working. So she moved another pawn—a useless move to take attention away from an important conversational shift. "You mean like Samantha, right?"

His expression darkened some as he used one of his rooks to slide past her defenses and capture another pawn. "Yes. Just like her." None of his pieces were vulnerable.

Nibbling on her thumb, she continued to split her focus between the game and the interrogation. It was like a powerful hose splitting its stream in two. She moved one of her bishops into a position where it could neither capture nor be captured. "I'm glad she's gone. I was stupid to put faith in her, and it got me injured. That Sam of Spades is a blight on humanity." Tania believed Sam of Spades was actually a *loa* possessing Sam. Dixie wasn't sure what to believe there.

Dr. Klein's sneer vanished. "Yes, Sam of Spades is evil. But don't beat yourself up over it, Lieutenant. We all make mistakes. Zat is part of being human." He moved a pawn into position.

By now, she could clearly see his overall strategy. Only one more move and she could begin her attack. Sliding one of her pawns into another useless, easy-to-capture position, she said, "True, but I want to make sure that such a mistake will never come back to harm me, my friends, or my family. I want to know that she's no longer a threat."

He captured that pawn with one of his knights. "I would not worry about zat, Lieutenant. Sam of Spades will never see the light of day again."

The utter finality in which he said that grabbed her heart in an icy clutch. "Wait, is Sam—er, Samantha—dead?"

Her flub hadn't gone unnoticed. For a long moment, he regarded her, narrowing his eyes. As gingerly as she dared, she swallowed. It felt like a lump of coal was lodged in her throat. Had she just blown it?

And then he shook his head. "Oh, nothing like that. Zis is not a police state. We do not euthanize someone because they are criminally insane. No, I mean that Sam of Spades is in a place where she cannot ever escape."

She silently exhaled. She was certain he hadn't seen the panic she had felt. *Don't do that again, dummy!*

Looking back over the chess board, she realized that she needed to stall until she got her head back into the game. Slowly, trying to look unsure, she moved a pawn far away from the action. "Not to be distrusting, but are you certain? I would rest better knowing that you are guaranteeing this."

He shrugged and then captured that pawn with one of his knights. "Lieutenant, I give you my word. I see Samantha every day. The place she is at is both remote und secure."

I need to get rid of that knight. Nibbling on her thumb again, Dixie changed her strategy, moving out a rook as bait. "That's really good to know. I haven't much faith in the psychiatric hospital system. No insult to you intended."

Dr. Klein captured her rook with his knight, exactly what she wanted. "None taken. I have very little faith in them as well. Zat is why I choose to treat my patients outside of the system."

Although she didn't show any signs of it, she felt a rush within her. He had fallen for both traps. His chess pieces were now vulnerable, and he had let slip that Sam was being treated outside of a real hospital. Now Dixie just had to confirm that the plantation was the sanatorium.

With a sudden confident push, she went on the attack, capturing that very same knight with a bishop. "Sounds like you have an optimal system. Do you find that the air out in the country helps with the treatment?" *Come on, you prick! Be distracted by the game.*

His face registered surprise at her move on the board. Quickly, as if trying to cover up for a mistake, he moved out his other knight and captured that bishop. His back-line defenses were getting thin. "Well, I do not know about ze patients. They are kept underground. But personally, I find the countryside to be very relaxing."

Dixie kept up her poker face. He was slipping. Badly.

Not letting up the pressure, she captured that other knight with a rook. Her offense was falling into place just as quickly as his defenses crumbled. "Sounds wonderful. There are times I wish I could live out there, perhaps in the plantation country."

Visibly shaken by the loss of his second knight, Dr. Klein clenched his jaw and then cleared his throat. "I highly recommend it, Lieutenant. You will feel like you are king of your own domain." He then moved out his queen and captured that rook, completely removing his queen from his defenses.

Now it was a struggle to hold back her excitement. He was falling completely into her trap. All she had to do was get a name to confirm the location. "Sounds lovely, truly. I might want to move to someplace like that one day. Is the area expensive?" She moved out one of her knights, capturing a pawn.

Take the knight. Take the bait. Come on, you creepy son-of-a-bitch.

Growling under his breath, he moved his remaining bishop to capture that knight. "Of course. Edgard has such beautiful plantations. Of course, I live in one for free as a caretaker. Ze arrangement works out very nicely."

Her pulse raced all the way to her hand as he fell completely for her strategy. *That's it! Sam's gotta be at the Evergreen plantation. This game is mine!*

Then she picked up her queen. "I'm envious. Oh, by the way . . . Dr. Klein . . .?"

"Hmm. Yes?"

Dixie slid her queen into place, right next to his king. None of his pieces could capture it, and the king couldn't move without getting captured.

She smiled sweetly. "Checkmate."

Chapter 11
Cold November Rain

Date: **Saturday, October 31, 1992**
Time: **5:00 p.m.**
Location: **Esplanade Apartments**
New Orleans City Park

The warm, rose-scented water sloshed around Dixie as she rested in her bathtub. Along with the wet heat, a calm, subtle euphoria ebbed over her, tingling at every nerve. With every gentle breath, the worry and stress of the past few days slipped away. Finally, she felt at peace.

She slid down, her bangs dipping into the water.

Dr. Lazarus was pleased with her report. It was in his hands now. Although she wanted to go to the plantation herself, she couldn't ignore Dr. Kindley's warning. If running afoul of the Knight Priory would put her, Gino, or her baby at risk, then she would have to be content on the sidelines.

I'm sorry, Sam. This is the most I can do right now.

Sitting up, she dipped her hand in the water and smoothed back her bangs. Then she rubbed her forehead, feeling those final lines of stress vanish.

There was a gentle knock on the bathroom door. It was Gino. "Dixie? Dinner is ready, my love." He had insisted on cooking tonight instead of going out, which was odd, since going out on Halloween had become a tradition. But she was excited nonetheless. "I'll be right out!"

She then drained the tub and tiptoed into the bedroom. The smell from the front of the apartment was amazing, making her mouth water. First, she got into a simple slip dress, and then she dried and styled her hair. After a check in the mirror and a nod of approval, she headed out front.

When she saw what Gino had done, she gasped.

The front room was lit entirely by dozens of candles resting on everything from bookshelves to countertops. The dining-room table, which was usually littered with both of their work, was cleared off and decorated with a white tablecloth and a lit candelabrum. A dinner of filet mignon with sautéed mushrooms, served with red potatoes and asparagus, lay there. A bottle of wine rested in a bucket of ice, opened and breathing. The Fantasy Overture from Tchaikovsky's *Romeo and Juliet* played in the background.

Gino stood before the table, dressed in a suit that Dixie had bought him for Christmas. He held out his hand. "Dinner is ready, my love."

She nearly swooned.

My God, look at all this! Gino, you . . . you . . .

"I love you." It was all she could say.

Once he had helped her sit, he poured the wine and held his cup aloft. "To you, Dixie."

Her cheeks felt as red as the wine as she clinked her glass to his. Then she drank—it was full-bodied and dry, perfect for steak. She reached for the fork. Almost immediately, she saw a problem. "Gino. The filet mignon looks perfect. But I don't think I can cut it with one arm."

"Just try your fork," he said gently.

She blinked and pressed the utensil into the meat. It easily sliced through. With an exhale of anticipation, she took a bite. It melted in her mouth, the flavor like ambrosia from heaven. She closed her eyes and slowly chewed. Everything was perfect.

"Dixie, I have to apologize to you."

She opened her eyes and then swallowed. "Apologize for what, Gino?"

His face was wrought with melancholy. "When I first met you, I fell completely in love. I was young and full of pride and the desire to make you mine. I pursued you until you relented. And since then, I have given you no other option but to be with me."

"What do you mean?"

"Every time we've been together, every time we've made love, I've only thought of how I was with the woman I wanted. I have lived for nothing but the desire to love you. It is like a drug I cannot live without."

Putting down her fork, she tried to catch his eyes. She had never seen him so serious.

Their eyes met. His were already overflowing. "Now I have created a life within you, one that came without any plan, one that was born of a desire that could never be quenched. Dixie, my love, I am so sorry for doing this to you. I . . . I have given our situation so much thought. There is only one way I can make this right."

Her mouth was dry as he came to her side, got on his knees, and took her hand. Tears spilled down his cheeks. "Dixie, I swear to you, from this moment onward, everything I think, everything I do, it will be with your desire, your plans in mind."

She dared not breathe, her heart punching against her chest. *Is he about to—?*

And then he was holding up a beautiful diamond ring.

"Dixie Olivier, please marry me."

Dixie didn't move. She didn't blink. She didn't think.

And then, a moment later, she squealed and hugged him as tightly as she could. "Yes! You big idiot! You had me so worked up, I could hit you. Yes, yes, you . . . you beautiful man, you!"

Gino started laughing and embraced her back. "I am sorry for being so dramatic, Dixie. I really did not know how to do this. I do feel at times like I was using you, and—"

"Just shut up and kiss me," she interrupted. And they kissed for a very long time.

After dinner, they made love right there on the couch, with him treating her with great gentleness. The candles were nubs by the time they were done. With a happy sigh, she lay her head on his chest while he stroked her back. They cuddled in silence until each candle was dark.

Fairy tales really can come true.

Then her pager went off.

"Mmmm. Can we ignore it?" He rubbed her arm, her back, her butt.

She kissed him and sat up. "You know I can't ignore it, Gino. It's probably just Landry or Rivette misplacing something. I'll be right back."

She checked the number. It was indeed Rivette. Yawning slightly, the wine and sex tugging at her eyelids, she placed the call. Gino lounged on the couch as if he were Dionysus, staring at her until her cheeks lit on fire.

Then Rivette picked up. "Dixie? Thank God you're there!"

He sounded so panicked that she snapped to attention. "Um, what's wrong? Please tell me it's Paul choking on a po'boy again." At the couch, Gino quickly sat up.

"It's bad. Real bad," Rivette said. "Ouellette wants you at Tulane Hospital right away."

A chill washed over her. There was only one reason for her to go there. "What happened with Hannah?"

"She went on a rampage. She murdered most of the people at the psych ward and then ran off into the city."

The receiver shook in her hand. All she could hear was Hannah's threat to stomp out her baby.

"Dixie? Dixie! Are you there?" Rivette was shouting.

Taking a deep breath, she steadied her grip on the phone.

Then finally, she spoke, her voice barely above a whisper. "Yeah. I'm here. I'm on my way."

Any hope Dixie had that Rivette was exaggerating vanished when she saw the dozen or so police cars and ambulances outside of Tulane Hospital. Seeing almost as many covered bodies getting loaded for transport to the morgue was like a kick in the gut. It was like the wharf all over again.

Oh, Hannah. What have you done?

She waded through the police, searching for Ouellette. She found him talking with Dr. Kindley and an older African American gentleman, whom she recognized as District Attorney Harry Connick.

He stared down his nose at Ouellette. "I thought this crazy stuff was over when the Castille girl went away."

Ouellette unflinchingly matched his gaze. "With all due respect, sir, we don't know what happened tonight. Dr. Kindley was in his office, and the only patients who survived are a catatonic and man who speaks solely in Bible verses."

With a grumble, Connick rubbed the back of his head. "Dammit, Louis, the mayor's office wants answers. They went on about the Castille family legacy and getting these events under control. Then they wanted to talk alone to Dr. Kindley. I just don't know what they're all about anymore."

Dixie stood by her commander's side. He glanced at her in acknowledgement but said nothing. Poor guy was stuck playing the middleman again, just like after the wharf.

Connick folded his arms. "So what did they want to talk with you about, Kindley?"

Almost as if on cue, Dr. Kindley adjusted his glasses. "They wanted my opinion on Miss Davis. I told them I believe she suffered an acute psychotic break that resulted in overstimulation of the adrenal glands. She will be dangerous to apprehend until she calms down."

Although Dixie saw no outward signs or tells, her gut told her he was lying.

However, that explanation appeared to sate Connick. "Right. So, Louis, before the mayor's office puts both of us up on the cross again, let's find this little nutcase and take her down. And try not to kill her. The last thing we need is the

Picayune running a story on the white, ex-military police commander having his men gun down the little black girl."

He headed off with Ouellette muttering. "That's not offensive. Not at all. Asshole." Then he turned to Dixie. "So here's what we do. You find out where Hannah Davis is and bring her in alive. Use any means you have at your disposal. I don't care how unorthodox. Let me repeat that again. No matter what you have to do, bring her in alive. I'll go deal with the press, the mayor, and anyone else who gets in your way."

"Yes, sir!"

He turned to leave, but then he stopped. "And by the way, congratulations."

"Pardon?"

"The engagement ring you're wearing. Congratulations."

This time, he left.

Her brow furrowed. "I hate it when he does that."

Behind her, Dr. Kindley said, "Yes, yes. Ouellette is simply amazing, isn't he? Even after all these years, he impresses me when he takes the stage." His voice was thick with contempt.

"Hmph. And how long have you known him, to speak of him in the familiar?" She glared back at him.

He smirked. "Perhaps even longer than you, Lieutenant." He shrugged and pushed up his glasses. "But what do I know, right? I'm not nearly as intelligent as you, after all."

A bad taste rose in her mouth. She really disliked him.

"You know, Dr. Kindley, I was going to ask your thoughts on Miss Davis, since you obviously lied through your teeth to the DA just now. But then I realized I just don't care what you have to say."

"Oh, I think you should. But then again, you don't believe in ghosts and goblins, do you? And magic is something akin to pulling a rabbit out of a hat."

His glasses began to shimmer as if filled with their own light. "A lot of people died tonight. That's an awful lot of energy for someone with the right tools to use."

She shook her head. This guy was supposed to be a doctor. Why was he spouting nonsense?

The shimmer faded. "I wonder how much will be released when Miss Davis dies."

Her skin crawled as if covered in a hundred tiny bugs. "Only a sicko would see benefit in a child's death."

As he walked past her, his voice got low, almost threatening. "I'm practical with my new tools, nothing else. But what I do is none of your concern. If I were you, Lieutenant, I'd start believing right here, right now."

He sauntered off, whistling. She glared at his back.

What was he up to? Were these "new tools" he was bragging about the ones Ouellette was searching for? *If so, Landry needs to know.*

The inside of the psych ward reminded Dixie of the wharf. Blood was everywhere, caking the floors, walls, and ceiling like a macabre coat of paint. Some of the bodies were so badly mutilated that, more than likely, they'd only be identifiable by their dental records.

She frowned as she worked her way around the crime lab people. How could a ten-year-old girl be capable of this much brutality?

She entered the common room, where the fluorescent lights flickered. She saw dozens of bodies—some orderlies and some patients. She recognized a few of them: the short patient who had told her where Sam was and the older woman who had quoted Martha Stewart. Like with the Davis family, there were few defensive wounds.

"Serious mess here, eh, Dixie?"

Rivette and Landry had joined her. While Landry looked around horrified, Rivette said, "We came over as soon as I got off the phone. Ouellette just filled us in on our 'mission.' So we're supposed to capture a girl who can do all this without killing her?"

"Yes," she said, trying not to lose her balance on the gore-covered floor.

"Well, Dixie, I gotta say that I hate the position we're being put in."

"Duly noted."

He folded his arms and scrutinized her. Then he grunted. "So what do we do?"

Finally steadying herself on a pillar, she said, "Go up front and see if there's any security-camera footage. Maybe we can get an idea of where she went."

After giving a dramatic bow where he nearly slipped, he headed off.

"Landry?" Dixie called.

He was chatting with one of the crime lab specialists, so she shouted his name again. "Hey, Landry!"

"Yes, Dixie," he said, carefully walking over to her.

She lowered her voice to just above a whisper. "I don't know if it means anything, but Dr. Kindley's been acting very strange. I suspect he may have whatever it is that Ouellette has you searching for."

His voice lowered just the same. "Are you sure?"

"No, I'm not. I don't even know what tool you're looking for. It's just a hunch."

He locked eyes with her and then nodded. "Thanks."

As he walked away, Dixie scanned the room for any information that could lead to Hannah. She was just about to leave when a familiar white flash caught her eye. She turned just in time to see that same small orb float to the far wall of the room. What she saw took away her breath and made her heart race.

The letters for "Crazy is only in your mind" had been cut, torn, and rearranged to spell "Stomp out the baby."

"Oh, my God," she said, shining her flashlight on it. "Paul, look."

The moment he saw it, he put his hand on her back. "Dixie, we need to get you out of here. Right now."

"Yes, please. Get me out of here."

They stepped out into the front lobby, which was swarming with uniformed officers and medical personnel. Rivette was on the phone. As soon as he saw her, he asked, "What's wrong?"

Her heart was still racing as Paul said, "Hannah left a written threat for Dixie, Scott. We need to get her to safety."

At once, Rivette hung up the phone and took her arm. "Let's get you out of here now. We can form a plan later."

She suddenly thought of Gino. He'd be alone and very vulnerable. "Um, guys, can one of you please go get Gino?"

Landry waved. "I'll call him and let him know what's going on. Then I'll go get him. Scott, can you bring her to the precinct?"

Rivette tugged on her arm. "Yep! Let's go, Dixie. No time for chances."

Breathing a sigh of relief, she said, "Thank you, Paul. Right, Scott. Let's get going."

While Landry got on the phone, Rivette led her to the exit. They met Ouellette at the front door.

"What's going on here?" he asked, looking at the two of them. "We have an investigation to run. No time to get coffee, children."

Without skipping a beat, Rivette said, "Sir, we believe that Miss Davis is going to target the lieutenant directly. We want to take her and Gino into protective custody."

Thanks, Scott, for handling this. She hated feeling this vulnerable.

Again, Ouellette looked back and forth between them and then said, "Fine. Get them to the precinct. We'll figure things out there. We'll—"

"Lieutenant!"

Landry was waving frantically. "You need to come and listen to this right now!"

As if the devil himself were after her, she rushed toward Landry, pushing past other police, hospital staff, and patients, until she was able to snatch the phone away. "Hello? Gino?"

She was answered with a recording of a song.

"*So never mind the darkness, we still can find a way.*"

A cold needle pricked her heart.

"*'Cause nothing lasts forever, even cold November rain.*"

"Hannah!" she screamed into the phone. Almost everyone in the room turned to her. "Hannah! Don't hurt him! Don't hurt him, please!"

Girlish laughter, followed by Gino crying out in pain, was her response.

"Gino!" Her throat was parched and her temples pounded. "Please! Hannah! Don't hurt him!"

This time, Hannah said, "Hurry home, bitch!"

Then the line went dead.

Her balance dropped and so did she, sliding to the floor. Wrapping her arm around herself, she shivered uncontrollably. All she could think about was Gino's body, bloody and broken.

And then Rivette was at her feet, gently shaking her. "Dixie? Lieutenant, what's going on?"

But she could barely hear him, just as she could barely hear Landry relaying what was going on, or even hear Ouellette barking orders. All she could hear was Gino's cries.

He's going to die! God—someone—what do I do?

Anxiety flowed through her like a river. She never felt so out of control.

Then she saw Dr. Kindley staring at her from across the room. She instantly remembered his words: " . . . start believing right here, right now."

Believing. I've refused to believe she's possessed.

Then Rivette's words followed: ". . . go with whatever solution has the least assumptions."

She closed her eyes and inhaled deeply. *If all I assume is that Hannah is possessed, this entire case makes sense.*

And finally, Tania's words rang in her head: "If she's possessed, I'll know, and I can help."

Opening her eyes, she pulled herself to her feet. She had to take a stand. "OK, I know what I need to do." She grabbed the receiver, tucked it under her chin, and dialed Tania's number.

"Dixie?" Rivette asked. "What do we do?"

The other line started ringing. "I want you to bring the car around so I can get home. I'm sure that by the time we do, Ouellette will have the entire SWAT team there. But I need to meet someone."

"What are you doing?"

She didn't answer him because Tania had picked up. "Thank you for calling La Croix Voodoo Shoppe. How may I help you?"

Dixie breathed a sigh of relief. "Tania? This is Lieutenant Olivier. I'm going to need your help with Hannah Davis after all."

She swallowed hard.

"I'm ready to believe."

By the time Dixie got back home, being driven by Rivette and Landry, at least a dozen police cars, an ambulance, and an armored SWAT vehicle surrounded the upscale apartment building. A police helicopter was flying around, shining a spotlight on the upper windows. Several news stations and a growing crowd of people were gathering outside.

As soon as they parked, she headed to the mobile command center. Among the several officers, Ouellette was inside, standing near a hostage negotiator. Ouellette was wearing his Kevlar jacket and looked ready for war.

"He's pulling out all the stops," Rivette said.

Dixie tapped her commander on the shoulder. "Expecting another wharf incident?"

He spun around. His face had the same intensity as it had that night. "Not taking any chances. But enough of that. Gino's still alive. The negotiator is on the phone with him right now."

She hurried over and grabbed the phone from the negotiator. "Gino, baby?"

"Dixie?" He sounded pained and weakened.

"Baby, what's going on? Are you OK?"

"I've been better. But I'm alive." He sounded hoarse.

In the background, the negotiator and Ouellette started arguing over procedure. She shut them out. "How badly are you hurt, honey?"

His chuckle turned into a coughing fit. "That little girl. She really beat me. I think she broke my arm. She didn't get you, though, right? That is all that matters."

Her hand started shaking. It was a struggle to keep the phone still. In the background of the call, she could still hear "November Rain" playing.

Calm down. If you panic, he's dead.

"What is Hannah doing right now? Can you see her?"

"Yes. She's in the front room. She's dancing. Lewdly."

Tears dripped down her cheeks. "Can you get into another room?"

"I'm trying. I'm in the hallway. Crawling to the bedroom. Will—AHHHH!"

She cringed as his cry was cut short, her throat constricting until she could only breathe tiny huffs. For an awful moment, there was total silence. Then someone picked up the phone.

"Is that you, Lieutenant?" It was Hannah.

With every ounce of will she possessed, Dixie steadied her nerves. "You know it's me, Hannah."

"Good. I was just about to break your boyfriend's neck, and I wanted you to hear."

"No!" she wailed into the receiver.

Everyone in the command center stopped what they were doing. You could hear a pin drop.

Then Hannah laughed. "Gotcha! Happy Halloween!"

Every nerve in Dixie's body tingled. Every part of her shook. She was certain that her heart had stopped and then restarted.

Ouellette reached over and flipped the call to speakerphone. Then he gently took the phone from her hand.

"Listen, Lieutenant, it's really simple," Hannah said. "Come see me alone, and your bo-hunk lives. I get so much as a hint of the police coming up here, and he'll be dead before you blink."

Then the line went dead. Slowly, Dixie turned to face everyone. They were watching her with concern.

"What does she want with you?" Ouellette asked.

Her voice shook. "I think . . . I think she wants to kill me."

The look on his face became almost murderous. "No way are you going up there, then."

"Lieutenant, if you can get Miss Davis to release the hostage, we can proceed with a raid," the hostage negotiator said.

Just when it seemed like Ouellette was about to tear into the man, Rivette said, "Actually, Commander, it's a valid plan. No one can get into a suspect's head like Dixie. All she has to do is distract her until we get Gino to safety. Then we can nail her."

Dixie's lips quivered as she smiled. *Thanks, Scott. You're a great guy.*

Ouellette clicked his jaw several times. "Fine, but we do this by the book, or our careers are dead. You, negotiator, get your ass back on the phone and get the hostage ready for release. Rivette, you and Landry cover Olivier and wait to extract Gino. First sign of trouble, though, go in with maximum force. And I don't care what Connick said. If you have to, bring the girl down."

It took only a few minutes for Dixie, Rivette, and Landry to get into their Kevlar vests, both men helping her get dressed. By the time they were done, the negotiator had an answer from Hannah.

"She's agreed to let Gino go but demands that the lieutenant go unarmed."

Ouellette said, "Bad idea. But it's your ass, Olivier, so it's your call."

Putting on her badge, she said, "I'll be OK. You do your part, Commander. I'll do mine."

Then she motioned to the negotiator. "Tell her I'm coming in, unarmed."

As Dixie, Rivette, and Landry stepped out onto the top floor, they saw Tania leaning against the wall. She was in a full indigo-colored bodysuit and had a dangerous look in her eyes. All hints of charm and sweetness were gone.

"You didn't tell me it would be this hard to get up here, Lieutenant."

"I didn't know. Sorry."

"Who the hell is this?" Rivette asked as both he and Landry reached for their sidearms. "How the hell did she get here? The whole floor is shut down."

Dixie held out her arm. "Stand down, men. I invited her. I think she can help."

"A civilian? Really?" Rivette sounded disgusted.

She ignored him. "Tania, tell me you can help."

Tania folded her arms under her chest. Her gaze was intense. "I can't guarantee yours or anyone else's safety, if that's what you're asking. But I can feel it. You've got a *krabinay* in there—a real strong one. And it wants to kill."

"What the hell is a *krabinay*?" Now Rivette sounded even more frustrated. "Will someone tell me what's going on?"

"I think we should just let the lieutenant do her job," Landry said. He seemed very calm for someone usually so nervous.

Nodding, Dixie said, "Landry's right. I need to try this out first. Tania's coming with me. Stick to the plan. If this goes bad, do what the commander ordered, even if you have to kill the suspect."

Rivette gritted his teeth, his face getting red. "Fine! But be careful, OK, Dixie? You aren't just risking your own life anymore." He motioned toward her stomach. "Don't be stupid."

She was grateful to him once again. "I won't take any risks, Scott. Thanks. Just watch my back."

"You know I will."

As Dixie headed toward her apartment, she filled Tania in on the situation. When she was finished, Tania said, "This is unusual behavior for a *krabinay.* It sounds like someone forced it into Hannah and is ordering it to kill specifically to send life energy back into the spirit world. Like a ritual of sorts."

Dixie nodded, remembering Occam's razor. She'd just have to trust that Tania knew what she was talking about. "Hannah wants me to go in alone, so wait until Gino's out before you do anything."

"All right. But you must keep the *krabinay* busy. I have to touch the host in order to do anything. If it sees me coming, we'll have a bloody fight on our hands, one I can't guarantee you'll survive."

"Understood." Something told Dixie that wasn't a bluff.

Once at the apartment, Tania hid behind some nearby potted plants while Dixie gingerly opened the door. "Hannah, it's Dixie. I'm coming in, alone and unarmed."

Hannah was in the hallway, standing on an unconscious Gino, his right arm unnaturally bent. Her hair covered much of her face, showing only a wide, sick grin.

"Hey, there. Thanks for stopping by. I got bored playing with your man-steak. So, here!"

Jumping off, she pushed him across the floor like a curling stone. Dixie barely stumbled out of the way, landing against the dining-room table as she lost her balance. Gino slid out into the hallway, hitting the wall with a heavy thud. He groaned and then fell silent.

"Gino!" Dixie staggered toward the doorway, only to find Hannah suddenly blocking her path.

"Nope. That's against the rules, bitch." She cackled as she jumped and punched Dixie in the face. The impact was enough to send her flying, momentarily knocking her out. When she regained consciousness, she was slumped against the entrance to the hallway. Hannah, who had a chef's knife, was stalking toward her, licking the flat of the blade.

God, she's fast. OK. Engage her. Distract her.

Leaning against the wall, Dixie held out her hand. "I don't get it. Why do you have to kill? I thought *krabinay* didn't normally do this." Her vision blurred in and out.

A few feet from Dixie, Hannah hunched down. She seemed a bit disappointed. "You know what I am? Bah! This host musta spelled it out for you with that Scrabble board."

Then she twirled the knife around. "I guess it can't be helped. The girl's will is shit, but psychoactive drugs can weaken even the strongest possessions. I remember the good old days when all they had were leeches and smoke from burning dung."

Taking the knife, she pressed it against her throat. "I guess at some point, I need to make her commit suicide. That's what she wanted anyway, eh, mortal? To end her life 'cause of what happened to Granny?"

By then, Dixie's vision had fully returned. She saw movement go past the doorway. It seemed like this interrogation could actually work. "But why are you doing this? *Krabinay* don't usually kill mortals. So why are you?"

Leisurely, Hannah slid the knife's blunt end over her body. "You know what it's like to follow orders, don't you? Of course you do! That's why I love you cops. You obey without question."

"What does that have to do with anything?" Dixie asked.

Without warning, Hannah stabbed at her, stopping less than an inch from her eyes. While Dixie stared back without flinching, she shrieked in terror on the inside."I'm the same way, mortal," Hannah said. "When our king, the Lord Baron, tells us to do something, we do it. I'm not one to question why he's become such a prick. None of us are. Maybe he's not getting some with the queen. Who knows? Point is, when he says to kill, we kill."

Who is this king and queen? Dixie suddenly wished she had taken voodoo more seriously.

Hannah kissed the knife and then exhaled to mist the blade. "But every time I kill on an order, the life energy that flows from death goes right back to him. That's the sweetest of ambrosia to us, but I don't get any. How is that fair?"

"Sounds very unfair," Dixie said, having no idea what Hannah was talking about.

But then Hannah's sick grin returned. "But that's where you come in, Lieutenant. You really pissed me off with that music stunt, so I got special permission to kill you. And you're pregnant. So when I off you both, I'm going to get double the ambrosia. And I'll savor every single drop."

"Special permission? From your king?"

"Yup."

"So, then, you were told to murder Hannah's family?"

"You guessed it."

"And all those people at the hospital?"

Hannah stood up and bowed and then twirled around as if she were a ballroom dancer. "Correct on all counts. And the mortal who placed me inside this girl didn't specify when I could leave. So now I'm stuck here until she dies."

Dixie's eyes widened. She sat up. "A person did this? Who? Who put you inside her?"

With a giggle, Hannah twirled one more time and reclined against the couch. She ran the knife up and down her small body. "Dunno the guy, but he's a real pill. He'll likely waste away with how much he hates living. But he has our king's pen, so what he writes, we have to do."

What is she talking about?

Dixie saw that she and Hannah were alone. Outside, the helicopter flew around again, shining its light momentarily into the room. Surely they were getting ready to strike.

Yawning, Hannah gripped the knife. "But enough talk. I'm hungry. Time to perform an emergency C-section." With a suddenly menacing expression, she crept forward, brandishing the knife.

Just then, "November Rain" restarted again in the background.

As Hannah continued to stalk toward her, Dixie inhaled and then started singing. "*And when your fears subside.*"

Suddenly, Hannah stopped, her body jolting. "What are you doing?"

Dixie swayed side-to-side with the music. "*And shadows still remain.*"

Hannah's face tightened into a frightful grimace. "Shut up, you twat!" She again stabbed at Dixie, but this time, her hand jerked. She ended up stabbing beside Dixie's head, embedding the knife in the wall.

Dixie locked eyes with her. "*I know that you can love me, when there's no one left to blame.*"

Hannah's fighting it.

With the knife stuck, Hannah stumbled back, her hands shaking. "Damn it! You're connecting to this little bitch with music. Does her heart find that much peace with this song?"

Keeping her eyes on Hannah, Dixie pulled herself to her feet. "*So never mind the darkness. We can still find a way.*" Silently, she begged Hannah to fight back.

Hannah's entire body started to tremble. Blood dripped down her cheeks. "Fuck you! I'll kill you with my bare hands."

But as soon as she took one step toward Dixie, Gino rushed into the room and grabbed her with his good arm.

"Ugh! You?" Hannah said. "I'll kill you both, I swear it!"

"Tania!" Gino said. "I have her like you asked."

Coming out from the hallway behind Dixie, Tania clasped her hand over Hannah's face, her pupils so dilated that they were almost completely black.

"*Pa volonte m 'yo, pa pouvwa mwen, parte sa a soti nan pitit! Vini non nan m '! Trase nan m '! M 'mande nou antre nan m' koulye a*!" Tania's voice, heavy with authority, reverberated throughout the apartment. Her hair blew around as if from an invisible wind, just like when Sam and Blind Moses had fought on the wharf.

The helicopter started coming back around.

Gino pulled Dixie away. "We must give her space!"

By then, Hannah's body was twisting and writhing as she foamed at the mouth. Tania's eyes widened until they were like the sockets of a skull, her teeth bared until they were like the fangs of a wild beast. Only when Hannah went limp did Tania let go. Then she roared in agony. Her veins went black and bulged. Then they subsided and then bulged again.

"It's in me! Stay back while we destroy it! Stay back!"

With another screech, Tania stumbled back into the hallway, convulsing as if having a seizure.

"Tania!"

"No! Don't follow me! Stay back!"

The sound of the helicopter grew louder.

"Lieutenant!"

Rivette and Landry were at the front doorway, their pistols drawn and aimed at Tania. Now standing, she started foaming at the mouth before rampaging toward the back of the apartment, punching holes into the walls. Her bellows were like a beast from the depths of one's nightmares.

"Stay back!" Dixie ordered her men. "Leave her alone!" Suddenly, her apartment was flooded with light. The helicopter hovered right outside, turning so that its side faced the window. The sound was almost deafening.

"Lieutenant," Rivette said, his voice barely audible, "look out!"

Dixie turned to see Hannah stagger back on her feet. The girl looked around, her body shivering. Her eyes were no longer bloodshot. Her pupils were no longer dilated. She held out her hand, her face clouded with confusion and fear.

Smiling gently, Dixie reached for Hannah. *She's OK! My God, Tania, you did it! She's—*

Then the side of Hannah's head exploded, blood, bone and brain matter spraying the dining-room table. Her fingertips grazed Dixie's as she fell to the ground. Outside, the helicopter turned away as a police sniper lowered his rifle.

For a few seconds, Dixie watched Hannah's lifeless body, her eyes wide and her lips trembling. Gino, Rivette, and Landry all had horrified expressions. Then Ouellette rushed into the room. The moment he saw what had happened, he hit a wall, making the panels shake.

"What the fuck is wrong with them?"

Hannah's eyes were still open, a look of innocence there. Trembling, Dixie slid to the ground, reaching over and pulling Hannah to her lap. The girl was still warm. Cradling what was left of her head, Dixie screamed as loud as she could. When her vocal chords started to ache, she cried, rocking Hannah's lifeless body back and forth.

It started to rain a cold, cold rain.

Dixie's Epilogue
Nothing Lasts Forever

Date: **Friday, November 6, 1992**
Time: **12:00 p.m.**
Location: **Desire Street Cemetery**
New Orleans Ninth Ward

A cold November rain sprinkled the cemetery as Dixie lay flowers upon Hannah's grave within the Davis family mausoleum. Then she caressed the plaque, her fingertips lingering over the memorial etched in bronze, which said, "It is nothing to you, all you who pass by."

"They murdered her," said a voice behind Dixie.

She turned to face Tania. "They had no idea she wasn't a threat."

Tania wore a black dress with high heels and a small jacket, seemingly unaffected by the weather. Her eyes narrowed. "After everything you saw, you still want to believe that?"

With a defeated sigh, Dixie shook her head. "I don't know what to believe anymore, Tania. You obviously got rid of that *krabinay* and saved her. Yes, *loa* and ghosts exist. I can't deny that. But to suspect that the people in charge of this city willingly executed a ten-year-old girl? That's a lot to swallow."

Tania snorted with disdain. "And what about her social worker? Didn't she say she was going to the press about this? Where is she now?"

Dixie scowled. "Miss LeBeouf? She had a nervous breakdown and was committed for treatment."

"And you honestly believe what they tell you? Where's that detective's intuition you supposedly possess?"

At that, Dixie said, "Tania, I'm not a detective anymore. The mayor himself had me placed on indefinite leave. And after what happened, I don't know if I want to go back. I don't even know if I want to stay here in New Orleans."

Tania firmly tapped above her heart, getting her attention. "This, right here, will never stop being a cop. And you've never struck me as the kind to lie to it."

"Thanks. I'm sure I'll figure it out in time."

With a much gentler pat on the shoulder, Tania turned to leave. "You may not have time. There's an ugly storm coming. If you ain't gonna fight, you need to get out while you can. For you and your child's sake. Me? I plan to find others like me. Then I plan to fight."

Others like her?

Before she realized what she was doing, Dixie took out Dr. Lazarus's business card and presented it to Tania. "Here. Call this guy when you get a chance. I'm sure he could use someone with your, um, talents."

Tania looked at the card as if it were a trick. Then, with a sigh, she snatched it away. "Not promising I'll call it. But thanks."

Dixie watched as she left. Then the same white orb that had helped her several times before appeared and floated around Tania, who shooed it off. For a moment, it formed the ghostly shape of an unrecognizable older man in a trench coat. Another ghost. Why did this one seem familiar?

It gazed in her direction and then faded into mist. She frowned, turning back to Hannah's grave. *This is how the world is now—an ugly, unkind world. Can I run from it just because it terrifies me?*

Running her fingers over the bronze plaque again, she sighed. "What kind of a person would I be if I ran away? For the sake of all who've died, I need to fight, too."

Then, closing her eyes, she fondly thought of those who had died: Hannah, who would have been a bright, talented member of her community; Mama and Papa Olivier, who gave her a chance to live; Rodger, a friend and partner who never stopped believing; and Michael, who was always with her through thick and thin.

And then she remembered going out with Michael to the French Quarter—the night they shared their only kiss.

Dixie's memories stopped short with that one. *Wait, we kissed?*

Her face grew flushed as she remembered. *At the beginning of July. We had worked all night. We went drinking. We were sloshed and . . . something happened. He had a breakdown. He wanted to know if he was truly . . . Did we . . .? Did we sleep together?*

She placed her hand over her stomach. *Is it possible?*

Closing her eyes, she trembled. *Is my baby really Michael's?*

"Dixie, honey, are you OK?"

Opening her eyes, she saw Gino waiting out in the rain, his arm in a cast. Even in the cold weather, he looked as enchanting as the day they'd met. She melted into that smile. *Does it even matter? If I knew, would it change how much I love Gino and will love my baby?*

Holding out her hand, she said, "Yes. I'm OK. Just memories."

With a tender gaze, he kissed her hand. "Let's go, then, shall we?"

"Yes. Let's go." They walked away together. She stole only one last glance at Hannah's grave.

No, it doesn't matter. What matters is that I'm alive. And to honor those who have fallen, I will fight as well!

The sun broke through the clouds, ending the cold November rain.

Chapter 12
Always With You

Date: **Tuesday, October 13, 1992**
Time: **7:00 p.m.**
Location: **Evergreen Sanatorium, New Arrival Block**

Several weeks before Dixie learned of her whereabouts, Sam awoke in total darkness to the sound of someone whispering her name.

"Sam, honey, you need to wake up."

With a groan, she rolled her head to the side. Cool fingertips gently caressed her cheek as two other people spoke.

"We need to talk to her before they arrive. Just shake her!"

"Hey, don't treat my niece like that!"

"Shhh! Give her a second, you two! Sam, honey, please wake up."

Feeling groggy and sluggish, she looked up, and her heart ached at what she saw. In the darkness before her were the ghosts of Rodger, Michael, and Richie. They were mostly solid, with a white glow around them.

"Guys . . ." Her throat tightened. Tears came to her eyes.

"Shhh." Richie leaned down and pressed his lips to hers. They were like a cool breeze. "Sam, honey, we're here."

Michael folded his arms. "We finally secured Edward. He's chained in Papa Ghede's meadow now. Now he can't get to you, even if Vincent commands it."

Rodger kneeled down next to her. "Edward says he's sorry, Sam. He wants you to know that he loves you and that he'd rather stay bound forever than be able to hurt you."

She tried to wipe away her tears but found that she couldn't move her arms. She sniffed. "I'm sorry, guys. I'm so sorry. I love you three. I'm so sorry you died—"

"Shhh . . ." Richie stroked her face again. "It's not your fault. It's Vincent. It's always been him."

Michael knelt beside her. "Listen, Sam. Right now, we need you to be strong. Strong and brave."

"Why?" She wanted nothing more than to hug each of them.

"Vincent's hunting for us," Rodger said, running his fingers through her hair. "We have to stay on the run. But if we can find a way to save you, we will."

"Stay on the run? Save me? Wait, what's going on?" She struggled to move.

Michael suddenly looked around. "Vincent found us. His *loa* are coming. We have to go."

She strained against what felt like invisible chains. "No! Please don't leave me again!"

"Don't worry, Sam. We'll find someone to help you." Rodger rubbed her head as he used to in the old days. "Be brave and don't give in."

Richie kissed her once more. She could almost smell his manly scent. "I hope you find someone who will make you happy," he whispered, cupping her belly. "And love our children."

"No! I don't want anyone else. Please! Don't leave me!"

And then Sam was alone in a dark and quiet room, lying on the floor. Beads of sweat poured down her brow and the back of her neck. Her mouth was open so wide, the sides of her face hurt. Her entire body shook as if she were freezing. Her cry for her friends cracked out like a dying lamb's bleat.

It hadn't been a dream. It couldn't have been a dream. It had been too intense, too real.

"Richie. Michael. Rodger." Just speaking their names hurt. For a few more minutes, she dwelled on their words, the sight of them, their touch and smell. Then she tried to make sense of her situation.

Clearly, she was in some sort of dark room. She could feel her children inside of her. And she was wearing something that not only kept her from moving her arms but also wrapped them around her and secured them at her back. It took her a few more seconds to realize that it was a straitjacket.

Carefully, she shuffled to the side until she felt the soft material of a wall.

I'm in a padded cell.

Leaning against it, she pushed herself to her feet and then carefully walked along the walls. She felt light-headed, and it was difficult to concentrate. After several attempts that ended with her falling on her face, she figured each wall to be about ten feet. She also found a single metal door in the middle of one.

She rested her head against it. "Hey! Hey, I'm awake! Who's out there?"

Nothing.

"Hey, dipshits! Let me out!" She felt woozy, her knees buckling.

Suddenly, there was a loud clanking sound. Then, as the door opened and light poured inside the room, she was blinded. With a cry, she fell back to the farthest wall.

"Where am I?" She squinted, trying to see.

"You are finally where you belong, Sam," a voice speaking in a thick German accent said.

Blinking a few more times to chase away the light spots, she gazed at the doorway once more. What she saw made a bitter taste rise in her mouth. Standing in the doorway, flanked by two large, muscular men, was someone she both loathed and feared.

"Dr. Klein," Sam said. "I had a feeling it was you."

From where he stood, peering at her from behind his glasses, Dr. Klein looked like a veritable cock-of-the-walk. As he entered the cell, his smile was one of boastful conceit.

"I told you that I would eventually get you, Sam. Zat hack Dr. Lazarus could only stop me for so long."

She exhaled and pushed down the bitter soup in her throat. "Hack? What are you blabbing about?"

"I am talking about his ridiculous belief zat you are possessed. Und after working things out with ze local magistrate, we got his protection on you revoked. Now you are mine."

Her bangs fell over her face as she shook her head again and again. She couldn't focus, and she couldn't activate her power. It was all she could do to stay standing.

"Maybe I am possessed. You ever see me run up a crane? Or dodge bullets? You think a normal chick can do that?" She could feel the local spirits around her. Like her, they must have been repulsed by Dr. Klein, for they were keeping their distance. Richie and the others were gone, on the run from Vincent's *loa*. She really was alone.

He snorted. "Normal? Sam, you are anything but normal. You are an aberration created by sweet little Samantha because she could not handle what her grandfather did. Ze only demon here is you, Sam of Spades."

Recalling that Dr. Klein was convinced that Samantha, her "good personality," was subverted by Sam of Spades, her "bad personality," she felt that arguing it was a moot point. *He'll never believe that Sam of Spades was just what Marinette called herself because the drugs he gave me made her forget she was even a loa.*

"All right, I'll bite. How do you know I'm Sam and not Samantha?"

He snapped his fingers. At once, the two men were upon her.

"What the hell?"

Each secured one of her legs and shoulders, pinning her to the wall. As Dr. Klein approached, one of them grabbed her head while the other held one of her eyes open.

"Have you lost your mind?" She gnashed her teeth, panting. Her face flushed with the rush of blood. She strained against her bonds and tried to tap into her power, but she couldn't focus. She felt powerless as Dr. Klein shined a small flashlight into her eye.

He smirked.

"Your pupils are dilated beyond ze acceptable range. At the wharf, when you showed the strength of your madness, they were dilated. Therefore, so long as your pupils are dilated, you are Sam und not Samantha."

The two men tossed her to the ground. She yelped as she hit the floor. As Dr. Klein walked back to the doorway, she realized that with her being Bridgette, she'd probably seem possessed for the rest of her life.

I am screwed.

With a grunt, she struggled to her knees. "That's a crackpot theory."

He shrugged. "I think it's quite sound."

She spat. "Fine. So what happens now?"

At that question, he grinned cruelly. "I have already told you. I am going to use every technique I know to destroy you so zat Samantha can be whole again."

Cold descended through her. "You're gonna torture me?"

Waggling a finger, he said, "'Torture' is such an ugly word. My experiments will not only remove you as ze dominant personality, but also provide valuable data in treating future patients."

"But I'm pregnant!"

He sniffed the air with disinterest. "Normally, I wouldn't care. But my benefactors have forbidden me from doing anything to harm those twin inconveniences. So, for now, the treatments vill be mild."

Benefactors? Oh, the Knight Priory.

But then his expression darkened. "After they are born, however, ze real therapy begins."

The look in his eyes made her heart race. She struggled to stand, jerking her head back and forth to try to focus. If only she could activate her power and increase her strength, she could break free. But even as she reached her feet, her legs gave way again. With another cry, she fell down, hitting her chin. Colors and lights exploded around her.

"Having trouble, Sam?" Dr. Klein's voice was filled with glee. Then he snapped his fingers. A moment later, she was roughly pulled to her feet. "Your little displays of psychosomatic superhuman strength have forced me to be cautious. What you're feeling is a special drug of mine that acts as a muscle relaxer und a mild anesthetic. You will find concentration and exertion to be impossible."

Approaching her, he stroked his beard. "I want to run a few tests. Don't worry, they won't endanger your little inconveniences." He poked at her stomach.

Her body heat rose to a boil, and her muscles, despite being like jelly, quivered with rage. She growled at him. "Don't you dare touch me there, you son-of-a-bitch! Never touch my children again!"

He pulled his hand back as if it were in the mouth of a lioness. "My apologies. Gentleman, bring her zis way."

A moment later, they were dragging her down a dimly lit hallway lined with condensation-laden pipes along the ceiling and dirty, stained tiles on the floor. They passed a few other large orderlies and armed guards. Some were even escorting other patients, all of whom looked as bleak as she felt. One of the guards was dragging an unconscious, badly bruised girl whom Sam instantly recognized.

"Meghan? Meghan!"

Although she bubbled up some blood, Meghan didn't respond. The guard dragged her around the corner.

Sam tried to pull free but just couldn't. "You bastard! What did you do to her?"

Dr. Klein again sniffed the air in disdain. "I did nothing. Twice now, she has beaten herself against the walls of the treatment room. I am sure that is what happened."

She tried to glare holes into the back of his head. From the short glimpse she'd gotten of Meghan's injuries, they didn't look self-inflicted.

Several twists and turns later, they entered a well-lit room. "Here we are, Sam."

In the center was a table with leather restraints in each corner. Nearby lay a tray of medical equipment with everything from syringes to scalpels to forceps. Next to that was a small side table with a notebook, a pocket watch, and a pen.

The two men unfastened her jacket and strapped her down to the table, her jelly-like muscles making it impossible to struggle. "You realize that you're acting just like Vincent and Dallas, right?"

"Except I'm not going to kill you, Sam," he said with disinterest as he jotted down some notes. "Not until there is no other course of action." He took out a syringe and a small glass bottle, which had only a numbered label on it.

She craned her neck and eyed it warily. "What is that?" The question came out more shakily than she would have liked.

"A concoction of my own design," he said, tapping the excess liquid from the needle. Then he nodded, and one of the men exposed her neck. "It will cause you some, well, discomfort. But the idea here is to gauge your reaction."

A moment later, she felt a pinprick and then the rush of warm fluid enter her. Crying out, she bit at them, wanting nothing more than to feel their flesh tear beneath her teeth. "Fuck you!"

They backed away without concern. Dr. Klein clicked the side of the pocket watch. A ticking sound started.

Laying her head back, she stared up at the ceiling. "I hate you all so much."

No one replied.

Weariness washed over Sam. With it came a sense of resignation. "When will it take effect?"

"Pretty soon," Dr. Klein said, opening the notebook.

She gazed at the light fixtures above. "Will there be pain?"

"Most likely."

Asshole. But she said nothing else. She just wanted it to be over with.

Minutes passed with no result, and she had just started dozing off when her skin began itching as if it were dry. It started at the injection point and then spread along her veins and arteries. Soon, every inch of her body was covered in the unpleasant sensation. She shifted side to side on the table, trying to get even a second's relief.

"Crap, it itches!"

"Good." He scribbled in the notebook, glancing occasionally at the pocket watch.

Then the itching penetrated deeper until the rawness in her flesh felt like fire. She panted and arched her back. "What the hell? It's starting to burn."

"That's what it's supposed to do," he said clinically, his eyes never leaving the notebook. "It's purging your body of toxins und old medication."

Every nerve was alight, as if someone were rubbing a red-hot iron over them. She screamed until her throat ached. Tears ran from her eyes. Snot dripped from her nose.

"You bastard! It hurts! It hurts!"

"Understood, Sam. Thank you very much." Dr. Klein closed the notebook and watched her writhe about. "It should end in a few minutes. Then you will urinate ze toxins out. Just go when you must. There is no shame here."

Sam shrieked again. It felt like she was burning from the inside out. Liquid streamed from her nose and eyes. "You're crazy! You're evil and crazy!"

Then her body started shaking, and she felt her jaw lock. Spittle started foaming out as she convulsed. Her vision took on a red tint as the liquid pouring from her eyes turned thick and hot.

One of the men said, "Doctor, her eyes are bleeding." He sounded nervous.

Panic grew in Dr. Klein's voice. "Get me the number twenty-five bottle. Hurry!"

As her rose-tinted vision grew dim, her thoughts numbed. The tremors strengthened as her throat relaxed and her stomach tightened. The iron taste of blood filled her mouth as she vomited into her throat. Then she started choking on it, her lungs gasping for air. The last thing she felt before blacking out was someone grabbing her head and jerking it to the side.

Then all was dark.

When Sam finally awoke, it was from a nightmare of Dallas torturing her. His maniacal laughing as he cut into her flesh rang in her ears as she sat up, crying out.

Her cry died into silence as she realized it was just a dream. She rocked back and forth. Then she tried to reach for her face but couldn't move her arms. The straitjacket was back on.

With a groan, she leaned to the side, her face resting on the padded wall.

"Damn it. That crazy bastard."

She closed her eyes, realizing that her future now was a lifetime of pain, one she couldn't even escape through death. "So, Vincent, is this what you envisioned when you bound Baron Samedi to you?"

No one answered. She tasted more blood and spat it out.

"Jesus. Why is it that so many men in my life are such assholes?"

A voice from behind the wall said, "Men just suck in general, Sam."

The voice was muffled, likely from the padding, but Sam knew who it was. "Meghan?"

"Yeah."

She breathed a sigh of relief. "I'm so glad you're OK. I was so worried about you."

"Me, too. About you, I mean."

She slid down until she was lying on her side. Just knowing that Meghan was still alive was enough for now. After a few moments of silence, she closed her eyes, imagining she was back at Tulane, in her comfortable dorm room.

"Hey, Sam?" Meghan asked, sounding tired.

Sam opened her eyes as if she could see her friend. "What? Yes, what is it?"

"I just wanted to apologize."

"For what?"

"For not being more honest. Ya know, about everything with Dr. Kindley."

"What was really going on?" Sam asked, stretching out to get comfortable.

Meghan frowned. "It's just . . . he knew I couldn't help myself. And he exploited it. He wanted me to keep an eye on you and report things you did or said. In return, I got to do stuff with whomever."

It was what Sam had figured, but knowing it did nothing to dull the pain of betrayal. "So that's why you became chummy with me."

"At first, yes. But after a bit, I told him to go screw himself."

"You broke your deal with him?"

"Yes."

"Why?"

"Because you became a friend. A real friend. Probably the only real friend I've ever had."

Sam rolled on her back. She wanted nothing more than to believe Meghan's story. She just didn't know whom to trust anymore.

After coughing a few hard, hacking coughs, Meghan said, "So I don't expect you to forgive me, Sam. But I'm sorry."

Lying in silence, Sam closed her eyes and sorted through the aching that swelled in her heart. Kent Bourgeois. Jacob Heuber. Louis Ouellette. Dixie Olivier. Vincent Castille. All those people and more had betrayed her trust. It seemed that now, only the dead and the spirits were honest. Even Vincent, as a ghost, had never lied to her.

"I guess you'll hate me forever," Meghan said. "I deserve it. Take care, Sam."

Opening her eyes, Sam decided to give the living one more chance.

"Meghan, I forgive you."

There was a long pause, and with it the sound of weeping. Then Meghan asked with a shaky voice, "You do?"

"Yeah. The things you told me outside Dr. Kindley's office. About us being friends. That's the Meghan I know. Not the one who was told to spy on me."

Again, there was a long pause. "Thanks, Sam." Meghan was obviously crying.

Sam cleared her throat. "Just do me a favor, OK, Meghan?"

"What's that?" Meghan asked as she sniffed wetly.

"Live, OK? Live until we find a way out of here. I want to take my friend out to eat. Maybe we'll go to Arnold's. Or Commander's Palace. Or maybe just Popeye's."

"Heh. I like Popeye's."

Chuckling, Sam asked, “It’s a date, then?”
“Yeah. It’s a date. I’ll do my best to stay alive. You, too, OK, Sam?”
In the darkness, she smiled.
“Yeah, Meghan. Me, too.”

Chapter 13
An Apple Peel

Date: **Thursday, March 11, 1993**
Time: **10:00 a.m.**
Location: **Evergreen Sanatorium, General Population Block**

Staring at the ceiling and imagining the condensation patterns to be passing clouds, Sam gently stroked her belly, which was now several times larger. She could feel the two lives growing inside. It was moments like this, when she was allowed to bond with her unborn children, that kept her from losing what little sanity she had left.

The first few weeks under Dr. Klein's care had been pure hell. Enduring his treatments, which seemed focused solely on bringing discomfort and pain, was bad enough. However, ten days after her arrival, she was moved to a different block from Meghan. She hadn't seen her friend since.

When Sam had asked where Meghan was, Dr. Klein had grinned maliciously and said, "That girl has such a severe case of nymphomania zat isolation is the only possible treatment. I've moved her to a place I call 'the tombs.'"

That made her hate him all the more, but there was little she could do about it. His anesthetic mixture, which he injected regularly, along with vitamin shots for the babies, kept her unable to concentrate long enough to use the powers she had gained from merging with Bridgette. And, just as bad, her senses were dulled to the point where feeling for spirits gave her a pounding headache. So, to protect her mind, she mentally retreated, focusing every free moment on the twin lives within her.

And that was her life, month after month.

The sound of sliding metal latches pulled Sam back into the hell around her. The door to her cell opened, and the two large orderlies who had been assigned to her entered. They never spoke directly to her, and she didn't know their names. So she'd made up nicknames for them.

"Hello, Dick and Dock," she said. "Here to take me to my daily torture session?"

Without a word, they pulled her to her feet. She groaned as her back muscles pulled against the bones, throbbing like hot coals. It was hard to stand with jelly for legs and a belly full of babies.

"Easy there, fellas. Mama's got buns in the crockpot, and they are getting heavy."

The three of them silently walked along the hallways, Sam's bare feet slapping on the ground with every step. Dick and Dock supported her in a surprisingly gentle manner. And even if the only reason was that the Knight Priory wanted her children unharmed, she was grateful.

They passed by another patient, a mocha-skinned woman being carried by two other orderlies. One of them was talking to her. "Well, Miss LeBeouf, you need to start responding to your treatment soon. Dr. Klein's getting impatient. It won't be too much longer before it's time for a little brain surgery, you know?"

The woman looked terrified. "Not that! I'll get better. I promise I'll improve!"

Poor bitch, Sam thought. It was common knowledge in Evergreen that once Dr. Klein gave up on a patient, they were lobotomized. She couldn't think of a more horrendous fate.

A few minutes later, they entered a treatment room that had a video camera and a surgical table with stirrups. She frowned. Dr. Klein had begun filming their sessions a few months earlier. Everything, from talk therapy to his many painful injections, was recorded. Sometimes she was clothed, and other times she was naked. She had long ago replaced her dignity with sarcasm and disdain.

"So how's the home movie coming? Getting good wank time?"

Dr. Klein was busy putting on a surgical mask and gloves. As was typical for him, he didn't react to her comment. "Very educational, Sam. Very much so, indeed."

"So what's on the menu today?" she asked as she waddled over to the table. Dick and Dock helped her up and strapped the restraints over her arms and chest. "I know it's not to check my burns." They were all healed, with only ugly scar tissue remaining.

Remaining quiet, Dr. Klein motioned toward her legs. Dick and Dock strapped them into the stirrups.

Feeling herself exposed, she gulped. "You're not going to do anything sexual to me, are you?" The very notion made her stomach turn, anxiety fraying her carefully knitted curtain of apathy. She pushed those thoughts away and spat out some more sarcasm. "Because I probably stink to high heavens down there."

"Zat is very insulting, Sam," he said, flipping her gown past her knees. "I'm checking on your pregnancy. Some important people want a status report."

She looked away from him as she felt cool metal against her genitals. A moment later, an instrument was probing her insides. Sucking in her breath, she tried to focus on something else—anything else. Even the thought of him seeing and touching her was more than she could bear. After a few seconds, her stomach gurgled like a clogged drain.

"I think I'm gonna puke."

"Get Sam a bucket, please," Dr. Klein said.

"Oh, you don't have to—"

Dick grabbed her head and pushed it into a tin pail.

You're kidding, right?

Her body tensed as she dry-heaved in rhythm with Dr. Klein's probing. Nothing came out.

This could not get any more degrading.

She did it a few more times and then leaned back. She burped hard and then shrugged.

"False alarm, Dick. Sorry about—"

Then it hit. With another loud belch, she projectile-vomited all over Dick's uniform. The vomit was green and smelly. As he swore and jumped back, she felt a bit of satisfaction. When the last drop was out, she looked back up at the ceiling and began to laugh.

"Seems like you find this amusing, Sam." Dr. Klein withdrew the instruments from her and wiped them off.

She continued to giggle, feeling strands of sanity snapping one by one. *How is any of this supposed to fix me again?*

He came around to her head, avoiding the puddles of puke and ignoring Dick's swearing.

Wiping her mouth on her shoulder, she asked, "So will you please tell me how my babies are? We do have an agreement that if I let you do whatever you want, you'll be careful with them."

"As far as I can tell, they are fine. Someone will come by tomorrow und do an ultrasound."

Then he leaned down until his beard was touching her face. She moved her head, repulsed. "But Sam," he said. "You're not responding to my treatments. My benefactors want Samantha back. Und if I cannot succeed in bringing her back, their focus may shift only to the health of the children."

For the first time since she'd met him, he sounded tired. "I vant this to work, Sam. I need you to let Samantha go. Don't humiliate me in front of them, or the consequences will be dire."

Sam looked back up at him. "Listen, I can't just stop being—"

Then her eyes fell on his pen. It was red, one of those expensive fountain pens with a beautiful luster.

Wait. I had one like that.

As she stared at it, a horrible memory resurfaced—a memory of a focus used to direct the *loa*, one that was used to cause the deaths of Michael and Rodger and many others.

A silver fountain pen.

The pen! How could I forget that?

"Sam, you were saying?"

She shook her head, too lost in thought.

Did I succeed in destroying it?

Dr. Klein sighed. "So much for an accord. Take her back to her cell."

She closed her eyes as she was helped up.

God, I hope I did. Otherwise, we're all in trouble.

The following day, the ultrasound technician came. Sam, who was allowed to watch the monitor, saw both of her children resting within her. It looked almost like they were holding hands. She didn't need someone to tell her their gender. She just knew it was a boy and a girl.

Shutting out everything else, she reached out and touched the monitor's surface. *My babies. My little girl and little boy. You are both so beautiful.*

She wanted to cry. She wanted to feel the raw, unmitigated happiness that was supposed to come with motherhood. But she couldn't. She had turned off that part of herself months ago.

I'll cry when I hold you, little ones. I promise. Her fingertips grazed the images, touching their small, round heads. Tapping the glass to the rhythm of their heartbeats, she focused on them. For the moment, they were all that existed.

Then the monitor shut off. Her fingers stayed on the blank screen. *My babies . . .*

"This has gone very well, Dr. Klein," the ultrasound technician said. "I'll let them know that the children are fine. They'll contact you when they're ready to visit the Princess."

She regarded him with scorn. *Princess. I am so sick of being called that.*

After the ultrasound technician left, Dr. Klein instructed the orderlies to take Sam to the interview room. Once there, she was given her vitamin shot and a slice of apple. It was her first piece of fresh fruit since her time in Tulane. Without a thought, she wolfed it down, hardly tasting it.

Dr. Klein entered and sat across from her. "Looks like you were hungry, Sam. Would you like some more?"

She wiped the juice off her mouth and licked her hand clean. "Yes, I would."

With a smirk, he placed a whole, plump apple and a knife on the table. She watched as he picked up the knife and started to peel the apple, the deep red skin pulling away to reveal the flesh underneath. She licked her lips, salivating.

He locked eyes with her as he dropped the peelings onto a plate. "You've been a very good sport these past few months, Sam. I know you are frightened, but if all goes well, then there vill be no more need for suffering. You'd like that, ja?"

She glanced back and forth between him and the plate of apple peels and nodded enthusiastically.

"So I need you to do something for me when ze Knight Priory comes. I need you to pretend you are Samantha. Can you do that for me?" The plate was now covered in apple peelings.

Again, she looked at the plate, her mouth watering. He could offer any terms he wanted right now, and she'd agree to them.

"Yes, sir, I can do that. I'll pretend to be Samantha. Promise!"

Chuckling, he slid the plate over to her. As she dug into the peelings like a ravenous animal, he sat back and cut himself a piece of the fruit's pulp. Then he popped it into his mouth and chewed, watching her with a smug expression.

Sam stopped eating, her fingers half-crammed into her mouth. The smug guise on his face said it all: she had become his "good little Samantha" once more. Swallowing the peel, she felt her self-respect drain along with the blood from her face.

"What have you done to me?" Her lips trembled.

"What have I done? I've given you something to eat, because you've been a good girl. My good, sweet little Samantha."

She looked down at her hands. They were shaking.

He sliced off another piece of fruit and ate it. "Sometimes you use vinegar to catch your prey, und sometimes you use honey . . . or an apple peel."

That son of a bitch. After months of hurting her, he showed one act of kindness, and she did exactly what he said, just like when she was ten years old.

"You know, Sam, the skin of an apple is just the trash. As are you. But these people want you to be more, so become that, and next time, I'll even let you have a slice."

Finished with the apple, he tossed the core into a wastebasket. Then he left, his expression still smug.

Alone now, she tightened her fists as much as she could under the effects of Dr. Klein's drugs. Barbs of humiliation and degradation tore through her being. Her entire body shook with rage.

Dr. Klein.

She ground her teeth until she felt pain in her gums.

One day, you will die.

Chapter 14
Enter the Oracle

Date: **Sunday, March 14, 1993**
Time: **8:00 p.m.**
Location: **Evergreen Sanatorium**
General Population Block

The evening the Knight Priory came, Sam awoke to a freakishly loud storm. The thunder and roar of the rain pounded around her, despite her certainty that she was underground. Sitting up, she pressed her ear to the wall. The rumblings outside rattled through the plumbing, creating a symphony that was both dark and foreboding.

She swung her legs around and rested them on the floor. It was wet. The water must have been seeping inside. Rubbing her face, she muttered, "Something's gonna go bad. I can feel it."

The door to her cell swung open, and in came Dick and Dock. "All right, 'Princess,'" Dick said in a mocking tone. "Time to meet your people." He grabbed her head as Dock took out a small case.

"What's in there?" she asked, eyeing it warily.

"Relax, bitch," Dock said. "It's just contact lenses. You know, so your pupils don't look dilated."

They were surprisingly gentle as they put the lenses in, coating them with saline solution and making sure they were in place. It felt like there were two bits of dirt in her eyes, but she did her best to ignore it. Then the orderlies helped her stand.

"Good dog," Dock said, patting her head.

Better watch it, Dock, or you'll pull back a stump one day.

As she walked along the hallways, she passed a pair of guards carrying a female patient who was so thin and pale that she looked like she'd break at any moment. Sam gulped as she recognized her.

"Meghan!"

Meghan glanced up, her face bruised and her lips cracked. "Sam," she said weakly before being dragged around a corner.

"Meghan! Meghan!"

Sam called out her name until she was in the treatment room.

Except for the video camera, the room was empty. They led her to the center of the room and then left. For a moment, she was alone.

Then the door opened, and Dr. Klein entered. "Good evening, Samantha."

Remembering the deal they had made, she smiled meekly. "Oh. Good evening, Dr. Klein." All she had to do was endure this meeting, and she'd finally be safe.

Dr. Klein smiled back. "Come in, everyone. As you can see, Samantha Castille is here, und not Sam of Spades. Your Princess is waiting."

A dozen or so figures entered. Each one was wearing a black, hooded cloak and a stylized voodoo mask. Each one bore an ornate gold pin on their cloak: the symbol of the Knight Priory of Saint Madonna.

Despite being prepared for meeting them, she felt her heart rate spike. The last time she had seen those masks, they were hovering around her terrified five-year-old self as Vincent pushed the *loa* Marinette into her tiny body.

As they gathered, she blinked a few times. The contacts were bothering her.

When they were finally settled, one of the hooded figures spoke. It had a female voice with a cultured air. Sam was certain she had heard that voice before.

"Good evening, Princess."

"We are glad to see you have chased your demons away," a male with a thick Cajun accent said.

"Before we celebrate, we must test her," a third, a male with a deeper timbre, said. "We must make sure it's really her."

Sam eyed the third figure, certain his voice was familiar, from either the radio or television. It was someone famous in New Orleans. But who?

"Ladies and gentlemen, please." Dr. Klein held up his hand. "I promise you that I've made sure that—"

"Let Ignatius examine her," the female interrupted. The others nodded as a general murmur of consent arose.

One of the hooded figures removed his mask. It was Dr. Kindley. He approached and smiled in his trademark hollow fashion. "Good to see you again, Samantha. Would you kindly please step forward?"

Blinking again as the left lens slid to the side and then back into place, she obeyed. Her feet slapped against the tile flooring as she moved directly under the light. It was uncomfortably warm.

He leaned forward and pressed his hands to the sides of her head, squeezing against her temples just enough to cause discomfort. Then he whispered, "The rest of the Priory doesn't believe in possession. I do. You will be useful to me back outside, so play along and I'll have you released tonight. But don't think for a moment I won't throw you to the wolves if you fail."

She whispered back, "Please don't let them hurt my babies."

"Then obey."

"What are you muttering to the Princess?" the female figure asked.

Taking out a small pen light, he checked her eyes. "I am telling her to behave while I perform my tests."

She blinked a few more times. The lenses were becoming very irritating.

"Contacts so you won't look dilated," he whispered. "Very sneaky."

Then he spoke out loud. "Pupils are normal."

Next, he took Sam's pulse, then her temperature, and finally, her blood pressure. "Core temperature is normal. Heart rate and blood pressure as well."

Once more, he whispered, "I'm lying. You are showing all the physical signs of possession on a massive scale. What's inside of you, I wonder?"

Sam remained still, wondering how he knew all of this.

"What's going on, Ignatius?" the man with the deep timbre asked.

From the back of the room, Dr. Klein anxiously watched.

After patting her shoulder, Dr. Kindley turned around. "Everyone, it's Samantha. All of the symptoms she displayed at the wharf while being Sam of Spades are gone. We can conclude that the Princess is clean."

"Can we trust that?" the man with the Cajun accent asked. "Is she cured?"

"Ignatius is one of the few purebloods left," the man with the deep voice said. "I trust him, and so should all of you." Then, without another word, he sank to one knee.

Sam's mouth opened as, one by one, every hooded figure in the room, as well as Dr. Kindley, knelt before her. Soon, the only person standing was a very relieved-looking Dr. Klein.

The man with the deep voice bowed his head. "Princess. Forgive us for putting you through this, but our predecessors did terrible things to you. They broke your mind and turned you into something unworthy of your name. But now we have come to take you home. The Castille family has always led the Knight Priory, and we believe that tradition should not be broken. You will finish your healing outside. We will groom you into a public figure fitting of our regime. And with your children, the Knight Priory will once again flourish. Please, Princess, lead the Knight Priory of Saint Madonna into the twenty-first century."

Her head spun as the rest of the Knight Priory repeated, "Princess, come with us." The group seemed like a full-blown cult. *What have I gotten myself into?*

Dr. Klein puffed out his chest. "I told you I could cure her. I will relish continuing her treatment back at—"

"Shut your mouth, Lucius," the hooded female said. "You have done your job, and now, Ignatius will take over as her physician. Remember, it is we who allowed you to claim her as your patient when Vincent was arrested, and it is we who have kept you connected and in power. You owe us. Never forget your place."

His face turned red. It was then that Sam noticed he was not wearing the ornate gold pin. Suddenly, all of his comments about "benefactors" made sense. He was trying to join the Knight Priory.

But they never let him into the big boys' club. How pathetic!

The man with the deep timbre rose, as did everyone else. "Then it's settled. We leave with the Princess and her children—"

A series of heavy footfalls shut him up.

From the crowd, a lone, hooded figure stepped forward. He was no bigger than the others, but somehow, he made everyone else seem small. Sam couldn't get a read on him. It was like his very presence shut down her senses.

He stopped right in front of her, staring at her. His mask was Baron Samedi's, and behind it was a steely gaze that bore into her. Her thoughts slipped back to when she was five years old. She remembered seeing that same mask and those same eyes on the night that Vincent had called Marinette down to possess her. They had remained in the back of the room, silent and stoic, watching the ritual and the chaos that followed.

"I know you, don't I?" she asked, blinking like mad as her eyes watered from the lenses. Try as she might, she couldn't discern the face behind the mask.

He said nothing, just headed back to the man with the deep voice and whispered.

A moment later, the man with the deep voice said, "Are you sure, Oracle?"

The Oracle nodded and walked back into the crowd.

"Dr. Kindley. Dr. Klein. One more test, if you will indulge us." The man with the deep timbre leaned over to the man with the Cajun accent and whispered.

"What the hell? Are you sure, sir?"

"Just do it."

“Lordy. All right, just a moment.” The man with the Cajun accent took a deep breath and walked up to Sam. “Sorry, Princess.”

He slapped her across the face so hard her ears popped.

A collective gasp rippled through the crowd. Her head rocked to the side as the pain exploded. Slowly, she looked back at the man before her.

Then she saw red. *How dare that little maggot!*

All of her feelings of indignation and anger hit a crescendo with that slap. Every injustice and indignity she had suffered—every insulting and degrading act—hit her at once. For one brief moment, even the haze of the medication burned away. “You impudent little prick! You dare strike a queen!”

Tightening her fist, she punched him in the face as hard as she could.

His face caved in, his mask wrapping inside of it. He flew back several feet, brain matter and blood spurting out along with bits of ceramic. He was dead before he hit the ground.

Pandemonium ensued.

The members of the Knight Priory swarmed, falling over each other as they scrambled out of the room. Several of the members surrounded the one with the deepened timbre, escorting him away. The one with a woman’s voice admonished Dr. Klein. “You liar! You told us the Princess would be ready by now! Why can’t you cure her? You are false, Lucius. You will never be a member now!”

Sam fell to her knees as the medication seized control again. Her great strength was gone once more. Just before she passed out, she saw Dr. Kindley staring at her.

He looked bitterly disappointed.

When Sam awoke, she was momentarily blinded by lights around her. Then, her senses returned. She was secured to an operating table, nude and gagged, with an IV stuck in her arm. Immediately, she broke out in cold sweats, expecting Dallas to come into view. Nearby, a heart-rate monitor started beeping wildly.

Instead, Dr. Kindley approached. She screamed into the gag.

He ran his fingers through her sweaty hair. “You’re awake. Good. I wanted to talk to you before the operation began.”

Removing the gag, he tapped her lips.

“Operation?” she asked, searching for some hint to her fate. “What operation?”

“Don’t worry. You’ll be put completely under before the procedure.” He kept stroking her hair, rubbing the strands together as if he were her lover.

She felt revulsion. “What procedure?” The monitor continued its rapid beeps.

“Do you remember when I told you that you made me a believer?”

“What of it?” she asked, glaring.

"As a pureblood of the Knight Priory, I was always taught that what Vincent did to you wasn't supernatural. But after seeing you in action back in Tulane, I had a change of heart. I came into something one of the original members had—a collection of amazing information. Now I understand the nature of your possession. One gone wrong would weaken the host, but one done correctly strengthens it."

He lifted her hair, sniffed it, and let the strands fall free.

"I guess." The monitor continued to beep wildly. What were they going to do to her?

"But you're something more than just possessed now. Only the Oracle has ever shown so much power. I still have so much more to learn. Think of what I could do with that knowledge!" He twirled her hair in between his fingers again.

Without warning, he tugged hard, lifting her head off the table.

"Ouch!" she cried.

"I wanted that power. And you were going to help me get it all. But you blew it. You blew it! And for what, an insult?"

She winced. "Stop it!"

He let go. "The Oracle was right. You're not how I'll take over the Priory. You're just a liability. But no worries, this will only set me back a few years. See, I've struck a deal with our leader. She gets something she wants, I get to keep the grimoire a while longer."

"Grimoire? What grimoire?"

"Don't worry about it, Princess—Sam," he said, stroking her bulging belly. "Sadly, I've done all I can for you. Soon, your real nightmare will begin. We won't be seeing each other any longer."

He leaned down and kissed her cheek. "Farewell, Sam."

Then he placed the gag back on and left.

A few minutes later, Dr. Klein, Dick, and Dock entered the room in full medical scrubs. Dr. Klein started whispering instructions.

Sam struggled and groaned against the gag.

Dick took a syringe and measured a dose of pasty-looking liquid while Dr. Klein took out a marker and then felt around her belly. A moment later, he drew a line beneath her navel, right above her pelvis.

No! she thought as the beeping of the monitor spiked. *Not that!* The type of operation was now obvious.

She suddenly felt the area around her chill, the sounds begin to mute, and the world start to slow down. With the rush of anxiety came the familiar sensation of her power coming forth. The power of Bridgette.

Then Dr. Klein looked up. "Do it now."

Dick injected the pasty liquid into the IV.

Sam pushed against the straps and started to feel them pop—when suddenly everything began to go black.

No! She struggled to stay awake. *Don't do this! Please!*

Dr. Klein took out a scalpel, and then all was dark once more.

For a long time, Sam floated in that darkness, the memories of merging with Bridgette playing before her like an old 8mm movie.

We are now one being, Bridgette and I. And because of Vincent, neither of us can die until we free Baron Samedi. But once I free him, I will have to die for us to separate.

The film showing her making the pact played over and over.

I am fighting a war to earn the right to die. How messed up is that?

It was raining again when Sam woke up, still in darkness. Her head ached, and the taste of bile was in the back of her mouth. She tried to sit up and touch her face. But then she realized she couldn't. She had been restrained.

She shook her head many times to clear the haze, but try as she might, she couldn't focus or call upon her strength. She could feel Dr. Klein's mixture coursing through her, clouding her thoughts and relaxing her muscles.

"What happened?"

As if on cue, the door to the cell opened, flooding the room with light. She was back in her cell, still nude and bound with leather straps.

"You're awake? Good."

Dr. Klein entered the room, sneering cruelly. "You are now mine for life. Und now that the inconveniences are gone, we can focus on your real treatment."

"Inconveniences?" She furrowed her brow. A moment later, she realized that her belly was no longer bulging. A post-operative bandage was wrapped around her abdomen.

Her world went red, and her throat went raw. "What have you done to my children, you sick fucking bastard?" Muscles and veins all over her body started bulging and pulsing, and her jaw locked. The sedation started burning away again.

But even as the leather straps groaned under her strength, Dr. Klein snapped his fingers. Dick and Dock emerged from the doorway and fired what looked like pistols. She felt two sharp pains—one in her shoulder, the other in her thigh. Looking down, she saw two darts sticking out of her flesh.

"What is this shit?" Her throat tightened as she struggled to break free.

"Tranquilizers. The kind we use on large, wild animals. Because zat is all you are now—a wild animal."

Sam felt dizzy as the chemicals surged into her bloodstream, but she continued to strain against the leather straps, feeling the one around her right wrist snapping. "Where are my babies, you worthless speck? Where are they?"

Dr. Klein shrugged. "It is out of my hands. The Knight Priory felt they were worth keeping but felt that you were no longer fit to carry them. So I removed them, und they took them away. They were a bit premature, but a team of physicians will ensure their survival. They should thrive as their Prince and Princess. But you will never see them again."

She started frothing at the mouth. Her vision doubled. "I want my babies, you psycho! I will kill you and the entire priory!"

Leaning over her, he smirked. "Doubtful. I will hurt you until you break, Sam. Und once you are gone and all that is left is Samantha, I will finally earn my place in the social elite. You will be my magnum opus, the culmination of my life's work."

The restraint around her right wrist finally snapped. She roared and grabbed him by the throat. He grabbed her arm, his face getting pale. For one moment, he looked terrified.

But then the tranquilizers kicked in, and her grip loosened. Dick and Dock rushed forward and pulled him away. She glared at him. One more second, and she would have broken his neck.

"Dr. Klein," she said, spittle flying from her lips. The world around her started melting.

As he rubbed his neck, his color returning, he glared back.

With all the effort she could muster, she pointed at him.

"One day, I swear I will kill you."

Then she passed out once more.

Chapter 15
A New Neighbor

Date: **Saturday, April 3, 1993**
Time: **3:00 p.m.**
Location: **Evergreen Sanatorium, Treatment Room**

"Increase ze voltage."

"Yes, sir."

Sam screamed against the wooden dowel in her mouth as the electrical current ran through her. The electrodes on the sides of her head felt like molten lead as they seared her skin. Every muscle in her body seized, her feet curling until her calves charley-horsed. Her shoulders pulled up until they locked. She bit down until she felt her jaw pop.

Then the current stopped. She continued to shake, her muscles quivering as she convulsed on the table.

"Anything?"

Dick roughly grabbed her now-clean-shaven head and shined a light into one of her eyes.

"Nothing, sir. Pupils are still dilated."

Dr. Klein stood nearby, scribbling in his notebook with a silver fountain pen. He looked annoyed.

"Increase the voltage und try again."

"But, sir," Dock, who was manning the machine, said. "This is already past the recommended—"

Slapping the notebook, Dr. Klein said, "Increase the voltage und try again!"

"Yes, sir."

As the current tore through her, Sam shrieked again. Ever since her children were cut from her womb, this was her life—electroshocks, experimental injections, overstimulation, sensory deprivation, and more. Every day was a new "treatment." Dr. Klein was as vicious as he had once threatened to be.

The electricity stopped, and she continued to convulse. Ever since the surgery, she kept waiting for an opportunity to strike. But one never came. After she had choked Dr. Klein, security with her had become impenetrable. Every time someone came for her, she was tranquilized, and she was constantly kept on that concoction that relaxed her muscles and muddled her mind. Her restraints were steel chains.

But she was patient. She was immortal, after all. She could wait.

"Check her again. Any changes?"

Once more, Dick checked her eyes. "Nothing. It's like we're not doing anything to her."

Dr. Klein closed the notebook, placing the silver pen inside. "Unhook her, und take her back to her cell."

As they unfastened her and administered more sedative, he leaned down almost nose-to-nose with Sam. His breath stank of eggs. "Sam, I must warn you. I am losing hope that I can cure you. You don't want zat."

"Go to Hell."

He sighed. "Well, it can't be helped. If I lose all hope, we can always try brain surgery."

"Just try it. I'll rip your throat out." She exposed her teeth to emphasize the point.

As they dragged her out of the room, she noticed a surgery scheduled on the whiteboard. "LeBeouf, Transorbital Lobotomy." It was the sixth surgery she had seen that week. It was like Dr. Klein wanted patients to fail. Why would he do that to so many people?

Along the way back, they passed a surgical technician, someone Sam didn't recognize. And to her, he seemed out of place—a Middle-Eastern-looking man with a military haircut and a tightly trimmed beard. He had to be in his mid-to-late twenties.

They stopped, and Dick asked, "Hey, new guy. Is the machine ready for that girl? The nympho? Dr. Klein wants to put her on it tomorrow."

Sam gasped. *Meghan!*

"Yes, sir," the technician said. "It's ready."

"Good, good." Dick seemed quite pleased.

Dock tugged on Sam. "Whatever, man. You just want to be there and help stretch her out. Come on, let's get this one back."

My God, what are they doing to her? Just thinking about it made her stomach ache.

Once in her cell, Sam rolled to the side and rested her hands on her stomach, her fingertips brushing over her caesarean scar—the place where her children had been taken from her. Gritting her teeth, she placed both palms over it and pressed gently. It had healed to a thin line within days. The loose skin and detached muscles had healed back to a tight abdomen within a few more. It was like she had never been pregnant.

Hours passed. Several times, she broke into tears, sobbing softly into the mildew stink of her cot. She was finally settling down to sleep when the cell next to her opened.

She craned her neck and listened. Someone said, "Well, this one's a hard nut to crack. What's he in for?"

"Murdered one of his own," someone else said. "Claimed the Devil made him do it or something. Who cares?"

In the other cell, someone landed hard on the cot. Then he moaned with pain.

"Sleep tight. Tomorrow's going to be real fun. Dr. Klein's going to shock you back into sound mental health."

The two men laughed as they left.

For a while, there was only silence. Sam lay there, listening for movement. It seemed like she had a new neighbor. Maybe this one would last longer than a week.

After a few more minutes, the springs of the other cot creaked. The man, whoever he was, moaned again.

Finally, Sam said, "Sounds like you've had a tough time of it."

"Ah, what? Who's there?"

"On the other side of the wall." She tapped it a few times with a metal restraint. "Here."

He tapped the wall, presumably with a fingernail. "I guess they don't make cells like they used to, do they?"

She hummed and then said, "That's a funny thing to say. Who are you?"

"Does it matter?"

"I guess not."

"All right, then. Leave me alone."

She stayed silent for a long time, just tracing mindless patterns on the wall of her cell and scratching the annoying stubble on her head. Finally, she asked, "So you killed someone?"

"Is everyone here this nosey?" He sounded both annoyed and tired.

For what felt like the tenth time that day, she ground her teeth. "Look, you ass, you may not realize it, but you're stuck in Hell. Now, I don't know what you've done, and quite frankly, I don't care. But let me tell you, the days of torture and the nights of solitude wear on your sanity. So, unless you think you'll be out in a few days for good behavior, you'd better get used to talking to someone. And, unfortunately, you're stuck with me."

There was a long pause before he said, "Sorry I was rude. And, so you know, I'm not getting out. I'm here for life. Might as well be a prison."

Relaxing her jaw, even popping it a few times to help the muscles relax, she leaned her forehead against the wall. "You, too, eh? So what did you do?"

"I killed a cop."

"Really? That's pretty serious."

"And you're pretty observant."

Sam chuckled. It was refreshing to hear someone else's sarcasm. "So why did you do it?"

"To stop him from killing someone I love."

Part of her wondered what this guy looked like—if he was handsome and good in bed. He sure sounded that way. Then she remembered that it was Bridgette who gave her such sexually aggressive thoughts. Pushing back those urges, she asked, "So, what, was it one of those bad-cop-holding-a-gun-to-your-girl's-head things?"

"No, nothing like that at all."

"Then what was it?"

"You wouldn't believe me if I told you."

She snorted. "Bub, I've been through shit you wouldn't believe. Try me."

The springs creaked again. "Fine. The cop got his hands on something that lets you kill people just by writing about their death."

Sam froze, her forehead pressed against the stone masonry as she broke into a cold sweat. She knew something that could do exactly that.

"What . . ." Her throat tightened. "What are you talking about?"

He sounded tense as well. "A pen. A goddamn silver pen. Possessed by the devil himself. The Bourbon Street Ripper. Vincent Castille."

A Shield That Protects

(Kyle Aucoin's Story)

Chapter 16
Fat City Stabber

Monday, March 19, 1993
Time: 8:00 p.m.
Location: New Orleans Police Department
Precinct Eight, French Quarter

A few weeks before Sam met her new neighbor . . .

"Kyle, I'll be in town on Friday to close my Whitney account. Do you, um, want to have lunch afterwards?"

What Detective Aucoin wanted to say more than anything else in the world was "yes." But as he sat at his desk, the floor all but empty, he just couldn't bring himself to.

"Kyle?" Cathy sounded more desperate.

He rubbed his face, spreading his sweat. It made him feel greasy. "I'm sorry, Cathy. I don't think that's a good idea." He just couldn't face her, not yet.

She sighed. "I understand. Are you at least sleeping well? Taking care of yourself?"

"Yes and yes." He hated lying to her, but the truth would hurt more.

"All right. Hun, you take care. I'll call you when I'm in town, just in case you change your mind."

"Cathy, I really don't—"

But she had already hung up.

With an exasperated sigh, he hung up the phone. She had asked for a divorce six months ago, and they had finally gotten around to officially filing the papers. Even though they agreed to do it "no-fault," the cost and time was making every day drag out.

At least that's how it felt to Aucoin, and having her continuously try to get together "for lunch" made it much worse.

"Well, seeing her would give her closure. I owe her that much."

He was still mulling it over when Rivette sat down across from him at the desk that used to be Dixie's. He put his feet up, fiddling with one of his action figures. "Ya know, if you ever need someone to talk to or just wanna yell about how much your ex-wife sucks ass, I'm here."

Aucoin raised an eyebrow and stared at Rivette as if he was about to wind up his head with a clock key. "I don't even talk to Dix about Cathy. Why would I talk to you?"

Rivette shrugged and dropped his action figure into his lap. "Probably because I'm the only one who will talk to you. The lieutenant is about to pop, the commander wants nothing to do with you, and Landry, Gravois, and Breaux are convinced you're gonna go on a killing spree any day now."

"Wouldn't that be something? Give you guys a reason to put me down."

Frowning, Rivette said, "Man, don't even kid like that. Look, if Rodger or Michael were still alive, they'd be taking you out for drinks at Jean Lafitte's. But since they're not, I'm more than happy to treat you to a few pitchers."

Aucoin grunted. It was always tedious talking to Rivette, whom he regarded as a child. "Thanks, but all the same, I'm gonna finish this up and go home. I have a crossword puzzle with my name on it."

"Fine," Rivette said, getting up. He shook the action figure as if it were talking. "But the captain says that the invitation is out there for ya."

With a murmur, Aucoin waved him off.

A moment later, though, Rivette cleared his throat. "Hey, Kyle."

"What?" He didn't try to hide his annoyance.

Stroking his goatee, Rivette said, "Real talk time. Just remember, no one can go it alone, OK?"

For a few seconds, Aucoin gawked at Rivette, his mouth open. Then he said, "Why, thank you, Scott. I have seen the light and am now a changed man. Truly, you are an amazing individual with the ability to save the soul of even the most embittered person with just a well-rehearsed philosophical line or two."

Rivette ignored him the rest of the night.

When Aucoin got home, he jerked off and then took a long, hot shower. Then, dressed in his robe, he fixed a microwave dinner and sat down in front of the television. The scent of pine cleaner and fresh carpet surrounded him. The few containers he had managed to stack up on the coffee table were gone, and there wasn't any dust anywhere.

Damn maids were here again. Jesus, Dix, I told you once a month was fine!

He considered calling her to complain, but he knew she wouldn't listen. She had made it perfectly clear that if he didn't allow a maid service, she'd come and clean his house herself—pregnancy be damned.

"So much for not helping until I ask for it." But despite it all, he couldn't be angry. She was only looking out for him, and he knew it.

He turned on the television. The rerun of the evening news had just started.

"Tonight, another murder in Metairie. Police are looking for any leads in the stabbing death of local teenager Luane Calvin. Luane, who had been in and out of drug rehab since last Christmas, was found in an alleyway behind the Ship's Wheel Gentlemen's Club in Fat City. He had been stabbed thirty-seven times."

Aucoin shook his head in disgust. Over the past month, five teenagers had been found stabbed to death in Fat City, Jefferson Parish's version of the French Quarter. The media was already giving it the same level of coverage that they had given the new Bourbon Street Ripper back in August.

"A memorial service for the sixth victim of what is being called 'the Fat City Stabber' will be held this weekend. Jefferson Parish Sheriff Harry Lee has also issued the following statement."

The report cut to a portly Asian man standing behind a podium. He had the look of someone who did not play around. "We're devoting full-time resources to finding this killer. For now, I urge all Metairie residents under the age of eighteen to stay inside after nightfall unless with large groups or parents. I've also spoken with Commander Louis Ouellette of the New Orleans Eighth Precinct. Commander Ouellette oversaw the new Bourbon Street Ripper case last year. He has promised to bring in additional, specialized resources. I'm sure with his expertise, he'll—"

Muting the report, Aucoin said, "Well, I don't know what resources the commander's bringing in, Harry. They're all either dead or on medical leave."

He rifled through a stack of notebooks and picked one out, opening it up. Inside was page after page of personal thoughts. They were all extremely dark—some of them outright murderous. Then he took out a silver fountain pen that he had recovered from the ashes of Sam Castille's home. "All right, time for some therapy."

After his mental breakdown, he'd started seeing a city-appointed therapist. One of his exercises was learning how to admit to his feelings. The counselor suggested that he write down every twisted thought that came to mind in stream-of-consciousness writing to "get it all out" instead of bottling it up inside.

After six months, he had filled up over a dozen notebooks with some of the sickest shit imaginable. It started as a rambling narrative and transformed into full-blown prose, focusing on his rage. Just as he hadn't been able to save his daughter, he fixated on others dying violent deaths that could have been avoided if they had just listened to their fathers.

"Let's see."

After a few seconds of thought, he began to write:

> The killer skulked about in the shadows like a plague waiting to be unleashed, stalking his prey with murderous intent. Betty had gone out for a pack of smokes, disobeying her parents' pleas for safety. Betty's father, Mike, had even offered to take her to the gas station himself, but she was too cool for that. And so, poor Betty arrived at the gas station alone and got her pack of cigarettes, tucking one behind her ear and lighting another. She thought she was fine as she headed home, but the killer was already waiting for her in the alley behind the comic shop. Before she even knew it, he was upon her, stabbing her again and again, slicing through her arteries and cutting into her heart. She was dead before she could even gurgle.

Aucoin shivered as a tingle rippled down his spine. He put the notebook and pen away without reviewing his story, thinking about something else instead. It was what the therapist had suggested, getting the negative thoughts out and then forcing them away. Then he quietly ate his now-cold dinner. Eventually, he fell asleep in his chair. It wasn't a choice so much as a necessity. Cathy had taken the bed when she'd left.

"Sir, you're doing what?"

Aucoin sat across from his commander, staring in disbelief. He hadn't even gotten to his desk before Ouellette had called him into his office.

Ouellette stared back, arms folded and as dour-looking as ever. "Believe me, Aucoin. If there was any other way, I wouldn't. But Connick's kicking up shit, and the mayor's seat is up for election next year, so Barthelemy don't give a crap. And seeing as how everyone else is working triple overtime, you're the one. So, instead of sitting there bitching like a little girl, how about you find your balls and start being a cop again?"

Under normal circumstances, Aucoin would enjoy every second of Ouellette's tough attitude. It was the one thing about his boss he'd always loved. But with his own life falling to pieces, he just wasn't into it. He especially didn't feel up to the task he'd been given.

"Sir, I get that we're understaffed. But asking me to go help the Jefferson Parish police find the Fat City Stabber?"

With a snort, Ouellette said, "Who else do I send? Bergeron and LeBlanc are gone. Olivier is about to drop her baby. Rivette is constantly acting up. Landry is occupied with personal assignments. Breaux and Gravois are doing more work than everyone else combined. There's no one else. You're it."

As Aucoin opened his mouth to protest, Ouellette held up a hand and locked eyes with him. "Look. I know you're in pain. I get it. No father should ever have to bury a child. I've been there. And also, like you, I've had a marriage ruined by a child's death. So I know you're suffering. I know it better than you can ever imagine."

He leaned forward, putting his elbows on the table. "But I also know that you're a detective and a damn good one. You squeeze this last one out for me, and I'll make sure you get on paid leave for a month. Deal?"

After a few seconds, Aucoin nodded.

"Good," Ouellette said. "Report to Harry Lee's office tomorrow. You'll work there until the Fat City Stabber is caught."

"Yes, sir," Aucoin said. "I'll make sure Dix knows what's going on. Otherwise, she might worry herself into labor." He smirked. It was a joke. His former partner was anything but weak.

Ouellette snickered. "And she'd beat the crap out of you with her one hand if she heard you say that. Now get going. I've got too much to do. That fat-ass Landry needs to report on a special project, and he's running late."

However, Aucoin didn't want to leave yet. His commander's comment about burying a child brought forth something he'd been holding in for months.

"One question, sir, if I may?"

"Yes?"

"I was just wondering, given what happened to your son, Jason, and all . . ."

That made Ouellette scowl. "Your point, Aucoin?"

Asking the question was harder than he had anticipated. "How long does it take to come to terms with your child's death? How long does it take to forget the pain?"

For a moment, Ouellette looked old and tired. It was the first time Aucoin had ever seen his commander with that expression.

"You never get over it," he said. "A parent shouldn't have to bury their child for any reason. Even if you start another family, the pain doesn't go away."

Aucoin blinked. "Start another family? I thought Jason was your only child."

With another scowl, Ouellette waved him off. "I try offering counsel, and you pry into my past. Get your ass back to work. Focus on your fixing your own life instead of sticking your nose into mine, all right?"

He then turned his attention to the reports on his desk, leaving Aucoin to wonder just what past his commander was hiding.

Once back on the floor, Aucoin saw Detective Landry on the phone, cupping his mouth around the receiver. He wiped sweat from his forehead. As Aucoin approached, all he heard was "keep an eye on her" and "do my best."

Coming up behind Landry, Aucoin squeezed his shoulder. "Hey, Paul. Everything OK?"

Landry squeaked and hung up the phone. "Yeah! Yeah, Kyle. Everything's fine." He grinned nervously, avoiding eye contact.

"Right. Hey, man, you know if you're ever in trouble, you can give me a call. I'll help."

Throwing on his overcoat, Landry said, "Yeah, thanks, Kyle. No, I'll be OK. I was just talking to my, um, mother. My little sister's dating another deadbeat, and Mom wants me to keep an eye on her."

He gathered his belongings and waved goodbye. "So I'll catch you later, right?" He was gone before Aucoin could respond.

With his hands on his hips, Aucoin said, "Right. So what was that all about?"

Then something on the ground caught his eye—a scrap of paper that had fallen from Landry's coat pocket.

Aucoin skimmed the room, but the only other person around was Rivette, and he was having a fight with the coffee machine. Nonchalantly, Aucoin snatched up the paper. Then he went back to his desk, smoothed it out, and looked it over. It was a series of street addresses and times.

Well, this is nothing special.

A moment later, his detective instincts kicked in, and he realized what he had. Confusion settled within him.

I don't get it. Why does Landry have Dix's daily schedule?

Chapter 17
Enter Caroline Saucier

Date: **Wednesday, March 21, 1993**
Time: **6:00 a.m.**
Location: **Severn Avenue, Fat City, Metairie**

The sun hadn't risen yet as Aucoin headed out to Fat City, a large, square area of bars, clubs, and restaurants in the heart of Metairie. In many ways, it was the little brother of the French Quarter—it was a place of vices that stank of well-seasoned bodily fluids. But unlike the Big Easy's main attraction, Fat City was filled with low-rise buildings and cheap expectations, with only the occasional drunken bum or high teenager to show what it wanted to be.

To Aucoin, it was a punishment just having to be there.

His check-in with Harry Lee was brief and uneventful. He learned that the Fat City Stabber had struck again the previous evening. He was also informed that he'd be working with Detective Bradley, who was heading up the investigation.

As he pulled up next to a police car, which was silently flashing its lights, he saw several trucks from the local television stations and a growing mass of pedestrians. At the outer edge of the crowd was a truck from the *Times-Picayune*, and behind it was a red Cadillac convertible with a white hood and tinted windows.

Aucoin got out and pulled his overcoat around him. The air was still chilly, and the humidity was as terrible as always. As he passed by the Cadillac, his gaze lingered. He could just barely make out someone inside and heard NPR playing. He nodded briefly at whoever was inside and moved on. "Now that's a gorgeous car."

Sparing a glance at the reporters and the crowd, he slipped under the police line and headed down the alleyway toward the crime scene. A uniformed officer stopped him about halfway.

"Who are you?"

He showed his badge. "Kyle Aucoin, New Orleans Eighth Precinct Homicide. My boss has me helping your boss with this mess."

The officer nodded at the badge and then motioned for him to follow. "This way, sir. I'll introduce you to the detective on scene."

He led Aucoin to a tall, suited man with a beer gut and a dangerously receding hairline. "Detective Bradley, this is Detective Aucoin. He's the guy from New Orleans."

They shook hands. "Aucoin, eh? Glad you could make it. It's a shit sandwich here, and I'm about full." He slapped his bulging stomach.

Aucoin scanned the scene. A single body lay underneath a white sheet with pools of blood leaking out from the sides. Several smaller puddles of blood led from a nearby wall toward it. "Looks like the victim was attacked over by the wall there and made it about four yards before being overtaken." It felt good to be a detective again, even if he was stating the obvious.

Bradley cleared his throat and spit a wad of phlegm to the side. "Excuse me. Yeah, it's disgusting. This is the seventh victim of the Stabber. The son-of-a-bitch is getting bolder, like he's daring us to catch him. But there's no trail and no evidence. Whoever this guy is, he's good at covering his tracks."

Kneeling down next to the body, Aucoin gingerly picked up the corner of the sheet. "May I?"

With a shrug, Bradley said, "Sure. I'll guess you've got the stomach for it, based on your work on the Ripper case. So be my guest."

Aucoin peeled back the sheet. It was an awful sight. The victim was a girl in her mid-teens with chestnut-brown hair and too much makeup, like she was rebelling against being a child. From the denim jacket to the pack of cigarettes clutched in her hand to the Walkman buds in her ears, she had stark similarities to Cheryl. Her chest and abdomen were covered with blood, her eyes were open, and her mouth was stretched into a frozen scream.

For a brief moment, he was standing in the morgue over the tortured remains of his beautiful daughter, the pieces of her that were left detailing the hours of relentless agony that Dallas had made her suffer.

Dropping the blanket, Aucoin rushed behind a dumpster. He barely made it before vomiting. It wasn't the brutality of the crime, as he had seen far worse over the course of his career. If it had been a teenage boy, or an older girl or an adult, or even a girl who dressed differently, that would have been OK. But to see a girl who reminded him of his Cheryl was way too much.

"Hey, whoa, you OK there?" Bradley stood behind him. He sounded concerned.

After he had emptied his stomach of the store-bought waffles he'd had for breakfast, Aucoin wiped his mouth and said, "Yeah. Just, long story. I'll be OK."

Bradley jerked his head toward the alleyway's exit. "Why don't you go chill out at the street? I'll come join you in a bit. Then we'll go have breakfast, and I'll fill you in on the case."

"Breakfast?" Aucoin spat out the remaining vomitus. "Yeah, sure, whatever. I have room now. I'll wait for you by the cars."

He hurried out of the alleyway, images of the dead girl still fresh in his mind. His thoughts then wandered to how much he wished Dallas was still alive. He often fantasized about how he would torture him slowly over a period of days or even weeks, taking care to ensure he didn't die until all that remained was a lump of flesh and organs that could barely be called human.

By the time he reached the street, he was so firmly entrenched in his elaborate revenge fantasy that he didn't realize he'd walked straight into a group of reporters. The next thing he knew, several microphones, cameras, and lights were in his face. Questions were being fired off at him.

"Excuse me, Detective, but what can you tell us about the death? Is it being ruled another homicide?"

"Is this another victim of the Fat City Stabber?"

"What is Sheriff Lee doing to keep the teenagers of Metairie safe from this killer?"

Aucoin stood in shock as the half-dozen reporters waited for an answer. Luckily, his training in dealing with the media kicked in after only a few seconds. "Sorry, I'm not authorized to comment on the case. You'll have to wait for Detective Bradley."

More questions flew at him anyway.

"Are you working with Detective Bradley?

"You're Detective Aucoin from Downtown, correct?"

"Why have you been assigned to this case?"

Starting to sweat, he noticed the passenger-side door of the Cadillac open and a feminine hand gesture to him.

"Sorry," he said. "Again, no comment." He slipped through the crowd into the car. Once inside, he closed the door and adjusted his overcoat. "Thanks. Can you drive me around the block?"

Then he got a good look at the person behind the wheel. He had thought it might be someone he knew, but he had never seen her before. Dressed in a charcoal business suit, she was in her early forties with dark auburn, bob-cut hair and cold, blue eyes. There was something about her that just said "bitch." She flipped a switch, locking the car, and then put it in drive. "Buckle up, Detective."

As she drove off and began circling the block, she added, "You owe me. I was going to grill you the moment you left the alleyway, but when I saw you getting mobbed, my conscience, or whatever, got the best of me."

Aucoin regarded the woman, wondering who she thought she was to act so familiar. "And you are?"

"Caroline Saucier, Editor-in-Chief of the *Times-Picayune*," she announced.

His brow furrowed. The last thing he wanted was to talk to someone from the newspaper. That was Harry or Bradley's job. "I think you better let me out, Miss Saucier."

She turned the corner, heading toward a traffic light. "You wanted a ride around the block, right?"

"Yeah, well, now I want to walk. And I've asked you to let me out."

As they approached the traffic light, which was red, Caroline slowed down to a stop.

He tried to open the door, but it was locked, and this model of Cadillac could only be unlocked by the driver. "Miss Saucier, if you don't let me out, I'm going to arrest you for unlawful detainment."

Flipping the door switch again, she leaned back and gazed at him, amused. "Detective, you're about to enter the game, like it or not. Pick your side wisely. Here, take this." She flicked a business card at him. "Contact me when you have a few free hours. I'd like to chat."

For the first time, he noticed an ornate golden pin on her suit's lapel. It bore the crest of a red cross and a golden crown. He took the card and pocketed it, figuring he might need to follow up on her at some point. "Right, I think maybe I'll just forget I ever spoke to you. Have a good day, Miss Saucier." He got out of the car. As soon as the traffic light turned green, it sped off.

"Fucking weird-ass chick."

Shaking his head, he turned around and promptly froze. He was facing the storefront opposite the alley where the girl had died. Right in front of him was a sign that read "Big Carl's Comics."

"What the hell? Didn't I write that someone would get killed outside a comic book shop?"

On the phone, Dixie asked, "So, Ouellette has you working on the Stabber case for now?"

Aucoin held his phone to his ear while flipping through the television's channels. Nearby, steam billowed up from a half-eaten Hungry Man dinner. "Yep, Dix, that's right."

She sounded pleased. "Well, I don't want to annoy you, but you sound more alive than you have in a while. Maybe all you needed was a case to work on."

He wolfed down a forkful of mashed potatoes that had mixed in with the corn. He didn't want to admit it, but she was absolutely correct. He hadn't felt this good in months.

"It is what it is, Dix. So how are you doing? The baby's coming soon, right?"

"Yes. Dr. Cambre is still saying April 7th, but it could be any day now."

Shoveling down a few more bites of dinner, he asked, "You have a name picked out yet?"

"Hmm. Well, we think it's going to be a girl, and if it is, we're going with Felicia. If it's a boy, we'll call him Felix."

Aucoin chortled and then guzzled down a glass of water. "Sounds good. You call me when you're going into labor. If I can, I'll join you."

She chuckled, too. It was the first time in a while that they had conversed so casually. "All right, Kyle. All right. Now, concerning what we were talking about earlier?"

He stood up, taking the empty dinner tray to the kitchen and tossing it out. "It was just eerie. Miss Saucier was acting like she knew something. And when I talked to the commander about her, he said that he'd take care of it."

"This is the first time in a while I've heard Caroline's name come up. I know she's one of the wealthiest women in southern Louisiana. And I recall Sam mentioning that she couldn't stand her."

Hearing Sam's name made his gut tighten. He had never gotten a chance to apologize to her—or, rather, to give her a chance to spit his apology back in his face. "Right, well, Sam couldn't stand a lot of people, me included. I'm just curious as to why this Saucier woman is singling me out."

"Honestly? I don't know. That pin on her lapel, I think that's the Knight Priory."

"Knight Priory? I thought they were destroyed."

"Yeah . . . Long story. They're just not who they used to be, that's all."

"Right. And the commander's comment about him 'taking care of it'?"

Her voice dropped to a whisper. "I don't know for sure, Kyle. I trust him, and I know he hates the Knight Priory, but I get the feeling there's more to it than that. It's almost like it's . . . personal."

Aucoin closed his eyes. Ouellette's most recent comments confused him, too. More and more, it seemed like he was living several lives at once.

Finally, he said, "I have a feeling you shouldn't go poking around in his business, Dix."

"You, too. Just keep your eyes open and your ass covered."

He opened his eyes. "Will do. You take care."

"You, too, Kyle—oh, one more thing. Can you talk to Scott tomorrow?"

"Really?" He hardly ever spoke to Rivette unless it was to berate him. "And why am I doing this, Dix?"

"Yeah, listen. He's been really angry about the budget cuts, the lack of manpower, and how all that's been translating into the increase in violent crime. You know him, he's a pacifist who'd never hurt anyone. He barely made it onto the force because he's so kind-hearted. So can you please just sit and talk with him for a bit, just so he can blow off steam?"

Aucoin grunted, preferring not to act as counselor to the younger detective when he was messed up himself. But it was for Dixie, so . . .

"I'll do it."

"Oh, thank you! Kyle, I really appreciate this. I mean it!" She sounded ecstatic.

Rubbing his face, he said, "Well, I'm going to get going. I need to do some catch-up and read through these old case files for the Stabber."

"All right. Keep in touch. And Kyle?"

"Yeah?"

She giggled the same way she did when they were partners. "Good to have you back."

"Heh, OK, you. Good to be back." He hung up the phone and then turned off the television. "Time to go to work."

It took Aucoin several hours to sort through all the information on the Fat City Stabber. While he had hoped Bradley would tell him about the case throughout the day, all he had done was give an overview during breakfast.

"Well, at least I have all night to work on this."

He had been expecting to work late into the evening at the department with Bradley. Around five in the afternoon, however, Bradley had gotten a page on his beeper from home. His daughter had been caught pinching a beer. Aucoin had told Bradley they'd meet up again in the morning, having been in similar situations with Cheryl before.

So, sitting on his couch with notes spread out on the coffee table, he leaned back and went over what he felt were the most important facts.

Each victim was between fifteen and eighteen years old, female, and Caucasian. Each one was what would be considered a delinquent—indulging in vices such as alcohol, drugs, and promiscuity. Each girl was killed between eleven at night and four in the morning, and each murder took place within the confines of Fat City.

He opened the folder containing pictures of the victims. As soon as he saw their faces, his hands started shaking. "Good God. These girls all look like my baby."

Spilling the photos onto the floor, he hurried to the kitchen and poured a glass of water. Then he started rummaging through the cabinet of medication he kept near the sink. A moment later, he took out an anxiety pill prescribed in case of a panic attack.

As he held it, an image flashed in his head—Cheryl's eviscerated body lying on the coroner's table, her face stuck in a cry of anguish. Most of her teeth were gone, having been pulled or chiseled out, and the side of her eyes had crusts where her tears had dried. Her hands, her cute little hands that used to grab for him when she was a child, were ground into the same type of pulp one uses for hamburger.

Aucoin slid down to the floor, his knees buckling for the second time today. Grabbing the sides of his head, he screamed. He had been fighting back those memories for weeks, and with one look at the Stabber's victims, they came rushing to the surface. Now they wouldn't leave.

He popped the pill and gulped it down with a glass of water before heading back to his comfy chair. He needed his notebook, and he needed his pen. He needed to get the dark thoughts out before they drove him mad.

With a heavy plop, he sat down, threw open his notebook, and started writing.

> Marilyn was not a good girl, and that's why the killer chose her, because all bad girls have bad things happen to them. Her dad, Jim, just wanted her to go to school and find a good husband, but she didn't listen. Marilyn never listened. She dressed like a whore and flirted with every older guy who'd pay her attention. So it was no surprise when the guy she picked up behind the sports bar turned out to be the killer. She thought it was someone she could trust, but he had evil plans for her. Raping her was enjoyable, but stabbing her was even more fun. When he finished, he stuffed her dead body into

the dumpster behind the bar so she could lay with the rest of the garbage.

Aucoin squeezed the silver pen as he dotted the last period. He was breathing heavily and sweating profusely. A sudden chill and a tingling down his spine brought him back to his senses. He started to close the notebook but then stopped. A bitter taste in his mouth and a feeling in his gut told him to open it back up. Putting down the pen, he read what he'd just written instead of pushing it out of his mind like he usually did.

What he saw appalled him. "Damn, that is sick. God help me if anyone ever reads this. I'd be locked away for life."

He put down the notebook and got up. "I need a drink. I deserve a drink." He was halfway to the kitchen when a white flash caught his eye. He quickly turned, ready to defend himself. All he saw was a small, white orb floating over the notebook. It quickly vanished into mist.

What the hell? Wait, Dixie mentioned seeing something like that during the Hannah case!

Heading back to the notebook, he scanned the entry from the night before, frowning as he read over the details. They were similar to the case from this morning. Then he flipped back and read another previous story and then another. An uneasy feeling descended over him.

The details of all three of those stories were similar to victims of the Fat City Stabber.

Flipping back further, he read through each story from the past couple of months—seven total. They were all about teenage girls being brutally stabbed to death. He didn't even remember writing some of them, although they were clearly in his handwriting.

"What the hell is going on?"

Now sweating, he returned to the case notes and read over each murder, comparing it to the entries in his notebook. Not only were they remarkably similar, down to details such as locations and certain items like cigarettes or condoms, but each murder occurred within a few nights of his writing down the story.

Both the notebook and the case file fell to the floor. He tried to make sense of it but found that he could not. If he hadn't already encountered something like this during the new Bourbon Street Ripper case, he'd think he was being paranoid.

But this wasn't the first time.

"This is exactly what happened with Sam and her stories!"

Chapter 18
Lunch at Morning Call

Date: **Thursday, March 22, 1993**
Time: **10:00 a.m.**
Location: **Corner of Division and 18th Street**
Fat City, Metairie

Aucoin watched with a grim expression as two men from the coroner's office zipped up a body bag. Another victim of the Fat City Stabber had turned up, and somehow, the circumstances were just like what he had written the previous night. The victim was about seventeen years old, was skimpily dressed, and had a reputation for promiscuity. Her body, which showed signs of sexual assault, had been found in a dumpster behind a seedy local bar.

"Have you ever seen anything like it?" Bradley stood with his arms folded. He looked like he hadn't slept.

With a shake of his head, Aucoin turned away. "Too many times. Whoever this person is, they're escalating their violence."

They headed out of the alley. Bradley lit up a cigarette. "Well, you worked the Ripper case last summer. I remember that. Fucked-up bit of shit that was. Harry had us on watch the entire time. Crazy stuff."

"Is there a point to this?" Aucoin was starting to feel annoyed. He just wanted to clear his head and try to figure out why the murders were like his stories. There had to be a correlation between what had happened to Sam and what was happening to him.

Bradley blew out a stream of smelly smoke. "I was hoping you'd have some insight into what was going on here, seeing as how you've already dealt with a serial killer."

As they reached their cars, Aucoin glowered. "You listen to me. There is nothing similar between this sicko and Dallas. This guy is a nutcase who is going to get caught because he's getting careless. Dallas was methodical and carefully planned his killings months in advance. You want my insight? We stake out every corner of Fat City and watch every girl who fits the killer's MO while she's here. Sooner or later, the killer will screw up, and we'll grab him."

With a final puff of his cigarette, Bradley tossed it to the side. "All right, let's get back to the building and run the plan by Harry."

"Actually," Aucoin said, holding out his hand to stop Bradley, "there are a few things I need to handle back in New Orleans first. I'll come meet up with you afterwards."

After staring at him for a couple of seconds, Bradley said, "All right. But don't be gone too long. It'll take several hours to put together what you're suggesting, assuming it's approved."

After leaving Fat City, Aucoin headed back to his precinct. The door to Ouellette's office was closed, voices coming from the other side. Rivette had his feet up on his desk and seemed annoyed with the world.

Remembering his promise to Dixie, Aucoin sat across from him. "Hey, Scott. You look agitated."

"I'm annoyed as hell, Kyle," Rivette replied, sliding over a photograph of an adorable child no more than two years old with dark skin and curly, black hair.

"Cute kid, Scott. Is she yours?"

Rivette snatched it back. "No, you ass. She's the kid of a woman who was beaten to death by her boyfriend a few nights ago."

Aucoin frowned, not trying to hide his disgust. "Good old Nawlins. Murder capital of the South. So was the girl kidnapped?"

"No, and thank God."

"Then why do you have her picture?"

Raising his voice, Rivette said, "To remind me of what was left behind after her mother was killed. It's getting worse out there, Kyle. We're unable to keep up, and the bad guys know it. The murder rate has never been this high!"

Shifting in his seat and glancing back at the photo, Aucoin asked, "So this is what's been pissing you off these past months—that we can't keep up with the rising crime rate?"

"The rising *violent* crime rate," Rivette clarified. "We've struggled ever since the massacre at the wharf. The peeps in charge keep saying we'll get priority on the recruits coming out of the academy this summer, but you and I both know that it takes years to train competent detectives. So we won't be up to snuff until at least 1995. And here, the commander is sending you off to go play in Metairie with Mister Harry Fucking Lee. How long do we have to endure this?"

As he sat there, watching Rivette's feet shake from an excess of nervous energy, Aucoin felt like he genuinely understood. It was what every good cop wanted, from rookie to veteran—to keep the good people safe and to stop the bad guys.

"Ya know, Scott? I get it. And all I can say is to trust in Dixie, trust in Ouellette, and trust that the top brass won't leave us hanging."

Rivette sighed. "Trust, right. How much longer until someone takes matters into their own hands, I wonder?"

That took Aucoin by surprise. "Not thinking of going rogue there, are you, buddy?"

With a snort, Rivette said, "No. You know I hate violence. But I can dream, right? Anyway, Kyle, thanks for listening."

Getting up, Aucoin patted his foot and said, "You're welcome, Scott," before heading back to his desk. As he sat down, Landry came out of Ouellette's office, looking hangdog.

I wonder what's up with him.

Shrugging it off for the moment, Aucoin called Dixie. After a few rings, someone picked up.

"Hello. How may I help you?" It was Gino.

"Gino, hey. Is Dixie available?"

"Ah, yes. She's right here, Kyle."

A few moments later, Dixie said, "Hey, Kyle. What's up?"

"Hey. This is going to sound weird, but I need to talk to you about something important. Do you have a minute?"

He heard her shifting in bed and caught her muttering, "I don't need anything right now," to Gino. Then she said, "I've got some time, Kyle. What do you want to talk about?"

"Sam."

Immediately, her breath got shallow. "Yeah. So maybe we should meet up and have lunch somewhere."

That caught him off guard. "You sure you're up for leaving the apartment?"

"Kyle, I'm pregnant, not stricken with polio."

With a laugh, he said, "All right. Let me get out of here before Ouellette sees me. I'll meet you at our usual place?"

"Sounds good. Do you mind if Gino comes?"

"Sure. I'd like to see the big guy. I'll meet you there in an hour."

"All right, hun. See you soon."

Hanging up, he saw that Landry and Rivette were gone and the door to Ouellette's office was still closed. The floor was quiet save for Breaux working on some reports.

Aucoin pulled his jacket on and called out, "Gary! Hey, man, when the commander comes out, let him know that I checked in but then went out to lunch with Dixie. Afterwards, I'll head back to Metairie."

Breaux nodded and went back to his work. Aucoin slipped out, but not before stopping by Rodger and Michael's old desk, which had remained enshrined since their deaths.

Wish you guys were here.

When Aucoin arrived at the Morning Call café in City Park, it was already noon. The café was packed, with very few places to sit—only a few tables outside and the bars inside. All around, the picturesque beauty of the park, from the green, drooping cypresses to the blossoming magnolias, was just starting to take on color. Winter was over, and spring was struggling to be more than a cool, wet season.

He searched for Dixie and Gino, first out on the patio, and then inside.

"Kyle! Over here!"

Dixie was waving from one of the corner tables, a coveted spot. It wasn't the least bit surprising. Despite being a bustling city with a rising crime rate, New Orleans was in the South, and Southern hospitality would always give the best seat in the house to an expectant mother.

Gino was sitting next to her, protectively holding her hand. Her midsection was bulging, and she looked both fatigued and radiant at the same time. For a moment, it reminded Aucoin of when Cathy was pregnant with Cheryl. He pushed that memory away, shaking Gino's hand and then hugging Dixie. "Good to see you."

"Good to see you, Kyle. Have a seat. We've already ordered lunch."

He sat down and skimmed the menu. Other than beignets and coffee, the Morning Call also served gumbo, jambalaya, and a few other hearty items. Between the atmosphere and the lovely view of the park, this had been their favorite place to eat when they were partners.

He ordered the jambalaya and a coffee and then leaned back. "So, Dix, you don't mind if I just get straight to the point, do you?"

When she shook her head, he started. "So, I want to talk about Sam—specifically, about how her stories paralleled Dallas's murders. What did we discover?

It was a modem in her copier that was transmitting her stories to Kent and Nick Bourgeois, right?"

"Correct," Dixie said. "She would copy her manuscripts, and the copier would send a fax to Kent, who would then forward the information to Dallas. Dallas would then pattern his crimes off her stories. This was, of course, to frame her for the murders, isolate her from her friends, and make it easier to take her in the end."

Aucoin nodded. His jaw locked tightly as he remembered. Everything about the case was screwed up. Richie, the prick from Pittsburg, turned out to be the subservient personality of Dallas, the monster who killed his Cheryl.

"So, Kyle, why did you want to talk about this? Just wanting to clarify things?"

Coming out of his thoughts, he realized that both Dixie and Gino were waiting for him. "No. I was wondering how you thought it could be replicated. You know, if someone else could do it again, maybe with something other than a copier."

"What do you mean?"

He shrugged. "A silver pen, perhaps?"

She blinked. "A what now?"

"Heh . . . just humor me, but what if there was a pen, and whatever you wrote with it, it happened?"

For a few more seconds, she nibbled on her thumb. He knew that meant she was in deep thought. Then, quite suddenly, all color drained from her face. "Oh, my God, so that's what the *krabinay* meant by 'magic pen.' Kyle, what have you done?"

Her reaction caught him completely off guard. "Um, Dix, you're making no—"

"I've got to go," she said, getting paler. She struggled to stand, getting help from a concerned-looking Gino. "Sorry, Kyle. I need to call Dr. Lazarus."

"Dr. Lazarus? Dix, what did I say?"

"You didn't say anything, Kyle. It's just that . . . if I'm right about this, you're in serious danger."

Sweat broke out on his brow. "Um, what? Dix, you're starting to scare your old partner."

She grimaced, her face wrought with anxiety. "Let me think on things. I'll call you in a few days. For now, don't write anything with that pen, OK?"

As she started leaving, she added, "Gino, can you give Kyle Tania's card?"

Gino reached into her purse, took out a business card, and slid it across the table. "If not for that woman, we'd be dead right now."

Aucoin read the name on the card out loud. "Tania Patterson. That's Blind Moses's sister, right?" It had a phone number and an address for Jackson Square.

"Yes," Dixie said. "I'll call you soon. If, um, weird, crazy things start to happen, you contact her immediately." Gino led her away.

He called out after her. "What crazy things?"

"You'll know, Kyle," she said. "You'll know."

After leaving Morning Call, Aucoin met up with Bradley and received news that Harry had approved his plan to stake out Fat City. He spent the rest of the day setting it up with the Jefferson Parish police. By that evening, Fat City was as secure as the French Quarter had been after the mayor had declared martial law back in August.

When Aucoin arrived at home, there were two messages on his machine.

The first was from Cathy. "Kyle, I'll be in town tomorrow around noon. I'd really like to meet you for lunch. I'm going to the Copelands on Carrollton Avenue. I'll be there until two o'clock. If you show up, lunch will be on me."

He deleted it, pushing thoughts of her from his mind for the moment. He had other, more pressing concerns.

The second was from Dixie: "Hey, I've been thinking about what we talked about today. Can you do me a favor? Please check whatever you wrote back around the end of October. I mean your therapy writings. I'm specifically searching for anything around or before the twenty-sixth. And remember, don't write anything with that pen tonight."

He deleted the message. "This is freaking crazy."

After taking a shower, he sorted through his notebooks, finding the one he had been writing in near the end of October. Flipping through the pages, he found an entry on the twenty-fourth.

> Little Lindsey hated her family. She blamed them for the death of someone she loved. Lindsey wanted revenge, but it had to be complete. No loose ends. So Lindsey waited one night until the family was busy. Her father was watching the big game, her mother was crocheting, and her brothers and sisters were preoccupied. The perfect time for the perfect crime. Grabbing a kitchen knife, Lindsey slit their foul throats and bathed in their blood. A fitting end for a fucked-up family.

Aucoin said, "So whatever, right? I mean, why did she want me to look at—oh, my God . . ."

His detective skills, which had atrophied in the months succeeding Cheryl's death, were reawakening. "I wrote something very similar to the Davis family murders only two days before they occurred."

He scanned the pen he had used to write that story. It was silver, with the name "Castille" etched into the side. It was the pen he had taken from the ashes of Sam's townhome, a pen he had felt oddly obligated to pick up.

Come to think of it, whenever I want to write, I feel compelled to use it.

He uncapped the pen, sniffed the ink on the tip, turned it around, and examined every aspect of it. Nothing really stood out. It was a nice pen, obviously well-made and expensive, but there wasn't anything he could see that was special about it.

So Aucoin spent another hour going through each notebook, comparing each of his stories with murders that had happened throughout the city. What he soon realized made him feel sick to his stomach. Almost every story was similar to a real-life murder, some of them as far away as Alexandria and Grand Isle—all parts of southern Louisiana. The parallels, while not as concise as they had been with Sam, were still too alike to be coincidence. And, as each month passed, the areas affected were farther away. Was its sphere of influence growing?

He picked up the pen and examined it again. The light sparkled off its surface.

With a sigh, he added, "Can this pen only do evil? Or can it do good as well?"

That was something he wasn't about to leave to chance. Flipping to a fresh page in his notebook, he wrote:

> The Fat City Stabber cornered his latest victim, a girl who had just had a fight with her father. He took out his knife and lunged at her, but before he could cut her, he was shot and then arrested by Detective Mike Bradley.

Capping the pen, Aucoin closed the notebook. He then felt a chill as well as a tingle rippling down his spine. "There! If this pen can actually make things happen, then tonight, the Fat City Stabber will be arrested."

Chapter 19
Another Chance

Date: **Friday, March 23, 1993**
Time: **4:00 a.m.**
Location: **Kyle Aucoin's House**
St. Bernard, New Orleans East

Aucoin dreamed of running down a long, lonely hallway, his footfalls reverberating all around. From the darkness ahead, he heard Cheryl calling out, her voice sounding the same as before she had died.

"Daddy? Daddy, please help!"

"Cheryl?" Sensations of panic welled up until they choked him. He willed himself to run even faster.

"Daddy! I'm so scared." Cheryl now sounded younger, like a tween.

"I'm coming, honey! Daddy's coming!" He went even faster, pushing himself until he felt like he was running on all fours.

Then he broke out of the darkness and into a mist-covered forest, the shadows around him moving as if they were alive, and the haze was like a thick blanket. Cheryl's sobs came from up a large hill. "I'm coming, baby!" Going up felt like moving through syrup.

"Daddy! He has a knife!" She now sounded like a child.

He reached the top of the hill, his throat tight with panic, where a lone chapel stood in a small graveyard. With a roar, he burst inside.

Cheryl, no more than five years old, was tied to a cross. All around were men and women wearing devil masks and holding torches. A masked man stood before her with a dagger.

He took off his mask. It was Dallas.

"Hey, Daddy. We're gonna carve your baby girl up and eat her for dinner, all right?"

He stabbed into Cheryl's heart. Aucoin reached out, unable to move, and cried, "Nooooo!" The grisly scene stretched away until it was a single, white dot in the distance. Then the dot spread into a slit, which turned out to be his eyelids opening as he woke up.

He was sitting in his chair, reaching out to the darkness and sweating so badly, he felt soaked. His throat hurt. Next to him, the phone rang, but he didn't answer it. Instead, he continued reaching out to where his dream of Cheryl had been. *I couldn't save her. Even in my dream, I couldn't save my daughter.*

Then his answering machine kicked on. "Hey, this is Kyle. Leave a message."

It beeped, and then Ouellette's voice spoke up. "Aucoin, when you hear this message, get your ass down to the station. We need to talk. Something happened in Fat City a little while ago."

Aucoin finally settled back down. It took a few more minutes for the shock of the dream to fully wear off. Then he got up and listened to the message again.

He was perplexed. "What the hell happened?"

"Come in, close the door, and sit down." Ouellette looked exhausted. The bags under his eyes were heavier than usual.

Aucoin did so. "Am I in trouble? Do I need to get my union rep or something?"

Ouellette shook his head and chugged a cup of black coffee. "No, you're not in trouble. But you are going to get grilled later today by Harry Lee."

"Why? What happened?"

"You worked with Detective Bradley these past few days. What did you think of him?"

His brow tightening, Aucoin shifted in his seat. Had Bradley shot the killer, like in his story, or did something else happen, debunking his theory about the silver pen? "I saw him as a good cop, like most of us here. I think he was a bit tired all the time because of his daughter, but I'm sure he'll be the guy to catch the Fat City Stab—"

"Excuse me one second," Ouellette said, getting up. He stormed over to the door and threw it open. "Landry, what is your major malfunction? I called you in here early to find that goddamn book, not to eavesdrop on my conversations."

As Ouellette stormed out, Aucoin caught a glimpse of Landry tripping over desks to get back to his. He couldn't figure Landry out. *How did the commander even know he was there?*

Shrugging, Aucoin turned away. It wasn't any of his business. As he heard Ouellette reading Landry the riot act, his eyes fell upon a folder on his commander's desk. It was simply labeled "Castille." Sucking on his bottom lip, he checked back outside. Ouellette was still reaming Landry. *Well, Dixie did say she wondered what the commander's up to, so . . .*

As quietly as he could, Aucoin slipped over to the folder and peeked inside. Within were dozens of old newspaper clippings. A couple of them were from the original Bourbon Street Ripper case, including photographs of Vincent Castille during his trial. Some were of the old Knight Priory of Saint Madonna. There were also a few articles on Guinea during the First World War and a photograph of Ouellette and his platoon during the Vietnam War.

Aucoin touched the photo and snickered. "The old son-of-a-bitch looked the same back then. Some guys have all the luck."

The sound of someone clearing his throat caught his attention. Ouellette was standing in the doorway, looking irritated. "Getting in some casual reading, Aucoin?"

Holding out his hands, Aucoin backed away. "I didn't mean anything by it, sir. I just . . . Well, I just . . ."

"You were just snooping around in my shit. I swear, you and Landry are like two little fucking kids." He slammed the folder shut and then waved toward the chair. "Sit your ass down. I catch you on this side of the desk again, and I'll suspend you for a month."

Without a word, Aucoin did as he was told.

"Right. So I asked you about Bradley because he was killed last night."

The shock was so sudden that he just sat there, mouth agape. Then he asked, "Who did it? Was it the Fat City Stabber?"

Ouellette got a thoughtful look and then said, "Yes. Yes, you could say that."

Something about how he phrased that didn't sit well with Aucoin. "What do you mean, sir? What exactly happened?" Did he somehow cause this with the silver pen?

Leaning forward and staring into his eyes, Ouellette said, "Bradley shot himself in front of his seventeen-year-old daughter last night."

Aucoin felt a chill descend upon him. The words he had written—"cornered his latest victim" and "shot and then arrested by Detective Mike Bradley"—resounded mercilessly in his skull.

"Commander, what are you saying?" He covered his face, feeling panic, anxiety, and even anguish. His stomach felt like it was in knots.

With a sigh, Ouellette said, "I'm saying that Detective Bradley was the Fat City Stabber, and when he realized he had chosen his own daughter as his next victim, he blew his own goddamn brains out."

Sitting back, Aucoin stared ahead, feeling what little sensation he had left drain from his face.

What have I done?

"Thank you for having lunch with me, Kyle," Cathy said, seated at a booth in Copeland's. She was already on dessert, with the check waiting on the table. She watched him softly, with the gentlest expression she had given him in many years. She was lovely, especially with her hair recently colored and styled, and with new earrings in her ears.

"Well, it turns out I'm not as busy as I thought," he said, taking off his jacket and sitting across from her. He had spent most of the morning dealing with the fallout from Detective Bradley's death, all while trying to sort through the revelation about the pen. Finally, he decided to ignore the issue until he could speak with Dixie again. Any other way would likely strip him of his sanity.

She smiled. "I'm glad, Kyle. I wanted to see you. So how have you been holding up?"

He recognized that she was trying to reach out again. The last few times, however, it hadn't worked out. When he had needed her after Cheryl's death, she had pulled away. And then when she'd come to him, he'd pushed her away. It was a sordid dance that had contributed heavily to the end of their marriage. But now she wanted to reconnect.

So he smiled back. "I've been OK. Ouellette has me working a new case, so I feel . . . well, I feel like my old self again."

"Oh that's wonderful!" She reached over and placed her hand over his, squeezing. He knew she wanted him to hold her hand, but he didn't move.

Her expression faded. "What's wrong?"

"Things have been happening that have brought back a lot of memories about, um, Cheryl."

Cathy squeezed his hand a little harder. "What happened?"

"A girl named Misty watched as her father, a cop, committed suicide in front of her. She's gone completely crazy. I'm told she'll be committed. Anyway, the fact that I couldn't save this girl reminded me of how useless I was with our daughter."

She rubbed her thumb over his hand. "Oh, Kyle."

He clenched his jaw. "I think what's really gotten to me all this time isn't so much what happened but that I felt completely helpless. When she needed me, when it really counted, I couldn't be there for her. I couldn't protect the one I love."

For a few more seconds, Cathy was silent. Then she covered his hand with both of hers and squeezed. "Kyle, you're a good man and a good cop. You always have been."

"But I haven't been a good husband or father." He looked away from her.

She leaned over and captured his gaze as she always did. "You'll get better at that again. But right now, you are a good man, and you are a good cop. You love helping and protecting people. So I think that when it matters—when it really matters—you'll be a shield that protects the ones you love."

With a gentle tug, she brought his hand to her lips. "I believe that."

She kissed his fingers and then let go. Getting up, she said, "I need to head out, but I'll be in touch. Remember what I said, and maybe, after some time, we'll try this again."

As she left some cash for her meal and started to leave, she turned to him and winked. "That is, if you want to give this train wreck of a marriage another chance. I know I do."

Aucoin watched as she left. Then he laughed. "That woman is unbelievable."

It was the near the end of the day when Aucoin finally went to the La Croix Voodoo Shoppe in Jackson Square. When he entered, he caught a sweet, spicy scent in the air. Other than himself, however, the store was empty. He frowned. If not for everything that Dixie had told him about the Hannah Davis case, he wouldn't even be there. He had no time for superstition.

A voice from across the shop caught his attention. "May I help you?"

His breath was nearly taken away. Standing there with her hands on her hips was a chocolate-skinned woman dressed in a dark red bustier and a long, black skirt. Her black hair was braided in locks and draped over her shoulders. She wore golden loop earrings and a red headscarf. She had a sensual air about her. Clearing his head of indecent thoughts, he glanced again at the business card Dixie had given him. "Are you Tania Patterson?"

"I am," she said. "And who wants to know?"

Showing her his badge, he said, "Detective Aucoin. Dixie told me to contact you if strange things started happening. You helped her with the Davis case, and I was hoping you'd help me."

Tania folded her arms. Then she said, "One moment." She moved past him like a summer breeze and turned the store's sign to say "Closed." Then she leaned back on the door. "So, tell me about your problem, Detective."

He hoped this wasn't a waste of time. "All right, so here's what's been going on. For weeks—months, even—things I've been writing down have been coming true. Not word-for-word, but they've been pretty accurate. I'm . . . I'm pretty sure I'm somehow responsible for what happened to Hannah. And I'm pretty sure I'm responsible for other things. The problem is that I just don't, well . . . I'm not a very religious man, but—"

"You don't believe in voodoo," Tania interrupted.

"Pretty much. But from what Dixie told me, and from what I've seen lately, I don't know what to think."

She straightened up and locked eyes with him. Her look was intense, her pupils were dilated, and the area around her eyes was slightly bruised. It was similar to how Sam was during the wharf incident.

Finally, she spoke. "Hmmm. Well, you're clean. There isn't a *loa* attached to you or inside of you."

Nodding ever so slightly, he backed up. "Right. So, Tania, any idea what's going on?"

Walking over to the sales counter, she said, "Not at first glance. For *loa* to affect the physical world, which is what your story suggests, there needs to be a ritual, an action that's done repeatedly—like dancing or chanting. And there needs to be a focus."

"A focus?"

"A magic wand. A ritual dagger."

A light suddenly went off in Aucoin's head. "Or a pen?"

Leaning against the counter, Tania said, "Yes. A pen would make a good focus. The monotonous strokes of ink on a page could be the repetitive motion of the ritual. This would fit with what you've described. Have you always used the same pen?"

"I have." The pieces of the puzzle were falling into place. He had known it was something about the pen, but he hadn't expected it to be a voodoo ritual.

He hurried out the door. "Thanks, Tania. I know what I have to do."

She called out after him. "Wait, what do you need to do? Let me help you!"

"No time. I'll be in touch tomorrow."

When Aucoin arrived at home, it was well past dinnertime. The afternoon traffic had been thick, matching the heaviness of his thoughts.

The pen. The silver pen. All this time, it had been the cause of untold suffering.

I destroy that thing, and we're done. It's over.

His house was quiet and dark when he got home. As soon as he closed the door, he flicked on a light switch.

Nothing.

That's odd.

He flipped it a few more times and then felt his way into the living room, figuring the light bulb had burned out. It was surprisingly cold, although there was no draft, and the air was stale. He reached the lamp by his chair and tried to turn it on.

Nothing.

"OK, something squirrelly is happening here."

Taking out his gun, he headed to the kitchen and felt around the cabinets. It wasn't long before he had what he was searching for—a flashlight. Shining it around the kitchen, he saw some light glinting off the metal of his empty sink and the glass of the window above it. Otherwise, the room was completely dark.

"Right, let's go check the fuse box," Aucoin said, turning around and coming face-to-face with what looked like a rotted corpse made of smoke and mist.

The creature's jaw unhinged, and it shrieked right in his face. With a cry, he fell back, landing on his rear. His tailbone exploded with pain, but his instincts and training kicked in, and a moment later, he was aiming his gun at . . . nothing.

The creature was gone.

He sat there, holding out his gun and panting heavily. He heard feet padding behind him. It reminded him of when Cheryl was a baby, crawling on the floor. Only the sensation he felt wasn't heartwarming. It was dreadful. Taking a deep breath, he turned around.

Crawling toward him was a creature that looked like a nutria with human feet. Like the corpse from before, it was smoky. It stopped when it met his gaze, and then it stood up on its hind legs. On its stomach was a single giant eyeball, which scowled at him.

"Oh, the fuck," Aucoin said as he stumbled out of the kitchen. When he reached the living room, he ran right into his comfy chair and flipped to the ground. The flashlight rolled across the carpet.

"Excuse me," a voice behind him said. Sitting on his chair was a skeleton wearing a bathrobe. On the couch was another skeleton wearing a dress, and a third, smaller one wearing jeans and a tank top and listening to a Walkman.

"Please be quiet. We're trying to watch the movie." The skeleton in the bathrobe pointed at the television. It was on, and the screen was covered with static, periodically showing scenes of Dallas torturing Cheryl.

"Oh, Daddy," the skeleton with the Walkman said. "Do we have to watch a documentary tonight?"

"Shh, mind your father," the skeleton with the dress replied.

"What the fuck!" Crawling to the flashlight, Aucoin grabbed for it, but odd little creatures that looked like black clothespins with large, white eyes at the tips carried it away. He swatted them to the side, grabbed the flashlight, and spun back around to see that the skeletons were gone, and the television was off. Every muscle in his body shook, and sweat poured down the sides of his head. With every breath, he felt his grip on reality strain more and more.

"OK, if this is real. If this is really real . . . if I'm not crazy . . ."

Without another word, he scrambled to the table next to his chair and dug out the notebook and the silver pen. By the light of the flashlight, he wrote down what he hoped would be the end to this madness:

The spirits stopped haunting Aucoin and turned his power back on.

Within seconds, the lights flickered on, and the temperature rose back to normal.

Leaning against his chair, he rubbed the sweat off his face. "Thank God that's over."

Then all around him, a deep and cultured voice spoke. "I assure you, Detective, God had nothing to do with it."

Chapter 20
The Silver Pen

Date: **Saturday, March 24, 1993**
Time: **1:00 a.m.**
Location: **Kyle Aucoin's House**
St. Bernard, New Orleans East

The silver pen fell to the carpet with a soft thump, and Aucoin stared at it. *Did I just . . . did it just talk to me?*

For a full minute, he sat motionless, unsure of what to do. When a few minutes passed and nothing happened, he picked it back up. Almost immediately, the voice spoke again. "It's really rude to cut me off like that. Please don't do it again."

Aucoin leaned against his coffee table. If not for his experiences over the past few days, if not for Dixie's story about Hannah, he would think he was dreaming. But he knew this was no nightmare. This was real.

"Who are you?" he asked.

"Is it important? The point is that you've used this focus so much that now I can communicate to anyone holding it. My strength is growing every day, and I have to thank you, Detective."

"Tell me who you are! I want to know what's going on."

"Oh, me. Oh, my. So full of questions. Very well. As for my identity, I am the king of the *loa*. As for what's going on, we're having a conversation on your living-room floor."

Aucoin realized he was, indeed, on the floor, so he got up. "So you're the one who's been killing folks in New Orleans and Metairie and other places all over southern Louisiana?"

"No, I didn't kill anyone . . . this time around. Other people did. More precisely, people my *loa* were either riding or possessing. Consider Detective Bradley, for example. It was written that he'd shoot the Fat City Stabber. But he was always the Stabber—an amazing coincidence, to say the least. So all the *krabinay* within him had to do was drop the possession right before he attacked his own daughter. Then the weakness of human nature kicked in, and bang—a dead serial killer. You're welcome."

Seeing how that fit into what he already knew, Aucoin said, "Yes, but you were the one leading them. The *loa* possessing Hannah said they had to do what their king commands, and since you're their king and you commanded them, that makes you the main conspirator."

The voice chuckled . Then it said, "My, my, but you are entertaining. But, then, following that logic, you were the one giving the requests to me through the pen, so doesn't that make you a conspirator as well?"

Shaking the pen in the air, Aucoin said, "Don't try to turn this back on me! I had no idea what I was doing."

The voice grew darker and more sinister. "Isn't ignorance of the law no excuse for breaking it? You see, your will has powered these commands, these rituals. You wanted others to suffer because your daughter suffered. I merely translated those desires into actions. So don't act like you're innocent, Detective."

Closing his eyes, Aucoin focused, remembering what Dixie had told him. "The *loa* possessing Hannah said it needed lives. Why do your *loa* have to kill?"

"Because the amount of energy a person releases when they die is necessary for my plans."

"What plans?"

"You wouldn't understand, Detective."

Aucoin tightened his grip. "What plans?"

The voice laughed and then said, "To extend my reach to every part of the world where the voodoo gods reign and to be able to send my *loa* into the physical world without needing this pen."

"Why would you do that?"

"I want to destroy the Knight Priory of Saint Madonna and end their use of the *tkeeus* so I can control this city alone from beyond the grave!"

Pieces of the puzzle started falling into place. "Knight Priory? *Tkeeus*? Beyond the grave? Were you a part of what happened back in August?"

Laughing, the voice said, "Isn't that wonderful? Despite having been only on the periphery of the investigation, you're figuring out the mastermind. Yes, that was all me."

The rest of the pieces fell into place—comments made by Sam and Rodger, snippets of notes from Michael, and even the methodologies of Dallas. If one accepted that spirits existed, there could be only one person on the other side of the silver pen. "I know who you are now. Oh God, everything that's been happening makes sense. Poor Sam."

"Poor Sam?" the voice said in an incredulous tone. "Poor Sam? That ungrateful child is why I'm having to make do with a depressed, washed-up cop like yourself."

"Shut up," Aucoin said, putting on his jacket and heading out. He felt an ember of rage igniting in his heart. "Because of you, Vincent, so many people have suffered—Cheryl, Dixie, Sam, Rodger, Michael, and who knows who else? Whatever you're doing, I'm sure Tania Patterson can stop it!"

"Hmph! That dumb dog? I'd like to see her try."

Aucoin held on to the silver pen securely as he drove back to Jackson Square. Vincent spoke the entire time. Nothing he had to say was particularly flattering.

"You're wasting your time, Detective. That Patterson girl was the weaker of the two sisters. Even now, with the power she has gained, she'll never be able to stop me."

Rolling his eyes, Aucoin said, "It doesn't matter, you sick son-of-a-bitch. You've been hurting people for far too long. It's time we put an end to you."

"Detective, you have no idea what I've become or what I've done. You're just a small piece in this sordid puzzle—a disposable piece, at that. But work with me, and I can help you become something amazing."

Aucoin turned off the interstate and drove down Decatur Street. He'd be at the shop in just a few more minutes. "I'm not interested."

"Think about it, Detective. Think long and hard. If you work with me, think of all the good we can do."

"There's no good that can come from you."

"Just hear me out. You know how the pen works now. You can just use it to kill criminals. Murderers. Like how you killed the Fat City Stabber."

The desire was there, and Aucoin couldn't ignore it. Now that he knew what the pen could do, the craving to punish those who harmed others was almost overpowering. But he thought of how much Sam had suffered and how children like Hannah were being hurt by the pen. So as he drove on, he pushed those desires down with every ounce of will he possessed. He was an officer of the law, and he had come too far to fall again.

"That's enough! I may hate those scumbags, but I will not become one of them."

Vincent growled. "Your will is much stronger than I thought. How? Has your suffering made you tougher, or is it your convictions? No matter—someone out there is willing be judge, jury, and executioner. All I have to do is call them to me, and I'll have my way. It's human nature to harm."

"No, that's your nature, you sicko," Aucoin said, putting the pen in his glove compartment. "And I'm through listening to your poison."

Up ahead, at the entrance to Jackson Square, were the flashing lights of a dozen police cars at a blockade. A uniformed cop was redirecting traffic down a side street.

Aucoin rolled down the window and flashed his badge. "Hey. What's going on?"

The officer moved the barrier. "Some shop caught fire. Occult store. Real bad, too. A woman was killed."

The blood began to drain from Aucoin's face, and a sickening feeling grew in his gut. As he passed through the barricade, all he could think about was Tania. Driving along the cobbled stones of the square and approaching the voodoo shop, he could see the blaze. A pair of fire trucks in front had it mostly under control. He parked next to Rivette and Landry's car—he could tell it was theirs from the Power Ranger on the dashboard. Ouellette's car and an ambulance were nearby.

At the shop, Rivette looked pissed, Landry shuffled about anxiously, and Ouellette stood over a body bag. As Aucoin approached, Rivette said, "Isn't this great, Kyle? Paul and I are being sent back to the precinct to work on reports. I guess a woman being burnt to a cinder ain't important enough for two homicide detectives!"

"Shut up and get your ass back there, Rivette," Ouellette said. He motioned Aucoin toward the bag. "You think this is the proprietor?" Inside were the charred remains of what used to be a human being. The skin was black as soot, the hair was gone, and what little clothing remained was more like a burned paper bag. She was unrecognizable.

Maybe it's not Tania. He scanned the gathering crowd and didn't see her. Wouldn't she be around if her store had caught on fire? If she wasn't here, though, where was she?

"Well?" Ouellette asked.

"Where was she found?"

"In the middle of the damn inferno. Do you think it's Tania Patterson?"

Looking over the crowd again, Aucoin said, "My gut tells me that she's alive."

Folding his arms, Ouellette said, "Humph. All right, then, Detective. Poke around and see if you can find something to corroborate your gut." He headed off to talk to the fire chief.

Aucoin hunched down and examined the woman's remains once again. There was no way to determine if she was Caucasian, African-American, or something else. The damage was too severe. Carefully, so as to not further damage the body, he opened the bag. The smells of burned human flesh, muscle, and fat were nauseating. Shining his flashlight into the mess, he searched for something—anything—that could clue him in as to who this was.

Was the fire an accident or arson? Who would want to kill Tania?

His musings were interrupted by another flash of white. The same white orb as before was floating over something in the bag, something made of metal. After a second, the orb vanished like mist.

What the—? Crime Lab had missed something. He plucked it out. It was partially melted, but he could make out the basic design—a crest sporting a cross and a crown. He flipped it over a few times before realizing where he had seen it before. "Caroline Saucier, the editor-in-chief of the *Times-Picayune,* had this same design on her lapel!"

He headed back to his car. Rivette and Landry were gone, as were a number of uniformed officers. When Aucoin saw that his passenger-side window was open, a surge of panic gripped him. Rushing inside, he checked the glove compartment. It was open.

"No, no, no!" Nearly falling over himself, he searched the glove compartment, then the seat, and then the floor for signs of the silver pen.

"Vincent! Where the hell are you, Vincent?"

But it was no use. The pen was gone.

Beating the roof of the car, he cried out, "No! No, damn it, this is not happening. No, no!"

"What the hell is the matter with you?" It was Ouellette, standing behind him and looking as dour as ever.

"Sir, someone robbed my car. I had a pen. A silver pen. Very dangerous. It's how Vincent uses the *loa* to—"

"The shit did you say?"

Aucoin stopped, realizing how crazy he must sound. "Sorry, sir, I'm just hysterical. My car, and—"

Ouellette said, "You are just starting to get your shit together. Don't lose it now. Do you have any leads from the body?"

It took a few deep breaths, but Aucoin calmed down. He'd deal with finding the pen as soon as he could, even getting help from Dixie if he had to. Showing the destroyed crest, he said, "I don't think it's Tania. See, I found this in the bag. I remember seeing one like it on Miss Saucier of the *Picayune*. I'm fairly certain rich socialites like her wouldn't associate with Miss Patterson."

When Ouellette examined it, his expression grew dangerous. Then he said, "Right. Best you back off this one. I'll get Olivier on it tomorrow."

Aucoin shook his head. "Sir, with all due respect, she can hardly walk. She's in no condition to—"

"And you think you are?" Ouellette eyed him harshly. "You've been a fucking mess for over half a year. You've only started becoming a non-mess the past few days. Listen, these people are dangerous, especially Saucier. She will ruin your world if you cross her."

As his commander said that, another piece fell into place for Aucoin. Given what Vincent had said, he had a pretty good hunch as to who this group was.

"This is the Knight Priory, isn't it?"

With a harrumph, Ouellette said, "Hell of a time to make a comeback, Aucoin. Yes. The Knight Priory of Saint Madonna. But unlike the old one, these guys aren't some elite social club. They're vicious, power-hungry psychopaths. And Caroline is one of the worst."

"Sir, I can handle this. Please don't put Dixie in danger. Not when she's so close to having her child."

The two stared at each other for a full minute. The last time Aucoin had seen Ouellette's gaze so intense, it was during the wharf incident. It was like looking into an angel statue at a church—strong, imposing, and more than a little frightening.

Finally, Ouellette sighed. "Fine. But this is the only warning you get. Run afoul of the Knight Priory, and I will not be able to save you. Tread lightly."

The sun had risen by the time Aucoin was admitted to see Caroline. A clerk announced him, as her secretary's desk was empty, which seemed odd. As he entered, she was on the phone. She sounded annoyed.

"Yes, Ignatius, I know I promised you full use of that book, but it's been months. You aren't going to find any secrets in it. It's just an old tome that crackpot Russell used to own. No, we need to make sure that the Oracle doesn't find out until I take charge."

Oracle, huh? Must be Knight Priory stuff. He filed that name away for later and then took in her office. Besides being posh and well decorated, it showcased headlines from the newspaper's illustrious history. Everything from the Challenger shuttle explosion to the JFK assassination to Martin Luther King's most famous rally was hanging on the wall. The two that caught Aucoin's eye were "Bourbon Street Ripper Executed" and "New Ripper Killed. Castille Mansion Burns."

"Have a seat, Detective," Caroline said as she hung up the phone and sat back down behind her desk. "Do you want a coffee? A latte perhaps? There's a PJ's in the lobby, and they deliver."

As she picked up her phone, he said, "A latte sounds great. Maybe a slice of banana bread as well." It would have been rude to turn down her offer.

While she called it in, he scanned her desk for something—anything—that could clue him in on what happened last night. With luck, she would also be involved with the silver pen. He hadn't forgotten about that.

All he saw were some pictures. One was of a younger Caroline with a pretty girl her own age, labeled "Allison—1971."

"OK, your order is placed, Detective." The leather in her chair creaked as she leaned back. "Do you know why I want to talk to you?"

"I'll be honest," he said. "I haven't got a clue."

With a smirk, she said, "I want to hire you. You're smart, you're resourceful, and now that you've gotten yourself back together, you're the best choice."

Leaning forward, he examined her face. She had that same stern expression as before, but now it was accented by a cocky sneer. Everything about her was off-putting.

"I really rather like my job, Miss Saucier. I'm not a journalist."

She sniffed contemptuously. "I don't mean for you quit your day job. And you know that. I want you to work for me on the side."

"So brazen," he said, leaning back. He tried reading her, but all he got was a detestable cockiness. Still, she might know something. He started playing his cards. "So is this for you personally or for the Knight Priory?"

Touching the crest on her lapel, she said, "Well, well. You're even smarter than I thought. Yes, Detective. This is for the Knight Priory, but mostly to help me. See, I'm tired of being Connick's number-two, and I'm tired of competing with the remaining purebloods. I want to move to the top of the ladder, and you can help. It will pay well. Very, very well."

Her mention of Harry Connick took him by surprise. "What? The DA is in the Knight Priory?"

She shrugged. "We let him in as a bribe of sorts right after the Hannah Davis incident. But he's become popular. Too popular. If he wasn't the District Attorney, I'd have had him killed already."

Aucoin couldn't believe her. But he held his tongue. He needed information. "So let's get down to brass tacks, then. Why me and not someone else? I've been a washed-up excuse for a detective since my kid died."

Snickering, she waved him off. "The only other person we'd want is Lieutenant Olivier. But our recruiter blew that one so badly, she won't come near us, which is why we have an idiot of a detective working for us right now."

He blinked. "You have a cop working for the Knight Priory?"

"Of course."

"Who?"

"Not your concern," she said.

"Right. So this business relationship includes me operating in the dark."

She leaned forward, resting her elbows on the desk. "If I don't think you need to know, you won't."

He leaned forward, too. "And you want me to help the Knight Priory, but also help you take control?"

"Exactly."

"I thought the Castille family ran the Knight Priory. That would mean Sam."

Now her expression darkened. "Humph. Screw Sam. Her grandfather murdered the only woman I've ever loved. And Sam is a committed psycho with no future. So the new Knight Priory needs a new leader."

With an unkind grin, he said, "And you're that person?"

"You catch on quickly."

"All right, Miss Saucier. I have only one question."

"Oh?"

He tossed the burned crest onto the desk. "Who died in that fire last night?"

The room grew quiet as she examined it, tapping her fingers on the wooden surface of her desk. Then she picked up the crest and pocketed it. Her voice was low. "My secretary. She wasn't supposed to die."

"What happened?" He wanted nothing more than to cuff her right then.

She closed her eyes. "The cop who works for us is an idiot and gave her bad information. She died as a result."

"Who is this cop? Someone burned to death last night, Miss Saucier. I need to know."

When she opened her eyes, they had a look of cruelty and malice that took Aucoin by surprise. She pointed over his shoulder. "Look behind you, and you'll see."

He turned around. At once, his mouth hung open.

Standing at the entrance to the office, holding a tray of PJ's coffee and several slices of banana bread, was Detective Paul Landry.

Chapter 21
A Shield That Protects

Date: **Saturday, March 24, 1993**
Time: **8:00 a.m.**
Location: *Times-Picayune*
Central Business District, New Orleans

Landry looked as stunned as Aucoin felt. "Mistress Saucier? Wh-what's going on? Wh-why is Kyle here?"

Suddenly, everything about Landry's behavior made sense. The skulking about, the interest in Dixie's schedule, the eavesdropping, the sudden bouts of nervousness—everything seemed clear. It was likely that Landry was a double agent against Ouellette, too.

With that revelation came anger at the dishonesty, the disloyalty, and the treachery of a fellow detective. Aucoin got up so fast, he felt static charge around his shoes and pants. With a roar, he knocked the tray out of Landry's hands and pushed him against a wall.

"What the fuck is the meaning of this, you piece of shit?"

"Kyle! It's not what you think! It's not—"

"It's not what I think?" Aucoin felt his face getting hotter, redder. "You fat, stupid son-of-a-bitch, what do you mean? How long have you been selling us out? How long have you been spying on us for the Knight Priory?"

"Oh, I can answer that," Caroline said in a cold voice. "Paul has been working with us since about the time Sam was committed. In fact, he's the one who helped Dr. Klein push that through by delivering messages and payoffs to the judges. Didn't you, Paul?"

Landry squealed in terror. "Miss Saucier? Why? I've always done what you asked. No, I didn't do that. Kyle, you have to believe me!"

Again, Aucoin pushed him against the wall, slamming him hard. "You make me sick, sick, sick. You can't even admit you were a traitor. You gutless, spineless twerp!"

Caroline chuckled darkly. "Oh, Paul, you may be easy to control, but you are an idiot. I have no need for someone who can't do even the simplest task. My poor secretary was supposed to go in, light a fire to kill the Patterson girl, and get out. But you got cold feet, and she ended up trapped. How does that further my plans, again?"

Looking panicked, Landry struggled in vain to escape Aucoin's grip. Finally, he said, "It wasn't my fault. Something happened. Something ghostlike scared us so bad that she spilled the accelerant and it blew up on her. I woulda gotten burnt, too, if I hadn't run!"

She harrumphed. "Ghosts? How lame. There are no ghosts, Paul. Just a fat, stupid loser. Detective Aucoin, if you kill this waste of life, the Knight Priory will not only make sure you get away with it, but we'll also set you up with a million-dollar-a-year salary, with bonuses from me for our special side project."

Aucoin could tell she was completely serious.

As Landry hyperventilated, the air around them started getting cold. Then he started to shake, making it harder for Aucoin to focus on Caroline. He ignored it for the moment and said, "I'm afraid you have to do better than that if—"

He stopped when she suddenly looked terrified. He glanced back at Landry, who was bleeding from his eyes, his ears, his nose, and his mouth. He was convulsing, and his face was contorted in terrible pain.

"What the fuck?" Aucoin backed away as Landry fell to his knees.

"Help me, Kyle!" He doubled forward and puked blood, the stinking mess so hot it steamed. Grabbing his throat, he started frothing foamy red suds, gagging. His veins grew darker until the blood started oozing out of his pores. With a final tortured cry, he fell to the ground, dead.

Caroline screamed. "What the hell just happened? What did you do?"

Aucoin didn't respond. His heart was racing as he stared at the bloody mess that was once Paul Landry. There was only one thing in the world that could kill like that.

Whoever had the silver pen was already using it to kill.

It took almost three hours to deal with Landry's death. Rivette finally arrived and, regarding his partner's body with surprisingly little emotion, stayed with him until the EMTs took him away.

Despite her icy demeanor from earlier, Caroline was a mess. Eventually, a man named Dr. Kindley arrived, examined her, and recommended she be taken home and sedated.

As she left, led out by two uniformed officers, she shot Aucoin a poisonous look. "You can bet I'll get to the bottom of this."

Aucoin couldn't believe her audacity. *Uppity bitch.*

Dr. Kindley flashed a vicious grin as he passed by. "Making friends and influencing people, eh, Detective?" He left with Caroline, whispering in her ear.

When Aucoin got back to the precinct with Rivette, he went to Landry's desk. "Hey, Scott. Do you need anything?"

"No, I'm all right. I just need to think." Rivette rubbed his face and sat down heavily.

Seeing him like this made Aucoin sigh. Poor guy had to be in shock, losing his partner like that.

While Rivette withdrew, Aucoin went through Landry's desk. Amongst the piles of post-it notes and takeout menus was a small, red booklet. Inside were detailed notes on every detective in the precinct, including Dixie and Ouellette, with potential threat levels to the Knight Priory. Theirs were rather high, while his was insultingly low. Also detailed were everyone's movements over the course of months, from where they had lunch to when they went to the bathroom—a complete record of the movements of the eighth precinct.

"This is un-fucking-believable," Rivette said. "I would not have believed it in a million years."

Looking up from the booklet, Aucoin said, "Man, I'm really sorry. I promise I'll catch the guy who did it."

"I just want to fix it. I want him to be alive."

"I know, Scott. Be strong, buddy." Although he felt he understood Rivette's pain, Aucoin put his sympathetic ear aside to finish scanning the booklet. Two phone numbers on the inside cover caught his eye. He picked up Landry's phone and dialed the first.

A woman picked up. "Dr. Klein's office. How may I help you?"

He hung up. *Holy shit! Is Dr. Klein in the Knight Priory?*

Hands shaking, he dialed the other number.

A man picked up. "Evergreen Plantation. Who do you want to speak with?"

Aucoin hung up even harder. His hands were trembling so badly, he could barely hold on to the booklet. *Evergreen? That's where Dixie said Sam was!*

"I'll be right back, Scott."

Rivette, who had taken out a notepad and was reading over some scribbles, nodded sadly. Aucoin stopped long enough to pat him on the shoulder and then rushed to Ouellette's office.

The door was closed. He could hear Ouellette on the phone. "No, Douglas, you listen to me. You need to gather up Mabel and Boudreaux, pack your bags, and get the hell out of New Orleans for a while. . . Right. I have a cabin up in Ponchatoula. It's stocked with cans and dry goods. . . Yes, dog food, too. . . Stay there for at least a few weeks. . . Good. Hugs to Mabel. Take care, and later."

Knocking on the door, Aucoin entered the office and slapped the booklet on Ouellette's desk. "That belonged to Landry. It contains detailed information on everyone in the precinct, especially in our division."

Ouellette swiped the booklet and read it, his expression never changing. "Well, this is a steaming pile of shit. Looks like Landry had himself some balls after all."

Although he didn't want to argue with his commander, Aucoin couldn't have disagreed more. "Sir, he was spying on us all. I don't see how you can compliment him for that."

With a wave, Ouellette said, "Take a seat, Aucoin. Let me tell you something."

"Sir, this is hardly time for a story," he said, sitting down.

Ouellette rubbed his hands together and leaned forward. "I'm about to tell you something I've never told another living soul."

That got Aucoin's attention. He sat up straight.

"Before my marriage to Nina, and before Jason, I used to be married with a family."

"What?" As far he knew, Nina and Jason, who was killed by Dallas back in the eighties, were his only family.

"Dear, sweet Constance. She was a socialite, one of the New Orleans high society, and a member of the original Knight Priory. My kids were wonderful. One boy and two girls. Smart, beautiful, pleasant children. In many ways, I was king of my own kingdom." The fondness in Ouellette's eyes was as unmistakable as it was unusual.

"But then the war hit, and I went over there thinking I was going to earn glory. The whole thing turned into a fucking nightmare. When I finally got back, my family was in ruins."

"What do you mean?" Aucoin leaned forward, trying to see what this had to do with Landry.

"My wife was dead. My children were a mess. It was awful. The Knight Priory slid into shit, and every time I tried to fix it, I got laughed out of the room."

"That's harsh."

"Those in power aren't forgiving, Aucoin."

"Sir, I'm not following what this has to do with Landry betraying us."

Leaning back, Ouellette said, "I can't influence the Knight Priory like I used to, and I'm aware that this new incarnation wants to screw us up. So when I caught Landry snooping around and made him confess about working for them, I turned him into a double agent of sorts."

That last statement made Aucoin sit up straight. Blinking, he said, "Wait . . . what? Landry was working for you?"

"Yes, indeed," Ouellette said. "His fat ass was a terrible spy, but he was pretty solid at following my instructions. I had him tracking the Knight Priory's plans for the city."

"There was no way I could have known that." Now Aucoin felt bad about tormenting Landry in his final moments.

"Yes, well, that's because, unlike everyone else in this city, I can keep a secret, and I play my hand close to my chest."

"Jesus, Commander. What's going on here?"

Once more, Ouellette leaned forward. "An ugly game that people have been playing for decades, one you don't need to be involved with. Now get going and forget about Landry. And watch your ass the next few weeks. Like I said, I can't help you if the Knight Priory wants you removed."

Without another word, Aucoin left. This was unbelievable. He took a few months off from the world, and everything went crazy.

When he got back to his desk, he and Rivette were the only people on the floor. Rivette was scribbling in his notepad with all the secrecy of a child cheating on a test. Aucoin was about to head over to him when his pager went off. It was his house.

Cathy! He detoured back to his desk and called.

She picked up after two rings. "Hello? Kyle?"

"Hey, Cathy. What brings you, um, home?"

With a gentle laugh, she said, "Well, I needed to pick up some clothes from the attic. And I thought we could have dinner. My treat."

Despite everything he had been through lately, he liked that idea. It would give him a chance to mentally re-center before trying to track down the silver pen. "Sounds great. Where to?"

She hummed happily. "Let's go to Antoine's."

He couldn't help but smile. That's where he had proposed to her. "Sounds wonderful, hun."

"Great! I'll see you there at six?"

"Six sounds perfect. See you then."

He had just hung up the phone when a uniformed officer ran in, out of breath. "Detectives! Commander! You've got to see the news, now!"

As Ouellette came out of his office, the officer turned on the television. A newscaster was seated at the studio with the headline "Vigilante Riots Downtown" at the bottom of the screen.

"Reports keep coming in," the newscaster said, "but it seems that there's been an unprecedented number of vigilante attacks. So far, we have twenty-six confirmed deaths. Sources in the field indicate that each of the victims were wanted killers, rapists, or other violent criminals. Each death is being caused by different groups of a dozen or more individuals who have been reported as being crazed, unresponsive, and with heavily dilated pupils."

Someone handed the newscaster a piece of paper.

"OK, I am now being told that the death toll has spiked to fifty-three. Both Orleans and Jefferson Parish are being affected. The police are urging citizens to stay home and lock their doors. The mayor has reached out to the governor to request assistance from the National Guard."

Ouellette turned off the television. He was sweating profusely. "Goddamn it. I am sick and tired of the damn news finding out about these things before we do. They are not, I repeat, not supposed to be first responders."

He exhaled deeply. "I did not need this."

Then he paced back and forth a bit and then said, "We're so badly understaffed, all we can do is damage control."

Aucoin was also sweating. He knew what was causing this nightmare. "Sir, it's the—"

Holding out his hand, Ouellette said, "Give me a second."

Then he turned to the officer. "Lenny, get all available persons in the precinct assembled. I'll call the mayor and ask where he wants us. Get everyone in here. We don't have time to fuck around."

The officer nodded and ran off. Ouellette then turned to Aucoin. "Now, what is it?"

"Sir, it's the silver pen, the pen Vincent Castille used to record his murders. Look, this will sound insane, but his ghost is using that pen to somehow control voodoo spirits, *loa*."

He half-expected Ouellette to glare at him, call him crazy, and tell him to get his act together. Instead, he just frowned. "She was trying to tell me that months ago. Damn it."

It didn't take long to figure out who he was talking about. "Sir, do you mean Sam?"

"Yes. Damn it. I need to think this over. Give me a minute." He headed back into his office.

Aucoin returned to his desk. He was gathering his belongings and getting ready to call Cathy when Rivette sat down across from him, pale as death.

"Kyle. I need to talk to you."

"Not now, Scott. We have an emergency." Aucoin dialed his home. The phone rang.

Without a word, Rivette took out a small notepad and the silver pen. He showed what was written:

> Cathy was alone in Kyle's house when a pair of rioters broke in and strangled her to death

The story was complete except for the final period at the end.

Aucoin's heart pounded in his throat, and he clenched his jaw tightly.

"Hello? Hello, Kyle?" Cathy had picked up.

Rivette's lips were quivering. "I think you should talk to me, Kyle. Vincent's not going to wait." Then he moved the tip of the pen toward where the period should go. "You know that if I do this, the ritual will complete and it'll actually happen."

"Kyle? Is that you? What's going on?" Cathy sounded concerned.

"I love you, honey," Aucoin said and hung up. He focused all of his attention on Rivette. "It was you. You killed Landry."

"And the others," Rivette said. "Everyone who's died in the past few hours." He was sweating. He looked sick, and his hands shook.

"Why?" Aucoin could barely speak. He could try to grab the pen, but if he messed up and Rivette touched the pen to that page, Cathy would die.

All Rivette could do was titter anxiously. "This pen is fucked up. It summoned me to it. I felt compelled to break into your glove compartment and steal it. And Vincent started talking to me, promising me I could make a difference."

That was something Aucoin knew all too well. "So then what happened?" He had to keep him talking until the pen was no longer almost touching the page.

Tears formed in the corners of Rivette's eyes. "I found out that Landry was betraying us. I was so angry. Everything that we've dealt with—children getting orphaned, violent crime going up—and then his fat ass is a turncoat. I just snapped. So I . . . I . . ."

"You wrote about his death, right?"

"And once I started, I couldn't stop. I just wrote down every horrible thing I'd been holding inside."

Again, this was something Aucoin knew all too well. "The pen is like a drug. You think you're controlling it, but it's controlling you."

Rivette was loosening up. Aucoin was almost ready.

Rivette's hands continued to shake. "I can't stop. I . . . I must be weak. God, Kyle, he's so powerful. So insanely powerful. He terrifies me. He's already influencing everything I do."

"I know, Scott. I know. OK. I'm going to take the pen from you. Just stay still."

Flinching away, Rivette said, "He's mad at you. Real mad. Right now, he's telling me to kill Cathy."

Aucoin grabbed for the pen, but Rivette pulled it away.

"Rivette, stop. This is not funny." Aucoin reached for it again.

Sliding farther away, Rivette's eyes rolled back and his eyelids fluttered. Then his voice deepened. "My strength grows. Look at what I can do now. You could have had this power, Detective. You shouldn't have opposed me. This is your punishment."

Hearing that voice made Aucoin stumbled back. "Vincent? Vincent, stop this!"

But Rivette's eyes had already returned to normal. Backing up, almost tripping on the other desks, his hands started moving as if against his will, placing the tip of the pen back at the end of the sentence. "I'm sorry, Kyle. I'm so sorry. I can't stop. I'm too weak to resist. Forgive me."

Aucoin slowly stood. "Scott, please don't do this."

"He's too strong."

"Scott, you need to fight it." Carefully, he unfastened his gun.

"Please, Kyle, forgive me."

In one motion, he pointed the gun at Rivette's chest. "I said *stop*!"

The door to Ouellette's office burst open. He came out at the same moment that every officer in the precinct arrived. Everyone focused on Aucoin and Rivette.

"Aucoin! What the hell!"

The officers drew out their weapons and pointed them at Aucoin. Ouellette held out his hands and approached slowly. "Aucoin. Rivette. What's going on?"

Keeping his eyes on Rivette, Aucoin said, "Sir, Scott has the pen. He's written down that Cathy dies. All he has to do is end the sentence, and it will happen."

"Is that true, Rivette?"

"Y-yes, sir."

Ouellette looked between them. "Aucoin, put your gun down. Rivette, put down the pen."

"I can't, sir," they both said at once.

"Vincent's possessing me," Rivette added. "I can't fight it."

Ouellette grimaced. "It doesn't need to end that way. Kyle, put down your gun. Scott, I'm going to come behind and restrain you." It was the first time in years he had used their first names.

"I'm trying to fight him, sir, but he's going to make me do it." Tears ran down Rivette's face.

Aucoin cocked the hammer back. "For God's sake, Scott, stop. I will not let you kill my wife."

Ouellette shouted, his voice reverberating, "Put down the gun, Kyle!"

His finger on the trigger, Aucoin trembled. "Please, Scott, fight him. I don't want to kill you."

Now Ouellette was halfway to Rivette. "For mercy's sake, Kyle, stop it. There is no going back from this."

Rivette continue to weep, his hands shaking and then steadying, then shaking again. Each time, the tip of the pen got closer and closer to where it would finish the deadly sentence. "I can't fight him. He's got me, and he won't let go. Please, Kyle, don't let me do this. I beg you. Please kill me before I hurt anyone else."

And then Rivette's hand suddenly grew still. His eyes then fluttered back again. Almost in slow motion, he moved the pen right toward the page. Vincent had won control.

"No!" Ouellette rushed toward him.

Aucoin felt cold. He knew Ouellette wouldn't make it in time. Every moment he and Cathy had spent together bled into a collage of memories, sweet and bitter. And then, clear as a bell, her voice resonated in his mind: "When it really matters, you'll be a shield that protects the ones you love."

He closed his eyes. She would survive. That was enough.

"I love you, Cathy."

Aucoin pulled the trigger. And as he emptied his gun, bullets tore into him.

Aucoin's Epilogue
A Good Cop

Date: **Thursday, April 1st, 1993**
Time: **12:00 p.m.**
Location: **Tulane University Hospital**
Downtown New Orleans

The coldness of the hospital room bit at Aucoin's skin, and the blanket hardly helped. Handcuffed to the bed with an IV in one arm, he lay there, staring into space. His body ached from the dozens of places where he had been shot. He still couldn't believe he had survived. The doctors had even said it was the devil's luck that none of the bullets had struck vital points.

Aucoin wasn't sure what to believe.

"You're awake. Good." It was Ouellette, wearing his commander's uniform. He stood by the bed, pity on his face. "I just got back from Rivette's funeral."

"Here to fire me, then?" Aucoin asked weakly.

Ouellette's expression remained stern. "Among other things. You're in a very unique kind of trouble. The powers that be think you know too much and want to make you disappear."

"Know too much? That's funny." It was hard to speak. Every word was labored and painful. Then he asked, "Did you know that Connick is in the Knight Priory?"

When Ouellette didn't say anything, Aucoin rolled his eyes. "Fine. Keep your secrets. Can you at least tell me if Cathy will be kept safe?"

"Yes. As per your plea agreement, she's been taken into the witness protection program. She's far away from here. She won't be dying from any home invasions anytime soon."

Aucoin exhaled with relief. He hadn't even been allowed to see her one more time. But at least she'd live. "And Dixie?"

"She's fine. She's the mother of a beautiful baby girl named Felicia. And she'll be moving up to New York where the Knight Priory can't touch her."

"And the riots?"

"Over. You killing Rivette ended them. Without a human's will behind the pen, Vincent's influence isn't as strong. But that won't last. A storm is coming, and it's only a matter of time before he doesn't need it anymore."

"Is the pen destroyed?"

Shaking his head, Ouellette said, "The Knight Priory has it, which is bad for everyone. Fortunately, they gave it to someone who is completely incompetent, which gives us a chance."

"Us?"

Silence.

"Commander, who are you?"

With a sigh, Ouellette said, "Someone who has been trying to keep the new Knight Priory in check for years. I, and others who are struggling to keep this storm from coming, want to stop them before they kill millions. And that's all you need to know."

It would have to be enough. "So what happens to me now?"

"You're going someplace from which you'll never return. They are going to do terrible things to you. I'm sorry. Your life will suck until they end it."

Aucoin didn't feel a hint of fear or anxiety. He'd figured as much. "And you can't help me?"

Ouellette shook his head. "I told you that if you ran afoul of the Knight Priory, I wouldn't be able to help. I am sorry, Kyle." He turned to leave.

He was at the door when Aucoin called out. "Sir!"

Although Ouellette stopped, he didn't look back. "Yes?"

Weakly, Aucoin asked, "Am . . . am I a good cop?"

Now Ouellette turned around. For the first time ever, he smiled—slightly, but genuinely.

"One of the best I've ever known."

Then he left without another word.

Lying back, Aucoin closed his eyes and waited for either sleep or death to come for him. Nurses came in to check on him, and police came to make sure he was secure. But no one spoke to him, and when the lights finally went out, he was completely alone.

"So this is how my life ends," he said to himself. "You know, I just don't care."

"You should," a voice whispered.

Aucoin opened his eyes. The white orb from before was floating over his bed.

A month ago, he would have freaked out. Now he just asked, "So what the hell are you supposed to be?"

"You need to care," it whispered. "She needs you. Help her, please."

"What? Who needs me? Cathy?"

"No. Sam . . ."

"Sam? What do you mean? What—"

But then Aucoin realized whose voice was coming from the orb.

"Rodger?"

The white orb then vanished like mist, leaving him alone in the room once more. He laid his head back and started laughing.

"Me help Sam? What good can I possibly do?"

Chapter 22
Worthy of Hating

Date: **Sunday May 2, 1993**
Time: **7:00 p.m.**
Location: **Evergreen Sanatorium, Isolation Chamber**

Sam was cold to the point where she couldn't think straight, and there was no escaping it. The freezing water bit deeply, deadening all sensation of life in her limbs. With only her head above the surface, and in total darkness, she had never felt more alone. She had been placed in what Dr. Klein called "the water coffin" soon after waking up. There was no light and no sound, only her ragged breath keeping her company. At first, she focused on her rage to try to stay warm, but after a while, thoughts, feelings, and even time became a jumbled mess. Before she knew it, she was hallucinating.

It started as a few spots here and there and the sounds of bells and static. Then, shapes started to form, creeping across her vision like insects and worms. Then, finally, a pink-and-purple caterpillar started to inch around and make funny gestures. With nothing else to do, and in the vain hope of keeping her sanity, she started talking to it.

"Is death anything like this, Mr. Caterpillar?"

It shrugged and then crawled onto a mushroom, curling up comfortably next to a tiny campfire.

"I guess death would be like this."

It smiled sleepily.

"I wonder if I'll ever actually die. I'm immortal, you know."

It stuck out its tongue.

"Oh, come now, Mr. Caterpillar. Be nice!"

It blew a kiss and went to sleep.

"Now my imaginary caterpillar is taking a nap, and here I am floating in my own piss. God help me, if I wasn't nuts before they put me in here, I am now—"

Suddenly, the sound of metal screeched all around her, and her world was flooded with light, making her yelp from the abrupt overstimulation. She shut her eyes tight, her head almost immediately throbbing with pain. Then she was roughly lifted out of the water coffin. Sounds of what might be speech were drowned out by loud bells and harsh static. Someone's fingers roughly pried open her eyes one at a time and shined a light directly into them. The agony in her forehead increased as she cried again.

Through the pounding headache, she heard a voice say, "No change."

Whoever was holding her let her go, and she fell to the floor like a rag doll, hitting her chin. The impact made her world explode like fireworks. She couldn't move at all. For a few minutes, she lay there weeping, unable to focus. Finally, her vision returned enough to make out shapes, and she saw Dick, Dock, and Dr. Klein conversing over a clipboard. Through the static, she made out words like "condition worsening" and "running out of options."

As she lay there, colored lights and shapes still dancing around her, she smirked. *Haven't broken me yet, you bastards.*

Right before she passed out from exhaustion, she saw the caterpillar reappear, wink at her, and then crawl off into nothingness.

When Sam woke up, she was lying on the cot in her cell, back in her gown. Her throat hurt, and her nose was runny. Her head still pounded, and she felt a shiver running through her. She hacked several times. Her chest burned.

And now I'm sick.

"Hey, you OK over there?" It was the man in the other cell.

When she heard his voice, she started turning over. However, her limbs were still weak from the water coffin, and they ached whenever she moved. It took her a minute to face the wall. "I feel like shit, but I'm alive."

"You were making a lot of noise over there a little while ago. Had me worried."

Despite the numbness that blanketed her heart, she was touched by his concern. They had been chatting almost every day through the wall, mostly about the state of New Orleans since her commitment. Her conversations with this mystery man were one of the few things that helped her keep her sanity.

"I must have been having nightmares. I've gotten those all my life. What did I say?"

"I don't know. I don't speak Creole."

Sam frowned. "I was talking in Creole?"

"I'm pretty sure. Yeah."

I don't know Creole. It must be Bridget.

"Oh, well." She rested her forehead against the cold stone. It actually helped alleviate her relentless headache.

Then he asked, "You've always had nightmares, right? What were they about?"

She blinked. "You're asking me something personal? Just the other day, didn't you say that would be a bad idea? That we might get attached to each other?" He still wouldn't tell her about the silver pen, shutting down the conversation whenever it went there.

His bed creaked. "Honestly, I don't know. Maybe it's because I've run out of things to talk about. Maybe it's because the electric shocks are scrambling my brain."

She rubbed her head against the wall, trying to get as much coldness against it as possible. "Fair enough. I'd have nightmares of my father."

There was a long pause. "You didn't get along with your father?"

She thought of Vincent and then snorted. "No. I hate him with all my heart." The snort vibrated in her sinuses, making her sneeze until her nose was sore.

"Ouch," he said after she had quieted down. "That's kind of rough. I mean, fathers aren't perfect, but they're far from monsters."

Guy, you have no idea . . .

Sam coughed a few more times, her throat scratching. "So I take it that you're a father?"

Silence.

"Hello, you there?"

More silence.

"Come on. You asked me something personal. Play fair or piss off."

A few more seconds passed. "Yes. I used to be a father."

She coughed again. Her lungs burned. "So what happened?"

His voice sounded strained, then angry. "Someone killed her, OK? She was murdered!"

"Shit, I'm sorry." She was sure she had pneumonia.

"It's fine," he finally said.

Closing her eyes, her heart ached at the memory of her children being taken from her. She couldn't even imagine what it would feel like if someone had murdered them.

Finally, she said, "Hey. Just so you know, how I feel about my father is pretty unique. He wasn't even the man I thought was my father—his son was. So my situation is pretty screwed up. I'm sure you were a wonderful dad."

There was a long pause before he said, "Thank you. It's taken me a while, but I'm sure my baby girl loved me to her last breath."

Then the door to his cell opened. Someone said, "All right, you. Time to meet with the doctor. You're the last one tonight."

As she heard her neighbor being carried away, she grimaced.

I hope this guy lasts. He's possibly the only friend I have.

She settled down into her cot. In a few minutes, she was asleep.

The following week consisted of even more electroshocks, injections, and sensory deprivation—sometimes several treatments in one day. By the time Sam was seated before Dr. Klein, her face puffy and bruised from an hour in the "correction chair," she was so tired that she could barely keep attention.

Tapping the clipboard he held, he said, "It has been seven days since ze water coffin. I have upped the treatments more than with any other patient. Und yet you still aren't responding. Sam, I am very disappointed in these results."

She rolled her head to the side and peered up at him. With the concoction keeping her too weak and muddled to act, it was all she could manage. "You're disappointed? I thought you hit harder than that."

Dr. Klein nodded to Dick, who punched her so hard that the fireworks went off around her again. She leaned forward, spit up some blood, and then started laughing, well past her breaking point. "You don't get it, do you, you stupid shit? I'm fucking immortal! Vincent murdered all those people to bind Baron Samedi to him. So no matter how much you hurt me, I'll just keep getting better."

Smiling viciously, Dr. Klein jotted something down, the light shining off the silver luster of his pen. "Of course you are immortal, Sam. Und I was foolish to assume otherwise."

She shook off the last of the colored explosions. "Taking down notes on how much you're hurting me?"

"No, these are notes on your healing rate. Ze Knight Priory has decided to use you for experimentation on how quickly you recover from trauma."

Spitting again, she said, "Heh, and here I thought this was to get rid of me and get Samantha back."

"For me, yes. For them? They are convinced the *tkeeus* has given you superpowers. They refuse to accept it's your psychosis. They plan to mass-produce it und use it to further spread their control."

With a derisive hoot, she said, "That's stupid! The *tkeeus* just makes it easier for a *loa* to possess someone. All they're going to do is make . . ."

Then the reality hit her. It would be a situation where people would, just by inhaling a powder, become susceptible to possession—possession by *loa* that were now under Vincent's control. Things could get bad in a hurry.

Her attention returned to Dr. Klein as he sighed. "I tired of these conversations of ghosts and possessions. Crackpots like Dr. Lazarus und lunatics like yourself just love to blame madness on demons. Utter rubbish."

She glowered. "Then why would someone like you do research for the Knight Priory if you don't believe in the *tkeeus*?"

"Because, Sam, they are the ones who have been funding my research. So if they want to mass-produce ze *tkeeus*, then I will provide them that service. It amazes how little you understand the way this city works. Why, you probably don't—"

But she interrupted him by throwing her head back and howling with glee. When she stopped, he was glaring at her. She then shook her head. "Amazing. After all these goddamn years, I see you for what you truly are. You aren't some psychopathic psychiatrist. You aren't even a good shade of Vincent Castille."

As she spoke, Dr. Klein's mouth tightened and his face grew red.

"You're a sad, pathetic puppet of the Knight Priory who's not ever going to be allowed to join. You must have some dirty blood in you. You're not even worthy of hating. I pity you, Dr. Klein."

She spat in his face, and as the glob slid down his beard, he went from red to purple. Standing up, he screamed, "Get this bitch out of my sight!!"

Sam continued to laugh as they dragged her down the hallway. On the way back to her cell, they passed the Middle Eastern technician again. He regarded her cautiously and then stepped in front of them.

"What are you doing, new guy?" Dock sounded irritated.

The technician leaned in and squinted. "I was just wondering if she's gone mad."

She blew a raspberry at him. "Hun, I am well past crazy."

Dock pushed him out of the way. "Of course she's mad. Now don't ever do that again!"

"I'm not mad. I'm having too much fun. It's a vacation here, handsome!" She winked at the technician and then continued giggling all the way back to her cell.

"You're in a good mood," the man in the other cell said.

Sam snickered as she lay chained to her bed. The image of Dr. Klein's outburst, his saliva forming strings across his lips as he screamed, was still fresh in her mind. She rested her forehead against the cool stone wall. It felt like victory. "I just made Dr. Klein lose his shit."

He started laughing. "That's brilliant! Someone needed to put that prick in his place."

She took a moment to catch her breath. "He's probably going to go on a rampage now. Sorry in advance if he hurts you worse than normal."

"At this point, I don't care," he said with a snort. "Don't you dare regret it. Not even for a second."

Snickering again, she rubbed her puffy face on the surface of her filthy cot, scratching her skin, which itched as it healed. "Hun, I don't regret a damn thing in my life, not a thing. Nothing except . . ."

Then she stopped, the memories of Richie, Rodger, and Michael gnawing at her.

"Except . . . ?" His voice had lowered.

With a sigh, she traced designs on the wall again, something she did whenever she became introspective. "Some people very close to me—people who I loved very deeply—died because of me."

"How do you mean?"

It took her some effort, but she rolled on her back, staring at her shackled wrists in the dim light of the cell. Thinking about it was still painful. "My father did terrible things to many people in order to fulfill a wish I'd made. If I hadn't made that wish, the ones I love would still be alive. They all died because of me. If I had never been born—"

"Don't you dare say that!" he yelled harshly.

She stopped. "Say what?"

"You listen to me, girl, and you listen well. You are not responsible for what other people do. You say people died because of your father? Well, you aren't your father! Why should you have to pay for what he did? That's ludicrous!"

Now it was her turn to be silent.

He continued. "I've seen some sick shit in my days. I have seen evil that would make most people run home to their mamas. So before you go blaming yourself, just remember that you aren't the reason they're dead. You didn't kill them. He did!"

Looking back up at the ceiling, she said nothing, deep in thought. Even if her wish to live without the fear of death is what had set everything in motion, she hadn't actually killed anyone. Even with the silver pen, she wasn't aware of what she was doing.

For the first time in years, she searched inside herself and saw something other than a blight against God and humanity. *This guy is right.*

Closing her eyes, she said, "None of this is my fault." A weight, one that felt like it had been on her chest all her life, vanished with those words.

"Hey," the man in the other cell said. "I'm gonna get some sleep. You think on all that."

She rolled over and pressed her lips to the wall, kissing it. "Good night. And thanks."

Dr. Klein leaned over Sam, who was strapped to a table, and scribbled furiously on his clipboard with a silver pen. "Now, Sam, I'm going to try something new today."

She sniggered, unable to take him seriously anymore. "What? You gonna let me go for a walk, maybe get a bit of fresh air?"

His pen stopped mid-stroke. Then he grinned wickedly. "No. I am going to blind you."

Her smile vanished. "You're gonna what?"

"Like we talked about, you've exhibited an amazing ability to heal. I want to see if you can regrow tissue." Then he nodded to Dick and Dock, who secured her head in a vise and administered more sedative.

Struggling against the restraints, she scowled at him. "You really are a sick fuck, you know that? Did having me call you a puppet piss you off that much?"

"I do not know what you are referring to, Sam. I have never lost my temper before in my life." He sniffed with contempt and drew liquid from a bottle labeled "HCl" into a syringe.

"Acid? You're going to use acid?" Despite the courage and cockiness she'd felt so far, this provoked a fear response unlike before. She thrashed in her restraints as Dock held her right eye open. "You goddamn, in-denial, booger-bearded shit! This isn't treatment! This is torture! Why are you doing this?"

Dr. Klein held the syringe over her. She could see the clear liquid bubbling from the needle's point. For a moment, his eyes rolled back, and he said in a deeper voice, "When you are in pain, Princess, you are the most alive."

The way he said that, the words he used, reminded her of Vincent. Her eyes rested on the pen he was holding. It was a silver fountain pen, and on the side was etched a single word: "Castille."

Oh, God! How did I not notice that? But she already knew the answer. For weeks, she'd spent every moment fighting for her sanity. It was an easy detail to overlook—a small but vital one.

"Dr. Klein, you need to get rid of that pen. It's pure evil!"

Then his eyes went back to normal and he said, "You're stalling, Sam. Let us begin."

Dick and Dock held her eyes open. The drops of acid splashed in and immediately starting sizzling away the tissues. Despite all the suffering she had been through in the past, nothing could have prepared her for that pain. She shrieked without restraint as her vision was agonizingly eaten away over the long, drawn-out treatment.

When Sam was brought back to her cell, the world of light and color was gone. She was shivering as they secured her to her cot, pain still searing through her ruined eyes. She lay there and cried.

Finally, the burning ebbed, and the queasy sensation of tissue rebuilding began. It itched like mad. She reached up and touched where her eyes used to be. They were regrowing. Was it Bridgette, her immortality, or both? She didn't know any more. All she knew was that no matter how badly she was hurt, she'd heal and live on. That thought made her feel sick to her stomach.

"Are you OK?" It was the man in the other cell.

She sniffled and then wiped her nose. "No. I'm . . . blind. He squirted acid in my eyes."

"He did what?"

The itch grew outright painful. She scratched at her eyes to no avail. "It's OK. I'll be OK. I can recover from this."

"Recover from . . . are you out of your mind? How can you recover from that?"

She started cackling. It was all she could do to keep the pain from driving her over the edge. "You wouldn't believe me if I told you. It's crazy. All of it."

"Oh, yeah? I've seen my share of crazy, too. Try me."

"All right, you want my story, Bucko?" She rocked from side to side, forcing herself to think of anything but the horrendous itch in her eyes. "When I was a child, my father put something inside of me. Something powerful. Ever since then, I've always been able to heal quickly. And then one day, I made a pact with something even more powerful. I can get hurt, but I always recover. Always. And now I'm immortal and I can't die, and oh God, this hurts so much!"

There was silence as she continued weeping, jerking against the restraints, anything to alleviate the pain.

Then he said, "I believe you, Sam."

She froze in place, the pain momentarily forgotten. "You know who I am?"

He chuckled. "I sort of figured it out a while ago."

Try as she might, she couldn't place his voice. "I'm sorry, do I know you?"

His bed creaked as he sat up. "I met you very briefly when I arrested you."

Almost at once, she knew who it was. The shock only aggravated the itching. "Detective Aucoin?"

"Yeah," he said. "Call me Kyle."

"But I don't understand. Why are you here?"

"Because I killed someone over the silver pen. Before I was sent here, however, I was visited by Rodger's ghost. He told me that I'd be helping you."

"Rodger," she said, remembering how he, Michael, and Richie said they'd find a way to assist her. She scratched at her eyes as they continued to regrow. "But wait, I thought you hated me."

"I did. For the longest time, I thought you were responsible for Cheryl's death."

She knocked her head on the wall. It helped with some with the discomfort. "What happened to change that?"

"Dallas happened. I realized that I had been focusing my anger, my sadness, and my confusion on the wrong person. I persecuted you unfairly. So there's something I want to say, and I won't blame you if tell me to fuck off."

"Go ahead." She was pretty sure she knew what Aucoin would say next.

"Sam, I'm sorry for accusing you of killing my daughter, and I'm sorry for trying to get you executed."

Now she chuckled. "I think we're long past that bullshit."

Silence.

Then she cleared her throat. "All the same, you're forgiven. Apology accepted."

"Thank you."

"So where do we go from here? How will you help me?"

"I don't know yet. I'll think of something. I hope."

As he grew silent, Sam continued to scratch at her eyes. There wasn't anything to think about as far as she was concerned. She knew what she had to do.

I have to get out of here, get that pen, and destroy it!

Chapter 23
Queen of the Loa

Date: **Monday, May 10, 1993**
Time: **4:00 p.m.**
Location: **Evergreen Sanatorium, Treatment Room**

"Sam, I think it's safe to say zat we're disappointed it has come to this."

Secured to a chair while Dr. Klein paced before her, Sam only glared with defiance. Even when Dick and Dock took turns beating her for over an hour, she never took her recently healed eyes off him. "I mean, your eyes grew back, Sam. That is an impossible miracle! Und yet they are still dilated! After all my treatments, you still will not give up und return little Samantha to us."

He snapped his fingers, and Dick pulled back her head so he could lean in close. His rancid breath splashed over her face. "Do you know what I think? I think zat Samantha is gone. I think you murdered her."

She felt nothing but pity, having seen through the façade of his convictions. With his arrogance stripped away, all that was left was a pathetic little man who had spent his life as the Knight Priory's puppet and then Vincent's puppet.

"Have you nothing to say for yourself, Sam?"

She spat on him. "You're trash."

He wiped away the spittle and then slapped her across the face. "Und you are a shade Samantha created. Und tonight, I will carve you out of her soul."

Then he tapped her forehead. "Right here. Let's see you recover from that."

Like a wolf baring its fangs, she gnashed her teeth. "Just remember. I am going to kill you."

"Of course you will. Take her out of here und prep her for surgery."

She was taken to a large shower. There, she was hosed down, her head was freshly shaved, and she was put into a surgical gown.

As he changed her clothes, Dick said, "You know, we've never raped this bitch. Should we do it now?"

Dock injected a dose of the sedative. "Nah, wait until after the operation. Then you can fuck her all you want."

Rolling her head back, she said, "You boys realize I'm going to kill you as well, right?"

Dick laughed. "Did you hear something?"

He and Dock started dragging her back to her cell.

"Nope. Nothing. The dead don't talk."

Once on her cot, Sam lay there for a long while, reflecting on her fate. She wasn't sure if she could heal from such an injury. Finally, she tapped her shackles on the wall. "Kyle. Are you there?"

Silence.

She cleared her throat. "Kyle!"

Aucoin sputtered. The springs of his cot creaked. "Yeah? Sam, what's going on?"

"I just wanted to say thank you for everything. After tonight, I may never be able to speak to you again."

"What do you mean?" he asked, sounding concerned.

"They're going to lobotomize me."

The cot creaked more loudly. "What? Are you serious? Why?"

"They've given up on me."

"Jesus. Sam, I am so sorry."

Now it was her turn to be silent.

After a few seconds, he said, "If it makes you feel any better, none of us ever gave up on you."

"What do you mean?" Sam pressed her head against the cool stone, knowing it could be the last time she felt such a sensation.

"Myself, Dixie, Gino. Hell, even Ouellette, in his own way. We all believed you would come out of this thing."

Hearing that made anger well up inside of her. She hit her shackles against the wall. "The hell they did. Ouellette's hated me for years, and Dixie betrayed me!"

The cot creaked again. "What do you mean, Dixie betrayed you?"

"Back at Tulane," she said. "She knew I was going to be committed, and she said nothing. And after all the bullshit about her being my friend."

Aucoin sounded disgusted. "Seriously? You really think that? Sam, did it ever occur to you that she was told not to say anything?"

It wasn't something she had considered. After mulling it over for a bit, she asked, "OK, so what do you mean?"

"The mayor's office put a gag on her. Sam, the entire administration has wanted you out of the way for years."

That was news to her. "Why?"

"Haven't you figured it out? It's the Knight Priory. They're the ones that run the city."

Suddenly, many things made sense. From the forced solitude and persecution during the new Ripper case to the years of surveillance, it was all because of the Knight Priory. They wanted to control her and the Castille name, just as they controlled the city. Dr. Klein's involvement was just so her commitment would look legit. "They're the ones who wanted me committed."

"Yes. They want your power. They want your wealth. They want your influence as the last Castille in New Orleans. And they used the mayor's office to stop people like Dixie from warning you."

She thought on that. *Dixie didn't betray me. They threatened her. It's been the goddamn Knight Priory all along.*

"The guilt has been tearing Dixie up. She cares about you."

Sam rubbed her face. This was almost too much to deal with. "And Ouellette?"

Aucoin sighed. "I don't know. He's definitely against them. But sometimes I wonder if he's with people like Dr. Lazarus or if he's with someone else."

"Well, that will have to do," she said. Then she touched the wall. "Kyle. Thanks for telling me about Dixie."

"No problem. You want to talk about anything else?"

She shook her head. "No. I want to rest. I need to prepare myself for what's coming."

"All right, just remember one thing."

"What?"

"You're a fighter. You proved it at the wharf. You proved it in your townhome. No matter what happens, never stop fighting."

With effort, she said, "All right. Thanks, Kyle. Goodbye."

"No, not goodbye. See you soon."

She said nothing else, eventually falling asleep.

In the darkness, Sam felt cool arms slide around her body. Then she felt a kiss on her ear. She blushed, knowing who it was. "Richie."

"Hey, beautiful." His voice was weak, even for a ghost's.

She felt tears coming on. "What's wrong, baby?"

He stroked her hair. "Running from Vincent has exhausted us. We split up months ago, and I've only heard rumors of what the others have been up to. Rodger helped Dixie and Kyle get to you, but he nearly spent all his energy. To avoid dispersing into nothingness, he had to settle down in one location for a while."

"And Michael?" She nuzzled back against him.

"He took the brunt of Vincent's wrath. Last I saw him, he was hobbling off. Said something about his sister."

Things seemed rather grim. "And you?"

"I'm looking for our children." He kissed her ear again. "Someone has them, and I'm going to find out who."

She held him tight, pulling his arms around her like a blanket. "When you find them, stay with them. Please. Let them know that their father is there and that their mother loves them."

"I will. And Sam?"

"Yeah?"

"I will always love you. No matter what, I swear I'll be there when you're finally able to die."

"Oh, Richie, I—"

The sound of loud, metallic clanking woke her up. Before the door to her cell flew open, Richie was already gone.

"Wake up, bitch!" Dick exclaimed. "Time to choppy-choppy your brainy!" He and Dock picked her up and carried her down the hallway. She took in every detail down to the moisture damage on the floor, since it could be her last time.

As they reached the operating room, the Middle Eastern technician stepped out.

Dick stopped. "Hey, new guy."

"I have a name, you know, sir. It's—"

"Whatever. Did you get the drip set up?"

The technician just smiled and bowed his head respectfully. "Yes, sir. Everything is in place. Just how the doctor ordered."

As he said "just how the doctor ordered," he stared right into Sam's eyes. Dick grunted and waved him off.

She wrinkled her brow as she was carried into the operating room, wondering what the technician had meant by that.

It took them several minutes to secure Sam to the operating table and put the IV in her arm. Then Dick shined a bright light on her as Dock placed instruments that looked like long ice picks in a disinfectant solution. Cold air hit her from all around.

"Is the sedative dripping and the anesthetic ready?" Dock asked as he attached the heart-rate monitor pads to her.

Dick tapped the IV bag. "The new guy set it up perfectly. The sedative is in the IV, and the anesthetic is over here. See?" He held up a bottle filled with whitish liquid.

"Good."

Sam glanced between them both. She was awake and alert. Usually, she'd be getting drowsy by now.

Half an hour passed before Dr. Klein entered in surgical scrubs. "Is ze patient ready?"

Dock nodded.

"Good, good. Well, Sam, this is ze last time we will speak. I am going to perform a transorbital lobotomy on you." He held up one of the instruments and said, "This will enter into your brain from the eye. Then I will sever the nerves leading to the frontal lobe. When it is done, there will be no more you, Sam."

He put it down. "You'll be under anesthetic, of course."

"How thoughtful," she said. Her heart wasn't pounding. In fact, she had never felt calmer. With every passing minute, he senses were becoming more acute. The fog that had been clouding her for months was breaking apart. Whatever was in the IV, it wasn't the usual stuff.

"Do you have any last words for me, Sam?"

She hummed and then said, "Yeah. Remember how I promised to kill you?"

He seemed bored. "Yes. How predictable."

"I just want to clarify what I meant."

At that, he arched an eyebrow.

Licking her lips, she said, "I'm going to rip out your heart and show you how black it is right before you die."

All he did was harrumph. "Such a waste for final words. Farewell, Sam of Spades."

He nodded at Dick, who injected the white solution into the IV. Seconds passed as it slid through the tube and into her bloodstream.

Nothing happened.

OK, I should be asleep by now. Did that technician do something to—

Then Sam felt a tremendous surge of energy, like someone had kickstarted her adrenaline production and then thrown it into overdrive.

That technician had to have removed the sedative from the IV and replaced the anesthetic with something else She didn't know what it was, but she felt great.

She closed her eyes and tightened her fists. Her veins bulged and her muscles coiled. The heat of raw energy rippled through her. It was the same powerful feeling she'd gotten when she had obliterated those *loa* in her townhome.

That's why the technician had looked at her when he'd said "the doctor." He wasn't referring to Dr. Klein. That could only mean one thing.

Her lips parted in a wide grin.

That technician works for Dr. Lazarus!

At that moment, the lights went out, and a second later, red emergency lights came on. A siren blared in the background, and a voice over the PA system said, "Patient and test-subject release has been activated. Warning: both the patient and test-subject release has been activated. All security personnel, initiate lockdown sequence."

"What is going on here?" Dr. Klein demanded, his face turning red.

Sam tugged at her shackles, feeling them pop under her newly restored strength. With this energizing mixture coursing through her veins, she felt even more powerful than when she had punched Herpin's jaw off. Her strength was increasing with every breath.

Let's dance.

With a guttural cry, she tore through the shackles and ripped the IV out of her arm. As all three men turned toward her, she felt the world around her slow down. Once more, every sound was enhanced and every visual detail was sharp. As she ripped the shackles off her legs, she once more felt like a god.

Dr. Klein backed up, his expression one of growing horror.

She felt Dick's fingers brush her head in an attempt to grapple. It was as if an insect were crawling on her. Grabbing the two lobotomy instruments, she drove one of them up through his chin and into his skull. The impact pushed him into the ceiling. Then she turned and saw Dock, his eyes wide with shock, as he reached for his tranquilizer. She threw the other one with exact precision, embedding it through his right eye. He flew back and collapsed, dead.

As Sam jumped off the table and rushed at Dr. Klein, time returned to normal. Before he could blink, she had him pressed against the far wall of the operating room with her forearm. He was trembling.

"My, my, what a pretty pickle we're in, eh, Dr. Klein?" she asked.

His lips began to dry as he stammered, "Please. Don't kill me."

She tsk'd several times. "Don't kill you? After everything you've done to me? Really, now?"

He struggled against her. He might as well have been a gnat.

Lifting him up until his feet were dangling off the floor, she asked, "Where are my babies, asshole?"

"I told you. The Knight Priory has them." His face started to darken as he struggled to breathe.

She tilted her head to the side. "Where? I want answers, you insolent prick."

"I don't know . . . I swear . . . They don't tell me . . . anything . . ." His face deepened in color.

Sam gazed into his eyes. She saw shock, confusion, and even fear. Everything she wanted to see in him. But she didn't see deceit. She lowered him to the ground, keeping him pinned. "You're completely useless."

As the deep color left his face, Dr. Klein said, "Yes, I am very useless. I am just a pitiful old man. Please let me go, Sam. Please, I beg you."

Watching him beg for his life, she felt nothing but a deep disgust. It was hard to believe he had once held her in such a grip of terror. "You know, you really are a pathetic loser. You never cared about helping me. I was just another experiment, no different from vermin. And you couldn't even get that right. No wonder the Knight Priory rejected you."

"Yes, that's me," he said with a titter. "I am just as pathetic as you say. I am a worthless man who disappoints everyone. I am—"

"Not to mention all the other patients you 'helped.' Meghan. Miss LeBeouf. What you did to them was unforgiveable."

Before he could say another word, she thrust her hand through his sternum. It split like a twig. His eyes widened from the shock, his body started to shake, and he began to spit up blood. Reaching around in his gooey chest cavity, she felt what she was searching for, a small muscle pulsing with a rapid, terrified beat. Blood spilled over her wrist.

With a yell, Sam pulled out Dr. Klein's heart.

Holding it up to his face, she said, "So let's make sure that you never help another person ever again!"

His eyes transfixed on it even as they started glazing over.

She squeezed, squishing the heart into pulp. Blood squirted over both of them.

"Farewell, Dr. Klein."

She waited until his eyes went dark before dropping him, allowing herself only a moment to relish her revenge. Then she shook the blood off her hand. It was time to find the others and escape.

As the sirens continued going off, she knelt down and rummaged through his coat. A moment later, she found a small pen case. Opening it, she once again came face-to-face with a source of untold misery and pain in her life.

The silver pen. She finally had it again.

As soon as her fingers touched it, she felt the oppressive, evil presence of her father. A moment later, she heard Vincent say, "Hello, Sam."

Just hearing his voice made her jaw tighten. "Hello, Vincent. So, you're strong enough to take control of others now?"

He sniggered. "You cannot imagine how powerful I am becoming. With every death caused by my *loa*, I grow even stronger. And please, call me 'Father,' my little Princess."

She stood up. "I'm no longer your Princess."

"My mistake, Sam. I am the king, and you are now my queen. I would say 'isn't it wonderful,' but you tend to lose your shit whenever I do."

"I'm not your queen, your princess, or your daughter, you son-of-a-bitch."

"Semantics, Sam. But we can argue those later. For now, please be careful. I'd hate for you to *die* in such a place."

Sam closed the container. Her hands were shaking. *Oh, God, how I hate him.*

She rushed out of the operating room, down the hallway, and toward the cell blocks. Along the way, she heard dozens of shouting voices along with gunfire. It sounded like they were shooting patients. But what she saw was far more disturbing.

Dozens of nude patients with frothing mouths were rushing at armed guards. Their pupils were fully dilated, and each one had a large number tattooed on their back. Some of the guards pulled off a few shots, dropping one or two, but they were soon overcome by the mobs and dragged to the ground in a squealing pile of teeth and claws.

Sam could feel evil spirits within each of the feral patients. They had to be the test subjects. *What was done to them?*

But then, Aucoin's voice, shouting in fear, seized her attention. She rushed down another few hallways, moving far faster than normal, and found him near the cell blocks. He had taken a gun off a dead guard and was waving it at several advancing test subjects, howling at them to get back. Behind him were a few normal, terrified patients, including an emaciated girl Sam immediately recognized as Meghan.

"Kyle! Meghan!"

Then the test subjects swarmed them.

"No! Damn it, no!" Sam activated her power. The world around her slowed down to a crawl. Dashing forward, she burst into the group of test subjects like a bowling ball, throwing a punch at one of their heads. That one's head cracked open like a watermelon, while the others flew in different directions. Viscera coated her to her shoulder. Aucoin fell back, crashing into Meghan and the others.

The test subjects then got back up, screeched at her, and attacked again. She scanned them as they approached. These were human beings, not *loa*. She wasn't a murderer, but they were giving her no choice.

As they reached her, she fought back, punching the head right off one and then spin-kicking another into a wall, where it splattered like a water balloon. She elbowed a third one in the gut, folding it in half. White energy coursed through her limbs, and as she killed each one, she felt the *loa* inside being destroyed as well.

These are innocent victims. Damn it, damn it, damn it!

Her frustration at being forced to kill normal people grew with each victory. When there were no more attackers, she dropped to one knee and took in a deep breath.

Then she screamed in rage. It reverberated through the corridors like a monster's roar, shattering the light fixtures above.

Aucoin limped out in front of her. "Jesus fucking Christ, Sam. What the hell are you?"

She stood up, holding on to the pen's container with a death grip.

"I'm Bridgette, Queen of the *Loa*."

"Sam!" A small waifish set of arms wrapped around her midsection. It was Meghan, as thin as a skeleton, hugging her and crying. "I missed you so much! I missed you! Oh, Sam!"

Sam put an arm around her but said nothing. *What did they do to you, Meghan?*

Meanwhile, Aucoin was helping up the other patients, a teenage girl and boy. "Any idea what was with those, um, people?"

She continued holding Meghan close to her, afraid she'd break her if she hugged too hard. "I think they've been experimented on with the *tkeeus*. They were all possessed by malevolent *loa*. I think it was permanent."

He nodded. "And Dr. Klein?"

"Dead. I ripped his heart right out."

With a smirk, Aucoin checked the gun's ammo. "Wish I'd seen it."

Then he wiped the sweat off his head. "Someone triggered the cell release system. All hell's broken loose. And with crazy possessed patients and gun-toting guards, this is going to be a shitty escape."

Grinning cockily, she asked, "What? Wanna wait back in your cell?"

"Ha! Not on your life. I may not be one hundred percent, but I can still shoot straight."

She took a few seconds to look him over. He was older, skinnier, and sicklier than she remembered, but he had the same grit from when he'd arrested her at the wharf.

"All right, Kyle. Let's go raise some hell."

Chapter 24
Darkness Once More

Date: **Monday, May 10, 1993**
Time: **11:00 p.m.**
Location: **Evergreen Sanatorium, Underground Facility**

The sirens continued to resound as Sam and Aucoin worked their way through the corridors of the sanatorium. All around, gunfire, shouts, and the shrill, high-pitched squawks of the test subjects created a warlike backdrop. By the time they found a large storage closet to duck into, it was clear that there was no more social order in Evergreen. It was every man for himself.

Other than them, there were only six other patients who were not possessed—Meghan, one middle-aged women, one young man, an elderly woman, and two teenagers—one boy and one girl. They were as diverse in both ethnicity and structure as they could be, except for two things—they were all malnourished and shaved bald.

"Sam, can you give us a minute?" Aucoin said as he ushered the last person into the closet. "Some of us are about to pass out."

Browsing the shelves for anything useful, Sam said, "Sure. See if we have any water left."

He tended first to the elderly woman, then the others, offering sips from a bottle of water they had managed to salvage from the cafeteria. The others coughed and shivered, pressing against each other for warmth and comfort.

Sam took one of the boxes off the shelf and opened it. Inside were uniforms for the medical staff. "Hey, we can wear these. Kyle, please help Miss Ester get dressed. Meghan, I'll help you. Misty and Lester, you help everyone else. These should keep us warmer and . . ."

She gazed around the closet. Seven mostly nude people, whose dignity had long since been stripped away, looked back. She smiled softly. " . . . help us to feel like human beings again."

As Aucoin and the two teenagers passed out the clothes, Sam helped Meghan to the farthest end of the closet. Then she stripped off her own surgical gown. Her body was covered with cuts, bruises, and sores. The burns from her townhome were ugly, caked scars.

"I'm so gross."

"No, you're not, Sam," Meghan said, leaning against the wall. "You're still beautiful."

"Thanks," Sam said, despite doubting it. "I guess I don't feel like a woman right now. Too many scars." She finished getting dressed.

Meghan coughed a few times and then asked, "Help me change?"

When Sam got her gown off, she saw damage that made her own seem mild. Meghan had patches of skin missing from what looked like self-inflicted wounds. Her ribs were all but showing. As Sam knelt and helped her slip on the uniform bottoms, she noticed that her genitals had been mutilated and then sewn shut.

"Oh, Meghan, what did they do to you?"

"Things I'd rather forget. Dr. Klein's theory was that if I was over-exposed to sexual stimulation, I wouldn't want it."

She chuckled morbidly. "He's right. I don't ever want to be touched again."

Sam pulled her into her arms. As soon as she was nestled against her, Meghan started crying. "I'm not a woman anymore, Sam. I want to die."

"Shhh," Sam stroked her hair. "No, Meghan, honey. No."

"There's nothing left of me. I'll never be normal again. I have no family. I've got nothing."

"You have one thing."

"What, Sam? What do I have?"

She gazed into her friend's eyes. "You have me."

Meghan sniffled. "What do you mean?"

Leaning down, Sam kissed her forehead. "You're one of the few friends I've got left. I've been worried sick about you. I'm never, ever going to let you go. We'll be like sisters."

"Sisters?" Meghan asked. She then dried her tears. "Yes, I'd like that."

Someone nearby cleared his throat. It was Aucoin. "Need a few more minutes?"

"Cute," Sam said, kissing him on the cheek. "And for you—that's for keeping me sane all these months."

He patted her shoulder. "Thank me when we escape. For now, let's go."

He turned back to the group and cocked his gun. "All right, let's keep to the formation. Sam will take point, I've got the rearguard, and everyone else in the middle. Move out!"

A minute or so later, they passed an open security door and entered the office hallways. Just as Sam turned the corner, she came face-to-face with four armed guards. For a moment, they stared at each other, blinking in shock.

Then one of the guards cried out, "It's the Castille bitch! Shoot her!" They pointed their weapons at her while she focused on her power. Time once again slowed down. Quickly, she pushed the group of survivors back. A moment later, she heard a loud pop and felt an incredible pain in her gut.

Meghan cried out, "Sam!" Her voice was low-pitched and drawn out due to the time distortion.

Two more shots were fired. Sam fell back as the bullets impacted her left side and the top of her right breast. Pain tore through every nerve as she felt the projectiles rip through her flesh and tear out the other side. As she landed on the ground, Aucoin ran past the front of the group, steadying his pistol. All four guards aimed at him. But before any of them fired, a loud series of shots rang out, and one of their heads exploded in a bloody mess. Then several things happened at once.

Aucoin fired into the chest of a different guard, who flew back. Sam grabbed the gun of another and easily crushed it. Then she kicked him in the groin and launched him into the ceiling, where his feet flailed a bit before going still. A few more shots rang out, and the last guard fell forward with holes in his chest.

Time returned to normal.

At the end of the hallway was the Middle Eastern technician. Only, now, his beard was gone, and he was in a black military uniform, wielding an assault rifle. He approached the group, looking right at Sam.

"Sam Castille?"

Aucoin aimed his pistol at him. "Who the hell wants to know?"

The man ignored him and shouldered his weapon. "Can you stand, Sam?"

"Hey, asshole," Aucoin said, "I swear I will blow your damn—"

"It's OK, Kyle," Sam interrupted. "This guy helped orchestrate our escape. You're with Dr. Lazarus, correct?" Even with her strength, standing after getting shot three times was tough, so she leaned against a wall.

The man nodded. "Call me Meyer. I've been ordered to bring you to him. Can you run?"

She shook her head. "I'm immortal, Meyer, not invincible. I don't have long before I pass out from blood loss."

"I understand," Meyer said, motioning down the hallway. "It's just a short way to the elevator. We have a helicopter waiting for you and any other survivors. You, with the gun, can you fight?"

"I was a cop," Aucoin said. "Anyway, we've been through the whole facility. We are the only ones left alive."

"Copy that. Then bring up the rear. Make sure no one falls behind. Samantha, you're with me. Everyone, listen up! This place has become overrun by the test subjects. I know you're tired and scared, but we have got to run. Let's move out!"

As Sam limped along the hallway, supported by Meyer, he explained everything. "After Dixie Olivier determined this was where you were being held, Dr. Lazarus had us do reconnaissance to gather intel. We then verified that the Evergreen Plantation was actually being used by the Knight Priory as a place to send their enemies. However, they've also been using it as a testing facility for experiments with the *tkeeus*. When Kyle Aucoin was committed, they brought on new staff. That's when I joined. We've been spending weeks planning your escape. I'm not proud of having worked on those so-called treatment machines, but it was necessary to keep my cover."

Sam took in all the information, ignoring the sirens and other noises. "So I take it that you triggered the release?"

"Affirmative," Meyer said. "We had no idea it would be this chaotic. We were taking time to plan a more structured raid, but when we learned about your lobotomy, we knew we couldn't wait."

As they reached the elevator, he punched the "up" button. "The Knight Priory has found a way to induce a permanent state of possession. The test subjects are first lobotomized to remove any will. Then, using the *tkeeus*, they are taken over by malevolent, low-level spirits. Their crazed state makes them look like they have a form of rabies."

Aucoin and the others reached the elevator. "So the Knight Priory is building an army?"

"In a manner of speaking, yes. They want to take over the entire region. More than likely, their next goal is all of Louisiana. But Dr. Lazarus can brief you on what we know when we get to base."

A sick tightness spread in Sam's gut as she got into the elevator. Vincent's words resounded in her mind. *There is a storm coming—a bad one.*

Aucoin hit the button for the ground floor. "How widespread is this thing?"

"For the moment, we're only aware of this facility. That's why as soon as we're at a safe distance, a missile strike will be ordered to wipe this place out."

"Lord, save us," the elderly woman said.

"A missile!" Aucoin exclaimed. "Who has that kind of firepower?"

Meyer checked his rifle. "Someone of the highest authority who has deemed this place unrecoverable."

Sam said nothing. The loss of blood was starting to get to her. Her head felt light, her vision was going out of focus, and her knees were getting weak.

The elevator door opened, and then a panel slid to the side, revealing the interior of a plantation home. Gunfire and the rumble of a helicopter could be heard from outside.

"I'm scared," Meghan muttered.

Meyer pulled out a radio. "This is Lone Soldier to Blackbird. The Queen is secured."

It crackled to life. "Roger that, Lone Soldier. Blackbird is setting down."

He tugged on Sam. "OK, let's go. We're heading to the rear of the plantation."

As they headed through the building, past antique furniture from the antebellum era, lavishly beautiful rugs, and paintings from the Civil War, Sam started feeling faint. She knew she only had a few more minutes before she collapsed from blood loss.

Outside, a group of sanatorium guards was fighting a horde of test subjects. Above them, a black helicopter circled around. A pair of 50-caliber machine guns stuck out the side.

"Fall back," a voice said from the helicopter. "We can't cover you if you're that close to them!"

Suddenly, the test subjects broke through the line of guards, tearing them to pieces. As soon as every one of them was dead, machine-gun fire poured from the helicopter onto the remaining test subjects, dropping them like flies. As it landed, Meyer led the group out to it.

Sam fought to stay conscious. The world was already fading,

Two more people in black uniforms, one Caucasian and one Jamaican, were in the helicopter manning the machine guns. While Meyer helped her on board, Aucoin helped the others. Whatever group it was that Dr. Lazarus led, they weren't messing around.

"Welcome aboard, Your Majesty," the Jamaican man said with a pearly white grin. "Just buckle up and hold on tight. We'll get you someplace safe in just a few—"

"We gotta go!" Aucoin said in a panic. From the plantation home, an even larger horde of test subjects rushed at them, shrieking in their shrill, high-pitched voices.

Oh, shit! Sam felt her pulse quicken, and with it, a boost in focus. For the moment, she could disregard the loss of blood.

"We need to go, Mister Rabbi, sir!" the Jamaican man said as he started firing. Several of the test subjects fell within seconds, some cut in half by the high-caliber weapon. But they kept coming.

"Take off!" Meyer called out, helping Aucoin on board. "Take off now! And tell Command that this place is lost!"

As the helicopter started rising, Sam heard a squeal. Meghan was being pulled out of the helicopter by two test subjects. They were already biting her.

"Meghan, no!" Activating her power, Sam dove at them. In the blink of an eye, she crushed the skulls of both patients and rolled on the ground, holding Meghan in her arms. The helicopter was already over twenty feet off the ground.

Oh, this is bad.

"Sam!" Aucoin leaned over the edge as if intending to jump, but Meyer was holding him back. "Get off me, you son-of-a-bitch!"

"You can't do anything right now!" Meyer pinned him and then shouted, "Sam! We'll meet you at the river. It's due east about five hundred yards. Go there!"

She nodded and pulled Meghan to her feet. "Hey, you OK?"

Her neck and shoulder were bleeding profusely from the bites. "God, I hope this isn't contagious like in the movies."

Sam quickly examined them, frowning. They were pretty deep, and blood was flowing freely from Meghan's neck. Pulling her onto her back, she said, "I don't think it's that kind of thing. Spirits don't transmit through bites."

Sounds of gunfire and shrieking caught her attention. Dozens more test subjects were rushing toward them. Bullets hailed down from above, but it wasn't nearly enough.

"Sam, they're almost here!" Meghan gripped Sam in a panic.

Focusing on her power, Sam pressed a palm to the ground. "All who hear my voice, help me! Your queen commands it!" Her voice reverberated.

Even as the flood of test subjects drew near, a large, white sigil appeared around them.

"What is this?" Meghan wailed.

But Sam didn't reply. Instead, she closed her eyes and pushed her will into the earth, beckoning every free spirit in the area to her side. A moment later, loud cries issued forth from the ground and hundreds of *loa* rose into the air. They circled around the test subjects, tearing at them with bony hands and snapping jaws.

Meghan cried in terror. Sam exhaled and felt her strength ebb. She still had control over some of them, but it wouldn't last for long. Not if Vincent kept gaining strength.

Then she heard a jet approaching. With her senses still acute, she caught sight of an incoming missile speeding toward them. "Oh, shit, I think this is the 'blow it up' part! Hold on, Meghan!"

She was almost spent. But once more she felt the world slow down and the pain vanish. The muscles on her legs bulged as she rushed forward, the cool night air splitting like water. She heard Meghan wail, she felt the missile get closer, and she tasted the moisture in the air.

With a final cry, Sam closed her eyes and leapt.

Behind her, the world exploded. She could felt the heat as the missile hit its mark. She smelled the debris from the plantation buildings as they ignited an inferno. She tasted the sulfur.

When she finally opened her eyes, she looked down. She was hundreds of feet in the air.

"Holy shit!"

She and Meghan both screamed as they came down, landing at a boat dock nearly a mile south of the plantation. The mighty Mississippi River spanned before them.

With an "oomph," Sam hit and rolled, cradling Meghan protectively. They lay there for a few seconds to catch their breath.

She limped over to the pier and laid her friend against one of the pylons. Then she searched for the helicopter, finding it in the distance. "We're off course. It's gonna take them a few minutes to reach us."

"Hey, Sam," Meghan said. Her voice was weak.

Sam knelt down beside her and examined her wounds. They were bleeding even more, likely torn open from the escape. *Shit! She needs first aid.*

"Don't talk, Meghan. I'm gonna find something to stop the bleeding."

Meghan was barely able to look up. "Did you mean it? We'll be together? The two of us?"

A rush of emotion she hadn't felt since she was with Richie filled Sam's heart. "Yes. So hang on, OK?"

With a soft, weak smile, Meghan said, "OK."

There was a fisherman's shack nearby, so Sam headed toward it to search for something to stop the bleeding. The weakness in her joints was so great, she had to lean on the pylons to walk. She was only a few feet away when Meghan asked, "Hey, are you really immortal?" Her voice was very weak.

"Yeah. I am. I can't die."

"Lucky you."

And then silence.

"Don't worry, Meghan. We'll get through this, and . . ."

But Sam felt that something was wrong. She turned around. Meghan was sitting there, still smiling softly, her eyes glazed over.

Sam fell to her knees, tears pouring out as she crawled over to Meghan and shook her. "No, no, no! Come on, damn it! Don't go! Don't do this to me!"

But it was too late. Meghan was already dead.

Rocking back and forth, holding Meghan's head to her chest, Sam cried out in agony, a long roar that carried years of frustration and pain. *I can't save anyone! Not Michael, Rodger, Richie, or even Meghan. Everyone I love keeps dying!*

She darted to the edge of the pier and puked into the water. Then she howled again. "What use is any of this?" The wooden pier cracked, parts of it crumbling.

From above, the helicopter roared and a light shone down upon her. Sam stood up, leaning on one of the pylons. She felt weak. She felt cold. She felt like any moment could be her last.

I can't go on like this. I can't live while everyone around me dies.

"Sam!" Aucoin called out, signaling to the riverbank. "We'll circle around and land. Just hold on."

Hold on? What a joke. It all ends the same way. People die because of me.

She glanced back over her shoulder. The Mississippi River was dark, cold, and silent.

Maybe if I go down there and can't come back, the Baron will have to dig my grave.

Then she looked back up at Aucoin and smiled, stepping back to the edge of the pier.

His eyes widened. "Sam? Sam, what are you . . ."

Take care, Kyle. I hope you find happiness someday.

Spreading her arms, she leaned back.

"Sam! NO!"

Then Sam knew only darkness once more.

Part Two

Chapter 25
Two Years Later

Date: **Sunday, April 16, 1995**
Time: **1:00 p.m.**
Location: **Penthouse at 740 Park Avenue**
Manhattan, New York

"Are you working late tonight, Gino?" Dixie asked as she lay Felicia on the floor, her daughter still groggily rubbing her face after waking from her nap.

Her husband's voice rang out from the speakerphone, as sexy as ever. "Unfortunately, yes. We start filming for the new season next week. I'll be working late every night."

Upon hearing his voice, Felicia called out, "Daddy!"

Dixie's smile deepened as she gazed affectionately at the toddler, lightly tickling her little feet until she started giggling.

Gino chuckled. "Hey, baby girl."

Felicia said, "Daddy," again before rolling to her feet and toddling toward the table where the phone lay. She patted it repeatedly. "Daddy, Daddy, Daddy!" Fortunately, she kept missing the buttons.

He continued to laugh. "Sounds like our girl is in a good mood."

"She is, indeed," said Dixie, going to pick her daughter up. "And she misses her daddy. So don't come home too late, Mr. Soap Opera Director." In her arms, Felicia wiggled, wanting to get free and back to her father.

"All right, my love. I'll make it in for a late dinner."

"Thank you, honey." She put Felicia into her high chair, laying out some animal crackers. At once, the toddler was distracted with consuming the snack.

As things quieted, Gino cleared his throat. "Dixie, have you thought about Commissioner Bratton's offer? For the job?"

She sat down, her smile dwindling. "Not yet. While I'm not ready to retire, and 'captain' has a nice ring to it, I don't think I'm suited to a desk job. I work best out in the field, solving cases."

"I know, but . . ." There was always a "but" when they talked about this. "Don't you think you've taken enough risks? Aren't you ready to be safe?"

There were a few loud voices on the other end of the line. Then he said, "Sorry, love. They need me on the set. It was so much easier when I was just writing these. We'll talk more later. See you tonight?"

"I'll be here when you get home." She hung up and for a long while stared silently out of the large, wall-length window overlooking Park Avenue.

Gently, she stroked Felicia's hair until her daughter said, "Cracker!" She was offering a cracker in the shape of a horse.

With grin, Dixie leaned down and nipped it out of her daughter's small hand. She gazed lovingly at her. With her blond baby hair having turned dark, and with her smooth pale skin, Felicia looked more like her father each day.

"I wish you could have met him, honey. He was a good man."

It wasn't something she and Gino discussed. Either he just accepted that their child hadn't inherited his swarthy skin, or he was too much of a gentleman to ask uncomfortable questions. Regardless, she wished there was someone she could talk to about it, but there was no one. Sam had vanished two years ago, Aucoin's whereabouts were unknown, and everyone else who had known Michael was dead.

Dixie was just about to pick Felicia up when the phone rang. Glancing at the caller ID, she saw it was from Arkansas. "Huh? I don't know anyone there."

A few rings later, the answering machine responded. Then a familiar voice spoke up.

"Dixie? This is Dr. Lazarus. When you get this message, pl—"

"I'm here!" Dixie said, slapping the speakerphone button so fast, Felicia jerked, sudden anxiety on her little face. Rushing back to her daughter, she rubbed her head reassuringly. "Sorry, honey."

Once Felicia had gone back to eating, Dixie said, "I'm here, Andre. You caught me feeding Felicia her afternoon snack."

Instantly, his voice warmed up from its usual professional tone. "Hello, there! And how is little Felicia?"

"She's fine. About to have a story read to her."

"Wonderful! I take it that your nanny is not there?"

"Yes, today is Miss Abercrombie's day off." She had a hunch why he'd asked that. "I'm effectively alone, if you need to discuss something sensitive."

"Indeed, I do." His voice grew serious. "Dixie, I hate to ask you for anything, especially after all you've done. But I need your help."

For a moment, her heart skipped a beat. "Is it Sam? Have you found her?"

"Unfortunately, no," he said. "There is no trace of her. But I require someone with your analytical mind to assist some colleagues of mine on another task."

"OK. What's going on?" she asked, munching on a lion cracker offered by her daughter.

"We've been tracing how Vincent came across the *tkeeus*. I believe we've discovered who introduced him to it."

Dixie swallowed. "You're kidding."

"No, I'm not. We believe that a member of the Knight Priory called the Oracle brought the *tkeeus* into the United States back in the 1960s. Before giving it to Vincent, the Oracle used it some other place. Unfortunately, the people who are investigating that other place—associates I've known for many years—have run into difficulties."

"And you'd like me to help them?"

"I would."

"Is it dangerous?"

"It is, but no more so than your experience with Hannah."

Again, Dixie grew silent. As boring as her life had become, it was safe. *But I'm not ready to be safe, am I? Does that make me irresponsible?*

She looked down at Felicia, who was smiling up at her with eyes like jelly beans, her bowl of crackers empty. Picking her daughter up, she realized that if Michael were alive, he'd tell her it was illogical to risk her life when she had a child to raise. And she was certain Gino would say the same thing. She should probably sit this one out. Maybe in a few years, she could be useful again.

But before she could speak, Dr. Lazarus said, "The people who need help are at Emory University in Atlanta."

That meant nothing to her. "OK, and?"

"You don't know? That is where Alexia LeBlanc attends school."

That made Dixie stop in her tracks. *Oh, my God. Michael's little sister! I'd forgotten about her.*

Suddenly, she had someone she could talk to about Felicia, about what had happened with Michael. Finally, she could get some closure.

I'll have to get Miss Abercrombie to cover full-time, and Gino will be worried, but . . .

Before she even realized it, she said, "Count me in, Andre."

"Wonderful!" he said. "I'll arrange everything. I'll also send you what we know about the Knight Priory, especially on members like the Oracle, Miss Saucier, and Dr. Kindley. Thank you so much, Dixie. I promise to make it up to you."

After he disconnected, Dixie stood there for a while, absently rocking Felicia back and forth until the toddler leaned against her, nuzzling affectionately.

Did I make a mistake? Should I do this?

She walked to the window and gazed out over the Manhattan skyline. As peaceful as her life was, she wasn't happy. She needed to be useful again.

Her thoughts turned to Alexia. Michael's little sister. The one person he'd loved more than anyone else. She had known the girl through her brother and knew her to be as headstrong as he had been. A bit of a tomboy, too, from what she recalled.

Dixie kissed the top of Felicia's head.

I wonder what kind of woman she's grown into?

The Scent of Fear

(Alexia LeBlanc's Story)

Chapter 26
Postcard from New York

Date: **Friday, April 21, 1995**
Time: **2:00 p.m.**
Location: **School of Medicine**
Emory University, Atlanta, Georgia

Alexia LeBlanc didn't consider parties, dancing, or clubbing to be a good time, even though all her friends claimed a woman with her figure should. Loud music, alcohol, and charming boys did nothing to excite her. Instead, what she found stimulating were martial arts, fencing, good books, and lengthy lectures. And nothing titillated her more than when Professor Templeton, her forensics pathology instructor, went over recent tragedies like the Oklahoma City bombing.

"So, as you can see from the aerial photos, the blast at the Murrah Federal Building caused massive damage to its structure. Now, we know from early reports that several thousand pounds of ammonium nitrate were used, but what can we tell by looking at the picture?" Pointing at the projected photographs, Templeton, who was only five feet tall with a receding hairline and always a tweed suit, looked around the auditorium from behind his Coke-bottle glasses.

Alexia, who was sucking thoughtfully on her pen cap, raised her hand. She was sure she knew the answer.

"Yes, Miss LeBlanc," he said.

She stretched her jaw, clicking it. "The destruction, while heavy, isn't spread out. If you detonated several thousand pounds of ammonium nitrate, the radius would have been immense, but there would have been significantly less structural damage."

A nearby student who looked like his study guide was a Playboy spoke up. "Huh? Do you mean that something other than aluminum nitrate was used?"

Every word he spoke made her cringe. "Ammonium nitrate, you dolt!" she exclaimed. "No, of course not. Look at the photos. They tell the entire story!"

There was a general murmur in class as Templeton nodded. "Miss LeBlanc is correct. The photographs almost always tell what happened. Now, Alexia, what do the photographs tell you?"

She spun her pen around. It helped her think. "The bomb was created as a shaped charge, directing the blast directly into the structure, in order to cause the highest possible level of damage."

He smiled proudly. "Exactly, Miss LeBlanc, good job! So while the FBI hunts for the culprits, likely a fundamentalist terrorist group, we can be certain that these are absolutely not amateurs. We can—"

"I don't think that's accurate at all," she interrupted.

His brow tightened into a familiar wrinkle. "What do you mean?"

Most of the class was now looking at her, but she didn't care. As she continued twirling her pen, she mentally laid out a roadmap of the evidence. She had her theory a few moments later. "The blast is not just controlled, it's too controlled. There's no hate or rage in this crime. No passion, no pathos. There's only cold and emotionless conviction. That's not the work of an extremist. They were making a statement, simple as that."

Templeton cleared his throat. "Yes, well, that's good and all, but—"

She interrupted again. "I'm not done. The bombing date is suspicious, too."

"As in?"

Closing her eyes, she thought back to April from two years ago, recalling a headline that had stuck with her. "The date coincides with the two-year anniversary of the Branch-Davidian compound fire in Waco, Texas. So you have the cold, calculated destruction of a federal building two years after federal agents purportedly botched a standoff that resulted in dozens of deaths. It's possible the two events are connected."

Leaning on the projector as if this situation were routine, Templeton frowned. "What do you think this is, Miss LeBlanc?"

Annoyed murmurs about "Awesome Alexia" started rising from the other students.

She absently nibbled on her pen cap. The answer seemed obvious. "Only one or two people did this, and they'd have knowledge of demolitions. They're either military or ex-military, maybe a Gulf War veteran. They consider themselves at war with the United States government. They'd be psychologically unstable, perhaps a sociopath, and . . . and . . ."

She trailed off, going deeper into thought and trying to profile the bombers.

The same male student from earlier called out in a sing-song manner, "And what? What? We're waiting for you to solve the crime, Lexi!"

Snickering rose around her. Without looking, she threw the pen at him. It whizzed right by his nose. "Don't ever call me Lexi, you dick."

"Shit! Forget Awesome Alexia. More like Angry Alexia!" He scooted away. Several other students muttered in disdain.

Then the campus bell rang, signaling the end of class. Everyone got up and started shuffling out.

Templeton tried to speak above the clamor of their departure. "OK, class. Remember that Monday is when we start preparing for the semester final. Also, if you're leaving campus this weekend, remember to stay in groups. The Druid Hills police are still searching for those students who vanished. And finally, don't forget that this Sunday is a special medical lecture by visiting New York University professor Mathi—"

But the class was already empty. He sighed, his shoulders sagging.

Alexia felt a sinking in her stomach. She had promised him she'd try to not take over the lecture again. But just like before, she had gotten so caught up in solving the puzzle that she had forgotten she was in class. The ill feeling increased as she realized she wasn't living up to the values taught by her faith. *By sinning in pride, I am rejecting His love.*

Mentally berating herself, she headed down to him. He stopped stuffing his portfolio. His disappointed expression was as prominent as his Brut aftershave.

"I'm sorry, sir," she said. "I know said I wouldn't, but . . ."

Templeton closed his briefcase. "But you did. And you lost your temper again. You know you're on permanent probation for what you did during your first year."

She looked down, her ears on fire.

"Look, Alexia, you're quite possibly the most gifted student I have ever had. But the sooner you realize that no one can ever do it all alone, the sooner you start accepting the help of others, the sooner you'll find where you truly belong."

"Yes, sir," she said, still flushed. Pride was the sin she fought against every day. It was also the sin that had taken away the person she loved the most.

Templeton, having gathered his belongings, threw on his jacket. "Anyway, you usually end your theories with a profile. Do you have one this time?"

His question pulled her from her brooding thoughts. "I would look for one or two men, ex-military with a general discharge and possibly a Bronze Star or Purple Heart. They'd have a grudge against the current administration and would have been outspoken against the Branch-Davidian compound incident. That's all I've got."

With a chuckle, he patted her shoulder. "Well, like always, you're probably pretty close. Have a good weekend, Alexia. Hope to see you at the lecture on Sunday. I think you'll appreciate Professor Mathias. He's renowned for his study in psychology, especially the fight-versus-flight phenomenon. I'm sure you'll enjoy it."

The thought of a lecture from a famed professor made her tingle. "I'll be there so long as Serge doesn't have me wrapped up in practice. Championships are coming up soon."

Templeton shot her a thumbs-up and then headed off. "And remember to watch that temper. You're supposed to be Awesome Alexia, not Angry Alexia."

As he left, she gripped the silver, cross-shaped locket that always dangled around her neck, savoring its coolness against her skin. She clicked it open and gazed upon the picture of the handsome man inside—someone she loved very much, but whose pride had led to his death. And his death had torn her family asunder.

Michael. Brother. I miss you.

A few minutes later, Alexia was heading across Emory. It was the afternoon, and the campus was alive with activity. Students were lounging around the quad, groups of guys were playing football in an open field, and a band was playing a charity concert at one of the amphitheaters.

While she stopped at a crosswalk and waited for a large truck bearing the insignia of the Kappa Sigma fraternity to pass by, the members hollering about the big off-campus party that evening, something caught her eye. She turned to see a woman standing on the far side of the street staring at her. She was dirty and dressed in a long overcoat, her short, blond hair matted and filthy. As Alexia scrutinized her, pegging her as some kind of derelict and wondering how she'd gotten onto campus, the Kappa Sigma truck passed between them.

"Come to our party, everyone!" one member shouted.

"We will have, like, all the beer!" another shouted.

Then the truck passed, but the blond derelict woman was gone.

Uh, what the hell?

By the time she got back to the dorms, though, she had all but forgotten the blonde woman.

It was late in the afternoon, and Alexia was reclining on the lower bunk of her dorm room bed, nose-deep in her forensics textbook. She had just gotten to an exciting section on blood splatters when her roommate, Patty O'Brien, leaned over from above. Her short, red hair was still damp from the shower, the smell of Head and Shoulders as prevalent as the freckles on her face.

"Hey there, girlfriend! Whatcha reading now?" Patty asked in a boisterous voice. She snatched Alexia's book.

Caught off guard, Alexia tried to grab it back. However, Patty sat up so quickly that Alexia ended up falling on their ten-dollar fleur-de-lis rug, landing right on her substantially endowed chest. The pain was explosive.

"Ow! Dang it! My boobs!" She clutched them and writhed around, trying to fight out the sting.

Patty read out loud. "'Descriptions of an abnormal fluidity of blood seen at autopsy in asphyxial deaths are part of forensic mythology and can be dismissed with little discussion.' Jesus, Alexia, can't you just read *The Golden Compass* or *The Wheel of Time*?"

By then, Alexia was sitting. "Don't take His name in vain," she said, pulling herself to her feet, snatching the book back, and tossing it on her bed. "And I can't expect a computer science major to understand forensics. All you have to do is punch code into a server. I have to figure out how crimes were committed."

She folded her arms underneath her chest and grinned cockily. It was a jest meant for the girl she saw as a sister—Patty's brilliance on computers was without peer.

But instead of taking the bait, Patty messed up her hair and then pulled out her shirt as if she had unreasonably large breasts. "Duh, my name is Alexia LeBlanc. I'm a genius that knows everything about everything. I've never blown off a single class. Ever. I could be a world-famous neurosurgeon or beat Stephen Hawking in a wager about black holes, but noooo! Instead, I want to work in a lab with dead bodies and bones. I get insulted when other people have trouble figuring out really complex problems—because, genius. I have to wear specialty bras or I suffer from chronic back pain, and I've never heard of Vidal Sassoon because my hair is always a fricking mess. But don't you dare make fun of God, Jesus, or Christianity because I'll karate-kick your butt through your moooooth."

As Alexia stared incredulously at her roommate, Patty chortled and pointed. "Seriously, that's what you sound like. Just like that. Vocal inflections and everything. Honest to goodness."

And then, Alexia burst out into laughter. "I'm so going to kick your butt—through your mouth—right now."

Without another word, she pounced on her friend and tickled her until she was begging for mercy. A few minutes later, she was sitting in victory on the soft, flannel sheets of Patty's bed. Her friend was on the floor, catching her breath and sniggering.

"That . . . was not fair . . . Alexia . . ."

From her perch of victory, Alexia beamed. "Didn't you say you wanted to take a sour, dour, boorish, and angry girl and make her more fun? And for your information, I did blow off one class. Emory History. Because it bored me to tears!"

Patty blew a raspberry. "I remember. I had to help you pass that class." Then she winked up at her. "And you're no longer sour, dour, boorish, or angry. You're a lot of fun in your own way."

Alexia's smile widened. Patty always made her feel right about herself. If not for her, she would have left Emory after the first time her temper got the better of her. Hopping off the bed, she helped up her friend. "Thanks. But honestly, I need to get ready for practice, so it's good you got me away from the book. All's well."

The phrase "All's well" was her way of saying that as far as she was concerned, the matter was settled, and the conversation was over.

Grinning cheekily, Patty lit a stick of incense on the bedside table. The sweet smell of jasmine soon flooded the room. "Aw, you're gonna miss the Kappa Sigma party to go . . . what do you have today, karate or fencing?"

Alexia stripped off her shirt and shorts and tossed them into their hamper. "It's not karate, it's savate. Sah-vat. Two totally different things. And it's fencing today. Besides, you know I don't do parties. All that drinking and dancing and fornicating like Sodom and Gomorrah. Doesn't ring my bell."

"But I like drinking and dancing and fornicating." Patty giggled, nibbling her bottom lip and swaying her shoulders back and forth.

That display made Alexia roll her eyes. Once she'd figured out that Patty was one of those childlike, carefree girls who just couldn't make good decisions on their own, she'd decided to protect her like a big sister would. More often than not, "protecting" would end up meaning "bailing out."

"I know there's no use in asking you to wait until I can go or just stay home, so I'll show up after practice. Please behave until I get there, OK?"

Patty waved her off. "Fine, fine, fine. I'll stick to beer and mild flirting until you arrive."

"And stay with a group, all right? Remember that several students have gone missing over the past few weeks. The police still haven't ruled out foul play."

"Yes, Mommy."

With a sigh, Alexia headed into the bathroom they shared with the adjacent dorm room. "I can't slack off. Serge will kill me if I get lax this close to a championship."

Patty leaned against the bathroom wall. "Right, you're going for team captain this time, right?"

"Yes, and Leona's not just going to let me beat her," Alexia said. Then she looked at herself in the mirror. At nineteen, she was about five feet six inches tall. Her black hair was constantly unkempt, since she had no inclination to style it. Her hazel eyes had the same intensity as her late brother's. She was well-toned: her muscles were more pronounced than most other girls', her hips were a bit larger, and her chest was like her mother's, one size too big. She self-consciously cupped them, feeling their weight, and groaned. They made physical activity even more of a challenge.

Lord, you certainly have a sense of humor, giving a fighter like me DDs.

Patty started cleaning her face in the sink. "Seriously, though. If those midgets get any larger, you're going to want to see a doctor about reduction surgery. There's a fine line between an hourglass figure and looking like Jessica Rabbit on steroids, and you're about to cross that line, girlie."

Alexia made a face and adjusted the strap of her rather pricey bra. "Heck, no! I'm not chopping up the body God gave me no matter how much they hurt when they bounce."

Looking at her own chest, Alexia caught sight of her locket and thought again about her brother.

As Patty chattered on about the advantages of small breasts, Alexia closed her eyes. Thinking about what had happened with Michael always brought her anger to the surface. He had left Shreveport after a falling out with their father, a Southern Baptist minister. But it was his death that had destroyed her relationship with Reverend LeBlanc.

It had been over Michael's sexual orientation, as she was taught he was damned for it. But she couldn't accept that someone as selfless as her brother would go to hell, and the conflict between doctrine and emotions rocked her otherwise unshakable faith to the core. When she finally confronted her father about the issue, his answer did even more damage.

"I love your brother," he had said. "But he has chosen to reject God. I can do nothing for his soul. Don't do the same thing yourself, Lexi."

"I can't believe that," she had bawled. "I can't believe God would condemn someone that good for just one sin!"

In the end, she left home after graduating from high school, going to Emory on a full scholarship. While she still talked to her mother every weekend, she hadn't spoken to her father in three years.

"Hey, Alexia, are you OK?" Patty sounded concerned.

It pulled her out of the mental beat-up session. She nodded, noticing that she had sunk her fingernails into her palms. "Yeah. Just. No worries. All's well."

Patty hugged her gently. But then, loud techno music started up from the adjacent dorm room. Like a ferret distracted by a sock, she started slapping and kicking the door. "Oh, come on! Damn Marcie! She always plays that when her and Chuck are screwing!"

She then pressed her face against the door. "We all know what you're doing, Marcie! You can quit blasting the floor with your industrial noise."

Alexia cleaned off her face with strawberry-scented soap. "She can't hear you. That's why she plays the music, not to disguise the sounds of copulation." As if on cue, a girl moaned in pleasure from behind the door. "See what I mean?"

Making a face, Patty started brushing out her wet, tangled hair. "Yuck. Not that I totally wouldn't sneak my boyfriend in if I had one, but geez, at least I'd be tasteful."

"Uh-huh," Alexia replied as she got dressed in black jeans and a cream-colored blouse. "How many times have I had to 'go run to the store' for a few hours? Hypocrite much there?"

"Ouch!" Patty replied. "Fine, hit a girl below the belt." She slipped into a cute, tie-dyed dress with spaghetti straps. "At least I don't cut my boyfriend off at second base."

Alexia's face and ears burned before Patty even finished. "That's not fair. Besides, Mark is very understanding. He doesn't push."

"He's gotta be getting something, because he's been with you for years. Come on, you let him rub those casabas of yours once in a while, right?" Patty nudged her, waggling her eyebrows.

"So crude!" Alexia said, swiping at her with her fencing bag. "I told you, we fool around some, not that it's your business. He's just . . . he's really sweet, and he knows I want to save myself for marriage. He's never forced the issue. He just wants to love me."

Markus Eversoll, a Danish student and member of the fencing team, had proved that on their first outing, a hiking trip through Fernbank Forest. After she'd twisted her ankle at one of the old settler's stone monuments, he had carried her back to campus. He then spent the two weeks she was recovering seeing to her every comfort. From that point onward, he was as protective of her as she was of Patty.

"So, yeah, none of your business. What we have is love—true love. Understand?" Her cheeks and ears were positively burning.

"Whatever you say, Princess Buttercup," Patty said, who then slipped over to a stack of mail, most of it containing applications for student credit cards. "By the way, you got a postcard from New York."

That got Alexia's attention. "New York? I don't know anyone there."

Waving it around, Patty said, "From someone named Dixie. Dixie Eliopoulos. She says she needs to talk to you."

Alexia blinked "Dixie? Dixie. Where have I heard that name before?"

With a shrug, Patty said, "I dunno. Maybe someone you knew back home?"

Snatching the postcard, Alexia examined it front and back, nibbling on her bottom lip. She was just about to put it aside when the recollection came crashing back. "I met her in New Orleans. Dixie Olivier. She was my brother's best friend!"

Chapter 27
Alexia's Unfortunate Evening

Date: **Friday, April 21, 1995**
Time: **5:00 p.m.**
Location: **Woodruff P. E. Center**
Emory University, Atlanta, Georgia

"*Arret*!" Serge Eversoll said, calling for the match to stop.

Alexia out held her rapier in a perfect lunge, its blunted tip resting squarely on her opponent's chest.

"Touch and bout!" Serge said in his thick Scandavian accent. "Alexia wins."

She relaxed her posture, saluted with her blade, and removed her mask. Her opponent, the student instructor, did the same, her long black hair spilling down her shoulders. Both of them were covered in sweat.

Her opponent spoke in a French accent. "Very well done, Alexia. It seems that I cannot beat you today, *oui*?"

Grateful for the praise, Alexia bowed her head. "Thanks, Leona. Coming from you, that means a lot." She had just beaten her toughest opponent in the class—a senior with several championships—and all but secured her position as team captain. But it had been a hard-won victory, for during the match, all she could think about was the postcard from Dixie. Her brother's best friend wanted to meet her tomorrow. Alexia couldn't wait.

She was jarred from her thoughts as the applause and yells for "Awesome Alexia" rippled through the rest of the class. The pinkness in her cheeks continued rising as she and Leona quickly stepped off the mat. Serge called the next two opponents.

"Just don't let it go to your head. Next time, I plan to win." Leona winked and headed toward the water cooler

"I won't," Alexia said, laughing. Leona, like Serge, was someone whom she greatly respected.

A bubbly girl's voice caught her attention. "Hey, Alexia!" Helen, one of the freshman students, came over. Her honey-brown hair was tied back in a tight ponytail. "I just wanna say that, oh, my God, if you become our team captain, we are so going to rule the circuit this year!"

Alexia chuckled, fighting back more heat in her cheeks. "Thanks, Helen. You're doing well, too, you know."

Helen beamed. "So, are you going to the Kappa Sigma party tonight? I heard that's the place to be."

Alexia shrugged. "Yeah, Mark and I will stop by at some point." After all, she had to check on Patty.

That seemed to be good enough for Helen, who shot her a thumbs-up. "All right. Keep it real, girl. Later!"

The sound of more clapping got her attention. Mark had just won his match and was bowing with a flourish. After he and his opponent clapped each other on the back, he came over to her, his bright, blue eyes shimmering behind his floppy, dark brown bangs. "Good job there, Alexia," he said in that Scandinavian accent she found simply adorable. "Everyone loves you. And my uncle says you're all but guaranteed to lead the team this time."

Her blush, which had yet to settle, spread to her ears. He could charm her with just a few words. She leaned against him. "Thank you, Mark. Although I still haven't beaten you."

He stroked her hair as if he didn't mind the sweat. "I'll never be as good as you, baby. Beating me will just be a formality."

Her cheeks grew even hotter until she thought she would burst into flames. She closed her eyes and rubbed her face against his chest until she felt like she could sink into him. Never before had she felt so much emotion for one person.

They stayed in that embrace for several minutes, until someone shouted, "Excuse me, is there an Alexia LeBlanc here?"

She glanced up from Mark's arms. "Yeah. I'm Alexia."

It was a member of campus security. "Miss LeBlanc. We just got a call from off-campus. Someone from the Kappa Sigma party."

Alexia felt a chill. She already knew who it was about.

"Yeah, apparently a friend of yours, Patricia O'Brien, got into a situation. The police were called and some guy was arrested. Anyway, she refused to let an officer drive her back and wants to know if you'll come get her."

She felt her world spin. "Oh, my God. She can't even . . . what the . . . oh, I'm gonna be sick."

Mark squeezed her arms and gazed into her eyes. "Your friend needs you. Want me to come along?"

With a weak nod, she said, "Yeah. I have a feeling Patty's going to need two people to carry her home."

"All right. But let's get changed first. We are quite sweaty."

"Yeah. Good idea." She sulked. Her evening was ruined.

It was close to ten when they arrived. Alexia, who had changed back into her blouse and jeans, with a pair of boots and her cross locket, regarded the converted party house. It belonged in a John Hughes film, decorated with Christmas lights and tinsel, all in the Emory colors, with two mini spotlights beaming the Kappa Sigma logo onto its side. The front lawn had two kiddie pools filled with ice and beer bottles. The main attraction was the lawn chair attached to the roof, which featured Lord Dooley, the skeletal mascot of Emory, in a flowing black cape and top hat, lounging like a boss.

A soft moan from a nearby tree caught her attention. She recognized Marcie, her dorm mate, and her boyfriend Chuck, behind it. Chuck's hand was up her shirt and his tongue was down her throat. Alexia rolled her eyes. *Babylon's whores are the first to go.*

Mark, who was wearing jeans and a t-shirt with his letter jacket over it, pointed toward the driveway. "There she is."

Patty was leaning against a Druid Hills police car, talking quietly with a balding officer.

Rubbing her arm, Mark said, "Let's go." He headed toward Patty.

She started following when something to the side caught her eye. Staring at her from across the street was the blond derelict woman from before. As soon as their eyes met, the woman hurried away down the street.

What? Is that bum following me?

As she approached Patty, she saw that her friend's lovely tie-dyed dress was torn in several places. Without a word, Mark slipped his letter jacket over her shoulders.

Alexia felt her pulse and temperature increase. She was sure that if the culprit was still around, she'd cave his head in with a kick. "What happened?"

The police officer pushed his glasses up on his nose. "Are you Miss LeBlanc? I'm Officer Ernest Penfold."

"Yes, I am," Alexia said.

Patty had buried her face in Mark's chest and was sobbing.

"What happened?" Alexia asked again.

"Your friend here had a bit too much to drink and started fooling around with one of the fraternity boys. Things got a little heated, and he went overboard. You know how guys can be."

She felt her temperature rise even more. "Wait, he tried to rape her?"

Officer Penfold shrugged. "I don't think it got that far, Miss LeBlanc. Your friend here screamed so loud, half the party came running. They pulled him off and gave us a call."

She looked at the house. Music and artificial fog were pouring out. She harrumphed. "Doesn't sound like they stopped the party for long. Can't you shut them down?"

"For what? They're keeping the noise at ordinance level, and there aren't so many in there as to break fire codes. The guy has been arrested for drunk and disorderly conduct. All we need is for you to get your friend home."

Feeling her blood pound in her veins, she said, "And that's it? Some drunken douche tries to rape my best friend and this is all you do?" She stuck her finger under the officer's nose. "I want that son-of-a-bitch arrested for sexual assault, do you hear me?"

With a scowl, Officer Penfold said, "I'd put that finger down before you end up spending the night in jail. No one saw what happened, and there's no evidence of an assault. Now, she has the right to press charges, but without witnesses, it's gonna be a tough case."

"No evidence?" Alexia said, incredulous. "Her fucking dress is half ripped off!" She only swore when truly enraged.

Mark cleared his throat. "Alexia, please."

Grinding her teeth, she glowered at him.

He ignored her. "Officer, forgive her. Patty is her best friend. Let us just take her home and call it a night."

Officer Penfold looked back and forth between her and Mark, then snorted. "Fine, but just watch your asses going back to campus. Remember, some Emory students are still missing." He spat to the side and got into his car.

"We will, Officer. We will."

Alexia was still glaring as the officer drove off. When Mark approached her, half-dragging Patty along, Alexia pointed at him. "And you! What the spit was that about? I'm trying to look out for my friend here."

Although Mark stepped back, he locked eyes with her, his gaze unflinching. "I'm not your enemy, Alexia. I know you're angry, but you were about to get in serious trouble. Don't you remember you're on permanent probation? You know, from kicking that sorority girl in the head during hazing? One more slip-up, on or off campus, and you're done. No more scholarship and no more Emory."

She sighed, feeling the will to argue drain from her. It was why she made sure to miss when throwing pens at people. She was constantly walking the line. "Fine. Let's just get Patty back to the dorm. Think we can get those frat boys to call us a cab?"

Patty, who was still sniffling, looked up from Mark's shirt, which was now soaked. "Actually, Alexia, can we walk?"

Shaking his head, Mark suddenly sounded nervous. "Um, that is not a very good idea. You heard what the policeman said. It's not safe."

"Please, Mark. Pleeeease!" Patty eyes were pitiful and doe-like. "I need the fresh air and a chance to clear my head."

When Mark looked helplessly at Alexia, she said, "I think we'll be fine. We can cut across the Druid Hills Golf Course."

"But, Alexia . . ." He was so anxious, his forehead was sweaty.

What's with him? She put it aside for now, figuring that if there was something going on, he'd tell her. After all, they didn't keep secrets. "Don't worry, honey. No one will mess with us. I am in a right good ass-kicking mood."

Mark sighed, defeated. "Fine. Just . . . let's be careful, OK?"

She clenched her fist. "Like I said. This is the wrong night for someone to mess with me."

The Druid Hill Golf Course, a private country club, had a tall wall around the property to ward off intruders. However, the locks on the gates were perpetually broken, and it was common knowledge that although Emory students were forbidden to go there, pretty much everyone used it as a shortcut late at night. And at that moment, Alexia couldn't care less about school rules. All she cared about was getting Patty safely home.

Walking along the fairways, the scent of freshly mowed lawn all around her and the grass crunching at her feet, she could see house lights on one side and the darkness of Fernbank Forest on the other. Ahead was Emory's campus. She figured that they had about an hour before they got to their dorms.

Mark quietly walked by her side, holding her hand, while Patty was on her other side, hugging her arm for protection. Suddenly, Patty stopped walking. She just stood there, her head down. "Hey, guys?"

Alexia, who had been keeping an eye out for potential threats, let go of Mark's hand and rubbed Patty's shoulders. "Yeah? What's up?"

Patty's lips were trembling. "Thank you. Ya know, for always being there for me. I know I'm a dummy. I always make terrible choices like tonight. But whenever you two are around, I feel like I can make it."

Alexia's heart swelled. She kissed Patty on the top of the head. "I'm here for you. All will be well, I promise. You'll be OK."

Mark came up behind Patty, still seeming nervous. "Yeah. You'll be fine, Patty. Let's get back to the dorm and make some of Alexia's special herbal tea."

"Yes," Alexia said. "We can listen to your favorite music, too. Anything you like."

Now Patty smiled, soft and trembling. "That would be nice." Then she started shifting from foot to foot. "Only one problem. I really, really gotta pee."

The sudden change in topic was so abrupt, Alexia couldn't help but laugh. Seeing that they were at the ninth hole, she scouted ahead until she saw a set of restrooms. They were unlocked, with the doors open and the lights off.

"We can use those," Alexia said, leading the others over.

Mark bit his bottom lip, eyes darting around. "All right, but hurry up."

She tapped his shoulder. "You OK?"

He nibbled his lip. "Just don't want to get in trouble."

But she could tell he was hiding something. She frowned. "What's wrong, honey?"

When he shook his head, she said, "Humph. Fine. Let's just go to the bathroom. Then we can get out of here, Mister Nervous Nelly."

It only took them a minute to do their business. The bathrooms were surprisingly spotless and smelled of pine cleaner. Mark, who said he didn't have to go, kept a lookout. That only made Alexia frown more. She felt like he was hiding something.

Outside, Patty was cocking her head toward the men's room. Curious, Alexia went over and did the same. Inside was heavy breathing, followed by a deep guttural groan.

What the heck? Is it a wild animal?

Alexia gathered her nerve and crept forward. Patty grabbed her hand and pulled back, terrified. "No. Don't!"

"It'll be OK. I'm just going to look. If it's some sort of dangerous animal, we'll need to call the police." She patted Patty's hand, then held it and glanced back toward Mark, who was several yards away and scanning the course. "Come on, before he notices and gets all anxious or something about us going into the men's room."

She slipped forward along a short stretch of interior wall that opened into the main restroom. Patty snuck along beside her, clutching her hand with a vise-like grip. At the edge of that wall, Alexia steeled herself, said a quick prayer, and peeked around the corner.

She was not expecting what she saw.

Chuck was standing at the far wall while Marcie was on her knees in front of him. Even though her head obfuscated what she was doing, it was absurdly apparent. His moans of pleasure, resonating in the bathroom's acoustics, made the low guttural groan Alexia had heard.

Her cheeks were burning as she ducked back behind the wall.

Patty's expression instantly went from scared to inquisitive. She ducked under Alexia and stuck her head around the corner. Her shoulders dropped. "Jeez, Marcie! Can't you wait to get back to the dorm?"

Alexia heard Marcie cry out in panic and Chuck stumble around. Rubbing her face, she then joined Patty. Marcie was busy trying to fix her hair, and Chuck was zipping up his pants, irritated. "Fucking hell, Mar-mer. You said no one would come by here."

"Oh, screw you, Chucky-Chuck!" Marcie washed out her mouth in the sink and glared at Alexia and Patty. "What the hell are you two doing here?"

The fire still glowed in Alexia's cheeks as she looked away.

"We were using the other bathroom," Patty said, folding her arms. "Although we were being quiet compared to you two."

Alexia's cheeks just grew hotter as Marcie paused and then slowly grinned.

Oh, come on. That's not what we—

"Oh, I get it now," Marcie said, smirking in a rude and condescending way. "Now I see why you won't let poor Mark into those pants of yours. Awesome Alexia is a carpet muncher."

Slapping her palm to her forehead, Alexia said, "No, you dumbass, that's not it at all. Tell them, Patty. Please."

Instead, Patty put an arm around her and started running her fingers around her stomach. "Oh, yes, you know it, Marcie the Martian Man-Mounter. Alexia and I are so gay, we make Ellen Morgan look like she loves the dick. And Alexia here is so butch. Can't you tell? Did you know she had a tattoo of Emily Dickinson on the inside of her right thigh?" She quivered and sucked in a shudder.

"Are you out of your freaking mind?" Alexia pushed her away, glaring.

Patty shrugged and motioned at Marcie as if to blame the entire thing on her.

And Marcie apparently bought the outrageous story as she laughed cruelly. "Wait until I tell everyone tomorrow. Oh, this is going to go in the campus dirt rag. I can see it now, 'Awesome Alexia Digs Skinny Chicks.'"

Chuck laughed as well. "No, no, wait! How about this: 'Angry Alexia Now Lesbian Lexi.'"

"Uh-oh," Patty muttered.

Alexia's jaw tightened and her temples pounded. That nickname was one of the few things that could make her lose her temper. She rushed over to him, grabbed his collar, and pulled his nose to hers. "Never call me Lexi, you dick!"

Just then, a loud, deep croaking sound tore through the night air like the rumble of approaching thunder. The fluorescent lights of the restroom flickered on and then went off. Alexia was momentarily blinded.

Marcie cried out. "What the hell was that?"

Alexia let go of Chuck, who stumbled back into a stall, yelping. "Ah! Mar-Mer!"

The air started getting chilly, more so than usual for a spring evening. In the dark, Patty grabbed her arm. "Alexia? What's going on?"

"I don't know! I don't—"

The lights flashed on again, and Alexia saw Marcie stumbling around, crying out, "Chuck? Chucky-Chuck?"

Then the lights went out, and Alexia was blind again. She heard Mark from the entrance of the bathroom. "Alexia! Patty! Where are you?"

"We're in here!" she yelled.

Again, Marcie called out, "Where are you, Chucky-Chuck?"

The lights flickered on again, and Alexia saw Marcie in the center of the restroom, her hands out as she blindly moved forward. Chuck was staggering at the entrance of the stall where he had fallen. The lights went out again, and Alexia was blinded once more. Patty buried her face against her arm.

This is freaking me out! Alexia thought.

As Marcie continued to plead for Chuck, another loud, deep croaking sound flowed through the air. Marcie and Patty squealed, and Alexia's body locked up as fear rippled through her very being.

Then Mark shouted, "Get out of there, now!"

The lights flickered back on. Chuck was nowhere to be found.

Patty bawled, "What the hell? Where did he go?"

"Chuck? Chucky-Chuck?" Marcie continued tripping as the lights went out again.

"Alexia! Patty! Please come out!" Mark sounded frantic. "I'm coming in!"

This time, Alexia had been ready, closing her eyes as the lights went on and then opening them right after they went out. The result was that she could see better in the dark than before. She met Marcie, who was stumbling blindly around, in the center of the restroom.

"Who's that?" Marcie whimpered.

"It's me, Alexia!"

"Where's my honey? Where's my Chucky-Chuck?"

Alexia couldn't see him. "I don't know. He was right there, and now he's gone!"

Patty whined. "Alexia, let's go. I'm scared!"

Closer now, Mark said, "Everyone, please listen. We have to leave."

Another deep croak rumbled throughout the room, making the light fixtures shake. Marcie stomped her feet. "Enough! Enough! Enough!"

Then the lights came back on, and Marcie grabbed Alexia's shirt. Mark was to the side of them both, his face pale with terror, reaching for them.

Alexia pulled back. "Let go, Marcie!"

"Shut up, you psycho-bitch! Everyone's right, you're a damn time bomb waiting to go off. You tell me where my Chuck is, Lexi, or so help me—"

Marcie stopped as liquid started dripping on her and Alexia's faces. Alexia smeared some off and inspected it. It was hot, had a pungent, metal smell, and was a deep, dark red.

Blood.

Patty started blubbering, "No, no, no, no, no, no . . ."

Slowly, their faces paling, everyone looked up.

Chuck was pressed up into the ceiling as if his body was a part of it. His arms and legs were pulled back and covered by a pool of deep red blood. His skin was as white as porcelain, his veins as black as pitch, his eyes bloodshot, and his jaw opened so wide that it seemed unhinged. All around him were tiny black tendrils worming in and out of his flesh like maggots eating carrion. His eyes were filled with pain and panic as he focused on everyone. His throat tensed, his tongue dripped down like a droplet of water on a string, and from his mouth issued forth the most disturbingly deep and rattling croak.

Alexia, Patty, Mark and Marcie all shrieked as the lights went out.

Still screaming, Alexia and Patty stumbled back. In front of them, Marcie screeched even louder as the blood dripped down on her like a deep, crimson shower.

As Patty trembled against Alexia, Mark grabbed her shoulders. "We gotta go."

Then Alexia's survival instincts kicked in. She scrambled to her feet and yanked Patty with her. "Patty! Run!"

Mark grabbed her hand and pulled her toward the exit. All three of them stumbled out of the bathroom into the cool night air. They tripped at the entrance and fell over each other. Her breasts impacting the ground was painful, and she rolled to the side, crying out. Someone had hit Mark in the groin, and he fell back and retched. Patty clung to Alexia, crying like a little kid. "Ohmigod, ohmigod! What was that?"

Scooting away from the door and gripping her cross locket, Alexia fought to stabilize the shakes. Despite the courage she thought she had always possessed, this was something she wasn't prepared for. Every part of her shook with terror. "I don't know, Patty. I don't know!"

From inside the restroom came another cry. Alexia felt helpless as she realized that Marcie was still in there.

"We need . . . to run," Mark groaned.

Alexia struggled to her feet. "Marcie's trapped! I gotta get her. I can't leave her!"

Patty clung to her and pulled. "Nooooo! Don't go in theeeeeere!"

"I have to! I have—"

She stopped as Marcie staggered to the door of the restroom. She was covered in blood and had a large gash along her stomach. She held her guts with one hand and reached out with the other.

"Alexia . . . Help me . . . ," she said. Then suddenly, she was thrown to the ground as if someone had grabbed her feet and pulled.

Falling to her knees, her body locked up again. Alexia watched in horror as Marcie tried to crawl out. All she could do was reach out to her. "Marcie . . . ?"

"Help . . . me . . . ," Marcie said once more, her voice weak. Saliva dripped from her lips. Then she let out a blood-curdling squeal as something yet unseen pulled her back into the darkness of the restroom. The door swung shut.

Then there was silence.

Trembling, Alexia stared at the door. Patty was sobbing into her arm. Mark was throwing up. Pushing her fear down into her stomach long enough to engage the flight response, she got up and then helped both Mark and Patty stand. "We're going. We're going now. Run. Just run."

The three of them sprinted all the way back to campus.

Chapter 28
Lullwater

Date: Saturday, April 22, 1995
Time: 9:00 a.m.
Location: Druid Hills Police Station
Druid Hills, Atlanta, Georgia

Officer Penfold stopped writing long enough to rub his balding head, scratch his thick, trimmed mustache, and push his glasses back up. "So you saw the first student get sucked inside the ceiling of the restroom and saw the second one dragged back into it by an unknown assailant?"

Alexia nodded, straining to keep her eyes open. It was nearly nine in the morning, and she hadn't slept yet. As soon as they had reached the dorms, Mark had told them to stay put until he returned. Then he'd run off.

But Alexia knew she couldn't wait. Something inhuman had murdered Marcie and Chuck, and it was likely the same thing behind the other student disappearances. Thinking about what Michael would have done, she contacted campus security, who immediately brought them to the county police.

Now she was sitting in the open area of a police station across from the same officer she had copped an attitude toward the night before, holding a cup of long-cooled coffee. Nearby, Patty was curled up on a row of seats, fast asleep.

Clearing his throat, Officer Penfold asked, "So you're sure that you saw this instead of, say, nothing? I mean, I did clearly instruct you to bring your friend home, but if you had decided to detour for, you know, a bit of toking—"

"We weren't doing drugs, Officer," Alexia interrupted. "I know what I saw. If you just go to the men's restroom on the, um, the ninth hole, you'll see that I'm not joking. There should be blood positively everywhere. I'm sure that any moment, they'll call about it!"

He grunted and rubbed his scalp again, muttering to himself before heading over to the water cooler. He took his time getting a cold drink from a paper cup. When he finished, he tossed his cup into the trash, went back over to his desk, and sat on the edge. Thumbs hooked on his belt, he leaned down and gazed into her eyes.

Is he sizing me up?

"You haven't touched your coffee," he said. His breath stank of it.

"I hate coffee," she replied, recoiling from his smell.

With a shrug, he said, "All right. Let's go check out this bloody shitter you saw. You can let your friend sleep there on the chairs. Someone'll bring her home."

Sighing, she rubbed Patty's shoulder and then followed him outside.

Once she got outside, she felt someone staring at her. Looking across the street, she saw the same derelict blond woman as before, sitting on the curb and holding a Styrofoam cup in her hands. Alexia locked eyes with her just before Officer Penfold helped her into the car.

Huh . . . who is that woman?

"I just want you to know," he said as they drove, "that it's a bad idea to lie to an officer. Just remember that."

She scowled. "I try never to lie."

"Humph."

When they arrived at the golf course, there were already three other police cars. Immediately, Alexia felt vindicated. They must have found the blood. Now they would know she wasn't lying.

The inside of the clubhouse boasted of its class with shiny, wooden floors; soft, plush rugs; and sparkling chandeliers. The scent of wood polish wafted through the air. There were three policemen already inside, talking to an older gentleman in a tailored suit. He had an air of importance. Near him was a woman with shoulder-length, auburn hair, wearing a trench coat. She was writing in a small notebook at a desk. Alexia looked from the man to the woman and back again, certain she had seen both of them before but unable to place where.

"Mr. Candler." Officer Penfold cleared his throat and placed his hand firmly on Alexia's shoulder. His grip tightened. "This is Miss Alexia LeBlanc. She reported an attack on two Emory students in the men's restroom at the ninth hole last night. She claims there was blood everywhere."

The auburn-haired woman quickly glanced at Alexia, her eyes widening. Then, as if masking her reaction, she quickly looked away.

Um, that was strange.

"Is that so, Officer?" Mr. Candler asked. Approaching Alexia, he regarded her with what could only be curiosity. Then he smiled in a grandfatherly fashion. "I'm Asa Griggs Candler the Fifth. Why don't you tell me what happened last night, Miss LeBlanc?"

Alexia, who was still scrutinizing the woman, balked at the man's introduction. "I recognize you! You're the descendant of Asa Griggs Candler, the founder of Coca-Cola. Wow." He was quite possibly the wealthiest and most influential man in Atlanta.

"Now there's a bright girl, one who knows her history," he said, removing Officer Penfold's hand from Alexia's shoulder and patting her upper arm. "Yes, Miss LeBlanc, you are correct. However, right now, I'm less of a businessman and more of a concerned citizen."

He turned toward the auburn-haired woman. "That should be enough for your report, Miss Carter. Have a nice day."

"Nice to meet you, Mr. Candler," the woman said. She slid her notebook into a coat pocket. "Please call me if there are any new developments. Have a good day."

As the woman passed her, Alexia noticed that her left arm never moved and that the fingers were motionless inside a leather glove. She figured it had to be a prosthetic.

Who is that woman? It was maddening that she couldn't place her.

Once the woman was gone, Mr. Candler leaned inward. "Now, please tell me what happened last night."

Taking a deep breath, Alexia recounted what had happened the night before, finishing with, "So, then, Patty, Mark, and I ran back to the university. When I went to the campus police, they sent me here." She folded her arms under her chest.

Mr. Candler's expression had turned serious. "Officer, I think you need to bring Miss LeBlanc with us."

"Yes, Mr. Candler," Officer Penfold said. Again, he grabbed her shoulder.

Unsure of what was happening, Alexia fidgeted as she was walked outside. "Hey, am I being detained? Don't I have any rights here?"

"Shut up if you know what's good for you," Officer Penfold said.

"That attitude won't be necessary at this time, Officer," Mr. Chandler said.

They got into a golf cart and rode along the course.

"And as for your rights," Mr. Chandler continued, "you only need worry if I press charges. Right now, we're just going for a friendly drive to the ninth hole. You like drives, don't you, Miss LeBlanc?"

Why are the police treating this guy like he owns them? Alexia was starting to get nervous. This scenario was well outside how she felt the world should work. She didn't like it one bit.

When they reached the ninth hole, she saw police tape over the entrance to the men's room. There was no blood trail from where Marcie was dragged inside. Ducking under the tape, all three of them entered. When Alexia saw the inside, her mouth dropped open.

Nothing. Not a speck of blood. The faint scent of pine cleaner was the only thing she could smell. Otherwise, the bathroom was completely clean, except for one thing—every single mirror was broken.

Mr. Candler motioned around the room. "So, as you can see, Miss LeBlanc, there is no blood. Just some vandalized mirrors and broken glass. Wouldn't you say that's odd?"

"You think I did this?" she asked, feeling sicker every moment.

He tousled her hair as if she were a child. "Well, I think that if you didn't do it, you saw it happen. Our security cameras caught you and your two friends running out the back gate. You all seemed positively terrified. Maybe there were dangerous people here and you concocted that ridiculous story because you were frightened."

Then he leaned down. He sounded like a wolf cornering its prey. "Is that what happened, Miss LeBlanc? Were you frightened?"

Fear indeed ran through her—fear of getting arrested, fear of getting expelled, and fear of being sent home in shame. Tears started welling up in her eyes. She didn't know what was going on, if this was some sort of conspiracy or if she had just imagined the whole thing. Her normally iron-clad will was fractured from trauma and lack of sleep. All wanted was to go to bed.

Lord, I'm sorry I'm not strong enough to endure this. Forgive me for lying.

"I couldn't really make them out. One of them kept turning the lights on and off. But there were two or three of them. Big guys. Didn't look like Emory students." She had never hated herself so much. Pressing her hands to her face, she started sobbing.

I wish Michael was here.

Mr. Candler ruffled her hair. "Awww, now, don't cry. You're being more helpful than you realize. Officer, I think we're done. You can take Miss LeBlanc back to the station. She's been through enough today."

Officer Penfold nudged her. "All right. Come on. Let's get you back to your friend."

Alexia nodded and wiped her eyes. As she started leaving, a flash caught her eye and what looked like a small, white orb flitted past her. No one else seemed to notice. Blinking away the tears, she saw it float toward the middle of the room. It circled around the drain and then vanished. A moment later, she realized that the area immediately around the drain was stained red.

Oh, God. It did happen. I didn't imagine it.

As she continued staring at the stain, a raspy voice bubbled out, "Lullwater."

She jerked to a stop. "Did you hear that?"

But Mr. Candler pushed her hard and said, "Let's go, young lady. Time to leave."

They took her back outside. As she stumbled into the golf cart, she searched her repository of knowledge for anything about Lullwater. But it was no use. Her thoughts were too muddled, too murky. She was just too worn out.

As soon as Officer Penfold brought her back to the police station, Alexia woke Patty up. She was still preoccupied with what the voice had said. *Lullwater. What is Lullwater?*

After she awoke, Patty hugged Alexia and whispered, "I wanna go home."

Alexia hugged her back. "Anything else, Officer?"

He shook his head. "Nah, you two are free to go."

As they started leaving, he said, "Oh, Miss LeBlanc."

"Yeah?"

"If I were you, I'd watch myself for a few weeks. You're lucky as hell you're not in jail."

She sighed, tired of being bullied. "Sure thing, Officer."

Once outside, standing amongst the hot stink of streets in the mid-morning, Alexia tried to flag down a cab. As she waved her arms to no avail, someone grabbed her shoulder. She turned, ready to kick whoever it was. Then she stopped. It was the blond derelict woman. The left side of her face was covered in burn scars.

"Are you Alexia LeBlanc?" she asked.

Staring at her, Alexia blinked, unsure of how to respond.

The woman positively reeked of booze and garbage. "Are you Alexia LeBlanc?"

"Alexia, who is this?" Patty said from behind her.

Alexia tried to pull away, but the woman held on tight, her strength like a vise.

"What the heck?" Alexia asked. "Lady, who are you?"

Gnawing on her bottom lip, the woman looked past Alexia and then back at her. She mumbled to herself for a few moments, rubbing her filthy face.

Oh, crap! It's one of those crazies.

"Lady, I've had a shit day. Let me go or I'll scream. I swear it!"

"What?" the woman said. "No. You're in serious danger. It's marked you. It senses your will. It wants to consume you. It—"

Then the woman looked past her again. This time, her face paled. "No, I can't stay here," she said to no one in particular. "That wasn't the deal. I'm only dealing with Alexia, not anyone else. I won't do it!"

Before Alexia knew what was happening, the woman was running away.

Patty shivered. "Who the hell was that? What's going on?"

Alexia opened her mouth to answer, but nothing came out. She couldn't think of a single thing to say. All she could do was watch the blond woman vanish into the morning crowd of people as if she were a ghost.

My poor, tired brain can't handle this anymore.

Before she could reflect on it any further, another voice called out. "Excuse me, are you Alexia LeBlanc, the sister of Michael LeBlanc?"

She jerked her head toward the voice, unsure what to expect. It was the woman Mr. Candler had called "Miss Carter." She was driving a black Porsche convertible.

"How does she know your brother?" Patty asked.

Through the exhausted haze of her muddled mind, Alexia somehow put two and two together. "You. You're Dixie, right?" No wonder she had seemed familiar earlier.

"Yes. And since you've figured out who I am, I assume you got my postcard?"

"Yeah, I did." *Was the blond woman afraid of Dixie seeing her?*

Dixie smiled broadly. "Well, hop in, you two. I'll give you a ride back to campus."

Taking the back road to Emory, passing through Fernbank Forest, Dixie went slowly enough to talk to Alexia and Patty, who was sitting in the back. The first thing Dixie did was have Alexia recount what had happened the previous night.

When the story was over, Dixie said, "So that's what happened. No wonder Mr. Candler is keeping a gag order on the police and the media."

"He can do that?" Alexia asked. Such a thing seemed like fantasy.

"He is one of the most powerful men in Atlanta, if not Georgia," Dixie said. "Trust me. I know a lot about the power men can wield with money. You'd be surprised."

"I guess. So, you posed as a reporter for the *New York Times* to speak to Mr. Candler about last night?"

"Yes. I may live in New York, but I still maintain contact with people in New Orleans. One of them in particular, a Dr. Lazarus, is good friends with the president of Emory. So a group of us are investigating what's been going on around here."

"A group of you?"

"Well, the others have been here for a while. They called me down here when the students started vanishing. The whole case is rather complicated, actually."

"So what's going on?" Patty asked.

"That's just it," Dixie said. "We're not completely sure. This is the first time we've had an eyewitness account."

"What about Mark?" Alexia asked. "He was there. Have you spoken to him yet?"

Dixie spared her a quick glance. "Mark is one of us. He's how I knew about the attack last night. He told us after dropping you off at the dorms."

Alexia felt her mind hit a brick wall.

"Oh, my God, are you serious?" Patty started laughing. She sounded a little unhinged by all that had happened. "You're kidding. Mister Super-Straight Always-Serious Mark is investigating crazy, bloody boo-doo murders?"

Dixie brought the car to a stop. They were just outside of Fernbank Forest. She half-turned in her seat. "Mark. His uncle Serge. Even Leona. All three of them are investigating Druid Hills."

As Alexia wrapped her arms around herself, unsure how to feel, Patty shook her head. "Man, this is crazy. This can't be happening. Why are you even telling us this?"

"The two of you, whether you like it or not, have gotten drawn into this. And I believe you deserve to know the truth."

But Alexia could only focus on what she had learned about Mark. *Was that why he was acting so weird before the attack?* Her head had started pounding. She needed to sleep. She needed to think. And she wasn't being afforded either luxury.

"Anyway," Dixie said, starting the car moving again, "I spoke with the others. We want you both to lay low. Go about your normal lives and make sure to stay on campus. You're safest there."

"Sure thing," Patty said.

Alexia kept quiet, still processing everything. The rest of the ride back to the dorm was in total silence.

When Dixie stopped in front of the undergraduate residences, she rested her hand on Alexia's shoulder. "Listen. I did come here on business, but I also wanted to meet you. I never intended for you to get caught up in this. I'm sorry."

Feeling what little patience she had for the world slipping, Alexia managed a small nod. She needed to sleep soon or she was going to start kicking faces.

"So when we get a chance," Dixie said, "I want to talk with you. Alone. About Michael."

That got her attention. "OK. Lemme sleep first. Brain shutting down."

Dixie patted her hand. "I understand. Go rest, hun. I'll contact you later."

Students were already heading out to enjoy their Saturday. As Patty and Alexia went inside, Patty asked, "So why do you think she wants to talk to you about your brother?"

Alexia's head was really starting to throb. "I don't know. I hope it's good. I'm tired of bad news."

Holding her dorm room phone to her ear, Alexia fought back rising tears.

"Hello, Mark? Are you there? Please pick up." There was no answer, just as there hadn't been the last three times. Alexia hung up the phone and dried her eyes.

"Give it up and get some rest," Patty said. She was in her nightgown and hugging a pillow to her chest. "He's probably busy with whatever this secret group is doing."

"He's not supposed to keep secrets from me." Alexia sniffled loudly. At that moment, she utterly hated herself. Gone was the self-control and ironclad will. Gone was the keen intellect she had spent years honing. And gone were the walls around her heart she had erected since her brother had died. The stress and emotion of the night before was ebbing it all away. Now she only wanted someone to protect her, like Michael used to.

Patty moved behind her, hugging her gently. "Hey, you're gonna be OK, right? Awesome Alexia is always OK, right?"

Shaking, Alexia turned around and pulled Patty into her arms. Her carefully constructed paradigm of how life should be was falling apart. It was no longer about going to class, excelling in fencing and savate, and dating a cute guy. It was about a murder that seemed right out of a horror movie and a secret group investigating it.

Real life was not supposed to be this way.

She began to sob silently.

Patty led her to her bed, sat her down, and rubbed her shoulders. "Man, this is weird. Every other time, it's been you comforting me."

"I'm sorry I'm so weak," Alexia said between sobs. "I'm supposed to be the strong one."

"Strong one? Weak one? You've got to let that go." Patty softly chuckled. "We're none of that. We're friends. That's all there is."

"Yeah?" Alexia dried her eyes.

"Yeah," Patty said. "I don't know why you get hung up on labels of weak and strong. Actually, I think I do. I'm a screw-up, and you want to protect me. Heck, maybe by saving me, you can somehow make up for Michael dying."

With a hiccup, Alexia giggled uneasily. "I didn't know you were a psychologist." The assessment was perfectly accurate.

"I read a lot," Patty said. "But I want you to know that when it comes to us, there doesn't have to be a set role. Nothing says that sometimes I can't guide you or teach you or comfort you. That's what it means to be friends, Alexia. We do whatever the other needs when it's necessary."

Alexia sniffled again—hard—and rubbed her nose. "Are you sure?"

Moving to her side, Patty smiled up at her. "I'm as sure of that as I am of anything. I know I make terrible decisions and often need you to bail me out. But I'm not so pathetic that I can't save you from time to time."

Slowly, Alexia smiled back. It was like Patty had grown up right there in front of her. *Or maybe she's always been grown-up and I didn't realize it.*

Leaning down, she kissed Patty gently on the forehead. "Thank you, Patty. We are best friends. And I do love you."

Blushing a little, Patty said, "Love me? Ya know, we could become lovers. Two girls and a dozen cats. All the pussy we could wa—"

With a groan, Alexia hit her best friend with a pillow. "Oh, shut up. Seriously, you keep talking like that, and I'm going to think you really are gay." But her dark mood had lifted.

Patty rubbed her nose. "Now that's the Alexia I know and love . . . in a totally celibate way." She waggled her eyebrows.

Snickering, Alexia said, "Fine, I'm in a better mood, you dork. Now, enough talk. Let's get some rest."

She lay down on the bed with Patty settling next to her.

Yawning, Patty rested against her arm. "Hey, Alexia, can we make a promise?"

"Hmmm? What?"

"Can we always stick together?"

Alexia put her arm around Patty. If there was one thing she could count on now, it was her best friend. And with the adrenaline of the morning finally gone, the muddled mess in her head was back in full force. She needed sleep.

"Sounds good," she said, pulling a blanket over them both. "Wherever I go, Patty, I'd like you with me."

It was as good an oath as any between friends.

Chapter 29
Eversoll

Date: Saturday, April 22, 1995
Time: 7:00 p.m.
Location: Undergraduate Residences
Emory University, Atlanta, Georgia

"Oh, wow, that pizza really hit the spot." Patty leaned back in the cafeteria, rubbing her tummy.

Alexia finished the last of her grilled chicken salad. "That was an extra large. How do you eat so much?"

Patty gulped down her third Dr. Pepper and then belched into her hand. "With my mouth!"

"That's not what I meant!" Alexia snickered. The eight hours of sleep, the hot shower, the food, and Patty's general cheerfulness had helped her a lot, despite the horror they'd witnessed.

"So, about the douche who tried to rape me," Patty said, popping open another can of soda. "I want to file charges, but not until after this weird stuff is done. I don't want a battle on two fronts."

Sipping her iced tea, Alexia said, "Good idea. The statute of limitations on sexual battery is like six or seven years. We've got time." It felt good to be able to think clearly again. Now she could finally focus on the night before.

The clue that stood out the most was the word "lullwater." It sounded familiar, and Dixie and the others needed to hear about it.

"Hey, Patty, I want to go to the Woodruff Center and speak to Serge."

Patty blinked. "Who what now?"

Snickering again, Alexia leaned forward. "Let me say it slowly. I want to tell Serge about something I saw. Something important."

"Oh! Didn't Dixie tell us to stay here?"

Alexia scowled. Her sense of justice wouldn't let her sit idly by. "Others could die in the meantime. You heard the rumors about Marcie and Chuck—people think they went to Atlanta to go clubbing. There's a conspiracy covering up the truth, and that's not OK. So it's our duty to tell whoever's trying to solve this everything we know."

Patty laid her head on the table and groaned. "And I was hoping to watch a good chick flick with you tonight."

Reaching over, Alexia tousled her hair. "When we get back, I'll watch any movie you want. Sound fair?"

Patty stood and stretched. "All right, girlfriend. Let's toss our trash and go for a walk!"

They had just exited the residences when Alexia heard a boisterous voice call out, "Alexia! Over here!"

It was Helen, the freshman, waving at her with an exaggerated motion.

"Oh, hey, Helen. Good to see you." Alexia waved back. "What's going on?"

Helen bounced over, looking way happier than any person ever should. "Just finished dinner and heading to the quad. What're you up to?"

Sweating a little at the younger girl's exuberance, Alexia said, "Um, you know, just going for a walk. Gonna stop by the fencing hall to talk to Mr. Eversoll about . . . stuff."

"Ah, cool!" Helen slipped up beside her and grabbed one of her arms in a hug. "Let me tag along. I left my foil in my locker, and I need to clean it. Otherwise, Leona's gonna skin me."

From Alexia's other side, Patty peered at her. "And how long has this bit of cheating been going on?"

Alexia sweated more. "It's not like that, Patty. Helen's on the fencing team with me."

"Yeah!" Helen exclaimed. "So I've got just as much a right to Awesome Alexia's arm-space as you do, whoever you are!" She stuck her tongue out.

Patty stuck her tongue out as well. "Oh yeah? Well, I'm Alexia's best friend and roommate. You ain't got a prayer, girlie!"

Rolling her eyes, Alexia mumbled, "This is ridiculous." Still, the banter of the two girls for her attention was a welcome respite from the stress of the night before.

Finally, she tugged both of them down the road, heading toward the campus park. "Look, we can all be friends. Let's just have fun and enjoy the evening, OK?"

While Patty and Helen nodded in agreement, they stuck their tongues out at each other once more.

The campus park was as well-lit as the golf course. All around the concrete pathways were gas lamps made to look like old-fashioned streetlights. No one else was around, since it was a Saturday night and most of students were in town or at the quad. The fresh scent of spring woods filled the air, reminding Alexia of the pine groves and babbling brooks of Shreveport.

Helen had talked the entire time. "When my friends are all busy, I like to come here and draw birds at the lake. This has got to be my favorite part of the entire campus. Well, other than the cafeteria on Taco Tuesday!"

As Helen and Patty laughed together, Alexia felt herself relax even more.

"And Lullwater Park Trail has got to be one of the most peaceful places in the evenings," Helen said.

Hearing the word "Lullwater" made Alexia stop short. She jumped in front of Helen. "Wait!"

Helen stumbled. "What is it, Alexia?"

Patty watched curiously.

"You said 'Lullwater Park Trail,' right?" Alexia asked.

Looking around as if expecting a prank, Helen said, "We're walking on Lullwater Park Trail right now. It cuts through the park. How did you not know that?"

Alexia stepped back. *She's right. How could I not know that?*

Patty snorted. "Oh, right, because the one class you blew off was Emory History. And God knows you never do something as simple as read a campus map. That's Alexia for you. Can't see the forest for the green."

A surge of panic rose up inside Alexia. Patty was right—she had failed at something so simple. What else did she not know? She grabbed Helen. "What can you tell me about Lullwater? Where did 'Lullwater' come from? Tell me!" Such an amateurish failure was unacceptable.

Suddenly, Helen was wailing and trying to pull away.

Patty yelled, "Stop it! You're hurting her!"

There was fear and pain in Helen's eyes. Alexia realized that her fingers were digging into Helen's shoulders, and she let go.

Helen stumbled back, clutching her shoulders. "What the hell is wrong with you? I thought those rumors about Angry Alexia were stupid, but you really are nuts!"

Instantly, Alexia felt sick to her stomach. She held out her hands. "I'm sorry! I swear it's not like that. It's just—"

"Leave me alone!" Helen ran down the trail.

Patty regarded Alexia with concern. "Hey, you OK? I know we saw two people die horribly last night, but you've been freaking at the drop of a hat."

Holding her arms around herself, Alexia closed her eyes and imagined all of her wild emotions being heaps of loose packing peanuts. Then she gathered them and pushed them into a box, compressing them until she could close the box. The shivering stopped. Then she said, "I'm not dealing with this very well, am I?"

Once again, Patty put her arms around her. "I never thought I'd see you like this. What will it take to help? Talking to Serge? Finding Mark? Going off with Dixie? Tell me, and I'll make it happen."

Alexia hugged back. Again, Patty was taking care of her. "I just want things to make sense. Even what happened last night has to have a rational explanation." Once more, she found herself wishing that Michael were still alive. He'd solve this like he solved the new Bourbon Street Ripper case.

"Well," Patty said, "despite believing in fairy tales and fables, I know reality doesn't allow for people to get turned into bloody ceilings. But that's what happened. We have to trust that Dixie and her people will—"

A shrill squeal split the night air. Alexia felt her blood chill.

"Oh, crap. Patty, it's Helen!"

They sprinted toward the cry. When they reached a bend in the trail, the lights along the path started to flicker just like the bathroom lights at the golf course.

Cupping her hands to her mouth, Alexia shouted, "Helen!"

Patty joined her. "Helen! Where are you?"

"Help me!" Helen called from the wooded area off the trail. "Oh, God, Alexia, please help me!"

They both stumbled into the brush, the twigs and overgrowth slowing them down. "Helen! Helen, can you hear me?" Alexia's heart was pounding.

"Help me, please! Oh, God, help me! It's right behind me!" Helen was crying.

Patty grabbed Alexia's arm. "I'm scared!" Alexia squeezed her hand, now protecting her.

"Helen! We're coming!" She ran as fast as she could, Patty in tow.

When they came upon Helen, it was in a small clearing lit only by the moonlight. The area was as cool as an autumn evening. She was pressed against a tree and staring out into the open. Her face was terror-stricken.

As soon as she saw Helen, Alexia yelled, "Helen! We're here!"

She ran forward . . .

. . . and stopped when Patty pulled her back.

"What the heck? Patty, let go!"

Patty's face was pale, and her eyes were wide and glassy. Her voice cracked. "Alexia. It's looking right at you."

Alexia stared back into the clearing. It took her brain a few moments to register what she saw.

Floating in mid-air was a pale, white entity that looked like it was made of fog. It was wrapped in a tattered, full-body, hooded cloak. Its bony hands and legs stuck out, and the hood barely showed its face—a skull. It smelled of death. It was watching Alexia, its bony mouth grinning. Then its jaw unhinged and let out a long, loud, deep, rattling croak, the same sound as at the golf course.

Next to her, Patty trembled.

God help me, Alexia thought, too terrified to move.

It started floating toward them and then stopped. Its grin turned to a grimace.

Christ have mercy on me. Alexia put every fiber of her being into her plea.

Snarling, the entity let out another horrible croak. As it did, Helen screamed again. Looking back, it rushed at her. She threw up her arms in defense just as the entity flew into her and vanished completely.

Alexia felt faint. She smelled piss as Patty started urinating.

Helen slowly turned toward them, her skin turning bleach white. She held out her arms, looking down at them, as her veins turned pitch black, growing and pulsing wildly through the skin. As the blackness crept up her face along the vein lines, she looked back at her friends. Her face was constricted in agony.

"Alexia. Please . . . help me . . . !"

With a sickeningly wet sound, Helen's veins exploded in a shower of dark blood. She let out a deep gurgle that turned into a croak, just like the entity, as the blood solidified and turned into wormlike tendrils. Each tendril then buried itself in the ground.

Alexia watched, her heart pounding in her throat, as the dying figure of Helen was pulled into the earth by her own blood.

Sliding to her knees, Patty whimpered. "Mommy, Mommy, Mommy . . ."

Her knees shaking, Alexia's body jerked, then lurched. But it was rooted to the spot.

Move, Alexia. Move, damn you!

With a hard push, she willed her legs forward. "Come on! We gotta run! We gotta run!"

But Patty just knelt there, stinking of piss, gibbering to herself. "Sunshine and castles and pretty maidens and kitty cats . . ."

"Come on!" Alexia said, shaking her. "We have got to go now!"

Patty stared at her blankly, her lips trembling. "I made a tinkle."

Another long, loud croak drew her attention. The entity rose from the ground, its hollow sockets boring down on them. It pointed at Patty. The intention was clear.

That knocked Patty out of her shock. She shrieked.

Alexia stood between them. "Leave her alone!"

It sneered at her and let out another awful rattle.

Oh, dear Lord. She grabbed the cross locket around her neck.

It reared back as if about to charge.

She closed her eyes and prayed, "Although I walk in the shadow of the valley of death, I shall fear no evil." Then she steeled herself for death.

But death didn't come. Slowly, she opened one eye, then the other.

It still hovered before her. And once more, it was gritting its teeth.

My prayer? Oh, sweet, merciful God, please protect me.

She continued praying. "I shall fear no evil, for you are with me. Your rod and your staff, they comfort me."

It shifted and let out a low growl. Its tattered cloak started peeling away.

"The Lord is my shepherd, I shall not want," she said. Her head was starting to throb. She didn't know if she could keep this up.

The entity spoke in a deep throaty voice. "I felt your will last night, mortal. It insults me. Your life is mine."

Hearing it speak took away all will to fight. She just wanted to run.

A white flash caught her eye, the same kind that had drawn her attention to the blood-stained drain in the golf course. Off to the side, she saw a small, white orb floating in between a set of trees. Something about that light felt safe. She grabbed her locket and squeezed once more.

As the entity let out another loud croak, Alexia said, "This way!" They ran after the orb. She heard the apparition behind them, giving chase.

As they ran through the brush, the small, white orb stayed just barely within view, leading the way. Behind them, she could feel the entity, hear its croak, and smell its stench of decay.

Suddenly, light burst forth as they exited the brush and stumbled into another person.

"Alexia? Patty?" It was Mark.

Patty wrapped her arms around his waist and wailed while Alexia pulled on his hand. "We gotta go! We gotta—"

At that moment, the entity burst from the woods. Patty screeched and buried her head in Mark's chest.

"Alexia, stand back!" he said. Only then did she notice he was dressed in a dark set of clothing: a tight-fitting shirt, leather pants, boots, and gloves. A pair of rapiers hung from a large belt on his hips.

"Mark? What's going on?"

With one motion, Mark pushed Patty into Alexia's arms and drew out his swords. In the moonlight, they almost seemed to glow. The entity locked eyes with him and let out its terrible rattle, its unhinged jaw dropping past its hood.

Patty, who was clutching Alexia for dear life, sobbed and then went limp. Alexia sank to her knees. Her strength was exhausted, and her momentum was gone. All she could do was watch in disbelief as Mark faced off against it.

Yelling in Scandinavian, he rushed forward, swinging both blades. With a surprised look, it drew back from the blows. Then it grunted hollowly and, diving into the ground, vanished like mist. "It is the girl, not you, who repelled my power. She is marked. I will have her life!"

As Mark turned back toward her, sheathing his blades, she felt the final threads of her strength break. With a weak exhale, she fell to the ground.

Mark. You saved me.

He ran to her as her mind was engulfed in darkness.

After what felt like hours, Alexia awoke on a cot in a small, dark room that felt eerily familiar. Outside, she heard the sound of metal hitting metal in rapid succession.

She sat up and felt a painful pulling on her side. She found that her ribs were taped. Also, she was only in her underwear. Sitting still, she listened. Other than the distinct, metallic clanking, she could also hear gentle snoring no more than a few feet away. The room was cool and smelled of bandages and antiseptic. She began to comprehend where she might be.

Let's see, there should be a string for the light . . . right . . . here.

The light came on in the trainer room of the fencing hall. It was the place where team members were sent to rest and recover from injuries. Patty was sleeping on a nearby cot, curled up in a ball. Their clothing, mended and cleaned, lay folded on Serge's desk

Alexia knelt at her best friend's side. *Patty.* She smoothed back her hair, kissing her forehead. Watching her sleep like that made her feel more protective than ever. Once again, she was the big sister.

I'm so glad you're OK.

She quietly and carefully got dressed. Heading out to the fencing hall, she saw that it was still nighttime. Serge and Leona were hard at practice, their masks and suits off. They moved without effort or constraint. Watching them like this was like watching a choreographed dance.

On the other side of the room, Mark practiced with two foils on a padded dummy. The two rapiers rested on a bench nearby. Dixie sat at what was often used as the judge's table, which was covered with notes. She was talking on a phone while nibbling nervously on her thumb.

"Dr. Lazarus, please listen. I think Dr. Kindley has the book. Remember when Hannah wiped out Tulane? I talked to him for a short while then, and parts of his clothing were glowing. . . I think he made what you call talismans. . . No, I don't know where he got the souls for them. . . No, I haven't told Ouellette. I'm not sure how he'd react. . . All right, I'll call him tomorrow."

That's some crazy talk over there, Alexia thought as she watched Serge and Leona. As their practice concluded, they leaned in until their lips were almost touching. Leona's cheeks were furiously rosy, and Serge's face had an intense expression. Alexia's mouth gaped open as she saw that they were both wearing golden wedding bands.

Just as their lips were about to touch, Alexia cleared her throat. Immediately, Leona pulled away and headed toward some bottles of water, blushing to her ears. Serge had a pleased, if not guilty, smile. Mark put down his foils while Dixie used her one arm to stand.

Alexia limped over to everyone, her ribs hurting. "Hey. How's it going?" She had no idea what to say in this kind of situation.

Serge wiped the sweat from his brow. "Good to see you are well, Alexia." His accent was so thick from his physical exertion that she had to strain to understand him.

"I'm well as can be expected, sir."

"Mark told us what happened," Leona said. "What do you know about that creature?" Her French accent was also thick from being out of breath. She handed out cool bottles of water.

Alexia sipped hers. It felt good. "Nothing, I'm afraid."

Mark pulled her into his arms. "I was so worried about you, baby. I was so scared."

She rested her head against his chest and held onto him. "Thank you for saving me." She wasn't sure what else to say, to him in particular.

Dixie finally came over. "Serge, I spoke with Dr. Lazarus. We need to tell Alexia everything. Considering what she's been through, she deserves to know."

"All right," he said. "Alexia, please pay attention."

Looking up from Mark's chest, she stepped away and drained her water bottle. Then she folded her arms under her chest, trying to sound strong again. "I'm listening, sir."

"*Ja*," Serge said. "My father, Dr. Oskar Eversoll, runs a group based out of Copenhagen called the Eversoll Institute for Paranormal Research."

Alexia shrugged. "I never heard of them before."

Shaking her head, Dixie said, "You wouldn't have. They're privately owned and stay out of the news. They even have a convenient cover at the University of Copenhagen."

"That sounds . . . ," Alexia wasn't sure how not to sound cheesy. "Like a plot from a really bad horror novel."

Leaning back, armed also folded, Serge let out the merry laugh he was known for. "Yes, I agree that it sounds ridiculous. But I assure you . . . ," His expression grew serious. "The Institute has been around in one form or another for centuries. And what we do is very real. We investigate paranormal activity and, if necessary, try to neutralize it."

If she had heard that a day ago, she would have dismissed it as nonsense. "But you've been here for years as the fencing instructor. And these crazy things started only a few weeks ago."

Mark gently rubbed her arm. "Actually, baby, the real bad stuff started three years ago in New Orleans. When that happened, Uncle Serge and I were sent here."

"Why here?"

"Someone linked to the case in New Orleans came to Druid Hills many years ago. Gramps—Dr. Eversoll—wanted us to find out why that person was here."

She leaned back against him. It felt nice. "A case in New Orleans? Wait, the new Bourbon Street Ripper!"

Dixie nodded. Her expression was serious. "Yes. So while a friend of Dr. Eversoll's, a man named Dr. Lazarus, focused on New Orleans, Serge and Mark were sent here. Two sides of the same overall investigation."

"OK. So how is this linked to what happened in New Orleans?"

"Back in the sixties, a key component of the original Bourbon Street Ripper case, a compound called the *tkeeus*, was used in Druid Hills."

"The what?" Alexia's head was spinning.

Reaching over, Leona pulled her into a hug, stroking her hair. "Dixie, you should probably start by explaining the entire Bourbon Street Ripper case, *oui*? It might help her understand better."

"You're right," Dixie said. "Alexia, I'm sorry. I've told this story so many times, I've gotten sick of it."

With a nod, Alexia pushed back from Leona. She needed to stand on her own. "Well, I'd like to know everything. Is the story a long one?"

With a smirk, Dixie said, "It could fill a book or two."

Chapter 30
Will to Power

Date: **Sunday, April 23, 1995**
Time: **3:00 a.m.**
Location: **Woodruff P. E. Center**
Emory University, Atlanta, Georgia

"So then, Samantha Castille learned that it was really her father, Vincent, the original Bourbon Street Ripper, who had been manipulating events in order to bind Baron Samedi to him so that she would be unable to die."

Alexia sat there, slack-jawed and arms folded, as Dixie finished. The story was both long and complex, but it answered every question she had concerning her brother's death. Finally, she felt she understood what Michael had been going through.

"And that brings us here," Serge said. "In 1967, someone calling themselves the Oracle used the *tkeeus* in Druid Hills for some kind of ritual. This was the first time the *tkeeus* was recorded as being used."

Dixie picked right up where he left off. "And soon afterwards, the *tkeeus* was used on five-year-old Samantha in New Orleans."

"Which is when she was possessed by Marinette and this whole thing started," Alexia said. When the others nodded, she rubbed her chin. As unbelievable as the story was, she couldn't refute it.

"So, Mark, you and your uncle originally came here to focus on that part of the *tkeeus* story, but then, when students started disappearing a few weeks ago, you all shifted your focus."

"Exactly," Mark said.

"So you contacted Dr. Lazarus, who had Dixie come down because of her familiarity with the New Orleans case, right?"

"More like I was the only one who could come," Dixie said. "Kyle is busy working on another project, and Ouellette is doing all he can to keep New Orleans together. Otherwise, I never would have left my husband and two-year-old girl."

"Right. And Leona, you . . . ," Alexia stopped. "I have no idea why you're a part of this."

With a curt laugh, Leona winked. "Besides being secretly married to Serge for the past year? *Oui*, I am very spiritually sensitive. I figured out something was going on some two years ago. I confronted them, and they let me in. It's as simple as that!"

That settled all the loose ends for Alexia. "So now what? I mean, obviously, this thing that tried to kill us is somehow linked to all this, right?"

Mark slid his arm around her. "Correct, baby. And since you have seen it up close, we wanted to include you in the Institute's investigation."

"Agreed," Serge said. "Both Father and Dr. Lazarus had agreed to let you join. Seeing as how you've exhibited both an intellect and an instinct for this, we're certain you can help us crack the mystery of that creature, the Oracle, and the *tkeeus.*"

"So why is the *tkeeus* all that important, again?" she asked. "Doesn't it just make summoning spirits and possessions much easier?"

Dixie shook her head. "It has caused unbelievable havoc in southern Louisiana. A group called the Knight Priory is using it for everything from animating dead bodies to murdering their enemies. And a man named Dr. Kindley—well, I'm certain he's learned how to bind ghosts to him."

"The Knight Priory," Alexia repeated. They seemed like the real villains. "Well, here's something creepy. At the golf course, something—I think it was that thing—said 'Lullwater.' When I mentioned it, Mr. Chandler seemed taken aback. Do you think it's connected to all this?"

Raising his eyebrows, Mark said, "Lullwater? There are many parts of Emory and Druid Hills called that. Even the university president's home is called Lullwater House."

Part of Alexia was still shocked she had blown off those classes.

Serge and Leona glanced at each other. Then he stood up. "There's a campus function there tomorrow afternoon. We'll attend and see what we can learn."

"Of course, Uncle," Mark said. "And I'll go to the library to research the name Lullwater. Maybe there is more to it than meets the eye."

"I'll help you," Alexia said.

A voice from off to the side spoke up. "And me, too!"

Everyone turned to see Patty, dressed and grinning cheekily.

Dixie's eyes widened. "How long have you been there?"

Patty sauntered over. "Long enough to know that if I'm not included in this awesome cloak-and-dagger stuff, I will never speak to any of you again." She giggled and leaned on Alexia.

The sudden intrusion made Alexia chuckle. "Gee, Patty! Well, to be fair, she is amazing on computers."

"I have mad, crazy hacker skills." Patty flexed her nonexistent muscles.

Mark shrugged and said, "Patty is actually the best I've ever met."

After a few moments, Serge sighed. "Fine. Just. No one else. This is not a game."

Patty fist-pumped and then leaned on Alexia. "So when do we leave? Are we going to break into the library?"

"No," Dixie said firmly. "This thing attacks at night, and we now know that the campus grounds aren't safe. You'll sleep here, and in the morning, you'll go to the library in a group."

Patty sat down heavily, pouting. "Fine, ya ol' one-armed party pooper."

Dixie rolled her eyes and muttered to herself.

That only made Alexia laugh more. For a sweet, singular moment, life was back to normal. It was a welcome respite.

After the meeting, Serge and Leona set out cots while Dixie returned to her mountain of notes, mentioning to Alexia that they'd talk one-on-one tomorrow. Patty went to the restroom while Mark returned to the practice dummy. Alexia sat on the bench nearby and watched. Soon, however, her eyes wandered toward the two swords he had used against the entity.

The guards were made of the purest silver and their grips covered with the smoothest leather. She touched them and gasped—they were warm to the touch. Glancing over at Mark, who didn't seem to be paying attention, she started drawing one out of its sheath. The blade was sharp and shone with an amazing luster.

She had just started seeing that gold letters were etched into the blade when the tip of one of Mark's foils patted her hand. She looked up, heat spreading across her cheeks.

He was smiling. "No touching. Even for you, hun."

She slid the sword back into the sheath and moved away. "Sorry. It's just that they're beautiful. Are they . . . um, magic?" Even after all she had seen, saying the word "magic" still felt unusual.

He guffawed and sat down beside her. "I guess you could say that." Taking out a silk cloth, he unsheathed the two swords and laid them side-by-side on his lap. He slowly turned them around so she could see the gold lettering inscribed on each side.

Our Father Who Art In Heaven
Hallowed Be The Name Of The Lord
Thy Kingdom Come, Thy Will Be Done
The Kingdom, The Power, and The Glory

"The Lord's Prayer." Alexia was in awe. She was certain these had to be holy weapons.

Mark returned the blades to their sheaths. "There are very dark things in this world, baby. Things that would snuff out mankind's light. My ancestor, Abraham Eversoll, fought one of those evils. Family legend says that the Vatican itself gave him these weapons to battle his enemy, and when he was triumphant, they let him keep them. They are now a family relic of sorts."

"Wow. Just, wow." She didn't know what else to say. Surely they were imbued with her God's power, regardless of the church it came from. Doctrine hadn't meant anything to her in years. *He is my savior, and these feel imbued with His power.*

"My uncle used to wield them. But after Aunt Eydis died, he lost his faith. So Grandfather has me training to use them. I am to take over as the 'paladin' of the family when I get older."

"Paladin, eh? Sounds nice." That just made him all the more beautiful. Memories of how badly she had handled herself with the entity, however, made her heart heavier. "You'll do better than I did. I nearly died from that thing."

He put his hand on her leg. "No, not at all, baby. You're the reason I was able to repel it."

Remembering that the entity had said as such, she asked, "But how? My prayers?"

"Ah, yes, how to explain it without offending you," he said, taking her hands into his. "You have great faith, but it is your will that gives your faith power."

"My will?"

He slowly rubbed his thumbs over the tops of her hands. "It's hard to describe. Just accept that one's will is what enables them to fight off evil. It gives priests the ability to exorcise demons, saints the ability to perform miracles, and people like us the ability to touch and injure otherwise intangible spirits."

"I see," Alexia said. That made sense. "So you say my will powers my faith?"

"More like your will manifests itself as your faith. Will is the most powerful weapon any human can ever possess."

That didn't make any sense. She tilted her head to the side. "Jesus said, 'Without Me, you can do nothing.' You've known me for years, Mark. You know I won't even consider anything else."

Cupping her face, he said, "I know, baby. I'm a Christian too, and I believe the same thing. But if our faith was the only thing in the world that repelled darkness and evil, then only Christians like us would be able to fight. But I have seen men of other religions, as well as those who don't believe, do the same thing. So, your faith sustains your soul, my love. And you use your faith to fight evil like that creature. Ergo, your will manifests itself as your faith. Your will can overcome any obstacle. And your will is strong—the strongest I have ever seen."

Squeezing his hands, she nodded again, fighting back the urge to argue that it was her faith in God that did all the work. But she held her tongue, believing she had it figured out. *I have this power because I unconditionally accept God and Jesus's love. If I try to rationalize it, then I will compromise that power.*

"All's well?" he asked, stirring her from her thoughts.

She blushed. The way he used her trademark line was endearing. "Yes."

"I love you, baby."

"I love you, too. Now shut up and kiss me."

They only stopped kissing when the heat between them grew so great that their hands started wandering. It was then that Alexia remembered that there were others in the room, and they were all trying to ignore them. She gently pushed back.

"Can we pick this up another time?" She was out of breath.

"Yes," he muttered, his eyes an inferno of passion. "The greatest challenge I will ever face is waiting to make love to you."

Still blushing, she leaned up and licked the tip of his nose. "You know what you have to do, Mark. Until then, just keep being the perfect gentleman."

They kissed and parted ways.

The cots were laid out, Serge and Leona were finishing the equipment clean-up, and Dixie was already lying down, gazing at a series of small wallet photos.

Going back to where Patty had arranged two cots beside each other, Alexia slipped out of her pants and her bra and slid under the covers. Lying on the cot next to her, Patty grinned. "Your willpower is of biblical proportions, girlfriend."

Alexia stuck out her tongue. "Uh-huh. Actually, I kind of like feeling the tension slowly subside. It's amazing."

Snorting, Patty pulled the covers up. "You're crazy." Then she rested her hand on Alexia's. "Thank you for saving me, though. I love you so much."

Clasping hands, Alexia said, "I love you, too. Now let me sleep."

As Patty left her alone, she put her hands behind her head. Her thoughts were awhirl.

People keep talking about my will. Even that thing mentioned it.

She turned over and settled under the covers.

Is my will really that strong?

"Within the animal kingdom, the greatest of all senses in distinguishing between predator and prey is smell. The scent of fear is what designates a creature as prey, while the scent of aggression is what designates a creature as a predator."

Alexia sat in the lecture hall, listening to Professor Mathias Drakos, the guest lecturer from New York City. After cleaning up and changing clothes back at the dorm, she had learned that Mark wouldn't be ready to go to the library until later in the day. So after a brief conversation with Dixie, she decided to go to the lecture. However, as Professor Mathias, a tall, hairless man with a skinny frame and hollowed cheeks, engaged the full lecture hall in a treatise on the study of fear and criminal behavior, she was as unengaged as she could be. She was thinking about everyone's plans for the day. Serge and Leona were heading to the Lullwater House to speak to Emory's president, and Dixie was checking in with Dr. Lazarus. Everyone was trying to stop this before someone else died.

Professor Mathias continued. "This phenomenon extends to all members of the animal kingdom. In fact, some academics, myself included, believe that fear is one of the few chemical scents that humans can both emit and smell. We don't emit pheromones when sexually aroused. We don't emit a territorial odor. But we do emit fear. And fear we can smell."

She stirred from her thoughts. If she hadn't spent two nights in a row running for her life, she'd be skeptical about that. But now? What he said made perfect sense. Taking out a pen, she sucked gently on the cap, paying attention.

He put his hands on the podium and leaned forward. "So when we look at the chemical outputs of fear and death, can there be any doubt that some people are just born to kill? And following that logic, can you not say that some people are born to be victims?" His countenance darkened as everyone in the auditorium inhaled deeply.

With a chuckle, he leaned back. "Of course, I jest for the sake of shocking you into thinking. But consider this: when a crime involving multiple potential victims is committed, the offender will often go for the person who exudes the strongest fear scent. So in many ways, one can say that the perpetrator of a violent crime is drawn to the person most likely to be their victim."

Alexia exhaled along with everyone else. This guy was creepy. Brilliant, but creepy.

"So, now we come to the crux of the matter. The idea that being predator or prey is as much a matter of chemical release as it is size or strength. In no species other than humanity is that more prevalent. Take the case of the new Bourbon Street Ripper from three years ago. The copycat killer, Dallas Christofer, was killed by Samantha Castille, his intended final victim. Why?"

The example couldn't have been more personal to Alexia. All of her attention was on Professor Mathias.

"Samantha was being tortured by Dallas when something inside her changed. Now we know that Detective Rodger Bergeron was there. But while he fought Dallas, she freed herself from metal shackles, overpowered Dallas, and killed him. How was this possible? She was smaller and suffering from both locked-in syndrome and blood loss. How was she able to overcome this and fight back?"

Someone in the audience shouted, "Magic?"

A general laugh rippled through the audience. But Alexia said nothing. Her paradigm on magic had already been shifted. For now, she was riveted on what Professor Mathias might say.

"Perhaps," he said. "Someone once called it 'magic in your mind,' after all. But the truth is stranger than fiction. Samantha, through what appeared to be sheer force of will, changed her scent from fear to aggression. No doubt, when Dallas no longer sensed a victim, his resolve to murder her faltered. And when Samantha began to overpower him, no doubt his own fear scent gave her the edge to finish him off."

Placing his hands together and smiling wolfishly, he said, "So the next time something frightens you, remember, it's your fear that marks you as a victim. Therefore, fear really is what kills you. Thank you for coming."

He left the podium, and as Professor Templeton concluded the lecture, the audience applauded. Alexia drew back into her thoughts. Was that what happened to Michael and what happened to her? Could she use her will to change her scent like Samantha did?

Those thoughts brought out a sigh. Maybe her brother would still be alive if he had known the truth about *loa*.

The lecture hall began to clear out. She grabbed her books and got in line to speak with Professor Mathias in person. She ended up being last in line and waited over thirty minutes. By the time she got to him, he was packed up and ready to leave.

Templeton motioned toward her. "Ah, Mathias. Before you go, I did want you to meet my best forensics pupil. This is Miss Alexia LeBlanc."

"LeBlanc," Professor Mathias said. He put on his coat and regarded her. His expression never faltered. "You wouldn't have any relation to Detective Michael LeBlanc, would you?"

She felt a bit overwhelmed by his steady scrutiny. "Yes, sir. He was my older brother."

"I thought so. You are the spitting image. My condolences on his death. I studied the case in New Orleans as it broke, and I believe that had he survived the Bourgeois arrest, the case would have had a less . . . messy outcome at the end."

"I've often felt the same way. Thank you, sir."

He picked up his briefcase. She quickly re-captured his eyes. "Sir, I have a question about what you said regarding switching from prey to predator."

"Go on, Miss LeBlanc." His gaze penetrated her.

She swallowed. "So, if a person can theoretically switch between emitting fear to aggression, then a person can stop being the prey and start being the predator. Is that correct?"

"It is."

She shifted from foot to foot. More than anyone, even her father, he made her feel like a green student. "So, then, how does one do that?"

With a gum-filled smile, he said, "My dear Miss LeBlanc, to do that, one must completely believe, with every fiber of their being, that they can rip the other to shreds." He leaned forward and nearly growled as he said "shreds." "You have to know you're going to kill them, destroy them. Then they will be afraid of you."

Then Professor Mathias leaned back. "I hope that answers your question. Good luck with your final exams, Miss LeBlanc." He gestured toward Templeton. "Come, Irving. I am starving, and I still have several hours before my flight leaves. Take me to the Lullwater social. I heard they're serving lamb chops at the buffet."

"Absolutely, Mathias," Templeton said. He patted Alexia's shoulder as he passed.

Soon, she was all alone in the lecture hall.

Change myself to predator. Make the other fear me.

Holding her cross locket, she said to herself, "If my will is strong enough, if my faith is strong enough, then I should be able to do that. Right?"

She was alone as she walked down the hallway, her footsteps resounding loudly. Sucking on her pen cap and thinking, she stopped by a corkboard where various student and school activities were posted.

Whatever this thing was, it killed by some sort of exsanguination. But it was more than that. It couldn't get Chuck up into the ceiling, so he and Marcie got sucked into the drain. And Helen's body was pulled into the ground.

A flash of white light caught her attention. That small, white orb from before floated around an advertisement for a concert at the park. The opening band was called "Earth Gods." Just as quickly, the orb vanished.

Seeing those words made a light go off in her head. "Wait! What if this entity is somehow related to the earth? Could it be linked to Emory, or even Druid Hills?"

"That's just what was I was thinking," Dixie said, coming down the hallway.

Alexia jerked back in surprise. "What're you doing here?"

"Picking you up. I figured we could go for a coffee or tea or whatever you drink. And I see that I'm not the only genius with an oral fixation."

She glanced down at the pen, the cap wet with spit, and felt her ears get hot. "It's just a nervous habit, sheesh!"

Dixie laughed and patted her on the back. They both headed down the hallway. "I know. I know. I nibble my thumb. I'm just playing with you. You're as bad as your brother."

Putting the pen away, Alexia asked, "So, I take it that my brother is what you want to talk about?"

"Yup. I figure this is the last chance we might get. And I have a story about Michael that you need to hear."

She nodded. "Is it sad?"

Dixie squeezed her shoulder. "No. But it will make you cry."

Chapter 31
A Truth Revealed

Date: **Sunday, April 23, 1995**
Time: **4:00 p.m.**
Location: **Rise-and-Dine**
Druid Hills, Atlanta, Georgia

Steam rose from the cup of hot chocolate in Alexia's hands, caressing her face. Throughout the diner, groups of students were either conversing without a care in the world or getting a jump-start on studying for finals. She ignored them all, concentrating on the sensation of heat rolling over her skin. It was a welcome feeling. With a heavy sigh, she raised the cup to her lips and drank, enjoying the sweet, rich flavor.

No matter what, her life would never be the same again.

A few days ago, life was perfect. She was on track for acing her finals and taking on the state fencing championships as team captain. Now, she was just happy to be alive and sitting in a booth in the corner of a diner, drinking hot cocoa.

Across from her, Dixie watched in silence, nursing a cup of coffee. Her expression was tired, the lines showing on her brow. Her left arm rested limply at her side. Finally, she spoke. "What's on your mind, Alexia?"

Looking up, Alexia tried to appear pleasant, but it was too much effort. "I'm annoyed with myself."

"Why?"

She put down the cup and rubbed her face. "I should have known more about Lullwater. I always do this. I discount things that aren't in my spectrum of interest. I must be pathetic."

To her surprise, Dixie cackled. "My, my. If you don't remind me of your brother right this moment."

Alexia stared, taken aback.

Dixie gingerly sniffed her coffee, then sipped it. "Michael always beat himself up when he didn't realize something."

"I guess I shouldn't be surprised," Alexia said. "It all goes back to our father."

"He caused a lot of problems for you both, eh?"

Still rubbing her head, she murmured, "You have no idea, Dixie." Even thinking about him was upsetting.

"Oh, I think I do."

Slowly, she lowered her hands. "Do you, now?"

"Michael and I were best friends. He told me everything. How his father blocked his entrance to the FBI, how the schism with his family never healed, and how you were the one ray of light in his life."

Alexia felt her cheeks get hot. "Big Brother said that about me?"

Nodding, Dixie said, "On more than one occasion. He told me that if you hadn't been there for him all those years, he'd have killed himself."

This was the first time Alexia had ever heard that Michael had contemplated suicide. "Oh, wow. I don't know what to say."

Smiling gently, Dixie said, "Don't let it bother you. Michael loved you more than anyone else in the world. Even me." Her voice choked a bit.

Her eyes watering up, Alexia sloshed around her now-cool chocolate. "So that's what you wanted to tell me, then."

"Not entirely."

"What do you mean?"

Dixie's expression was pained, and she forced a smile. "What I'm about to tell you is something I have kept to myself for years."

"All right. Go on."

With a brief but sharp inhale, Dixie shifted in her seat. Then she gently traced the lip of her coffee cup. "About a month before the new Bourbon Street Ripper case began, Michael and I got stuck on duty finishing reports. Sometimes, the precinct would get a backlog, and the junior detectives would be stuck doing paperwork for several days."

Alexia nodded. Michael had mentioned such things before.

"This one stretch had us pull close to a twenty-four-hour shift. Luckily, our boss let us take our work home. We took it back to your brother's apartment and didn't stop until sometime around two in the morning."

Recalling past conversations with her brother, Alexia said, "Right. He told me about that, Dixie. He said the two of you ended up going to the Cat's Meow, a gay bar on Bourbon Street, and getting drunk."

"Yes, but did he tell you what we talked about?"

She shook her head.

Dixie leaned in. Her voice grew hushed. "We talked about him being gay. It all started when we saw this adorable college guy. I suggested that Michael should ask him to dance. The next thing I know, he's bawling like a little kid. I had never seen him like that before."

"Why?" The only time Alexia had ever seen him cry was after the fight with their father, and those were tears of betrayal.

"His heart was in pain, Alexia. Constant pain. He wanted so badly to have a family, to have a father who loved him, to feel free to go home and see his mother and little sister. He told me that the more he pretended things were OK, the more he felt dead inside."

Alexia pushed her chocolate away, no longer interested in drinking it. "So, what happened?"

"Well, we walked back to his place—stumbled, actually," Dixie said, reclining once more. "All the while, he was carrying on, letting out years of pent-up pain. He poured his heart out until four in the morning. At the end of it, he admitted something he'd kept to himself his entire life."

Now it was Alexia's turn to lean forward. "Please tell me."

"He said he honestly didn't know if he was truly gay, or if he was broken, like your father had said. He believed that he had to be broken for his father to hate him so much."

Tightness grew in Alexia's throat. Her father calling Michael "broken" is what had pushed him out the door.

Dixie paused, slowly inhaling and then exhaling. "So, he asked me if he could try to see if he really was broken. He wanted to know for sure if he was gay."

"Wait a second," Alexia said, staring with wide eyes. She pretty much knew where this was going. "You mean he asked you to . . . you know?"

"Yes," Dixie said, her cheeks a deep red. "It wasn't the first time someone has asked me to have sex just to see if they were gay. All those other guys were creeps who just wanted to get in my pants. But not Michael. The confusion. The pain. The inner turmoil he kept buried deep inside. That was all real. He truly wanted to know if he was lying to himself about being gay. He really wanted to know if he was broken like your father said and if sleeping with me would fix him."

Alexia felt a lump in her throat. She struggled to swallow the now-cool cocoa. It tasted bitter. "So, you slept with my brother, then?"

Nodding once more, Dixie wiped away a few tears. "Yes. Now don't get me wrong. I love Gino. And never before or since have I cheated on him. But for Michael, someone I loved that much, I did it. Just once."

For a long moment, Alexia stared into Dixie's eyes. In her heart, she knew what resulted. "In the end, he realized he was gay, right?"

"Yes. Queer as the day is long. Poor dear stuck with it until he finished, but in the end, he said it didn't feel natural. He said he felt gross sleeping with a girl, even one he loved."

It was almost too much for Alexia. Her sweet big brother had bottled all that pain and confusion, and she never knew. "Was he OK with himself after that night?"

A sad expression crossed Dixie's face. "He never talked about it. I don't know if he even allowed himself to think about it. But yes, he was no longer confused. He knew what he was, and he was OK with it. He was 'fixed' from needing to be 'fixed.' I think he even started looking for a boyfriend. I seem to recall him mentioning a cute cop in Lafayette."

With a soft sigh, Alexia felt the tightness loosen from her throat. "Well, then, all was well." She wiped away the few remaining tears.

To her surprise, Dixie started laughing.

"And what's so funny?"

Instead of answering, she took out her wallet and fished out a picture. Then she slid it over to Alexia. It was Dixie with a handsome, olive-skinned man and a beautiful toddler with dark hair.

"That's Gino, right? And who's the kid? Congrats, by the way."

"Thank you," Dixie said. "That's my daughter Felicia."

She leaned forward. "Your niece."

"My what?" Alexia jerked so hard she hit the table with her knees. Dixie's coffee spilled.

Picking the picture back up, Dixie smiled apologetically. "I had a paternity test done without Gino's knowledge. No match. So Felicia is Michael's child." She cleaned up the spilled coffee.

Now Alexia gaped. "You did what?"

Dixie shrugged. "I guess everyone has to have a skeleton in their closet. This one is mine. And if Gino ever figures it out, I'll deal with it."

Alexia continued to stare. Part of her wanted to slap Dixie across the face and proclaim her a whore. The other part of her understood it was sometimes best to leave things alone. Once again, her strict upbringing and her common sense were at odds. Finally, she asked, "You weren't married when it happened, right?"

"Wasn't even engaged."

She frowned. "For Michael's sake, I won't say anything else. What's done is done."

Locking eyes with Dixie, she asked, "So why did you tell me? Was it to unburden your soul? I really hope not. That would cheapen Michael's memory."

"No, not one bit," Dixie said. "I've already sought guidance, counsel, and absolution. I told you because, through Felicia, a part of Michael lives on."

She rested her hand on Alexia's. "And I want you to be her godmother."

Hearing that was more than she could handle. Turning away, Alexia wept.

It was later in the evening when they arrived back at campus, having stayed at the diner a while longer, sharing stories about Michael. It was only when Dixie's pager went off with an Emory phone number that they returned.

Serge and Leona met them at the entrance to the library.

"Talk run a bit late there, Dixie?" Serge's arms were folded. He seemed annoyed.

Dixie held out her hand. "I apologize. Don't blame Alexia, Serge. It was all on me."

Leona pressed her fingers to his chest. "Serge, my love, let it go. They had their own demons to exorcise."

With a grunt, he waved everyone off. "I must call Father and report in. Dixie, Dr. Lazarus wants you to call. Leona, please take Alexia to Patty."

Before Alexia could speak, Dixie hugged her and said, "I'll see you in a little while. And I'll introduce you to Dr. Lazarus next time. He does want to meet you." Then she left with Serge.

"Um, bye?" Alexia waved to the air.

Covering a giggle with her hand, Leona led Alexia into the library. "Come. Your friend Patty is like a supercomputer. She's all but solved this Lullwater mystery herself."

Even though it was after hours, the library was unlocked. They slipped into the main floor and headed to where the computers were set up in small alcoves. Patty was rapidly typing on one of them, and Mark, standing next to her, was giving advice on where to check next.

"Hey, guys," Alexia said.

Mark pulled her into his arms. They kissed with no sign of stopping.

"Ugh, get a room, you two!" Patty said.

Leona nudged her. "Ah, love is beautiful, *oui*?"

"You're not helping," Patty said in an intentionally nasal voice.

Breaking the kiss, Alexia nuzzled Mark's face. "So, honey, I hear you all but cracked the case?"

"Yes, baby." Mark kissed the tip of her nose and then guided her over to Patty. "So, we're ready to show you what we've discovered."

Patty was grinning cockily. "He means what *I've* discovered. Because I humbly submit that I am Patty E. Coyote, super-genius."

Alexia laughed sharply at the cartoon reference. Feeling herself blush in embarrassment, she playfully smacked the back of her friend's head. "Can you be serious for one moment?"

"Hey, I peed my pants last night. I get to crack jokes so long as evil death monsters aren't trying to make my blood explode."

As Patty opened a series of windows on the computer, Leona leaned against the side of the cubicle. "Your friendship is wonderful. But now it is time to focus."

"Right. Sorry, Leona." Alexia rubbed Patty's shoulder. "Show us what you discovered."

Patty began sifting through several articles. "Well, the case started back the 1940s when a man named Henry Heinz was murdered at what is now called the Lullwater Estate."

"Lullwater Estate," Alexia repeated. "Is that the same as Lullwater House, where the president of Emory lives?"

"No," Leona said. "Serge and I confirmed that the two properties are different."

"OK," Alexia said, glancing back to the computer screen. "So, what's so special about Lullwater Estate?"

"Well," Patty continued, "the family that owns Lullwater Estate is none other than the Candler family."

A light bulb went off in Alexia's head. "Asa Candler the Fifth. The guy I spoke with back at the golf course."

Kissing the top of her head, Mark said, "Precisely. Old Asa Candler built it for his daughter, Lucy Bell Candler."

"So who was this Henry Heinz guy?"

Patty brought up a black-and-white image of a man with a considerable forehead. "That was Lucy's husband. Her second husband, to be precise. He was allegedly shot by a burglar in 1943. A house servant confessed to the crime, but it was bogus."

"The servant was sent to jail, and the matter was swept under the rug by the authorities," Mark said, now rubbing Alexia's shoulders. "So that's when Patty dug further and discovered that when Lucy Bell's first husband died, that was also covered up."

Alexia patted Mark's hand to indicate she was done being rubbed. "And how did the first husband die?"

Flipping to another article, Patty said, "The official report said he died of influenza. But there was no medical examination, no doctor to verify cause of death, nothing. Even for the time, that's a bit odd. It was like they wanted both husbands' deaths to just be forgotten. "

An ugly pattern was starting to emerge for Alexia. "So both deaths were covered up?"

Mark slipped out from behind her. "That's right. And both funerals were closed-casket. However, the coroner's reports for both men mentioned 'heavy blood loss.'"

That got her attention. "Wait, heavy blood loss? Technically, that's how the entity killed Marcie, Chuck, and Helen."

"Exactly what we were thinking." Patty said. "And those weren't the only bizarre deaths with similar coroner's reports, they were just the ones that got us looking. But starting from when settlers first arrived at Druid Hills until about 1967, there have been one or two of these strange deaths every year. Each time, there was a cover-up, no investigation, and a closed-casket funeral."

Alexia whistled. "So, for as long as this place has been inhabited, people have been getting killed by exsanguination? But can we actually link this to the entity?" She folded her arms under her chest. Hunches were fine, but her forensics training taught her to look for evidence.

Mark leaned on the desk. "Well, normally, you wouldn't pay attention to conspiracy theorists, right?"

"Right."

"Well, one theorist back in the sixties started publishing papers about everything we just talked about. He even managed to sneak into the morgue and take a few pictures of the caskets. They were all filled with sandbags."

Leona gasped. "*Ah, non*!"

It was enough to turn Alexia's hunch into a hypothesis. "They'd use sandbags if there were no bodies. And there'd be no bodies if that creature pulled them into the earth."

"And the conspiracy guy vanished soon after those pictures were printed," Mark said. "He was never seen again."

She gulped. "They killed him to shut him up."

Then Patty brought up an article that looked over a hundred years old. "So then I did more digging, because—super genius. The entire area of Druid Hills was once home to members of the Cherokee Nation. And guess what the settlers back then called it?"

"Lullwater," Alexia said. That much was easy to figure out.

"Yup," Patty replied. She turned around and stretched, looking very pleased with herself.

Clearing her throat, Leona spoke up. "This is what Serge and I discovered when we were at the Lullwater House. According to the president of Emory, soon after he was inaugurated several months ago, someone from a group called the Lullwater Society came to him and offered a great sum of money to 'take away' one or two students a year. He refused, of course, but when he reported the incident to the police, they told him to 'not worry about it.'"

"Oh, my goodness," Alexia said. "Maybe the police are in Candler's back pocket?"

Leona said, "*Oui*, I was thinking the same thing. It's *tres mauvais*."

Then Mark said, "And Alexia, do you remember when we first went hiking years ago to Fernback Forest? To the settler's stone monument?"

She nodded.

"The real reason I went there was because Uncle wanted me to investigate that place for supernatural activity. I found traces of something we call a seal. However, it was considerably weakened. And over the years, it's just gotten weaker."

She huffed. So that was why he wanted to go there so badly! "Is the seal still there?"

His shoulders dropped. "Actually I don't know. It's too weak for me to tell. I was hoping to bring Leona there tomorrow."

"*Oui*. I should be able to tell."

"So that's it, then," Alexia said with a soft sigh. "Give me a moment, everyone. I need to think."

Moving to a separate part of the library, she found a chair, sat down, and took out her favorite pen. Then she leaned back and started sucking on the cap, closing her eyes and sorting through the facts.

The murders stopped in 1967, only to pick up again a few months ago, right around the time that the new president of Emory was approached by the Lullwater Society asking him to hand over one to two students a year.

An awful theory began to form. Alexia opened her eyes. "What if all of those deaths were actually human sacrifices to this entity?"

"Well, that would be pretty screwed up, wouldn't it?" Mark came around the corner.

She yelped and threw her pen at him. "Hey! Sneaking up on a girl is a bad idea."

Dodging the pen, he chuckled pleasantly. "Sorry, baby. Patty is taking a bathroom break, and Leona went to check up on the others. I just wanted to see how you're doing."

She shrugged and leaned forward. "Oh, you know me. I won't be happy until I solve the puzzle."

He placed a gentle kiss on her cheek, then crouched in front of her and took her hands.

Her breath unexpectedly taken away, she swallowed, gazing into his beautiful eyes.

His voice got serious. "Alexia, baby, I'm sorry I kept my business with the Institute a secret. I know we promised never to keep things from each other. I broke that promise, and I regret it."

She squeezed his hands. "Mark, honey, it's OK. I understand why you did it."

"Still, it's unforgivable to keep secrets from you. I'll never do it again, I promise." He looked upon her with the same intensity Serge had given Leona.

"Mark?"

"I want to include you in everything I do, no matter what. So from this day forward, if something is happening in my life, or with the Institute, I'll tell you right away."

Gazing at him, she broke out into a smile. He smiled as well, his bangs flopping to the side. He looked so handsome.

I feel safe with him. If there's anyone I'll marry, it'll be him.

Still holding hands, they gazed into each other's eyes until they felt the attraction between them light up. Her cheeks got warm. Slowly, she moved in for a kiss, her lips parting.

Then his eyes bugged out and he vomited blood all over her.

Alexia's body seized and her throat clenched shut. All she could do was watch as he slid back, his body moving like a puppet as mist gathered from the floor. It flooded into him. His expression was one of pure terror.

"A . . . lex . . .ia . . . ," he said in a helpless voice.

"Oh, God, no!" She grabbed at him.

An instant later, his flesh started paling to that bleach white, and his veins started turning black. Just by touching him, her hands started suffering a similar fate, like she was losing all sensation, all life.

"Run . . . A . . . lex . . . ia." His voice was thick with agony.

She held on until she saw that his body was completely changed. Her beloved was already doomed. She couldn't save him.

Leaning in, she pressed her lips to his, the coldness spreading. She couldn't let him die without hearing her feelings.

"I swear, Mark, I will always love you."

They kissed and parted ways.

Alexia fell back with a cry as Mark's veins exploded and his tendril-like blood started pulling him downward, the mangled, gelatinous mess that was once her love emitting that awful croaking sound. However, just like with Chuck, his body couldn't go through the artificial flooring.

She didn't even realize Patty was beside her until she heard her say, "Mark, no!" Grabbing Alexia's arm, Patty pulled. "We gotta run! We gotta run!"

But Alexia refused to move. "I can't leave him! I can't let him die alone!"

"He's already dead, Alexia!" Patty cried. "We have to run!"

As Patty pulled, Alexia watched what was left of Mark slide to the window. The tortured mass hit it several times until the glass broke. The last she saw of her boyfriend was his terror-filled eyes glazing over. Then the ooze slopped outside.

"We need to go now!" Patty shouted.

Alexia ran. As she sprinted along campus, she kept her mind blank so that the fear, the hurt, and the rage wouldn't cripple her. Pushing all of her emotions aside, she simply focused on running for her life.

As soon as they were outside, she saw the same small, white orb from before flying toward Candler field. "That way!"

Another terrible, low croak rattled behind them. The entity was once more giving chase. Its jaw unhinged and it spoke her name. "Aaaaallleeexxxiiiiaaaa . . . !"

"Why does it want you so badly?" Patty wailed.

"I think I hurt it!"

As they turned a corner, heading toward the field, they ran into someone's arms. They both screamed.

"It's OK! It's OK!" It was the derelict woman. She reeked of booze even more than before. The white orb floated around her head for a moment and then vanished into her clothes.

She pushed both girls away. Her strength was incredible. "Alexia, right? Run. Run as far away from campus as you can! I'll come find you later."

As Alexia stumbled back with Patty in her arms, she asked, "Who are you?"

"Run! Run, you stupid girl! I'll hold him off! I'll—"

With a loud croak, the entity rounded the corner. Its eyes fell upon the woman. "Another who is like a god? You will not seal me again!"

Through her fear, Alexia felt vindication. She was right—someone had sealed this thing away once before.

The woman stomped her foot so hard, the ground cratered and rocks flew up into the air. "Back off! You can't have her."

A shot rang out through the night. And then another. The woman wailed as bits of her legs blew off. She fell to her knees.

"What's going on?" Patty asked, panicked.

Alexia's legs seized again as fear coursed through her. "I don't know. I don't know!"

Looking back at her, the woman smiled with pained resignation. "Run. Please. For Michael's sake."

Then the entity drew back, snarled, and flew into the woman. At once, her body started turning pale. She shrieked so loud, the glass on the nearby building shattered.

With the shock blasted out of her, Alexia grabbed Patty's hand and they ran until they were in Chandler Field.

Another shot rang out, and suddenly, dirt flew up in her face. With a cry, Alexia landed hard on her chest. Pain exploded in her head like stars. She rolled around, holding her chest. *I've been shot!*

It took her a couple of seconds to realize that she hadn't actually been shot, only the ground before her. She felt Patty trembling next to her. Then she heard footfalls crunching the grass of Chandler Field. Still clutching her chest, she saw Mr. Candler standing before her. Behind him were Officer Penfold and another police officer. Both were holding scoped rifles.

"You've been a very bad girl, Miss LeBlanc," he said, pointing a silver pistol at her.

She glared at him, blood trickling from her busted lip.

"How about another friendly drive? You like drives, don't you, Miss LeBlanc?"

"Leave us alone!" She spat at him.

"My, my. How rude. Not a lady at all. We've already grabbed your other friends. Now be a good girl and pass out quietly."

Then, Officer Penfold stepped around her and covered her mouth and nose with a cloth. It stank of alcohol. She fought against him, but he pressed his knee onto the small of her back.

Within seconds, her head started spinning and she felt faint.

Chloroform!

Her eyes began water and her vision blurred. In the distance, headlights approached.

And then all was darkness.

Chapter 32
The Scent of Fear

Date: **Monday, April 24, 1995**
Time: **3:00 a.m.**
Location: **Fernbank Forest**
Druid Hills, Atlanta, Georgia

When Alexia came to, her vision was blurry. But as it refocused, she realized she was in a limousine, her hands cuffed behind her back. She glanced around, fighting panic. Patty, Leona, and Serge were all seated next to her, and all three were bound and unconscious.

They didn't get Dixie. It was a small relief.

"You're awake," a voice said. "Good." It was Mr. Candler.

"So what do you want?" She felt a burning ember of rage growing within her.

"Oh, my, you have dirt on you." He took out a handkerchief, licked it, and wiped her face.

She felt utterly repulsed and tried to pull away. "Hands off, creep!"

He grabbed her head and forcefully wiped off rest of the dirt, making her flinch. "You know, despite having a curvaceous body, you are quite the tomboy. How very unsexy. There. All done."

Alexia felt sick to her stomach.

Stuffing the handkerchief into his coat pocket, he asked, "Do you know why we've taken you and your friends?"

As he spoke, she tried to wipe the wetness off her face with her shoulder but couldn't. "We're trying to destroy that thing that's been killing people."

He gawked at her a moment before bursting into laughter. "Destroy it? Destroy Lord Dooley? You're joking, right?"

"Lord Dooley?" she asked, her eyes widening. "The Emory mascot? Are you serious?"

"Well, not exactly. The society calls it Lord Dooley because its real name is lost to time. You see, the Cherokee here had bound it, and when the settlers came in and took over, they accidentally released it. It's an old and very powerful spirit. The settlers called it Lord Dooley in honor of their own legends. The name just stuck."

The pieces of the puzzle started falling into place. "Now it all makes sense. Every aspect of Druid Hills and Emory were crafted to contain and pay homage to this thing."

"You are correct. Even the school mascot."

"So it's true. All those mysterious deaths were sacrifices."

He clapped his hands together, "Indeed. Correct again, Miss LeBlanc. My, you are brilliant."

The whole ugly picture was coming into focus. "That was the purpose of the Lullwater Society. To make sure that thing, Lord Dooley, was satisfied. Right?"

"Another one spot on. It told us who it wanted, and we provided. In return, it would protect us from harm."

Closing her eyes, she let the rest of it come together. "But when Lucy's two husbands became sacrifices, it got unwanted media attention. And then the conspiracy theorist died. That's when things started to change. You all were able to hide it for decades, maybe even centuries, but not anymore. You were in danger of being exposed."

"Quite right again!" he exclaimed. "Oh, I am impressed. Yes, the husbands were unfortunate, but Lord Dooley chose his sacrifices, and we obeyed. So, to cover it up, we started bribing city officials, federal investigators, and even judges. Getting rid of that idiot theorist took money to the mob. Really, it all started turning into a very big mess."

"But then, in 1967, you all found a way to seal Lord Dooley away, right?"

Mr. Candler leaned forward. "We didn't. Someone else did. Did you figure out who?"

For a few seconds, Alexia said nothing, feeling only the rhythm of the limousine as it rode along. She thought back to the year, 1967, and who else might have been in Druid Hills. Then the answer hit her.

"It was the Oracle."

With applause, Mr. Candler said, "Yes! You are a brilliant young lady. A shame you weren't born part of the society. We could have used someone like you."

She narrowed her gaze him, hating him more and more each passing moment. "So who is the Oracle?"

"That, I don't know," he said, shaking his head. "He hid his face behind a mask and kept incognito. All I know is that he originally came from New Orleans."

She sighed. Another dead end. "So, how did he seal away Lord Dooley?"

Leaning back in his seat, he said, "It was . . . unusual. He went to the sacrificial point, burned some pink incense, and waited. That ritual summoned Lord Dooley, and when it arrived, he physically beat it down and sealed it in the stone."

The very thought seemed as ridiculous as it sounded. "So this Oracle sprinkled some pink powder and then just beat up Lord Dooley like it was nothing?"

"Yes. I've never seen anything like it. Lord Dooley is very powerful. This guy easily defeated him."

"Did he say why he was doing this?"

He rubbed his chin. "He said the whole reason he came to Druid Hills was to test out the pink powder, which he called the *tkeeus.*"

The tkeeus! Alexia recalled the others mentioning it. "Did he say why?"

"He wanted to see if it could summon spirits as well as aid in possession. Then he mentioned something about a sick child needing help."

Alexia gnawed at her bottom lip. Why did the Oracle care about helping young Samantha? "What happened to him after he was done?"

"He returned to New Orleans. I never saw him again."

The limousine finally stopped.

As the door opened, Mr. Candler said, "The end result, Miss LeBlanc, is that Lord Dooley was sealed away for years. The seal only recently started weakening. By the time we realized it was due to the overdevelopment of land around Fernbank Forest, it was too late. Lord Dooley was out."

Officer Penfold and several other officers pulled her and the others out. They were in Fernbank Forest only a few hundred yards from the settler's stone. Dozens of cars were parked in the clearing. The air was cool and thick with springtime humidity.

Patty moaned and muttered, "What's going on?" Leona and Serge looked around with fear in their eyes.

But Alexia, for the moment, was focused on the conversation. "So you asked the president of Emory for sacrifices, and when he didn't agree, you just let Lord Dooley randomly kill students anyway."

Mr. Candler nodded, heading toward the monument. They were forced to follow. "Exactly. Lord Dooley is out and wants to catch up with his missed sacrifices. But wouldn't you know, I was able to bargain with it, and we're going to quell its bloodlust."

"How?" she asked. But she already knew the answer.

He turned and pointed at her. "It wants you, Miss LeBlanc. You really angered it. So I give it you and your friends, and everything can go back to normal. One or two victims per year instead of per week. All's well, don't you think?"

That jerk used my own line—

A blow to the back of her head sent her world into darkness once more.

When Alexia finally came to, she couldn't move. But as the grogginess cleared, she realized that she was tied, standing up, to a large stone. She tried looking around, but at first she saw only blurs. As her eyes started to refocus, she saw many people, all of them wearing drab, gray robes and holding torches. The back of her head ached, and her thoughts were foggy.

She shook her head until the cobwebs vanished.

When her thoughts and vision finally returned to normal, she saw she was at the settler's stone in Fernbank Forest, the place where she had sprained her ankle when she was out with Mark years ago. This was the sacrificial point.

And then she realized who the people surrounding her were—the Lullwater Society. All of them were chanting in a strange language. Officer Penfold and other Druid Hills police were walking along the edge of the clearing. Patty, Leona, and Serge were on their knees nearby. Patty was sobbing, her face wet with tears and snot. Leona shook with fear, and Serge, who was trying to appear strong, was glancing around anxiously.

Directly before Alexia was Mr. Candler. He was reading from an old scroll, raising his voice to the sky. "Lord Dooley. We have brought the one you asked for. Come and receive her blood and her flesh. Accept this sacrifice!"

"Accept this sacrifice!" the entire society proclaimed.

At once, mist started to gather from the trees, the moss-covered ground, and the canopy above. It grew cold, and the wind turned foul with the stench of decay. Alexia struggled with her bonds, trying to loosen them and get free. The sickness in her stomach rose. Her heart pounded in her chest, and her body shook. She had never been so frightened. It wasn't supposed to end this way. They were supposed to stop this time.

Her thoughts were interrupted by that deep, loud, croaking sound that rattled her bones. The mist had gathered into a writhing morass.

It's here!

The shifting bulk of mist coalesced into the form of the entity Lord Dooley. Its hollow eyes focused upon her, its jaw unhinged, and once again, it let out that awful, rattling croak.

She screamed into her gag. Everything that she had learned was forgotten. Fear had taken control.

Mr. Candler called out. "Lord Dooley! We have brought you these four. Now, we beg you to honor our agreement!"

It regarded each of its sacrifices. Its voice rattled like bones in a cage. "Very well, mortal. No more lives until the following thaw. But try to seal me again, and I will bring death to your entire house!"

Mr. Candler bowed on one knee, lowering his head. "Of course, Lord Dooley. We will never betray you again. You are our master!"

"Good!" Lord Dooley floated in front of Alexia, lowering itself until it was eye level. "I want to hear you cry. I want to hear you beg. I want to hear you suffer."

It ran its bony fingers down her cheek. Its touch was freezing cold. She felt the veins in her face start to pulse as it tore her gag off. "Beg for your life. Admit your God cannot protect you, and in return, you'll get a swift death."

It was hard to talk. Her throat was so dry, and she felt like she would vomit at any moment. She closed her eyes, wishing she was anywhere in the world other than where she was. *I'm going to die. Give . . .me . . . God, give me strength . . . to die loyal to you and my beliefs.*

It roared. "Beg for your life!"

She could smell the scent of death oozing from it. Opening her eyes, she tried to speak, her chapped lips quivering in the night air.

It moved closer. "What was that? Louder, pathetic mortal."

Alexia swallowed and steadied her breath. "The Lord . . . is my Shepherd, I shall not want . . ."

It reared back and roared. "You think prayers can save you? Empty, meaningless words! Now you will suffer like no one before! Die!" With another loud croak, it flew directly into her. She felt it enter her body in a splash of cold, foul air.

She gasped and shook. Pure and unrelenting coldness consumed her. It was like something was congealing all the fluid in her body. Looking down, she saw her arms start to turn bleach white and her veins start to turn black. Her heart beat wildly, trying desperately to move the solidifying blood. Her throat burned as she tried to take air into lungs that would not expand. The saliva in her mouth turned into icicles that sliced into her gums, and the fluids in her eyes started to freeze, hazing her vision into darkness.

The pain was utterly consuming.

Oh, sweet God, help me!

She knew what was next. Her veins would explode, and her blood, somehow possessed by Lord Dooley, would pull her liquefied body into the earth.

She reached into her mind for something, anything. The surge of panic and the waves of pain made thought difficult. She knew she had seconds to live.

Then Alexia remembered:

"Your fear marks you as a victim."

"Change your scent from fear to aggression."

"Turn from prey to predator."

"Will is the most powerful weapon any human can ever possess."

"Will can overcome any obstacle."

"Your will is strong."

Remembering those words, she focused.

The fluid in her ears froze, deafening her. The pain was excruciating. The flimsy walls of her veins were moments away from giving way to the pressure.

With a silent cry, Alexia pushed her mind forward until she found Lord Dooley inside of her. Visualizing her hands grappling his, she focused on pushing him away with her beliefs.

Even though I walk through the valley of the shadow of death, I will fear no evil, for You are with me!

She felt its focus shift to her resistance. For a moment, it stopped attacking. Then she felt it push back, snarling at her. Visualizing her hands locked with its, she pushed harder.

The LORD is my strength and my song; He has become my salvation.

Feeling it slide back, feeling its surprise as it renewed its efforts, she struggled to close her mouth until she was gritting her teeth. She felt warmth as blood poured out of her mouth. She imagined herself hitting the entity and continued to focus her will into her prayers.

The LORD is my strength and my shield; my heart trusts in Him, and I am helped.

She felt it cry out in confusion and push back with even more of its strength. Forcing herself to grin with confidence, she visualized ripping its cloak off, crashing into its rib cage with blow after blow, all while pushing it back.

Be strong in the LORD and in His mighty power.

It roared in pain. She visualized breaking off its rib bones, ones by one.

He gives strength to the weary and increases the power of the weak.

Feeling it pull back, feeling her skin and veins start to return to normal, her vision and hearing restoring, she released a deep and guttural howl that came from her innermost depths. She visualized gathering its broken bones and casting it from her body.

I can do everything through Him who gives me strength.

As Lord Dooley roared once more, Alexia summoned forth all of her will and gave one last, decisive push.

"The LORD is my Shepherd! Amen!"

Her vision, hearing, and sensation in every part of her returned. Her body was normal once more. Then she saw that Lord Dooley was floating around, its ghostly body broken, its cloaked ripped to shreds.

Mr. Candler cried out. "What happened? Lord Dooley, what—"

It roared, "Lives! I need lives!"

It reared back and flew right into Mr. Candler. Several people screamed, but none as loudly as he, who fell to his knees. As his skin bleached and as his veins blackened, he looked at Alexia. "Who . . . the hell . . . are you?"

Then his veins exploded, and he was pulled into the ground.

Shouts of panic filled the air. The Lullwater Society members started scattering as Lord Dooley reappeared and dove into another man, a police officer. He suffered the same fate. Most of the other police ran away as well, leaving Officer Penfold looking lost and bewildered. Serge struggled to his feet and helped Leona and Patty stand as the clearing descended into utter bedlam.

A flash of white caught Alexia's eye, and she saw the white orb fly toward a group of trees. Behind one was Dixie, holding the twin rapiers in their sheaths. It seemed like she was waiting for a chance to get to Serge.

Lord Dooley dove into another victim.

"Serge!" Alexia shouted. "Dixie's over there! With the swords!"

He followed her gaze. Then he nodded and nudged Leona and Patty out of the clearing before running toward Dixie. A few moments later, his bonds were cut and he was armed.

Lord Dooley dove into yet another victim.

Serge dashed back to the stone. With a single stroke, he cut Alexia's ropes. Then he helped her down. "Run to Leona and get out of here," he said. His eyes were almost glowing with fire. "I'll destroy this thing. We'll meet back at the—"

Then the top of his head blew off in a shower of blood and brains.

Alexia stumbled back.

As his lifeless body fell to the ground, she looked up. Officer Penfold was holding his rifle. With a hateful sneer, he reloaded it and aimed right at her.

"Murderer!" she yelled. "I'll kill you!"

But she didn't have to do a thing. Before he even laid his finger on the trigger, Dixie appeared beside him, her gun to his head. Tears of rage were in her eyes.

"Protect and serve, asshole." She pulled the trigger, splattering his brains on the nearest tree.

Then Alexia heard Lord Dooley's awful croak. It was re-forming and going for another victim. She felt her own rage focus on it. So long as that thing existed, people would keep on dying.

She kneeled down by Serge's body and briefly touched his chest. "Goodbye, teacher." She fastened the rapiers around her hips and stood to face Lord Dooley.

As God is my witness, I will purge the earth of this . . . thing!

Without a word, she drew the weapons. The steel and silver glinted in the moonlight. To her, it was like what the angels would bear, and it matched the furious rush of blood through her veins.

Lord Dooley turned to her and snarled again. As light reflected from the rapiers, it recoiled. Seeing this, she brought them together and formed a cross. It thundered in pain as the cross-shaped light pattern shone upon it.

"Who the hell do you think you are?" It glared at her, but this time there was fear in its voice.

Alexia smirked.

"My name is Alexia LeBlanc," she said, getting into a fighting stance. She felt like the hunter cornering its cowering prey. "And I'm the pathetic mortal who's going to rip your sorry soul into oblivion."

The fury within her heart burst forth as she rushed forward, brandishing her weapons at Lord Dooley. Once more, she was so angry she swore. "So repent now, motherfucker!"

Jumping on the settler's stone, she flung herself at Lord Dooley. As soon as she was within range, she swung both weapons in a series of arcing blows. With every swing, she envisioned herself cutting its ghostly form.

It bellowed in pain again. As she landed, she saw that her blows had indeed managed to damage it, producing massive gashes upon its spectral body.

Then it dove at her, but she jumped to the side and rolled. The entity flooded into the ground, leaving a small puddle of mist that quickly dissipated.

"Where did it go?" Alexia scanned the glade. Her body ached from exertion, but she forced herself to ignore it. This was a life-and-death struggle, not a fencing bout. There'd be no do-over.

A moment later, a skeletal arm burst through the ground and grabbed her ankle.

"Damn it!" She swung at the bones and shattered them.

Four more erupted forth, then a dozen more, and then two dozen more. As if the earth were water, the bony arms waded toward her, grabbing and scratching. Their bony fingertips were like razors, cutting into her jeans and flesh alike.

Wincing, she swung at them, breaking each with a single hit. But for every one she destroyed, more would take its place. As she flipped back in hopes of getting away from the clawing hands, she saw the white orb swooping through the air again. It made a few tight circles around the settler's stone and then vanished.

The stone! Its strength comes from the stone! Jumping and cartwheeling over the bones, she headed toward the center of the glade and leapt into the air. With a shout, she stabbed both swords into the top of the stone.

Then several things happened at the same time.

The stone started glowing, radiant etched carvings that looked like pictograms appearing. The grasping bony hands all shattered into dust. And mist gathered from the stone as that horrid croaking sound reverberated across the clearing.

Alexia skidded back, digging her heels into the ground, and watched as Lord Dooley formed above the stone.

"I've existed since before your ancestors walked this land, mortal. Do you think you can really destroy me?"

She tightened the grip on her weapons, seething with concentrated fury. "I don't think anything, Lord Dooley. I *know* I can destroy you!"

It roared, cupping its hands above it. The pictograms upon the stone shimmered, and energy poured from them into its hands. Within moments, there was a large rotating sphere of sizzling energy above it, made of hundreds, if not thousands, of faces wailing in agony.

What . . . What is that? She gripped the pommels of her rapiers.

Yet another flash of white caught her eye, and once more, the white orb appeared, flying right around Lord Dooley's chest. She immediately saw what it was pointing out. Unlike before, this time there was a pale, ghostly, beating heart visible within Lord Dooley's bony chest.

That has to be its weak spot!

Lord Dooley centered the sphere toward her. She sprinted forward, concentrating on its heart. It pushed its hands together, and the sphere exploded into a wide cone of energy that blasted right at her.

For Mark! For Serge! For everyone!

Alexia howled as she ran directly into the blast. Her flesh and hair burned from the flare of energy. She felt like she would burst into flames at any moment. But she didn't falter. The moment she was close, she hurtled into the air. And with a deep breath, she thrust both of the rapiers into Lord Dooley's heart. "He is my sword! He is my shield! He is my strength! Now begone!"

The blades tore through its heart, ghostly fluids spilling out as it ruptured. Then, she passed through it and landed in a heap on the other side. For a few seconds, her skin started to bleach and her veins pulsed, but it quickly subsided.

Lord Dooley arched its back and screeched, "No! How can a mere mortal destroy me! This cannot be!" Bright light poured from every crack in its body.

Energy arced from its eyes, mouth, and fingertips. "This cannot be!" Then Lord Dooley exploded, utterly annihilated for all time.

The force of the blast flung her back, the rapiers flying into the brush. The stone cracked and then shattered with a shockwave of concussive force. Dixie, who had been running toward her, was knocked against a tree. She cried out and collapsed. Leona and Patty, who were watching from the edge of the clearing, were flung into the forest. Serge's body caught on fire from the heat.

Then the ground started caving in.

Alexia stumbled to her feet and started running just as the entire glade collapsed beneath her. With a shout, she grabbed onto the edge of what was now a giant hole, watching helplessly as Serge's remains fell into the darkness below.

She grabbed at the earth with both hands, straining to pull herself back up. The ground started crumbling. With another cry, she made a final, desperate grab. Her fingers sank into the moist soil. It was terribly unstable.

"Crap!" Her arms burned so badly, they felt as if they were on fire. "Someone please help me!"

Then her fingers slipped and she fell . . .

. . . only to be caught by someone's hand.

"Ahhh!"

Whoever it was, they pulled her up with ease. Only once she was safe did she look at her savior. It was the blond derelict woman from before.

Alexia blinked, her mouth open. "You? I thought Lord Dooley killed you."

"I underestimated his strength, and he splattered me like an ink blot." The woman sniggered and sat back, running her fingers through her filthy hair. Then she took out a cigarette, lit it with a match, and took a long drag. "But I got better."

As Alexia continued staring at the woman's profile, she started to recognize her. She was older, her hair was shorter, and her eyes were harder. But it was the same woman as from the various articles about the New Bourbon Street Ripper that she had read.

"You're Samantha Castille."

The woman puffed on the cigarette and then winked at her. "Call me Sam."

Alexia sat up. "But why are you here?"

She shrugged. "Just passing through. Heading north. Getting away from the fucking coast."

A million thoughts went through Alexia's head. This was Sam Castille. The woman people had been searching for since 1993. "But the reports said—! I thought you died after—! No one has seen you in years. Oh, I have so many—"

Sam pushed her hand right in front of Alexia's face. "Stop."

"But, I . . ." Then Alexia closed her mouth. Something in Sam's eyes told her not to push.

Sighing, Sam rubbed her forehead. "You want to know why I'm here? Someone wouldn't leave me alone until I made sure you were safe. You could say that I brought your guardian angel to you."

"My guardian angel?"

As if on cue, a white flash again caught her eye.

She looked over . . . and then stared.

Kneeling next to Dixie's collapsed body was the ghostly form of her brother, Michael. He smiled at her and then stood.

"The sooner you realize that no one can ever do it all alone," Michael's apparition said in a whisper that carried on the evening breeze, "the sooner you'll find where you truly belong. Don't close your heart, dear sister. Open it and allow others within."

Then it faded down into a small, white orb and floated off into the forest.

Sam flicked her cigarette into the giant hole in the ground and stood as well, dusting off her rear. "You're a lucky girl. Most people's ghosts wouldn't travel five hundred miles just to check up on their sibling. It takes a lot of energy to do that, even with someone like me helping."

She walked away, twirling a silver pen between her fingers. "I guess you could say Michael loved you more than anyone else. His little sister."

As the cool evening breeze blew through her messy hair, Alexia wept once more.

Alexia's Epilogue
All's Well

Date: **Friday, May 26th, 1995**
Time: **12:00 p.m.**
Location: **Atlanta International Airport**
Atlanta, Georgia

Alexia held the payphone to her ear, watching the airport traffic. "And that's the entire story."

"This is amazing, Miss LeBlanc," Dr. Lazarus replied. "Not only does this conclusively prove that a spiritual entity can be fought and destroyed merely with will, but it shows that even a powerful one can be defeated."

"It was powerful, yes, but I think you're overinflating its ability."

"Oh, no, I assure you that I am not. This Lord Dooley was higher on our rankings than you think. Not a high-born spirit, but definitely one of the stronger ones."

She had no idea what that meant. "I'm still learning about spirits and rankings and stuff. So you lost me."

"Let's just say that your will must be amazing, Miss LeBlanc. What you did should have taken significantly more people."

The tips of her ears grew hot, and she hastened to change the subject. "And Sam? I lost sight of her."

"Yes, Miss Castille. We've been trying to find her for years. With your intel, I believe we'll be able to locate her."

"Good. Just be warned. I don't think she wants to be found."

"I understand. Thank you again for everything. Especially for confirming that the Oracle was involved. Since I sent Dixie over, I've been struggling with how the situation at Emory was linked to New Orleans, and now I know for certain. The Oracle is behind everything, and I suspect that his power comes from something other than the voodoo pantheon. I'm going to work harder at cracking his identity."

"Pantheon? Lost me again, Doctor."

"Sorry," he said. "The point is that all of this will aid my organization greatly in the coming days. Speaking of which, have you considered my offer?"

"I have, indeed. And while I'd like to join in the future, for now I'm going to have to decline."

"Oh?" He sounded disappointed.

With a gentle chuckle, she said, "I need some time to find myself. Plus, I want to finish my education. I can't stay at Emory, not after all that happened. Not after losing Mark and Serge."

"Ah, yes. I understand."

"But having said that, when you're ready to destroy the Knight Priory and stop the Oracle, I'll go there and fight. You have my word."

"And I'll take you up on that. So what will you do, Miss LeBlanc? Go with Dixie to New York?"

"Not exactly. Leona is heading to Denmark. Now that she graduated, she'll be teaching fencing at the University of Copenhagen. Since she's Serge's widow, she pulled some strings with the Eversoll Institute and got both Patty and me accepted."

Dr. Lazarus sounded joyful. "Oh, Miss LeBlanc, that is wonderful! Yes, my dear friend Oskar will take good care of you and Miss O'Brien. You will get a top-rate education there."

"Thank you."

Leaning into the payphone stall, she lowered her voice. "So, about my brother. Did you figure out . . . why?"

"Ah, yes. Michael died in New Orleans, so one would think that his soul would be bound there. However, Miss Castille has . . . well, a special connection to the spirit world. It's easy to imagine that Michael's ghost could piggyback on her all the way to Atlanta."

Her throat tightened. "So why did he only appear as himself, instead of that orb, once? Why not more?"

There was a pause and the sound of shifting papers. "My research so far indicates that ghosts like his require a certain amount of energy to manifest completely. I believe that Lord Dooley was siphoning the energy of the region, being some sort of site-bound earth-based entity. So when you annihilated it, that energy returned to the spirit world, and Michael was able to tap into it to appear."

"So where is he now?"

"My guess is he will return to New Orleans. I am sure you will see him again one day."

She hoped so. She wanted one more chance to say goodbye.

"So he can't move on to . . ." She paused. After what she had experienced, she knew there could be only one place for Michael to go. " . . . Heaven?"

"I'm sorry, Miss LeBlanc. Because of reasons I cannot speak of, the dead under the care of the voodoo pantheon cannot move on. I'm afraid your brother will be on this earth for a long time."

She grimaced. That was entirely unacceptable. "Then one day, I will discover what is holding him here and destroy it."

"You aren't the only one with that goal."

Someone tugged on her arm. It was Patty. "Hey, Alexia. The flight's been delayed. I'm gonna go get an ice cream. Wanna join?"

"All right," she said, winking.

As Patty gathered her luggage, Alexia spoke into the phone. "I've got to go, Dr. Lazarus. I hope the invitation to join your organization will still stand in a few years. I'm definitely interested."

"It'll be a pleasure to have you, Miss LeBlanc."

She giggled. "All right, then. Need to run. Please take care and good luck."

"You as well, Miss LeBlanc. Take care."

She hung up the phone and gathered her bags. Then she stopped. There was something else she had to do.

"Hey Patty?"

"Yeah?"

"Go on and get your ice cream. I'll join you in a bit."

Patty looked her over. "Are you sure?"

She nodded. "Yeah."

Leaning up, Patty kissed her cheek. "See you soon, Awesome Alexia."

Alexia blushed as her best friend left, showing not a care in the world. Of everyone touched by the events at Emory, Patty seemed the best adjusted. *Her will is pretty amazing in its own way . . . when you think about it.*

Focusing back on the phone, she inserted several coins and dialed a number she hadn't rung in years. A few seconds later, an older woman answered. "Hello?"

Alexia inhaled and then exhaled. She could do this.

"Mom? It's me, Lexi. Let me talk to Dad."

She held her locket. "I want to tell him that all's well."

Chapter 33
A Year After Emory

Date: **Saturday, May 11, 1996**
Time: **12:00 p.m.**
Location: **North River Pub**
Murray Hills, Chattanooga, Tennessee

"All right! Rack 'em up, boys. Mama's gonna kick all your asses today!"

Sam chalked up her favorite pool cue, a red one with two black stripes, and sneered across the table at the men challenging her. Each one of them was sneering back, with teeth missing or wrinkling their noses to look tough. Although none of them was older than twenty-three—more like boys than men—they were known for being the toughest in town. She thought it was just plain adorable.

Bill, the oldest, who also had the least teeth, spat a wad of black tobacco juice into a nearby spittoon. "Fine, Sara, but you're gonna face us all at once. We decide who shoots each turn."

"Three guys on one girl? Bill, I had no idea you were that kinky." Sam had gone by the name Sara since she'd settled in Murray Hills, a rural section of Chattanooga.

Adjusting himself rather lewdly, he said, "Me 'n my friends would tear you up. But we don't need Caleb running us down just for porking your big ass."

His younger brother, Will, who was built like an ox and just as smart, set up the table for a game of eight-ball. Their friend Macky, a skinny fellow with the face of muskrat, passed out their pool cues.

She leaned on the table, bored. "Tch. Caleb doesn't own my ass or any other part of me. He's just the only guy in town who can handle it."

Shouldering her cue, she added, "I'm gonna get a drink, boys. Let me know when you're ready."

As she headed to the bar, Bill called out, "Hey! How much we playin' for today?"

"As much as you're willing to lose."

At the bar, Sam adjusted her tank top and took a seat. The feeling of sobriety was starting to wear on her nerves. Slapping a ten-dollar bill on the counter, she said, "Horace, gimme a Sara Special."

Horace, who could tell you the name of every person in Murray Hills, peered at her with a squinty eye. "Caleb know you're hustling the Hickerson boys again?"

Shrugging, she scratched the tattoo of a thorny rose on the small of her back. "I don't think Caleb cares who I play, so long as I play fair and pay up when I lose."

Then she winked. "Of course, I never lose."

Another patron entered the bar, a trucker who passed by the route every week. He flashed her a smile, but she ignored him.

"That's what I'm saying," he said, mixing what she called a "Sara Special," a concoction of grain and sour mash alcohols that was as thick as motor oil and tasted just as foul. "You've drained over a dozen guys close to what, two grand in the past six months? You've gotten about two hundred from Bill alone."

He slid her the drink. Some of it spilled on the bar and began eating at the varnish.

"Three hundred," she corrected him, dipping her finger into it. It stung one of her hangnails.

"Right, like that's any better. Look, Sara, maybe you need to haunt a new bar. There's several here in Murray Hills. Hell, go over to Hixon or Big Ridge. Tons of dives there."

Sam swished her finger around the glass, feeling the liquid burn her flesh. "Are you kicking me out, Horace?"

Sighing, he shook his head. "No, I'm not kicking you out. You're one of my best customers, and you always keep your peace, even if you get liquored up more than the men. Just please be careful. Some fellas just don't like to lose, especially to a girl."

She nodded and pushed back her bangs, which were longer than the rest of her hair. Then she swallowed the drink in one gulp. It was like sucking on a hot coal. "Thanks for the warning, Horace. But I'll be fine. Trust me, I've been through worse."

Then she tipped him a five, slid off the stool, adjusted her shorts so they'd stop invading her privates, and then headed back to the pool table. As she walked away, the trucker said, "Hey, isn't that Caleb the mechanic's woman? Sara, right? Why does she always look so angry?"

"I dunno," Horace said. "She came into town about a year ago and hooked up with him. As far as I know, she's never opened up to anyone. I get the feeling that whatever past she's running from is real ugly."

Horace, you have no idea.

An hour later, she was two drinks drunker and three hundred dollars richer. As she stuffed the money into her front pocket, she said, "Thank you much, boys, for contributing to tonight's party fund. When I'm getting drunk and laid, I will think of absolutely none of you."

"Hey, now," Bill said. "Just because you won don't make it right to say stuff like that. It ain't natural for a woman to be that good at pool, especially when drunk."

"I'm not drunk. I'm just better than you." She leaned on her pool stick and blew kisses at him.

He started blowing up, as did Will and Macky. That's when a deep voice came from the doorway. "You fellas aren't thinking of swinging at a lady, are you?"

Caleb's impressive form shimmered in the afternoon sun. Sweat beaded up on his bald head and ran down the milk chocolate texture of his skin to the white tank top that barely covered his broad chest. As far she was concerned, he was the only good-looking guy in all of Murray Hills. She watched him appreciatively.

Bill said, "It's not like that, Caleb. She just gets so arrogant sometimes. Like she thinks she's better than us!"

Caleb slid an arm around her, putting his hand possessively on her hip. Sometimes, she'd slap it away to remind him that he didn't own her. But for now, she wanted it there.

"If you boys are so tore up over Sara beating you, why do you keep playing? Don't treat her like you gotta beat her. She's one of us now."

The young men started leaving, with Bill furrowing his brow. "No, Caleb, that's where you're wrong. That woman will never be one of us. And she needs to watch that big ass of hers if she knows what's good."

Once they were gone, Sam glanced around the bar. Everyone, including Horace, had been watching with anxious expressions. It was more attention than she would have liked. She was, after all, trying to leave the life of Sam Castille behind her.

"Gettin' into trouble again, hun?" Caleb let go and leaned against the pool table. Some of his sweat splashed on the green fabric.

She shrugged. "I don't see what the big deal is. It's just money. I don't complain when they beat me at darts. And . . . my ass is not big."

Laughing loud and hard, he patted her back and led her out of the bar. Above, the sun was beating down on the dirt and concrete roads, but in the distance, rain-clouds were already forming. It was springtime in the Appalachian Mountains.

"Well, just remember that Deputy Hammond is watching you after that business with the rum bottle and spittoon. Try not to get in any fights this time, all right? My business can't handle that kind of heat."

As they walked down a dusty road toward his home, where he ran his garage, she wrapped her arms around herself. "Well, I'll try. But when they start acting like they're better than me just 'cause they're guys, it really pisses me off."

I am a queen, after all.

He rubbed her shoulder. "Don't let them get to you. They're just boys. They don't know how to handle a real woman."

They walked in a silence a bit more.

"Caleb, you don't think they're right, do you?"

"Hmm? About what, hun? About you not belonging?"

"No. I mean, do I have a big ass?" She snickered.

He chuckled and carefully placed his hand on her backside. It felt nice, and when she didn't protest, he squeezed. "Seems perfect to me."

She grinned at him, her hormones flaring up like a volcano. "Wanna take it for a spin?"

He grinned back, making him even more handsome. "All right. But first I need to shower. Then afterwards, I have a ton of work to do."

She pulled him closer. "Fair enough. I'll try not to tire you out."

"Oh, damn . . . Sara . . . That's amazing . . ."

The sound of approaching thunder concealed most of Caleb's moans. Lying next to him and feeling his fingers work their magic on her, Sam drew her mouth away. "Lay back and I'll do something really incredible."

Given her strength, she could easily overpower him, but she never had to worry about that. He always allowed her to have sex however she wanted. She felt in control with him. She felt safe with him.

As he lay back, she settled on top and rested her hands on his muscular thighs. After taking a few seconds to get comfortable, she started moving her hips.

"Ah, fuck! Sara! Ah, baby!"

Once he started moaning, she let her mind go blank. He was now just a piece of meat to her. It's how she wanted it, to feel the physical sensations without a hint of emotion. After exhausting him to the point where he could no longer perform, she finally allowed him to rest. Lying next to him, she opened a bottle of

Jack Daniels and took a swig. The alcohol mixed with the endorphins to numb a growing ache in her heart. Thoughts of Richie had kept entering her mind while they screwed.

Rolling on her back, she glowered. Caleb rolled to his side and stroked her hip. "You're upset. Thinking about 'him' again?"

Tolerating him touching her, she gazed out the window. "Yeah. Sorry, hun. It wasn't on purpose. You know you're my only guy now."

"It's a'right," he said, stroking her stomach, his hand getting a little too close where her caesarian scars had once been. She slapped it away. "Hun, when're you gonna tell me about him? About your life before here? I know it was a serious thing and something terrible happened, but what?"

She regarded him for a moment and then rolled on her side, facing away. Then she drank more whiskey. The pain wasn't deadening fast enough. "Caleb, don't. We've got a good thing here. I help you around the shop and let you fuck me several times a week. You let me live here and make sure my . . . needs are met." She sloshed her bottle around.

From behind her, he sighed. "I know, hun. I know. And I hate to bother you about it. But I see you hitting the bottle sometimes as early as ten in the morning. It's hard to watch someone you care about destroy themselves."

With a scowl, she downed more whiskey. "This is exactly the cuddly shit I told you I didn't want when we hooked up. If it's such a big deal, maybe I should look for another arrangement."

"Oh, hun, don't say that. You know that ain't right."

She glanced back at him and arched an eyebrow. "Then what do you want from me?"

"Like I've always said. I just want us to be friends."

Placing the whiskey bottle to his mouth, she held it there until he drank. Then she leaned in and kissed him passionately. "I'm gonna work out for a while. See you at dinner time."

Stopping by the mirror in his bedroom, she examined herself. The burn scars were gone now, as were the ones from Evergreen. Other than her hips and chest being larger from the pregnancy, she looked the same as she had in 1992. The biggest difference was her eyes.

Her pupils were no longer dilated. For whatever reason, they had returned to normal.

As she got dressed in her tank top and shorts, she could feel his eyes gazing sadly at her. It was times like this when she wished he had just left her on the side of the interstate where he'd found her after she got hit by a truck. Those kinds of wounds healed much faster than the ones inside her heart.

And she wasn't about to allow another wound there.

By the time she got outside, the rain was coming down in a steady downpour that reminded her of New Orleans. Even though it had only been a few years, that life seemed so far away. At times, when the booze was really strong or the sex was really good, she actually felt like she had been born and raised in Tennessee.

"Christ. It's gonna be a two-bottle night if I keep thinking about the past."

So she distracted herself by working out in the large barn behind Caleb's house, where he had a weight set, a pull-up bar, and a punching bag. The local spirits floated around her, some sniffing curiously, as she concentrated on bench presses and squats, adding weight after weight until there were no more—five hundred total. Without focusing her power, she'd barely break a sweat on the presses, but not even feel it on the squats.

Her strength was still increasing. Soon, she'd have to find new ways to train herself.

When she finally looked at the time, it was nearly six in the evening. Her stomach rumbled just as Chris Jenkins, the teenage boy who worked for Caleb, stuck his head through the doorway. "Hey, Sara, the boss is going out for Chinese across town. Whatcha want?"

She sat up and wiped the sweat off her hands, chest, and face. Then she thought about it a moment. "Sweet and sour pork. And egg rolls. Lots of egg rolls."

He saluted. "Yes, ma'am!"

As he ran off, she smiled, watching him go without a care in the world. He was good-natured, simple-hearted, and treated her politely no matter how drunk or crass she got. Outside of Caleb and Horace, he was one of the few people she liked—a living reminder that some people were just good folk.

The rain was pouring down in torrents when Sam came out of her thoughts, realizing that she had tightened her fists until her fingernails cut the flesh. Too many thoughts of New Orleans were coming back, spiking her anxiety. She knew what she had to do to set her mind at ease.

She needed to check on her father.

At the back of the barn, underneath a heavy cement block, was a small safe, one she had bought after settling down. Her lips were tightly drawn as she entered the passcode and opened it. Inside was a scrap of Meghan's gown, a battered copy of Richie's books *Darkness Rising* and *The Pale Lantern* that she got from a second-hand store, and a plastic container.

She drew her lips tighter as she opened the container. Inside was the silver pen. Sucking in her breath, she touched it.

"Hello, Sam," Vincent said. Despite the pen being isolated, his power hadn't diminished. If anything, he felt stronger.

"Hello, Vincent."

"Checking on your old man? I'm touched."

"Don't flatter yourself. I'm just making sure you're here."

"Of course I'm here, Sam. I'm always here, watching you while you drink yourself to death and screw that lowborn trash. You must love wounding your father by polluting your body—"

"Shut up!" Her body temperature and blood pressure rose before she finished shouting.

"Is that any way to talk to me?"

"You've caused me nothing but pain. I swore I'd find a way to destroy this pen and cut you off from our world. I haven't forgotten that!"

"Ah, yes, and so successful it's been. The axe that couldn't cut it, the cinderblock that couldn't crush it, the fire that couldn't melt it. Your attempts at destroying this pen have been so successful."

At once, she realized she was grinding her teeth. "One day, I'll find a force strong enough to destroy it. I promise that."

"Of course you will, my beloved daughter," Vincent said, his tone utterly condescending. "Meanwhile, you'll form great strategies by boozing up and sleeping with that monkey. Tell me something, Sam, do you want to lay with that youth also? Because you might as well go all the way into debauchery and screw a t—"

Sam shut the container closed, cutting out his voice. By the time the safe was locked away, she was in a furious mood. So she spent the next thirty minutes beating the hell out of the punching bag, using only a fraction of her strength so as to not rip it in half. When she was done, she stank of perspiration and needed a shower.

Outside, she held up her arms, leaned back her head and let the fresh rain of the Appalachians pour over her body. She never felt more alive than when water was running upon her. It reminded her of the time she'd spent in the Gulf of Mexico after being washed out of the Mississippi. A rebirth in which she realized that if she couldn't die, she could run away from living.

"Hey, Sara!"

Opening her eyes, she saw Bill coming toward her. He had a lead pipe in his hand and a drunken sneer on his face. His intention was clear. She wasn't the least bit surprised. *Boys gotta do dumb shit.*

"Well, hello, Bill. Did you need your car fixed?"

"No," Bill said, tapping the pipe against one of the junk cars out in the yard. "But I do need that money back you stole from us. We're broke and can't do a thing until next Friday when we get paid."

She laughed, lowering her arms. "Not my problem."

He tapped the pipe a lot harder against one of the cars. "Oh, I think it is your problem. And don't go sobbing for Caleb. Unfortunately, he got himself a flat and will be gone awhile."

She frowned and cracked her neck. Fighting wasn't how she wanted to spend her Saturday evening. "Bill, you don't want to do this. Tell you what, walk away now and I'll forget this ever happened."

"Oh, I don't think so. See, we got insurance."

Then she saw it. Off to the side, Will and Macky had Chris. The boy was beat up, blood all over his face.

"Oh, no . . ." Her shoulders sagged. "That poor kid. Bill, why'd you—"

Bill slammed his pipe onto one of the car's windshields, shattering it. "I'm tired of you, Sara! You come walking around here like you're something special. The way you walk, talk, act. You make me sick, you bitch!"

Watching Bill make a spectacle of himself, she couldn't help but feel pity. What a pathetic mortal.

Holding up her hands, she walked slowly toward him. "All right. All right. You can have the money. Just please, don't hurt Chris anymore. He's just a boy."

"Sixteen ain't no boy," Bill sniffed. "I was hunting raccoon and getting poon when I was his age."

At that, she rolled her eyes. "Yeah, well, thanks for sharing your sexual prowess with weasels. Chris is a good kid. Please let him go. You can have the damn money."

"And what else?" Now he was smirking and regarding her as if she were a piece of meat.

She felt nauseated. "You wanna fuck me? Seriously? Can I go screw a raccoon instead?"

He snorted. "We each take a turn. Then you give us our three hundred. Then you never go back to the North River Pub. Chris keeps his teeth."

As she looked between him and Chris, she realized that she was on her own. There were only three options: she could give into their demands, she could let them hurt Chris more, or she could slap the taste right out of their little insect mouths.

The third option felt like the best one. She hadn't gotten into a fight in months, and her conversation with Vincent had her in a foul mood. Stepping forward, hands still out, she spoke in a sexy, sensual tone. "Come here, Bill. Let's have some fun."

Bill licked his lips and rotten teeth and then dropped the pipe and waltzed over. As soon as he was within reach, she focused her power just a tiny bit and slapped him across the mouth. It was still enough force to send him head over heels through the air. As Will, Macky, and Chris stared in shock, she focused more, slowing down time around her, and then rushed toward them in a way that must have been like an oncoming train. Then she stopped in front of them, her fingers outstretched menacingly. "Boo!"

Will and Macky dropped Chris and ran off screaming. From a few yards away, Bill burbled out his own blood. Powering down, Sam knelt in front of Chris and smoothed his hair off his face. He was staring with wide, terrified eyes.

She smiled softly. "Hey, you OK?"

But it wasn't Chris who answered. Instead, a voice behind her said, "Freeze! Hands in the air!"

Swearing under her breath, she stood with her hands up, then turned around. Deputy Hammond, of all people, was there with his gun on her. He looked triumphant. "When I saw the Hickerson boys come here, I thought I might catch them making trouble. But then, lookie-lookie, I bagged me a slut with an assault-and-battery charge."

Sighing, she closed her eyes. *Typical. Just when I start getting comfortable with living, something happens to fuck it all up.*

Chapter 34
A Dinner Meeting

Date: **Sunday, May 12, 1996**
Time: **8:00 a.m.**
Location: **Murray Hills Police**
Murray Hills, Chattanooga, Tennessee

Sam was awoken by Deputy Hammond banging the cell bars with his night-stick. "Hey Sara, wake up! You've got a visitor."

She had been dreaming that she was back in Evergreen Plantation under the "care" of Dr. Klein. So as soon as Hammond awoke her, she sat up, ready to fight. But when she saw him standing there with a smug expression, she relaxed. "Who is it? The district attorney from Chattanooga to pardon me since I'm so sexy?"

He cleared his sinuses and then spat at her. "No. It's that squeeze of yours, Caleb."

Then he shouted down the hall, "Hey, boy! You got five minutes to see your woman. And no funny business. Come up front when you're done."

Adjusting his britches, he sauntered off. A few moments later, Caleb came into view, looking as hangdog as a man could. "Hey, Sara."

She went over to him, reaching through the bars to touch his face. "Hey. I'm sorry. I didn't mean for this to happen."

"Those jerks had it coming," he said. "Wasn't enough to mess with you, but to beat up a kid? That wasn't cool."

Resting her head on the bars, she asked, "He'll be OK, right?"

"Yeah. But my business ain't. I'm gonna have to pawn quite a bit to cover your bail."

Feeling a tightening in her throat and a souring in her gut, she gazed into his eyes. Once again, her inner demons had caused her to wreck the life of someone else. "Oh, Caleb, you can't. You're barely making ends meet as it is."

With a resigned expression, he said, "Well, we'll find a way. Sara, I really like you and—"

Holding out her hand, she covered his lips. "Hey, before you start professing your love to me, just hear me out," she said, gripping the bars as if her life depended on it. "I've fucked up a lot in my life, and other people have always paid for it. Caleb, I like you and Chris too much. What's best is . . ."

She locked eyes with him. "What's best is if you just forget about me. Go and find your happiness with someone who isn't so screwed up."

Caleb stared at her like she had told him he was about to die, which made her guts hurt even worse, the pain crawling up into her chest. *Fuck! I don't want to feel bad about this. I don't want to feel anything.*

"I can't do that," he said, backing away. "I can't do that, Sara. You mean too much to me. We'll find a way to make it work."

With that said, he hurried out of the room. She pressed her head against the bars once more, swallowing her tears. "You fool. You stupid, beautiful fool." She closed her eyes. Although she felt dozens of spirits around her, some rubbing against her in an effort to bring comfort, she ignored them all. She wanted to be alone.

After Caleb left, Sam had many hours to think about what to do, indulging in daydreams from riding the situation out to going on a murderous rampage. But they were just fantasies.

Eventually, she decided the best course of action was to break out and run. While she couldn't summon *loa* any more, as Vincent was now too powerful, she could summon a ghost to distract the guards. Bending the bars on the outer wall would be easy. Then she could slip into Caleb's barn, get the safe, and go. No one would ever find her again. She'd just vanish. Maybe try Mexico.

Her thoughts were interrupted by the sounds of footsteps and rolling wheels. As she sat against the back wall, she imagined Dick and Dock coming into view with a gurney and Dr. Klein claiming it was time for another experiment. It was a morbid thought for a morbid afternoon.

But it was a man in a suit pushing a man in a wheelchair. A moment later, she realized who they were.

"Hello, Sam." It was Dr. Lazarus, being pushed by none other than Kyle Aucoin.

For several long seconds, she just regarded them both in silence. They were almost the same as she remembered, only a bit older. Dr. Lazarus had a blanket over the parts of his legs that still remained, and Aucoin had a few wrinkles. But despite that, they were healthy and in good spirits.

"Um. Hi." She didn't know what else to say.

"Good to see you, Sam," Aucoin said, his eyes showing considerable relief. The last time she saw him, she was plunging into the Mississippi in a suicide attempt.

"Um. Hey," she said again. A moment later, she shook her head violently and then slammed her palm against it. "This is some kind of a messed-up dream, isn't it?"

Dr. Lazarus chortled. "Dream? No, Sam, this is very real. We've been searching for you since you vanished. We wouldn't have even known where to start if not for Miss LeBlanc. But it has still been an exhausting search. We thought we'd never find you."

By then, the shock had worn off and the defiance had kicked in. "Maybe I didn't want to be found. In fact, I'm certain I told little Miss LeBlanc that much." The utter hopelessness she had felt that night at the pier had long been replaced by self-loathing.

He frowned. "Part of this is my fault. I didn't succeed in getting custody of you after your townhome burned down. I underestimated the reach and strength of the Knight Priory. I just didn't do enough. Sam, I'm sorry."

She spat. "Sorry? You're sorry? That lunatic tore my children out of my womb and tortured the shit out of me. You want sorry? I've got your sorry right here." She tilted up her hips and patted her crotch.

Shaking his head, Aucoin said, "Sam, come on. We've all been worried sick about you. And you have no idea what's been going on back home since you—"

"I don't fucking care!" She shouted so loud, her voice reverberated. The bars rattled, and the birds outside flew away.

As the two men recovered, Sam shut her eyes and let out all she'd been bottling up. "This cursed life of mine has been a goddamn nightmare. I thought I could die if I got swept out into the Gulf, but no! I spent a year in that dark abyss. Do you have any idea what it's like to drown, slip into a coma, then revive a few days later, only to drown again? It's horrible. I would have stayed down there forever if not for some shrimper from Grand Isle. Imagine their surprise when a wasted-away, naked woman puked up water and mudbugs that were trying to eat her insides and stumbled off, mumbling like a nutcase."

They both stared at her, horrified.

"So I wandered about aimlessly until Michael-fucking-LeBlanc's ghost found me. He told me he'd throw everyone off my scent if I'd just take him to see his little sister. Of course, I have no money, and I can't exactly reveal who I am, so I have to hobo across the South. I did things to survive that I never thought I'd do. By the time I got to her, I was a full-blown alcoholic."

Sitting up, she put her elbows on her knees. "But Michael kept his word. After we helped Alexia, he made sure no one could find me. I don't know how, and I don't care. So I headed up here to the mountains. And everything was going great until I lost my temper. So, as you can imagine, I'm not keen on being Sam Castille anymore."

"I understand how you feel," Dr. Lazarus said. "I can't imagine what you've gone through. However, I need to ask you something very important. Do you still have the silver pen?"

She snorted. "So that's all you care about? Fine! I've got it hidden. Why do you ask?"

Aucoin, who had been mostly silent, said, "So long as that pen exists, Vincent can influence our world. We want to destroy it."

That made her laugh hard. "You don't think I haven't tried? The damn thing is unbreakable. I've cut it, smashed it, burned it, frozen it. Not even a scratch!"

With a nod, Dr. Lazarus said, "Well, we want to try. Between myself and several colleagues, we have some ideas. And we want you to come with us, too."

"Why the hell should I do that?"

He blinked. "Sam, a lot of people are dying. We could use your help."

"Why the hell should I care?"

Now staring at her crossly, Aucoin asked, "Sam, what has happened to you?"

"What has happened to me? Are you fucking serious? Everything I have ever loved is gone. Michael, Rodger, and Richie are gone. I tried to care again with Meghan, and she's gone. Countless people have died so I could live forever. My children are gone, and I can't get pregnant ever again. Everything I touch turns to shit. The world would be better off without me!"

"Stop," he said. "Just stop. You should listen to yourself. You've been given a gift people only dream about. Not only are you immortal, but you have a goddess inside you. You could do so much good in a world that really needs someone with your power."

She just glared at him, tightening her fists.

"But you go ahead and pity yourself. I thought for sure that Sam Castille was a fighter who wanted to make everything right. I guess that was all bullshit. You may have the queen of the *loa* inside you, but you're nothing but a wild animal."

With a roar, she rushed to the edge of the cell faster than either man could blink. She growled, squeezing the bars until they squished in her hands. "You listen to me, you little shit! Don't you ever presume for a second that you understand what I feel. I want to free Baron Samedi, I want to destroy the Knight Priory, and I want to stop all of this before it hits a downward spiral. But I . . . I . . ."

"You're afraid of something bad happening again?" Dr. Lazarus asked.

She turned away, shedding her first tears in a long time. She wrapped her arms around herself.

"Sam, listen," Aucoin said. "Someone once told me that no one can go it alone."

A few stray tears rolled down her face. "Who said that? Rodger? Michael?"

"No one you know, but he was one of the bravest cops that ever lived. He chose to die instead of harming an innocent. He was right. We need to work together to stop Vincent and the Knight Priory."

"Sam, I understand your caution," Dr. Lazarus said. "I've gone to great lengths to ensure that nothing like Evergreen happens again. Will you hear me out?"

Wiping away her tears, she glanced at him, her bangs covering her face. "Yes."

"I'm going to pay your bail. I want you to get cleaned up and have dinner with us. All you have to do is listen to what I say. If you don't like it, you're free to go."

"So, a dinner meeting and that's it?"

"That's it."

With a sigh, she said, "Fine. I'm not promising anything. But I'll listen."

"Thank you, Your Majesty. Kyle, let's go post Miss Castille's bond."

As they left, she peered after him in confusion. *He called me "Your Majesty." That's two people now.*

It took a few more hours for Sam to be bailed out and head back to Caleb's. He and Chris, who were going over what they could sell to raise the money for her bond, were shocked. She hugged them both and briefly explained that some old friends had bailed her out and that she had to have dinner with them. Caleb voiced concern that they'd try to take her away, but she assured him that she'd be home before nighttime. It was five o'clock when she, completely clean and changed into a nice pair of jeans and a button-down shirt, hugged them both again, hopped on a dirt bike, and rode into downtown Chattanooga for dinner.

She met them at a local steakhouse, one of the nicer ones in town. A few of the locals pointed at her and whispered things like "Caleb's tramp" and "white trash," but she didn't care. She had ceased giving a shit about how people viewed her a long time ago. And yet, the moment she heard the music inside the fancy restaurant, a part of her old self crept forward—one of the social elite. *You can't completely kill a part of yourself you grew up with, no matter how hard you try.*

The host regarded her with disdain. "She's with me," Aucoin said. "We'll go take our seat now." Watching appreciatively, she followed him to a private booth where Dr. Lazarus was tasting a glass of white wine. His wheelchair rested in a corner.

Her eyes fell back on Aucoin as he helped her sit. *I have to admit, Kyle looks good in a suit.*

A few minutes later, a waiter presented her with a menu. It took her only a few moments to decide what she wanted. It was something she hadn't eaten since before the fight at the wharf back in 1992. "I'll have the filet mignon, medium rare, with a loaded baked potato and a broccoli-and-cheese casserole. Oh, and a glass of Inglenook 1990 Cabernet Sauvignon. Not a 1991. Don't you dare give me a fucking 1991, or I will bite out your soul."

She handed the waiter back the menu and smiled sweetly. "Thank you."

After the waiter had hurried away, Aucoin said, "Lord, Sam. Do you have any manners left at all?"

Already scarfing down the complimentary rolls, she shrugged. "I still hold in my burps and farts. Does that count?"

He rolled his eyes and returned to nursing a glass of ginger ale.

"Sam, I know you've been through a lot, so it's OK," Dr. Lazarus said gently. "Just be yourself."

"Well, thank you, Dr. Phillip Fucking McGraw. So, you said you wanted to talk to me about something?"

Dr. Lazarus gathered his thoughts. "Since your disappearance, the Knight Priory of Saint Madonna has gained considerable power. They are using the *tkeeus* in experiments like the one at Evergreen, and they've slowly been turning New Orleans into a place you'd read about in horror novels."

"Like what stuff?"

Aucoin twirled his finger around. "Walking corpses. Haunted houses. Maniac killers with chainsaws. Fun times."

"Just like Kyle says," Dr. Lazarus said. "Basically, while they can't control the *loa*, they're able to put them in people with the *tkeeus*. Vincent's evil influence does the rest."

"Huh," she said, leaning forward. "I thought the Knight Priory didn't believe in voodoo?"

"Sam, thanks to you, me, and Dixie, they now believe," Aucoin said.

Sitting back, she said, "Unbelievable. But why hasn't this been all over the media?"

"Because Caroline Saucier, who is a part of the Knight Priory, controls the media. Not just in New Orleans, but most of the Gulf South."

"Not only that," Dr. Lazarus said. "But high-ranking members of the United States government work with us to keep this kind of information from causing widespread panic."

Suddenly, something Meyer had said from the night she escaped Evergreen made sense. "So, those missiles that hit Evergreen. That came from the president?"

"Correct," he said. "When we determined that Evergreen was lost, we gave him the information, and he called the strike."

She grunted. Things were once again complicated. "So, how do you guys all fit into this?"

Dr. Lazarus leaned forward. "I head up an organization, a privately funded one that works with the US government, especially the FBI. We were formed based on research from the new Bourbon Street Ripper case. Our job is to investigate and remove threats like what's in New Orleans. So while the FBI investigates the members of the Knight Priory for illegal activity . . ."

"We're trying to cut down their supernatural operations before it spreads out of control," Aucoin finished.

Closing her eyes, she rubbed her forehead. "So, the Knight Priory has become a threat to America, and you guys are shutting it down."

She was interrupted as her wine arrived. She sniffed it and then glared at the waiter. "This is a 1991." As he began to stammer, she waved him off. "Whatever. I'll drink it even though the grapes were crap that year. Just go."

After he had served the salads and then left, she sipped her wine and grimaced at the bitter taste. "So what would you have me do?"

Dr. Lazarus crunched on a crouton. "Well, Sam, my organization has many layers of employees. There are agents, who do general missions and interface with the FBI; investigators, who gather intel on a situation; and operatives, who deal with the stronger paranormal threats. Kyle here is an investigator."

Aucoin, who had dug right into his salad, said, "My detective skills are best used that way. Only people with extraordinary talents like yourself are made into operatives."

She folded her arms. "Like that Meyer guy?"

Dr. Lazarus said, "Correct. He's my first operative, actually."

"And that's what you want me to be?"

He nodded.

"And I'll help you guys in New Orleans?"

He nodded again.

With a chuckle, she sipped more wine. "Hilarious. I go to great lengths to stay away from that city, and now I'm being told to go back with some secret organization."

They remained completely serious.

Sighing, she asked, "So what do I get out of this? Other than the satisfaction of putting down the Knight Priory?"

Dr. Lazarus leaned back, very matter-of-fact. "I'll erase your past. When this is over, you can go wherever you want and restart your life. I'll do everything in my power to help you destroy the pen and Vincent. And, one more thing."

"Yes?"

"I'll help you find your children, Sam."

Putting down the wine glass, she gazed at him as if she could see into his soul. "God as my witness, you had better not betray me, Dr. Lazarus."

He shook his head. "Sam, I am one of the good guys. So many times in your life, I have failed to help you. Now, I will do everything I can for you and those children."

Once more, she closed her eyes. After years of learning not to feel, of trying to forget her children, she was being given a chance to make it all right. *OK. One more time. I'll try just this one more time.*

Opening her eyes, she said, "I'll do it."

With a smile, Dr. Lazarus nodded to Aucoin. "Give it to her."

Aucoin, who seemed very relieved, slid something across the table to her. She instantly recognized it as her mother's shoe charm, the one she hadn't seen since her time in Tulane. "By the way, Sam, happy Mother's Day."

As she took it into her hands, feeling the melted plastic against her skin, Dr. Lazarus said, "And welcome to GEIST!"

Chapter 35
GEIST

Date: **Monday, May 13, 1996**
Time: **2:00 a.m.**
Location: **GEIST Headquarters**
Southern Arkansas

"Welcome to GEIST headquarters, Miss Castille," the tall, pale man said. He had white hair and wore a uniform, white gloves, and an officer's hat. "I'm Assistant Director Abel."

"Um, thanks. Just call me Sam." She was still a bit distracted by the sudden turn her life had taken. The goodbye with Caleb and Chris had been mercifully short, with her only returning long enough to pack her few belongings into a duffel bag. Both had been devastated, as she'd known they would be, but she hugged them, kissed them goodbye, and promised to return one day if she could. They would have to wait. Her children needed her.

With the silver pen secured, she was put on a truck and driven south to the Atlanta airport. Within minutes of arriving, she was on a private jet to Shreveport, and then on another truck north into Arkansas. By the time they entered the underground GEIST facility, she had realized the enormity of Dr. Lazarus's operation.

"So, what do you think?" Aucoin asked as Abel led them both through the loading bay. Several other trucks were being fueled up. Nearby, a group of uniformed men pushed the large metal crate containing the silver pen toward a door marked "Lab and Quarantine."

Looking around, she sucked on her bottom lip. The moment she had entered the base, she had felt the ambient spirits pull back. "Well, the entire place is sterilized. It's a bit annoying, like you just took away one of my senses. But, yeah, I'm impressed."

Aucoin chuckled. "You can't run an operation against the supernatural if your home base is open to attacks from them."

"That is correct, Miss Cast—er, Sam," Abel said. "The director, Dr. Lazarus, has worked hard to make GEIST safe. The electromagnetic field generator ensures that the only spirits or ghosts inside are the ones we allow."

They walked through a hallway and then to an elevator, which had four buttons and a card reader. Abel swiped his badge, and the doors closed.

"How does he pay for this?" Sam asked.

"GEIST is fully funded by a private entity in Europe. The director can tell you more about it during your briefing tomorrow morning."

She nodded and leaned against the wall of the elevator. She felt like she had just walked into *The X-Files*.

The elevator door opened to a well-decorated and comfortable hallway, complete with carpet and wood-paneled walls. Pointing at the décor, she said, "When did we get to the Hotel Monteleone?"

"These are the apartments for our operatives and administration. I'll show you to yours," Abel said.

She followed him out, but when Aucoin stayed on the elevator, she stopped. "Kyle, are you coming?"

"Sorry," he said. "Only operatives and special personnel are allowed on this floor."

"Oh, that's bullshit," she said, yanking him with her. "Abel, this guy is one of the few friends I have. He's coming with me."

Abel bowed respectfully. "If that is your wish, Sam. This way."

He led her down the hallway to a room with a plaque reading "Operative #000." Then he swiped his badge to unlock the door. Finally, he bowed again. "I suggest you get some rest. See you tomorrow morning, directly after breakfast." He left without another word.

"Strange guy," Sam said.

Aucoin shrugged. "Abel is like most of the people in Dr. Lazarus's inner circle. Creepy but well-intentioned. Just wait until you see his friend from New York. That guy is like a mummy."

Then he motioned toward the door. "Do you want me to show you in?"

She pulled him inside. "Yes, dumbass. I don't want to be left alone in this insane asylum until I feel safe."

Despite all the fanfare, it was actually a pretty normal room, reminding her of a Holiday Inn. There was a queen-sized bed, a desk, a dresser with a television on top, and a wardrobe. An alcove to the side opened up to a vanity, and from there, a door led to the bathroom.

"A bit nicer than my room," Aucoin said. "I have to bunk with a guy who snores like a whale."

In spite of herself, she laughed, tossing her duffle bag on the bed. "Sounds terrible." She spent a few minutes taking it in. While it didn't compare to her old townhome, it was far better than any place she had lived in for years.

Leaning against a wall, Aucoin asked, "So, what do you think?"

"It's nice."

"I mean about GEIST."

That question made her pause. She had learned that GEIST was short for Global Extermination Initiative of Supernatural Threats, and despite sounding like something that belonged in a comic book, it was a legitimate group. She had also learned that other forms of supernatural activity, besides just voodoo, were starting to surface around the world. She wondered if it was all because of her and Vincent.

She leaned on the wall next to him. "It's OK. You're sure these are the good guys, Kyle?"

"Yeah," he said. "I was distrustful of them for a while, too. I mean, seriously, it sounds just so incredible. But the more I've seen these past few years, the more I realize that without GEIST, the world as we know it would be in serious trouble."

Nodding back, she started taking off her clothes. She didn't even realize she was stripping in front of Aucoin until he cleared his throat and said, "I should probably go."

Quickly, she pulled her clothes back on. "Sorry! I'm just so used to no privacy or shame. These past few years . . . have changed me."

She looked at her hands. The injuries from her incarceration were already healed. With a heavy sigh, she went into the bathroom and closed the door. "I need to crap and then shower."

"Right," he said. "Um, now I should leave, right?"

"No. Please stay. I need someone I trust near me for a while."

"OK. I'll be here when you come out. I promise."

By the time she got out, snug in a robe with her hair wrapped in a towel, she was righteously tired, but she and Aucoin stayed up for a little while longer, chatting about everyone they knew.

New Orleans had a new mayor, Marc Morial. Harry Connick, who was now known to be in the Knight Priory, had changed from the outspoken man of justice into a ruthless politician who ensured that the Priory's enemies disappeared. Caroline had become increasingly reclusive, gathering only for Priory business. And Ouellette, who was still trying to keep New Orleans from falling apart, was as secretive as ever.

Sam shifted the conversation over to people she actually liked.

Dixie had married Gino and then moved to New York shortly after the birth of her daughter Felicia. Cathy had been placed in the witness protection programs. Tania had vanished without a trace. The surviving patients of Dr. Klein were either being treated at Acadia Vermilion Hospital or had since gone home—except for Misty and Lester, who had joined GEIST as part of the technical staff. And Aucoin himself had made sure Meghan was buried in her family gravesite soon after the escape from Evergreen Plantation.

By the time Sam was ready to go to sleep, her opinion of Aucoin had shifted completely. Gone was the man who had been like a lunatic when he'd arrested her, and in his place was one of the most level-headed and amazing people she had ever met. As he left, she watched him fondly.

Ya never know how someone will end up. Go, Kyle.

She closed her eyes and slept well for the first time in years.

"Sam, Kyle. Please, come in!" Dr. Lazarus motioned them both into his office, one of the few parts of the facility above ground. Large windows overlooked some of the rolling hills of southern Arkansas. Abel was there, standing beside him, along with several other people. A red-headed woman in a nurse's outfit served coffee.

As soon as Sam entered, she gasped, recognizing one of the guests as someone from her time in Tulane hospital. "Miss Dumont?" The woman with blue-gray hair pulled back into a bun was like a younger version of her social worker.

The sudden shock made Sam feel dizzy, and she leaned against Aucoin, who said, "Sir, with all due respect, I think you should explain things to Sam before she passes out from shock."

"Yes, yes," Dr. Lazarus said good-naturedly. "Sam, let me introduce you to the person who was helping me keep an eye on you. You knew Veronica as Miss Dumont. She's an expert in infiltration, disguise, and espionage."

Veronica smiled gently. "I love the new hairstyle, Sam."

Sam was still floored. *I knew there was something about her, but wow.*

Sitting across from Veronica was a lovely French woman with long, black hair. And sitting across from Dr. Lazarus was a tall, hairless man.

"This tall gentleman is one of my closest friends, Professor Mathias Drakos from New York," Dr. Lazarus said.

Professor Mathias stood and shook her hand. "It is a pleasure to finally meet you. I have studied your case since the very beginning. An amazing story."

Kyle was right. He did look like a mummy.

Finally, Dr. Lazarus motioned to the woman with the long, black hair. "And this lovely lady is Leona Eversoll from the Eversoll Institute for Paranormal Research."

Leona bowed her head politely. "*Bonjour.*"

As Sam took a seat, he continued. "Our original plan was to keep you at Tulane and use the legal system to get you out. But Dr. Kindley trumped us before we could complete the plan. That's when Dixie stepped in."

The red-headed nurse, with light skin, blue eyes, and blood-red lips, leaned over and offered Sam a cup of coffee. "You like Community coffee, Your Majesty, isn't that right? Cream or sugar?"

Sam shook her head, still feeling overwhelmed. Beside her, Aucoin squeezed her shoulder. "Sir, please, let's wait until she recovers. She's adjusting to a lot."

"Quite right, Andre," Professor Mathias said. "Let the poor girl absorb everything first."

Closing her eyes, she inhaled the coffee-and-chicory scent, her favorite in the world. She sipped the brew, savoring the sharp, bitter taste. It was one she had sorely missed. Everyone was quiet as she took a minute to calm her nerves.

Finally she opened her eyes and gazed at Leona. "So is the Eversoll Institute a part of GEIST?"

"*Non*," Leona said gently. "The Institute is in Demark, outside of GEIST's current jurisdiction. We are, how do you say, its benefactors, *oui*?"

"Correct," Dr. Lazarus said. "The Eversoll Institute is one of the oldest paranormal research facilities in the world. I've known its director since childhood. When he read my reports—"

"You mean all the stuff that happened with me?" Sam asked.

"Not just you. With everyone affected by the *loa* during the new Bourbon Street Ripper case. When Dr. Eversoll saw tangible proof of malicious supernatural activity, he immediately began funding our organization."

"And through my connections to the federal government, GEIST got sanctioned to operate within the United States," Professor Mathias added. "You probably recall the missile strike at Evergreen? I'm the one who passed that information on to the president."

Sam skimmed everyone in the room. "So, how big is GEIST?"

Chuckling again and rubbing the back of his neck, Dr. Lazarus said, "Well, GEIST itself is only about a hundred people. Kyle, you know. Veronica is one of my best agents. Mathias here is more of a consultant, while Leona is a representative of the people funding us. Abel and Camellia are my assistants."

Camellia leaned back over, her red lips forming a saucy smile. "Is your coffee to your liking, Your Majesty?"

Putting down the cup, Sam exhaled loudly. "Why the hell do people keep calling me that?"

Several people in the room, especially Leona, recoiled at Sam's outburst. Showing no emotion at all, Professor Mathias sipped his coffee. "Andre, I think we're done with formalities. I suggest you explain pantheons and fusion to her."

"Pantheons? Fusion?" This was starting to sound like a bad TV show.

"Quite right," Dr. Lazarus said. "Sam, do you know what a pantheon is?"

"You mean like the Greek gods of Olympus?"

"More than that. In our line of work, a pantheon refers to a belief system that a regional culture subscribes to. Like voodoo in the southern US and Haiti, or the various Native American animal spirits, or the Celtic pagan mythos."

"OK. So what about them?"

He leaned forward, tapping his fingertips together. "Well, the spirits that make up each pantheon have a dominion of sorts over those regions. So, in the South and Haiti, the voodoo pantheon rules. In the Midwest, a sort of totem pantheon rules. In Ireland, what you would call a pagan pantheon rules."

Mulling over that, she asked, "So, basically, most religions that we would call polytheistic are pantheons of powerful spirits that watch over their part of the world?"

"In a simplified manner of speaking, yes." He leaned back. "Now, you know how there are two levels of possession, right? Riding and full possession?"

This was something she knew well. "Yes. Riding is when a spirit, like a *loa*, attaches itself to your spine and influences your actions and augments your body. That's how Michael, Rodger, and Dallas were able to have enhanced abilities. Full possession is when a spirit is resident inside a body for a longer period of time. It's stronger but can cause permanent damage to the host, such as mental degradation and insanity. Basically, what happened to Blind Moses. I didn't suffer those effects from Marinette because of the drugs Dr. Klein gave me. And a willing, symbiotic possession can be long-term without any damage to the host."

"Correct," Dr. Lazarus said. "And any kind of spirit from any pantheon can be used. *Loa*. Animal spirits. Fairies. You can even use ghosts to ride or possess someone."

She nodded. Things were rapidly falling into place. "So I'm guessing that fusion is a special type of possession?"

"*Oui, oui*!" Leona said charmingly as she sipped her own coffee. "It seems Her Majesty understands."

Nodding, Professor Mathias said, "Correct. But it can only be done with a high spirit such as Madame Bridgette. Basically, a god or goddess within a pantheon. High spirits can enter a pact with a human and merge their souls together. That is fusion, and that is what has happened to you. When a person becomes fused, they obtain godly power and stop aging, becoming technically immortal. They can still die from trauma or disease, but not age. And only when they die is their soul and the high spirit separated."

"It was Mathias here who actually discovered fusion, so to speak," Dr. Lazarus said.

"Less discovered and more quantified, Andre."

While that explained why her body hadn't aged in the past three years, it conflicted with what her father had said. "But I thought I was the only person who was immortal. Vincent. I mean, he . . ."

Leaning forward, Dr. Lazarus locked eyes with her. "That's what confused everyone for so long. You kept saying that Vincent made you immortal. When we finally understood the ritual he had performed, we realized the severity of your condition. Yes, you are immortal due to your fusion with Bridgette, but you are also incapable of dying from trauma or disease, as Mathias said. To understand why, you need to accept a basic tenet: because of the pantheon you were born under—voodoo—your version of the Grim Reaper is Baron Samedi. As you die, he is the one who removes your soul from your body."

"How does that even work?"

"We don't know," Professor Mathias said. "We're only beginning to understand it."

She slowly exhaled. "So no matter where I am in the world, Baron Samedi is my 'Death,' correct?"

"Correct," Dr. Lazarus said. "But because of Vincent's ritual, Baron Samedi cannot come for you, and neither can any other pantheon's Grim Reaper. Therefore, no matter how hurt or sick you get, you cannot die. And the power from being fused with Bridgette will eventually heal you of any injury."

Closing her eyes, she shuddered. It was exactly how Vincent explained it, and she knew it to be true from the year spent in the Gulf of Mexico. She simply could not die.

"And the reason I can't get pregnant?"

"Our research indicates that every person who becomes fused gives up something, depending on the deity they make a pact with. You were pregnant before becoming fused, but afterwards, you could not become pregnant again. More than likely, that is what you gave up—being able to carry any more children."

"That really, really sucks. And I take it being unable to die is a rare thing?"

"Never in recorded history has there been a person with your condition, Your Majesty," Professor Mathias said. "There have been many wonderful and terrible people who were fused—Alexander of Macedonia, Peter the Great, Mahatma Gandhi, Cao Cao, even Emperor Nero. People who have shaped history for good or worse have often been fused. But you? You are unique."

"Right. Any other fused people running around that I should know about?"

"None that I know about," Dr. Lazarus said. "Because the spirit combines with its host's soul instead of being a mere possession, a fused person doesn't even appear possessed."

"Their pupils are dilated for the first year or so, but then, even that goes away," Professor Mathias added.

Sam nodded. Her eyes had gone back to normal.

"Anyway, that is why we call you 'Your Majesty.' You are the queen of the *loa*, and we are showing you respect."

She tittered. "All right. Well, don't. Just call me 'Sam' from now on, OK?"

All in the room nodded.

Sipping her coffee, she thought about what else she wanted to ask them. One question stood out. "So, since you all are experts in this stuff, how do I get to where Vincent is to destroy him?"

An uncomfortable silence blanketed the room, with everyone else shifting their gaze away. Finally, Professor Mathias said, "I'm sorry to say, we don't know of any way to do that. We can assume Vincent is deep within the spirit world. As how to get your physical body there to fight him? I'm afraid we don't know."

With a soft sigh, she sipped her coffee and then popped her jaw. Part of her knew that she was attempting something impossible. "So, I may never be able to end this?"

"We need to destroy the silver pen," Dr. Lazarus said. "We may not being able to defeat Vincent, but if we sever his connection to the physical world, then his *loa* will not be able to wreak such havoc. The naturally malevolent *loa* may still pose the occasional problem, but . . ."

"But not like they are now?" she asked.

He nodded.

She sipped her coffee again and then she asked, "So is that what GEIST is doing?"

Abel stepped forward and bowed respectfully. "Yes, Your Majes—Sam. As you no doubt realize, his power is rising. As his power increases, the damage and harm he can cause grows. If his link to the physical world is not cut soon, untold disasters will occur."

"Yay, as I feared." Even if she couldn't figure out how to get to him and destroy him, she had to sever his connection to this world.

Taciturn as ever, Abel continued. "But for the moment, we're investigating the various experiments the Knight Priory is performing with the *tkeeus*. Investigators like Kyle find out where these experiments are being done, and then agents go in and shut them down. If the situation proves to be serious, we send in operatives."

At that, Dr. Lazarus chimed back in. "Including you, we currently have four operatives. One of them is deep undercover in New Orleans, trying to locate where the Knight Priory is headquartered and where they have your children."

That got her attention.

"You see, Sam, the experimentation with the *tkeeus* all started when Vincent injected it into Dallas. The effect was that Dallas had a permanent ability to attach spirits to him whenever his adrenaline spiked. Since then, the Knight Priory has made exponential strides. But it hasn't been without its problems. You've seen their failures up close at Evergreen."

"I remember them," she said. "So, then, my job will be to shut down Knight Priory operations that are too big for agents to handle?"

"Yes."

Once more, Professor Mathias spoke up. "We should tell her about the Oracle."

"I met him," she said, her body heating up. She gritted her teeth as she remembered how the Oracle had destroyed her chance to leave Evergreen with her children. "I hate him."

Abel cleared his throat. "We know very little about the Oracle. He has gone through great lengths to hide his identity. What we do know is that he is an honorary member of the Knight Priory and the one who brought the *tkeeus* to Vincent years ago. Throughout the years, he has assisted them as an advisor of sorts."

Still grimacing, she said, "Sounds like this Oracle could be fused, yes?"

Leona finally spoke up. "Considering that he once sealed away a very powerful spirit called Lord Dooley with his bare hands, I would say that's a fair assumption."

"Thank you, Miss Eversoll," Abel said. "Sam, our secret operative has been trying to ascertain who the Oracle is, but with no success."

"So there you have it," Dr. Lazarus said. "That's the current state of affairs. Do you have any other questions?"

"Will this secret operative report in as soon as he finds my children?"

"She has several other objectives, but yes, she's been told to contact me when she finds them."

"Then my only question now is 'when do I begin?'"

Dr. Lazarus grinned. "Excellent. Kyle, can you get her started?"

Aucoin, who had been silent the entire conversation, stood up. "Yes, sir. Sam, come with me. Abel will handle orientation, while Meyer will assess your need for combat training."

"Assuming you don't require any training," Dr. Lazarus said, "we'll start you on missions as early as this week. And by the way, your operator number is zero."

"Yeah, I saw that on my door. Why zero?"

"You aren't the first operative, but without you, GEIST wouldn't exist. So think of it as another way to honor you."

Finishing up her coffee, Sam smirked. "With a zero, eh? Cute."

The actual orientation to GEIST was more like starting a new job than Sam had expected. There was a photograph for a security badge, a series of forms to fill out, and even an explanation of salary and housing allowances.

"So what about health benefits?" she had asked Abel, mostly joking.

"If you get sick, we have an on-staff physician. If you die, we pay for your funeral or cremation. That's pretty much it." He had said it very matter-of-factly.

"What about child care?" Sam had asked, pushing to see how far this would go.

"We need to recover them first."

She stopped pushing after that.

Her training assessment went much more quickly. When she showed that she was able to hit the bulls-eye on every shot and could punch holes in concrete, Meyer just checked a box marked "No Training Needed" and sent her off to dinner.

By the time her day was over, she was exhausted, and Aucoin had to help her into her room. She flopped onto her bed. "You know, this is pretty amazing. I'm still expecting to wake up and learn this is all a dream."

Aucoin unlaced her boot and tugged at them. "I know what you mean. The world is different than it was years ago. We have to accept that."

As he helped her out of her boots, she examined him. He was smiling kindly and with a sort of sad strength to his face. He was so different from the angry, bitter man she had known as Dixie's partner. And despite being many years older than Sam, he had handsomeness that shone through his face.

Without even realizing it, she was blushing. "Hey, Kyle, can you come here a second?"

"Hmmm?" He put her boots down and slid over. "What's wrong, Sam?"

Without a word, she grabbed the collar of his jacket and pulled him down, covering his lips with hers. He tasted like ginger ale, and she held him in place until he finally pulled back. He was blushing furiously.

"You wanna stay with me tonight?" she asked, sliding her fingers over her hips.

He looked away and exhaled heavily, gripping her hand with his. "I'd love to, but I don't think that's a good idea."

She frowned, feeling an unpleasant ache in her chest. "What? I'm no good for you?"

Shaking his head, he looked back. "No, I'm no good. Maybe one day I will be, but not yet."

Then he kissed her hand. "Remember, you can trust me. I will never turn my back on you."

A glint of metal caught her eye. He was still wearing his wedding band. Staying loyal to his wife, even though he could never be with her.

"Sleep well, Sam."

She watched him as he left, her face still flushed.

Feeling good, she turned off the light.

There goes a real man.

For the next year, Sam's life and everything she did was directed by GEIST. Her missions took her all over the South. She was even able to go back to Tennessee just long enough to properly say farewell to Caleb and Chris.

They were among the hardest goodbyes of her life.

Chapter 36
Just One More Time

Date: **Thursday, October 31, 1996**
Time: **10:00 p.m.**
Location: **Penthouse at 740 Park Avenue**
Manhattan, New York

It was on the anniversary of Hannah's death when Dixie finally called Dr. Lazarus.

She had just put Felicia to bed when she realized how she could best help GEIST. So while Gino queued up a movie for them to watch in their media room, she grabbed their cordless phone and dialed Dr. Lazarus's number.

"Who are you calling this late, Dixie?" Gino asked. He was in his bathrobe and looking particularly gorgeous. It was the one night of the week they could be alone together.

"Andre," she responded. After achieving closure in her heart regarding Michael, she'd sworn never to lie to Gino about anything again.

He frowned and poured a glass of wine from a bottle in an ice bucket, draining it in three swift gulps. "Whatever you want, Captain Eliopoulos."

She grinned apologetically at him as the other line picked up. It was Camellia. "Office of Dr. Lazarus. May I help you?"

Dixie was glad she had a direct line. "Camellia? It's Dixie. Is Andre there?"

"Well, hello! Yes, one moment."

A few seconds later, Dr. Lazarus answered. "Hello? Dixie? It has to be late over there. Is everything OK?"

"Yes, it is late, but don't worry. Do you remember how you said if I helped out at Emory, you'd pay it back?"

"I did, indeed. Anything you want."

"And is GEIST close to defeating the Knight Priory?"

"We're getting there. My operatives are doing well enough. I'm certain we'll be ready to strike a decisive blow against them within a year. Why?'

She grinned. "I know exactly how I want to help put those bastards down."

Thirty minutes later, the arrangements had been worked out, and Dixie hung up with a feeling of triumph. Heading back to the couch, she saw that Gino looked disgruntled.

"Not pleased with me?" she asked, already knowing the answer.

He took her hand. "Dixie, I thought you were done with all of that after Atlanta. You promised no more chances. No more risks."

Squeezing his hand back, she gazed into his eyes. "I know you're trying to look out for me and our family, but honey, you've got to understand. If the Knight Priory isn't stopped, if their power and influence reaches New York, then we won't be safe."

"Then we'll move to Europe," he said. "We'll move to my villa in Ath—"

She interrupted him with a long kiss. When she leaned back, she saw tears rolling down his cheeks. "Gino, this isn't something we can run from. You were there in New Orleans when it started. You know what the Knight Priory is capable of. We have to destroy them to be safe."

"But, Dixie. Our marriage. Our baby girl."

"That's why I'm fighting. One more time. For you and for Felicia."

"One more time?" He put his arms around her. She hadn't seen him this vulnerable in years.

She kissed his tears away. "One more time. After I've helped GEIST finish off the Knight Priory, I'll get out of it all. I'll focus on being a captain, a wife, and a mother."

Gino nodded, rubbing his face against her head. "Then one more time, Dixie. Just one more."

Chapter 37
Finally Found a Home

Date: **Friday, June 13, 1997**
Time: **7:30 p.m.**
Location: **GEIST Headquarters**
Southern Arkansas

"I'll tell you what, Victor," Sam said as she limped out of the elevator to the domicile floor. Pain rippled through her shoulder from a bullet wound caused by a *tkeeus*-powered super-soldier in the Knight Priory's privately contracted army. "I am going to eat every damn thing in the cafeteria tonight. But first, a shower."

Victor Bane, a fellow operative, said nothing as he headed toward his room. At six foot three, with a red glass eye and the unkempt appearance of a bum, right down to the dirty brown duster and matted hair, he wasn't known for being either conversational or charming.

"Right," Sam said. "Well, good job today, Big V."

He half-turned as he swiped his badge, mumbling "you, too" under his breath and vanishing inside.

She snickered and gestured firing a gun at him. "Got you to say something. I win."

Once inside her own room, she stripped off the twin pair of .45 automatic pistols GEIST had armed her with, placing them on her desk. Then she popped a few hydrocodone painkillers and went to the bathroom mirror.

She had kept her hairstyle from Tennessee, short in the back and long in the front. The black army pants and black camo tank gave her ease of movement, and the black fingerless gloves gave her a great grip.

"Well, Sam," she said as she peeled the compress off her left shoulder, "you'd be the hottest chick on base if not for the large hole right here." The wound was still oozing blood. She had refused medical attention on the ride back, making sure it was concentrated on anyone else who was injured. Even when she was told to report to the staff physician, she said she'd "take care of it."

"Well, let's get this sucker out before the hole closes back up. Would hate to go through that again." She unsheathed the combat knife she kept strapped to her pants, as well as a field suturing kit. Then she bit onto a hand towel she kept at the sink. Lastly, she sterilized the blade with some alcohol before unceremoniously jamming it into her wound and rooting around for the bullet.

The pain was excruciating, and blood poured out as she dug around the wound, finally finding and popping the bullet out. It was a sizeable caliber and covered in chunks of meat and skin. Then she sewed up the wound and placed a fresh bandage over it before spitting out the towel and hollering in pain.

It felt good to scream.

By the time she stripped off her clothes and got in the shower, the painkillers were kicking in, and with it the desire to sleep. She took her time to wash away the grime from the mission. When she got out of the shower, most of the hydrocodone had burned out of her system, leaving a dull ache in her shoulder. They'd offered her stronger stuff before, but it didn't work. Even when she overdosed during Christmas, the medicine was gone before the wound healed.

Sam had since learned to deal with physical pain by just enduring it, and it ended up being one of the best ways to know that she was alive.

"You ended up being right, Vincent. You are the most alive when you're in pain. Fuck you."

A few minutes later, dressed in a pair of casual shorts and a T-shirt, she was in the cafeteria picking double portions of everything she wanted. It was dinnertime, so most of the personnel on base were eating. Scanning the room, she spied Aucoin eating with a dark-skinned Middle Eastern man dressed in a dark blue, gold-trimmed *bisht*, an Islamic robe. Away from everyone else, Victor ate alone, peering at the world with what could only be called suspicion.

She joined Aucoin and the new guy. "Hey, Kyle. Hello, person I've never seen before."

Aucoin motioned to her. "Hakim, this is Sam Castille, the one Abel told you about during orientation. Just remember, she doesn't like to be addressed as 'Your Majesty.'"

With a polite smile, Hakim tapped his fingers to his forehead and said, "*Assalamu alaykum*, Lady Castille. This one's name is Hakim Hassan. It is an honor for him to meet you."

Smiling back, she said, "I'm gonna take that as 'hello,' Hakim. Pleased to meet you. I'm gonna guess from your get-up that you're a Muslim, right?"

Again he bowed his head respectfully. "Indeed. This one is a follower of Allah and the prophet Muhammad. He is also a brother to all men and women and desires only peace and friendship. This one has seen the terrors that lay in the darkest parts of the world, so when Master Abel came to him, he agreed to join."

His manner of speech caught her off guard. "Um, Hakim, why do you refer to yourself as 'this one' and speak in the third person?"

"Ah, apologies, Lady Castille. This one struggles with the sin of pride. He speaks in this way as a constant reminder to him to put himself last."

She stifled a giggle as his cheeks flared up in embarrassment. *We are truly a multicultural organization. That's awesome.*

"Hakim is going to be an operative," Aucoin said, breaking the silence. "Operative number four."

"Oh? That's wonderful! What can you do?"

The blush on Hakim's cheeks continued to flare up. "This one is forced to confess that he was blessed with precognitive abilities. Lady Castille would call him a 'seer' in her language. Also . . ."

He held up his hand, showing off a beautiful golden ring set with a large ruby. "This one made a pact with the spirit that resides in this ring. While this one's guardian is not nearly as powerful as Lady Castille, he hopes it will serve him well."

"That's great, Hakim." As she moved her fork around her food, she took a few moments to scan the room, even watching Victor as he ate hunched over his plate. This had become her family, and while they had gained and lost people over the past year, never once had she felt unsafe among them. *I've finally found a home.*

"Meyer should be back from his mission soon," Aucoin said, pulling her out of her thoughts. "How about we get some practice in the gun range and give Hakim a few pointers? His assessment came back stating he'd need considerable training in firearms."

Again, Hakim blushed. "This one is terrible with guns."

Looking down at her food, she realized that she hadn't eaten a thing on her plate yet, just played around with it. And she was very hungry. "Ya know, Kyle, I'm gonna pass. I think I wanna gorge myself, check on Vincent, hit my G-spot like a maniac, and then sleep until noon."

Instantly, she could tell from Hakim's expression that she had made him uncomfortable. "Sorry, Hakim," she said gently. "They did tell you that I'm fused with a goddess of sexuality, right? And my social skills aren't so great?"

He cleared his throat and then said, "This one will remember that we are all different and yet equal under Allah's eyes. He will also never pass judgment on his brothers or sisters. He will have to get used to such open talk, however."

With a laugh, she reached over and patted him on the back. "Hakim, my friend, you are OK in my book. Welcome to GEIST!"

After stuffing herself until her stomach ached, Sam headed back to her room. Her camos and pants had been replaced by a fresh pair of the same style. Although operatives were allowed to dress in whatever they wanted, most opted to walk around in their field clothes while on base—it showed everyone else, who had to wear some sort of uniform, that no one was better than anyone else.

Before changing, she took a moment to check the wound underneath the bandage. It had mostly closed up with just a puckering to the flesh. She put the bandage back in place.

I'm healing faster.

After putting on fresh clothing, she headed through a security checkpoint to the lab and quarantine section. Inside, a dozen or so experiments on supernatural items and entities, ranging from testing the brain activity of animated corpses to analyzing the containment of ghosts, were taking place in secured glass compartments. Everything was kept sealed off through an elaborate series of lasers, ionized air curtains, and electromagnetic fields.

She didn't understand the science behind any of it, only knowing that GEIST was using research from the Eversoll Institute to figure out how to properly ensnare and destroy supernatural threats. Visions of the containment unit from the *Ghostbusters* movie always flashed in her mind when she thought about that.

After a minute of walking around the lab, even tapping on the glass of a particularly vicious ghost she had help capture, which made it wail at her, she came upon a man in a slimmed-down version of a white hazmat suit. The helmet was fitted with a porcelain face that was almost creepy. A voice box was attached to the front.

Tapping his shoulder, she asked, "Julius? Do you have a moment?"

The man in the suit, Julius Boucher, turned around. A moment later, a mechanical-sounding voice rang out. "Good evening, Sam. How may I help you?"

Seeing him always made her feel a bit sad. He had been brutally burned by Dallas during his youth and was like a simpleton for many years thereafter. But it had been a single outcry from Julius that had helped Rodger break the new Bourbon Street Ripper case. After that, Dr. Lazarus had worked tirelessly to restore his mind to normal. During his therapy, it was discovered that his mind was sharp as ever, and his aptitude for solving puzzles made him perfect to lead GEIST's science team.

"Any luck on figuring out how to destroy the silver pen?"

He shook his head. "Unfortunately, no. We have even tried cutting it with our new CO2 laser. Nothing has worked."

"Damn. Well, thanks for the update. I'd like to check on it, though, if I may."

"Of course, Sam. If you wish. Follow me."

Leading her through the lab, past more experiments and contained creatures, he headed toward the back. There was a vault door marked "Quarantine" which required both of their badges be swiped at the same time to open. The inside was freezing cold, and despite her power, she started feeling numb within seconds.

The vault was still under construction and had only one item in it. Sitting on a metal block and surrounded by several panes of glass was the silver pen. Dozens of cold lasers were trained on it, keeping its temperature as far down as possible.

Pressing her hands to the glass, she felt the evil energy emanating from the pen. Julius spoke. "His influence and power is increasing because of his connection to the physical world. Even with the pen in frozen isolation, his ability to exert his will over his pantheon has grown. If the pen is not destroyed soon, who knows what he'll be able to do?"

"I won't let it get that far," she said. The truth was, however, that due to its extensive use, by herself, Aucoin, and even Rivette, it had no longer needed someone using it to extend its reach. It was growing on its own. For now, destroying it was a priority over destroying Vincent.

"What is needed to destroy it, Julius? Do you know?"

"An enormous amount of energy and pressure."

"How much? Are we talking coal to diamonds here?"

"I don't know for sure, Sam. I'm sorry."

"No worries. I'm certain you'll find something that can get the job done."

"Thank you. Although for now, we should leave. Your lips are turning blue."

He was completely unaffected, the insulation of the suit protecting him from the extreme cold. But she was shivering, so she left the vault. Once outside, she warmed up within seconds. Then she cleared her throat. "Hey, Julius. I never apologized. You know, for everything that happened back at Acadia Vermilion when we were kids."

Again, he shook his head. "You have nothing to apologize for, Sam. We were all victims. Even Dallas. The real villain has always been Vincent."

"Thanks, Julius," she said, feeling a weight lift off her chest. Walking along the hallways, she decided that she needed some fresh air, so she headed up to the roof. It offered a lovely view of the stars at night, and she often went up there to think.

As soon as she stepped outside, she felt the spirits around her once again. A few of them nudged against her, a few more circled around her like wisps of smoke, and one or two tried to get her attention. She smiled to herself, reaching out and letting them swirl around her arms and between her fingers. When they weren't under someone else's control, most spirits were playful. They felt like children that just needed love.

Then she went to her favorite spot, the parapet on the far end of the roof. She wasn't the only person up there—Aucoin was quietly gazing at the stars. She watched him a few seconds, admiring his posture. He hadn't drunk or smoked anything in the past year. Most members of GEIST used vices to help cope with their constant battle against the Knight Priory. Even she still drank when off duty. But not him—somehow, he managed to stay straight and narrow.

He's turned out be my best friend. Heck, I even drink less because of his influence.

Inhaling the warm evening air, she approached him. "Nice night, eh?"

He jerked, probably out of deep thoughts. "Oh! Hey, Sam. Yeah, I just needed to get out here and clear my head."

Leaning against the railing next to him, she looked up as well. At times, she felt like she could reach up and grab them out of the sky. "Thinking about Cathy again?"

"Yeah," he said. "Found out that she finally remarried. Nice guy, too. He'll take care of her."

She noticed that for the first time he wasn't wearing his wedding band. "Oh, Kyle. I'm sorry."

"Nah, don't worry about it. She needs to be happy. I'm just glad we reconciled before ending it."

Hearing that made her think of Richie for the first time in almost a month. *I still miss him, and I always will. But he wants me to be happy, right?*

"So what brings you out here?" he asked, pulling her from her thoughts.

"I dunno. I just was tired of being cramped in that bunker. Aren't you supposed to be working with Hakim on 'that one's' firearms skills?"

"Ha, 'that one.' Yeah, Hakim is awesome," he said. "But no. Turns out Meyer works better alone. Amazing, though. Their religions usually don't get along, but here in GEIST, they are brothers-in-arms."

"We all are," she said. "United against the Knight Priory and Vincent." Then she leaned back on the parapet, her chest sticking out. "Kyle, the world is changing, isn't it? And not for the better."

Getting a thoughtful expression, he gazed back up at the sky.

She stood beside him in silence for a while. Then she said, "I mean, well, these dark things are coming out of hiding and hurting people. And we're stopping them."

"You want my honest opinion, Sam?"

When she nodded, he said, "I think those dark things have always been a part of our world. We've just refused to notice. People who experienced them were called crazy and locked away. And why? Because these incidents have been so isolated. But now, because of what's happening in New Orleans, they're getting widespread and more commonplace. Perhaps in time, we'll realize that the people we called crazy were the sane ones, and we were crazy for not believing them."

Slowly, Sam turned toward Aucoin. He was watching her. She smiled. Of all the things she'd heard since that night in August when Rodger and Michael knocked on her door, this made the most sense. It was never crazy to believe in *loa* and voodoo—it was crazy not to.

"Kyle . . ." She leaned over and hugged him. "Thank you."

He hugged her back. "You're welcome."

They stayed that way for a while, the wind blowing over them, the sounds of crickets keeping them company.

Their respite was interrupted by the sound of someone stepping out onto the roof. It was Abel. Under the moonlight, his pale skin nearly glowed, making him look otherworldly. She had once asked him what he was, and he had just said he was "no different than you."

"Sam, Kyle, the director wants to see you. It's of paramount importance."

When Sam entered Dr. Lazarus's office with Aucoin and Abel beside her, she noticed that he and Camellia were making calls on cordless phones. Abel cleared his throat. "Sir, they're here."

Dr. Lazarus held out his hand and spoke into his phone. "I understand that you cannot make it, Mathias, but thank you for your support. Yes, it will be enough that she comes. Yes, Sam will be pleased."

He hung up and motioned for Sam and Aucoin to come forward. "Thank you, Abel. Please inform the other operatives that we'll be having strategy meeting at noon tomorrow and that it will last several hours. Everyone will want to take an early lunch."

Abel bowed politely and left.

Sam approached. "Um, so what's going on?"

A smile that wouldn't fade parted Dr. Lazarus's lips. "Sam, we're ready to make our move. The secret operative I've had working for me? She's back, and she discovered where the Knight Priory holds their secret meetings."

Aucoin whistled. "That sounds huge, sir."

"It is, Kyle." Dr. Lazarus got Camellia's attention. She was speaking in Scandinavian.

"Camellia, please finish that in the other room."

"Yes, sir," she said and left.

Sam folded her arms. She didn't know what to think. During the past year with GEIST, Dr. Lazarus had kept only one secret—the identity of the operative who was working undercover. As far as she was aware, no one but he and his innermost circle knew her identity—all to keep her safe.

"So the Knight Priory's headquarters has been located? Great. But what about my kids?"

Still grinning, Dr. Lazarus leaned forward. "Yes! That, too. She found your children!"

Her pulse spiked. "Are you serious?"

"Absolutely!"

She could have started dancing right then and there. "So, where are they? What's the story?"

He cleared his throat. "It's better if she explains it."

She looked around. "OK. Well, where is she?"

"I'm right here, Sam." The voice was so steady and measured that it sounded threatening, and Sam felt a cold presence emerge from behind the curtains.

It was a figure dressed in a dark indigo robe, her face covered by a skull mask. An assault rifle was slung over her shoulder. The stance, the arrogant air, and the feeling of coldness were unmistakable.

But it was also impossible. This person had died by Sam's own hand.

"Blind Moses? But, how?"

Her Sister Was Home

(Tania Patterson's Story)

Chapter 38
The New Blind Moses

Date: **Tuesday, June 10, 1997**
Time: **3:00 p.m.**
Location: **Office of Harry Connick**
District Attorney, New Orleans City Hall

And this is the story Blind Moses told . . .

"Mr. Connick, the mayor is on line three about your meeting with him tonight."

"Oh, right. Send it over, Petunia. I'll talk to him myself." Connick's voice had a deep timbre to it, especially when on the phone. "And once you complete those reports, you can clock out for the day."

"Thank you, Mr. Connick. Transferring him now."

Tania Marie Patterson, operating under the alias Petunia Evans, exhaled tiredly. Although it was necessary that she worked for the district attorney's office as part of her mission, she couldn't stand the day job. But it was necessary to keep abreast of the political winds in New Orleans if she was to discover where the Knight Priory gathered.

Finishing the last report, she turned off the radio, which was playing the latest pop hits by artists like the Spice Girls and Jewel, bid her co-workers good evening, and left.

Like always, traffic was bad going to the West Bank. When she got home, the neighbors of her rented duplex were arguing, as they typically did. And as usual, dinner took longer to cook than she wanted to wait with her increased appetite. By the time it was dark, and her food was settled, she was outright grumpy.

You really are a bad influence on me, she thought to other residing within her.

"*So you say*," said the voice in her head. "*Let's just get going.*"

Mmm. Right. Since you're so eager to atone for your sins.

"*Just shut up and get dressed.*"

She went to the attic of her duplex, pulling back several floorboards until she uncovered a large, black box. It was only thing left from the night her store had burned to the ground, and she had nearly died saving it.

Taking a few seconds to run her fingers over its surface, remembering the life she'd left behind that night, she then unlocked it with a key she kept around her neck. Inside were several hooded indigo robes and black bodysuits, a skull mask, and a semi-automatic sniper rifle given to her by Dr. Lazarus.

Good thing you kept more than one bodysuit. They tear so easily.

"*Good thing you widened the bust and hips on all of them.*"

Hmph!

In a few minutes, she was dressed in her sister's Blind Moses costume. Against the bodysuit, she strapped a pair of binoculars, a lock pick set, and a medical kit. Then, kneeling down, she made the sign of the cross and prayed. "Lord, forgive me for what I have done and what I am about to do. Amen."

Standing up, she closed her eyes and focused. *All right. Let's go.*

"*Finally!*"

Her body shook, and her eyes rolled back as she felt the other presence move, coming forward and giving her power she never had on her own. When she regained control, she felt stronger, faster, and more focused, but she also felt crueler and more vicious, her own mind altered by the possessing soul. For five years, it had remained within her, gradually wearing down her once-cheery disposition until she was perpetually moody. But despite that, she was closer to it than anyone else in the world.

It was the soul of her twin sister, Violet Patterson, who had been the original Blind Moses before Sam killed her. Together, they were the new Blind Moses, a secret operative of GEIST.

Above the streets of New Orleans, Tania leapt from rooftop to rooftop, keeping clear of the police below. As Blind Moses, Violet had massacred dozens of officers, and Tania herself had broken into more than enough places during her year-long investigation of the Knight Priory. Oftentimes, the roofs of the city, the suspension cables of bridges, and the darkness of back alleys were the only safe way to travel.

"*Do you know our destination tonight, dummy?*" Violet asked impatiently.

Yes, Tania responded, although it was difficult to think in full sentences while dashing along the girders of the Crescent City Connection. She stopped at the top of one of its apexes. *Mayor Morial has been meeting every night with Connick, who we suspect is the leader of the Knight Priory. I want to spy on their meeting tonight.*

She continued on to the other side of bridge, heading toward Poydras Street and the Central Business District.

"*Right, well, keep on your toes. You almost got us arrested last night.*" Being dead had done nothing to make Violet any less antagonistic.

We'll be fine. And stop distracting me!

Tania felt Violet settle down as she leapt onto the rim of the Superdome. Running up to the top, she hung on the flag pole, took out her binoculars, and then scouted out her target several blocks away—City Hall. Due to the increase in supernatural activity, as well as successful missions by GEIST, it had become one of the most guarded buildings in New Orleans. She spotted two armed guards on the roof and six more inside.

Any loa? They've gotten better at using them as sentries. Ever since Evergreen Plantation, the Knight Priory had fully embraced the supernatural.

"*The spirits in the area are acting normal. I'll know more once we're inside.*"

Satisfied for the moment, Tania secured her equipment and took a deep breath, measuring the distance across Poydras, one of the largest streets in the city, to the building right next to City Hall. When she was ready, she sprinted down the side of the Superdome, gathering up speed until she was moving in a blur. When she reached the very edge, she jumped. Her robe's material rustled as she sailed over the highway.

A moment later, she landed on the side of the building, planted her heels on the nearest windowsill, and pushed. Her legs, augmented by her sister's power, were like springboards. After a few well-timed jumps, she was on the roof.

"*Someone's looking this way!*"

Sliding toward the parapet of the roof, Tania hid herself. When she glanced back up, binoculars in hand, she saw it—a sniper on City Hall, a third guard she had missed.

"*You don't have a choice. He dies.*" Violet almost seemed to be snickering.

Tania grimaced. She disliked killing, but this was a war against the Knight Priory. They had crushed countless lives in order to obtain dominion, including murdering young Hannah Davis even though the *krabinay* possessing her had already been absorbed and devoured. As far as Tania was concerned, everyone on the Knight Priory's side was a threat.

You're right. He won't give a second thought to killing me. He goes.

While on her back, she attached the silencer to her rifle and then set up the shot. There were lights and a strong headwind—a normal human had virtually no chance of hitting a target under those conditions. But Violet's soul made her senses far more acute.

Keeping the sunguard over the scope to prevent the sniper from seeing her, she waited. The moment the traffic on Poydras got loud, horns honking as commuters expressed themselves, she flipped open the sunguard and lined up the target. The sniper must have seen a glint, because he jerked in surprise. Without hesitating, she pulled the trigger. A moment later, his head burst open like a melon.

Tania licked her lips. "Tango down."

"*You are such a nerd.*"

Knowing she had only a few minutes before the dead body was discovered, Tania leapt down to the lower roof of one of City Hall's annexes and rushed across to the main building. A few more seconds of leaping from ledge to ledge and she was on the main roof next to the dead sniper. Hiding the body, she lay low and waited. A few minutes later, the other two guards on the roof came over.

"Hey, Rob, where are you? You're supposed to be watching this side of the building while the mayor—"

Before he could finish, she knocked out one with an elbow to the back of the head and another with a spinning kick to the face. Then she tied them both up.

"*Hmmm. You're gonna let them live, eh?*"

Sorry to ruin your fun, Sister! Tania smirked as she slipped inside.

Once on top floor, she felt Violet prickle up. "*Hey, be careful. I feel a guardian spirit.*"

Any idea what it is?

"*If you're talking about those classifications Dr. Lazarus came up with, then no. I told you, dummy, we ghosts don't care about that. But it's a loa, it's big, and it's hungry.*"

Keeping watch for signs of spiritual activity, such as drops in temperatures or the hairs on the back of her neck standing up, Tania snuck along the corridors of City Hall. Her movements were fluid and quick. The only sound she made was the rustling of her robe. Several times, she heard the footfalls of guards as they came near, forcing her to duck into an office or restroom and wait for them to pass. By the time she reached the doors outside the mayor's office, she had been inside for over half an hour.

"*The guards on the roof will likely be discovered soon.*"

I know.

"*When that happens, they will raise the alarm.*"

I know, Sister. Tania was starting to get annoyed.

The doors were guarded by two armed men, so she slipped back around the corner and into a nearby, smaller office. It wasn't the first time she had snuck through buildings, so she knew exactly what to do. Removing a panel of foam insulation from the ceiling, she slipped inside, making sure to put her weight only on the support beams and cross-sections. Silently, she made her way through the ceiling.

"All right. I'll admit that you've gotten pretty good at this."

Thanks! As good as you used to be?

Violet snorted. *"Don't press your luck, dummy."*

As Tania passed over the threshold to the mayor's office, she felt a sudden chill. Along with the sound of voices, she heard heavy breathing and the rattle of chains. Then she felt something searching for her. The sensation of dread was overwhelming.

"Damn it! Sister, it's a bakulu!"

Tania froze in place. *Bakulu*, like *krabinay*, were petro *loa*, the malicious and dangerous spirits of voodoo. But unlike the kind that possessed Hannah, a *bakulu* was a greater *loa*—too powerful, too wild, and too violent to safely possess anyone.

Those things eat lesser loa, don't they?

"Yes. And it can sense me. I'm going to withdraw before it detects me and blows our cover."

Before Tania could protest, Violet pulled back deep inside of her, which caused her powers to fade away. Gritting her teeth, she struggled to stay stable on the ceiling's support lattice, the only strength she had now from hours of yoga each day. But it worked. A moment later, she felt the *bakulu*'s attention shift elsewhere. Sweat was already dripping down her face and the inside of the mask. Stilling herself as best she could, she concentrated on listening to the voices.

"You've made a wise decision, Marc." It was Connick, his deep voice very distinct.

"I hope so, Harry," Mayor Morial said. "Those Republicans are throwing everything they can at me to discredit my administration. I need the backing of the elite to make a difference."

A woman spoke up. It was a cold voice that Tania didn't recognize. "Mr. Mayor, let me assure you that the Knight Priory of Saint Madonna will give you its full support. All we ask in return is that you let us use the New Orleans police to crush a group that's been . . . hindering our scientific research."

Tania gulped. The woman had to mean GEIST.

"Scientific?" Morial sounded incredulous. "You call this floating . . . thing scientific? You call any of this voodoo-hoodoo science?"

They could see the *bakulu*. It wasn't a surprise. The ambient energy of New Orleans had gotten so strong that spirits and ghosts were able to manifest with ease.

Connick chuckled deeply. "Our resident researcher, Dr. Kindley, has done extensive study on the *loa* and their composition. While we cannot control them, we can influence them. Isn't that accurate, Miss Saucier?"

Caroline! I remember her. Tania took off her mask and flicked the sweat away. Then she wiped her face dry.

"Yes," Caroline said. "So, Mayor, if you agree to our terms, we can induct you into the Knight Priory the night following the next."

"Right, so the immediate things. Apart from signing the order to demolish old Jonathon Russell's mansion, what else did you want me to do?"

Jonathan's mansion? Why did they want to tear that down?

"Well, we lost control of the Castille accounts a few weeks ago, so we need to file an appeal—"

The door to the office burst open. Several people trampled inside, and someone said, "Mr. Mayor, Mr. Connick! We have an intruder in the building. He's already taken out three of the guards on the roof. Sirs, madam, you have to come with us!"

Lovely. Just lovely.

Tania knew that in less than a minute, the entire building would be swarming with guards. Human and spirit guards.

Sister, we need to get out of here.

When Violet didn't respond, Tania reached down within herself and pulled her forward. *Damn it, Sister, I need your power now!*

"*No! Don't! The bakulu—*"

Forget the bakulu, Tania thought as she put on her mask. *I'm going to smash through the window and run down the side of the building.*

"*What? Have you lost your stupid mind?*"

She didn't answer. Instead, she focused on bringing Violet as far forward as she could. As she heard the *bakulu* snarl, she said a quick prayer and dove through the ceiling, landing right in the middle of six armed guards escorting Mayor Morial, Harry Connick Sr, and Caroline Saucier out of the plush, well-decorated office. Nearby was the *bakulu*. Translucent and glowing a pale, sickly white, it had a thick chest and a massive head that was mostly mouth. Two beady eyes rested on its low-hanging tongue. Its tree-trunk-sized arms ended in huge, clawed hands, and it was shackled with ghostly chains wrapped around its entire body.

The moment it saw her, it let out a roar so load the pictures on the wall shook.

"*Run. Now.*" For the first time since Violet had possessed her, she sounded frightened.

"Who is that?" Morial cried out. "I thought we were secure!"

Caroline stumbled back against a wall. "Isn't that Blind Moses? Isn't she dead?"

Tania didn't wait, springing to her feet and rushing toward the window with the *bakulu* right behind her. As it let out another horrifying roar, she fired at the glass. In just a few shots, it shattered, brightly lit particles of glass dancing through the air. With a cry of her own, she dove through.

A moment later, her feet touched the side of the building, and she ran down, focusing each step to control her fall. By the time she reached the overhang at the entrance, she had slowed down enough to jump, flip, and roll. She landed in front of the steps, and then glanced back up. The armed guards were pointing at her and shouting into walkie-talkies. The *bakulu* was staring at her and breathing heavily, its mouth foaming.

"*OK. I'll admit it. You did really well just now.*"

But don't let it go to my head, right?

"*Exactly. Now let's get out of here.*"

Tania harnessed the rifle on her back and ran off down the street as fast as she could. Then she jumped onto the roof of a nearby parking garage. Within a few minutes, she was far away from City Hall.

Chapter 39
A Cuff Link

Date: **Tuesday, June 10, 1997**
Time: **11:00 p.m.**
Location: **Russell Family Mansion**
Lake Pontchartrain in Slidell

Despite being exhausted after getting back home from City Hall, Tania immediately threw a fresh costume into the backseat of her car and headed toward Slidell and the Russell family mansion. There was no way of knowing when it would be torn down, and her gut said that there was an important reason the Knight Priory wanted it destroyed.

Sipping on some convenience store coffee, she turned off the interstate and onto the side road leading to the mansion. She had been there once before, soon after the fire in Sam's townhome, but the police had locked it up on account of it being a mechanized death trap.

"*There's something about Connick that concerns me.*" Violet had been more talkative than usual.

Oh? What's that ?

"*I'm not sure. The way he talks and acts is so different from before. He seems like an entirely different person.*"

Tania pulled up to the gates of the Russell estate and started getting dressed.

You think he's possessed?

"*That's the thing. If he was possessed by a* loa, *then I'd know. If he was being ridden by a* loa, *then I'd know.*"

She slipped out of the car, secured her rifle to her back, and got ready to pull Violet forward.

So what do you think it is?

"I'm not sure. Only a high loa *could evade my senses, but there aren't any left. Baron Samedi is bound, Madame Bridgette is fused with Sam, and Papa Ghede is pure benevolence. Besides, high* loa *can't normally possess a human. It's too unstable."*

Donning her mask, Tania thought, *Ponder on it later, Sister. Let's go!*

Violet moved forward until Tania felt the power flow through her. The coldness, the focus, and the energy were intoxicating. With a single leap, she soared over the gates and toward the mansion. It was still shut down, boarded up tightly with thick metal sheets at every entrance. There were also warnings, like "Stay back" and "Dangerous machinery." Tania had heard reports on the traps that Jonathon had installed to ward off and maim intruders. It was the very definition of overkill.

After circling around the mansion twice and not seeing a viable way in without tearing through walls, Tania finally climbed up to the roof. The skylight above the foyer hadn't been boarded up.

"You sure the traps are disabled?"

Yes. The house has been off the grid and without generators for years. I think this place is as safe as a baby's crib.

"I'm certain Rodger Bergeron thought the same thing."

Snorting, she held her breath and jumped through the skylight. She landed gracefully on the carpeted floor below, shards of glass sprinkling around her like droplets of rain. Giving her eyes a moment to adjust to the light, she moved out from under the broken glass.

The air was dusty, and the stench of mildew was suffocating. All around, the walls and wooden fixtures were covered in mold. The staircase on one side of the foyer was flattened into a slide, leading down into a pit of spikes, the chandelier lay broken in the middle of the room, and at the front doorway, a guillotine blade lodged into the floor.

"I like this guy's style."

Hush it.

She carefully crept up the other staircase, which was normal. There were faded footprints in the mold—someone else had been here quite some time ago. At the top of the second floor landing was a set of metal bars separating it from the hallway. Several of the bars had been cut away, probably when the police removed Jonathan's body. The footprints headed through that gap and down the hallway to the left.

"I don't sense anyone, but be careful."

Now moving more cautiously and with her rifle out, Tania snuck down the hallway, the flooring loose as if it had once moved on its own. Following the footprints, she came upon a room that she recognized as a study. The ceiling, which had spikes on it, was retracted by several large metal bracings. It looked like a section of the wall had been pried open. Inside was an empty desk.

I think that's where Jonathon was shot.

"*Look over at the other wall, dummy! I think someone searched there, too.*"

Sure enough, part of a side wall had also been pried open. Inside was a small bookcase with rotted black velvet drapery. It had been picked clean, save for a few scraps of paper. She kneeled down in front of it, searching for a clue as to what had been there.

She was just about to leave when a glint caught her eye. Moving aside some of the dust, she pulled out a small button made out of copper or brass. The face of the button had the letters "NOPD" on it.

The police. I wonder whose it—

"*Shh! Quiet! I feel something.*"

A groaning sound disturbed the still night air. Pocketing the button and rushing out to the landing, she saw a translucent figure in an elaborate feathered headdress with an animal-skin shield and a spear. Its face was puckered tightly, with oversized eyes and pierced ears. As it spotted her, it let out a piercing war cry that made her teeth clatter.

"*What the? An* ogoun*?*" Violet sounded shocked.

Ogoun*? What's that?*

"*An African war spirit, from the Nigeria and Guinea regions. Roughly as strong as a krabinay.*"

The *ogoun* throw its spear at Tania, the ghostly blade nicking her cheek. Its movements were surprisingly fast.

What is something from the African pantheon doing here?

"*I don't know. Someone must have summoned it.*"

It stomped its large feet in a trampling dance and let out another battle cry, never taking its eyes off her. Then it pulled out another spear from behind its shield and took aim.

I'm a sitting duck up here. I need to get down there and fight it on equal terms.

"*Just remember what we learned from the Alexia Report. It's your human will that allows your physical attacks to damage spirits. Focus your will to overcome it.*"

Tania laughed as she jumped down to the foyer, landing with the grace of a cat. *Sister, I lived through Vincent's abuse, mother's death, and your grumpy ass. I have will to spare.*

Feeling Violet channel her power into her, she rushed at the *ogoun* as it threw another spear. This time, she was ready and rolled to the side, coming up in time to jump onto the side of the staircase and push off, flying right at it. With a yell, she kicked it square in its head, focusing herself into the attack, visualizing it connecting. Instead of her foot passing through, it made physical contact. The *ogoun* screeched and flew back, landing near the front door.

"*Keep it up!*"

With a frustrated glare, it let out another battle cry, drew out two spears with one hand, and threw them at her. She spun to the side and dodged one, only to be sliced across the stomach by the other. It felt like she had been cut by an icicle. As blood started to trickle, she unharnessed her gun and focused Violet's energy to steady her aim. Then she fired off several shots, forcing her will into each one. Some of the bullets passed through it and sank into the wall, but one embedded itself in its chest, making it stumble back.

"*Bullets aren't as effective as close combat, dummy!*"

You think?

Rushing at it, Tania focused her will through the butt of her rifle and hit it with an arcing uppercut swing. As it flew up into the air, she jumped after it, hitting it a dozen more times, and letting loose with a battle cry of her own. When she landed, she heard a wailing shriek. Above, the *ogoun* was arched back, white light pouring from it as it vanished into misty vapors.

"*I am impressed,*" Violet said. "*You defeated it. Its energy has returned to the spirit world.*"

Hey, you helped. I couldn't have done it without you. We're a team, Sister!

When Violet didn't respond, Tania sighed. Violet had killed her heart while they were still children. It was the only way she could survive Vincent's cruelty. That aversion to emotion carried into her death. While most ghosts oozed pathos and passion, Violet always grew silent.

So instead of pushing, Tania took that time to exit the house through the broken skylight. She headed back to the car and got out of the costume.

"*So where to now?*" Violet asked.

Whoever was here and took whatever was in those bookcases was a member of the police. We have only one contact with the police that we can trust. We go to him.

"*Ugh. I hate visiting him. His dog is so damn annoying.*"

Compared to how the rest of the evening had gone, breaking into their contact's house was easy. Sitting in his easy chair, she fixed up her injuries with her medical kit and then let Violet contact the ghost that resided in the house. She had to go about it carefully, or her sister would wake up the family Shi Tzu, which would blow any secrecy to the meeting.

Ten minutes later, an elderly man in a pair of shorts came out, rubbing his eyes. "Mmmm . . . what's going on? Who's that?"

"Douglas, it's me, Tania."

Douglas Dugas groaned. "You couldn't wait till morning?"

She turned on his light. "You know I couldn't. Did Rodger wake you up?"

Sitting down and rubbing his face, he said, "Of course he did. Otherwise, he just sits in the bedroom rocker and watches over us while we sleep. Mabel, bless her heart, thinks he's a guardian angel. Boudreaux now loves him and never leaves that chair at night. It's a sight, watching him get petted by a ghost."

Tania nodded. Thankfully, Douglas had adjusted to the reality of the supernatural very well, while most people were like Mabel, either ignoring it or losing their minds. "Well, he nearly spent all of his energy helping Dixie and Kyle while evading Vincent. This is probably all he has left. You're lucky to have him protecting you. He must love you very much."

With another yawn, he said, "I know he does. His death all but broke Mabel, so having him here is a kind comfort. Anyway, not to be rude, but it's two in the morning. What brings you here?"

She leaned forward. "I'm onto something big. Remember how you swore you'd help me if it would stop the Knight Priory?"

"Tania, you don't have to remind me of our agreement. What they've done to our city is plain criminal. And after talking to Rodger—well, his ghost—and finding out the whole story about Vincent, I'll do whatever I can. So what do you need?"

Taking out the button, she tossed it to him. "I found that at a place of interest. Jonathon Russell's old mansion. What is it?"

Catching it, he held it up to the light, squinting. A moment later, he said, "Well, I'll be. It's a cufflink for the NOPD."

"Any guess what kind of cop would have one?"

"I don't need to guess. I know. This cufflink is only given to commanding officers. Was offered a pair of them myself when I retired, even though I never made officer."

That clinched it. In her mind, only one police commander could be involved in this sordid tale. "Ouellette."

"Excuse me?"

With a shrug, she said, "It has to be Ouellette's. There's no one else."

His expression immediately showed irritation. "Are you saying that Louis is working with the Knight Priory?"

At that, she shook her head. "No, my boss made it clear that he's not. But listen—years ago, he told both Dixie and Kyle he was searching for something, and they believe that something was of interest to the Knight Priory. So one way or another, he's involved."

Sitting at the edge of his seat, he pointed his finger in her face. "Now you listen to me, you fool. He may be a great many things, but he is not a bad guy. He—"

Not flinching, she calmly lowered his hand. "All right. I apologize. Help me to search his office for information on what was taken out of the mansion. If he's clean, then I won't find anything."

He tightened his fist around the cufflink. "How am I supposed to do that? I'm retired going on twenty-five years now."

"Simple. You have lunch with him and get him out. I'll handle the rest."

He frowned, rubbing his head again. "Fine! But after this, no more nonsense connecting him to the Knight Priory."

Smiling, she said, "Done."

Chapter 40
Sobs of Sorrow

Date: **Wednesday, June 11, 1997**
Time: **12:00 p.m.**
Location: **New Orleans Police Department**
Precinct Eight, French Quarter

"*We're going to get caught, dummy.*"

No, we won't. And get back. We don't know if Ouellette can detect you or not!

As she squeezed through the air ducts of the eighth precinct, Tania again took off the Blind Moses mask. It was difficult to see where she was crawling with it on, and unlike her sister, who had been guided by the *loa* Bwa-Cheh, she actually needed her eyes.

"*I'm telling you, this is a bad idea. You shoulda just gone to work.*"

I took the day off to do this. Gracious, Sister, why do you have to be so negative?

When Violet didn't respond, Tania continued onward until she was over Ouellette's office. Breathing slowly and softly, she peered inside. Ouellette was at his desk, going through the contents of a file folder. When he stopped and looked forward, she held her breath, ready to scoot back in case he glanced up. But instead, he went over to the door just as someone started knocking on it.

Is he precognitive?

"*Not sure. He's not being possessed or ridden.*"

"Douglas, you old bastard," Ouellette said as he let Douglas in. "What brings you here today?"

They sat back down. Douglas laughed. "Oh you know, just keeping myself busy. Mabel's wanting to spend more time with the grandkids, and little Boudreaux has maybe a good year or two left. Can't complain."

"That's wonderful, Douglas. And for the record, I think you and Mabel should go out of town and visit the grandkids more. They're up in Chicago, right?" Ouellette, who usually sounded harsh and gruff, was being friendly.

"Yup, Chicago. That's right."

I can't get a read on this guy, Sister.

"*Neither can I.*"

Tania exhaled in frustration. Aucoin had made it very plain that he didn't trust Ouellette, but Dr. Lazarus stated he had complete faith in him. She didn't know what to make of him.

"So, there's been something that's been weighing on my mind for a while. I was hoping we could go to lunch and talk." Douglas's expression was serious.

Ouellette put down the folder. "This sounds important."

"Yeah. It's everything that's been happening. You know, since Rodger died. Everything's going nuts. And with the Knight Priory making a comeback, I just don't feel as safe as I once did."

"Yeah, we need to go out. My treat. I'll—"

Abruptly, Douglas leaned forward. "I just need to know one thing. Are you one of them?"

That question seemed to stun Ouellette. He looked hurt. "Why would you ask that?"

"I just need to know. Look, the Knight Priory used to be a good thing. Even back when Vincent was running it, they did a lot of—"

Ouellette stood and shouted, his voice reverberating. "Vincent screwed the whole thing up!"

Tania's ears rang for a few seconds, making it hard to focus. When she looked back, Douglas was leaning back, his face pale.

"Sorry," Ouellette said, sitting back down. "It wasn't really Vincent's fault. Someone, years ago, gave him something. That thing destroyed his life."

He means the tkeeus.

"*It destroyed his life? What kind of crap is that? It destroyed my life.*"

Tania shifted her perception away from the conversation to focus on Violet. Deep inside, she felt her sister's soul aching, helplessness pouring out. Compassion overwhelmed Tania as she reached within, visualizing her hand stroking Violet's hair. She imagined it would be stringy and matted, as it usually was, but underneath was a softness wanting to come out.

"*What are you doing?*"

Loving you, Sister.

"*I . . . We need to focus on the mission.*" Violet pushed her hand away, as she had done every day of her life.

Despite that, Tania felt like she had just touched a part of her twin. It was almost like they had, for a brief second, connected. And while Tania knew that such behavior during a mission was inappropriate, she didn't care. She might never get a chance to connect with her sister again.

But, pushed away for the moment, she focused again on the conversation below. Ouellette was finishing up an explanation that she missed while Douglas sat there in deep thought. Finally, he spoke up. "That makes sense. So because of what this Oracle guy did back in 1962, everything that we've suffered through happened. And now you're working to fix it."

"Pretty much," Ouellette said. "Someone with a clue needs to stop this thing before it spirals out of control. I'm figuring out a way, but for it to work, I need the Knight Priory to trust me. So I kept my older membership and just played along for now. But enough of this crap. Let's go do that lunch."

"All right."

The two headed out of the office. For a moment, Ouellette stopped at the door and looked toward the vent. Tania pulled back so that she wasn't visible.

"Everything OK?" Douglas asked.

"Yeah. Just thought I saw a rat."

Then the door closed and all was silent. After a few minutes, she slid forward, unfastened the grating, and slipped out. Then she started digging through Ouellette's desk. There were old notes dating back from the early eighties and take-out menus from every restaurant in the French Quarter. One drawer held a bottle of half-drunk whiskey and two glasses. The only drawer she couldn't get into was the main one right under the desk. It was locked.

"*We can break it open easily.*"

And then he'll know someone was here.

"*Who cares? Once this mission is over, we're heading back to GEIST.*"

She knew Violet was right. They were running out of time. Focusing her sister's power, she yanked the drawer hard. It popped right open. Inside was a .40 caliber pistol—standard issue for police—and several clips of ammunition. Also, there was a small notebook. Tania flipped through it to the last page, where she found a note that looked several years old: "Knight Priory leader has Russell's book. Lets Kindley use it." It was signed, "Landry."

She grinned. Something had, indeed, been taken from Jonathan's mansion.

So the Knight Priory's leader has the book and lets Kindley use it. It has to be Connick!

"Likely, yes. But what is the book?"

I have no idea. Let's go find out.

Putting everything back and closing the drawer, Tania stepped on the desk to get back into the vent. As she grabbed the rim to pull herself up, her foot tapped the folder Ouellette had been reading. She glanced down to make sure it hadn't moved.

One of the papers was now sticking out a little. The header bore the name "Castille."

What the heck?

Jumping back down, she opened the folder. Inside was the genealogy of the Castille family for the past several generations. Starting with Louis Castille, it spread down to Vincent, Gladys, and Marguerite.

Louis was Vincent's father, right?

"Yes. He fought in the First World War and then vanished, leaving Vincent in charge of the family at a very young age."

How do you know all this, Sister?

"I paid attention when Mother tutored us. She often believed that life without a father made Vincent into the man he became."

Tania continued following the family line. From Vincent came two children through two separate wives—Edward through Grenadine and Samantha through Mary.

Right. Vincent remarried Mary and had Sam.

The line continued from Edward and Maple, leading into Dallas, and from Dallas and Samantha leading into Alice and Eugene.

Oh, my goodness!

"What? What is it?"

Sister, those are Sam's children! The ones the Knight Priory took from her!

"So?"

We have their names now. We can find them, too!

"Again, so?"

Tania scowled.

Now is not the time to be pissy at Sam. You said yourself that it was never her fault that—

Footsteps and a voice outside interrupted their conversation.

"Is the commander in? I have his report ready."

Another voice spoke. "No, Gravois. Just leave it on his desk."

Tania closed and straightened the folder, then slipped into the vent shaft before the doorknob even started to turn. The grate was back in place by the time an older detective entered the room. He didn't seem any the wiser.

We made it, Sister. Now, as I was saying—

"Just drop it. Let's go. We can check Connick's home tonight for that book. If we're lucky, we can find out where they hold their meetings, too."

Even though Tania did drop it, she noted that Violet felt a little less chilly than she used to.

By the time Tania cleaned up, finished dinner, and got back into her Blind Moses costume, it was already past eight o'clock and dark outside. Running along the rooftops and bridges, she headed toward the one place she was certain the book would be—Harry Connick Sr.'s home. They had to be near the end of this investigation. They just had to be.

"We've been through his mansion once before, remember? Around Christmas. We know it's not their base."

I know. But all the same, we have to get that book back.

When she reached Connick's home, she easily scaled the outer wall of the property, thanks to Violet's power. About ten or so armed guards were patrolling the property—likely an increase in security from what had happened at City Hall the previous night.

"Watch it! Someone's coming this way!"

Hiding among the shrubs and trees, she watched as a red Cadillac convertible drove down the driveway and out to the highway. Caroline Saucier was at the wheel.

Hmph. Wonder why she was there.

"Never mind that. Look! There's only one light on, and it's from the second floor study."

Tania scanned the mansion with her binoculars. Sure enough, it was the only lit room, and Connick was at his desk. Creeping around back and waiting for a break in the guards, she ran up to the mansion and, with several leaping bounds, reached the second floor balcony. It took her only a minute to unlock the door and slip into the study.

Connick sat behind his desk, but something was wrong. He was completely motionless, his eyes were half-lidded, and he wasn't moving. If not for the way his nostrils flared with every breath, she would think he was dead.

Um, this is strange. Normally, people don't do that.

"Get closer."

Why? I mean—

"Just do it, please." Violet sounded hushed, almost frightened. And she never said "please."

Swallowing hard, Tania snuck closer, ready to run the moment he reacted. But he never did. It was like he was in some sort of trance.

"*Touch the sides of his head. Very carefully. And look into his eyes.*"

Her heart raced as she slid forward, feeling every vein in her body pulse. From the way he sat motionless to the increased feeling of dread, she knew something was very, very wrong. When she placed her hands on either side of his head and looked into his eyes, however, she saw that his pupils were heavily dilated.

Then she felt Violet come forward until she was almost taking control.

Sister, what the—

Immediately, her consciousness slid forward, and she felt like she was falling through a black void. All around, she heard children laughing in unison, a musical symphony of happiness that slowly turned to sobs of sorrow. Then she landed in the darkness, a single spotlight shining on them. But she was no longer her adult self. Instead, she was young Tania Patterson, dressed in her servant's clothes from the Castille household. Next to her, holding her hand, was an equally young Violet, whose eyes were a healthy, soft gray-blue.

"Sister?" Tania squeezed her hand, fighting back the urge to panic. "What's going on? Why're we children again?"

Violet squeezed her hand back. "I think I know what's going on. Just trust me." She ran forward, tugging Tania with her. Her hand felt warmer than ever before. For whatever reason, in this black void, Tania's sister was more alive than she had ever been in life.

Tania squeezed her sister's hand, afraid to let go, afraid of losing her again.

They ran in darkness for what felt like a long time, the sounds of laughter and sorrowful sobs growing. And then, a light began expanding before them, more and more, until it engulfed them. In contrast to the darkness, it was warm and comforting. Tania felt like she could bathe in it forever.

Then, suddenly, they were standing in field with a magnificent cypress tree. In its shade were hundreds of children of all ethnicities, merrily playing and singing with a kind of innocent joy that Tania had rarely known. Chained to the tree, however, was someone sobbing uncontrollably. He was a short, dark-skinned man wearing a comically tall top hat and a tuxedo with tails. A cigar was hanging out of his mouth, and an apple rested at his feet.

Instantly, Tania knew who that was: the chief of the *loa*, who aided the king and queen in all their affairs, and the protector of children. Next to Baron Samedi and Madame Bridgette, he was the most important high *loa* in the voodoo pantheon.

"Papa Ghede?"

Violet nodded. "As I feared. Someone possessed this man with Papa Ghede."

That went against everything Tania knew. "But, you can't do that, can you? Didn't you say that just the other day?"

Gnawing anxiously on her bottom lip, Violet said, "Someone forced it inside. That would require a powerful magic, stronger than any I've ever seen. But that's why Connick is acting different. Taking a god like Papa Ghede and cramming him into a mortal body . . ."

" . . .would drive both of them insane." Tania now understood why Connick, a man who had once been a proponent of justice, suddenly became a conniving politician over a year ago. "Poor Papa Ghede's been trapped in here all this time. We need to free him."

Violet's gaze narrowed. "That has to be what the book stolen from Russell's house is. A ritual book. A grimoire. Someone used it to forcibly place Papa Ghede inside Harry Connick. That means he isn't calling the shots. Whoever did this to him has to be the one in charge."

Before Tania could respond, Violet abruptly snapped her head toward the sky. "We have to go. Now." Her voice cracked with an unexpected fear.

"But, Sister, I—"

Violet grabbed her and yanked hard. "I said we have to go now!"

Tania's head whipped back so hard, she saw stars. When she recovered, she was back in her body, stumbling away from Connick.

"*Run.*"

Blinking, Tania steadied herself. She wasn't sure what was going on.

"*Run now!*" Violet sounded utterly terrified.

But—

Suddenly, Tania felt her consciousness get pulled until she was seated in the back of her mind, forced to watch through her eyes as if she were a third party. She felt Violet up in front. Her sister had taken full control of her body.

Sister, what are you doing?

Violet didn't respond. Tania watched, as if on a movie screen, as she rushed toward the window and crashed through, shards of glass spilling out in slow motion. Then she watched as she sped along the mansion's lawn, hearing the shouts of guards and the firing of guns. She felt a few bullets buzz past her head, but the sensation was numb and distant. A moment later, she jumped over the wall. Only once she was a nearly a mile away did Violet look back at the mansion.

What Tania saw made her mind shriek with fear.

The ghostly shape of a skeletal face and large, bony hands reached out, fingers curling around the mansion. It wore a top hat on its head and was sneering at them, its eyes like balls of fire.

Baron Samedi!

It opened its mouth and whispered in her mind, "Come here, dog," before shifting back into the clouds in the sky and the mist on the ground.

Tania watched herself run until she was on the West Bank.

In a park, Violet dropped control, and Tania fell down and skidded until she came to a stop by a pair of swings. She laid there for a long time, out of breath, the effects of full possession utterly exhausting.

"*You dummy! You stupid girl! Why didn't you run? Why didn't you listen?*"

I'm sorry! I just, I didn't—

"*You didn't think. You never have. That was Vincent, and he could have killed us both.*"

I didn't know! How could I have known?

"*Vincent is the king of the* loa *now. Being that close to Papa Ghede must have tipped him off. Oh, God have mercy, I felt his evil all over me again!*"

As Violet wailed on, Tania suddenly realized that her sister wasn't yelling at her. Violet wasn't even mad. She was scared. And she was crying.

"*You could've died. You hear me, dummy, you could have died!*"

And as Violet called her "dummy" once more, Tania suddenly remembered every time her sister ever called her either that or "stupid." Each time, it was because she had done something to put her in danger. And as she recalled that, she also realized that every time Violet said it, it wasn't being mean, it was showing concern. Finally, the meaning of her sister's abusive words made sense.

Sister . . . you really love me.

Violet was still sobbing. "*What? What are you babbling about?*"

You really love me. All these years, I thought you hated me. But now I realize you've been protecting me. Even from myself.

And once more, Violet was silent.

Sister? Tania was almost desperate. She had to know.

"*Of course I love you. You're my sister. My stupid, clumsy, obnoxious twin sister. And . . .*" A moment passed. Finally, she said, "*I'd never forgive myself if someone hurt you.*"

There in the playground, Tania hugged herself. *Thank you.*

By the time Tania got home, she was so tired that she could barely move. The Blind Moses costume was wrapped around her rifle and mask. To anyone watching, it would seem like she was just carrying some indigo cloth. When she got to her front door, she heard a man's voice behind her. "There you are. I've been waiting half the night for you to return."

She turned around. It was Douglas Dugas.

"You're out late," she said, exhaustion making her voice frail.

"I have something important to tell you. Something Ouellette told me at lunch today that should solve your little investigation."

She looked him over and then said, "Go on."

He folded his arms. "He went to Jonathon Russell's home soon after he died and took out a bunch of books. He intended to give them to Dr. Lazarus. Well, one of those books was a grimoire, a spell book that the Knight Priory owned. Supposedly, it's the one that Vincent used for his rituals."

"*Ah-ha! I was right!*" Violet said.

"So, what happened to it?"

He scratched the back of his head. "Well, most of the stuff got to Dr. Lazarus just fine, but one of the Knight Priory members stole the grimoire. Now they lent it to a Dr. Kindley over the years, which is why Ouellette had such trouble tracking down who actually took it. But he finally figured it out, thanks to one of his detectives."

Tania's pulse raced. That had to be the person who was pulling the strings, the leader of the Knight Priory. "So who was it?"

"The editor in chief of the *Times-Picayune*, Caroline Saucier!"

Chapter 41
Not What You Think

Date: **Thursday, June 12, 1997**
Time: **8:00 p.m.**
Location: **Caroline Saucier's Mansion**
Garden District, Uptown New Orleans

Tania called in sick once more and spent the entire day preparing to infiltrate Caroline's mansion that night. She did yoga for four hours, meditated for three, performed preparatory rituals for two, and prayed for one. When she was finally ready to don the costume and bring Violet forward, she was as ready as could be.

Throughout the day, Violet had been very quiet, a peaceful vibe coming from her that filled Tania with harmony. Whether last night's brush with Vincent had changed her, or whether the icy covering had finally cracked, she finally felt like the sibling Tania had always wanted—strong but loving.

As they prepared to leave, Violet said, "*When this is over, Sister, we'll have a lot to talk about.*"

She had never called Tania "Sister." That was enough.

Night had fallen by the time Tania arrived at Caroline's uptown mansion. A secluded estate, it was surrounded by high, vine-covered walls with a double wrought-iron gate. Trees dotted both sides of the wall, offering perfect cover. A single unarmed guard stood in the gatehouse, reading a magazine and looking both bored and inattentive. The apparent laxness in security was a welcome break from the security at City Hall and Connick's mansion.

"*Fortune favors us, Sister. This guy isn't paying the gate any mind.*"

Lucky us, for once.

Climbing one of the trees and perching in the branches, Tania surveyed the inside of the estate. A lavishly dense garden of bushes concealed most of the yard, leaving only the walkway and driveway uncovered. Looking through her binoculars, she surveyed the area. A few guards were inside and only one was walking along the path. Compared to the last two places she had snuck into, this place was relatively open.

She was just about to hop over the wall when Violet tugged at her. "*Sister, stop! Look up at the roof!*"

As soon as Tania did, she realized why there were so few human guards. Floating around the roof, a silent sentinel, was a *bakulu*, quite possibly the same one from City Hall.

Oh, heavens! This is the power of the grimoire?

"*Very likely. I'll need to pull all the way back so it can't sense us. Only call upon me if you need me.*"

All right.

"*And, Sister, please be careful.*"

Tania smiled. *I will.*

As Violet retreated deep within her, she felt all her power drain and all her senses dull. Just like at City Hall, she felt weak, with only her training keeping her nimble. It was a sobering reminder that without Violet possessing her, she was as frail and weak as anyone else.

Pushing those thoughts away, she concentrated on the training she received from GEIST—the hours of physical exercise to tone her body, the practice at the firing range, and the hand-to-hand training with Meyer. As Abel had said when he'd scouted her, her possession made her extraordinary, but solid physical conditioning would give her the edge.

Jumping over the wall, she grabbed the branches of another tree and flipped to the ground, landing with a soft thud. Then, creeping on her belly, she slunk through the undergrowth of garden until she reached the walkway. Staying perfectly still, she waited. A black, unmarked sedan drove past the gate and up behind the house.

Company? Give me a break!

It was disconcerting not to hear a response from Violet. She wasn't used to being alone in her head.

Above, the *bakulu* sniffed the air and then growled but made no other moves. Wondering what could have caught its attention, she scanned the area for other spirits. But there were none she could see or feel. With a sigh, she returned her attention to the guard walking the grounds, lying still and waiting until he passed her.

Quickly, she slipped out from the bushes and choked him with her rifle, applying the method Meyer had taught her to subdue someone without killing them. He wheezed, gurgled, and tried to get free. After what seemed like too long, he went limp. She sank to the ground with him and checked his pulse. It was still there. She had managed to take someone down using only her training.

Breathing a sigh of relief, she pulled him into the undergrowth, binding his arms and legs and gagging him. Then she snuck up to the porch. It was dark, save for the lights coming from inside. Starting far away from the front door, she checked each room. Every one of them had guards. Some were playing cards or otherwise engaging in recreation, but most were going through boxes of assault rifles and pistols.

What the heck? Is the Knight Priory planning something?

She was just about to head to the back of the house when she heard giggling. From the room closest to the front door came the sound of a child's laughter. Carefully, she peered inside. Two children, a boy and girl no more than a few years old, were playing with Caroline. The boy was sitting a few feet away, playing with blocks and holding a conversation with the corner of the room, while the girl sat in Caroline's lap and read a book along with her. The boy, who had short, black hair, laughed merrily as he built towers of blocks, only to smash them down, while the girl, who had long, blond hair, was quiet and attentive.

Caroline and the girl finished up the book. "Good night, stars. Good night, air. Good night, noises everywhere."

The girl looked up at her. "Mama, why say goodnight to the stars? They're millions of miles away!"

Keeping up a smile that was obviously fake, she said, "Well, Alice, the stars can hear the wishes and dreams of little girls like you."

Alice . . . then the other one was Eugene. *My God, these are Sam's children!*

Alice's expression never changed. "Well, that's not right, now, is it?"

Before Caroline could respond, an older woman in a maid outfit entered. "Madam, the Oracle is here."

"Good," Caroline said. "Tell him I'll meet him in the side room. And send out all the guards to patrol the grounds. Also, can you and Paula take care of the kids' baths?"

"Of course, madam."

Crap, this place is about to get unfriendly. I need to get in, now!

Still no response from Violet.

Rubbing Alice's head the way one would a dog, Caroline brought her to the maid. "Alice, go with Millicent and get your bath. Mama will come tuck you in when she's done."

"Yes, Mama."

As Millicent and Alice left, Caroline walked over to Eugene and ruffled his hair in the same manner. "Honey, stop talking to the wall."

"Just talking to Daddy," he said.

Tania focused on the corner of the room, detecting the minutest of spiritual presences. The girl seemed spiritually unaware, but the boy was amazingly sensitive.

"Of course you are, baby," Caroline said. "Now be good. Miss Paula will be here in a moment to bring to you your bath."

"OK, lady."

"Call me 'Mommy.'"

"OK, lady."

Caroline sighed and left the child alone in the room.

Feeling nothing but disdain for her, Tania shook her head. "Who leaves a little child alone like that?" Pushing her disgust aside, she started searching for an alternate way inside. She couldn't be on the porch when the guards came out.

But quite abruptly, Eugene went to the corner of the room, offering a block to an unseen entity. Slowly, something started appearing. At first, it was very faint, but then, ever so slightly, it began taking form. Up above, she heard the *bakulu* rumble as a spectral being shimmered before the little boy.

She gasped as she realized what it was—the ghost of Richie Fastellos. Now she knew where he had been all this time.

Richie's ghost glanced over at her, nodding. The locking mechanism on the window shook and then popped open. With an almost sad smile, he turned his attention back to Eugene. He knelt and made the block float. Eugene giggled and clapped his hands. Richie was distracting his son so that Tania could get in.

Moving as quietly as she could, she slipped inside, landing on top of a comfortable Victorian-style loveseat. Closing the window, she rolled to the ground and then snuck along the wall until she was at the doorway. She was about to slip out to the front hall when she heard a voice say, "Eugene? Little Eugene? Paula's coming to take you to your bath."

Tania slid underneath the loveseat so fast she almost got carpet burn. Once there, she lay very still. Richie's ghost vanished as a skinny, middle-aged maid with a veined neck entered the room. "Little Eugene, what are you doing?"

"Talking to Daddy, Pau-wa."

"Of course you are," Paula said as she took his hand. "Come on, little man. Time for a bath."

As they turned around, Eugene locked eyes with Tania. He pointed at her and said, "Scary woman under sofa!"

Tania tensed up, reaching for her rifle.

Paula chortled softly. "Of course, hun. Of course. Come on. Let's go play with Captain Ducky!"

As she led him out of the room, he repeated several more times. "Scary woman under sofa. Scary woman under sofa, Pau-wa!"

Once they were gone, Tania breathed a sigh of relief. *That was lucky.*

"You can come out now," a voice whispered. It was Richie's.

Rolling out from under the sofa, she looked around for him. He was in the corner, but without Violet's powers, she could only make out the faintest of outlines. "Richie, what's going on?"

"I swore to Sam I'd watch over them, but that creature above will destroy me if I fully appear. So all I can do is this." Richie's ghost gestured at his translucent form. "Look, I need to warn you. Please be careful. The Oracle. He's not what you think he is."

That wasn't particularly helpful. "What do you mean?" Tania asked.

"I mean he's actually—"

Above, the *bakulu* started rumbling, making the walls shake.

"I have to go," he said. "Please, Tania. Be careful."

He vanished. Pondering his words, she snuck out. *Damn it! Why don't we have any intel on this guy?*

The front hall was magnificent, from the sweeping staircase to the patterned rugs lying over the polished marble floor. But it didn't impress her, not anymore. Every mansion was starting to look the same. So instead of taking in the decadence of Caroline's wealth, she sought a place to hide. There was stuff everywhere, from statues of the Muses to potted plants to wall tapestries. She ended up choosing a wall hanging depicting two nude women intertwined in a passionate embrace. And there she waited.

A few seconds later, Caroline emerged from one of the side rooms. Walking alongside her was a figure in a black, hooded robe and a mask of Baron Samedi—the Oracle of the Knight Priory.

"After finding the ritual I needed, I returned the grimoire to you, as per our deal," the Oracle said in a mechanically synthesized, but decisively male, voice. "But you haven't heeded my warnings, Miss Saucier. The advanced spells are dangerous. You swore to only use the ones similar to Dr. Kindley's."

Caroline picked her nails. "Talismans made from the spirits of the dead are trite. What I want is real power."

"You are a fool. Magi who spend a lifetime in training wouldn't cast some of those spells. The one you used to place Papa Ghede inside the district attorney is unstable and potentially fatal. Spirits of that power aren't meant—"

With a condescending sniff, she said, "You know, I really don't care. Ever since I did that to Harry, running the Knight Priory through him has been easy. And after we induct the mayor tomorrow night, I'll simply transfer Papa Ghede to him. Then I'll control both the Priory and New Orleans safely from the shadows. See? Real power."

The Oracle was starting to sound exasperated. "But doing that will kill Mr. Connick and cause irreparable damage to Papa Ghede. You need to use something akin to a kabbalic seal to safely remove a high *loa*. Do you know kabbalic magic? Of course you don't. And you are going to end up murdering him."

Kabbalic magic? Tania thought. If she remembered properly, Meyer used that.

Shrugging, Caroline said, "I was thinking of running for district attorney. What do you think?"

He shook his head. "I think you are a terrible woman. When I agreed to help you, I never expected you to be so hateful. A heart filled with that much darkness is bound to—"

Once again, she interrupted him. "Spare me the lectures. You and I are using each other, and you know it. You want the children, and I want the Knight Priory. Don't play the morality card now."

Tania sucked in her breath. What did the Oracle want with Sam's children?

Then Caroline grinned wickedly, a dangerous glint in her eyes. "Or are you reneging on our deal? Perhaps I should tell the world who you really are?"

"Humph. You can't hold that over me forever, Miss Saucier."

"Watch me. So, are we still on? You get the kids, and I keep the book?"

"Yes. I must have the Castille children. They are vital to my plans. So, tomorrow night, we make the trade."

Caroline's hateful expression grew. "Of course. I'm even going to bring them to Deepwater Olympus for the ceremony. Eight o'clock sharp." She tapped the nose of his mask. "Don't. Be. Late."

Tania's eyes widened. She had just learned the location of the Knight Priory's base. Now she needed to get back to GEIST.

Suddenly, a woman's voice called out, "Little Eugene! Get back here! Get back here right now!"

Streaking across the front hall like an iguana running on its hind legs, a naked little Eugene rushed up to a shocked Caroline, grabbed her pants leg, and jumped up and down. "Lady, lady! Scary woman under sofa! Scary woman under sofa!"

Biting her tongue, Tania held back any reaction. She found the boy adorable.

Running up to him, Paula picked up the boy, who wiggled in protest. "I am so sorry, madam. He keeps insisting that there is a scary woman underneath the loveseat in the drawing room."

With the look of a pot ready to boil, Caroline rubbed her face. "Argh, Come on, you little fu . . . I mean, come on, sweetie. Let's make sure there's no monster."

She and Paula left with the child.

Still hidden, Tania waited for the Oracle to leave as well. But he didn't. She waited a few seconds more.

Then he spoke. "You might as well come out. I know you're there."

What the hell?

"Behind the tapestry. You've been there the whole time, listening. Come out or I'll come get you."

Unharnessing her rifle, she stepped out and pointed it at him.

He snorted. "Blind Moses. I thought you had died."

"Never mind that. How did you know I was hiding there?"

"Similar to you, I suppose. We aren't that much different."

"Indeed," she said. "So what happens now?"

The Oracle harrumphed. "You leave before I kill you. And tell Dr. Lazarus's little group to stay out of my way. There are more important things than the Knight Priory."

Tania growled. How did he know about GEIST? "Who the hell are you?"

"Someone you don't want to mess with. Leave now. New Orleans is my responsibility."

Smirking, she took the safety off her rifle. "So what is your stake in all this?"

Lifting his foot, he said, "You have no idea what's at stake. And I said leave, not talk. Goodbye." He then stomped on the ground so hard the room shook, and the floor exploded toward her in a shockwave. Before she could blink, the force lifted her up and threw her out of the house through the front door.

Pain tore through her, and she screamed as she landed on the front walkway, skidding so hard, the skin tore off her back. Her right shoulder popped out of its joint, and when she stopped halfway to the perimeter wall, she saw that the Oracle was already standing over her. He raised his hand to strike but stopped when a loud roar pierced the air. Up above, the *bakulu* was hurdling toward him, its mouth wide open.

"Insect," he muttered.

Through the agonizing haze, she heard Violet ask, "*Sister, can you hear me?*"

Yes. Help me, please!

"*I will. Just wait. As soon as I tell you, give me complete control.*"

Complete control?

"*Yes. Trust me.*"

Lying there in incredible pain, Tania watched as the *bakulu* fell upon the Oracle. He side-stepped with ease, and as soon as it snapped its jaws, he grabbed them and started pulling them apart.

He can touch spirits?

"*Yes! I think he's . . . just wait a few more seconds.*"

As the *bakulu* whined in torment, the Oracle slammed it into the ground. Then he punched it, white energy flowing through his arm. The moment his fist hit, it let out a horrific squeal and vaporized into black sand, which sparkled into nothingness.

Oh, my God. He obliterated it. That means—

"*Now! Do it now!*"

Closing her eyes, Tania willed herself back and her sister forward, the switch taking less than a second. Once again, she was observing her body from the back-seat, the pain numbed. She watched as she popped her shoulder back into place, jumped up, and sprinted faster than ever before.

There was a sudden rush of heat as the Oracle, holding out his hand, shot what could only be called a beam of white-and-black energy at her.

What is this?

Violet didn't answer, but Tania saw herself flip, twisting to the side as the beam passed underneath. She landed on a rooftop and started jumping across them.

Where are we going?

"*The river!*"

Behind them, a set of battle cries broke out. When her body glanced behind, she saw three of those African warrior spirits following her.

Ogouns!

They hurled their spears at her, the sharp tips cutting at her flesh. They were still chasing her when she reached the Mississippi River. Her body scanned the water, and when she saw a barge, she thought, *Sister, there!*

"*I see it!*"

Tania watched as her body took a few steps back and then leapt with every ounce of strength she had. The wind rushed through her robe as she sailed hundreds of feet through the air. Behind her, one of the *ogouns* stopped and threw spears while the other two also jumped.

One of the spears pierced her back. Violet shrieked as they slammed into the surface of the barge, rolling on the ground. With a pained groan, Violet returned control.

"*Spirit . . . weapon . . . you can resist . . . easier.*"

Tania knew Violet was right. Her back hurt, and blood trickled out, but the spiritual aspect of the spear would have been many times more damaging to her sister. Tania spun around in time to see one of the *ogoun* plop into the river. The other, however, landed before her, stabbing her right in the stomach. She cried out as the cold blade pierced her guts. As the *ogoun* thrust its spear at her again, she slapped it to the side with her rifle—but just barely.

Sister, are you there?

"*Only a little. These spirit spears really hurt!*"

Once again, the *ogoun* stabbed at her. And once more, Tania parried just in time.

We have to survive. GEIST needs this intel.

"*I know, Sister.*"

Her movements now sluggish, Tania groaned in pain as the *ogoun* attacked again, its spear sinking into her leg. She couldn't fight any more. They had exhausted too much energy escaping the Oracle.

I wanna try something. Can you focus your power in me once more, Sister?

"*Yeah, I think so . . .*"

Even as the *ogoun* struck at her heart, Tania felt Violet push every last drop of power into her. For a brief moment, time slowed down to a crawl. It was more than enough. She grabbed the spear, and as time returned to normal, she yanked it out of the *ogoun's* hands and stabbed it in the head. It convulsed and then fell off the barge in a small explosion of light and mist, its energy recycled back to the spirit world.

The spear disappeared, and Tania fell to the barge's surface. The sounds of the Mississippi were a peaceful contrast to the war they just endured.

Thank you, Sister. Everything was going dark.

"*No. Thank you.*"

Will we live? Sounds were becoming far away.

Tania felt Violet's arms around her.

"*Live or die, we'll do it together. As sisters.*"

As the world went black, Tania could swear she felt a kiss.

Tania's Epilogue
Her Sister Was Home

Date: **Friday, June 13th, 1997**
Time: **3:00 a.m.**
Location: **The Mississippi River**
Somewhere North of Baton Rouge

"*Wake up, Tania. You've overslept again, dummy.*"

Tania opened her eyes. The first thing she saw was how clear the sky was, the moon in its half-waxing phase. Then, as her eyes adjusted, she realized someone was sitting beside her.

It was Violet's ghost.

Sitting up, Tania glanced around. Except for the mask, her Blind Moses costume was gone. She was only in the bodysuit, with her wounds dressed and bandaged. The medical kit was opened to the side, nearly empty.

Violet's ghost sat there, legs in the water, smiling at her. It was the first time in too many years that Tania could remember seeing her sister smile.

"What—what happened?"

"While you slept, I took control and dressed your wounds." Violet's ghost could only speak in a whisper.

Tania examined the bandages. Violet had done a great job. "I appreciate this. By why exit me? You know you'll vanish to the spirit world if you're outside of me for too long."

With a wink, Violet's ghost said, "I wanted to see you. And I wanted you to see me. Just this once." Leaning over, she pressed against Tania. It felt like cool mist.

Tania reached up to put an arm around her, but without Violet's power, it just passed right through. But it didn't matter. Although they couldn't touch, they were truly connecting.

"Sister," Tania said. "I'm sorry."

"For what?"

"Vincent forced a lifetime of abuse upon you. I was so stupid, all I could do was pretend everything was OK."

"Oh, Tania."

"I guess what I mean is . . . I'm sorry I couldn't save you, Sister."

Once more, Violet's ghost smiled. "Stupid. You did save me."

"I did?"

"You saved my soul."

The moonlight sparkled off Tania's tears. She sat with her sister until the twilight of the dawn began and Violet was forced to possess her again. But Tania felt that that was where Violet belonged.

Her sister was home.

Chapter 42
The Conference

Date: **Saturday, June 14, 1997**
Time: **11:00 a.m.**
Location: **GEIST Headquarters**
Southern Arkansas

Whiskey bottle in hand, Sam strode into the conference room with Aucoin. Every important person in GEIST was there, including some members who had been on long-term assignments. There were even people she didn't recognize.

Meyer was with Abel near the front of the room, leaning over a transparency projector. Hakim was deep in conversation with Tania, who was in normal street clothing. Victor was sitting alone in a corner, oiling his revolver. Misty and Lester, the two teenagers from Evergreen Sanatorium, were busy setting up equipment for the meeting. And near a podium, a young woman with short, red hair was typing on a clunky laptop computer.

"Everyone and then some are here," Sam said as she gulped down a few swigs. She'd been drinking since last night to celebrate Tania finding her children, but she was hilariously sober. Even mixing up a "Sara Special" couldn't get her drunk. Her excitement was so great that she was just burning the alcohol away.

Aucoin leaned over her shoulder. "Keep drinking that much and your liver will fail."

She made a wet buzzing sound with her lips. "Back in September of 1994, both my livers died after a sixteen-day binge. I woke up two weeks later in a bus depot somewhere around Monroe, everything good as new."

"Morbid," he said, pinching the bottle out of her hand. "Well, these people are here for you, so act grateful. How about this—when the meeting is over, I'll share a drink with you for old time's sake."

That got her attention. He hadn't drunk since before Evergreen. It was a touching gesture, and her cheeks warmed. "All right, mister. You're on."

He tossed her a pack of Tic-Tacs. "And here. Suck on these. No nice way to say it. Your breath reeks."

With a snort, she popped a dozen or so in her mouth and crunched on them.

Then someone behind her said, "Oh, hey, Sam! How goes it?"

She spun around to see a woman in her early twenties with unkempt, black hair and a chest that could cause a concussion. She was wearing a cream blouse and a dark-brown leather corset with black straps, the kind you'd get from a Renaissance fair. She was also wearing tan cargo pants and a large black belt with two rapiers hanging from her flared hips. Black leather boots and gloves finished the ensemble. She looked like a Victorian swashbuckler.

However, Sam immediately recognized her. "Alexia LeBlanc, right? Michael's sister."

"Correct!" Alexia's smile was cheerful as she shook her hand. "I'm just glad to finally meet you when you aren't covered in filth. How have you been?"

Sam felt her cheeks heat up. At least Alexia was genuine. "I've been as well as I can be. How about yourself? When did you join GEIST?"

Now it was Alexia's turn to blush. "I'm not a part of GEIST. Well, not yet. I wanted to finish college first. I have a scholarship to the University of Copenhagen, and it just so happens that the Eversoll Institute is based there. Dr. Lazarus needed my best friend's computer skills for the operation, so I came with her and Leona."

That was a lot for Sam to take in at once, but she nodded along. "So, why are you dressed like that? Putting on a play or something?"

With her hands on her hips, Alexia winked. "This is my fighting outfit. It's the only thing I can wear that keeps my chest from getting in the way."

"Your fighting outfit?" Sam didn't like the sound of that. "Why are you wearing a fighting outfit?"

"Because, goofball, I'm helping out. You saved my life that day. And remember, I did destroy Lord Dooley. Ya know, 'destroy' as in, he cannot come back because his energy was broken down and returned to the spirit world? So like it or not, I'm doing this."

"Um, I don't think someone your age should—"

But Alexia tugged her through the room. "Right, because I've got no experience struggling against impossible odds? Whatever. Anyway, come with. Patty would never forgive me if I didn't personally introduce you to her."

"I'll keep your seat warm, Sam," Aucoin called out.

As she was towed to the front of the room, Sam couldn't help but feel good about Alexia. Not only was she Michael's little sister through and through, but she also had a lot of the same traits Sam had when she was her age. And despite the pushiness, Alexia exuded an honesty that was refreshing. But Sam did feel sorry for the guy who would fall for her someday. He would have his hands full.

Alexia stopped in front of the redheaded girl on the laptop. "Patty, this is Sam Castille. Sam, this is Patty O'Brien."

Patty spun off her chair and scrutinized Sam, poking at her with the eraser end of a pencil. "So, you're the immortal Samantha Castille? I've read a lot about you."

Sam swatted the pencil away. "Hey, stop that! So you're Alexia's best friend, then?"

"Patty E. Coyote, super genius," she said. Then she put her arm around Alexia. "This girl is my soulmate. I love, love, love her so damn much." She waggled her eyebrows and then smooched Alexia on the cheek.

Alexia said, "Ack!" and pushed Patty away, wiping off the kiss. "Sorry about that, Sam. Patty loves teasing me, but with how she acts, sometimes I wonder if she really is queer."

Leaning forward, hands on her knees, Patty made kissy faces at them both. "Only for you, Alexia, baby!"

As Alexia groaned in exasperation, Aucoin's voice rose above the clamor of the room. "Everyone, the director is on his way with Leona Eversoll and the operation's commander. Please take your seats."

Patty yanked Alexia over to some chairs. "Come sit with me! Nice meeting you again, Sam!"

"Kids these days," Sam said with a shrug. She then made her way back to Aucoin and sat next to him. "So, who is the operation's commander?"

Aucoin seemed pleased. "You'll see."

Suddenly, Abel said, "The director has arrived."

The door to the conference room opened. Camellia pushed Dr. Lazarus inside with Leona next to him. Behind them both was Dixie.

Sam gasped and ran to her. "Oh, God, Dixie!" she exclaimed, pulling her into a tight hug and squeezing as hard as she could without hurting her. "You have no idea how glad I am to see you."

Dixie put her one good arm around Sam and hugged back. "I'm glad to see you, too, Sam. We'll talk more after the meeting is over, I promise."

A few snickers around the room drew Sam's attention. She had just wanted to rekindle the friendship with Dixie that circumstance kept trying to squash, not make a scene. Now blushing wildly, she slipped back to her chair.

"That was adorable," Aucoin whispered.

"Oh, shut up," Sam muttered.

Dixie, Dr. Lazarus, and Camellia headed to the front of the room as Leona sat with Alexia and Patty. Once Dixie was at the podium, she tapped the microphone a few times and then said, "Members of GEIST and the Eversoll Institute, my name is Dixie Olivier Eliopoulos. I used to be a lieutenant for the New Orleans police. I am now a captain up in New York City. I am also one of the detectives who worked the new Bourbon Street Ripper case."

Sam squeezed her shoe charm several times. *Michael. Rodger. Richie.*

"We've all been briefed on the situation concerning the Knight Priory," Dixie said. "We all know the threat they pose. I've been asked by Dr. Lazarus and Professor Mathias to head up this operation. We've discussed it at length and have come up with what we believe is the best battle plan."

She then nodded to Abel, who dimmed the lights and turned on the projector. An image of an oil rig in the middle of the water appeared on the screen.

"The Knight Priory has been meeting in secret since the Evergreen incident. Thanks to the efforts of operative Tania Patterson, we have learned that their meeting place is the Deepwater Olympus oil rig in the middle of the Gulf of Mexico. They will be gathering there tomorrow night to induct a new member, the mayor of New Orleans, Marc Morial."

Abel replaced the slide with a new one that was split into four images.

"These four people are the high-value targets of the Knight Priory. The first is Marc Morial. Their support helped him secure his victory in the last mayoral election. Once he joins, they will be poised to take over the state government. The second is Harry Connick Sr. He is seen as their leader but is just a puppet. We know that at some point, someone forced the high *loa* Papa Ghede inside him. This is a very unstable possession that needs to be carefully removed or it could kill him and irreparably harm the *loa*."

Recalling Tania's debriefing from last night, Sam nodded. The only way something that powerful could safely possess a human was through fusion.

Dixie continued. "The woman is Caroline Saucier, who has been identified as the real leader of the Knight Priory. She is in possession of a grimoire that gives her undetermined levels of power. She is the one who put Papa Ghede inside Connick."

Sam glared at Caroline's image. She never would have guessed just how dangerous that woman would end up being.

"And then there is Dr. Ignatius Kindley," Dixie said. "He's a pureblood who has acted as a liaison for most of the Knight Priory activities. He has used the grimoire to create talismans from the souls of his patients."

Now I hate him even more, Sam thought, her lips tightening.

Waiting until similar murmurs of disgust died down, Dixie said, "The last person, we don't have an image of. He's called the Oracle. His role in the Priory is unknown. We do know that he's the one who introduced Vincent to the *tkeeus,* setting all that's happened into motion. We also have reason to believe that he is fused like Sam."

A hum of surprise rippled throughout the room.

"Are we certain of that?" Alexia asked.

Shaking her head, Dixie said, "We don't know for sure. Fused people are nearly impossible to detect. Only Tania has ever faced him."

Tania then spoke up. "He was immensely powerful. Even if he's not fused, he's easily the strongest person in the Priory."

Another mutter spread around, with lots of talk as to who should actually confront the Oracle. The volume was just starting to rise when Dixie slapped her hand against the microphone. The room settled back down.

"So we have three objectives. Abel, if you please?"

He changed slides to show a map of the Deepwater Olympus.

Leaning on the podium, Dixie said, "First, we are to go in and detain the members of the Knight Priory. The police will assist with this. Every one of them will be turned over to the FBI. Second, we're searching for two small children, Alice and Eugene Castille."

People in the room glanced toward Sam.

"They are being brought by Caroline to give to the Oracle. We are to intercept and take the children with us."

Despite having heard all this last night, Sam still felt her blood get hot and her pulse quicken. Those were her babies.

Then Dixie said, "And our third goal is to attempt to destroy the silver pen that links Vincent Castille to the physical world."

A loud rumble of voices again spread. Sam leaned over toward Aucoin. "Did you know about this?"

"No, not at all." His brow furrowed. "This is troubling. I thought Julius said the energy release would be like a nuclear bomb."

"He did."

Once more, Dixie slapped the microphone until everyone settled down. "After conferring with both Julius and Professor Mathias, we believe that Deepwater Olympus offers the best chance to do this. It is equipped with a plasma-cutting boring device—the only one of its kind. After we accomplish all other objectives, a select team will set the pen in the basin of the device and activate it. It will need to be on a special timer, because it's believed the explosion will be akin to a nuke."

"Glad they thought that out," Sam said.

Aucoin hummed. "More like a desperate gamble."

"Smartass," she said with a smirk.

Meanwhile Dixie scanned the room. "Any questions?"

"Yes," Hakim said. "This one would like to know who will be carrying the pen."

Without even thinking, Sam said, "I will. We need to cut Vincent off from this world. It's my father. It's my burden."

Once more, mumbling rose around the room. From his wheelchair, Dr. Lazarus said, "As you wish, Sam."

Leaning over, Aucoin whispered. "You better come back, or I'm taking your room."

Despite the situation, she chuckled. It was good to have him banter with her.

Dixie cleared her throat. "So, for the operation, we're going to leave the port of New Orleans in a squadron of helicopters. Once on the rig, you will split into seven teams. Please hold all questions until after I've assigned the teams."

Everyone in the room listened attentively.

"Team One, Kyle and Victor, will apprehend Caroline. Team Two, Gavin and Curtis, will seek out the children. Team Three, Chase and Noelle, will apprehend Mayor Morial. Team Four, Tania and Amelie, will apprehend Dr. Kindley. Team Five, Meyer and Hakim, will apprehend Connick. Team Six, Sam and Alexia, will apprehend the Oracle. Team Seven, Sebastian and Sheeree, will locate and prepare the boring device."

Clearing his throat, Meyer asked, "What do you want us to do with Connick?"

"You invoke kabbalic magic, right? And Hakim has a spirit guardian. He can distract Connick while you try to separate him and Papa Ghede. If that fails, subdue him. We'll place him in quarantine back here."

"Just don't dive into his mind," Tania said. "That will open up a direct link to Vincent."

"With respect, Lady Patterson," Hakim said, "this one has no intention of doing that."

"Of course," Tania said. "So Dixie, for my team, do we have any intel on Dr. Kindley's actual abilities?"

When Dixie shook her head, Tania sighed. "Fine, then. We'll manage."

Sam felt bad for her. She was still recovering from her ordeal in New Orleans, and now she was being asked to deal with a foe no one knew anything about.

Then Victor spoke up. "I have a question."

Everyone turned to him, as he rarely spoke. "So this Caroline woman is carelessly slinging around black magic and spirits. If she can't be subdued, can we kill her?"

"I hope so," Aucoin muttered. Sam was certain no one else heard him.

Dixie scowled. "We're not murderers. Defend yourself, but only kill if there is no other choice."

Victor nodded and returned to oiling his gun.

Standing up, Sam said, "Dixie, I mean no disrespect to Alexia, but why is she paired with me? If the Oracle is fused, she could easily die."

Dr. Lazarus spoke up. "Sam, I can personally attest to Miss LeBlanc's abilities. Not only did she destroy a powerful greater spirit by herself, but since she joined the Eversoll Institute, she has continued to prove herself on the field. She is the only person I feel safe pairing you with."

Sam frowned. While she understood that people who were not fused had to use their will to overcome spirits and magic and that Alexia's will was supposed to be amazing, something told her that the young woman couldn't handle a fused person.

"I'll be OK, Sam," Alexia said from across the room. "All's well."

With an audible sigh, Sam sat down. "All right, then. I'll trust you on this."

"Any other questions?" Dixie asked.

Aucoin stood up. "Yeah. Where is Ouellette in all this?"

Again, Dr. Lazarus addressed the room. "I know some of you don't trust Louis Ouellette, but he's helped me against the Knight Priory for years. If it weren't for his assistance, we wouldn't be this far along. He's allowing us to use the Napoleon Avenue Wharf as our command center and launch point. He'll be leading the police at the end of the operation to help round up the Priory members for delivery to the FBI. He's also providing medical support during the operation."

Sam hummed to herself. It was poetic that they were using the same wharf where she and Blind Moses had dueled.

Frowning, Dixie said, "I trust Dr. Lazarus. Anyone who has any issues with Commander Ouellette, leave them here. Any more questions?"

No one spoke.

"Good. So now we'll split into our teams and support staff to discuss strategies. Misty Bradley and Lester Martin. Where are you two?"

The teenagers stood up, waving and grinning cockily.

She motioned to both of them. "All right, you two, go with the pilots and make sure the helicopters are ready. All right, everyone. Let's do this!"

As the meeting ended and people got up to leave, Aucoin leaned over. "See you later."

With a wink, Sam said, "Drinks. My room. After dinner."

He laughed. "It's a date."

Chapter 43
It Was There

Date: **Saturday, June 14, 1997**
Time: **9:00 p.m.**
Location: **GEIST Headquarters**
Southern Arkansas

"So, how was it?" Dixie asked. "The bananas Foster, I mean?"

Sam clanked her spoon against the dessert dish. Not even a drop of cream remained. After the meeting, when Dixie had invited her to dinner, she'd figured it would be in the cafeteria with everyone else. She never could have imagined they'd share a catered dinner flown all the way from New Orleans. The expense must have been ridiculous.

But the food was as good as she remembered, and Dixie had gone to the extra step of decorating a spare office with drapery and lighting. As she leaned back from the meal, Sam felt a contentment that she hadn't felt in years. For just that moment, she could be her old self once more. "It was amazing, Dixie. Thank you."

Dixie, who was smiling radiantly, sipped her wine. "I wanted to give you something, no matter how small, to show you how much I care. I once added to your pain and misery, and for that, I can never apologize enough."

Sam swished her wine around the glass. "We're adults, so I'd like to think we've moved past that. But let's make it official: apology accepted."

"Good," Dixie said. "Once the operation is over, I'd really like for us to be friends. We've been so busy this past year. But I'd like to occasionally fly you up to New York to visit. I'm sure Gino and Felicia would love you."

Sipping her wine, Sam smiled back. Dixie had made it very plain that after the Knight Priory was destroyed, she'd be retiring from active duty with GEIST.

"Thank you for the invitation. I'd like that, to have a real friendship. And thank you . . . ya know, for finding out where Dr. Klein had me."

"You're welcome." Dixie gently squeezed Sam's hand. "And I'm not done yet." She leaned under the table, fiddling with something. A few seconds later, she slid Sam a large manila envelope.

"Here you go."

She arched an eyebrow. "What is it?"

"Open it and find out."

"Hmph," she said, opening the folder. Then she gasped. Inside was an official ruling from the state Supreme Court itself. All five billion of her estate, originally embezzled by Kent and then held by the Knight Priory, had been unfrozen and returned to her. "Dixie, this is . . ."

"Congratulations. You're a billionaire again, Sam." Dixie raised her glass.

Putting down the papers, Sam stared at Dixie, dumbfounded. "How . . . how did you do this?"

Dixie couldn't have been grinning wider. "Gino and I hired the best lawyers we could find. They appealed all the way to the Louisiana Supreme Court and won!"

"But that had to be . . . expensive," Sam said, still in shock.

"Bah! We can afford it. Gino is now the director of a prime-time soap opera, and I'm on a captain's salary. Besides, you saved my life. Back at the wharf, remember? I can never repay you completely."

Choking up, Sam quickly swallowed the rest of her wine. She muttered, "Thank you."

Toasting her, Dixie asked, "So, what will you do with all that money?"

"Uh, I really have no idea. Five billion is more than I can ever spend, especially with my Spartan lifestyle." Closing her eyes, she thought about it, the sound of Dixie sipping her wine accompanying her thoughts. After considering every option, she opened her eyes and said, "I know. I'll keep enough of it to live on and donate the rest to GEIST."

Mouth open, Dixie gawked at her. "Are you sure? I mean, what about Alice and Eugene? What if you have more children?"

Sam shook her head. "Dixie, I can't get pregnant again. And as for my kids . . ." Her voice trailed off. "You're right. I'll create a small trust fund for them, just so they'll always be OK. Other than that, I'm not sure I can be a good mother. I'm too messed up. Hell, I'm hardly human anymore. As long as they're away from the Knight Priory and with someone who can care for them, that's all that matters to me."

Dixie's lips twitched. "Well, do what you must. But trust me—no parent should ever forsake their children."

Pouring another glass of wine, Sam held it up to the light. It looked like blood. "Tell that to Vincent," she said, and then she drained the entire glass.

After finishing dinner with Dixie, Sam wandered through the hallways of GEIST headquarters, walking off the wine. Everywhere, people were either unwinding or still reviewing strategies for tomorrow. Her session with Alexia was short. They were just going to go in, find the Oracle, and beat him down.

When she finally arrived at the door to her apartment, Aucoin was nowhere to be seen. She hoped he hadn't been waiting for her.

Almost as if on cue, someone behind her said, "Kyle was here for a while, but then he went up to the roof." It was Tania.

"All right. Thanks," Sam said.

They stared at each other a few more moments, the silence between them getting thicker with every breath. Although she'd heard Tania recount her story, she hadn't spoken with her yet. She wasn't sure if Tania would want to talk to her After all, Sam did kill her twin sister.

Finally, Tania sighed and gestured toward the door marked "Operative #002." "Do you want to come inside and chat for a bit?"

Sam glanced away, unsure if she had the strength for any more emotional conversations, especially knowing that Violet was technically around.

"Please? It's important." Tania seemed pained.

With a sigh, Sam nodded. She'd do it for Tania's sake. "OK. But just for a bit."

Tania unlocked her door, and the two went inside.

The inside of her apartment was very different from Sam's. Black drapes lined the walls, and candles were lit on every bookshelf, desk, and drawer. Beads hung at the doorway to the bathroom. A small shrine to the Virgin Mary, Christ, and the voodoo deities rested discreetly in a corner—a reminder of the blend between Christianity and voodoo that Tania believed in. Overall, the room felt like the woman herself: dark, mysterious, and comfortable.

"I like it," Sam said.

Motioning toward her desk, Tania said, "Sit down, please."

When Sam did, Tania flipped three tarot cards in front of her, standing behind her. "The World Card reversed, your past. The Moon Card, your present. The Death Card, your future."

Sam skimmed over the cards. "These were from my reading back at your shop." She had expected an emotional conversation about Violet, not this.

But Tania didn't respond to that. She pointed at each card in turn. "The first one means success, but an unsubstantial one that lacks closure. That is where your life came from. You were given everything and did nothing with it. You just existed. The second card means a lack of clarity, confusion, and tension. This is where you have been all these years. You have been fighting your fate and all that goes with it. The third card means change, transformation, transition to a new life. That is where you are heading. Your entire life is about to change forever."

"But how is that still relevant?" Sam asked. "I mean, this reading was done five years ago. I don't get it."

"Because, Princess," Tania said, her voice suddenly reverberating, "you have yet to confront your destiny."

Sam jerked up and turned around. Tania's skin had taken on a pallor, and her pupils were dilated. It was no longer Tania who was speaking.

"Hello, Violet."

Tania—or, rather, Violet—bowed. "The thing about my readings is that they remain relevant until realized. It's part of my talent. Since we met that night in 1992, your hand has always been forced. The only choice you made was to fuse with Bridgette."

Tightening her fists, Sam said, "How can you say that? I've lived every day since then trying to—"

"Samantha, please. I'm not here to pick a fight with you."

Heaving a great sigh, Sam leaned back. "What do you want, Violet? An apology? Forgiveness?"

"I'm well past that, Samantha. I'm dead. Now I just want you to have closure. You've been given a terrible destiny, one I wouldn't wish on anyone. I don't know what that destiny will entail, but I believe you'll come to understand it tomorrow night. You'll also face a choice—a choice no one should have to make. And I believe that whatever you decide, it will affect the world for many years to come."

As Sam rested against the desk, she realized she was sweating. She could feel a sudden, heavy burden on her shoulders.

"I'm sorry I had to tell you this, Samantha," Violet said from within Tania's body. "You've suffered more than anyone else I know, myself included. But you've been given the power of a god. I just pray that when the critical moment comes, you'll use it the right way."

"How will I know?" Sam was still sweating.

The other woman tapped Sam's chest, right over her heart. "You'll know, Samantha. You'll know."

Nodding, Sam headed toward the door. She needed to get out of there.

She reached for the knob and then stopped. "Violet, you still there?"

"Yes?"

"Thanks . . ." She turned to face her old enemy. "And I forgive you. And I'm sorry."

With a smile, Violet said, "Same here, Samantha. Live well."

Sam smiled back. "Call me Sam."

Upon leaving Tania's room, Sam realized that she needed fresh air. Entering the elevator, she punched the button to go to the roof. The doors were just about closed when a big, black boot stopped it. With a gruff huff, Victor pushed his way inside.

She eyed him. "Um, going up?"

"Yep. Shooting range. Need to practice with my dead eye." He tapped the side of his red glass eye and then pushed the first basement button.

As the elevator went up, he glanced over, squinting at her. When he did that, he looked even creepier. "You're more tense than usual, Sam."

Leaning against the wall, she regarded him. While he always "had your back," he never asked about others' personal feelings.

"Just thinking about my fate, Big V. My destiny. Wondering what it could be."

"Load of snake shit." He took out his gun. With an extra-long and extra-wide barrel, it was more like a hand cannon than a revolver. Attached to it was a small, strong wire that ran to his holster—a way to ensure he was never completely disarmed.

She blinked. "Excuse me?"

With a loud snort, he said, "People are always talking about fate and destiny. Seems like an excuse not to do something difficult." He started loading his revolver, each slug like a shotgun shell. "I was once told I had a destiny. Followed it, too. Got my wife and son killed. Never again. I choose every inch of my grave that I dig."

Through that grizzled stare was a hint of regret, the first she'd ever seen. "People say those who go against destiny're damning themselves." He closed up his revolver and added, "If that's the case, then I'll be sure to shoot the devil right in balls with ol' Perdition here."

The door to the elevator opened up. Victor holstered Perdition, stepped outside, and then looked back at her. "You're a god, right? Start acting like one. Make your own damn destiny."

The door closed. Sam leaned back and laughed.

Who'd have thought, of all people, Big V would get through to me?

By the time she reached the roof, Sam felt better about her supposed destiny. Even though Violet and Victor's advice potentially contradicted each other, she felt more confident about her situation. And while she didn't know what choice she'd have to make, she knew she'd make it when the moment arrived.

Aucoin was at his usual spot. She slid up to the railing right next to him. "Hey."

He smiled. "Hey. Not busy anymore?"

"No, I'm free. For now." She chuckled. "Alexia has already booked my time when we get back. She's demanding we trade Michael stories."

"Ha! That girl is just like her brother: hard-headed and pushy but with a heart of gold. Whoever ends up with her? Good luck to him. He'll have his hands full."

Having thought the same thing, she hooted. Then she leaned against him. He jerked a bit, but a moment later, he put his arm around her. "You OK, Sam?"

She frowned. "Just. It's been a lot. You know? For me, this nightmare started when I was five years old. And it never ended. I'm still living in this constant Hell."

Aucoin squeezed her closer. "I can't even imagine that. I hope you find peace one day."

"I'll find peace when I can finally die," she said.

Immediately, he tensed up. "Why would you say that?"

With a grunt, she muttered, "Because everyone will be better off when I'm dead."

Before she could think, he pulled her back and stared into her eyes. "Don't you ever, ever say that again, Sam."

"Kyle?"

"You, you listen to me." He seemed hurt. Real hurt. "Life is way too precious. Way too damn precious. It can end in the blink of an eye. A trigger pulled and a seatbelt failed—that's how quickly Michael and Rodger died. And look at how their deaths have affected others. Mabel Dugas just about lost her mind when Rodger passed. Any chance of Alexia being a gentle girl went with Michael. Death always hurts the survivors the most. So to say that we're better off with you dead is just—ugh, have you learned nothing these past five years?"

She gazed up at him, unsure what to say or even feel.

"Damn it, Sam. We all care for you. We're all doing this for you. Tomorrow, we could all die to save your children, to stop your father, all so you can find a way to end this. Can't you see how much we love you?"

Tears trickled down her cheeks. The pain she had been suppressing the past few years was pouring out. "Kyle, I just . . . I'm so tired of all this pain. I live with it. I'm strong because I have to be, but I just want it to end."

The next thing she knew, he was holding her to his chest. "Sam, damn it. Life doesn't have to just be pain. There are good things as well."

"Name one," she said, sobbing into his chest. The floodgate was open. "Name one good thing that's come of me being alive."

"Your children."

"They don't even know me. I've already failed them."

"Then me, you . . . idiot!"

Her sobs stopped with a hiccup. "Kyle?"

His words caught in his throat. "Because of you, I went from being a hateful shell of a man into someone who wanted to live again. I found a reason to live. And so can you, Sam. So can you."

Slowly, Sam gazed up at Aucoin. Despite the wrinkles and the gray hair, he was handsome. It took her a few seconds, but she realized that behind that old face was a brightly shining light, the same kind of light she had seen in the eyes of another man who had once told her to live.

Richie.

Leaning up, she pressed her lips to his. She didn't know what to expect, but she was pleased when he kissed her back, wrapping his arms around her. Like she had kissed Richie outside her townhome years ago, she now kissed Aucoin, her arms around his neck, pulling him closer until she felt his heartbeat.

When they finally parted, she kissed tears off his face. "I don't want to be alone anymore. Please stay with me tonight?"

He nodded, blushing furiously, his voice barely above a whisper. "Yes. Yes, I will."

She took his hand, squeezed it gently, and started leading him off the roof.

"Sam, I just . . ."

"Hmmm? Something wrong, Kyle?"

"No. I just want you to know that I'm not using you tonight. That's all."

At the door heading back inside, she pulled him into another kiss. In her heart, she felt the same feelings she had felt for Richie so many years ago. Perhaps it had grown during the past year, or perhaps it had just formed. But it was there—love.

"Good," she said. "Because neither am I."

Several hours later, Sam and Aucoin finally settled down underneath the covers. As he lay back with an exhausted but happy expression, she sat up. She picked up her shoe charm and kissed it. Then she popped open a bottle of Jack Daniels. She paused, considering it for a few moments. With a frown, she closed it back up.

"What, you're not going to drink?" he asked, resting his hands behind his head.

Putting the bottle back on her dresser, she lay down next to him. "Nah. I think, for the first time in a while, I'm satisfied."

"Really?" He laughed softly, trying not to appear full of himself. "And I thought I was out of practice."

She hummed and leaned over, running her fingers down his hairy chest. While the sex hadn't been as physically intense as her encounters with men like Caleb, it had been far more emotionally fulfilling. "You're fine, Kyle. I think . . ."

She nuzzled against him. "I think for the first time in years, I'm happy being next to someone. I'm ready to open up again. Ya know, I'm ready to feel."

He put his arm around her and gently stroked her side. "So, what happens now? I mean, between us?"

Kissing his chest and then nuzzling it like a cat, she asked, "I dunno, what do you want?"

Resting his hand on her hip, he said, "For you to be happy."

"Happy. I like that." She didn't say anything else for a while, just snuggling him and occasionally kissing his chest. Hair aside, he felt like a leather jacket—smooth but tough. *That's how Kyle is—tough but comfortable.*

Finally, she stretched and rolled off, sitting up. "I'm going to take a shower. You're welcome to join." She posed demurely.

Sitting up, he said, "Sounds like fun."

He cracked his neck. "So, Sam, what do you want?"

Popping her spine in one last stretch, she reclined against the doorway to the bathroom and watched him fondly.

"I want you, and everyone I love, to be safe."

Chapter 44
The Operation

Date: **Sunday, June 15, 1997**
Time: **8:00 p.m.**
Location: **Napoleon Wharf**
Port of New Orleans Avenue

It was Father's Day when the operation began.

As Sam stood on the edge of the pier, grasping the steel container that held the silver pen and gazing off across the river, she thought of the upcoming battle. It was no longer about just her and Vincent—no, that fight might never even come. Now it was about one thing: making sure Vincent could no longer harm those within the physical world.

Back in 1992, when she had opened her door to Rodger and Michael, she couldn't have possibly imagined being at such a crossroad.

"Hey. Thinking about something?" It was Aucoin, handing her a cup of coffee.

She inhaled the chicory flavor and then drank it down. "Saying goodbye to the past. Come on, hun. Let's go." She secured the container with the silver pen in her cargo pants.

As they headed back into the GEIST camp, she took in the flurry of activity. People were preparing for the operation, and except for the operatives and admins, everyone was in a black or gray GEIST uniform. Misty and Lester were running checks on the helicopters, the black "doors off" kind that she first saw during her Evergreen rescue. Sebastian and Sheree, two young adult agents, were examining a map of the oil rig. Behind them were crates containing equipment to hack into the boring device's controls. Gavin and Curtis, two older agents, were arguing out a strategy. Chase and Noelle, two agents as different as night and day, down to one being a deep chocolate and the other being almost albino, were discussing details of their mission. Tania, back in her indigo robe, and Amelie, an agent skilled with throwing knives, were sparring. Hakim was kneeling on a prayer rug, facing the east. Alexia was in quiet contemplation. And Victor was lying on top of some boxes of machine-gun ammo, hat over his face and apparently asleep.

"This is the biggest operation GEIST has ever undertaken," Aucoin said. "And yet no one appears to be nervous."

"They're too focused on preparing," Sam said. She knew that come tomorrow morning, everyone else could be dead.

They entered the command tent. Abel and Meyer were at a large map, going over the initial approach to the oil rig, while Patty and Dr. Lazarus were conversing near several sets of computer screens. Off to the side, Dixie was speaking with Ouellette.

As Sam entered, Ouellette locked eyes with her. Then, without a word, he turned back to Dixie.

Sam started toward him, but Aucoin grasped her shoulder. "Sam, don't bother with him. There will be plenty of time after this is done."

"So you say." But he had a point. She headed over to Patty and Dr. Lazarus.

"Hey, Sam," Patty said, grinning up at her. "You and Alexia have a chance to talk strategy yet?"

"Yes, last night. Right now, she just wanted to pray."

"That's Alexia for you. That bullheadedness of hers is what gives her strength."

"So, what's the plan now?" Sam asked.

Dr. Lazarus flipped through pages on a clipboard. "The agents we sent to scout out the oil rig just reported in. The Knight Priory is still gathering, but they've already set up a defensive perimeter. That is not surprising, considering that we've been on their backs for over a year. But tonight, the stakes have been raised. We're going to have to go in low, fast, and armed."

Patty brought up a video feed from a boat. "This tech is so advanced, I wanna have its babies! But anyway, the four corners of Deepwater all have machine-gun nests. There's also some funky thing in the middle that's possibly a fifth one, so it'll be a hot insertion and an even hotter extraction."

"Lovely," Sam said. "So what are we waiting for?"

"As soon as the police and medical staff get here, we're setting off," Dr. Lazarus said.

"Right. Thanks."

Sam left with Aucoin. Outside the tent, they almost bumped right into Dixie and Ouellette, who were arguing.

"Sir, with all due respect, this is not your operation!" Dixie shouted, obviously agitated.

Ouellette was in her face. “I don’t give a rat’s ass whose operation it is. It’s my police, so it’s my call. Besides, need I remind you what happened the last time you didn’t take my advice, Captain? You lost half your goddamn arm.”

Tightening her fist, she reared back to punch him. “Why, you son of a—”

Moving like lightning, Aucoin grabbed her arm. “Dixie, stop it!”

Still kind of lost, Sam asked, “What the hell is going on here?”

Dixie pushed Aucoin away. “Commander Ouellette is insistent on sending the SWAT team directly to Deepwater after GEIST punches through the defenses, instead of intercepting the Knight Priory when they get back to land like he originally agreed.”

“You’re being stupid, Captain,” Ouellette said. “If they make it to land, catching them will be next to damn near impossible!”

“Why can’t you have faith in my leadership?” Dixie was near tears.

Aucoin stood between them. “Calm down. It’s not worth your career. Don’t hit him.” Then he added, “Let me do it.” Swinging a wild haymaker, he punched Ouellette right in the mouth.

Sam shuddered inside and out. *Oh! Yes!*

But just as fast, Aucoin recoiled from the punch, holding his hand and swearing. “Oh, fuck! Son of a bitch that hurt!”

Ouellette nonchalantly rubbed his jaw. “You’re lucky I rolled with that punch, Aucoin. Lucky as hell.” He returned to the command tent.

Dixie and Sam got Aucoin to stop hopping around in pain so they could tend to him. His knuckles already had a nasty black-and-purple bruise forming. Handing him off to Dixie, Sam said, “Get him some medical treatment. We’re launching any minute.”

“What are you going to do?” Dixie asked.

“Something I shoulda done years ago!” Sam stormed back into the tent.

No normal person is that strong!

Ouellette was talking with Dr. Lazarus. Grabbing his collar, she pulled his face to hers. “What the fuck are you, you son-a-of-bitch? Are you fused like me? Answer me!”

He angrily pushed her away. “Get your hands off me, Castille!”

Everyone in the tent was staring at her, but she didn’t care. Tightening her fists, she said, “Let’s see you shrug off a blow from me. How about it, Ouellette?”

“Sam, stop it,” Dr. Lazarus pleaded. “He’s just trying to help us with the—”

“Shut it, Andre!” Sam said. Years of frustration with Ouellette were finally coming to a head. She jammed a finger in his face. “I want answers. Answers, you prick. And I want them now!”

Glaring at her with an indignant expression, his brow wrinkled. Then he said, "Fine. When my work is done, we can have our little confrontation." Then he stuck his finger up in her face. "But you listen to me, Castille. I've got a personal interest as well. So like it or not, we're allies tonight against a common enemy. You have no idea what's really at stake here, so stay out of my way, or I will put you down."

She glared back a few more seconds, their gazes equally intense. Then she spat to the side. "Fine. But afterwards, me and you. One way or another."

She glanced over at Abel and Meyer, who were being cautiously observant, and Patty, who was watching with wide eyes. "I'm sorry you all had to see that." Sam left the tent.

Sam had just finished checking on Aucoin, whose hand had been wrapped in bandages by Camellia, when the New Orleans police arrived. SWAT team vans, ambulances, and squad cars flooded the pier—it seemed like every precinct was there. Officers blockaded the entrances to the wharf from pedestrians, escorting out ravers and partygoers who wandered too close.

"This is a screwed-up scene," Aucoin said as he tested his hand's range of motion. "The police of this city are going up against the mayor."

"Most of them probably don't know he's a target," Camellia said as she finished checking him out. "Only Ouellette is risking himself. And besides, the mayor will likely be allowed to testify against the Knight Priory in exchange for immunity."

"Typical politician," Aucoin said.

Sam gently touched his hand. "You gonna be able to shoot with this?"

"I don't have a choice."

Outside, Dixie's voice rang out over the camp's PA. "Everyone, gather into your groups. We'll be departing in ten minutes."

"This is it, you two," Camellia said. She smiled saucily. "Have fun storming the castle."

With a smirk, Sam said, "Cute movie reference."

Aucoin flexed his hand again. "I must have missed it. What movie is that?"

She tapped his nose. "You, sir, have just signed up for a date night when this is over."

Outside, agents and operatives alike were gathering near one of four helicopters. Sam hugged Aucoin and then said, "No matter what happens, thank you for teaching me to love again."

He hugged her back. "Yeah, well, stop acting like this is goodbye."

"All right, Kyle. See you later?"

"Yep. Still gotta share that drink."

They kissed and parted ways.

Joining Alexia at her helicopter, Sam was issued a headset. Alexia already had one on. "This will keep us in contact with Command."

When Sam put the headset on, she heard Dixie's voice. "Veronica, our infiltration specialist, has snuck onto the oil rig. We've received confirmation that the entire Knight Priory has arrived. They are just waiting on Mayor Morial to begin."

"Are my children there?" Sam asked.

There was no answer.

Alexia tittered and pointed to the "push to talk" button.

"Oh." Sam pushed the button. "Hey, are my children there?"

Patty's voice came up. "Sam, we've received visual confirmation of your children. Don't worry, I'll be personally guiding in Team Two."

Then Dixie said, "The Knight Priory arrived from several yachts currently docked below the rig. They were already wearing their masks. So when you get to the main meeting hall, scatter the Knight Priory, find your target, and apprehend them. Stick to your missions, people! Let the SWAT team and Ouellette handle the rest."

With a whine, the helicopters started. Meyer hopped onto one and shouted into a loudspeaker. "Teams Five and Six, board here now!"

Sam entered the helicopter with Alexia and Hakim. As she strapped herself in, she saw Misty, Lester, Sebastian, and Sheree loading up the equipment to hack into the boring device. Aucoin was getting into another helicopter with Victor, Gavin, and Curtis. She squeezed her charm as he vanished inside. *Good luck, Kyle.*

"Hey, Your Majesty! Welcome aboard!" It was the Jamaican from her rescue at Evergreen. She didn't even know his name. "Don't worry about a ting, Your Majesty. Anything comes close and I'll shred it wit' the fifty cal right here."

Being called that made her blush. "Thanks. But please, just call me—"

The helicopter engine roared to life.

"What was that, Your Majesty?" He held his hand to his ear. "I couldn't hear you."

She spoke a bit louder. "I said, call me S—"

And then the helicopter drowned out her words as it took off.

"All right!" he said, putting on his headset. "Let's go kick some Knight Priory ass!"

Despite getting cut off twice, she laughed at his enthusiasm. Much like Alexia's sincerity, his attitude was refreshing.

As they flew south toward the Gulf of Mexico, Sam steeled herself for the upcoming battle. The words of both Tania and Victor resonated within her.

Whatever your destiny is, you have to fulfill it.

Make your own damn destiny.

Sam closed her eyes and focused on what was ahead.

No matter what happens, this story ends tonight.

Chapter 45
Sounds of War

Date: **Sunday, June 15, 1997**
Time: **9:47 p.m.**
Location: **Deepwater Olympus**
Somewhere in the Gulf of Mexico

The rocking of the helicopter had just lulled Sam to sleep when she was jerked awake to the sounds of war.

Aucoin called out over the headset. "Dixie! We've got problems. Big ones!"

Sam started looking outside when an explosion rocked the helicopter, tossing Alexia against her. Grabbing her partner, she braced herself and held on tight. The Jamaican yelled, "Shit!" and started firing his machine gun. Outside, it sounded like the world was ending.

"Are you OK?" Sam asked, nudging Alexia.

"Y-yeah," she said, although her eyes were wide and she was almost hyperventilating. "What's happening?"

Instead of answering her, Sam pushed her back in her seat. "Hang on. No matter what happens, do not jump. If the helicopter crashes, wait until it stops moving, then unharness and swim to the surface."

"If it cra—what?"

Strapping Alexia in, Sam said, "Stay calm. If you panic, you're dead." Then she leaned out of the side of the copter to take in the scene. It was pure pandemonium.

The sky was illuminated with the hail of machine-gun fire, both from GEIST helicopters and the oil rig. Streaking by like lines of fireflies, they kicked up the water in splashes and bounced off metal hulls with sparks. The smell of gunpowder and oil was choking.

Aucoin called out again, "They have surface-to-air missiles. I repeat, surface-to-air missiles!"

Another explosion went off. Above them, one of the helicopters burst into flames. She gasped. "No!"

"Helicopter down!" Dixie cried. "Tania, Amelie, Chase, Noelle—anyone, answer!"

Then Alexia screamed, "Sam, we've got incoming!"

Joined by Meyer and Hakim, Sam saw a missile flying straight at them, streaking from a large vehicle with a radar dish situated in the center of the rig.

"An SA-15 Gauntlet," Meyer said, shouting over the sounds of battle. "Probably Russian black market. Sam, we need to take that or we're all dead!"

The missile rapidly approached

Suddenly, Sam had an idea—a bat-shit crazy, but entirely plausible, idea. Victor's words rang in her head. *You're a god, right? Start acting like one.*

"Meyer, Hakim, Alexia, can you three take that thing out if you get close enough?"

"Affirmative," Meyer said.

The missile drew even closer.

Tightening her gloves, she said, "Good! You three do that. I'll handle these."

"Right," Meyer said. "Keenan, we're going in. Shred everything on the ground!"

The Jamaican gunner shot him a thumbs-up. "Right as you say, Mister Rabbi, Sir."

As the missile neared, Sam focused her power. Time around her slowed down until even the rattle of machine-gun fire was like the tick of a metronome. With a quick inhale, she leapt out of the helicopter, swung from the landing skid, and landed on the missile. Then with a guttural cry, she punched the missile in half. Wasting no time, she scanned the battlefield. The helicopter holding Aucoin, Victor, and the others was approaching the rig, while the one holding the equipment to hack the boring device had soared upward. However, a missile was flying at it.

Damn it!

Even as the missile she had just destroyed started falling, she pushed off of it, hurtling toward the others. She visualized herself making the jump, and when she collided with the other missile, she knocked it off course. And as she flew past the helicopter, riding on the missile now, she caught a glimpse of the shocked expressions of Sheree and Sebastian. She shot them the victory sign.

I can do this!

Again, she glanced around. The helicopter with her team was beginning its approach, while the one with Aucoin, which was almost to the side of the rig, had two missiles flying at it.

No—Kyle!

Pulling on her missile with short, controlled tugs, she kept altering its course until she was flying straight at the other two. She took a second to assess their velocity, guessing as best she could, and then kicked hers like a soccer ball. It flew through the air in a tight spiral and hit, both exploding at a safe distance from the helicopter. Then she dove into the other missile, intercepting it just a few feet from impact. The moment she punched it in half, she realized that she had made a miscalculation. The head of the missile flipped up and hit the rotor mast. For a brief moment, she saw Aucoin, his face pale with fear. Then he closed his eyes as the top of the helicopter exploded.

Kyle! NO!

The concussive force blew her back. A moment later, she hit the water and blacked out.

"Sam! Come in! Come in, Sam!"

Sam awoke, face up in the water, to the sound of gunfire and explosions. Almost instinctively, she checked for the container with the silver pen. It was still in her cargo pants. Her headset crackled badly, but she could still hear Dixie. Tapping the "to speak" button, she groaned, "I'm here."

"Thank God," Dixie exhaled. "Listen, Meyer's helicopter went down, but he, Hakim, and Alexia survived and disabled the missiles. Both Kyle's and Tania's went down, and we don't know if they're alive. Ouellette and the police copters left and should be at your location soon. Sam, you've got to meet up with Alexia and continue the operation."

By then, Sam was swimming to the side of the rig. It was weather-worn but not yet rusted. Locating a ladder, she started climbing up. With her strength, she should have been able to go quickly, but she couldn't. Her heart ached too much at the thought of Aucoin possibly being dead.

"So why didn't we know they'd have a damn missile launcher?" she asked through gnashed teeth.

"Veronica just found out. It's Caroline. She has hefty black-market contacts. It appears that Tania's visit the other night stirred her up more than we thought."

"Damn it!" Sam climbed even faster. With every rung, the ache in her heart changed into boiling rage toward the Knight Priory. "Veronica should have dug deeper."

"We can worry about that later. Just remember that the Knight Priory employs a private army. Your orders to take prisoners don't extend to them. Kill anyone who tries to stop you."

As she reached the top of the rig, she took out her twin pistols. The feeling of righteous indignation within her peaked. "Good. That's what I was hoping you'd say. Fuck these damn insects!"

Rushing forward, she came across the remains of the helicopter. It was still smoking, flames coming out the cockpit. Keenan, the Jamaican gunner, was leaning out of the side, his eyes still open and blood dripping out of his mouth. He was grinning.

She closed his eyes. "Damn. Sorry, Keenan." At least she had finally learned his name.

Then she heard someone coming. Hiding against the tail of the helicopter, she waited. A few seconds later, two guards came into view. Immediately, she focused her power and side-kicked one of them in the gut. He folded in half with a sickening crack. Then she pointed a gun at the other guard's head. "Bang."

She pulled the trigger, and a moment later, he fell back with a hole in his head. Then she glared at his body. *Ya'll picked the wrong night to piss me off.*

Holstering her guns, she ran toward the center of the rig. There, she saw Meyer, Hakim, and Alexia pinned down against the Gauntlet by over a dozen guards. Most were firing upon them, but some were creeping around to get a better shot. She got as close as she dared and signaled for Meyer's attention. When he noticed her, he seemed relieved.

Knowing that she didn't have much time, she pointed out the guards approaching from the side and then pointed to him. He apparently understood, because he nodded and spoke to Hakim and Alexia. Sam didn't need to hear what he said. He was ex-Special Forces and understood the battlefield. So, taking her guns back out, she dashed into the open, hollering like a lunatic.

"Crazy blond bitch here! Shoot me if you can!"

Not surprisingly, the guards fired upon her, a few bullets grazing her arms and legs, slicing the tissue. But that wasn't anything new. Focusing until time around her slowed, she jumped into the air and started firing. Within seconds, she had killed eight of the guards and was landing by two more, one of them quite big. As time sped back up, she unsheathed her knife, sliced one across the throat, and then stabbed at the big guy. He blocked her attack.

"You aren't so tough," he said with a laugh.

Taken aback by his strength, which seemed to be at the pinnacle of human conditioning, she continued pushing forward. With a roar, he grappled her with both hands, forcing her to drop the knife. "Looks like you're done here, little girl."

His arrogance only made her angrier. Deciding she was done with him, she focused until her arms bulged. "No, you are!"

With a quick move, she snapped both of his wrists like twigs.

As he let out a shriek, she threw him to the ground and stomped on his shin. It also broke. Next came his collarbone.

"Oh, God!" the man cried. "You're a monster!"

"Shut up," she said, and she shot him in the head.

She panted as she looked down at his body. Suddenly, she felt sick.

Then the sounds of shouting caught her attention. Meyer, Hakim, and Alexia had pushed back the guards that were sneaking up on them. Alexia had disarmed two of them and was engaging them in close combat. Meyer was trading gunfire with the others while Hakim chanted and rubbed his ruby ring. Suddenly, a fountain of flame blossomed from it, and a creature made of fire and molten rock arose.

"What is your bidding, Master?" it asked.

Hakim pointed at the guards Meyer had pinned down. With a roar, the creature rushed at them. Moments later, they were reduced to ash.

Sam could only gape as the beast returned to the ring. *Holy hand grenade.*

"Repent!" Alexia said, doing a split in mid-air and stabbing both guards in the chest. They convulsed and then fell to the ground, dead. She got up and cleaned off her blades, regarding both men with regret.

"It looks like you guys didn't need me after all," Sam said.

"This one wouldn't say that," Hakim said. "He is just glad to see that Lady Castille will be joining us."

Sam said, "Good thing you have that fire beast going on. Meyer's powers are useless against pure humans."

Meyer glared at her. "No bantering during a mission, Sam," he said. As she stuck her tongue out, he tapped his headset. "Dixie, we've disabled the surface-to-air missile launcher. Ouellette and his people will still have to contend with the machine guns. Requesting permission to do a sweep of each of the towers."

"Negative." Dixie's voice was crackling badly. Sam tapped her ear piece to try and clear it up. "Go to the southwest door and rendezvous with Veronica. Then proceed directly to your objective. The Knight Priory is gathered, but they won't stay there when they learn about the fighting."

Veronica. Sam had a few things to say to her.

"Affirmative. Over and out." Meyer reloaded his rifle. "Ready, Hakim?"

Hakim bowed slightly. "*Na'am.*"

They headed off together.

Sam hurried over to Alexia. "Hey, you ready?"

Alexia was still staring at the men she'd killed. "This is my first time . . . ya know, murdering someone. Even in self-defense, it's not right."

They didn't have time for this. Sam was just about to say something when Alexia sighed. "It hurts, Sam, but I can't focus on it right now. We have to go. I'll pray on it later."

Sam began to understand what the others meant about Alexia's will being something amazing. She said, "All right, then. Did you hear what Dixie said?"

"Yeah."

"You ready to do this? It's going to be hell."

Alexia radiated confidence. "I'm ready. Let's do this."

As they ran toward the southwest door, machine-gun fire started up again. In the distance, Sam saw sixteen New Orleans police helicopters heading toward them, two from each precinct. They started firing on the machine-gun nests in the towers. *Well, I may hate Ouellette, but we need the police.*

At the doorway to the southwest tower, they met up with Veronica dressed as a member of the Knight Priory. Once inside a metal hallway, she pulled them into a small room. "OK, listen up. I've already sent Meyer and Hakim on. The only one I haven't confirmed is the Oracle, but he's likely in the meeting—"

Sam grabbed her collar and slammed her against the wall. The rage had returned. "You listen up, you worthless insect! You didn't do your job right, and because of that, Kyle, Victor, Tania, and the others are likely dead!"

"Sam, what the heck?" Alexia yelled.

"You deserve to die for what you did!" Sam screamed at Veronica.

Yet Veronica remained calm. "Yes, Sam, I screwed up big. I should have been more thorough, and I wasn't. If they're dead, it's on me." Then she grabbed Sam's hands and slid them to her neck. "You want to kill me over this? Go ahead. I can't fight you. You're a god. I'm nothing. Like you said, I'm an insect." She locked eyes with Sam, her expression firm. "And what are you? Are you a monster?"

"What are you two doing?" Alexia seemed completely shocked.

With her hands around Veronica's neck, Sam imagined squeezing. Veronica would gurgle, her eyes would bulge, and in seconds, she'd be dead.

But even as she stood there, she remembered the big guard from earlier. She could have let him live, but she'd chosen not to. He was just a soldier, and she'd chosen to kill him in cold blood, even after she'd rendered him helpless. She had one foot in her own damnation.

No. I am not going to do this.

Letting go and turning away, Sam leaned against the wall, her bangs covering her face. *I've almost become Vincent.* That realization made her tremble. She had come an inch away from losing herself.

From the side, Alexia looked back and forth from her to Veronica, her eyes wide.

Then Veronica straightened up. "Seems there's some part of you that's still human. Try to keep it that way." Putting on her mask, she slipped out the door.

Alexia gently touched Sam's arm. "Um, are you gonna be OK?"

Nodding ever so slightly, Sam said, "Yeah. I'll be OK." She had stopped herself from turning, from becoming another Vincent.

She smiled at Alexia. "I'll be OK."

Chapter 46
Knight Priory of Saint Madonna

Date: **Sunday, June 15, 1997**
Time: **9:52 p.m.**
Location: **Deepwater Olympus**
Somewhere in the Gulf of Mexico

With Amelie next to her, Tania pressed against the cool metal wall. Chase and Noelle were a few feet away.

"Damn, I am so lucky to be alive," Chase said, wringing out his clothing.

Noelle sniffed disdainfully. "You smell like a wet dog."

"Hush, you two!" Tania exclaimed. While they all had been lucky to survive the crash, they were now considerably behind. And being somewhere in the lower maintenance levels of Deepwater didn't exactly fill her with confidence about catching up. Even worse, they had all lost their headsets, so they couldn't contact the base.

"What do you think?" Amelie asked, nervously twirling her knives.

Tania hummed. "Well, people, any ideas?"

"Yes," Noelle said. "We find a radio room and contact Dixie."

"Then I get some dry clothes," Chase said with a growl.

Tania said, "Good idea. The radio, I mean."

As she started down the hallway, Amelie tapped her arm. "Hey, T," she said, using the nickname she had given Tania years ago, "are you sure those two will keep it together?"

Noelle and Chase were quietly arguing over which silenced pistol was whose.

Tania grunted. "This is no time for a discussion. Let's contact the base and then go from there." But still, she was nervous. Despite believing in her abilities as well as in GEIST, she was starting to get nervous. Things had not gone according to plan.

By the time they found the radio room, located in one of the sub-levels, the rig had gone completely quiet. Tania stood before the door with Amelie beside her. Noelle and Chase leaned on either side of it.

Sister, what do you sense?

"*There are two guards in the room and a third coming this way. That's all.*"

Tania cleared her throat, then pointed to the door and held up two fingers. Both Chase and Noelle nodded.

Then she whispered, "Amelie. Someone is turning that corner any moment."

Amelie nodded.

"Do we kill or not?" Noelle asked quietly.

While Chase grinned, Amelie sternly shook her head. Tania frowned.

I'm the operative, so it's my call.

"*Yes, well, make a decision now, Sister.*"

Sucking in her breath, Tania whispered, "We don't have time to fight. We kill. Sorry, Amelie."

"Very well." She seemed less than pleased.

"*You'd think a former CIA assassin wouldn't have trouble with that.*"

Some people join GEIST to escape their past.

Raising her hand, Tania counted to three and then dropped it. Noelle and Chase kicked down the door and rushed inside, where two guards were engrossed in a card game. They didn't even have a chance to blink before they were both shot in the head. Amelie knelt down, took aim, and threw a knife the moment the third guard ran around the corner. It embedded in his throat.

"I apologize," she said.

Inside the room, Chase worked quickly on the radio. "OK, I've cross-checked their frequencies to the ones GEIST is using. This channel should be secure."

"Thanks," Tania said, grateful for his expertise. Removing her mask, she spoke into the mic. "Tania to Dixie. Come in."

Dixie came through clearly. "Tania? Thank God you're all right. Who's with you?"

"Amelie, Noelle, and Chase. The rest are gone. What's the status?"

"Kyle and Victor's helicopter crashed on the side of the rig. We don't know if anyone survived. Sam, Meyer, Hakim, and Alexia have rendezvoused with Veronica and are heading to the main meeting hall in the center of the compound. Patty is guiding Sebastian and Sheree through the rig to get to the boring device."

"OK," Tania said. "So, any deviation to the plan?"

"None. Ouellette and the police just finished dispatching the machine-gun nests and are setting up a perimeter as well as seizing control of the yachts at the dock of the rig. You are to proceed to the meeting hall and complete your missions before the Knight Priory scatters."

"All right. Over and out."

As she spun the tuning dials to hide the GEIST frequency, Chase asked, "So, question: When Noelle and I grab the mayor, do we take him topside for a copter ride?"

"No," Tania said. "Once you secure the mayor, take him to the docks and requisition one of the yachts for transport."

"Hell, yeah," he said, slapping Noelle on the ass. "Party time with tequila and lime."

Noelle punched him in the mouth.

Heading up the rig was slower than Tania had anticipated, thanks to the many guards interspersed between the twisting corridors and small rooms. Moving two-by-two, they successfully took out every one of them without alerting the others. Even Amelie, who always apologized whenever she killed, admitted they didn't have the time or manpower to subdue that many people.

When they reached the floor containing the main meeting hall, the tight corridors and rooms were replaced by more spacious ones. With soft carpet and wood-paneled walls, it was obvious the floor plan was designed solely for comfort.

Chase, whose busted lip was no longer puffy, said, "Think they redecorated this place just for the Knight Priory?"

With a snort, Noelle said, "Obviously. How narcissistic of them, just like the elite."

Tuning out their banter, Tania focused on the area before her. There were about eight guards, some moving around and others standing idly. Beyond them was a set of double doors leading to the meeting hall, with two more guards on either side of it. And off to the side, in an alcove, was a smaller door marked "Balcony."

"Amelie, can you sneak onto the balcony with me?"

"Of course," she said. "We'll need a distraction for all those guards, though."

"Hmmm." Tania motioned to Chase and Noelle. "Any ideas, you two?"

Noelle's brow wrinkled. "It would be hard to distract them without raising such an alarm that Chase and I can't get to the mayor before he—"

"We can rig the water valves in the kitchen to flood!" Chase exclaimed.

Everyone stared at him.

"Think about it. A fire alarm will clear the rig, and if any of us blow our cover now, we may lose a chance to get our targets. But some broken pipes? That should get almost everyone on this floor concerned."

Tania had to admit that was a pretty good idea. "OK, you two. Go for it."

"This will all end in tears," Noelle muttered as she and Chase snuck off.

"What is her problem, T?" Amelie asked.

Frowning, Tania said, "Noelle's never been good at expressing her feelings, but I think she actually fancies Chase."

Amelie cocked an eyebrow at her. "Seriously?"

With a shrug, Tania said, "Despite everything, she always volunteers to partner up with him." That said, Tania turned her attention inward. *You've been awfully quiet, Sister.*

"*I'm worried about Sam.*"

What do you mean?

"*I don't know. I have a feeling. A bad feeling.*"

Sister, you're a ghost. You are nothing but bad feelings.

"*I'm being serious, dummy! I'm honestly scared that something awful is about to happen.*"

Before Tania could reply, someone shouted, "Busted water pipe in the kitchen!" With the exception of the two guards in front of the double doors, everyone else rushed out of the room.

"I'm impressed," Tania said. Then she nudged Amelie. "Your turn to shine."

"Of course. Follow me, T."

Amelie slid along the wall, inching toward the alcove with Tania carefully following. About halfway there, she stopped.

"What's wrong?" Tania asked in a whisper.

"There's no cover. We can slip along the wall, but if they look this way, we'll be caught."

Nodding, Tania weighed the options. They could kill the guards, but then they'd have to act quickly or lose the element of surprise. If they chanced it, it was possible they'd be spotted and an alarm would be raised. *No matter how I look at it, it's a no-win situation.*

"*Sister, I have an idea,*" Violet said.

Oh? What's that?

"*Let me out. I'll distract them.*"

But, Sister, you can't—

"It'll only be for a minute or two. I'll be fine."

Tania felt herself sweat. If something happened to Violet while she was outside, it could permanently destroy her.

"Trust me."

You're right. The last time Violet had asked for Tania's trust, things had worked out just fine. *Just be careful, Sister.*

"Good. I need to get some ghostly anger out anyway."

A moment later, Tania felt her strength and perception dwindle to normal as the sensation of another being within her vanished. The vacuum created an overwhelming sensation of loneliness. "Hurry back," she whispered.

"Hurry what back?" Amelie asked.

"Just wait. Violet has this one."

From the other side of the room came a strangled moan and then a wail. The guards jerked back when the ghostly figure of Violet Patterson slipped through the walls. Her sockets were twice their normal size, her jaw was unhinged, and her fingernails were long claws.

"Die . . . ," she moaned. "Die . . ."

"Oh, shit, what the hell!" One of the guards aimed his submachine gun.

The other one grabbed him. "Don't shoot, you idiot! Dr. Kindley told us to contact him if we saw any ghosts. He said—"

Violet suddenly shrieked and flew right into him. A moment later, his hair and skin started turning white as he foamed at the mouth. The first guard screamed, threw up his arms, and ran off, crying out, "They don't pay me enough for this shit."

Amelie grabbed Tania's hand and pulled. "We go. We go now."

As they rushed into the alcove and headed up the stairs, Tania watched the possessed guard writhing on the ground. She had never actually watched Violet hunt before.

You can be quite terrifying, Sister.

The interior of the main meeting hall was a richly decorated room of stone slabs and Roman columns. Red-and-gold tapestry proudly displaying the Knight Priory crest hung everywhere. The balcony itself held only a few cloaked members, and thankfully, none were near the door. Everyone was focused on the floor below.

Marc Morial, dressed in a hooded robe but with the hood pulled down, knelt in front of an altar that was covered in red velvet and adorned with a golden bowl filled with blood. Standing before him was a man in a voodoo mask, his hands on the mayor's head.

"Marc Morial," the figure chanted in a deep timbre. "You have been chosen by the Knight Priory of Saint Madonna to receive a mask of brotherhood. Will you keep our laws, our customs, our faith, and our covenant with the Virgin Mary and the Lord of Death, Baron Samedi?"

"I will," Morial said.

As the ritual continued, Tania felt Violet reenter her. It felt like her sister was gorged from a huge meal. *Did you have to feed off his fear during the operation, Sister?*

"*I was hungry. I only feed once every week or two. We've been too busy for me to hunt, remember?*"

Ugh. It's just your timing.

Amelie leaned over, pulling Tania from her thoughts. "What do we do, T?"

Tania watched the proceedings. "It's almost over. We have to stop them now."

"OK, how?"

As Noelle and Chase, who was soaking wet again, joined them, Tania got an idea. *It's a risk, but if it works . . .*

She cleared her throat and motioned for the others to come closer. "I'm going to snipe the mayor with a rubber bullet. It'll incapacitate him. When that happens, Chase, Noelle, go get him and run. Meanwhile, Amelie and I will find Dr. Kindley."

The others gawked at her. Then Noelle spoke up. "If we do that, every Knight Priory member may attack us. And if they use the *tkeeus*, we're dead."

"I know it's a risk," Tania said, sweating. "But I'm betting on them not having the *tkeeus* ready for use."

"That's a heck of a bet," Chase said.

"I agree with Chase," Amelie said. "But, you're the operative, so if you think it's best . . ."

This time, Tania didn't hesitate. "Yes. That's what we're doing."

"*Taking a gamble, Sister?*"

We don't have a choice. No one else is here.

"*Sadly, you're right. OK. Let's do this.*"

While the others got ready to jump down to the floor, Tania loaded her rifle with one rubber bullet. Then she adjusted the silencer and the scope. Finally, she slipped off her mask.

"*I'm behind you, Sister,*" Violet said.

With a deep breath in, Tania aimed, focusing the crosshairs on Morial's rear. *I didn't vote for you, anyway.*

Then she exhaled and fired. A moment later, all hell broke loose.

Morial hollered and fell forward, grabbing his bum and rolling around. Chase and Noelle jumped off the balcony and rushed toward the mayor, firing their guns into the air. All the other Knight Priory members stumbled back in a panic. Noelle grabbed Morial in a half-nelson. The figure who had been leading the ritual reached for the mayor, but Chase tackled him, knocking off his mask.

It was Connick.

"No," Amelie said. "This is bad. Chase can't handle him!"

The members of the Knight Priory started scattering out of room.

Tania, who had changed her ammo back to regular rounds, watched in horror as Connick picked up Chase by the throat. He started squeezing, and immediately, Chase started flailing and wheezing. With a shrill cry, Noelle charged him, firing her gun repeatedly. He dodged each bullet as if it were nothing and then caught her by the throat as well.

"No!' Tania yelled, aiming her crosshairs at Connick's heart. "Harry!"

He glanced up at her and sneered. Chase's struggle became more pronounced.

"Chase, honey, please," Noelle gasped.

Tania put her finger on the trigger. "Let them go or I'll kill you."

"Be careful, T," Amelie said. "He's fast. Real fast."

"I know. But I can do this!"

Connick sniggered maliciously. "Think you have what it takes, bitch? Try me!" He started squeezing Noelle's neck. "No? You can watch them both die, then!"

Noelle reached for Chase. "I . . . love . . ."

"*Sister, you have to—*"

I know. Guide my hand.

Focusing on Connick, Tania inhaled once more, and then exhaled.

And then she fired.

Chapter 47
Always a Smile

Date: **Sunday, June 15, 1997**
Time: **10:17 p.m.**
Location: **Deepwater Olympus**
Somewhere in the Gulf of Mexico

Aucoin awoke and immediately regretted it. His head felt like it was split open, and every joint in his body ached. His thoughts were foggy at best. Blinking several times to clear his crusty eyes, he finally saw that he was hanging a hundred feet above the Gulf of Mexico.

"Good, you're awake."

Looking up, Aucoin saw that Victor was holding onto him while grasping a steel beam. Way above them both was the platform of the oil rig.

"Arm starting to get tired," Victor said. "You need to climb on your own."

As Aucoin glanced back down, he tried to recall what had happened. The last thing he remembered was Sam pulling off some superhero stunts and then the helicopter crashing.

"How long have I been out?"

"Five, maybe ten minutes."

"And you've been holding me all this time?"

"Yep. Now here, grab on and let's climb."

With a sharp grunt, Victor swung him over to the lattice of the rig. Aucoin grabbed on and got his bearings, the confusion mostly cleared from his head. With ease, Victor started climbing the rig. *The difference between us and operatives is pretty intimidating.*

He started climbing. Within seconds, his arms started burning with effort. "Where are Gavin and Curtis?"

"Dead. Couldn't get to them in time. Only able to grab you."

"They were good men," Aucoin said, climbing. "I'll miss the hell outta them." After a few more yards, he tried calling Dixie, only to realize his headset was gone. "Crap. I need to get in touch with command."

"Here," Victor said, tossing him his. Then he started climbing again.

Catching it, Aucoin mumbled a "Thanks" and then put it on. "Dixie, this is Kyle. Are you there?"

Dixie came on. "Kyle? We've been so damn worried. What hap—"

"No time. Just Victor and I are left. We need instructions."

"It's chaos up there. Ouellette's arrived, and the police are securing the top and bottom of Deepwater. No sign of the Oracle. Children haven't been located. And I—"

Abel spoke in the background. He sounded as calm as ever.

"OK, update," Dixie said. "Shots have been fired in the meeting hall. The Knight Priory is scattering."

By now, Aucoin had stopped climbing. "Dixie, what's going on? Talk to me!"

This time, Dixie sound excited. "Veronica found Caroline! She and her guards slipped to the docks before the fighting broke out. Crap, how did she know about that attack? She's on board her yacht and leaving the docks right now."

Looking down, Aucoin saw a large luxury yacht sliding out into the Gulf. The deck was well lit. Caroline, flanked by several guards, was entering the cabin. He squinted and caught sight of someone in a Knight Priory cloak slipping through the shadows.

"I see it! And it looks like Veronica's there as well. What about the kids?"

"Veronica's saying that the children are not there. Kyle, you have to get on board by any means."

"What about the damn kids? Gavin and Curtis are dead!"

"They have to be on the rig. I'll send someone else. Just go get her! Over and out."

Aucoin roared in frustration and then said, "Victor, change of direction. Caroline's on board that yacht. Can you safely fall that—"

Victor grabbed him and jumped.

"—shiiiiiiiiit!"

Victor landed on the yacht, his boots cracking the deck, his duster billowing out, and his hat staying on. Aucoin kept hollering until Victor pushed him to his feet.

"Don't be a wimp," Victor said.

He then took out his oversized revolver, Perdition, and attached a long wire between the grip and the holster. "Any friendlies on board?"

Catching his breath, Aucoin said, "Yeah, Veronica."

"Right. Let's go." Victor cocked back Perdition's hammer and stomped off.

Although he was still rattled from the jump, Aucoin was grateful for his partner's quick thinking. Once he had gathered himself, Aucoin tapped his headset. "We're on board, Dixie. Going for Caroline."

"Good. Let Victor know that Caroline's private army is expendable."

Two loud blasts, like a shotgun, rang out through the nighttime air.

Taking out his own gun, Aucoin snickered. "I think Victor already knows."

Victor was leaving a trail of bodies, with Aucoin following behind. They met up next to the cabin door Caroline had entered. Nearby was a staircase going up to the bridge. Victor was reloading Perdition with its fist-sized bullets.

Aucoin couldn't help but admire his lethality. There was a reason Victor was codenamed "Death Adder."

"We need to stop this thing as well as locate Caroline," Aucoin said. "It'll be quicker if we split for a few minutes." Normally, he'd never suggest such a thing, but in this instance, he felt they'd be all right.

"Fine," Victor said, closing Perdition's barrel. "Pick one."

Looking from the cabin door to the staircase, Aucoin said, "You secure the bridge. Capture one of them if you can. Think you can handle that, big guy?"

Victor harrumphed and headed upstairs. Watching him leave, Aucoin shook his head. Only two people in GEIST knew Victor's past: Dr. Lazarus and Abel. No one else knew a thing about him. The common theory was that he used to be a professional killer. The second was that he wasn't even human. Aucoin believed it was best not to know.

Gun in hand, Aucoin entered the cabin. The hallway was decorated with track lightning and golden trim, and it smelled of fresh pine. His footsteps squeaked softly over the wooden floors as he crept as silently as possible. He paused at an intersection, hearing footsteps. Pulling back the hammer of his gun, he peeked around the corner. Two guards armed with rifles were heading toward him, checking rooms as they passed them by.

Aucoin pulled back before they could see him. He was both outmanned and outgunned, so rushing them would be suicide. Just as he began sorting through potential plans, three loud bangs from the floor above rang out.

"What the hell was that, a cannon?" one of the guards asked.

"No, it's a shotgun!" the other said.

No, it's just Victor killing your friends, Aucoin thought.

Then the first guard said, "Nevermind. Let's go!" Suddenly, the footsteps were running toward Aucoin. He had maybe a second or two before they'd round the corner. With nowhere to run, he did the only thing he could. As soon as the first one appeared, he punched him in the face with the butt of his gun, collapsing him into a heap. Then he shot the second one in the neck. Blood poured as the second guard fell.

Kneeling on the first guard's back, Aucoin pressed his gun to the man's temple. "OK, shithead. You've got one chance to get out of this alive. Where's Caroline?"

The guard spat out blood. "Fuck you!"

"Chance blown." Aucoin pushed the barrel harder against the man's head.

"Wait! Wait! In the middle of the ship. It's a panic room. She calls it the Vault!"

"How do I get inside?"

When the guard didn't immediately answer, Aucoin pulled his hair until the man screamed. "Once more. How do I get inside?"

Between sobs and labored breaths, the guard said, "Captain has the key. He's in the bridge. But you'll never beat him. He's . . . he was a Green Beret!"

"I don't care if he was 1st Goddamned Cavalry. We're GEIST. And we don't fucking play." With a hard swing, Aucoin knocked the guard out. Then he tied the man up with his own belt and dragged him into a nearby lavatory, securing him to the pipes.

"Lucky for you, I don't like killing unless I have no choice."

When Aucoin reached the bridge, he saw Victor leaning against the wheel, smoking a hand-rolled cigarette. The captain, who was tied up and on his knees, was beaten so badly, his face was a blackened, bloody mess.

"God, Victor. What did he do to you?"

Victor pulled back his duster to show a recently stitched-up wound. Nearby, an army-issue knife was blown to pieces.

Whistling, Aucoin asked, "Did you get him to talk?"

"Sang like a bird."

"Did he mention how to get into the Vault?"

Exhaling some smoke, Victor tossed him a keycard.

Aucoin pocketed it. "All right. Let's turn this tub around. Then we pay Miss Saucier a visit."

After turning the yacht around, something Aucoin had never done before, finding the Vault was easy. Mostly, that was because Victor, after having been stabbed, was particularly irritable. His red "dead eye" glowed constantly, giving him an unnatural, almost uncanny, aim and something akin to precognitive abilities. The guards always seemed to be a little too slow, and by the time they reached the Vault, there was a pile of dead bodies behind them. Even Aucoin, who had long since become desensitized to violence, still shivered at the efficiency of the "Death Adder."

The door to the Vault looked, indeed, like the kind found in a bank. Aucoin swiped the captain's card and then pressed the "open" button. Then he drew out his weapon.

"Get ready," he said. Victor reloaded Perdition and cocked back the hammer. Once the door was open, they stepped inside.

"Caroline Saucier, surrender and come with us or . . ."

Aucoin trailed off as he saw the room. Octagonal and covered in mirrors on all sides, it had only a chair and a small table in the middle. Caroline was sitting at the table, holding a glass of wine and grinning like a kid at a carnival. On the table was a wine bottle, another glass, and a small box with several buttons.

She toasted him. "Kyle Aucoin. And you brought a friend. Come in. We have much to discuss."

"I don't like this," Victor muttered. "She's got some hoodoo in here that's messing with the dead eye. Only gonna be able to use it once."

"Then we do without it." Aucoin aimed his gun at Caroline. "You, ma'am, are in serious trouble. I don't know what ways the government has for dealing with criminals like yourself, but you can bet it won't be pleasant."

Still smiling, Caroline sipped her wine. "You know, I think we got off to a bad start back in 1993. Want to start over?"

"Start over? Because of you, I was thrown into Dr. Klein's crazy house and tortured relentlessly. What do we possibly have to talk about?"

With a shrug, she said, "I now control all of the Knight Priory's assets. Let me go, and you can name your price."

He glared at her, insulted. "You think I can be bought off? You must be stupid."

"Hear me out," she said. "Believe it or not, we've both been victimized by Vincent and the Knight Priory."

"Enough of this shit," Victor huffed. "Can we just shoot her?"

"One second, Victor," Aucoin said. "What are you talking about?"

With a condescending laugh, she said, "Oh, how people forget their history. Does the name Allison Surrette ring a bell?"

The name sounded familiar, but he just couldn't place it.

"You don't remember?" She sighed. "Unbelievable. No one remembers Allison. Oh, sure, they remember Henrietta Babineaux, or Edward Castille, or even Maple Christofer . . ."

Just like that, Aucoin remembered who she was. "Oh! She was one of Vincent Castille's victims."

Caroline stood up. "Yes! That's exactly it! Victim number four of the Bourbon Street Ripper." Sitting down again, her voice was almost reverent as she said, "My beloved Allison. The most sensitive, beautiful soul I had ever known. She was perfect—not just to me, but to everyone. Always a kind word. Always a smile. A woman who loved everyone."

"I'm sorry for your loss," he said, keeping his gun on her. "But that doesn't excuse your actions."

With a snort, she said, "Actions. We're defined by them. Slaves to them. After Vincent was arrested, I swore I'd either rule the Knight Priory or burn it to the ground. I've obviously failed the first part. But I have the grimoire and can use powers beyond your understanding. So screw the Knight Priory. Let them burn."

She drained her glass. "So here's what I propose. Let me go, and I'll just disappear with my powers and my wealth. You can have what you want and be the hero who helped destroy the Knight Priory of Saint Madonna. Isn't that what you want, Kyle Aucoin?"

"What I want," Aucoin said, "is for you to go to jail for the rest of your miserable life."

Her expression slowly hardened. Sitting back, she glared at him. "I thought you might say that. So I arranged a different negotiation."

She tapped a button on the small box. Suddenly, one of the mirror panels slid open. In an alcove, inside of what looked disturbingly similar to an iron maiden, was a beaten and gagged Veronica.

"Aw, shit," Aucoin said.

"That's right! You'd be amazed how well spirit sentries can warn you about who is actually a spy." Caroline laughed cruelly, her finger hovering just above another button. "So, unless you drop all your weapons and kick them over to me, I press this button and end her life in a satisfyingly painful way." Her eyes were wide and her expression mad. "So, Detective, what'll be?"

Chapter 48
Worthy of Admiration

Date: **Sunday, June 15, 1997**
Time: **10:32 p.m.**
Location: **Deepwater Olympus**
Somewhere in the Gulf of Mexico

"Alexia!" Dixie called over the headset. "Come in, Alexia. Are you there?"

Alexia, fighting a trio of guards at the entrance to the meeting hall, was unable to respond. Even if she could, she'd have just voiced how chaotic the mission had turned out. The moment the Knight Priory had started using their surface-to-air missile launcher, things had fallen into chaos.

Lord, protect me, she thought as she swayed to the side, dodging the knife of one guard and parrying the other two. She and Sam had been fighting against groups of guards since splitting away from Veronica. Her clothes and blades were covered with blood, and despite her skill, more blades and bullets had grazed her skin than she would have preferred.

"Alexia," Dixie repeated. "Please come in!"

Swiping her blade in a double envelopment around one guard's knife, she thrust forward and into his throat. As he started gurgling blood, she kicked him off just in time to dodge a tackle from the other one. The third was reloading his gun. Quickly, she closed the distance to him and stabbed him through the heart. He shook and then fell. Then she spun around and cut the third one across the throat even as he rushed at her again.

"Forgive me, Lord," she whispered. She wasn't sure if she'd ever get used to killing.

Then she glanced over toward Sam, who had fought the rest of the guards. Most were dead, either broken in pieces or sporting sizable holes. Only one remained alive, and he was backing away from Sam, whose arms were covered in blood, whimpering "monster" over and over.

With a sigh, Sam shook her head and turned away. "Get out of here, insect."

Alexia winced. Although Sam had apparently stopped herself from descending into evil, she still seemed to struggle with her godlike powers.

Can a fused person ever live a peaceful life? Alexia wasn't sure.

"Alexia! Please answer!" Dixie sounded desperate.

"I'm here," Alexia said, wiping off her blades. "What's going on?"

"Oh, thank goodness! Listen. There's still no sign of the Oracle or Dr. Kindley, and about half the Knight Priory has already been rounded up. Kyle and Victor have gone after Caroline. Veronica's gone silent. Meyer and Hakim have engaged Connick, and Chase is after Morial."

Alexia exhaled. Things weren't as bad as they had originally seemed.

"Where are you and Sam?" Dixie asked.

"We're at the entrance to the meeting hall." From within were the sounds of fighting.

"All right, slight change of plans. Alexia, I need you to break away from Sam."

"What? Why?"

"Listen very carefully. Gavin and Curtis are dead. We need someone to go after the children. If they're moved off-site, we may never find them again. Give me a minute and I'll switch your headset over to Patty's frequency. She'll lead you."

"OK. I'll do it."

Just then, the doors to the meeting hall blew open with a fiery explosion. Meyer flew back with his arms crossed over his chest, engulfed in a glowing white-blue sphere covered with Hebrew symbols. Rushing after him was Connick, an aura of flame around his body, screeching insanely and frothing at the mouth. Alexia barely jumped to the side before they streaked by. She ducked into a corner.

Hakim ran out, holding onto his submachine gun as if his life depended on it. When he spotted Alexia, he headed over to her. "Lady LeBlanc, are you all right?"

She nodded, warily watching Connick as he crashed into Meyer, pummeling at his shield with flame-coated fists. "Yeah, I'm fine. I just almost got obliterated by those two."

"It is a terrifying sight to behold, is it not?" he asked. "This one is having a hard time figuring out how he can help."

She quickly assessed what was happening. Connick was wailing like a banshee and seemed to be summoning fire to aid in his attacks, while Meyer was focusing his will into some sort of shield. Closing her eyes, she hastily recalled the mission briefing.

Of course! Kabbalic magic is needed to safely remove Papa Ghede!

"Hakim, use the guardian from your ring to attack Connick," she said.

That appeared to confuse him. "But Lady LeBlanc, with all respect, this one's guardian is an *ifrit*. It cannot harm one who is adorned in fire."

"I know," she said. "You want to distract him and let Meyer recover. Give him a chance to use his powers to separate Connick and Papa Ghede."

The realization seemed to dawn on him. "Oh, of course. Meyer was trying to protect this one from battle by having him act as back up, since he only just joined GEIST. But this one has to fight with all his spirit if he's going to be of use." He ran toward Connick, calling back to her, "This one wishes you the best, Lady LeBlanc. *Fi Amanillah*!"

She smiled as Hakim ran off. "*Subhanallah* yourself." Then she turned her attention back to Sam, who was heading into the meeting hall. She needed to tell Sam about the change in plans.

The room was a mess, with rugs and tapestries on fire, columns and walls cracked, and craters in the floor—all likely from Meyer's battle with Connick. Tania was leaning against a busted column with Amelie next to her, binding up her leg. Tania's mask was off, and she was sobbing.

Near the altar was Noelle. Her head had been blown clean off.

Sam stopped in the middle of the room and stalked around, sniffing the air like a wolf on the hunt. "Where are you, Oracle? Come out!" Her voice reverberated.

Alexia knelt down beside Tania. "Hey, you OK?"

She wiped away some tears. "It was an accident."

"Accident? What happened?"

"She shot at Connick," Amelie said. "But he moved insanely fast and blocked the bullet with Noelle."

Looking back over at Noelle's body, Alexia felt her stomach churn. Compared to this operation, the slaughter at Fernbank Forest was nothing.

Tania continued wiping her face. "I thought I could handle it. We both thought we could handle it."

"You and Violet?"

"Yeah. She's devastated. She blames herself for Noelle dying. She keeps saying if only she had focused more."

"Then Tania attacked Connick, and he broke her leg," Amelie said, finishing the splint. "Ready to go?"

"As ready as I can be," Tania said. Amelie and Alexia helped her stand. Then she slowly put pressure on it. She sucked her teeth in pain.

"You need a doctor," Alexia said, frowning.

"No time for that. They've located Dr. Kindley heading toward a small helicopter at a side platform. Sister, can you focus into my leg?"

A moment later, Tania was able to walk with only a slight limp.

Alexia was amazed. Even with what she had learned at Eversoll about benign possession, seeing it in reality was pretty remarkable.

Finally, Tania put her mask back on. "I'll grieve properly later. For now, let's get that bastard."

Just then, the entire doorframe leading outside collapsed, and Connick, now surrounded by a small inferno, careened into the room and right into Sam. They both crashed into the altar with a sickening crack. Sam hollered and kicked Connick off of her.

As he slid along the ground, Sam rose up, an aura of energy gathering around her body. Both the muscles and the veins in her arms started bulging as she got visibly stronger.

Alexia gulped.

Another crash came from the hallway. Hakim's guardian grabbed both sides of the doorway, roared, and pulled itself through. Standing over ten feet tall, it stomped toward Connick. Hakim followed it, chanting in Arabic, his ring shining brightly.

Finally, Meyer entered, his hands and eyes glowing white blue. Holding up one hand, he chanted, "*Yesod, Shaddai el Chai! Netzach, Jehovah Tzabaoth!* Be weakened!"

Two intricate blue-white symbols, which Alexia recognized as *sephira* from the Hebrew tree of life, appeared high in the air, rotating slowly. Each one flared up in the center and then fired down thick beams of energy at Connick. He arched his back and yelped in agony. Watching this display, Alexia felt woefully underpowered. She just stood there as Tania, with Amelie's help, limped out of the room.

A voice spoke over her headset. "Alexia! Are you there, girl?" It was Patty.

She tapped it. "Sorry, Patty. Meyer just invoked the *sephirot*, and my brain froze."

"Well, unfreeze it. Sebastian and Sheree have set up the equipment to hack the boring device. We need Sam to find and apprehend the Oracle and then head down there. Meanwhile, I need to guide you to the children."

"Of course," she said.

"Just let me know when you're out in the main hallway, girl."

Alexia glanced back at Connick. Between Meyer's invocation and Hakim's guardian, he didn't seem to be faring very well. And when Sam grabbed him from behind, Alexia felt that the battle was nearly over.

Quickly, she hurried after Tania, meeting up with her in the antechamber. "OK, which way is it to Dr. Kindley?"

"That way," Tania said, pointing down a hallway.

Alexia tapped her headset. "Patty? It's me. Tania's been hurt. What's the status on everyone else?"

"Chase has apprehended Morial and is leading him up to the police helicopters. The mayor put up a fight, and I think Chase took out his anger over Noelle on his face. No word from Kyle, Victor, or Veronica on Caroline. Dixie's helping Meyer and Hakim with Connick. Sam's headset is busted. Still no sign of the Oracle. And Sebastian and Sheree are done, because I'm, say it with me, a super genius."

Snickering, Alexia said, "So humble. Look, Tania's injury might keep her from getting to Dr. Kindley in time. I'll assist her and then go find the children."

Suddenly, Tania spoke up. "No, Alexia, don't help us."

That got Alexia's attention. "Are you sure? I know I can do both."

"Stick to the mission," Tania said, resting her hand on Alexia's shoulder. "Listen to me. In all the card readings I've done regarding this operation, the common theme is those children. No matter what happens, you must keep them safe. Alexia, this may all hinge on you."

Alexia swallowed. Something about the intensity in Tania's eyes took away any doubt as to what she should do. "All right. I understand."

"Good. Don't worry about us. See you when this is over."

With a nod, Alexia ran off. She didn't know this Tania person very well, but she could feel the inner strength emanating from her. *I hope that I can one day compare.*

The sounds of fighting resonated in Alexia's ears as she ran down the hallways. With Patty guiding her, she was able to avoid any potential ambush. Soon, she found herself outside of the general manager's housing, where the children were supposedly being kept.

"Patty, I have to say this," Alexia said, sheathing her rapiers and trying the door. It was unlocked. "You and I make an unbeatable team. When I join GEIST, I want you with me."

Patty giggled. "Aw, shucks. You're gonna make me blush."

There was a pause, and then Patty added, "OK, now everyone's staring at me."

Alexia smirked and went inside. What she saw, however, wiped the expression off her face.

Seated in the middle of the living room of the tiny apartment were two four-year-old children: a blond girl with a copy of *Goodnight Moon* and a black-haired boy with a toy T-Rex. Kneeling before them, his back to Alexia, was a man in a hooded coat. He was holding a mask in his hand—a mask of Baron Samedi.

"Alexia, come in," Patty said. "Can you confirm that the children are there?"

The figure slowly stood and then put the mask on. Then, with the swish of his coat, he turned around. "And who might you be?" he asked, his voice mechanically synthesized.

At once, Alexia felt an overwhelming energy pushing down on her. It was as intense as Lord Dooley, but without all the rage. The expression in his eyes was both cold and calculating.

"Alexia?" Patty was starting to sound worried. "Can you con—"

Alexia turned off her headset. "My name is Alexia LeBlanc. Are you the Oracle?"

He nodded.

She drew out her weapons, glaring at him, her jaw clenched. The memory of what had happened at Emory started overriding her common sense. "Good. Because I have a bone to pick with you about Druid Hills."

"Oh?"

"Yes. A lot of people perished because of what you did." She shook with anger as she remembered Marc, Serge, and the others who died.

"No, I sealed Lord Dooley away. That fool Chandler weakened the seal with his overdevelopment."

Her grip on the rapiers tightened. "You could have just destroyed it. Then my friends would still be alive."

"You're misplacing your anger, child. I'm not your enemy. In a way, I respect you. Like your brother before you, you have a keen mind worthy of admiration."

He pointed at her. "So I'll let you leave now. The children are mine."

Quivering with emotion, she said, "Never! If I defeated Lord Dooley, then I can defeat you, Oracle."

"Doubtful."

Getting into a fighting stances, she said, "Enough out of you. *En garde*!"

Chapter 49
The Same As You

Date: **Sunday, June 15, 1997**
Time: **10:43 p.m.**
Location: **Deepwater Olympus**
Somewhere in the Gulf of Mexico

Sam's arms were starting to burn. "Hurry, Meyer! Connick is starting to break free!"

With a powerful kick, Connick knocked back Hakim's *ifrit*. It howled and crashed into the balcony, cracking the masonry into rubble.

"*Hod, Elohim Tzabaoth*!" Meyer lifted both hands in prayer, energy pouring from them like water and sparkling into the ground like droplets from a fountain.

Hakim's spirit guardian went still, energy ribboning out as it vanished. With a cry, Hakim fell to his knees, his eyes and nose bleeding. "With this one's *ifrit* banished, his own power fails!"

Connick continued to struggle, his strength as great as Sam's. Both of their bodies were engulfed with a fiery aura. He screeched unintelligibly, like a wild animal.

"*Netzach, Jehovah Tzabaoth*!" Meyer chanted.

One by one, three of those weird glyphs appeared around them both. Sam wasn't sure what they were. She just hoped they'd free Papa Ghede and Connick before either was destroyed.

"Lady Castille!" Hakim shouted, pulling himself to his feet. "Rabbi Gideon is almost done with his invocation. This one suggests you move away from Connick now."

"No way!" Sam yelled. She held on even tighter, feeling her back muscles bulge and the veins on her face and neck pop out. "Just hit him with it. You can't kill me, but if I let him go, he'll kill both of you!"

"This one understands. Please brace yourself, Lady Castille!"

"*Chesed, El!* Papa Ghede, be released!"

All three glyphs, vibrating with such intensity that the ground around them shook, bathed them in white-blue energy that burned even greater than the fire that had consumed her townhome. They both screamed in unison. The pain was all-consuming, burning her within as if someone had set her very soul aflame. When it finally passed, Connick was limp in her arms, and a powerful white light was gathering above them.

With the pain so great that she could barely move, she slid Connick to the ground and stumbled back. Then she regarded the gathering light, instinctively knowing who it was.

"Papa Ghede."

From the center of the white light blossomed the ghostly image of a short man with a tall top hat, a fancy tuxedo with tails, a fat, oversized face, and an almost comically large cigar in his mouth. In his hand was a huge apple. His expression, however, was not the jovial one Sam knew. It was angry.

"Well, this is a barrel of bad bourbon," Papa Ghede said. "Where is the woman who did this to me? I'll make her dance herself inside out!"

Meyer and Hakim carefully approached, but Sam motioned for them to get back. "This is a god. Let me talk to him. I need to calm him down, or he'll level this place."

The pain in her body was starting to subside. She cleared her throat. "Papa Ghede, the woman you seek isn't here!"

He gazed at her and then blinked. "Bridgette, darlin'? That you? What're you doing in a meat pack, love? You and brother had a falling out again?"

As if a part of her already knew what to say, she shook her head. "Papa, I forged a pact with this mortal to free my man. Don't you remember that he's been bound?"

Papa Ghede's fat face pinched in concentration. Then he said, "My word, my word, now I remember, Bridgette! The king's been trapped in that snake's coils. Oh, but I won't be able to free him. He's at the crossroads, love. Only mortals can go there."

Suddenly, his eyes lit up. "So dat's why you forged the pact, is it now, darlin'? If that meat pack can find a way to the crossroads, you can save Brother. Crafty as always, Bridgette, luv."

Sam nodded. What he said felt correct. "That is my plan, Papa. So for now, can you go and watch over our people?"

He sniffed, his expression finally relaxed. "Our people are in a bad way right now, love. That snake is using something to control them in this mortal world, ya."

Without thinking, she reached down into her cargo pants and gripped the container holding the pen.

His eyes glimmered. "You have it with you, don't you, love? Give it me, and I'll break it right quick."

Her heart racing, Sam took out the container. This could be the chance to put an end to the pen.

"Wait!" Meyer shouted. He came forward and got on one knee before Papa Ghede. "Oh, Chief of the *Loa*, please forgive this ignorant mortal's question, but what will be the damage done by you destroying that focus?"

Rearing back his head and laughing hard, Papa Ghede said, "Now, this one I like. He has manners and an eloquent tongue. To answer your question, mortal, the snake's focus has much of his own spirit in it, making it stronger than all but the strongest. The explosion will be enormous. Everything for a mile will be set aflame."

Meyer shook his head. "That will kill everyone, Sam. Only you'll survive. Maybe."

She rubbed her face. They were so close. "I'm sorry, Papa, I can't give it to you right now. If you can only wait—"

Again, he cackled, hard and long. "That wasn't a request. Now give it up, love. Our people are suffering something awful, and destroying that thing is the only way to free them from that snake's control."

She flinched. *I didn't know that. So the* loa *are, indeed, suffering because of Vincent's control over them. Benevolent or malevolent, the* loa *are my people now.*

Again, he cleared his throat and held out his hand. "Give it up, ya."

She put the container away. "As much as I want to free our people, Papa, I can't let you break it now. It'll kill too many mortals."

His ruddy, cheerful face changed into a glowering mask of fury. The air around him heated up as he snarled at her. "You testing my patience, luv. Give us the focus or I will take it!"

Gritting her teeth, Sam motioned Meyer and Hakim back. "Both of you, take Connick and go."

As they pulled the unconscious district attorney away, she held out both hands to Papa Ghede. Her words flowed naturally. "Papa, please. We are friends. Let's not fight over things. How about a drink of rum and a good dance?"

"I'm not in the mood for that," he said, his voice deepening. Around the room, fabric started smoldering and loose debris shook. "I want to free our children, luv."

Children? With those words, she knew what would disarm the high *loa*. "Papa, if you and I fight, or if you destroy this place, you'll kill two small children!"

His darkening countenance started to lighten almost immediately. "Come again, luv? Children is here?"

"Yes! This meat pack's two little ones. Can't you feel them? Their small beating hearts? Are you not the defender of children, the defender of innocents?"

He closed his eyes. A moment later, he said, "I'll be. Yes, I feel them. My anger was clouding my judgment. Oh, my, but I almost made a terrible mistake."

Breathing a sigh of relief, she smiled. "It's OK, Papa. I'll take care of the focus. Would you please go be ready to tend to our people? When it's destroyed, they'll need you to lead them."

"A'right, luv," Papa Ghede said. "But make sure you do that soon. All our children are suffering, light and dark. It ain't right."

As he started to vanish, she called out, "Papa, please watch over the spirits of the dead as well!"

Once more, he leaned back his head and hooted. "Always watching out for them mortals, eh, love? Don't worry. Them's a right angry lot, being unable to pass beyond. They'll fight for you if'n you ask."

And in a flash of light, he was gone.

By now, Meyer and Hakim were carrying Connick, who was groaning in pain.

"Lady Castille, what did Papa Ghede mean by 'unable to pass beyond'?" Hakim seemed concerned.

She glowered. It was exactly as she had feared that night in her townhome when she had fought off the ghost of Edward. "Until Vincent is destroyed, the souls of the dead under the voodoo pantheon cannot move into the afterlife. Rodger, Michael, dear Richie, and everyone connected to them will not be able to rest."

"Is there any other way around that?" Meyer asked.

"No, there is not," a synthesized voice said from the balcony. Before she even saw the Baron Samedi mask, Sam knew who it was.

"Oracle." The name felt like poison on her tongue.

With an effortless jump, the Oracle landed in front of the altar. He then casually approached them. "Good work on disarming Papa Ghede, Queen of the *Loa*."

Hearing Meyer and Hakim with their weapons, Sam waved them back again. "No, guys. This one is mine. Get Connick to safety. He's going to need medical attention."

"Sam," Meyer said. "You were weakened from my invocation, were you not? Can you fight him?"

She turned back and winked. "Don't worry, Meyer. I'm a goddess, remember?"

He frowned, but then said, "Come on, Hakim. We have to leave Sam to this alone."

Hakim bowed his head, "*As-salamu alaykum*, Lady Castille. *Ma'aasalaama*."

As they left, dragging Connick out, Sam chuckled. "I should have learned that language."

"He said 'peace be with you' and 'goodbye,' Sam," the Oracle said.

Turning back to him, she narrowed her eyes. "You sure know a lot of things about a lot of things. What are you?"

"The same as you."

"Fused?"

He nodded. "I see you also know Professor Mathias. He invented that term. I prefer the term *pact-holder*."

She snickered. "Or god?"

"You said it, not me."

Tightening her fists, she glared at him. "What do you want?"

He spread out his arms. "What I want, for the moment, is just to talk. I have a proposition for you, Sam. We are fighting for the same goals, believe it or not."

"No!" she shouted. "I am nothing like you at all!"

"Are you now?" he asked. "When you fought those guards, did you not feel the rush of power, the thrill of being omnipotent, and the self-disgust at enjoying it?"

Her heart beat faster as she realized he understood her feelings. It was like he knew her innermost thoughts. "How do you know that?"

"Because, long ago, I felt those same things," the Oracle said. "It's natural. We are gods, Sam. Gods among men. And now we have a chance to act as gods and save them from a terrible fate."

"What do you mean?"

He started walking around her, his eyes focused upon her. "I've found a way to open up a portal to the crossroad where Vincent has Baron Samedi bound. We can put an end to him together, freeing the *loa* from servitude to him, as well as the souls of the dead who are lingering. Moreover, we can relieve you of your cursed existence. You can die in peace, Sam."

She tilted her nose up, staring at him. "Who are you?"

"Someone who has been trying to erase the mistakes of the Castille family for a long time. And now, I can finally put to rest the sins caused by the family patriarch."

"Who are you really?" Sam narrowed her eyes. "Show me your face."

"Do you really wish to see it? Do you really wish to know the truth?"

"You're damn right I do, you jerk. Show me your face!"

"Very well, Sam."

Slowly, the Oracle removed his mask.

Chapter 50
The Mercy of Death

Date: **Sunday, June 15, 1997**
Time: **10:48 p.m.**
Location: **Deepwater Olympus**
Somewhere in the Gulf of Mexico

"Dr. Kindley, stop!" Stabilized by Violet's power, Tania aimed her rifle at his head. In the back of her mind, Violet wept bitterly, still distraught over Noelle's death. Beside her, Amelie had her knives out, ready to strike. The night air blew around them as they stood upon the side platform.

With one foot inside a small helicopter, Dr. Kindley seemed more irritated than worried. "What do you want, lowborn?"

Tania gritted her teeth. His arrogance disgusted her. "It's over. We're taking you into custody."

He smirked. "Oh, I don't think so. Tania Patterson, right? Do you know what I think you'll do? I think you'll let me go."

After what had happened with Noelle, Tania was in no mood for games. She shot at him, missing on purpose. "Or I could kill you. I think, given the circumstances, I'd be forgiven."

Holding up one of his hands, which was adorned with a signet ring bearing the Knight Priory crest, he asked, "Do you know what this is?"

Suddenly, Violet bellowed in anger "*Sister! Can you sense it?*"

The sudden change in tone took Tania by surprise. *Sense what?*

"*Close your eyes and feel that ring!*" Violet was absolutely livid.

Tania did so and extended her senses to it. Deep within, she felt a small, terrified soul shivering in constant torment. It was Hannah Davis.

"Hannah!" Tania yelled. She knew from Dixie that Dr. Kindley had used souls for talismans, but this was well beyond repugnant. "How dare you bind that poor child's soul!"

Dr. Kindley's grin widened. "It was easy. Each of these talismans is powered by one of my deceased patients. My lapel pin, my glasses. I even have someone in a porcelain crown on a lower molar."

Quivering with anger, Tania asked, "Talismans where an agreement has not been made are torture to the spirit. You're hurting them beyond death!"

He chuckled. "Oh, yes. Sweet pain. And I plan to make more when I've escaped. Many more."

Violet's voice began to deepen. "*Vile. A monster just like Vincent.*"

With a look of disgust, Amelie asked, "Why would you do this?"

"Mmm," he said. "Power, of course. Power to rule. It's my birthright, you see. I am destined to rule the Knight Priory. And once that Saucier bitch is gone, I will."

Tania was dizzy from the rage coursing through her.

All this suffering just to lead a group. I hate him, Sister.

"*As do I. People like him are mad with the delusion that they should rule. We should kill him, now*!"

Aiming at him again, she said, "My sister wants you dead, and I am sorely tempted. So unless you desire death, I suggest you put up your hands and surrender now."

Still grinning, Dr. Kindley raised both his hands. "You mean, like this?" The ring started glowing, and with a quick gesture, he shot a bolt of electricity at her and Amelie. She wasn't expecting that kind of attack, and it hit them both full on, flinging them back and scorching the skin where it passed through their bodies.

"Damn it!" Tania exclaimed. Next to her, Amelie struggled to sit up.

Then he jumped, the crest on his lapel glowing and his hands elongating into a pair of sharpened blades. Coming down, he stabbed both of them, Tania in her broken leg and Amelie in her stomach.

"Disgusting little lowborns," he said, twisting the blades.

Amelie coughed up blood, grabbing at the blade, while Tania cried out in pain. Through the agony, she heard Violet. "*Sister! I'll numb your leg. Fight him!*"

As she felt Violet's energy flow into her leg, strengthening it and taking away the pain, Tania pointed her rifle at him. He jumped back, his metal hands covered in blood.

"This has been fun, Tania Patterson. But, for now, I—" He stopped as several throwing knives embedded themselves in his legs. He fell to his knees.

Tania glanced at Amelie, who was sitting up and holding her gut, blood leaking from it as well as her chin. But she was smiling. "Kick that prick's ass, T." She passed out.

Standing up, Tania saw Dr. Kindley crawling toward the helicopter. With a guttural roar, she dashed forward and, focusing her sister's power into her strength, kicked the vehicle. With a loud screech of metal, it slid off the platform and fell into the Gulf below.

Dr. Kindley watched it fall, his eyes wide. Then he narrowed his gaze. "You damn piece of trash. I'll kill you for that."

Sniffing, Tania said, "Whatever." Then she gave him a hard right hook to the face, but at the last moment he caught it. His eyes started glowing.

"What the . . . ?"

"I am a pureblood of the Knight Priory of Saint Madonna! I will not permit garbage like you to defeat me." His glasses, lapel crest, ring, and even the inside of his mouth started glowing.

"*He's using every talisman at once to increase his power!*"

What can we—

Before she could finish, an invisible force emanating from Dr. Kindley knocked her back. Electricity crackled and fire blossomed around him as he started levitating, his hair standing straight up and his eyes shining. "I am the New Order here. I'll remake the Knight Priory into a force no one will dare oppose. I'll build it on the bodies of its enemies. And I will start with you!"

Stumbling back, Tania fired at him, but the bullet bounced off an unseen barrier. In all her years working with voodoo and magic, she'd never seen anything quite like it.

Lightning strike after lightning strike rained down upon her, each of her dodges more clumsy than the last. As she rolled from the third one into the center of the platform, a massive bolt struck her, searing her flesh and cooking her organs. Above her, he laughed. "How about we purify your dirty blood with sacred flame!" He then inhaled, the glow in his mouth increasing, and he spewed fire at her.

"Oh, bullshit!" she shouted, jumping out of the way and landing near the edge.

"*We need to find a way to use his power against him,*" Violet said.

How do we do that?

"*Hmmm. He's overusing those containers. If you can get me close, I . . .*"

There was then an uncomfortable silence from Violet.

What? Do what, Sister?

"Just get me close. Touch him, and I should be able to disable him." Something in her voice sounded resolute.

Tania didn't waste any time. As he inhaled deeply again, she sprinted. Rolling under the flame, she closed the distance in a matter of seconds.

"Come to meet your death, trash?" He whipped his hands, each finger elongating like razor wire, and cut into the ground around her. Some of the wires grazed her skin, slicing her, and some even cut her hair. But Violet continued to push energy through her, and a moment later, she tackled him.

"You're going down!"

"Get off me!" he roared, slicing at her with his razor fingers.

I've got him!

"I know. Tania, listen. I love you."

Sister? What are you—?

"It has to be this way. I've made too many mistakes. First you, then Sam, and finally Noelle. Goodbye, sister. You were the better one."

Sister?

With a flash, Tania felt Violet leave her body. The excruciating pain from her broken leg overwhelmed her, forcing her to roll away. Dr. Kindley started convulsing and screaming and writhing in agony. His ring, his lapel crest, his glasses, and even his mouth started smoking as if on fire.

She's overloading the containers to set the souls free. But the release of energy will—

And then his ring exploded, taking one of his fingers. His lapel crest exploded, burning the flesh from his face. His glasses exploded, searing out his eyes. His tooth exploded, and blood sprayed from his mouth. He continued thrashing back and forth, shrieking in pain, until he came to rest in the fetal position.

But Tania wasn't focused on him or her own pain. Instead, she was focused on the souls that had been released, flitting away into the night wind. Hannah, then a short man, a prudish woman, and man who looked similar to James Woods. What she didn't feel was her sister.

Violet's soul was no more.

Tania howled. "Sister? Violet? Noooooooo!"

For several minutes, she beat the platform, wailing. Her heart felt like someone had twisted a frozen knife into it. When she finally calmed down enough to think, she heard Amelie coughing.

"T, I think . . . ," Amelie muttered, slowly crawling toward her. "I think I need help."

"I'll radio Command," Tania said between sobs, the pain in her heart greater than any other. Then she heard Dr. Kindley whimpering.

"Kill me . . . ," Dr. Kindley sniveled, shivering. "Kill me, please . . ."

Standing up and supporting herself on her rifle, Tania glared at him. The freezing pain in her heart started to heat up into a fire. For a few minutes, she watched him writhing in agony, imaging the unforgiving sufferings she would love to inflict upon him.

But in the end, she said the only thing she felt was right. "I'm not killing you. No, I think you should live a long, healthy life to live with your defeat."

He moaned harder. "No! Kill me! I don't want to live like this. So much pain. So much shame. Please kill me!"

"Shut up! My sister, my beloved sister, was a tortured soul who only found peace in death. But because of you, she won't even have that peace, because she's gone forever! " Spittle flew from her lips. Just seeing him made her want to put a bullet in his head and be done with it.

"So you don't deserve an end to your pain. You don't deserve the mercy of death."

As he cried in anguish, flailing like an infant, she fell to her knees. Then she tapped her headset. "Dixie, Patty, someone? This is Tania. We've got Kindley. Please come get us."

"Tania?" Dixie replied. "Thank God! We can home in on your signal, but what's going on? Were there any injuries?"

"Two injuries," Tania said, tears rolling down her face. "One fatality."

Then she threw the headset to the ground. With a deep breath, she leaned back and cried Violet's name into the night.

Chapter 51
Being a Shield

Date: **Sunday, June 15, 1997**
Time: **10:53 p.m.**
Location: **Caroline Saucier's yacht**
Somewhere in the Gulf of Mexico

Aucoin and Victor kept their guns on Caroline. The standoff had only lasted a few minutes, but it had felt like hours. As Veronica struggled within the murderous device, Caroline swished her finger above a certain button on the console. "So, Detective, are you going to kill me?"

"Don't tempt me," Aucoin said with a snarl, his finger resting on the trigger.

"Do you think you can shoot me before I kill this woman?" She laid her finger gingerly on the button. At the same time, her foot slid over a discolored tile on the floor. "And what about this tile here? Could it be another trap? What could it do, I wonder?"

"Just gimme the word," Victor said, his red eye glowing and his hands steady.

Aucoin didn't answer. He looked from Caroline to the button on the console and then to the discolored tile. He wasn't sure what was what here. *This bitch is psyching me out. Damn her!*

Closing his eyes, he inhaled deeply and then exhaled. *I've seen Dixie do this a thousand times. I just need to get into her head, and when she lets down her guard, I'll nail her.*

Opening his eyes, he asked, "So if we put down our guns, you'll let Veronica go?"

"Yes."

"Then I only have one question."

"Oh?" She tilted her head to the side.

"What's the deal with Sam's children? Why did you have them all these years?"

She groaned. "It gave me status in the Knight Priory, which was barely worth the effort it took caring for the little brats. Alice is so logical, she's probably a sociopath, and Eugene is so sensitive to spirits, he'll never be normal. They'll likely both be as crazy as their parents."

"Hmph," Aucoin said. "Spoken like someone who has zero capacity to be a mother."

Grinning, she just tapped the button on the console lazily. "Some of us just don't have the instinct. Now, Detective, what'll it be?"

Aucoin nodded, noting that the button could press in just a little without setting off the device. He was pretty sure he knew how to stop her. "All right. We'll do things your way."

"The hell we will," Victor said.

Carefully, Aucoin said, "Victor, this is my call. We can always *pull back* and *take a hand* count later. For now, trust me."

As he emphasized "pull back" and "take a hand," he hoped Victor would get the meaning. He knew Dixie would.

Victor just snorted and said, "Smartass." He then put his revolver on the ground and kicked it over.

When Aucoin saw the wire still attached to the gun, he exhaled in relief. *He gets it!* He put his own gun down and kicked it over.

"Good, gentlemen," Caroline said with a triumphant sneer. "Now, if you two would join your friend over there, I can lock you away until—"

As quick as a rattlesnake, Victor yanked the wire and pulled the revolver back into his hand. His dead eye lit up as he aimed at Caroline's hand above the console. Less than a second later, he pulled the trigger, Perdition firing so loudly the mirrors shook, flame shooting from the barrel.

Aucoin momentarily lost focus, his eyeballs rattling. When his vision returned, Caroline's hand was gone halfway up the forearm. Blood was pouring out.

"Bye, bitch," Victor said, cocking Perdition's hammer back for another shot.

With a shocked expression, she stepped on the discolored tile. Aucoin heard a click and then a whoosh. Then he felt a hard blow to the side. Before he realized it, he was sliding along the floor, landing near his gun. The sound of meat tearing resonated in his ears, along with Veronica gasping.

"Damn it, woman!" Aucoin shouted. "What did you hit me with?" As he gathered his bearings, he realized it wasn't Caroline who had hit him—it was Victor. He had pushed Aucoin to the ground, and when he glanced back to where they had been standing, he saw why. Victor was impaled on several spikes that had shot through the flooring. There were more spikes where Aucoin had just been. Blood was trickling down onto the once sparkling floor.

Victor said, "Got your back." He bowed his head and died, still standing.

Aucoin glared at Caroline, who was gripping her bloody stump. When she met his gaze, she reached over to hit the console and trigger the device. In the blink of an eye, he had grabbed his gun and lined up a shot between her eyes. She glanced back, saw that he was pointing his gun at her, and froze. They locked eyes, his finger on the trigger and hers on the button.

"Please don't," she pleaded.

"Fuck you," he replied, and he pulled the trigger. Her head flew back with a hole in the middle of her forehead. Her fingers started pushing down on the button just a hair and then fell to the side. Then she slumped back in the chair, dead.

For a few moments, he just lay there, taking in what had happened. Then he got up, wiped off his jacket, and holstered his gun. "Are you OK, Veronica?"

But Veronica had passed out.

It took Aucoin a while to get Veronica out of the device. With all the rotating blades, corkscrews, and shredders, it looked like it would have made a bloody mess of her if it had been turned on.

The whole thing disgusted him. What kind of sick mind would create these death machines?

Once she was out and resting on the floor, he scanned the room. At the opposite end from the entrance was another discolored tile. "Veronica, do not move. I think I found a way out, but it could be another trap."

"OK," she said, watching him anxiously as he tapped it. There was a clicking sound, and then the mirror before him rose, revealing a small but comfortable bedroom. Inside were a full-sized bed and a garden bathtub, as well as a small vanity covered with images of a lovely young woman, Allison Surrette. Also on the vanity was a thick, black book—the Russell grimoire—and an open letter:

> Miss Saucier,
>
> I don't know how you learned about the grimoire. I suspect it may have been my fault, that I leaked too much to you during our conversations. Or it may have been that you learned of it from Jonathan himself before his passing.
>
> The fact is you know about it, and you chose to send Dr. Kindley to take it from me. Very sneaky, having him call me out about it during a Knight Priory gathering. Of course I had to hand it over.

> But you see, I know things about that book which you do not. I know its secrets. It's more than just lore of the Knight Priory. The grimoire can give you power beyond your wildest dreams.
>
> All I ask is that you lend me use of it. There is a certain ritual I am looking for, one that is vital to my plans. Give me access to the book whenever that fool Kindley is done, and I promise you true control over the Knight Priory.
>
> Signed,
>
> The Oracle

Aucoin harrumphed. "So the Oracle had the grimoire first, and he was willing to show Caroline how to use it in order to further his goals. What are his goals? What is his end game?"

"Well, it's likely from his tutelage that she figured out how to possess Connick with Papa Ghede." It was Veronica, limping up behind him.

"Very likely," he said. "This guy is dangerous. Whatever this ritual is, it must be huge."

She nodded. "Are we done here?"

He pocketed the letter and picked up the grimoire. "Yes. Let's go to the bridge, get this tub docked with Deepwater, and start loading people up."

Luckily, the same box that would have eviscerated Veronica also had the release button for the Vault. A short while later, they were pulling into the dock underneath the oil rig. The police were loading up two other yachts with Knight Priory members who had surrendered.

"So that's what happened, Dixie," Aucoin said into the headset, having recounted the entire story to her. "Victor had my back until the very end."

"My God," she said. "Kyle, I'm so sorry."

"Yeah, well, I'll mourn later. What else is happening?"

"Tania just captured Dr. Kindley. Meyer and Hakim just loaded up Connick to be flown to a hospital. Noelle didn't make it."

The news of Noelle's death was a surprise. "She was always so careful. Is Chase OK?"

"He goes between fits of rage and tears. But the one I'm really worried about is Tania."

"What's wrong with her?"

"I'm not completely sure. I think . . . I think something happened to Violet. She won't talk to anyone and just hugs her mask."

"And what about the children? Or Alexia? Or Sam?"

"Alexia was sent to find the children, and Sam went after the Oracle. We lost contact with them both over thirty minutes ago. Patty is pulling her hair out, and Dr. Lazarus wants to send everyone back in to search for them."

Grinding his teeth, he weighed his options. His body ached all over, and he felt fatigue setting in. But then he thought of Alexia and Sam. Unlike everyone else, they were alone. Sam might be able to handle herself, but Alexia was just a kid.

He sighed. It was a hell of a time for his paternal instincts to kick in.

"Dixie, I'm going after Alexia. Switch me over to Patty's frequency."

"Are you sure?"

He changed ammo clips. "Yes. That girl may be amazing, but she's still a girl. I'm not leaving her alone."

"All right, Kyle. Godspeed. And please, be careful."

As he left, Veronica, who was being examined by a medic, called out, "Wait! Kyle, you're going back in there? What are you doing?"

He cocked his gun as he ran inside. "Being a shield!"

Chapter 52
I'll Be There

Date: **Sunday, June 15, 1997**
Time: **10:59 p.m.**
Location: **Deepwater Olympus**
Somewhere in the Gulf of Mexico

"You know you're asleep, right?"

"Yes."

"Then why don't you wake up?"

"Because I want to talk to you. I miss you."

"That's sweet of you, Alexia. But right now, you have to wake up."

"But Michael, why? I've waited so long to see you again."

"Because if you don't wake up, those two children will die."

With a gasp, Alexia awoke and took in her surroundings. First, she saw that she was still in the manager's apartment. Next, she saw a ghostly hulk with a tiny, shrunken head and four massive arms, each holding a sword. Then, she saw three of what looked like African tribal warriors, down to the spears and shields, but with heavily pinched faces. Finally, she saw both children lying unconscious on the bed across the room from her. She recognized the large spirit as an *orisha* and the warriors as *ogouns*. They were similar to *loa*, but under the African pantheon.

Who did this?

Then she remembered. It had been the Oracle.

With that memory came the shocking realization that she couldn't move of her own accord. Horrified, she watched as her own body started walking toward the children. The four spirits started chanting.

What's going on?

As she slowly approached the bed, she drew out her rapiers, pointing one at each child. *No. Come on, stop it!*

It was like she was watching someone else control her body. The sensation of helplessness was just as bad as when she had been overcome by Lord Dooley.

OK, stop panicking and think. Think!

Forcing the fear down, she realized that she must be possessed. Somehow, the Oracle had put something in her. Recalling her encounter with Lord Dooley, she repeated the same steps as last time.

Our Father who art in heaven, hallowed be they name. As she prayed, she focused her will on pushing forward and tearing through the possessing spirit. She was sure it would be another arduous and difficult struggle.

However, a second later, she heard the spirit controlling her screech in agony and vanish. Her consciousness popped back into control so fast, she ended up stumbling, and she fell against the bed.

Compared to Lord Dooley, that had been extremely easy.

She glanced over at the *orisha* and *ogoun*. They seemed surprised. Grinning cockily, she pushed her will toward them, shifting her mindset from prey to predator. Her rapiers started glinting as if out in the sun.

"Repent now."

Rushing forward, she swung her rapiers at the first unsuspecting *ogoun* before it had a chance to raise its shield. As she focused her will through her attacks, her rapiers started glowing with a soft but steady white light, the blades shimmering with hundreds of sparkles. She slashed through it twice and then stabbed it in the chest. It yelped, light pouring from its wounds, and then vanished in a puff of misty, fog-like vapor.

The other two *ogoun* seemed jarred out of their surprise, raising their shields and stabbing at her with their spears. She bent back, the tip of one spear nearly cutting her chest, the other clipping her hair. Circling one rapier around in a double envelopment, she trapped the spear cutting at her hair and pushed. Then she knocked the spear near her breasts back.

"Leave my boobs alone!"

As she straightened up, the *orisha*, which had finally recovered from the shock, started digging its heels into the ground, preparing to charge as if it were a bull.

Keeping the *orisha* in her sights, Alexia slid in toward the *ogoun* who had stabbed at her chest. She trapped its spear between her blades and twisted, yanking it from its hands. It stumbled in shock.

She grinned. "Bye, now!"

Flipping in a back handspring, she kicked it in the face. Then, slicing up in the air, she slashed it several times and finally stabbed upward, impaling it on both of her rapiers. It shrieked, light poured out, and it vanished into misty vapor.

Suddenly, she felt a sharp pain at her side. The remaining *ogoun* had just missed sinking its spear into her ribs. "Dang it," she said. "You're next!"

But then she heard heavy footfalls. The *orisha* was charging right at her, its arms out and its swords swirling around. Throwing herself to the side, she twisted through the air as it flew past her, running into the dining-room table and cracking it in two, crushing several chairs. As she landed, the remaining *ogoun* jumped in, stabbing at her head.

She couldn't make it in time. She tried to parry, knowing she'd likely still get badly injured. But at the last moment, someone kicked the spear away.

It was Michael's ghost. He grinned at her and flicked his thumb over his nose. "Need some help, Sis?"

Alexia's mouth gaped as he rushed forward and attacked the *ogoun*. It stabbed at him, but he grabbed the spear, kicked it several times, and then broke the weapon in half. Then he said, "Alexia, finish it!"

That pulled her out of her shock. She rushed forward as Michael kicked it toward her. With her opponent completely open, she sliced in an x-shaped pattern. "Take that!"

The *ogoun* wailed and died, cut in half by her attacks.

Only the *orisha* was left, and it was preparing to charge again.

Michael stood next to her. "Remember when you fought Lord Dooley and you made a cross pattern with your swords?"

"Um, yes," she said, adopting a defensive posture. "Yes, I do."

"Whenever you have an opening on a strong enemy, do that," he said. "Project your will and faith into the pattern." He rushed toward the *orisha*, which was charging. The two met in the center of the room, its weapons coming down with such force that when Michael blocked the attacks, the floor around him cracked. He engaged the spirit in a furious frenzy, trading blow after blow.

The *orisha* seemed to get more agitated with every passing second. Finally, it chopped down all four weapons at the same time. While he blocked the attack, the force brought him to his knees.

Alexia gasped. "Michael!"

But then she saw it. With the *orisha* committing to such an attack, it was vulnerable. Bringing her blades together to form a cross, she focused her will and said in a commanding voice, "In the name of the Father and the Son and the Holy Spirit, begone!"

It screeched in a high-pitched wail and started pushing back, forgetting Michael. But as she pushed harder upon it, visualizing that she was making it disappear, its form started to waver.

"I said, begone!"

Finally, with its screech turning into a whine, it vanished like steam in a shower.

She stood there and breathed deeply. *I . . . I did it.*

Michael straightened his tie. Then he walked by and ruffled her hair. "Good job, Alexia. See you around, OK?"

She grabbed his jacket. "Please, don't disappear." Her messy hair covered her face, and a few tears dripped down the strands.

"I have to go."

"Why?" She looked up at him, crying. "Why can't you stay with me?"

Sighing ever so softly, he pulled her into an embrace. His hug was like a spray of cool mist, his arms partially going through her. "Alexia, I'm dead."

Then he knelt down and gazed into her eyes. Already he was fading. "It takes a lot of power to do what I just did. I could only do it because of Sam, and partly because a lot of energy is gathering. Whatever the reason, don't get used to me to appearing like this. It's a struggle sometimes, keeping my sense of self and my sense of ethics. Ghosts are sad, lonely, often angry beings. I'm doing all I can not to become that."

He wiped away her tears. "But I'm always around you. When you close your eyes and concentrate on me, I'll be there."

A lump had formed in her throat. With effort, she swallowed it. "What if I can't feel you?"

With a smile, he tapped just above her heart. "Then you're not using this."

Standing up, he said, "For now, I need you to be strong and get those children to safety. One night, when I can manage it, we'll talk again. A nice, long conversation."

She nodded and put away her swords. Then she hugged him one last time.

"Good bye, Big Brother!" She knew that she sounded like a little girl again, but she didn't care. "I love you!"

He stroked the back of her head and then vanished in her arms.

His last words lingered like mist. "I love you, too, Sis."

"Alexia, I'm here!" Aucoin burst through the door, gun out and ready to fight.

Alexia, who was by the children, said, "Oh, hey, Kyle. Give me a hand with Eugene here?"

Picking the boy up, he regarded the dusty residue from the spirits in disbelief. "I . . . did you do this? By yourself?"

She picked up Alice. "No. I had help."

"From who?"

With a joyous laugh, she blushed. "The greatest guy I'll ever know."

Chapter 53
Face Behind the Mask

Date: **Sunday, June 15, 1997**
Time: **11:01 p.m.**
Location: **Deepwater Olympus**
Somewhere in the Gulf of Mexico

Sam quietly gazed upon the Oracle's face. Part of her couldn't believe it, and yet part of her had always known.

"Ouellette. So you're the one behind everything."

He dropped the mask. "Behind everything? As if I purposefully masterminded this ridiculous crisis we're facing? No, I don't think so, Sam. It doesn't quite work that way."

She flexed her arms and prepared to strike. His posture, on the other hand, was relaxed and unassuming. It was rather disarming.

"But you're the one who introduced Vincent to the *tkeeus*, right?" she asked.

"I am."

"And you're the Oracle who has been manipulating the Knight Priory, right?"

"Yes."

She scratched the back of her head. "So, how does this not make you the mastermind?"

He folded his arms, sighing. "Because, you stupid girl, you're acting as if I'm the villain of this story, when I've been trying to set this whole thing right from the beginning!"

The conviction behind his response made her pause. "OK, let's start this over. First off, are you fused, like I am?"

"Yes. I am fused, but to a god of the African pantheon."

Placing her hands on her hips, she said, “Right. Who, then? Unless that’s a secret, too.”

With a shrug, he said, “Well, here’s no reason to keep anything from you, not at this point. He is named Orunmila, and he is the god of wisdom, divination, and foresight.”

That cleared a few things up. “Hence the whole Oracle thing and the summoning of *ogouns* and whatever, right?”

“Exactly,” he said.

“OK, so why did you introduce Vincent to the *tkeeus*, knowing the damage it would cause?”

Now he rolled his eyes. “I can only interpret prophecy, not see the future.” But then he sighed. “However, you want the truth about the *tkeeus*, so I will tell you. It’s a bit of a story, though.”

She relaxed her posture. “I don’t have anywhere to go. Spill it.”

Leaning back against one of the remaining pillars, he snorted in response. “Ah, Castille women, so sarcastic. Very well, here is what happened. You recall that I served as an officer in the big war, correct?”

She assumed he meant the Vietnam War. She nodded.

“My tour eventually took me to Guinea in West Africa. It wasn’t a great war, it was a great mess. I had already survived several dangerous situations, enough to earn a medal, but I was young and hungry for glory. The perfect setup for the gods to rain perdition on me.”

“So, why were you in Guinea? And how does the *tkeeus* figure into this?” She was still stuck on why he went from being stationed in Vietnam to Africa.

“I’m getting there, Sam. I went to Guinea because of the campaigns. I had aspirations of becoming a colonel, or even a general. But my lust for glory was my undoing. While out on patrol one evening, my platoon was ambushed by enemy forces. It was a bloodbath so brutal that by the time it was over, you could swim in the guts of my men. I, myself, was injured. Badly. I couldn’t even feel my lower body. I thought for sure that I was going to die.”

For the moment, she was enraptured in his story, not too dissimilar from how Vincent used to entrance her. “So what happened?”

“Some Yoruba priests found me clinging to life, and they took me to a holy place. There, they burned a pinkish substance, the *tkeeus*, and prayed for the local spirits to heal me. What they did not expect, however, was that a god would show up instead.”

“And that was Orunmila?”

"Yes. He was impressed by my will. He told me that he wanted to travel to distant lands, to learn of other pantheons. He had come to believe that the world was sliding into peril and wanted perspective on that. In exchange, he'd offer me his wisdom. And so we forged a pact, and just like that, I was a god among men. I spent a long time in Guinea, learned what it meant to be a pact-holder, and, more importantly, learned the secret of the *tkeeus*."

Sam harrumphed. "So, what is it? The *tkeeus*."

Slowly, Ouellette walked to the ruined altar, never looking away. "It's a compound created through dried fruit. Mango, papaya, kiwi, and such. It can be inhaled or burned as incense. But also included is an enzyme that comes from the blood of a living god."

"You mean the secret of the *tkeeus* is the blood of a Fused?"

"Exactly."

With a deep exhale, she started walking around the room. "And you brought it over from Africa."

"Correct. I brought over a sample. But once here, I made more. You used some of it the night you killed Violet, and Rodger used it to fight Dallas. Pure *tkeeus* is very powerful. Then the Knight Priory tried to synthesize it for their experiments. You saw how well that worked out."

Remembering what she had fought over the past year while working for GEIST—the hordes of test subjects and *tkeeus*-infused soldiers who had been driven insane—she shuddered. "Well, at least we know it can't be properly replicated. But now I'm curious. Are there other Fused?"

"Yes, but only a handful. People don't believe in the high spirits—the polytheistic gods, if you will—like they used to. I'm not claiming that there isn't a Christian, Hebrew, or Muslim God, mind you. There are mysteries out there that even the wisest cannot fathom. But high spirits have existed for as long as there's been a spirit world, and the Baron Samedis, the Orunmilas, the Thors, the Apollos, the Madame Bridgettes . . . all of them—they just don't receive the belief, the energy, or the will of mortals as they once did. So fewer and fewer of them have a reason to make pacts with us. The one other pact-holder I knew, the one whose blood created the *tkeeus* that saved my life, died many years ago by his own hand. He was just tired of living."

It was a lot for Sam to take in, the idea that high spirits, such as the high *loa*, relied on people's belief. But it made sense. A part of her just knew that everything Ouellette said was true. "So why did you share the *tkeeus* with Vincent?" She had to know.

"To save your life."

That was not the answer she was expecting. "What?"

Ouellette tapped his chest. "You inherited your mother's heart. A sickly, weak heart. After you collapsed at age five, Vincent became anxious over the possibility of losing you. At the time, I was . . . close to him. I even helped the old Knight Priory with some of their benevolence projects such as St. Jude Hospital. I wanted to spare him a pain no parent should suffer—the pain of losing a child. So during my tour of the Vietnam War, I returned to Guinea and learned how to make the *tkeeus*."

Now Sam was confused. She thought he had gone to Guinea the first time during the Vietnam War.

"Using the alias of 'Oracle,'" he said. "I tested it in Atlanta to compel a powerful and dangerous spirit to come forth."

"Lord Dooley?" She remembered that from the Alexia Report.

He nodded. "Yes. The *tkeeus* makes it absurdly simple to summon spirits, bind them to an object, or have them either ride or possess another. Lord Dooley couldn't resist. To show my thanks to the people of Druid Hills, I bound it into a sacrificial stone and sealed it away."

"But then he got free and murdered dozens."

With a disgusted grunt, he said, "I am so tired of people throwing that back in my face. The damn Lullwater Society overdeveloped the land and weakened the seal. That's why it's better for the secrets of spirits and magic to be kept out of the common man's hand."

"I agree, but for a different reason," she said. "Namely, because this shit hurts people. So after Atlanta, you went back to New Orleans and showed Vincent how the *tkeeus* worked. That's when he possessed me with Marinette?"

"Yes. Which leads us to the nightmarish life you've suffered these past thirty-five years. I never could've imagined that Vincent would do the things he did, especially discover and perform a forbidden ritual to make you unkillable. Had I known he was a sociopath who just needed a push to start murdering, I would have never enabled him."

Again she looked down, unable to hide the bitterness. "And I'd likely be dead."

"Very likely," he said. "But life is not fair. Michael. Rodger. Need I say more?"

Her brow furrowed, and she said nothing, absorbing all that she had learned. The sounds of battle had long since ceased. GEIST had won, and it was now truly down to her and Ouellette. But now that she knew the truth about him, she wasn't sure if she should hate him, forgive him, or what. Nothing was certain anymore.

Finally, she said, "So, tell me why you've been supporting the Knight Priory all these years? Especially with all the evil they've done."

He rubbed his forehead. "You're just like your father sometimes. You only see what's in front of you. Look, the original Knight Priory had its flaws, but they were good people. My people. After they fell apart, I hung up my Oracle robe until the shit with Dallas started and the new Knight Priory began making waves."

"Did you know that Dallas was the new Bourbon Street Ripper?" she asked. "Or what the silver pen did?"

"Of course not. If I had known, I would have done something." Then he frowned. "That doesn't mean I didn't keep information from people like Rodger, Michael, Dixie, or Aucoin—good cops I really respect. A few times, I'm sure I even slipped. But I kept up my cover and donned my mask in the shadows to infiltrate the group. That's when I learned about the synthetic *tkeeus*. And once you told me about Vincent and Aucoin told me about the pen, I used my connections to find a way into the crossroads."

"In the grimoire, right?"

"Yes. Russell's book is more than a history of the Knight Priory. It contains centuries of spells and rituals from three different pantheons. The ritual to make you unkillable is there, as is the ritual to allow living beings to enter the spirit world."

Sam slid down to the ground. "Now I get it. Everything you've done has been to undo your mistakes. Guilt and shame have been eating you alive for decades, haven't they?"

Ouellette choked, speaking barely above a whisper. "More than you can imagine."

With an exhale, she stood up. "This has to end. We have to enter the spirit world and destroy Vincent."

Nodding, he locked eyes with her. "Yes. It's normally nearly impossible for physical bodies to enter. We'll have a very limited time to destroy him, and it's possible neither of us will survive."

She knew that much already. Smiling softly, she asked, "All right, so what do we need?"

"The silver pen."

"Right here," she said, holding up its container.

"And the lifeblood of the youngest Castille generation."

Those words hit her like a freight train. She stumbled back, staring. "What. Did. You. Say?" She felt her teeth bare like fangs.

His face was pained. "Sam, you have to sacrifice your children in order for this to work. I'm sorry, there is no other—"

"Like hell you're killing my children!" Her voice tore out so hard, the stone pillars in the room cracked.

His face expressionless, he continued staring. "I could find no other way."

"Fuck this!" She clenched her fists, her muscles tightening and enlarging.

"Sam, please, don't get violent. If there was any other way, I—"

"You shut up!" she shouted, snarling at him. "You have no idea what you're asking me to do. You have to be goddamned insane. You wouldn't know what it's like to sentence your own kids to die, you piece of—"

"I know exactly what it's like!" Now he yelled loudly. Her ears stung, and she was pushed back. With a loud crashing sound, the wall behind her gave way and collapsed.

They glared at each other, their faces red.

Taking a single step toward him, she asked, "What the hell do you mean?"

As if answering her threat, he stomped toward her until they were nose-to-nose. "I know exactly how awful it is to sentence your child to die. I did it myself years ago, and it's haunted me every day of my damn life." His body quivered as much as hers.

Staring into his eyes, she saw how unhinged he was becoming. But beyond that, she saw a deep sadness and regret that seemed to consume him.

"Who did you kill?" she asked.

"My firstborn son."

"You mean Jason? I thought Dallas kill—"

"No, not Jason."

"Then who?"

Ouellette backed off, sighing again, his brow tight with a lifetime of worry. "You wouldn't believe me if I told you. Every pact-holder gives up something. I gave up my true identity so that no living person would ever recognize me. I lost my life, my family, and my legacy when I accepted Orunmila's power."

Watching the conflicted torment on his face, Sam felt a chill descend. Maybe it was Bridgette, but something told her that he was living more than just a double life as Oracle and police commander.

"Who are you . . . really?"

He took a deep breath and then said, "My real name . . . is Louis Castille. Vincent was my son."

Chapter 54
Sins of the Father

Date: **Sunday, June 15, 1997**
Time: **11:11 p.m.**
Location: **Deepwater Olympus**
Somewhere in the Gulf of Mexico

Her shoulders and jaw dropping at the same time, Sam stared blankly at Ouellette. His often strange behavior was suddenly reasonable. From his compulsion to help Vincent with the *tkeeus,* to the guilt of sending him to the electric chair, to his dutiful feelings about cleaning up the Knight Priory—it all made sense if he was a Castille.

After a long silence, she pointed at him. "You're Vincent's father?"

"Yes, I am."

The she pointed at herself. "You're my grandfather?"

"That is correct."

She leaned on the altar. "This is going to take a second to sink in."

But he kept talking. "I left New Orleans to serve in the First World War when Vincent and Gladys were small children and Marguerite was just a baby. I was critically injured in the West African Theater. That's when I became fused, as you call it. When I returned, because of my pact, no one was able to recognize me. So I reinvented myself as Louis Ouellette. The hardest part was forging documentation to establish a lineage worthy of joining the Knight Priory. Soon, I was working with my son and daughters to run New Orleans. It was hard at first, being so close and them not knowing me, but . . ."

He leaned next to her. " . . . at least I got to be near them."

Sam recoiled. Part of her wanted to call him a liar and slap his face. But the more she thought about, the more his claim appeared logical. Once she accepted that Louis Ouellette was actually Louis Castille, his entire involvement with her family fit into place.

"Then the second time you went back to Guinea, when you learned the secret of the *tkeeus*, was during the Vietnam War?"

"Yes," he said. "Louis Castille was a veteran. Louis Ouellette was not. You can't imagine how easy warfare is when you're a god. But this time, I had Orunmila's wisdom. I went there not for glory, but to understand human nature."

"How did that work out for you?"

"Not as well as I had hoped. Even with wisdom, I saw that one man could not change the world. So I thought of changing one group at a time. That's why I originally learned the secret of the *tkeeus*. To make the Knight Priory aware of the pantheons—to enlighten them. Once they were aware, we could use that power to bring harmony to New Orleans, then Louisiana, then the Gulf South, and so on. One region at a time."

"And it worked out so well," she said sarcastically.

"Your possession worked a little too well. I never intended for a petro *loa* to enter you. But one did. And you know the rest of the story."

"So you thought you could help the world, and you ended up making it worse." It was amazing that someone supposedly so wise could make such a miscalculation about human nature. "OK, so I get all that, but those years of persecuting Edward and hating me personally. What was up with that?"

With a grunt, he said, "Edward, my grandson, hung out with the Marcellos, a crime family, and that was bad news all around. He wouldn't listen to any of my warnings, so I used the law to scare him straight. And if you recall, it worked."

She nodded, hating to admit that he was right.

"As for you? I never really hated you. But when the new Bourbon Street Ripper stuff began, I suspected that the *loa* inside of you had made you a killer. It wasn't until your fight with Blind Moses at the wharf that I knew you were innocent. You see, Marinette was so affected by Dr. Klein's drugs that she only attacked in self-defense. When I realized that, I made sure Rodger, Michael, and even Dixie did whatever they could to find the real killer."

Despite his rationale, she still wanted to make sure he was telling the truth. "What you're saying makes sense. But it all hinges on you being Louis Castille. Can you prove it? Can you prove you're my grandfather?"

His expression was thoughtful for a few seconds. Then he said, "I have an idea. Hold out the silver pen."

"What?"

"No living person can recognize me. But the dead can. Vincent will know who I am."

With a sigh and feeling more than a little sick to her stomach, she popped open the container and took out the pen.

"Hello, Sam," Vincent said.

She held it out to Ouellette, frowning and unsure of what to expect.

As soon as he touched it, her vision tunneled in, and suddenly, she was standing in unending blackness. On one side of her was Ouellette, still in his Priory robe. On the other side was Vincent, dressed in the top hat and tails of Baron Samedi.

Vincent's eyes fell upon Ouellette. He snickered. "Hello, Father. Playing your trump card?"

"Hello, Son," Ouellette said weakly.

Sam glowered at her father. "Vincent, you knew who Ouellette was this entire time and didn't tell me?"

"A good card player never reveals his hand, my Queen," Vincent said with a catlike grin.

The muscles in her jaw tightened. *My whole family, from start to finish, are pricks.*

"So you see, Sam," Ouellette said, "I'm not lying. It's time we work together and end the nightmare my son has started."

"Sam, Daughter," Vincent said. "Are you honestly going to side with this bastard? Because of him, all this happened. I know you hate me, but you should hate him even more."

She opened her eyes, glaring at them both. "You two . . . make me sick."

First she pointed at Ouellette. "You made some really bad choices, Louis. Awful ones. But instead of making better ones to fix it, you continued to make bad ones. Your regret and guilt have ruined innumerable lives."

Then she pointed at Vincent. "And you . . . oh, you. You're just plain twisted. Torturing and murdering others and then damning me to live forever. The side effects of your ritual alone will continue to cause harm for years to come."

Finally, she looked at them both. "It's hard to decide which of you I hate more. If this is the Castille family legacy, then maybe it's best the line ends here."

Ouellette said, "Sam, I deserve to die for what I've done. And you cannot die until Vincent is destroyed. Let's end this together. Let's obliterate the Castille family and then die in peace. I agree. Let's wipe out the family line."

Vincent snorted. "Or you could just kill this no-account father of mine. Do that and I'll leave you alone. The real fun is on this side of the pond now, anyway."

"Do you see what I mean?" Ouellette asked with more urgency. "Vincent has no conscience. Death only made him worse. We need to destroy him. With two pact-holders, the battle will be short and decisive!"

Throwing his head back and laughing, Vincent said, "Of course! Pay attention to the man whose master plan included remarrying some tramp in Houma and spitting out a kid who drowned on his own birthday. Good strategy, Papa!"

"Jason was a son I could be proud of!" Ouellette exclaimed.

Vincent rolled his eyes. "And now we get to the real issue."

"Shut up!" Sam's face burned. "Shut up, shut up, shut up!"

When both men stopped, she took a deep breath. Then she said, "This is not some family therapy session. You two are bickering like children. All three of us are gods, and this situation is killing countless innocent people. You two are so out of touch with reality, it's disgusting!"

She glared at Ouellette. "I am not killing my babies. That is not negotiable. I am sorry you had to execute your son, but frying the Bourbon Street Ripper and killing two little children is about as different as you can get."

Then she glared at Vincent. "And I haven't forgotten you. First, I will destroy the pen and cut you off from this world, and then I will find another way to get to the crossroads and obliterate you. I'm immortal and can't die, asshole. I can wait a long time."

Pushing out the mountain of stress she had been accumulating, she said, "I'm done with you both."

Leaning toward her, his eyes glowing like fire, Vincent spoke in an enraged, low voice. "Now you listen to me, you ungrateful little shit. I am now the *loa* king, and I will always know where you are, because you are the *loa* queen. So if you break the pen, I will find a way to kill everyone around you that you care for. The detective you love so much? It better be a long-distance relationship, because as soon as I sense him near you, he's dead."

"And you're too late, Sam," Ouellette said, also glaring at her. "I've already had Alexia LeBlanc possessed. She'll be killing your children any second now. So we're doing this ritual whether you like it or not."

"Nope and nope," Vincent said with a sneer. "The LeBlanc girl broke free and tore your spirits up. She and the detective are taking my grandkids upstairs right now."

Ouellette drew back. "What?"

"Vincent, my children are alive?" Sam felt her heart skip a beat.

"Yes, they are," he said. "See? I want the children to live, too, Sam. That's why we should join—"

"Oh, go to hell!" She let go of the pen, her vision returning to normal. She then jumped and kicked Ouellette in the chest. It felt like slow-motion as he flew back, the pen spinning through the air. With a quick snap, she caught it in the container.

Thunder crashed loudly in the distance.

"You shouldn't have done that," Ouellette said, getting back on his feet. "Even if you destroy the pen, all you're doing is delaying a future disaster. Unless Vincent is destroyed, the dead of the voodoo pantheon will be unable to move on. Sooner or later, all that energy will break into our world. Do you know the chaos that will cause?"

"And when that happens, I'll figure out something else!" she shouted.

"You don't get to make that decision!" he bellowed back. "I know it's a raw deal for those kids, but they have to die for this to be over, to stop millions or even billions from dying. I'm sorry, but that's life—unfair and cruel. Oftentimes, the evils brought about by the parents are cleansed by the blood of their offspring."

Securing the container, she got into a fighting position. "The sins of the father are visited on the children?" Baring her fangs at him once more, she said, "What a load of shit."

"So we're really going to do this?" he asked. The dust around him, glittering with shards of glass, started to rise.

"I refuse to believe the rules of this world are so strict that there isn't another way to save it. Therefore, Grandfather, the only way you're getting this pen or my children is over my impossible-to-kill body."

He growled and, in one motion, ripped off his robe, revealing a black SWAT uniform underneath. Almost at once, his body started to glow, arcs of energy crackling around him. His eyes began to flare, and the air around him heated up. The ground at his feet crushed into a small crater as the debris continued floating upwards.

"So be it, Granddaughter," he said. The aura of strength coming from him was immense.

He's . . . so . . . powerful.

Casting aside all regret, she activated her power as well. Her muscles tightened, energy crackled, a glow surrounded her, and time began to slow down. She could feel the difference in power between them. The odds were definitely in his favor.

No matter. For my children, I have to beat him.

The crashes of thunder drew closer. A storm was almost upon them.

Roaring, Ouellette flew at her with a punch. She did the same, and their fists collided in the center of the room. A shockwave from the impact flew out, turning the pillars around them to dust. The walls crumbled like cards.

Sam's muscles ached and burned and then gave way—he was just too strong. As her arm gave out, his fist connected with her jaw, her vision exploding into starbursts. She stumbled as he punched her in the stomach several times, and then with a second roar, hit her with an uppercut hard enough to send her through the ceiling. She cried out as she flew through several stories of the rig, landing limply on the surface.

That freaking hurt! She spat up some blood as her vision returned. The SWAT helicopters were just taking off. In the distance, roiling storm clouds were rapidly approaching.

"Sam!"

She glanced toward one of the helicopters. Aucoin and Alexia were seated inside. Both were holding slumbering toddlers—her children.

"Kyle! Get out of here, it's—"

The ground besides her exploded as Ouellette burst forth, landing a few feet away. As he stood there, cracking his neck, his eyes fell upon the children.

"Damn you, Ouellette!" Aucoin yelled. "I knew you were trouble!"

Ouellette tightened his fists. "Give me those kids!"

The ground around his feet cracked as he rushed at the helicopter, moving like a blur. Bellowing, "No!" Sam, again, focused her power until time slowed to a crawl. He was still moving quickly. Concentrating on her children, she sprinted at Ouellette and caught him just a few yards away from them.

Time returned to normal as she grabbed his arms, struggling to restrain him in a full nelson. "You will not touch them!"

"Sam, hold him!" Aucoin lay down Eugene and aimed his gun at Ouellette.

"No, Kyle, that won't—"

But then Aucoin fired every shot at Ouellette, who threw her to the ground and then dodged each bullet with the speed of a viper. He even caught the last one and threw it back. It struck Aucoin's gun, sending it flying out into the darkness.

Aucoin pulled his hand back, his fingers singed. "Son of a bitch!"

"Kyle!" she cried. Flipping up, she donkey-kicked Ouellette hard enough to send him stumbling. "Kyle, Alexia! Get out of here! He's fused, like me. You don't stand a chance."

Aucoin's face was pained. "Sam, I . . ."

"She's right," Alexia said. "We need to go, now!"

The helicopter roared to life as Aucoin tried to yell something. Sam couldn't hear him, however, so, with an exasperated look, he threw her an oversized handgun. It was Perdition, Victor's weapon. *Is Big V dead?*

As the helicopter took off, she heard Ouellette charging. With a yell, he leapt toward the helicopter's railing.

"Oh, no, you don't!" She jumped after him and grabbed his feet. They both crashed upon the rig's surface as the helicopter flew out over the water. For the moment, the children were safe.

Thunder exploded all around them. Above, the boiling, black clouds, dotted with repeated lightning strikes, had formed a rotating tempest.

"Get off me!" Ouellette kicked her in the face so hard, she slid back, her nose breaking.

Getting up, she holstered Perdition and popped her nose back in place.

He raged toward her.

Taking out both of her .45 automatics, she said, "Dodge this." She then fired both at once, focusing so that every shot aimed straight for his heart. Again, the world almost moved in slow motion as he whipped out a combat knife and knocked every single one of them aside. By the time he reached her, her clips were empty.

Standing a mere foot away, he just puffed up his chest. That made her even angrier. She threw one gun at him, then the other, both bouncing off. When he started chuckling, she slapped him across the face so hard, she felt something crack in his mouth. Spitting out a few teeth, he then hit her in the forehead with the butt of his knife.

"You're making a fool of yourself," he said.

As she stumbled to the side, a nightmarish howl ripped through the night air.

"What the hell is this?" Ouellette asked.

The air turned cold, and a foul smell arose. Recovering from the strike, Sam looked around. She knew what it was. "It's Vincent! He's sending the *loa* here!"

Ouellette tensed up. "Which ones?"

From the center of the tempest, countless specks started falling, each one wailing and screeching in misery and rage. Alligators with human hands for feet and crawfish claws, skeletons with dozens of arms and legs, even hooded figures with glowing eyes—those and more fell upon them.

She gritted her teeth. "Looks like all of them."

A moment later, the *loa* were upon them. She punched and kicked, every strike crackling with white energy that reduced them to black dust. Claws tore at her legs, fangs sank into her shoulders, and daggers stabbed her sides. In seconds, she was bloodier than when she had fought Dallas years ago.

As she dodged a flurry of swipes from several hooded *loa*, her back touched Ouellette's. Immediately, she tensed up, ready for him to attack. But instead he spoke.

"Sam, a truce?" He sounded winded.

Her lungs burned. "Yeah. For now. So, any ideas?"

An alligator with crawfish claws jumped at them. She ducked, and he swiped at it with his knife, white energy flowing through the attack. The *loa* exploded in a shower of black dust. She watched as he sheathed his weapon, realizing that all Fused must be able to annihilate lesser spirits with one hit.

"I'll summon my *ogouns* and *orishas*," he said. "You summon whatever you can."

"Right," she said. As a six-armed skeleton with a second head in its ribcage jumped at her, she kicked it so hard, it exploded. Then she slapped both hands on the ground. "To all who would heed my command, your queen beseeches you. Fight for me!"

A large, white sigil appeared at her feet. Off to the side, Ouellette did the same thing. "Warriors of the dark continent, hear my plea. Come!" A sigil appeared beneath him.

In blinding flashes of lights, both sigils exploded, and a moment later, the air was filled with thousands of African spirits and an almost equal number of ghosts.

The dead of the voodoo pantheon? Just as Papa Ghede said!

Then she heard merry laughter. Floating dozens of yards away was Papa Ghede himself. "Ay there, luv, you and your grandfather split the attention of that snake what has me brother. Distract him enough, and I'll get our children away 'fore you destroy the focus."

"Right," she said. "Of course, Papa."

A massive *orisha* who wore a mask bowed before Ouellette.

"That meat pack has him a general," Papa Ghede said. "Here's one I know you'll like!"

The ghost of Edward Castille, covered in chains, appeared before her and bowed.

"Dad!" she gasped.

"My little Magnolia," he said. "Don't worry. I died for a child—you—so Papa Ghede now protects me. The dead will fight to contain Vincent. This is our battle, too. Let us be your sword."

Before she could speak, he took her hand. "I am so proud of you, my daughter." Kissing her hand, Edward took out a pair of machetes and rushed into the fray. She was so choked up with emotion that for a few seconds, all she could do was watch. It was pure pandemonium, with Vincent's *loa* fighting both African spirits and the dead of the voodoo pantheon. Even Papa Ghede got involved, firing bolts of energy from his apple that banished *loa* back to the spirit world.

"Whoa, ho, ho! This here be the most fun I've had since the Great Fire of '88, ya!"

Awed by the massive counterattack on Vincent's forces, Sam pushed her emotions back down and got swept up into the skirmish. For several minutes, she fought together with the dead, her comrades-in-arms now howling ghosts and enraged specters. She even saw Rodger and Michael, revitalized by the massive influx of energy, fighting alongside Edward. But as the battle grew the thickest, something caught her attention. It was Ouellette weaving his way through the fight toward the edge of the rig.

"Oh, hell, no!" she shouted. "Edward, Rodger, Michael! Hold the fort!"

Edward didn't answer, sinking his weapons into a pair of hooded *loa*. Michael saluted quickly and then spun around to kick a decayed hag on a skeletal horse. It was Rodger who responded, tipping his hat. "Go kick his ass, Sam. We've got your back."

"Thanks, guys!" Sam then dashed after Ouellette, grabbing him by the waist. They were right next to the holes they had made earlier.

"Stop it. Can't you see how this is escalating? We can end this!"

"Leave my children alone!" she shouted, suplexing him down one of the holes. As they hit the ground of the meeting hall, they crashed through to the floor below, then again, and then again. They broke through floor after floor, only stopping when they hit a hard, wooden surface. Looking up, Sam saw the bottom of the oil rig and felt the nighttime breeze. They had landed on a yacht at the dock.

"Cool," she wheezed. The sounds of battle were all around her.

Ouellette groaned and lay still. Slowly, she stumbled to her feet and assessed the situation. All around, New Orleans SWAT and GEIST agents were fighting Vincent's *loa* along with the African spirits and ghosts. Chase stood nearby, tearing into *loa* with his bare hands. He kept yelling, "This is for Noelle!"

Then the yacht's deck became illuminated by the lightning strikes above. It was moving away from the rig.

Hearing Ouellette bellow, Sam barely slapped aside a chop to the neck. He was back on his feet. "You're dead, Sam!"

"Let's finish this," she said, speeding herself back up. With everyone around them moving in slow motion, they engaged in a fierce volley of blows that did more to damage the yacht than turn a single wave in the tide of their duel. Finally, she jumped at him and punched as he rolled to the side. The impact of her fist on the deck was so severe that the entire ship started cracking. When Ouellette saw the damage, he got an angry expression and jump-kicked her right in the face. "You'll kill innocent humans, you psycho!"

"Sorry!" she cried as she flew back, skidding across the water like a skipping stone. He then leapt toward her, sliding across the Gulf as if he were skiing. She continued to skip, finally twisting her body around until her feet were pushing on the water. With a hard push, she changed direction, her feet catching the surface tension. Soon, she was heading right back at him.

Whoa, I'm running on water!

The two of them collided fist-to-fist a few miles from the oil rig, again causing a shockwave so intense, it made the water beneath them vaporize. As mist sprayed everywhere, she slipped in and kneed him in the gut, then elbowed him in the chin. He coughed up blood and hit her on the back of the head with both fists. For a moment, she blacked out, her vision vanishing in a sea of stars. Then she felt a punch to the chin—an uppercut. The next thing she knew, she was high in the air.

Nearby was the helicopter containing Aucoin, Alexia, and her children. It was struggling against the raging tempest. Shaking off the pain, she aimed herself at the copter and fell inside.

"Sam?" Aucoin said.

She shook off the pain and then reached out, touching each child on the cheek. She could feel Alice's intellect and Eugene's spiritual affinity. It was enough to know that they'd grow up to be exceptional. *I love you, my little angels. I'll never forget you.*

A flash of white caught her eye. A small, white orb flittered out from Eugene and into her back pocket. It felt warm and comfortably familiar. *I know that person, but—*

"Sam, what's going on now?" Aucoin asked anxiously.

Focusing on them, she said, "Kyle. Alexia. Tell Dr. Lazarus that Ouellette is Louis Castille. He'll figure out the rest. I need to destroy both him and the pen. Is the device ready?"

"I think so," Alexia said. "Here, take my headset. Dixie should—"

From outside, Ouellette called out, "Sam!"

He was hovering in front of her, his body engulfed in a fiery, white aura.

Sam's shoulders dropped. "You can fly?"

"Give me the children, Sam!"

Aucoin reached for her. "Look, Sam, I—"

She turned and kissed him. "Goodbye, Kyle. I love you."

Then she placed her forehead on Alexia's. "Make sure my children go someplace neither I or nor Vincent will ever find."

"I understand." Alexia smiled with a gentle strength. "You will win. I believe it."

Sam gazed upon her children one last time. *Goodbye, my loves.*

With a roar of her own, she hurled herself at Ouellette. As they flew through the air back toward Deepwater, she rained repeated blows upon him. "You – will – not – hurt – my – babies!"

Grabbing her neck, Ouellette flipped around and slid her across the rig's surface. The metal tore into her back, popping her back muscles and tendons out of alignment. She skidded to a stop in the center of the platform.

"Ouch."

All around, the *loa*, African spirits, and ghosts continued to fight, but it had become a blur. Ouellette was her only target.

He kicked her again, and she felt her ribs crack. Then he did it again. She felt her stomach rupture. And then he paused, regarded her with disdain, and then jumped so high, he became a dot.

Crap.

Suddenly, she felt a sense of peace, knowing she could never overpower him. At that moment, she realized her only chance was to outsmart him.

"Papa Ghede," she said, each breath more painful than the last.

He was busy banishing dozens of lesser *loa*. "Yeah, luv?"

"Remember the pen? The focus? I'm going to destroy it now like we discussed."

"Great gris-gris! My children can't survive that much power 'sploding out. Everyone, we retreatin'!" He tossed his apple into the sky, where it turned into a portal back into the spirit world. "Everybody get in here, or you done for."

Out the corner of her eye, she saw Edward start to run toward her, only to be grabbed by Michael and Rodger. "Let me go!"

"You fool!" Michael shouted. "You'll be destroyed."

"Good luck, Sam," Rodger said.

"My little Magnolia!" Edward cried they pulled him into the portal. "I love you!"

The African spirits and ghosts also started to retreat, pulling Vincent's *loa* with them.

Good. They'll be all right.

She looked back up. Ouellette was starting to descend. Putting on the headset, she hit the talk button. "Dixie? It's Sam." She felt exhausted.

Dixie picked up. "Sam? What's happ—"

"Listen," Sam said, gauging Ouellette's distance. "I'm not gonna make it out of here. But I need to destroy the pen. Is the device ready?"

Patty chimed in. "It's ready, Sam. Sebastian and Sheree put it on a one-minute cycle. Place the pen in the basin, hit the button, and in one minute, it should be destroyed."

Still falling toward her, Ouellette stretched out his hands as if cupping a large ball.

"Good," Sam said, standing up. Her chest and legs hurt. With every breath, she heard whistling in her lungs. She'd be unconscious soon. "Tell everyone to evacuate Deepwater. It's going down."

White and black energy started gathering into Ouellette's hands.

"I will," Dixie said. "And Sam?"

"Yeah?"

"Good luck."

Sam chuckled and spat up blood. "Thanks."

Tossing the headset to the side, she cupped her hands together like she did the night of the townhome fire. White and blue energy gathered. As soon as enough was there, she thrust her hands up at Ouellette. He did the same thing, and large beams of energy flew from both of them, colliding into a central point that grew larger and hotter with every second. All spirits and ghosts nearby were vaporized into black dust.

The remaining *loa* under Vincent's control shrieked in fear and retreated into Papa Ghede's portal.

Sam felt the ground around her feet start to break and the strength in her knees give. She could see the concentration on Ouellette's face as he neared her. Then the area where their beams converged exploded. For the third time in her life, Sam felt her flesh burn as she fell down the rig. And once more, she momentarily blacked out.

When she came to, she was in the drilling bay. In the center of the room was a massive cylinder with an equally immense conical plasma torch. She found it oddly similar to something she'd see in a science fiction movie. The hole it would normally descend into had been sealed off into a deep basin. Sebastian and Sheree's equipment—a console with a large, red button—was set up next to it.

She limped toward the basin, liquid sloshing in her lungs and giving her the feeling of drowning. Just as she reached it, Ouellette landed behind her. His face and arms were also badly burned. He seemed even more pissed.

"I tried to work this out with you," he said, stomping toward her. "However, you chose the hard route. But that's your way, isn't it? You've always been an entitled, spoiled bitch not worthy of the name Castille."

"I've got news for you, Gramps," she said, fumbling with the container. "Vincent might have been the Bourbon Street Ripper, but the one who truly brought dishonor to the Castille family was . . ."

He punched her in the face, breaking her jaw. The container flew into the basin. She looked at him and muttered, " . . . you."

For a brief moment, his face wrinkled in confusion and then regret. It was all the distraction she needed. Grabbing him and then kicking the large red button, she flipped them both into the basin. They landed right by the container.

Immediately, he pushed her back and scrambled over to it. With a triumphant laugh, he took out the pen and held it up. "Finally! I've got you, Son!"

Feeling her strength all but gone, she pushed everything she had into standing up. The machinery above clicked on and began sealing the basin shut. She had to finish this.

Then Ouellette's brow wrinkled. "What do you mean, I fell into her trap?"

He glanced up and gawked. "No! I won't allow it. I'll pulverize this thing first!" Holding out one hand, he started gathering energy again.

Tripping forward, she crashed into him shoulder-first. "No!"

As they slid back, he elbowed her in the face, shattering her left eye and breaking her nose again. She groaned and spat up blood as he aimed the gathering sphere of energy at her midsection. He sneered condescendingly. "I win, Granddaughter."

Heaving up blood and bile, she swatted weakly at his hand. She needed help.

Then a flash of light caught her eye as the small, white orb from before floated out from her pocket. With another flash, it turned into the ghostly figure of Richie Fastellos.

"You will not touch her," he said as a hooded coat appeared around him—the same kind worn by Dallas, the new Bourbon Street Ripper. He summoned a ghostly chainsaw.

"Tonight's going to be hard for you!"

As Sam staggered to regain her footing, Richie attacked Ouellette, forcing him back. Above, the device started coming to life, arcs of blue energy gathering into a tip. She then realized what Richie was doing—stalling for time.

"You pitiful little ghost," Ouellette said, swiping at Richie with his energy-gathering hand. Then he suddenly looked down at the pen. "Shut up, Son. Dallas was not your greatest creation!"

That distraction proved to be enough, however, as Richie stepped to the side and then slammed the chainsaw onto Ouellette's outstretched hand. The sphere of energy exploded, blowing them both back.

Stumbling back, her jaw now healed, Sam popped it into place. Then she took out Perdition and cocked back the massive hammer.

Ouellette cried out and fell to the ground, dropping the pen. It slid across the basin as he cauterized his stump with a crackle of energy. Then he turned on

Richie. A moment later, he had him pinned, punching him in the face repeatedly. Richie cried out and dropped the ghostly chainsaw. It clattered to the ground and vanished in a puff of smoke.

"Time to send you to oblivion, you pathetic copycat!" Ouellette took out his knife, white energy crackling through his arm and into it.

But this time, she was ready, aiming Perdition at him. "Grandfather!"

The moment he turned toward her, she fired. The roar of the gun was like thunder, and the massive bullet tore off most of his face. Blood and tissue went everywhere as he fell back into the center of the basin.

Seizing that moment, she grabbed the pen and jumped on top of him.

"Run, Richie!"

He struggled to his feet, the hooded coat gone.

"Run, you idiot! You have to be waiting for me when I die. You won't be able to do that if you get obliterated."

"Sam . . ."

"I said run!" she shouted so hard the basin shook.

He gulped. "A . . . all right. I'll wait for you, Sam. Goodbye. I love you."

In a flash of white, he was gone.

I love you too, you stupid kid.

She gazed back at Ouellette. Somehow, he was still alive, his face already reforming. With a groan, he tried to push her off, but now he was weaker than she was. Grinning madly, she held the pen above him like a knife.

"Time for us to die, Gramps!"

"Daughter, wait," Vincent said. "Don't! I'm not sure if you'll reform!"

"Isn't it wonderful, Vincent!" She stabbed the pen into Ouellette's sternum, making him cough up several kinds of liquid. Then she repeatedly punched the remains of his face until she felt his skull start to crack.

Above, the arcs of energy had flowed into a white-hot point. The machine above emitted a rising, pitched whine. It was almost ready to fire.

Ouellette burbled. "Sam . . . "

She grinned and started choking him. "Isn't this what you want, Gramps? To die and atone for your sins? Well, guess what, you get your wish!"

He gurgled again and then elbowed her in the chest so hard that her heart stopped. Blood poured from her mouth.

She spat on him and kneed him in the groin. As his eyes rolled up, she leaned back and screamed. All sensation in her arms and chest were gone, and with great effort, she took what could very well be her last breath. Then the whining above stopped, and the device began to fire.

She held up her arms. *Baron, if there's a chance in hell, please dig my grave tonight!*

"Let's do this!"

And then, all around them was white.

Outside, the dark, stormy night over the Gulf of Mexico was momentarily illuminated by a blast from the Deepwater Olympus rig. The light could be seen for hundreds of miles and was described as being as bright as daylight. The shockwave was so intense that it pushed away the clouds, and the sound was so loud that it shattered the windows of homes on the coast. The explosion lasted several seconds and then slowly flickered out.

The silver pen had been destroyed, and with it Vincent's influence in the world.

Epilogue

Date: Saturday, February 28, 1998
Time: 4:00 p.m.
Location: GEIST Headquarters
Southern Arkansas

"Are you sure I can't persuade you to stay, Kyle?"

"Too many things have happened here. I'm sorry."

"Will you at least consider remaining until after the move?" Dr. Lazarus frowned. To his side, Camellia silently poured him more coffee. "It's only a few more years, and it would be a shame to have the inauguration of our new headquarters without a founding member present."

"Always the diplomat, eh?" Sitting across from him, Aucoin offered the gentlest smile he could. "My mind's made up, Andre. I'd be a liability to GEIST if I knew where the new base was. I'd hate to be a reason for making it . . . fail." There was no other way to put it.

Dr. Lazarus seemed sad, but he nodded. "I do understand. With the Knight Priory gone and the crisis in the voodoo pantheon over, GEIST is ready to start working on a global scale. New investigators, agents, and operatives are coming in every week. Thanks to the Castille fortune, we can become what I envisioned."

Still smiling softly, Aucoin said, "You have good people helping you. Meyer, Hakim, Tania. That new girl from London, the ex-Triad from China, and isn't there a guy and his sister coming in from Ireland as well?"

"Yes. A lot of talented people are being scouted now," Dr. Lazarus said. "Even Miss LeBlanc and Miss O'Brien will be joining once they graduate. But, Kyle, you were one of the first and best. There will never be another like you."

Aucoin felt his ears heat up. "I did what I had to do to atone for my sins. But I'm not getting any younger, and I'm still not sure what I want to do with the rest of my life. So for now, I need to move on and see where else I can make a difference."

After a few moments of silence, Dr. Lazarus asked, "Are you going to search for Sam?"

"I thought about it," Aucoin said. "But something about the way she said goodbye seemed final. Besides, the destruction of Deepwater Olympus was so severe that even Julius thinks she may take years, if ever, to recover."

His voice cracked a little. "I don't think I'm meant to see her again."

"I'm sorry, Kyle. Is there anything that I can do?"

"Yeah, make sure you don't get complacent. Vincent's ability to command *loa* in the physical world may be gone, and Papa Ghede may be able to counter him, but he still exists. And he still has Baron Samedi bound. Because of that, the ghosts of the voodoo pantheon still cannot cross over. Not to mention that Papa Ghede and Vincent now fight in the spirit world. So while there's no immediate crisis, the world is far from back to normal."

Dr. Lazarus said, "You are correct. The constant influx of new ghosts under areas controlled by the voodoo pantheon, as well as the energy released from the war between Papa Ghede and Vincent, will eventually leak into the physical world. We'll see more hauntings and paranormal phenomena than even Hollywood could imagine."

He slowly spun a globe on his desk. "And this whole mess has encouraged conflicts in other pantheons. So, yes, the world may never be normal again. But don't worry, Kyle. Wherever the supernatural threatens humanity, GEIST will be there."

"Thank you. And Papa Ghede. Is he an ally?"

"Yes. I have made an arrangement with him. We will stay out of New Orleans—his headquarters, if you will. In return, he'll make sure that *loa* never attack humans again."

With an exhale, Aucoin said, "Then, as Alexia would say, 'All's well.'"

Smiling pleasantly, Dr. Lazarus asked, "Shall I see you to your car?"

Aucoin nodded and stood, taking his bags. Camellia pushed Dr. Lazarus along.

"It's been a long road, Kyle. Morial was able to dodge any blame, but his time will come. Connick is now an ally of ours, a sort of eyes on ground zero in New Orleans. And Dr. Kindley is locked away, deep inside an asylum, which I pray he never leaves."

They entered the elevator. Aucoin tapped the button to go up. "Amazing that Tania never killed him after what happened to Violet."

"Tania is a marvelous person. She's already found new ways to fight as an operative. I hope she stays with GEIST for a very long time."

"I'm sure she will."

The elevator opened on the ground floor.

"Anyway," Dr. Lazarus said. "We alone possess the secret of the *tkeeus*, which Julius has locked away in the vault. Before Dixie formally retired from GEIST, she delivered the Castille children to Mathias, who has assured me they will never be found by anyone who would abuse them. And Leona will continue to act as a liaison between us and the Eversoll Institute. So this chapter is over, and whatever storm may be coming, we're ready for it."

They stepped outside, where a black sedan was parked. Aucoin placed his bags in the trunk. "I wouldn't worry about it, Andre. I have faith in you and GEIST. And if Sam lives, I have faith in her. We may never see her again, but somewhere there is a god walking the earth. And she's definitely good."

"Yes, a goddess with a heart of gold. I'm certain that if she survived, she'll spend the rest of eternity finding a way to get to Vincent. Who knows, maybe one day after humanity has come and gone, those two will have a showdown the likes of which hasn't been seen since Zeus and his siblings defeated the Titans."

With a chuckle, Aucoin said, "A battle that shakes the heavens, right?"

Dr. Lazarus nodded. "Well, in any case, we'll still try to find a way to get there. If Sam is gone, then someone will need to take Vincent out."

Smiling again, Aucoin stuck out his hand. "If it comes to that, best of luck, Andre."

They shook hands. "And you, Kyle, if you ever need anything, anything at all, give me a call."

After Dr. Lazarus went back inside, Aucoin got into his car and drove off, heading northeast toward Tennessee. Once he was on the interstate, he took an envelope out of the glove compartment. It been delivered to him a few weeks ago. He rubbed his thumb over the Mexican postage stamp. There was no return address.

With a sigh, he re-opened it. Inside was a note: "I'm alive. Please don't come looking for me, but know I'll always love you."

Also inside was a melted red shoe charm.

Aucoin squeezed it as he drove off toward his new life.

"Yeah, the world's in good hands."

And so it was.

The End

Afterword

And now we're done—at least, as done as one story can be. That's the problem with stories. There's always room for more. But this story was about Sam and the silver pen, and that narrative is complete.

Now that I've finished a genre-bending trilogy with elements of thriller, mystery, and horror, I'm looking forward to trying something different. Fantasy, perhaps. Or science fiction. Or even urban fantasy. A world filled with uncertainty has been born from *Sins of the Father*, and an entire series could be written off of that.

Ideas, I have. Inspiration, I have. Next, I choose a direction to set sail. There are entire universes to explore.

Take my hand, and let's go together.

—Leo King

About the Author

Leo King was born in New Orleans, Louisiana, and moved to Houston, Texas, in 2005 after Hurricane Katrina. He works during the day and writes at night, usually juggling several projects at once.

He lives with his wife, his Playstation 3s, and more stuffed lions than an adult should probably own. His education is in game development, and he often uses the structured approach of game design in developing his stories.

Connect with Leo

Email
leoking@foreverwhere.com

Twitter
@leokingauthor

Website
www.foreverwhere.com

Facebook
facebook.com/leokingauthor

Grey Gecko Press

Thank you for purchasing this book from Grey Gecko Press, an independent publishing company that focuses on new and emerging authors, bringing readers the best in fiction and non-fiction at reasonable prices in all formats.

With books in nearly every genre of fiction and non-fiction, there's something for everyone, and you can be sure that buying books from us leads directly to the support of independent authors. Grey Gecko pays our authors some of the highest royalty rates in the business and strives to produce only high-quality books.

Visit our website to purchase our titles, pre-order upcoming books at a discount, sign up for our free monthly newsletter, and find out about two great ways to get free books, the Slushpile Reader Program and the Advance Reader Program.

And don't forget: all our print editions come with the ebook free!

Your Favorite New Indie Authors

www.greygeckopress.com

store.greygeckopress.com

www.ingramcontent.com/pod-product-compliance
Lightning Source LLC
Chambersburg PA
CBHW020603310726
48979CB00008B/1321/J

* 9 7 8 1 9 3 8 8 2 1 6 3 9 *

www.ingramcontent.com/pod-product-compliance
Lightning Source LLC
Chambersburg PA
CBHW020245030826
48979CB00030B/2626/J

* 9 7 8 1 7 3 9 2 6 2 5 0 1 *